My Dear Leo

Book Four

Elm Jed

ELM JED
Author ~ Creator

Contents

Content Warnings

This Book contains ON PAGE:
Death, gun & knife violence, kidnapping, explosions, various forms
of torture, heavy blood / gore, medical emergencies,
stalking / chasing, car & motorcycle chases, choking, attempted
sexual assault & rape, attempted murder, attempted kidnapping,
dismemberment, panic & anxiety attacks, attempted self-harm, and
medical mistreatment.

-Discussed-
Death, sexual trauma, depression, thoughts of suicide & self-harm,
domestic violence, medical malpractice, and family loss

BDSM Aspect of the Book:
bondage, loose restraints, sensation play, light role-
y, blindfolds, anal plugs, cock cages, gags, various
le clamps, spreader bars, dildos, strap-ons,
a rosary not being used correctly.
"stoplight method" are implemented.
words are used

Prologue

Five Years Ago

<u>Legacy</u>
Leo

THE VILLA IS quiet as Leo opens her bedroom door. It smells of lilies and peonies. Her favorite flowers. The room is dim as he enters, nodding once at the nurse next to the bed. There, almost too still, lays Rafaella Maria Salvadori under the covers with her chest rising faintly with each breath. The matriarch of the Luciano name.

He pauses before the end of the bed, looking upon his grandmother the only one left of his family he would ever return to Italy for. Precautions were taken for no one to know he was here at the secluded villa. Rafaella had requested the secrecy. Leo wasn't the only person who didn't trust their family.

An older nurse, approaches him and says in Italian, *"Evening Signor Luciano."*

"I want a moment alone with her before the doctor comes."

"Yes, of course." She nods, walking out of the room.

Leo quietly takes his suit jacket off, placing it on the bed covers as he gently sits on the edge. His hand lays against hers which rest upon her torso. Her age is shown in the wrinkles around her eyes and mouth. Her once dark hair, now grey and white, halos her head against the pillow.

"Nonna," he says gently. The vice grip on his throat and chest ease as she flutters her eyes open. A deep breath is taken as her hazel eyes come to his. A smile, albeit small, grows on his face as he caresses her hand.

"Leonardo," she whispers. "Sei venuto."

"*For you, always, nonna,*" Leo responds, speaking in her native language. "*I've missed you.*"

She brings a hand up, gesturing for him to come closer. Leo leans down to kiss her cheeks, pulling back as she pats his jaw lovingly. "*You're as handsome as your grandfather. His smile. Your mother's eyes.*"

Leo swallows hard, taking her hand and kissing her wrist.

"*My handsome pride,*" she continues, bringing his focus solely on her. "*We have not had time to discuss, but time is never on one's side.*"

"*What do you speak of, nonna?*"

"You *are the last Luciano.*" Her voice has more conviction in it, eyes hardening. The woman he's known his entire life, a storm to never tamper with, shown in her gaze. Bed ridden or not, she was still his iron-willed grandmother. The woman who had forged the foundations of the mafia in Rome and later in the U.S.

"*There's still Gabriel,*" he counters lightly.

"*No.*" She shakes her head. "*He is* Marchetti. *His father.*" Her voice becomes filled with disdain. "*He has become a stain, who my son ignores. He is no Luciano, you are.*"

"Nonna—"

"*It is yours.*" A hush comes between them as Leo stares down at her.

Understanding comes over Leo but it's instantly followed by confusion. "*The Luciano fortune is led by a matriarch, nonna. Not by the men. When Giovanna died—*"

"It came back to me, and now I give to you. You, my Leonardo, my grandson, my pride... I entrust the Luciano name to. Only you who took back the name."

"Renato won't accept it."

"Not his to accept." She waves her hand, looking away from him to the balcony where the last of day shines. Streams of sunlight pass through clouds over the sea the villa overlooks. *"He is my son, but he is a Salvadori, like his father. It was always his to continue, whilst Gigi's was for my family line."*

Her eyes begin to water and that strength of hers waivers before him. Leo leans over to the bedside table, grabbing a handkerchief and delicately wipes the tears from her cheeks. Rafaella brings her attention back to him, smiling warmly.

"You are all that's left of her," she whispers, clutching his hand. *"All who's left that I trust in what I created."*

Leo is quiet, looking away from her. What she wants may not be achieved. It was long instituted that only a matriarch, a woman, would remain as the sole proprietor of the estates under the Luciano family. Renato was still married, his wife Fiorella, should be next in line, not him.

"You shouldn't change what has been done for me, nonna," he says quietly. *"I am well off and have procured fortunes of my own. I do not need the money. I will protect the Luciano name to my last breath whilst I still have it, but I cannot agree to inheriting something that is not mine to control. Fiorella will do fine as the matriarch and charge of the estates."*

She hums, almost too thoughtfully as he looks back at her. Her smile almost a smirk.

"You truly are just like my Durante. Money and power will never sway you like your brother, uncle, or your father. My decision is final. You will be the one to secure the Luciano legacy."

"Renato will not agree and will fight me, along with Gabriel."

"I did not say I'd give my estates and fortune to you..." she pauses, pursing her lips as Leo's brows furrow, *"...I entrust you to marry a proper woman to inherit it all. Your wife will ensure the Luciano name. When you are married before God, vowing to another, she will become the*

matriarch and inherit all that is the Luciano name. That is how you will secure my legacy, Leonardo."

Leo stares at her, mouth almost gaping. Shock flicks through him.

A soft chuckle leaves her, coughing a little as he grips her hands. *"Nonna, no—"*

"You will find the woman who will guard the Luciano name with you. Promise me you will."

"Nonna—"

"Promise me. Promise me, you'll find a wife who will bring honor to my name."

Despair reaches over him, knowing his current situation in New York City with Gabriel and Matteo. The danger his own life leads along with the busyness of it. He has never thought of marriage or wanted it. It was not a future that seemed possible. Not after watching his own mother and then stepmother die.

Leo's jaw works, chest tightening knowing he can't refuse her. There's an ache that he may fail her after death, that what is left of her legacy will be given over to his uncle instead. Fiorella wouldn't be in control, his uncle would be. Yet, he cannot refuse a dying woman's wish.

"I promise, Nonna."

"Good." She pats his hand, laying back into her pillows. *"The others shall not know until it is time, when you are married. Until then, half the estates will go to Renato and the other half to you."*

"Gabriel and Matteo?" She shakes her head. *"Nonna…"*

"One has brought disgrace, and the other is a Marchetti," she spits the last name of his father, breathing picking up. *"He is not Salvadori or Luciano."*

"Very well," he whispers, an ache hitting him for his younger brother. Always left out. Always left behind.

"You will not fail me," she whispers, gazing out the balcony again. *"My blessed grandson."*

Quiet minutes pass by as the last of the sun disappears in the horizon. Leo remains silent, watching his grandmother as he feels the soft warmth of her hands beneath his calloused ones. Uncertainty engulfs him as the bedroom door opens, in walking the nurse and doctor. Behind them is Owen, who gestures for him.

Leo gets up as the staff check Rafaella, coming in close to Owen. "What is it?"

"Renato will be here tomorrow morning," Owen whispers.

"We'll be gone before dawn. Leave from Milan instead."

Owen nods, leaving the room as Leo moves over to the balcony. He watches them care for his grandmother, turning his gaze toward the soft brilliance of the evening and sea. A chill brushes over him as he inhales the calm scent of the ocean.

This would be the last time he'd see his grandmother. The last true matriarch of the Luciano and Salvadori family line. He was supposed to find someone to amount up to her legacy? Or someone he could love, but then the only ones he's known to truly love each other were his grandparents.

He opens his eyes, flicking them down towards a vase of lilies. He raises a hand, tracing the petals. His voice barely a whisper, "If that woman existed, where would she even be?"

There's some fussing and his grandmother calls out for him. "Leonardo."

Dropping his hand, he brings his mind to the present. "Coming, nonna."

Right there, Leonardo resigns that the Luciano name will eventually die with him—alone, like his mother had years before.

Across the Ocean
Autumn

Blood is splattered across my glasses.

The pounding of my heart echoes in my head as I stare at

the man crumpled before me. I'm certain he's dead. He hasn't moved. The bullet that hit him in the gut and chest stains his clothes crimson.

Swallowing hard, I glance down at the .45 in my hand.

Fuck.

Distant voices bring my attention back to my surroundings. I'm in a back alley near some warehouses. I'd been creeping through an underground club. And then this dude followed me, and then tried to…to…

The voices get louder, and I finally move. My body shakes as I shove the gun into the small bag I carry. I sprint from the dead body. No point trying to hide him when he's twice my size and has three of my bullets in him. The voices vanish as I keep running, heading for the commercial docks that are close.

My mind reels as I run, keeping my bag close and check over my shoulder. Anxiety ticks over me even when I see no one following, unable to shake the feeling that someone is. Heart racing, I cross behind another warehouse and turn towards the water glistening in the dark night.

Should've never listened to Roger.

Damn it, I knew going to that club was too dangerous, but he wanted *real* proof about Rossi's meth dealings with some big-time lawyer and judge. I don't remember who. Their names merge together as I struggle for breath. This isn't what I signed up for. This fucked up espionage shit. I was a hacker, a computer geek, not some fucking spy.

My lungs constrict, burning as I come to a stop next to some dumpsters. Panting, I check my surroundings then toss the gun and what ammo I have left into one when I see no cameras. I jog, aiming towards another warehouse as my feet ache and throb as I toss my now empty bag into another dumpster.

I pause, thinking of the quickest way back into Manhattan this late at night when I hear voices again. My shoes scrape against the concrete as I spin around. I run towards the end of the warehouse, wincing at the pain in my feet as I come upon the water's edge.

Swearing under my breath, I quickly look around and see some steel drums stacked against the back of the building. As the voices get closer, I scramble towards the drums, hiding behind them as I pull my legs in close and scoot my ass back against the cold asphalt. Cold creeps over my skin, hating I wore such a short skirt and barely a top with the stupid flats I'm wearing. There's even blood on my feet from running.

My throat is dry as I swallow, voices coming closer. They're far enough away I can't hear the words they say, but there's grunting as chains rattle. More scared than I was when I shot and killed someone barely thirty minutes ago, I press against the steel drums trying to be invisible. There's a splash.

Shit. I'm in mob territory still. Right now, I have no idea *who's* I'm in. Petrov's? Gallagher's?

The blood on my hands dries pulling my skin tight, which makes me stare down at them. I'd shot him so close, stupid move, but the fucker was choking me and trying to rip my skirt off. My tights were already torn. More bodies, I'm assuming, are dumped into the harbor. Shivers run over me, causing my stomach to clench. I try to remain still, hoping they'll leave soon. More splashes that vanish quickly. The cold air reaches my burning lungs, hoping six bodies were their max tonight. Voices mutter while footsteps fall away. My feet throb painfully, and I hiss low as I move them a little as I lose feeling in one of my legs. I curse the fact I need to find a way home tonight.

I accidentally bump into one of the steel drums, jostling one. In the quiet night, it rings with a clang that feels damning. Terror floods my veins as I freeze, staring at the dark water before me.

I hold my breath as I listen to someone shouting about checking out the noise. A whimper leaves me as I press further into the shadows.

I'm dead. I'm so fucking dead.

Footsteps come closer as they scrape against the pavement. My lungs ache as I hold my breath, burning as I await my doom that steps towards me. Dark, dress shoes appear. They shine against the low lights of the warehouse. My eyes travel up black slacks, paired with a button-up that's dark. My eyes shoot up to the man who's been sent to investigate the noise.

No.

Horror wraps itself around me, building tears in my eyes as I recognize the young man. He's shorter than his brother, leaner with brown hair that's shaggy and not a lick of facial hair on him. He turns in my direction, and it's then I notice the gun in his hand that points at the ground. In the low light, I make out those brown eyes as they find me.

Matteo Nicholas Marchetti.

I've landed in the worst possible territory—the Marchettis.

Panic encompasses me as my body shakes. My fate flashing before my eyes. I'll be dragged to his brother, Gabriel, the Mafia Don of New York City. Best case scenario he'll kill me quickly. Worst case…he doesn't.

Matteo stares at me, brows pinching together. His jaw works as someone shouts, "What the fuck is it? Matteo!"

I'm half-tempted to run for it, bloodied or not and see how far I get. I could jump into the water, drown myself before Gabriel nabs me and finds out who I work for. Before I can decide, Matteo answers, "Just a fucking cat."

Tears stream down my cheeks.

"All clear," he says, putting the gun away.

"Fine. Kill it or not, we're late for the meeting."

The young man, who's still a fucking teenager, gives me a brief sympathetic expression. He juts his head barely, flicking his gaze in the opposite direction of where the others are.

"Get out." His whisper pierces me before he turns away.

I can't move as I remain seated. Silent, flustered tears run down my cheeks as the noises dissipate. I'm not sure how long I remain there, shivering as boats and a siren sounds in the distance, water lapping. Finally, I stand using the drums to help me as I wince at the pain in my soles and legs. I stare out to where they'd been. Nothing is there.

No bodies. No blood. As if it was just a nightmare.

I shake my head, holding myself close as I go in the direction Matteo pointed in.

"Get out." My murmur is soft as I limp for home, wanting to forget this awful night ever happened. At some point, I think I truly did.

Chapter 1

Let the Games Begin

"Now."

I open the door, striding into the conference room filled with the most dangerous men of New York City.

A large rectangular table sits in the middle of the large room with those men sitting around it in their expensive suits. Four mob bosses; four underbosses. Each has a guard behind them, standing silently as I enter with Jameson following. Grey walls greet me with black tiled flooring that clicks under my heels. The far back of the room is all windows, the wall to my right has a couple of television monitors. A shelving unit is pressed against the window at the far end.

It's deadly silent as the men stare, scowling at me as I stride past to the head of the table and unceremoniously pull back what would be Leo's chair and sit down. I stack my array of folders onto the table. There're low murmurs.

"Gentlemen, if you could have your *personal* bodyguards leave the room," I say, focusing on the corset I wear, hugging my torso firmly. "This is private business for only the head honchos."

"What the fuck is this?"

My gaze lands on the one who spoke. Rossi.

"I called this meeting. Now if you want—"

"Where the fuck is Luciano?" Another questions.

"This is absurd," someone comments.

"Where's your boss, Vasquez?" Rossi asks, glaring at Jameson. "We had—"

"I was *fucking* talking," I interrupt angrily. "Send out your men, before I make you."

"You have no authority, what makes—"

"This does." I hold my left hand up, rings sparkling in the light reflecting off the buildings outside. The men murmur, exchanging looks. "I am Leonardo Durante Luciano's wife. So, I suggest you watch your tone."

The man I know as Nicki DeLuca tries to speak next, "What the fuck are you—?"

"Send out your men, and then we can discuss. *Now.*" All of them look to the other, and I give them the best customer service smile I can muster. I lean back in the chair, gripping the armrests to keep from trembling. "Unless you want to admit you're afraid of a woman."

That makes them rustle, but not obey.

Get the guards out. Another fear.

"Or perhaps you'd like your bodyguards to know some of your dirty secrets? Start some gossiping storms?" I ask, tilting my head. "Sure, you trust your man, but what about another's?"

That does it.

A flash of worry goes across some faces, glancing at one another. I'm about to start airing out dirty laundry anyways, until one of the crime bosses juts his head for his guard to leave.

Ralph Finstrum. Not a mafia boss per say, he's technically not part of the families, but he's been around for so long in the underbelly of New York, he practically is. He holds the most territories after the Marchetti Family.

Others follow Finstrum's lead, sending out their guards in a grumbling manner. It takes longer than I want, but then again, I've got a bit of time to wait on Leo's decision.

When the guards are gone, I'm left with just the bosses and their secondaries. Once the last man steps out, Isaac enters and closes the door to guard the entrance. All the bosses look at each other, then finally to me.

"See? Not so hard," I comment, opening the first folder, rifling through the contents.

"What the fuck is going on?" Rossi asks. "We were called together to discuss Luciano stepping down—"

"Oh, that was a lie." I pull out some photos. A few men scoff, while another grumbles. "You honestly think he's going to step down just like that after you helped sabotage his businesses or listening to a kid who can barely drink?"

"What the fuck do you know?" A different voice speaks, and I look up at Massimo Curione. I glare at him.

"More than you may think."

"Like…*what* exactly?" His voice could be smooth if he wanted it to. Given the defined cheekbones, dark hair, and eyes, he'd be a perfect candidate for a heart breaker. Well, he kind of already was. "Or you just some bitch that Luciano fucked and now he can't get rid of? A gold digger?"

Jameson tenses behind me.

I slide my hands over the table, bringing them back as I lean into my chair. They're brought to my thighs, hiding them underneath the dark tabletop. Calm trickles over me as I feel the "precautions" Chiari placed in here before anyone arrived.

"She's his wife," Jameson answers. "Although you're young Curione, there's certain etiquettes to be had with the wife of the Head Mafia Don. Whether you follow him or not."

"No rules state she can call meetings! Or sit in his fucking seat!" Curione argues, spitting as he looks at the others who sit quietly. Contemplative. I flick my gaze to Finstrum again, who's scowling at the folders.

For him and the others, this isn't the first-time things have been troublesome. There's a weariness on his and Rossi's face. Both of them barely made it with their businesses intact after what I did years ago. DeLuca just exchanges a look with his second in command.

Finstrum and I make eye contact. His frown deepening as I keep my composure. I hadn't taken him down because he killed two other underbosses for trafficking women. He's a slimy bastard, but one who has three daughters, which gave him a soft spot apparently.

Curione continues talking, complaining along with a handful of underbosses as I drown out their voices. Finstrum and DeLuca exchange a look.

"When were you married?" DeLuca asks, stopping the others from talking. The larger man glares at me.

"Before the hit was sent out on me if that's why you're asking." I move my attention to him. "Why? Were you a part of that?"

"Could be lying," Rossi's underboss suggests. "Some ploy—"

"They're married," Jameson states.

"Here. For your leisure." I pull out my copy of our marriage certificate, sliding it across the table.

"She's protected by silent laws older than anyone in this room," Jameson adds.

"We didn't know, no one did I'm guessing," Rossi spits. "If Luciano had said—"

"You'd have killed us together and not tried separately? Like Riccardo and his wife?" The men go still.

"That was his own son's doing," Finstrum says calmly. "And another, who Luciano killed years ago."

"But you're still *capable*…aren't you?" I ask. My heart thunders in my chest as Finstrum looks down the table at me. "Just as you know if you dethroned him, all of you would have a chance at the seat *I'm* in."

"Your husband's seat," DeLuca mentions, sliding those pale eyes at me. "*Now* who's dethroning him?"

"Yes, where *is* your husband…*Mrs.* Luciano?" Rossi asks, smiling like he caught me. "Married or not, you have no say. Unless *you* killed him."

The anger that's been simmering begins to boil. He pronounced 'Luciano' wrong, likely on purpose. They could accuse me all they want, it won't matter. Their condemnation, gaslighting, and lies don't affect me. It's the disrespect towards Leo that makes the shaking in my hands worsen.

"He's still alive. Be thankful that none of you succeeded in that."

"We had no part of what happened days ago." Rossi waves off. "His own men did that. Another reason why *he* should be here, discussing stepping down. He's losing control."

"Oh…really?"

"Yes, really, now call your fucking husband to get—"

"Are we really going to sit here—"

I ignore them as they talk over each other as I open a folder and glance at the photographs Chiari got for me. Evidence of one man's betrayal. My eyes flick up to who it is, grumbling along with the others.

There's movement at the door as Isaac opens it briefly and comes back in with a singular nod.

My eyes go back to the photos from the video footage of a few nights ago. To whom was there, almost killing Leo and some of the Crew.

It's not who I should be focusing on though. I should start tossing their dirty laundry at them; begin my plans for the black-mail that will consume them. Wait it out. I glance at the clock measuring how long I'd have to be in this room with these men. *If* Leo shows up. If not…

Stay on course, Autumn. You can't—

"This is ridiculous, having a woman telling us what to do," Curione speaks, starting to get up and I notice the tremor in his hands. "Luciano is a coward."

Fuck the original plan.

Without another thought, I reach under the table. My hands land on the two handguns Chiari taped underneath, and I roll the chair back. Somehow steady, I aim for Massimo Curione and fire.

I squeeze the trigger twice, hitting him square in the chest. He jerks back down into his seat, gasping as he clutches at the bullet wound. The room erupts as I aim my other gun at Rossi across from Curione. At the same time Isaac pulls out his 9-millimeters, aiming at Finstrum, who's closest, and at his underboss. Jameson does the same to DeLuca and his man across the table. A few minutes pass as the men yell in shock while Curione gasps for breath in his chair.

"A few things to know, *gentlemen*," I warn, glaring at Curione and the others. "One: I own *everything* my husband does, including the mafia and its affiliates. I have *every* right to sit here because he signed over equal control to me months ago. Two: do you really think I'd walk in here without any protection?" I let out an empty laugh, allowing my furious, possessive nature take control. The room goes quiet. "Three: I don't give two fucks about your rules. If I'm irrelevant to them, then they're irrelevant to me."

I look at every boss slowly. Curione last.

"You fucked over my husband," I growl. "You almost killed him, and men I trust and care about. You double-crossed him at that warehouse after using your meeting as a ruse."

He wheezes, pressing against the wound as his second in command next to him watches blankly. Of course, he's not helping, not when he gets what Curione owns if he dies. Or it's the gun aimed at him.

Blood seeps through Curione's suit. "I...I...didn't..."

"Don't lie, Massimo. It's not a good look." I set a gun down, grabbing the photos and toss them at him. I grab the entire folder of pictures of his betrayal, throwing them at the bleeding man. "Just admit it. You were being greedy, hoping to take his position when he died, right?"

Curione's lip curls in answer, and then coughs up more blood.

"Wasn't that the plan? For all of you bastards?" I grab the other gun again, pointing it towards Finstrum who goes still. "You help Matteo get rid of him, who takes over until one of you kills him next? How easy would it be to take out the young buck mafia boss when he isn't looking?" Finstrum's dark eyes meet me straight on.

My stomach churns, clenching onto fury. "You *are* capable but come on…it's practically a movie script."

"You wouldn't understand," DeLuca says, and my aim goes to him. "Luciano was a loose cannon."

"That so?" I suddenly put the guns down, my palms pressing into the table as I lean over the weapons, shielding them from being grabbed.

"If you knew what he was doing, then you'd know he was putting us all in jeopardy."

"I do know," I murmur, breathing deep as I grip my hands together. "And soon you'll be praying that he walks through those doors and beg him to never forsake his position here…especially to me."

"Cause you'll kill us?" Rossi asks, trying to sound cocky.

I smile and all the men jerk at the response. I open a folder, flipping through pictures and grab one. "Rossi…you have disgusting hobbies, I personally think. And I think Finstrum would agree."

Finstrum's brows pinch together as Rossi's face blanches. I shove the pictures across the table. "I think your wife and daughter would agree, knowing you've been screwing underage girls for over the past decade." I grab the last one, deciding to fling out the one that blurs out the girl's body mostly. "Including Finstrum's daughter."

The table shakes as Finstrum grabs the table, veins popping as he strains. I keep going as Rossi pales more.

"DeLuca," I say next, who's eyes snap to me in worry. "I think, there's a couple of politicians who'd *hate* to know you've slipped about their privacy at your clubs. And Hollywood execs. Or I wonder how pissed Rossi will be knowing *you* stole from his shipments two years ago. Oh, and six months ago."

I slide those photos next, and then the spreadsheets.

"Finstrum," I continue. "I believe the IRS will *love* to see all your tax documents of the last seven years. All those offshore accounts, illegal shell companies under certain closed businesses. You're behind on taxes." Those papers go flying across the table, and onto the floor. "I doubt you'll cry over Curione, giving that he was trafficking girls and giving you fucked up coke and weed, which is why your clients were dying."

The men are silent as they glare at each other, a few going pale; others going red with rage. Finstrum looks ready to kill. "Don't worry, I didn't forget your underbosses." I toss another folder, and then another. "From using products they shouldn't, stealing weapons, taking bigger cuts, or selling you out to other bosses."

There're some choking sounds of disbelief, chairs squeaking as they fuss.

"How?" Rossi croaks.

"Ghosts." I place my hand over one of the guns. "You may not remember some of them, but they remember you. Ghosts are very willing to talk, especially when you try to bury them alive."

One of the underboss' looks to where Isaac stands, watching the door.

"Your men won't help you," I announce. "No one will, except one. And if he doesn't walk through those doors in the next hour, *all* of this will be made public. Given over to authorities, news anchors, your associates, and your families."

Finstrum finally stares at me, fear flashing over him. "No, you can't, you'll ruin—"

"I don't care."

Curione chokes, and briefly I meet his dark gaze as he sneers through crimson teeth. "Monstrous bitch," he whispers.

Cold sweeps over me, feeling numb as I remember Leo's cries. The blood on his hands. The devastation in his eyes. All of it churning together as I reach for one of my guns. Jameson stiffens beside me as I aim it at Curione, willing to seal my fate.

Angry tears brim my eyes.

"I will make you all *beg* him to save you from me."

Gunfire splits the room.

Chapter 2

Make Me Your Villain

THE CLOCK TICKS LOUDLY as I sit back, watching the men squirm in their seats. Everything I had in the folders now strewn across the table for them to see. A few men grabbed a couple pages, trying to hide them. Others clutching them in rage. The bones in their closets were out for all to see. They were all fucking over the other. It's almost comical.

Curione slumps dead in his seat, mouth slack as blood drips to the floor.

A few tap their fingers on the table, sweating as they flash their eyes to me or Jameson. On the outside, I sit calmly, but on the inside, I'm trying not to hyperventilate as seconds tick by. Hate and wrath coil inside me, but so does anxiety. I couldn't care less about any of the men at this table, but it's what may happen before the hour is up that I worry. My hand runs over the boning of my corset, wondering what Leo will decide. I had been prepared for either choice, until I killed Curione.

The doors open and everyone jolts in their seats. Most look fearful when they see its Owen, who walks silently towards me and leans down near my ear.

"All their men have been detained. Keep them in the garage?"

"Any word?"

"No."

"Then yes. Easier to round-up." The last bit I say a bit louder. "Send in more guards if you could. Just in case."

Owen nods, walking out of the room. Not long after, the doors open again and in walks Michael with three other bodyguards. Two on each side of the room, keeping their guns casually in front of them.

"This is preposterous," Rossi mutters under his breath.

"Don't like being held hostage?" I ask.

"The disrespect! We are the most powerful men in the city—"

"And yet, a woman has you by the balls." I tilt my head.

"Exactly, you are just some woman Luciano fucks—"

"Shut up, Enzo," Finstrum interjects, fuming. "If you know what's good for you…keep your mouth shut, *pedophile*."

Rossi's eyes widen. "These photos are fake! She's lying—!"

"Shall I show the videos instead?" He better say no because I won't keep anything down.

Finstrum snarls, shutting Rossi up as DeLuca watches them silently. All the men at the table, including his own underboss, slightly move back from Rossi, giving looks of disgust. Rossi goes red, gaping at them and tries to stand, as if to attack me, but Michael quickly shoves him back down into his seat and points his gun at the man's temple.

"Orders, ma'am?" Michael asks.

I almost smile. Yeah, he's growing on me.

Finstrum speaks before me, "As much of a disgusting piece of shit he is, isn't one dead boss enough for today?"

"No." My answer is prompt. All the men at the table shift in their seats. "Unless you're saying that because *you* want to pull the trigger."

Finstrum and I make eye contact. I don't flinch, refusing to break the stare with the older man. His jaw tightens. Caught him. I say, "I would let you, but I'm not stupid enough to give you a gun."

He eases back, folding his hands in his lap. "Kill him yourself then. If you won't give me that dignity in defending my daughter's honor, kill him. As a woman—"

"What do you *fucking* know about being a woman?" I practically sneer. He quiets, but his jaw remains set.

We stare down the other, and I know he's trying to call my bluff as I just did with him— who has the balls to shoot Rossi? Or he wants to see how serious I am about not caring who lives or dies in here.

"What do you think, Sombra?" I ask quietly, glancing back.

"Already changed plans, why not have the bonus of less paperwork?" Jameson's answer is low, surprising me.

Part of me expected him to tell me to 'calm down' or wait for Leo. I look back, meeting his stony gaze, and realize he's testing me, too.

What is it with men and pissing contests?

"So, just kill him?"

His face shows no signs of emotion. Mine toil inside me as I stare at Leo's best friend, consigliere, and co-founder of the *Forgotten Demons*. He said he'd follow me, but to what end? Killing Curione, a newer boss and one who actually pointed a gun at Leo, was one thing. Killing Rossi? Even being a piece of shit, his death would cause a different ruckus. If I don't, my whole threat to them may dissolve. If I do…I'm cementing something I'm not sure of yet, but the anxiety ticking at the back of my neck is telling me no. Wait.

I've already fucked up my original plans by killing Curione, adding another body will complicate things if Leo doesn't show.

Not to mention…something is off. The look in Jameson's eye, similar to when he scrutinized me at the warehouse. Perhaps he's waiting to see if I'll snap like Leo or run screaming. Like he's asking: *Can you actually play boss?*

I look to Isaac, who tries to appear calm, but his eyes yell worry.

"Pull his chair back, Michael," I instruct. He does, and Rossi goes to fight, but the gun against his head makes him freeze. "Turn him toward me. Good, now step back."

Michael steps aside, and the three behind him, try to move

further away. Rossi glares at me, gripping his armrests as his chest rises heavily. Distress flashes as he glances at the gun I grab. Finstrum starts to smile in satisfaction, along with DeLuca.

"My people will come after you, unlike Massimo I have loyal people," he says.

"Not if I send them those pictures, the tapes, the cooked books..." his face falls, "...what? You think I'd have given you *any* respect after death? I'll make sure your wife knows first, so she can burn everything you've touched. Give her a chance to spit upon your ashes."

"You fucking *whore.*"

I aim and fire.

He howls, clutching his groin where blood spills. Thank goodness he was sitting to my right side, and I'm not a terrible shot to miss shooting his dick.

A bit of gratification trickles over me as he cries. That was cathartic.

All the men, mine or not, stare in horror as a few adjust their pants. Death is easy, but losing your cock? Well, that's a different nightmare.

"Satisfied?" I ask Finstrum, leaning back.

He gulps, staring at Rossi who groans and almost falls out of his chair. "For now."

I check the clock. Ten minutes left. Fuck.

DeLuca follows my gaze, and more sweat forms on his brow. Not only could I blackmail them now, but I could take their dicks, too. For these men, that's far scarier than death.

I put the gun down, going the route of appearing bored as the others become more restless. Rossi continues to whimper, holding onto what's left of his junk as I push down the want to hurl. My spine tightens, anxiety yanking at me as I feel sick. *Little longer. Keep it together, Autumn.*

I start to go over every detail on how to handle this if Leo doesn't show. I have a dead man now, and another who's bleeding from his groin, who could die from that alone. I could shove all the men into another room, distract the feds with *Castor 2.0* and the information I have on them. Let them focus on the big fish like Finstrum. My stomach twists as the clock ticks. Or I really could just shoot them. Handle the aftermath differently. Start over. Oh, fuck, I'm losing it if I'm thinking of killing all the men at this table.

I start to worry what Leo decided, wondering if he really did take the plane. Yet, I hope he did and got the fuck out of here. *No... he needs to decide. Finish them if you have to.*

"What if we made a deal?" Finstrum breaks the quiet. "I'm sure we can...give you whatever you want."

"You have nothing I want." I frown deeply. "What I *do* want, you conspired to take from me. If I must, I will do the same with you."

"What happens if Luciano doesn't show?" DeLuca asks. Finstrum soon adds in his own commentary on mafia uprisings, territories, etc.

I ignore his 'villain end speech', looking to Isaac. He opens the door barely, closing it with a shake of his head.

Shit.

I hope Chiari is ready for the hotel to be swarmed by police or help sink bodies into the Hudson. Did Chesty say he knew a pig farm up north?

"...besides, having a woman in charge doesn't seem appropriate."

Finstrum's words bring me back.

I raise a brow, and he holds his hands up. "You've shown you're...capable, Mrs. Luciano, but handling businesses take another skill. We could help provide you more money and power."

A smile forms on my face.

"We understand how serious you are," DeLuca adds, gesturing towards Curione, almost cautiously. The woman from years ago, left for dead, is cackling inside as these men practically beg me. "Even if you've broken rules to—"

"I don't give a fuck about rules, especially when they've been catered towards weak, sadistic *men*," I practically hiss.

DeLuca clears his throat.

"If my husband doesn't walk through that door soon…" I flick my gaze to the clock, then back at the table of mobsters, "…you'll play by *my* rules. Since you all seem so keen in breaking the ones you've made for your own greed."

I meet Finstrum's gaze, flicking them at Rossi next.

The gun is back in my hand, and all their eyes are glued to it. Sweat drips down their temples. I glare at the damning photos across the table.

"How does it feel knowing you're caught?" I ask in a rasped voice. "No way out? Like rats in a cage? Your money won't save you. Your choices have condemned you. All those skeletons out for the world to see?" I grab the final folder, tossing it and the papers scatter over the table. "I will use your secrets to hang you from the Washington Bridge."

Possessive wrath builds inside me, it flourishes through my veins after years of shoving it down. The pain. The fear. The fury. I let it all consume me as the clock ticks. No one gave me mercy when *I* begged.

"You can try to come for me when the clock stops ticking, but know that I will run circles around you, because you all need to learn that there is nothing you should fear more than a woman with years of rage in her."

The room goes cold. Every man frozen. Even Rossi doesn't make a sound as he stares in horror, holding tightly to what I took.

My gaze flicks to the clock. Two minutes.

He's not coming.

He left.

I straighten myself, preparing myself for the next steps. I tell Jameson, "Ve a buscar a la señorita Pierozzi, por favor."

He clears his throat, nods once and goes to the door. He disappears into the hall.

One minute.

I breathe in deep, focusing on the pressure of the corset.

"Mrs. Luciano," Finstrum tries again.

I ignore him, nodding at Isaac to come over. A guard takes his spot near the door, and he comes over for me to give him the gun I didn't fire. The other remains in my hand, oddly not feeling heavy like the one I shot years ago. My chest wants to cave in.

No point dragging this on. Chiari will be up soon, and I need to make my next move.

I'm about to speak, when there's loud voices outside the room, and the doors burst open. Ringer steps in first, and then Enigma. They move to the side as Jameson appears, and then finally…

"Gentlemen, it appears you've angered my wife."

Chapter 3

Lord and Lady

Leo steps into the room with that confidant, commanding air I know well. He's cleanly shaved, dressed in his signature black, the top buttons of his shirt undone. Not a flicker of the man I saw barely hours ago covered in blood. No, instead who stands before everyone is *the* Head Mafia Don of New York City, son of Riccardo Marchetti, Leonardo Durante Luciano with a dangerous gleam in his eyes.

He strides into the room, aiming for me as I begin to stand. Leo shakes his head once, and I remain seated. Rossi suddenly tries to get to his feet, deterring Leo's path. A few of the men stiffen, while others mumble under their breaths.

"Luciano, sh-she shot me…your w-wife—"

"For good reason, I presume?" Leo questions.

"He fucked my daughter!" Finstrum yells suddenly. "He black-mailed her and fucked teenagers!"

Finstrum continues yelling, DeLuca chiming in as Leo's gaze catches mine. I nod once.

Leo holds out his hand, and Michael hands over the gun I gave him. Without warning, Leo shoots Rossi in the head. Blood splatters over the documents and photos. Trickles of it hit the men as

Rossi's body slumps onto the floor. The room goes quiet. Leo gives the gun back to Michael, striding towards me. My heart pounds in my chest as I avert my gaze from Rossi's body.

Carefully, Leo brings his hand to my throat, lightly pressing his palm against the silk of the blouse I wear. I feel metal. He's wearing his wedding ring.

Leo brings his mouth to my ear, murmuring so very low, "Good girl."

The tightness around my chest vanishes as I grip the gun in my hand, smiling faintly at him. His hand lightly squeezes against my throat in a possessive manner.

"Leave us. Wait in my office," he instructs quietly, letting go and stepping back.

I stand, keeping the gun tight in my hand as I walk to the door. I don't look back as Isaac comes up behind me, and I avoid all eye contact as I make my exit.

"Gentlemen," Leo starts to say as the doors shut behind me.

I continue down the empty hall until I reach Leo's office. Isaac shuts the doors behind us. "Miss Autumn…"

I shove the gun at him. Bile builds up from my stomach as I sprint towards the bar area to the bathroom, barely making it to the sink as I hurl finally. My hands shake as I grip the porcelain, releasing what little I had in my stomach. Isaac comes rushing into the bathroom after me, grabbing a towel to help clean up any mess.

"Breathe, Miss Autumn."

My throat scratches as I dry heave, keeping a hand at the bottom of my corset as it presses against my stomach. I close my eyes as I finally stop, breathing through my nose and spit out the last of the bile. The water turns on, washing away what I puked up as I take the towel and wipe my mouth.

"Do you want me to take the corset off?" He asks.

I shake my head. He steps back as I stand fully, turning off the water and lean back against the sink. My hand continues to run over the corset, feeling the velvet and pressure around my body.

Yeah, it's harder to breathe given what I just did, but I don't want it off. I still need it.

"I'm alright," I murmur, tossing the towel aside. "Last minute there…really thought he left."

Isaac is quiet.

My breathing calms, but my hands still shake as well as my legs. Anxiety, pressed down and turned to anger, begins to crawl up my spine again.

"Did I make things worse?" I whisper, finally meeting Isaac's blue eyes.

"You made your point. Both of you. Potentially a new target on your back, but I think you garnered a different type of respect from them."

"Nice answer. Now be more frank, Pretty Boy." I half-smile at him.

He gives one back, leaning against the opposite wall. "You scared the fuck out of them. Including myself, and likely Jameson. But no, I don't think so."

"Jameson was testing me. Along with Finstrum."

"Yes, they were."

"Your thoughts?"

"You succeeded," he says, clearing his throat. "In more ways than one." It's silent a few moments as my limbs become less shaky. "Curione wasn't your first kill, was he?"

I shake my head. His face becomes somber.

"First guy tried to assault me outside a club. Shot him. Second guy, I stabbed after he killed another girl. Roger knew about both. Told me never to speak about it, and that it *happens* on the job." Isaac's eyes widen.

The memories slam into me. The blood on my hands and those lifeless eyes before me. I never truly gave them a second thought. A few times I'd think about those random moments, wondering if Roger would turn me in for murder. Maybe he forgot. At times I did. Blocked out like so many other nights.

"You never spoke about that," Isaac murmurs, voice despondent.

"None of you liked me discussing my undercover days, so murder was definitely off the table. Dr. Maxwell knows." Isaac's brows raise, and I shrug. "We've talked. I've long moved on. And he's a therapist for mobsters, so I'm not worried."

I stare next to Isaac at the cream-colored walls. The anxiety crawling up my spine disappears as I shut off those memories. A different time of nightmares where I did whatever to survive. Perhaps some of my nightmares and panic attacks were from those men, but I never felt sorry for them. Not when they would've done worse.

"None of y'all thought I was…*capable* of murder, huh?" I whisper, staring at the wall not fully present. "Then again, guess their underestimation kept me alive. Except Roger…he always knew. I think he always did."

Suddenly, Isaac comes into my vision. I jerk back as he approaches, but don't pull away when he clutches my shoulders. He strokes a hand over my hair as I stare up at him, seeing melancholy amongst his features, yet there's respect.

"I think you're capable of whatever you wish, Miss Autumn. You don't need to be a man to pull the trigger." Isaac briefly places a kiss on my forehead, pats my shoulder as he gestures toward the bar. "How about some tea? It may be a while until he's…done, well…"

"Renegotiating their lives?" I smirk.

"One way to put it," he mutters.

We walk out of the bathroom. Isaac goes behind the bar, pulls out an electric kettle, and starts to get tea started. He starts to pour himself a drink, and I almost snort when I notice it's a martini.

"We didn't know about Rossi," Isaac suddenly says. "Leo would've…none of us—"

"I didn't know until two months ago, after hacking into his personal mainframe," I interrupt, and he stops to stare at me. "Chiari nor I knew what to do but collected as much evidence as we could until we'd be able to nail him. It was two weeks ago I realized one of the girls was Fintrum's daughter."

Isaac sighs, then sips his drink. "There'll be some upset with his death, until Finstrum drags his name through the mud."

"Which he definitely will if he walks out of that boardroom."

"Curione's death will have less of an impact, given how new he still was. Either his underboss or another will take his seat, Leo may have more of a say on who now."

I lean against the counter, running my hand over my torso. I glance at his gun on the counter, next to the one I used. My stomach flips.

"He'll be seen as the savior as it were, they'll listen to his judgement now," Isaac says slowly. "Not to mention that amount of blackmail would keep anyone in line or the fear of his wife shooting off their cocks."

I smirk, but he winces.

"Wasn't the plan at first," I say. "Or Curione's death. See? Sometimes my plans don't go my way."

Isaac's quiet as he turns away, getting my mug ready as the water starts to boil.

"What would you have done if he hadn't shown, Miss Autumn?" He asks, and I inhale slowly, then let out the air in a controlled breath. He stops, turning around to face me with that worry in his eyes again. "You were going to kill them all, weren't you?"

I stare down at the counter, tracing a finger along the woodgrain.

"It crossed my mind." Few hundred times in five minutes. "But, no…I'd have fulfilled my promises of dumping everything onto public servers. Given over the men who were alive, let the feds take them along with all the information and bribe them with *Castor 2.0*, probably slip Curione's body out of the building. There's more blackmail for people not in that room, help distract them for me to get out of the state next if that was the case."

Isaac pours my cup of tea, then adds the proper amount of

cream and sugar before placing it in front of me. "How much exactly did you acquire with…*Eleanor*, was it?"

I nod. "Information on any association with the mobs or those who've done any dealing with them in the past. Such as politicians, real estate brokers, investors, CEOs, and whoever else fits the bill. Figured if the blackmail for the mobsters wouldn't work, then I'd go directly to another source that would fuck them over to save their own hides."

Isaac leans onto his elbows, putting his hands under his chin as he cocks his head at me. "How did you get all of this so quickly in only a few months?"

"*Eleanor* was built to be simple and quick once you know what you're looking for," I say with a shrug.

"Under all our noses, too?"

I lean in closer. "The last time I did this was on a battered Toshiba with the worst RAM and WIFI speeds. This time I had a high-tech laptop with software I've only dreamed of using."

Isaac snorts, then sips his drink. "That's what Enigma and Iron Buffalo get for gifting you a laptop."

I sit at Leo's desk, nursing the tea Isaac made for me over thirty minutes ago. Owen delivered my laptop back to me, along with my CDs. I didn't fully relax until I checked that all of them were accounted for, double and triple checking. The briefcase they're in sits before me, open with *Castor 2.0* sitting on top. I work on the laptop, making certain the blackmail I kept off the CDs are stored solely on this computer, cutting off any way of connection to networks. After I'd gotten the last of the tapes from Logan and Mikey, I had them destroy everything. What's left of the blackmail digital footprint was in that briefcase and on this computer.

All I'm missing is *Eleanor*.

I finish, then close the laptop and place it into the briefcase, locking it shut. There're two keys; one goes inside Leo's desk under a false bottom in his top drawer, the other goes inside my pocket.

My hand runs over my corset for almost the hundredth time as I sit back, taking a long breath. Anxiety pricks along my neck, unsure how much longer Leo will be. I should be thinking about what will happen after, but all I can think about is him. Questions whirl inside me, making my stomach twist.

Is he angry with me for hiding all this from him? Not telling him about the truth with *Eleanor*. Or perhaps pissed I used the hotel's security to help obtain information on dozens of people. Or will he not trust me after I lied? After me telling him not to hide things from me, I hid from him. Except, I knew he'd have stopped me, another attempt to protect me.

Tears threaten to brim my eyes, either from exhaustion that creeps along my skin or just the tumultuous day.

The door opens suddenly.

Jameson walks in, shutting the door behind him.

"Are they done?"

"They're leaving now," he answers roughly. "We have to take extra precautions given we disarmed their men. Leo will be taking you to the penthouse for a few days."

My brows scrunch. "Why?"

"Not safe at the hotel. Need you to stay low."

I scowl.

He stops before the desk, glimpsing at the briefcase. He begins to reach for it. "I'll put this in his safe—"

Abruptly, I stand and slap my hand upon the leather case. His gaze snaps to mine, frowning deeply.

"This needs to be locked up," he states.

"Not here."

"This office is the best place—"

"No. It's not." He starts to argue, but I speak over him. "*I* decide where this goes. Not you."

"Leo's still boss. He came back."

"This is *mine*, not his." The snarl in my voice is harsher than I intend. His eyes flare, jaw tensing. My chest tightens, and my legs suddenly fccl like jello.

Shit, I was more in control with those mobsters than with him. It's because he's Leo best friend and confidant. I *have* to work with Jameson, even if I don't agree with how he wants to help Leo. Or maybe it's because he can't seem to decide whether to handle me with kid gloves or not.

This time, he doesn't back down. "Autumn."

"Were you testing me in there?" I ask suddenly. His expression remains hardened. Time seems to stretch as we glare at each other. My hand flexes against the leather, stomach twisting. Finally, I whisper, "What do I have to do for you to trust me again with him?"

Those golden-brown eyes soften only a smidge, almost sad.

"I came back, just like him."

His throat works before his gaze goes back to being stern. He answers, "You weren't here the night before he met you."

Confusion contorts my face. What? "Jameson—"

The doors slam open. I jolt, standing straight as Leo enters with Rudy right behind him. Rudy's face shifts into a dangerous expression, glaring at Jameson.

"You were supposed to coordinate with Ringer and Enigma for a route to the penthouse," Leo states coldly towards Jameson. "Bond and I will finish up here."

Jameson barely flinches, putting his hands in his pockets with a stony expression. "Where do you want the CDs?"

Leo's brows furrow deeply, flicking his eyes to the briefcase where my hand still lays. He snaps his gaze back to Jameson. "She decides. Now leave."

Silently, Jameson strolls out of the office with Ringer close behind. Leo shuts the door as I remain in my spot, suddenly frozen as he turns back to me. The rigidness of his expression has somewhat subsided as he walks toward the desk, then stops a few feet from it. Those harsh hazel eyes remain on me.

If someone had told me I held this man while on his knees,

crying against my rain-soaked clothes, I'd have never believed them.

His expression shifts as he reaches into his suit jacket, pulling out a disc.

"You hid it inside Nicholas Cage's first movie," he says with such softness it startles me.

"Most think it's *Valley Girl*," I whisper. "But *Fast Times at Ridgemont High* is, just as—"

"Nicholas Coppola." I nod my head stiffly. "I know Castor is from *Face/Off*, but not sure which film Eleanor comes from."

I clear my throat. "*Gone in Sixty Seconds*. His car."

"Fitting."

"I thought so," I whisper.

He hums momentarily before stepping closer to hold the disc over the desk to me. "Take it. *Eleanor* is yours. Not mine."

I stare at the man across from me, glancing down at the ring upon his left hand that I've waited months to see. My program in his hands, more valuable than that ring. It's worth my life. My damnation. My queen piece in this game of chess.

Unexpectedly, I'm back to a moment in time that feels so far away. A time when I could pretend to be someone else, working in a café with nothing to her name. A stranger people rarely looked twice at. Until one evening, a man tried to pay me to dry clean my jeans.

The desk becomes a simple barrier between us as that counter had been. His hand is steady, holding it out for me to take. Instead, I wrap my hands around his, gently pushing it toward him. "Keep it."

The rigidness along Leo's face starts to vanish. "Autumn."

"Save it for a rainy day."

His stark expression disappears. I smile softly, knowing what I'm giving up, but also what I'm gaining. He made his choice; it's time for mine. "Checkmate, Leo."

"Autumn—"

There's a loud knock. Swiftly, that stony mask is plastered on his face again. He shoves *Eleanor* back into his jacket, then turns toward the door. "Enter."

They open to reveal Isaac. "Ready to go, Spartan."

"Good," Leo answers, then turns back to me. This time he holds out his empty left hand, eyes finding mine.

I grab the briefcase, come around the desk and slip my hand into his. His fingers grasp mine, leading us out of the office. Before we enter the main elevator, I hand the briefcase to Isaac, and say, "Give this to Bobby. Tell him I'll see him soon about it."

"Straight away, Miss Autumn."

Leo and I step onto the elevator, doors closing and leaving us alone. It's silent.

For the first time since I met him, I'm not sure how to talk to Leo.

Chapter 4

The Night Belongs to Us

The normalcy of the hotel lobby is surreal.

We pass people as they check-in, other groups are going to dinner or taking the elaborate stairs to the ballrooms. None of them know what happened at the top of the tower. What *could* have happened.

Animal and Chesty meet us at the main entrances, walking us through the revolving doors as I give a slight nod to the doorman working. Ringer waits in our SUV as Leo helps me in and then shuts the door after himself. Chesty gets into the front with Ringer before we drive off, leaving the hotel behind.

"Update on the others," Leo states as we pass the garage. I notice black SUVs leaving.

"DeLuca is the last to leave in five minutes," Chesty answers. "No issues, apart from some grumpy bodyguards who were detained for better than an hour."

"Finstrum's already asked for a meeting," Ringer adds.

"He can wait." Leo lounges back in his seat.

This feels more surreal than the hotel lobby. The odd calmness Leo possesses boggles me as I try to wrap my head around everything. Is this how he feels after one of my panic attacks? The way I bounce back sometimes? It's strange being on the other side.

His hand still grasps mine. It's the only reassurance I have that I didn't completely screw things up. My anxiety screams that he's angry, warning me to run. It takes all my willpower not to flinch every time he moves. I remain frozen as Leo converses with the other two, discussing plans for the next few days. I start to blur things out when they mention disposing of the bodies from the warehouse.

It's completely dark outside when we arrive to the penthouse building. The other two don't follow us out of the car as we exit, going inside the quiet building. I'm able to crack a smile when I see Xavier.

"Miss Watson, it's good to see you home safe," he greets, grinning. "Mr. Luciano, all security protocols have been implemented. If you need any more assistance, please let me know."

Leo nods at him as we approach the elevators, and they open for us. Leo instructs, "I want no disturbances, from *anyone* unless she or I give permission."

Xavier flicks his gaze between us. "Of course, sir."

We step into the elevator, doors closing once more to leave us on our own. Once the first light flashes to the next floor, Leo loosens a long breath and some of the stiffness in his body relaxes. His brows pinch close, looking up slightly at the ceiling.

I'm still unsure what to say, quiet as we ascend for home.

What the fuck are you supposed to talk about? Why wasn't there a manual on how to handle hiding top-secret information, including a hacking program you created from your secret husband after surviving several hits on both of you.

Face/Off was more believable.

We finally arrive, heading into the penthouse after what feels like forever since we were last here. Finally, I let go of Leo's hand, wrapping my arms around myself as I step into the living room space. Leo turns the lights on, bringing up only a few at a dim level.

I turn on the fireplace, allowing the crackling to bring noise to the space as orange flames flicker shadows.

After minutes staring into the flames in silence, I turn towards Leo who stands at the edge of the living room. Against the low light and dancing shadows of the fire he appears foreboding.

"I'm sorry." I break the quiet. Leo tilts his head in confusion, brows furrowing. "I lied to you for months, Leo."

"Technically you never lied." A half-hearted, exasperated laugh leaves me. Leo slowly pulls his suit jacket off, folding it over the sofa edge, then pulls out the disc. "It was smart for you not to reveal this. Keep *Eleanor* hidden, even from me."

"I never wanted to use it again," I say softly. "I'd have been buried with it if I could."

"I know."

"Except, I couldn't get the guilt in your eyes to leave me. The pain and struggle I saw. I couldn't keep watching you destroy yourself. I hoped I'd never use it, a precaution for years later maybe. I just couldn't not...*do* anything, but..."

I rub my hand over my chest, breath hitching as that anger comes back. That all-consuming anger I'd felt the last few days simmers with grief and terror. The scene of walking in on him at the warehouse comes back. The realization he was alone and shattering.

"They kept me away from you." My voice darkens, throat tightening. Tears form in my eyes as I clench my hands. "All of them. Mob bosses. Brothers. The Crew. I couldn't *get* to you, and when I finally did, you were *alone*. You were alone covered in blood and panicking. *They left you alone.*"

"Autumn—"

"It was a mirror, a horrific, agonizing mirror," I continue, hands shaking as I move towards him. "Someone forced to make impossible decisions that would make them the villain, it was cruel to leave you alone to take on those burdens."

"I ordered them to stay out."

"All the more reason for *someone...anyone* to be in there with you. I don't care what you did to those men. I have no pity or mercy left to give, but what that was…it wasn't business. It wasn't protecting me. It wasn't maintaining control. You were punishing yourself, and they were helping you do that."

The disc clatters to the ground. Leo's eyes widen.

My whole body trembles as that statement sinks. The lines between his brows soften as his face falls like I've found his final secret.

"You went from punishing every person who's ever hurt me to punishing yourself," I whisper, trying to keep my tears at bay. "The moment they said it was Matteo, I knew you'd blame yourself. You take *everything* upon your shoulders from the MC, the hotels, your brothers, the mafia, to me. And so many of them have deceived you, including me, even if you refuse to be angry over it. You've been betrayed. You've been blackmailed. And you've been coerced into a life you didn't want!" I throw my hand towards the windows. "Your own employees turned on you. But the worst is that your younger brother, whom you've done all that you could to protect from monsters like your father and Gabriel, backstabbed you." My hands fall. "I couldn't let you keep doing this alone anymore. So, I used what I had left, even if it meant keeping a secret from you."

His eyes glisten with tears, but they don't fall. We're both quiet, only the crackling fire filling the silence. He asks, "Did you want me to leave?"

"It wasn't my choice."

"Did you want me to leave, Autumn?"

"Leo."

"Autumn. Did you—"

"Why did you stay?" I counter. His jaw tightens, hand flexing at his side. "I made my choice, which was to follow you wherever you fucking go. Wherever you decided."

Leo steps closer, reaching for my hand and I feel him trembling like me. My breath hitches as a tear falls down my cheek, whilst his thumb moves over my rings.

His voice is soft; fragile almost as he looks into my eyes. "I couldn't leave you."

My throat goes dry as my stomach twists. Should I have given him the option of me leaving with him instead? Would that have changed his answer? Had I not given him a real choice? Questions whirl inside, wondering if I'd made things worse. His other hand comes up to cup my cheek.

"My dear Watson, if you told me to walk off a bridge, I would." My eyes widen in horror. This was *not* where I wanted this conversation to go.

"Don't say that."

"If you told me to walk through fire, I would."

"Leo, stop."

"I'd jump off a cliff or drive my last Harley off the end of a road if you told me to."

"Stop. No."

"Do you want to know why I'll never be angry with you? Whatever you do or hide, let it be mountains of documents, software you create with your brilliant mind, or handling a meeting of mobsters on your own?"

Trembling engulfs my chest as I clutch his hand, trying to focus on the touch of his other upon my cheek. I barely whisper, "Why?"

"You choose me first. Always." Leo's thumb strokes my face, while his other hand brings ours up to kiss my knuckles. "No one else truly has. Not ever for me."

He places our joined hands against his chest. His voice almost cracks as he speaks.

"Always family first. Always business first. Always money. Always something *from* me. But you...Autumn Watson Luciano choose me...*me* every time. Not the mafia don. Not The Spartan. Not the CEO. Not as a Marchetti or Luciano. Not as anyone else, other than the man you married."

My chin quivers, tears falling. Him and his damn declarations.

He lifts my chin, wiping away tears. "You would never ask me to do those asinine things for you, because I know how much you love me. I trust you with every fiber of my being, so that anything you say I'll do. Deep down, I know within my soul you'll protect me. It sounds incredibly fucking selfish, but I don't fucking care. Only for you, am I willing to go to my knees for. Happily, and in wanting of whatever you order of me."

The shaking stops. "Leo…"

"Did you want me to leave, dear Watson?"

My throat works, wanting to sob as I remember that fear in the boardroom. How much more terrified I was at the thought of him leaving, and how selfish that felt. I answer as more tears fall down my face, averting my gaze from his. "No."

His hand grips mine against his chest.

"Then I made the right choice." My eyes snap to his.

Leo frames my face with both hands, holding me gently. "Tear apart the mafia, I don't care. Scorn my family. Dismantle what I built for them. Destroy it all and do what I couldn't do. So, help me God, just allow me to remain at your side." The tears in his eyes finally fall, shining in the faint light. "My first choice will *always* be you. My dear wife. My Tesoro. My Dear Watson."

The tightness around my throat makes it hard to swallow, but I get past the lump and tell him in a rasped command, "*Never* tell me goodbye again."

"As you wish…" another tear slips down his face, "…Sarah."

My heart squeezes, breath hitching as I reach up to catch those falling tears. I move my hands towards the nape of his neck, gently pulling him down for a tender kiss. The last of the anger is drowned out by the feeling of him, striking through my core. Relief floods me as I kiss him fervently.

"I love you," I gasp against his lips. "You're not alone, baby. I love you."

"I know, dear wife."

We hold each other desperately, kissing feverishly as the past few days slam into us. The need for more with every touch. Leo's hands travel down the back of my corset, trailing over the lacing. My own hands dip under his shirt to feel his bare chest. Our movements are slow as hands roam over our bodies. I start to unbutton his shirt, going slow until I get to the last one. Leo, while still kissing me, undoes his sleeves and peels off his shirt. My hands press against the warmth of his skin, trailing over tattoos and muscles. His chest rises heavily with each long breath as Leo presses his forehead against mine. Our lips are barely touching, hot breaths mingling with the other.

"Check in," I murmur.

Leo takes my left hand, putting it against his beating heart. "Emerald."

My hands trail up towards his neck, gripping him as I go back to kissing him. Leo sighs against my mouth, hands roving over my corset.

"Turn around, sweetheart," he says against my lips. I do as he asks. In a silent command, he moves me forward to be more within the light of the fire. "Why the corset?"

"Helps anxiety," I answer, staring over at the flames.

I can just barely feel his fingers running down the lacing. His other hand strokes up over my shoulder, coming around to gently place the palm of his hand against the hollow of my neck.

A sigh leaves me as the familiar gesture tells me this is real. I'm home with Leo. I close my eyes as I begin to lean back into his embrace. Leo kisses behind my ear, my jaw, and along my neck. A resurgence of relief trickles over me with a longing that aches for him.

"Did you choose green for me?" He asks against my ear.

"Remind myself that I belong to you."

Leo carefully tilts my head, using the hand against my throat for me to look over my shoulder. Hazel eyes meet mine, glimmering from the firelight.

"We belong to each other, dear Watson."

A small smile is my response. He kisses my temple, loosening his hold on my throat as he steps back slightly. His free hand roams down the back of the corset, and there's a tug at the bottom. Keeping one hand upon the hollow of my neck, he unlaces the corset I wear. There's only the sound of our breathing, the fire-place, and the swishing of the laces being pulled free. Almost too slowly, the constriction around my torso is taken away. My chest expands and I breathe deep. The corset falls unceremoniously to the floor as my body shudders, going back to its natural state and not tightly kept together. My legs feel wobbly as I inhale long breaths.

Leo then starts to pull off my silk blouse, briefly taking his hand away from my throat before putting it back once the top is tossed aside. There's a soft snicking sound, and he undoes my bra single-handedly, which falls next at my feet.

My breath hitches. A shiver runs over my skin now topless like he is. Leo moves, pressing his chest to my back as he winds his arm around my torso then cups one of my breasts. His face nuzzles against the crook of my shoulder, inhaling deep as he holds me. I reach up, clutching the arm that's around me.

"I was afraid I'd never see you again. Hold you in my arms again." Leo's voice is rough and hoarse.

I lean my head against his. "So was I."

Leo lets go of my throat, placing his entire arm over the top of my chest. He holds me close, grasping me as I cling to his arms. Standing so close to the fire, sweat starts to form and I can feel it begin to trickle down my skin as we remain where we are. Almost too scared to move.

Finally, Leo starts to. His hands slide down the sides of my body, moving over my hips. I let go of him as he reaches around, undoing my pants to pull them down along with my underwear. I almost want to giggle at him on how he undresses me. I feel him kneel behind me, having me step out and away from the fabric. I hear them tossed aside, waiting for him to take his pants off next. Instead, Leo gently starts to turn me to face him.

About halfway there, I freeze remembering the blood. The sobbing. The anger. The horror.

I clutch his hands that now gently grip my thighs, not at all the frantic strength he had before. He's far more tender and practically delicate with me. Tears want to form as I stare into the fireplace with Leo still kneeling next to me.

"Stand up," I rasp.

"Autumn."

"Please."

"Dear Watson. Look at me." I close my eyes, hoping he'll stand up. "Please."

I open my eyes to the flames, unable to find refusal in my heart. Slowly, I turn the rest of the way to face Leo. His hands softly hold my hips with his head tilting back to gaze up at me. My throat tightens as I stare down at him. My hands almost shaking as I place them over his.

"Do not fear me in this position," he whispers. My chin quivers as those hazel eyes, gentle and longing look up at me reverently. "Because it's only for you, my dear wife."

Shadows play upon the starkness of his tattoos. Glistening tears, unshed lie within his eyes. Leo leans forward, kissing the top of my thigh and then to my stomach. My breath shudders as I place my hands on top of his head, clutching his hair. He continues to kiss my skin, moving over to the other side. The images of earlier start to vanish at his gentle touches. He kisses above my hip dip, and a giggle suddenly comes out of me.

"There she is," he murmurs against my skin. "La mia bellissima moglie."

My fingers thread through his dark hair. "Mio marito."

Leo looks up, giving me a faint smile. Finally, he stands, but swiftly picks me up in his arms. I almost giggle again as he walks over to the couch, sitting down with me straddling his lap.

My hands trail up his chest as his lips find mine. We kiss, hands running over the other's body and my hips begin to gyrate against his thighs. The fabric brushes against my skin as I push my chest closer to his in need. One of Leo's hands travels below my belly button, fingers skimming over my sex. My breath hitches as he continues to stroke with a singular finger.

"Check in," he says against my lips.

"Green," I rasp.

Leo brings his hand up, sucking on two of his fingers while keeping eye contact with me. A shudder rolls over me as he moves his hand back down again, slowly inserting a finger inside me. I grip his shoulders, bringing my head down into the crook of his neck. He begins to work me gently, thrusting his hand below as his thumb begins to circle and play with my clit. My legs start to tighten, but he opens his legs to keep mine apart. I'm panting, feeling the heat of the fire at my back as he pushes two fingers into me.

Soft lips kiss my neck while his other hand strokes up and down my spine. I sigh with contentment, holding onto him for dear life. He opens his legs more, making mine spread before him as he twists his hand inside me. His palm comes against my sex, pressing forward as he hooks his fingers.

My hips move on their own, trying to ride his hand as I start to lean back. My head tilts back, closing my eyes I cling to his shoulders for support. Leo's hand is placed at the center of my back, spreading his fingers as he leans in to start kissing the top of my breasts. His tongue slides over my skin, down towards my nipple and sucks. Entire body enflamed with pleasure; I jolt forward for his fingers to sink further into me. They work below as he licks and nips at my breasts, moving from one to the other. Nails digging into his shoulders, I grip him to keep from falling over, unable to keep my hips still. My legs try to squeeze together as pleasure zaps up through my spine, rolling over my skin as my muscles shake.

All of a sudden, Leo stops. His hand pulls away and I snap open my eyes to watch him lick his fingers clean. My chest rises heavily, trying to catch my breath as I wait for him to go back to what he was doing. A ravenous look is in his gaze as his mouth quirks.

"Stand up, sweetheart."

"Leo—"

"I want to be fully inside you when you come."

I blink at him, then my hazy, pleasure filled brain finally gets on board. I move off him, and he stands quickly shucking off his pants and underwear.

"Lay your chest onto the table," he instructs gently.

I get onto my knees next to him, setting my torso onto the stone coffee table that's between the couch and fireplace. The table is surprisingly warm as I wiggle a little on the textured surface. Leo kneels behind me, carefully taking my hands and placing them above my head to grip its edge. His hands run down my back, stopping at my hips.

"Check in," he whispers, as his warm body hovers over mine.

"Green."

"Good girl."

A whimper comes out of me, filled with want and anticipation. His hand trails around, stroking his fingers once more through my sex as he lifts my hips slightly. Leo positions his cock at my entrance, and then slowly pushes inside. I grip the table, arching my back as he pulls away and thrusts forward again. He continues at the slow pace, inching his way into me as I push back against him. Finally, his hips meet mine, filling me completely.

Sweat covers my body, droplets trickling to the table as I feel Leo's sweat sheen body slides against my skin. One of his hands is placed over mine, while the other massages his fingers into my hip and ass. I stare into the crackling fire as Leo thrusts his cock into me at a slow pace. He doesn't go hard, doesn't bang my hips against the edge of the table, instead he's tender and precise.

Leo fucks me on our coffee table before the fireplace. Shadows play upon the walls as I feel his sweat drip onto my back. My body shakes as his cock strokes inside me, ecstasy racing towards me. Kisses are placed at the base of my neck, trailing down my spine as I start to moan and grind against him every time he sinks back into me.

"Leo," I plead, grasping at the stone surface beneath me, clutching the edge for dear life. Pleasure courses through me, desire tingling at the base of my spine. Muscles clench around him, whilst my fingers dig into the stone as his hand grips mine. "Leo."

His tongue trails up my neck, kissing and nipping at my shoulder. "Come for me, sweetheart. Come with me."

My body tenses as he thrusts, hips flush with mine. The orgasm washes over me as Leo groans above me, everything going rigid as I vibrate with pleasure. Delight fills me as I struggle to breathe against the stone, screaming silently as he grinds his hips forward. My legs tremble, trying to remain where they are. Leo moans alongside me, and then starts to lift me up with him still inside me to sit back against the couch. Arms wrap around my torso as he leans me towards him. My head lolls back onto his shoulder as I clutch his arms.

I breathe heavily, blinking. Through my haze of euphoric bliss, I glance down at the table and see the imprint of sweat from my naked body on the stone.

Holy shit.

"I love you," Leo whispers against my ear. "I love you."

I close my eyes, and respond, "I love you, Leo…through heaven and hell."

Chapter 5

You're The Top

My eyes snap open.

I stare at the ceiling, short of breath as I shake off the feeling of falling and crashing. Clearing my throat, I sit up and glance over at Leo sleeping, facing away from me. I take a deep breath, smelling the familiar scent of our bedroom. We'd showered, had a brief dinner, sex again, and fell asleep promptly after. Apparently, distance doesn't just make the heart grow fonder, but hornier.

I step out of bed, pulling my robe on as I leave the bedroom. A couple lights are on low, the fireplace dark and cold, but I catch sight of the coffee table. The outline of my body is still there. I stare down at it, blinking in disbelief at the rough surface that now has… well, my boobs on it.

"Ohhh, you're gonna have some explaining to do Lucy," I mutter, hoping that fades before anyone else comes here.

My stomach suddenly grumbles, hunger pulling at me. I glance at the time, realizing its barely past midnight. I'd be surprised how early we went to bed, but who knows the last time Leo slept.

I go to the kitchen, grabbing cereal for a late-night snack. Once my bowl is made, I lean against the counter and stare at where we had our fiery sex session. We didn't talk about things I'd hoped to, but breakfast will no doubt be filled with 'wonderful' discussions. Or some stuff could remain boxed away. Or we stay up here forever. The sugary flakes crunch in my mouth as I try not to overthink.

I really should just go back to bed.

A warning prick slides along my neck, and I pause. My body straightens as I search around me, putting the bowl down. Anxiety crawls faintly, but it's there still as I step around the island counter and peer into the dimly lit space. My heartbeat quickens as I search the darkened penthouse. No noise. Nothing out of the ordinary.

"Shit, get it together, Autumn...no one's hiding in the damn penthouse."

The worry doesn't lessen. An odd horror that I'm alone again digs at my chest. I tiptoe back to the bedroom, peering through the darkness and find Leo's sleeping outline. A shaky breath comes out. He's fine.

See, you're awake, home, and not at Snake Eyes' bar.

Crud muffins. I rub my head and begin to head back for my cereal until Leo starts groaning. He grunts, then suddenly thrashes and grasps the blankets. More groans from him turn into whimpers. Quickly, I go to him and sweep my hand over his head, hoping to calm him.

"You're alright, baby," I whisper, putting my hand on his chest.

He goes still. Faintly, he murmurs, "Autumn."

I rub my hand on his chest, waiting to see if he'll wake up. He inhales deeply, but doesn't thrash again. I lean down, placing a kiss on his forehead. Leo's eyes remain closed as he begins to sleep peacefully.

Might as well make sure one of us gets sleep tonight.

I adjust the blankets to cover him more, beginning to leave the bedroom.

He mumbles, "Autumn."

I glance over my shoulder. He's still asleep. I sigh, leaning against the doorway as I debate bringing my cereal in here to keep an eye on him. About to leave again, his next mumbling makes me freeze.

"Mistress."

My stomach drops. A constriction forms around my chest as I stare at him. There's no movement, but he mumbles again, "Autumn...mistress."

There's a twist in my stomach as I try to decipher what he's saying, could be dreaming about. He'd never cheat, not after everything we've been through. Not to mention, why would he call someone...

The air whooshes out of my lungs as I scramble out of the bedroom. My feet almost trip over themselves in the hall as I rush to the bookshelves, frantically going through the titles. My fingers run over spines searching for the ones Dr. Maxwell told me to get. *"I think it'll help you understand him."*

Finally, I find the book on various power dynamics in BDSM and flip through the chapters. The pages come to the section I need, and I move closer to one of the lamps to read the words more clearly. My breath catches as I skim through the examples from Tops/Bottoms, Doms/Subs, Master/Servants, and...Mistresses.

I freeze, staring at a black and white photo.

Fragments of memories slam into me. Moments I overlooked or hadn't noticed because I didn't *understand* him yet. I was still learning.

"Only you, am I willing to get on my knees for..."

"...if the power exchange ever changes, you can."

"I belong solely to you."

"You own me."

"Don't fear me in this position."

All those declarations. In the shower at the estate. Yesterday and tonight. The fear in his eyes of me leaving. Every time he was on his knees.

The photo strikes through me. It's of a man kneeling with his palms facing up, while the handle of a whip lifts his chin. Eyes downcast as he wears nothing. Yet, all I can see is Leo on his knees before me; hazel eyes burning with desire.

Leo's not wholly a Dom.

After hours pouring over my BDSM books, I finally go back to bed. Except, I barely sleep. My mind searches through all the passages I read as if I was the Dom, not the Sub. Stricter protocols. Flipped dynamics. Common and uncommon needs. Tops versus Doms. Anything to help me talk to Leo and understand.

Light peeks through the windows. I check the clock, grumbling to myself. Of course, I'd squander the first real night being home. Giving up on trying for any sleep, I decide to go get a head start on coffee. Maybe watch *Secretary* for shits and giggles.

I slowly get out of bed, while Leo remains asleep. Right then, I decide if I ever need information out of him, I'm making him go to sleep since that's what gives him loose lips. I snort a laugh under my breath, covering my mouth as I leave the bedroom.

I rub my head as swirling thoughts plague me. Shaking my head, I start on the espresso machine and then the coffee pot. I'm half concentrating on making coffee when I hear a noise from the bedroom. I pause at the stove, scrunching my brows when I hear Leo's distressed call, "Autumn?"

I put the kettle down, about to answer when heavy footsteps sound next. Leo appears from the hall in nothing but his underwear. The instant he sees me, practically panting, he falls back against the wall in relief. His chest rising heavily as he scrubs his hand over his face. I practically rush to him.

"Fuck, I thought I was dreaming again," he mutters. "You're here."

"I'm here." I press my hands against his chest, feeling his erratic heartbeat. He releases a long sigh, wrapping his arms around me for a tight hug.

"Just making coffee," I say.

"Thank you." He kisses my head, then strokes my hair back, exhaling harshly as he pulls away. "I'll be right back to start breakfast."

"I could do it," I suggest, giving a cheeky smile. He raises a brow. "Cereal counts."

"Wait for me, dear Watson."

He disappears into the bedroom, and I hear the bathroom door close. A sharp exhale leaves me as I go back to the kitchen. While finishing his Americano, I'm back in deep thought.

Does he know he's a Switch? What if last night was really just a dream? And I'm overthinking...again? He may not know or wants to be dominated. No, he'd know. He was murmuring Mistress, he *has* to. He's a trained Dom, he *has* to know, right? But then why wouldn't he have brought it up? Then again, we've had other things to concentrate on lately. When do I even bring this up? Kind of got a whole other mess to worry about outside of here.

I put Leo's mug down, turn to grab mine and some creamer from the other counter. I'm so caught up in my head, that when Leo's hand touches my hip, I yelp and drop my mug of coffee. It clatters against the counter—coffee and creamer spilling. Leo yanks me back before it can drench me, liquid dripping onto the floor around my feet. My heart pounds as I stare at the small mess, swearing under my breath.

"Son of a cheese biscuit."

"Are you alright?" Leo asks, turning me around to briefly scan my body.

"Fine," I grumble, shaking my socked feet and realize they're already wet. Ew, great. Frustration bubbles up, tears threatening to come on top of everything else boggling my brain. "It's fine."

"I'll clean this up. Go change," Leo says softly. I don't move, staring down at my feet. Leo cups my cheek, caressing my skin with his thumb. "Autumn. It's okay, just spilled coffee, right?" I nod my head. "It's been a long week. We'll take it easy the next few days. Now, go change out of those socks."

He places a kiss on my forehead, and I avert my eyes still as I finally move. I head into the bedroom, close the door, and silently scream into my hands. Tearing off my socks next, I groan under my breath.

"For the love of Nick Cage," I grumble, throwing the wet socks into the hamper and then head to the dresser. I slam open the drawer, staring down at the array of fuzzy socks. I let out a long breath, gripping the edge of the wood as I shove away tears. "It's not that big of deal. The coffee. The fucking kink. Quit overthinking. You've barely slept, and it's been a long ass couple of days. From evil brothers, shooting crime bosses, motorcycle fucking chases, and near deaths, except hey let's talk about being a Sub or Dom. Sure, Autumn, let's ask your controlling, strict, mafia boss biker husband if he wants to be dominated. Can't be hard. Let's focus on that."

I lightly bang my head against the dresser.

"Couldn't have talked in his sleep before I had to leave New York? Or give me a couple days after the rest of this shit has settled. No, he had to do it during a night my ass couldn't sleep… *again.*"

"What did I say in my sleep?"

I shriek, grabbing a bundle of socks and throw them. They hit Leo's chest squarely, bouncing off to the ground. I clutch my chest as Leo glances down at the socks, then holds his hands up in surrender and gives a sympathetic look. Heart pounding, I stare at him as I swallow hard.

This morning is going fantastic. Not.

"Autumn?" Worry etches his face as he walks over, brows furrowing. "What's wrong?"

My mouth works, but words won't come out.

I've gone up against the most powerful men in the city, killed one of them, and shot another in the dick, but I can't seem to talk to Leo. What the hell happened the last few days that I keep finding it difficult to talk to him?

My chest constricts and the want to cry starts to come back. Panic rises as my hands start to shake, wishing I didn't feel like I was spiraling. Leo grabs my hands, kissing my knuckles before brushing his other hand over my hair.

"Breathe, sweetheart."

Stomach now twisting, I try to concentrate as everything feels like its crashing. Leo pulls me into his arms, smoothing his hand along my shoulders. He rubs my back, cradling my head against his chest.

"*Once upon a midnight…*" he starts to recite *The Raven* for me. I hug him, my arms reaching up to clutch his shoulders. The panic starts to subside as he caresses my back, slowly reciting the poem with me. The oncoming panic attack is gone by the time we finish.

"What's wrong?"

"I'm not sure if it's something we should talk about yet," I murmur against his chest, anxiety wanting to build again.

"Why not?"

"We've got bigger issues, and it's not really that big of deal. It's fine."

"No, it's not." Leo moves, gently grasping my chin to have me look up at him. "None of our bigger issues are going anywhere, Autumn. Whatever it is, it's bothering you enough to make you jumpy and cause a panic attack. It could be from the last 72 hours, but what's on your mind is likely part of it, too." He lets go of my chin, moving his hand to massage the nape of my neck. "We'll be home for the next few days, plenty of time to talk and allow the dust to settle. So, please, tell me what's causing you stress."

I lean forward, knocking my head against his chest in hopes it'll give me answers. It doesn't. Well, other than—*tell your husband, you wimp*.

"You're not a wimp." Nutcracker said that out loud. "Especially after yesterday shooting Rossi in the dick."

"And Curione." His fingers against the nape of my neck go still. "Both shots."

Leo moves back slightly, tilting his head with furrowed brows creating those little lines on his forehead. It's almost enough to make me giggle, until I remember *why* he's making the face.

"You...killed Curione?"

I nod, and then take a deep breath, swallowing hard. "Not the first person I've killed."

His fingers go back to massaging my neck. "Undercover?"

I nod. We're both quiet a moment. "Not as innocent as you thought?"

"Never thought of you as innocent, my dear Watson. I'm certainly not one to judge." He kisses my temple tenderly. "Is that why?"

"Weirdly...no. And now it feels even...stupider."

"I assure you, whatever it is, it's not. Even if you say you've actually been a double-agent this entire time from Genovia."

I try to stifle a smile on the brink of giggling. "Someone's been watching too many movies."

"I've learned from the best." A smirk appears on his face. He grabs both my hands, holding them gently. "What is it, Autumn?'

I lick my lips, swallowing hard again as I clench my fingers around his.

"In your sleep, you...you..." I sigh, telling myself to blurt it out while closing my eyes, "...said, maybe, called me Mistress. Couple times. Then I started to spiral, pieced together things from the past few months, and well...are you submissive? I mean, a Sub... Switch?"

Silence. Another beat. More silence.

I peek an eye open, then the other when I realize his furrowed brow is gone. He just stares, almost blankly before his jaw tenses a moment. I wonder if I finally overstepped, found the button not to push. Leo's quiet for what seems like forever, and anxiety gnaws at me.

Panic attack round two here we go. Before I can spiral, Leo finally speaks.

"Let's go have breakfast," he says calmly, beginning to lead me out of the bedroom.

I blink at him, wondering if he didn't hear me correctly. "Uhhh, Leo?"

"We always talk during breakfast, right? Best time." He glances over his shoulder. Still calm. Still aloof.

I nod, and he squeezes my hand in return.

Quietly, I follow him out of the bedroom. He lets go of my hand, gesturing for me to sit at my usual spot at the counter. He slides a new mug of coffee to me, and then pulls out ingredients to make pancakes, bacon, and eggs. Full Leo breakfast.

Once I finally get caffeine in me, I relax a bit more watching him cook. He's relaxed. Like…*really* relaxed as if a weight has been lifted off his shoulders.

"To answer your main question, yes I am a Switch," he says, piercing the silence as he focuses on the food. "I'm more of a Dominant than Submissive though when it comes to needs. I realized this soon after I started training as a Dom back in California."

"The, uh, early anger management?" I cradle my mug between my hands.

His eyes flick up to mine. "Yes."

"Did *they* know?"

"One or two came to the same conclusion around the same time I did. I craved a harsher setting within scenes, but couldn't follow through. As I've told you, I couldn't separate what I knew of, well, violence from role play or in a proposed setting, not as the one being in charge. I couldn't be a strict Dom without feeling tremendous guilt. On my own, I realized I was a Sub who wanted those scenes, not as a Dom or Top."

He pours the batter into the pan, forming perfect circles.

"For a time, I was fine always being the Dom. I'd find a Sub for a weekend at a club I frequented along with a handful of the Crew who are in the lifestyle as well." Least surprising thing I've heard today. "It worked, but I'd find myself wanting what I saw from others' scenes. A need to be ordered about and used. After some searching, I found a Dominatrix who could fulfill my desires."

Leo's voice quiets, brows pinching together as he frowns deeply. My stomach drops as I watch him pause. Already I know I'm not gonna like where this goes.

"What happened?" I whisper.

Whatever stupor he was in, he blinks out of it and saves the pancakes before they burn.

"We were play partners for almost six months. I'd vetted her heavily. Both of us professionals in the community, but I was becoming well-known as the hotel business grew. I wanted my private life to remain private and not deal with judgement from ill-educated vultures. And I needed someone who knew what they were doing. It was a good match."

I wait as he continues cooking, going silent suddenly. The lines on his forehead deepen as his jaw works. He's almost finished cooking, pulling plates out as the bacon sizzles. I watch him swallow hard a few times, and then turn the stove off.

I'm not sure I'll be able to keep any breakfast down as he speaks.

"She blackmailed me. She recorded, without my knowledge, several of our sessions. Then demanded money or she'd upload the videos to porn sites, news outlets, and send it to my competitors. I'm not ashamed of my kinks, now or even back then, but...information like that is damning for anyone. It was the violation of privacy and trust, using my desires as a weapon."

Leo finishes making our plates, then slides them to me. Stiffly, I set them in place as he grabs his coffee, but remains standing on the other side of the counter.

"Jameson and Waylon took care of it; I don't know what happened to her. Honestly, I don't care. Nor how they did it. The videos were destroyed, and I never heard from her again."

"When did this happen?"

"Two months before Gabriel tried to blackmail me the first time."

My breath shudders, remembering what Jameson told me about those months. How Leo's trust had been broken. How it almost destroyed him. I thought only his family betrayed him.

"The only reason I believed that...bluff of Gabriel's was because I thought she'd...he had..."

"The tapes."

He nods, coming around finally and sits. We drink our coffee in silence.

All of it made sense. The last piece of the puzzle as to why the seclusion. The paranoia. So many people he's been close to stabbed him in the back, and the hits hadn't stopped coming. No wonder he didn't introduce me to the Crew at first or anyone even before me. The world had made him defensive and cold.

Son of a nutcracker, I could never imagine having something so personal shown to the world without my permission. It'd be worse than *Eleanor* stolen from me.

"I swore to myself I'd let that part of me go," he says solemnly. I look over at him as he stares at his Americano. "I'd never let anyone in again. Too much of what I worked for was at stake, along with my own..." his voice trails off, clearing his throat, "...truly thought I buried it, even with you."

"Do you not want that anymore?" I ask tentatively.

Leo closes his eyes, giving a long sigh. "I've made my peace with it."

"That's not an answer."

"What I would want is not the same as you do in that role." He opens his eyes, finally looking at me and my heart aches. They're not fully sad, but there's a bittersweetness. "What I need is far harsher and rigid than what we've done, requiring different after-care not only for me, but for the Dom as well. I'm the type of Sub who wants to be used. Flogged, whipped, chained, or whatever comes to the Dom's mind. It's not an easy task to find someone who can do that, then trusting them fully in such scenes to give up that amount of control. I understand that. And so, I've made my peace with it."

"But you haven't."

The bittersweetness in his eyes diminishes, becoming pained.

After a short breath, I put my coffee down and get up to stand between his legs. I run my hands up his thighs, hoping to get rid of that pain.

"First off, thank you for telling me," I say, placing my hands on his chest. "Second, I'm so sorry that happened to you. No one you trusted like that should've used such a vulnerable part of you against you. She's a bitch, honestly."

He smiles faintly, bringing a hand up to place over mine.

"Third. I don't think you have made peace with it. There's still a side of you that wants that. Craves it even. I didn't notice before, but now I do. I can look back and see all the clues like at the estate in the shower, when you wouldn't move." Leo's jaw tenses. "Or how you always say *I* own you, not the other way around. Your comfortability on your knees. Asking me to be selfish or tell you what to do. Whether consciously or not, you're still grasping for someone to be that for you."

"I won't ask you to be something you aren't, Autumn," he murmurs.

I take his hand, kissing above his wedding band.

"You don't need to ask, Leo." I grip his hand. "But I'll ask the same question you gave me."

"Which one would that be?"

The anxiety from before is gone. It's replaced by that protective need for him again. Shield him from the world. Knowing all that's happened, the world rarely giving him a sliver of mercy, I knew what I wanted. Except, Leo would need to answer first.

"Leo, do you want to be my Sub?"

Chapter 6

Tails of Two Lovers

REEFER MADNESS: *The Musical* plays as I snack on chocolate ice cream.

Leo's been in his office upstairs for hours. Just because we're laying low at home, doesn't mean he'll stop working. We'll see how busy he'll become, while the Crew and Chiari handle the chaos outside. Curione's territories are being divided up between the other crime families, whilst Rossi's organization is another story. Apparently, there's already been some fights, but likely some guy named Petrinolli will inherit Rossi's. I was present for a couple of phone calls, but that was over an hour ago. I've no idea where Leo put *Eleanor*. Oddly enough, I don't care to know. Never thought I wouldn't.

Once the ice cream is gone, I put the bowl down and attempt to focus on the movie.

Leo didn't answer the question.

He wanted to think it over, so we tried to move on from the topic while having breakfast. Not long after, the phone calls from Jameson and the others started. All of them sounding agitated.

My fingers tap on my leg, trying to distract my running

thoughts with what movie to watch next. *The Wicker Man. Who Framed Roger Rabbit?* Or maybe—

My gaze flicks towards the playroom.

"I won't ask you to be something you aren't."

What if I was though?

Yesterday, I didn't necessarily hate giving him orders. The Autumn half a year ago would've screamed no at the idea of being a Dom, but now? Well…things change, including me and Leo.

I try to go back to watching the movie, but my gaze keeps going to the playroom. Pausing the movie, I take my dishes to the kitchen and head back to finish the movie, but stop. I glance toward the stairs. Quiet. He'll probably be busy until dinner.

Slowly, I turn and head down the hall, opening the playroom door and turn on the lights.

Stars in the ceiling twinkle as the lamps glow. I inhale deeply the warm scent the room has, taking in the comfort of the violet walls. Socks coming off, I sink my toes into the rug and smile. The thoughts start to quiet, slowing down as I look up at the St. Andrew's cross. The ropes on the wall arranged neatly behind.

Images from the books I read flash across my mind.

I walk towards the drawers, opening one to pull out a simple black leather crop.

Curiosity fuels me as I step back, giving myself space as I hold my hand up, palm up. Lightly, I tap the end of the crop on my hand, and then raise it to smack down. It slaps against my skin, stinging.

"Ow, holy cabooses, yup not for me." I shake my hand, flexing it as the sting subsides. "Crop works. Great."

I put it back, pulling out a flogger next. It's not thick with its tails, which are leather and thin. The handle is wooden with a leather loop at the end. I grip the neck, allowing the tails to dangle. It's not heavy as I gently swing it through the air, swishing back and forth. I walk around the room, swaying the flogger as I pace and think. After a while, I sit on the edge of the bed with a huff and lay it across my lap. Between my fingers, I play with the soft pieces of leather.

Staring at the flogger, I realize I *want* to be Leo's Dom.

I want him to feel safe; to find emotional release like I do with him in here. I want him to feel heard and cared for. For him to have those moments to let go of his ever-present control. But mostly, I want to be that person for him. Deep down, I think, I crave the kind of power it provides, too. That need to know he's truly mine to love, cherish, give pleasure to, and give what no one else can. To be trusted like that. Maybe I was always a Switch, too.

Except, he may not want it. Leo trusts me with so much, but this was different. I *know* it's different from experience. To give over control like that, and the vulnerability that comes with it. To have faith and so much trust in them. If he doesn't think he can, because of what happened in the past, then that means *I* have to be at peace with that. He's never forced me to do any of this, I did it willingly. He needs to be willing, too.

I loosen a sigh. Crud muffins.

Could I go back to dealing with crime boss secrets again? No, wait, no I don't.

Tingles run up my spine, tugging with warning at the back of my neck. I focus to not succumb to that feeling, knowing who's watching me. I look up, finding Leo standing casually in the doorway with his hands in his pockets.

"How'd the meetings go?" I ask.

Sure, we'll just act like I'm not petting a fucking flogger in my lap.

"We'll be staying here for the next week." He walks over, sitting beside me on the bed. "I'd prefer us stay at the estate, but given it's condition and location being compromised here is best."

"How's the hotel?"

"Crew is going through all employee records and backgrounds..." he clears his throat, gaze meeting mine, "...I want to give *Eleanor* to Julio to use."

"Okay." His brows furrow. "Gave it to you, Leo. It's yours. Want to take down the government? Fine. Dismantle Hollywood? Okay. Find out who really killed Tupac? Have at it. Just let me know when you do, there's a safety feature I created that will self-destruct the program if used without it."

Leo tilts his head, almost smirking. "Oh?"

"Not the only paranoid one in here."

He hums, nodding his head. "You're truly giving it to me?"

"I got what I needed, which was helping you, protecting your businesses—"

"Our."

"Our," I smirk, then shrug. "It was my last huzzah as a hacker. I'd like to go into the sunset with my movies. So, no leaving *our* castle…" Leo snorts, "…until it's a little safe?"

"Taking precautions and hoping that no one will retaliate. Although them fighting over Curione's and Rossi's territories should keep them content. Not to mention the promise of keeping their secrets safe and ours."

My brows come together. "What do you mean ours?"

Leo takes my hand, rubbing his thumb over my wedding ring. Oh.

"Our marriage will remain secret to the public," he explains. "Anyone else who knows will be sworn to secrecy, whether they helped you or not."

Likely threatened, but tomato, tomato.

"Why continue keeping it a secret?"

"Between the publicity of the public that will follow, angry lawyers and investors who won't be happy about the lack of a prenup, but mostly because of my family. I don't want them to know yet."

"You don't just mean your brothers, do you?"

He shakes his head. "I've never completely trusted Renato, but conversations of late have been concerning. It's best, I think, to wait and see what he does next."

Here I thought I was a good chess player. I'm certain Leo is steps ahead already.

I don't push further, not feeling in the mood to deep dive into the politics of his family tree regarding his uncle. He's supposed to be keeping an eye on Matteo in Italy, but seems to be doing a shit job. My gut churns, anxiety pricking at the bottom of my spine.

"Alrighty, keep it secret, keep it safe," I say, gripping his hand. "Anything else I should know?"

"We may have to go to Italy."

I blink at him.

Not even close to being on my bingo card. Maybe I *did* land in a Nick Cage film.

"It's not a certainty," he says, stroking my hair back. "If things worsen with my brothers, then I need to have a face-to-face conversation with Renato. It's not just family fortunes at stake, but businesses spanning internationally, too. Or to drag Matteo back to the states. Either way, I can't do any of that here."

"You'd take me with you?"

His brows raise. "I wouldn't go across state lines without you. No way in hell am I leaving the *country* without you."

I smile faintly, tightening my hold around his hand. I'm not sure what I'd do if he did leave without me.

"Could also use the trip as a vacation. Or honeymoon," he murmurs. I sputter out a sudden laugh. "I don't want your first trip out of the U.S. to be completely for my family's asshole behaviors. You deserve better than that."

The mirth I had turns into appreciation, knowing he's serious. He'd try to turn part of the trip into something for us, for me. His expression softens, brushing his thumb over my wrist. The emotions inside become a growing wave, gathering within as tears start to rush forward. My chest constricts, heart aching once again as I look at the man I know I'd die for. The revelation, real and all-consuming, hits me.

"So do you," I whisper.

A faint smile pulls at his lips. Leo sighs, head turning to look at the St. Andrew's cross. We sit in silence as his hand tightens around mine.

"Leo?"

He breathes in deeply. "Remember in Dr. Maxwell's session how you told me you were afraid I'd leave you? Replaceable was the word used."

I wait, gripping his hand back as he keeps his gaze on the cross.

"I worry I may ask too much of you," he says. "That in order to be with me, I will be your hardest burden to bear. At times, it appears I keep being the reason why you must change. To become someone else in order to…survive loving me."

I move my hand to touch his cheek, and he lightly presses his face against my palm.

"You haven't made me change, Leo," I say softly. "You helped me realize parts of myself that I didn't know existed. Parts that were either buried or I never felt worthy enough to be. You're not a burden to love."

A tear silently rolls down his cheek towards my hand.

Then, in an almost broken, soft voice he says, "Please don't ever leave me."

Wires wrap around my heart, squeezing as I watch another tear slide down his face. I'm unsure why he's saying this to me, not seeming that shaken this morning. Not even during our conversation which I knew for him wasn't easy. A thought flickers that something happened when he was working in his office. Or perhaps yesterday is catching up to him.

I set the flogger aside and climb onto Leo's lap. Straddling him, I wrap my legs around his torso and place his head under my chin. His only response is putting his arms around me as I cradle him in my arms. I hold my husband close, never wanting to let go.

"I love you so fucking much, Leo," I profess. "I'll love you through everything. I'll go wherever you want or need to go, for honeymoons or business. It's alright. You're not failing me, Leo." His arms tighten around me. "I promise to never leave you, my dear husband. And will always help drag you out of that damn, darkened well, as you've done for me." I kiss his forehead as tears try to escape my eyes next. "My dear Leo."

We clutch each other in the playroom. The only sound I seem to hear is the beating of my heart against his. One of his hands reaches up, grasping at the nape of my neck as he holds me firmly.

"I love you with everything I am," he says.

I lean back a little, feebly smiling at him as our eyes meet. He wipes the tears on my face, and then I do the same for him. The hand against the back of my neck brings me forward to kiss him. It's tender. Our mouths moving over the other in a gentleness that makes my heart ache. His fingers stroke down the side of my face, cupping my jaw as the kiss becomes deeper. Peace overwhelms me, finally a quietness calms my mind. He then lightly bites my bottom lip, causing me to smile at the flirting gesture.

We finally move apart, and he exhales warm breath across my skin. "Yes."

"Yes?" I ask, quirking a brow in question.

His eyes are clearer, gone are the tears and they're filled with relief. "Yes, I want you to be my Dom."

My body goes still. I stare at him, hands starting to shake as it sinks in that he agreed. Anxiety and elation war with each other. "Are you sure?"

"I am. If you're willing to try."

"Yes, I want to try…yes."

"We'll still have our other dynamic, that's not going away." He runs his hand over my thigh, while mine goes to his chest, moving my fingers gently over his shirt. "Given how long it's been for me and you being new, we'll take it slow. Should warn you, I'll likely not need that dynamic as frequently as being your Dom."

I nod. "I don't think I'd want to be a Dom more than a Sub either. For now, I guess."

"We'll keep learning together." We smile at each other, and he places another kiss at the corner of my mouth. He then lets out another long exhale, one of content. "You'll need to be taught and trained in some areas first."

"Such as?" I sit back in his lap, grasping his forearms as he grabs my hips.

"Impact play to start."

I nod, glancing at the flogger on the bed. "So, begin there? Go over list of limits, and then determine what to start training with first?"

"We could or..." he quirks a brow, following my gaze to the flogger, "...could both use the distraction, I think. Start teaching you now. If you're alright with flogging."

"As long as I don't legitimately hurt you."

"You won't." He kisses my cheek, pats my thigh and I get off his lap. He stands, walking over to the dresser and pulls out a few other floggers.

"Good thing I have a trained Dom to teach me."

I grin as he snorts at my comment.

Leo rolls up his sleeves, and my heart rate picks up at the small movement. I shake off the sudden arousal as he pulls out the velvet blanket, draping it over the St. Andrew's Cross and grabs clips to keep it from falling.

"First tip is to become more comfortable with every toy or piece of equipment you plan to use. Practice makes perfect, whether it's on yourself or on an object." He gestures toward the blanket after placing the floggers next to the other on the bed. "Flogging becomes simple once you learn the basics, from there it's just practicing your aim."

"Aim?"

He grabs one of the floggers with the longer tails and shiny wooden handle with a silver knob at the end. "There are spots on the body you need to avoid and be more aware of."

"Like with rigging?"

"Yes." He holds up the flogger, twisting his wrist. "Flogging has more to do with your wrist movement than the whole arm. Don't use your whole strength. It's easier to hit your target when you act as if the flogger is an extension of your arm, not just as an object."

Leo steps away, positioning himself before the cross. His arms hang loosely at his sides, relaxed. With his free hand he points to the middle of the cross and says, "Know where you want the tails to land, flick your wrist, then release as you move your arm."

He shakes out the flogger, then brings it up and moves swiftly as he hits the center of the X. There's no loud cracking sound, which I thought would happen, instead it's a thud that echoes through the room. My breath hitches as he continues, moving the flogger into a figure-eight pattern to continually hit the middle of the X. My mouth goes dry as I watch him flog the blanket easily, arm moving in a fluid motion. A zapping sensation runs down my spine, my body becoming very aware of what he's doing. I'm not at all enticed by the idea of being hit in any capacity, in fact I recoil at the idea. Except watching Leo is...exquisite.

I can't tear my eyes away from him. The controlled power he wields.

Holy crud muffins Alfred, Robin, and Batman. I'm supposed to do *that*?

He stops, bringing the flogger down and doesn't appear tired from what he just did. Leo turns towards me as I still stare at him.

"Your turn," he says.

I don't move, suddenly unsure as anxiety grips me. I must take too long because Leo walks over and grabs my hand. He gently pulls me to where he was, situating me before the cross. The flogger he used is placed in my hands. It's a touch heavier than the one I was fiddling with earlier.

I take a deep breath, telling myself I can do this. He trusts me, which means Leo knows I *can* do this. I face the cross more, letting the flogger dangle at my side. Leo stands close behind me, then leans down to place his hand over mine on the wooden handle. My breath catches as his brushes over my skin.

He gently instructs, "Don't grip the handle tight, keep it just loose enough. Start slow, and don't fight the tails."

Shivers run down my spine as I try to concentrate. Leo runs his other hand down my back, and I relax a bit more. "It's just leather, Autumn."

I nod my head. "Okay."

Leo steps back, letting go.

I exhale roughly, looking upon where Leo's hits fell. The velvet streaks in different directions, showing where the tails had landed. I shake out the flogger, then bring it up and do as he said—flick my wrist, while slowly swinging my arm. The leather snaps, most of the tails hitting where I planned. Quickly, I do it again, finding it easier than I thought. I keep going, feeling the weight of the flogger as each flick is easier than the next. After a few more times, I stop and stare at the crisscross streaks on the blanket. Not as perfect as his, but I hit where I wanted to.

A giggle comes out of me, realizing that was fun.

Leo wraps an arm around my middle from behind and says against my ear, "Good girl."

I smile, tilting my head back to look up at him. "Show me more."

Chapter 7

Ivory Tower

"WHEN CAN you leave your tower, Rapunzel?" Leanne asks.

"Very funny." I roll my eyes, adjusting the phone to my shoulder as I flip through another Italian language book. Figured it'd be a good idea to place it at the front of the language learning. Just in case. "Maybe 4-5 days."

"Wow."

"Lot of employees to go through."

Leanne lets out a shaky sigh. "I don't know how you're not terrified."

"Who says I'm not?" I try to be casual, but she remains quiet. I clear my throat. "Just gotta lean into the curve. Find hobbies to focus on instead."

"If you say so. What are your hobbies now since you're not at the hotel or working on motorcycles? Wait what am I saying, you get to watch movies all day and read."

I sit on the couch, and just hum in response. Technically she was right.

The rest of yesterday I learned from Leo how to flog and tie ropes, which kept me busy for hours. Learning more about how to use our sex toys will definitely become a hobby. She doesn't need to know that. Or that I jumped his bones after our lesson.

"And trying new skills. Like cooking."

"You? Cook?"

"Hey, it can happen."

"Here I thought your free time would be hacking more computers," she comments, and I snort.

Leanne mostly knows what happened, mainly that hitmen were sent after me and I kept intel from my days undercover. Figured *one* of my friends could know the truth, and Leanne would totally notice someone following her. Trix likely not. And Nan already had security surrounding her and the bookstore. Neither of them knew what truly happened, other than some potential threat and that's why I left town unexpectedly and now staying home because of "newspapers." One of the few times I appreciate Carrie.

"I'm officially retired," I mutter, rubbing my face.

"Maybe that's a good thing," she says almost too quietly.

"Yeah."

We're silent, and now I find myself in the same position as I had been with Leo—no clue how to talk to her. I thought my secret of being undercover was bad, but this weight feels worse upon my shoulders.

There's a knock and I glance at the front door, thankful for the distraction. "I've gotta go, pretty sure that's Isaac and Jameson."

"How is Isaac? I mean, all the Crew of course."

I pause standing up, eyeing the phone with a smirk. "They're good as far as I know. Could have Isaac come check on your little security detail if you want."

"Not what I meant!"

"Uh-huh."

"Just curious. Long week for them, you know?"

"Uh-huh," I say again, walking towards the door.

She sighs dramatically. "I have some work to do anyways. Lots of curriculum planning and stuff. Hopefully see you soon hun, stay safe and love you."

She hangs up before I can say anything else. I laugh under my breath, putting the phone away as I open the door. On the other side is Isaac and Julio. My brows scrunch surprised it's just them.

"Afternoon, Miss Autumn," Isaac greets as I step aside for them.

"Hey, Isaac."

"Buenas tardes, *hermana*…cómo está?" Julio asks as I close the door.

"Buenas tarde, eh…bien. Mejor."

Julio gives a warm smile, and then brings me into a hug. I melt into the burly biker's arms as he tightens his hold a moment. We let go and he winks.

"Café?" I ask.

"Sí, I'll take some, though won't be here long," Julio answers as I go into the kitchen.

"Would've thought Jameson would be here today," I comment.

Isaac clears his throat and starts to head for the upstairs. "He's busy. I'll tell him you're here, Enigma."

Julio nods as Isaac disappears. Confusion flits over me as I get the coffee to start brewing. I pause, glancing at Julio's concentrated face. He then scowls, shaking his head as he leans on the island counter.

"He okay?"

"Worried about everything, that's all," he answers, scratching the underside of his beard. "Spartan and Sombra squabbling ain't helping. Big fight yesterday."

Yup, that explains Leo's mood. And why Julio is here.

"It's because of me, isn't?"

"They just ain't seeing eye to eye. It happens with them two, they've always head butted."

I grab him a mug and then some creamer, remaining quiet.

"Just another hiccup, *hermana*. You'll be out of here in no time."

"Yeah," I whisper low, pouring his coffee and mixing in creamer. I slide it over to him, leaning on the counter next to him.

"Gracias."

"De nada." Julio gently grabs my shoulder, squeezing gently. I give him a small smile, hoping this tough patch will pass already.

"Be back down after the boss is done with me."

"He's giving you *Eleanor*," I say abruptly, and he blinks at me. I smirk. "Check in with me before you leave."

"Knew that thing would have more layers." He grins, clicking his tongue as he starts to walk away. "May teach me a thing or two, *hermana*."

I chuckle under my breath, starting to make myself an afternoon coffee until Julio pauses. "Hey, you know George? Nail guy at the hotel salon?"

"Yeah, why?" Please don't tell me he failed his background check.

"He's all good, by the way." The fear that must've been on my face disappears. "Just asked about you and hopes to see you soon or something."

A grin tugs at my lips. "He's a good friend and very sweet."

"Got that impression." Julio clears his throat, rolling his shoulders back. "Reminds me of a golden retriever though."

"They make the best cuddle buddies."

"Yeah, they can—" Julio narrows his eyes, and I grin.

Frowning only a moment, he starts chuckling and disappears next. He murmurs something in Spanish that I don't catch, which makes me giggle as I pour myself a coffee. I wonder who's gonna finally admit they have feelings first—my best friend or Enigma.

⸻

Leo

Isaac briefly knocks before entering Leo's office. It's been redone, now imitating the study he has at his estate— dark earthy colors with soothing browns and greens, shelves on the side with a window that illuminates an oak desk. Plush green chairs sit in front, which Isaac ignores as he stands behind them.

Leo doesn't look up, signing a couple of documents on his desk. "Where's Julio?"

"Autumn is making him coffee. She offered." Leo nods in return, flipping another paper. "How's she doing?"

Leo stops, finally looking up at Isaac with a rigid expression. "Fine."

"Fine?"

"Yes, fine," he says, finishing the last of the papers.

"After being chased out of the city *again*, comes back to save *your* ass, sits in a meeting of crime bosses, kills one and shoots another in the dick, and she's...fine?"

Isaac's tone is accusatory, the venom in it cutting at Leo, who scowls harder at the man. Leo leans forward on his desk, placing his elbows on the surface while folding his hands together. He strokes the ring on his finger, which he's refused to take off since putting it on, the smooth metal calming him.

A flash of memory. Chiari leading him into the first-floor office, gesturing towards the last of the paperwork. There, his ring sat, ready for him. Melancholy twisted in his stomach, wishing it'd been Autumn putting it on him. Only until he saw her, sitting upon his "throne" as it were, did the twisted feeling leave.

"Careful, Isaac," Leo warns. "I know how to care for *my* wife."

"Your track record says otherwise."

Leo practically snarls, defensiveness crawling up his spine as his hands clench together. "If you want to be pissed with me, go join Jameson at the *Italian Lily*. Otherwise, watch your mouth in *my* office. In *my* home."

Isaac stiffens only a little at the threat in Leo's voice. He fists one of his hands, frowning deeply as he exhales a sharp breath. Isaac murmurs, "You didn't watch her spiral for months. Trying to please you, only to—"

Leo's hands slam down onto the desk, standing as his rough voice argues, "You may be her bodyguard, but that does not mean you know her better than I. So, when I say she's fine...she's *fine*."

Blue eyes cut the tense air.

"Why don't you say what's *actually* on your mind?" Leo questions, cocking his head. The men glare at each other, until there's a quiet knock.

Both instantly school their expressions. Leo stands fully and Isaac adjusts his stance. The door opens with Julio holding his mug of coffee. He raises a brow, glancing between them as he sips his drink.

"Good thing I took the coffee," he murmurs, going over to sit in one of the chairs. "So you two can go back to your pissing match, you have something for me, boss?"

Isaac scoffs, looking away as he steps further from them. Leo glares at Isaac before reaching into his desk, walking around to hand it to Julio. The biker smirks as he takes *Eleanor*, and Leo leans back against his desk.

"Use *Eleanor* to help with the background checks. I want it done for everyone, and then for those in my organizations," Leo states. "Once you're done, get it back to me."

Isaac scowls at the disc, then to Leo. "She approved this? It's *her* program."

Leo ignores him. "Go to her before you leave. You need a code to keep it from self-destructing itself and any computer mainframe it's in."

Julio whistles low, putting the disc away as Leo flicks an angry look at Isaac.

"Neither of you breathe a word that it's being used. To *anyone*."

"Even the rest of the Crew?" Julio asks.

"Yes."

"More secrets, huh?" Isaac mutters. Leo snarls at him, face becoming stonier. Julio only shakes his head, sipping his coffee.

"*If I was an idiot, I'd sell this to the government, believe I'd be set for life,*" Julio speaks in Spanish, grabbing Leo's attention. "*But I wouldn't look good with a hole in my head.*"

"*Is that your only motivation?*" Leo asks.

Julio cocks his head, humming again. "*No. I have too much respect for our sister...and you.*" Leo's harsh expression doesn't change.

Isaac grumbles, turning away from them unable to fully understand the language switch. You'd think he'd learn by now, but knowing three other languages always kept him busy.

"Give them a few days, Spartan. Their ego and pride have been hit, but they're not gonna admit it," Julio says low.

"What about you?"

Julio chuckles, standing up and sipping his coffee again. *"Knew I met my match the day she escaped the hotel. And when it comes to you…I watched you make that decision. Not many men can say they'd choose what you have."*

Julio pats his leather jacket where the disc is. He says, switching back to English, "I'll keep it safe."

Isaac turns back to them with a sour look still on his face.

"Oh, and Matteo hasn't been seen now for over 72 hours," Julio adds before getting to the door. "Renato's trackers lost him. Think he landed in another mafia boss' territory."

"Renaldi?" Leo asks.

Julio shrugs. "Matteo would be perfect for him to use."

Leo nods, and then gestures for him to leave. Julio gives a small salute, walking out. The door shuts, leaving Isaac and Leo alone again. Both men stare at the other, scowling deeply. Leo straightens his posture, going back to behind his desk again.

"Want to continue this pissing match or you going to tell me what's really on your mind?" Leo questions, sitting back down in his chair.

Minutes tick by, before Isaac stalks to the middle of the room and stops. His voice is filled with anger and disdain. "How many times will she have to save your ass before you realize it'll be what kills her?"

Leo's entire body tenses. It's like a sword has been thrust into his gut. A snarl comes over his lips, gaze darkening as he glares at Isaac.

"I do not control her, *including* what she's done this week or the past several months."

"Except she wouldn't have needed to if you'd told her the damn truth. Like why you fucking married her...*Luciano.*"

Leo stands up suddenly, almost knocking back his chair.

"Watch it, Isaac."

"Don't pretend that you didn't think about how you'd screw Renato over and your brother by marrying her. She became another chess piece to regain your obsessive control."

Isaac's words cut, slicing at Leo. His hands fist upon the desk, trembling with anger and hurt. "Your opinion has *no* relation to my marriage. Or *why.*"

"Not even going to deny it?" Anger keeps Leo from answering, boiling through his veins. "Does she even know?"

"Get out, Isaac."

"She doesn't, does she?"

"*Get. Out.*" Leo prowls around his desk, knuckles cracking as he clenches his fist. Isaac flashes his gaze to Leo's hands, finally showing a twinge of fear at the thunderous rage on his face. "Leave before I do something I may actually regret. Unless you want to hand in your resignation, now."

Isaac stares at him. Leo stops just in front of his desk, waiting for an answer. Finally, Isaac clears his throat and starts to leave.

"It's crossed my mind," Isaac says roughly, and it's like a stake struck Leo's chest. "Except, technically, I solely work for her. And I promised to protect her...even if that means from you." He walks out, the door slamming behind him.

Leo's chest heaves, each breath heavier than the last as he moves rigidly to his desk and sits down. His hands shake, clenching and unclenching upon the surface. There's a roaring in his head as he stares at the papers on his desk he forgot to hand over.

A flash of conversation from yesterday comes back, Jameson's voice echoing in his head.

"Perhaps it's best if I went back to California. Keep watch over the West Coast operations."

Matteo. Jameson. Isaac. Who else will leave? Walk away?

Leo sits quietly, feeling the cracks in what he's built come closer to shattering. His secrets, his long plays now beginning to weigh heavy and taking casualties with them.

There's a knock at the door, but no one enters after a moment or two passes.

"Given my track record, it may be best to tell me I can come in," Autumn's voice sounds through the door.

A sudden snort of laughter hits Leo. "Come in, dear wife. It's safe."

Autumn enters, wearing one of her favorite sweaters and jeans. Her hair has grown out a little, just past her ears with its strands of light brown and auburn. When she looks at him, concern fills those chestnut brown eyes with gold. The small dimples she gets from smiling aren't there, instead she frowns as she approaches.

"Julio know what to do?" Leo asks.

"He shouldn't destroy the hotel's mainframe or ruin Owen's computers," she smirks, getting him to smile dimly. She comes around his desk. Autumn glances down at his hand, still fisted upon the desk. "Want to talk about it?"

"No."

Those beautiful eyes meet his, softening. "Okay."

Autumn takes his hand, putting it between hers as her fingers run over his wedding band. The constriction around his chest eases as he feels her hand upon his. They're quiet as she holds him, slowly his hands unclench.

"Let's go play hooky, meaning a bad horror movie marathon."

"Horror movies?" He asks, looking at her in confusion. "Since when do you watch horror films?"

"Older movies aren't that scary, and some are funny like *Army of Darkness*. Or emphasis on bad, to the point of laughing, not screaming like *Basket Case* or *Silent Night, Deadly Night*."

"All of those sound concerning." Leo stands up, following her out of his office as she tugs him along.

Elm Jed

"Don't worry, I'll hold your hand. Safe with me, mister."

"Yes, I am, dear Watson." She squeezes his hand, door shutting behind them.

Chapter 8

Time for Change

Autumn

NOT SURE HOW Rapunzel did it, but BDSM, languages, and bad movies is how I got through being stuck in *my* tower. A whole week we stayed home, not leaving. Then again it is a fucking penthouse not my old apartment we were holed up in.

My anxiety has waned through the days, but Leo has been unusually calm. He's taken a few calls here and there, but has barely spent over an hour in his office since Julio and Isaac visited. The only person we've seen since then is Xavier when he delivered groceries. No other sighting of the Crew. I'm unsure if that's a good thing or a bad omen.

I peek over my book about Italy to Leo in the kitchen. He's cooking pasta carbonara for dinner, wearing a t-shirt and slacks with a towel thrown over his shoulder. His brow scrunches in concentration, moving fluidly through the kitchen.

It's the most relaxed I've seen him in well…weeks.

I bring my legs up, sitting on the couch as I lay my head on my knees, watching him. A smile grows on me as he grabs a pan. Sweat glistens over his tattoos, making them shine in the kitchen's lamplight. I'm still very much staring when Leo pauses, looking over at me. A smirk plays over his lips. He brings a hand up, gesturing for me to come over.

Happily, I set the book aside and get off the couch to walk over to him. Halfway there, I run and slide across the floor in my socks. Leo smiles. When I'm close enough, he snakes his arm around my waist.

"Is my cooking fascinating you, dear Watson?" He brushes his mouth over the shell of my ear.

"One way to put it." I place my arms around his neck, hugging him. "You're just so pretty to look at, mister."

He kisses my neck. "And you're an enthralling beauty, my dear wife."

I giggle, leaning back to grin up at him. Although I'm giggling and smiling, my heart flutters as heat simmers low in arousal. My body thrums as his hand skims over my waist.

"Shouldn't you be paying attention to the food?" I ask, trying to act more interested in dinner.

"I'm not being a distraction."

I mock gasp at him. "I'm not a distraction!"

Leo swiftly grabs the back of my neck, gently yanking me to him and kisses me. His tongue skims over my lips, and I sigh as he deepens the fervent kiss. All of me wants to melt into his arms, but it's over too soon as he breaks away. Hazel eyes gaze down at me. I smile faintly, and then glance at the pasta he's making.

"Back to the real world tomorrow, huh?"

He traces a finger along my jaw, then nods.

I inhale deeply. "Well, knew it wouldn't last forever up here."

"We still have time," he whispers, kissing my cheek. Leo takes my left hand, kissing my knuckles and does it twice above my rings. A bit of sadness comes, realizing we'll have to hide the rings again. I take his left hand next, stroking my thumb over his ring, and kiss his hand like he did mine.

I remain next to Leo as he finishes dinner, watching him as I try to focus on the moment. In my heart, I know it's not our last dinner together, but warning prickles my skin. What's outside these walls could tear us apart again. Of course, I knew this peace was temporary, lucky we had this week to be together after such a horrific turn of events. I wanted it so bad to last longer.

I shove away the concerning thoughts, staying present as my husband and I have dinner like any other night. Except, I can't stop the quick looks to the door as if the wolves would arrive any moment.

* * *

The elevator doors open. Xavier stands in his usual spot, smiling with a nod as we exit. Leo's hand brushes over the small of my back, leading us into the lobby. I grin back to Xavier as we walk out into the rainy morning. Leo is dressed in his usual attire—black suit with a dark button-up and shiny black shoes. His severe expression and the stubble along his jaw are the perfect accessories. Meanwhile, I'm in jeans, an over-sized *Metallica* t-shirt, denim jacket, and converse.

One of us is going to a slew of meetings, while the other is having a salon day.

For the safety of clients and crime bosses, I'm the one with the hair and nail appointment.

Rudy stands outside our SUV, Chesty sitting in the front seat. Animal and Owen are in another car behind ours.

"Gutentag, *barchën*," Rudy greets, opening the door for us.

"Gutentag. Danke." I smile, climbing in.

Leo speaks a moment with Rudy, then follows in after me. Door shutting, Chesty looks over his shoulder and grins at me. "Hey sister, nice little break?"

"Yeah, it was. How's your injury?"

"Still kicking." He waves it off as Rudy gets into the car, who murmurs something to Chesty as we pull off.

"How many languages are you learning, dear Watson?" Leo asks faintly.

"Well, I'm already fluent in sarcasm," I smirk, and he snorts. "Mostly Spanish with Alba and Charlotte. Italian. And don't tell Rudy, but I'm behind on my German."

Leo takes my hand, holding it casually as he leans back. Suddenly, he starts speaking in German and Rudy chuckles in response. I lightly smack Leo's thigh. He smiles faintly, eyes glimmering with mischief.

"Show off," I grumble.

He presses his face against my hair, kissing there before he travels down to the crook of my neck. Leo remains nuzzled there as I look up, noticing Chesty glancing over his shoulder at us. He turns away with a smile.

My hand brushes over the pocket where my wedding band hides. Leo's is hidden inside one of his pockets, too. Neither of us could bear leaving them behind, both deciding to carry them close for comfort. Just hope it won't be another 3-4 months of hiding them.

The rest of the drive is relatively quiet. We arrive at the hotel, pulling into the garage where a handful of men stand along with Mila wearing her usual stoic attitude. I loosen a breath, preparing to separate myself from Leo again.

"I'll see you tonight," he says low as Chesty and Rudy exit the car. "If you need anything, call me or contact Ringer."

I give a puzzled look. I've never gone through Rudy to contact him before. It's usually through Isaac or Jameson. I quickly school my expression, nodding as I realize how strained the relationships may be.

"Okay," I say, kissing his cheek. "Maybe next time you see me I'll have long hair again." His brows shoot up, then scrunch as he stares at my hair. I start to giggle, getting out of the car. "Finally, something with fashion I can stump you on."

"Are you planning to wear a wig?" He asks, leaving the car.

I begin to walk around the car, noticing the small horde of

mobsters across the way. All of them stiffen when they see us, more so when Leo scowls at them before turning towards me.

"No, extensions," I answer as he comes closer.

"Whatever you decide, dear Watson," Leo murmurs, brushing a kiss across my temple. "Don't leave the hotel. I love you."

"Love you, mister."

Leo lingers a moment; hazel eyes look at me with concern. Gently, he brushes a few strands of my hair behind my ear. He then straightens, bringing forth that commanding presence of his in an instant. He walks away with Rudy, Animal, and Owen, who come up beside him as they reach Mila. She joins them as they head for the elevators. My chest tightens watching him leave, fear inching its way towards me. My breath catches as Chesty comes up beside me, placing a hand on my shoulder.

"How bad is everything?"

"It's not bad."

"Chesty," I mutter, folding my arms over my chest. "Come on."

He scratches his beard, adjusting his beard beads. "No, really. One dead boss, no one really had loyalties to. The other, well, would've been killed the moment Finstrum left this building. Mob families are inwardly fighting with each other, which means not our problem. For now. Still gotta watch our backs, always do, but they'll do whatever they're told not to lose more money or cocks at this point."

I snort with a small chuckle under my breath. "And everything else?"

"Change ain't easy, sister. Especially to a group of bikers."

We head towards the elevator, and I go to put my pin in, but remember it was changed. I redo it, getting on, and then hit the floor for the salon. "Where's Isaac?"

"Already up there," he answers. I glance over to him as he does. "Know what happened between him and Spartan?"

"No. Just that he was grouchy when he left."

Chesty hums, nodding a little. "Well, if you plan on goin' back to kicking groins instead of shootin' them, let me know. He does have a history with ya on that."

"You think it was that bad?" I ask. He shrugs. Great.

"He's been quieter than one of those European bikes he used to ride."

"Speaking of bikes..." and me not ready to tackle whatever happened with Isaac yet, "...any updates on what's salvageable up north?"

"Nah, not yet. We'll send someone trustworthy up soon."

The doors open and we walk out into the somewhat busy floor. Isaac stands quietly near the reception desk, eyes averting from mine as we approach. Oh, wonderful sign. Not.

Wanda sees me, giving a wide smile. "Autumn! Oh, it's good to see you! Are you alright?"

My heart drops. None of the hotel employees should know what—

"They think it was a normal attempted kidnapping," Chesty whispers near my ear.

Right. Yeah. *Normal*, meaning me being engaged to a hotel mogul. Don't need a reminder how normal *that* can be.

"I'm fine, long couple of weeks, but okay," I answer as she comes around to give me a hug. I gratefully take the warm gesture.

"There were rumors about hotel staff being involved," she whispers, pulling back as her copper hair bounces. "Is that true?"

"I can't really talk about it, but no...they just snuck in," I lie, not wanting more panic.

"Still, pretty scary," she grimaces, but quickly grins and takes my hand. "Well, George is ready for you along with Lisa. The entire salon will want the tea though."

I follow her with my bodyguards close behind as I'm sat in my usual spot, away from most clientele. Lisa then appears, practically squealing as she hugs me next.

"Thank *god*, you're okay," she says, while Wanda nods. "It's been so weird the past week. Is it true employees tried to kidnap you? Who'd do such a thing?"

This is gonna be a repeated question.

"No, no they snuck into the hotel, pretending," Wanda answers, nodding with wide eyes. "Which explains the new security measures and background checks."

"Yeah, *that* has been fun," Lisa mutters, sweeping back her dark hair. She glances at the men. "Speaking of, Wanda could you find two chairs for Autumn's bodyguards? Unless you want me to moisturize your beard, handsome."

"I'm good," Chesty answers, grinning.

"Something about burly, mountain guys," Lisa murmurs near my ear, leading me to her chair. I let out a laugh. "As for you Mr. Morton, don't change a thing." Isaac remains silent, which gives me pause.

Finally, I hear George's voice.

"One, did I hear something about bodyguards? Two, please tell me that's my wonderful Autumn, who desperately needs new nails." My sunshine filled nail tech comes around the corner, smiling and then playfully pouts. "Oh, not the bodyguard I wanted. I'll come back when he arrives."

"Hey!" I yell, starting to laugh.

He grins, coming over to hug me. Chesty chuckles, but nothing from Isaac. A part of me wishes he'd joke or smile, but whatever is wrong is eating at him. Not exactly the time or place to prod for answers.

George takes a seat next to me, lounging back. "Please tell me this horrid affair of being kidnapped, which led to being a polite socialite who disappears, is completely over." I raise a brow. "It's what they all do."

"Mostly," I answer.

"I'll take it, now how shall we pamper you for being such an adorable socialite." I start laughing, holding onto the armchairs. The worries I've had before vanish as George smiles at me. "Thought a good distraction would help you."

I smile, grabbing his hand and squeezing it. He winks with a knowing smile. "It does. And for that, I am finally saying yes to new hair."

He gapes, and then calls out, "Lisa! Happy early birthday! The boss lady finally wants new hair."

The next thirty minutes is a blur as we go over what I'm thinking, and they leave to gather materials, chatting away. Chairs are delivered for Chesty and Isaac, but only Chesty sits down while Isaac remains off to the side. I focus on the joy of George and Lisa, relishing the fun they provide. Wanda comes back, asking about refreshments. I take tea, while Chesty asks for a beer. Isaac scowls at him as Wanda walks away.

"You're on the job," Isaac mutters.

"A beer ain't gonna change anything," Chesty responds, then looks at me. "What say you, boss?"

"No beer pong."

"Darn." He leans back in his chair smiling. "You think Lisa is single? Haven't dated in a bit, but she's pretty. And funny."

I giggle at him, looking over at Isaac whose face is still a mask of seriousness. Suddenly he says, "I've got a call to make."

He walks away through the luxurious salon, disappearing through the crowd of people getting their hair and nails done. Chesty whistles low, grimacing almost as I give an incredulous look.

"Never thought you two would butt heads."

"Me neither. Be great if I knew what over," I say.

He tsks, shaking his head. "Well, whatever it is, keep me out of it. Already trying to keep Sombra and Spartan from throttling each other."

"Should I be worried?"

"Honestly, not sure. They've always been more like brothers, the kind that fight and argue, but make up once one of their ears get yanked. This time's a bit more serious."

"I sound like a broken record, but…because of me?"

"Yes and no. Not all about you, ya know?" I chuckle, and he grins as he rolls his chair over to me. He pats my knee. "Something for you to remember. Sombra's practically been taking care of the pres for almost two decades on his own. He's adjusting to new shit, like my buddies coming back from deployment. You get used to a cycle out there, and when you come back and ain't nothin' the same, it's hard. What you left behind changed, people moved on…but you ain't the same either. So, then where the fuck do you go?"

"Like being undercover for almost two years. You can't go back to the old life," I whisper, and he nods.

One of the assistants comes back with our drinks. He takes a swig of his beer, making a content sound.

"Is that what's going on with them? Fighting change?" I ask.

"Maybe. Perhaps, us both should remember what it was like coming home as it were. How hard that shit was."

"Pretty sure I'm still learning," I say, picking my tea up. "How'd you do it? Taking on change?"

Chesty strokes his beard again, giving me a half smile. "Can't go back to somethin' that's not there anymore. Whether it's places, people, or even you. And that change doesn't mean you're gonna forget, you just hold onto the memories tighter. I had to learn how *not* to be a Marine everyday anymore. Part of me will always be, but never like it was before. Hard to let go of that."

I clear my throat as his words sink in.

"And I think Leo and you lying to them…may have been the kind of change that they weren't ready for."

I meet Chesty's pale green gaze. There's no bitterness, just sympathy. "A price that I'm not sure he or I were ready for," I whisper.

Chesty pats my knee again, keeping his hand there. "Knew why you did it, sister. Both you and Spartan. Hurts, but that's reality. And honestly if you hadn't…we'd all be dead. And maybe that's what's pissing them off the most."

I bring my gaze up to meet his. My face filled with worry. My expression is shaken off when I hear Lisa and George coming back.

"I'm *so* excited. You're gonna love it," Lisa says happily. I put my tea down before she spins my chair around to face the mirror. Chesty scoots back to watch.

For the next couple of hours, I get my hair and nails done. George tries to convince me to get a full spa treatment, but I tell him next time. I still have errands to run.

"Maybe I should get my nails done," Chesty comments as I write out tips for George and Lisa, smiling down at my dark green nails.

"You'd look great in black polish," George says, grinning at Chesty. "Although, you could suggest someone else to come get their nails done."

I start laughing as Lisa rolls her eyes. I say, "You're insatiable."

"I am tenacious," George replies.

"And lovable."

"Yes, we both are."

"Hope you love your hair," Lisa says, winking. "Need to bring your Nan in next."

"That reminds me, when is she coming back? That woman fascinates me with her stories," George comments.

"Don't know, but I'll ask." I give them both a hug, waving at Wanda as she takes care of a customer.

"Love ya, darling, and behave yourself with that new hair," George playfully says.

"I'll do my best," I laugh.

I leave the salon with Chesty beside me, Isaac reappearing not far behind. I go through my head the schedule of the hotel, pausing in the hallway as I catch sight of my new hair. It's now a dark red with a much shorter pixie cut. While running my hand through the soft strands, I start moving and say, "Let's go check on my hotel."

Chapter 9

Below the Belt

NEVER WILL I make Alba cry again. I hope.

I fully believed that anyone within five rooms could hear Alba's cries and Charlotte's shouts from the *Lucca Suite*. Even Grant's professional mask cracked. They were surprised to see me, Charlotte the first to gasp, stumbling out of the bedroom. I was bombarded with questions, mostly by Charlotte. Not shockingly. It took Alba and Grant to slow her roll in order for them to get back to work before guests would arrive. I helped them with a few things while Chesty and Isaac stayed in the hall.

The small bit of normalcy was comforting, relief filling me as I followed them to the first floor afterwards. I received more joyous greetings from staff members as we made our way back to the main floor. I found Chiari briefly, who let me know where Bobby was, before disappearing to take care of some other matters.

My bodyguards are silent, staying in the hall, as I knock on the room door. Tears fill my eyes as I step inside, seeing him fix a heating vent. His beard is trimmed, along with his hair. I smile as he comes over to hug me. My arms shake a little as I embrace him, his own arms tightening.

"Thank fuck you're okay," he murmurs.

"Same to you. Not the one who stopped them." I try not to get choked up, remembering *who* he stopped. My stomach drops, holding him tighter. He squeezes me, and then pats my back before we separate. "Thank you, by the way."

"No need to thank me, kiddo. They were downright bastards." He looks past me to the hall. "Got two today?"

"Extra careful."

"Heard they were doing that." Bobby steps away, going back into the bedroom to work. I sit on the ground next to him.

"Mainly background checks. Double-checking everything," I say.

"Those uh, hitmen hired by some mob boss then?" He asks frankly. I half-smile. He grabs a screwdriver. "Didn't seem like somethin' to beat around the bush about."

"Yeah, but it's complicated."

"Should've known. Like the hair by the way, not trying to hide again, are you?"

I run my fingers through the darker short strands. "Needed a change. A real one."

"A real one?"

"My choice this time. Not someone else's," I murmur, staring at his tool bag. I watch him tinker, not quite sure what he's doing, but quiet as he works.

"You have the briefcase?" I ask softly.

"At home," he mumbles.

"I need you to do a few things."

Bobby pauses his work, brows raised in question. I flick my gaze to the bedroom door, just barely seeing the main door still open. Bobby clears his throat, scooting closer as he nods slightly. I pull out the briefcase's key hidden where my ring is inside my jacket, handing it to him.

"Take out the laptop, and then drop it off at the cafe's lost and found right before you clock in tomorrow morning. Tell them you found it in the lobby. Chiari will know it's there when you clock in."

"If someone else grabs it?"

"I input a code that makes the laptop seem like a dud and won't work again until a certain software program is inserted."

He nods, making a hard thinking face.

"Take the discs out, and put the empty movie covers back into the briefcase, and then bring it to the hotel and drop it off with Logan at security tomorrow evening. Say out loud, you found it in the lobby during your shift." He scrunches his brows. "He knows what to do next."

"And the discs?"

"Wrap them in a towel, put them in a brown paper bag. In four days, drop them off with Chiari directly and tell her you're finally returning the clothes you borrowed when you first arrived."

"Pretty specific there."

"If there's one thing I'm good at it…it's red herrings."

Bobby pockets the key. We glance at the shadows of my bodyguards in the hallway. He mutters, "Thought you trusted them. Something I should know?"

"It's who could be watching them I don't trust. And someone is. Problem is…I don't know who."

He grumbles low, exhaling harshly. "Never took you as a strategist, kiddo."

"I just watch too many spy movies." We chuckle, and I switch the topic as he goes back to work. "How's the apartment coming along?"

Perhaps, I'm overthinking from paranoia and anxiety, but I didn't care. The laptop and discs were damning if in the wrong hands, which is why I have extra precautions. I should've destroyed it all before giving it to Bobby, but I just can't yet. The potential power of those items could bring the last of the rats out of the walls. I can see a missing piece in the puzzle, but no idea what or who. Some things weren't adding up from the day I left the city, and deep down the feeling of being watched hasn't relented since I returned. Not all the enemies were in that board room, and I'm listening to my damn gut. Someone helped those mobsters into the hotel, and I need to find out who.

Bobby finishes his work as we talk normal stuff, and I give him a hug before he goes off to his next job. He winks at me before taking the stairs down a floor. I'm left standing with the other two in the hall, stretching my arms over my head.

"Well, I'm done today," I say, heading to the private elevator. "Wanna watch a movie?"

"Thought you'd be tired of 'em," Chesty comments as we get on and ascend. Isaac remains quiet.

"Never," I say with a grin, but my stomach churns as I feel Isaac beside me.

I'm gonna need to suck it up and ask what happened because I can't take this silence much longer.

The elevator stops, opening its doors to white lilies displayed on the foyer table. The two mutter to each other as I come up on the flowers, tracing a finger along some petals. I lean in to smell them, some of my unease disappearing. I take a deep breath.

"Chesty, I'd like to talk to Isaac alone please," I say finally. "I'll see you tomorrow."

"Sure thing, sister." He grunts, then disappears through one of the hall doors to the smaller apartments. I continue staring at the flowers.

"I'm gonna assume you're angry," I say, splitting the silence. "Is it with me?"

I turn, facing him as I lean back against the table as I grip the edges, preparing for a lecture. Maybe after a week, he decided he was angry with me and how I handled things. Except, Isaac just stares at me with a deep frown.

"No."

He speaks! It's one word, but he speaks!

"Then…with Leo?" His jaw tenses, blue eyes piercing mine as he straightens his posture. His hands go into his pockets, while he looks away, face contorting into anguish and ire.

I almost gape at him.

"You can't be *that* mad at him," I state. His gaze remains on the ground. "Okay, maybe you can be, want to tell me *why* to the point you won't talk or look at me?"

"Where would I even start?"

"Meaning?"

He exhales sharply as he finally looks at me. "You two may love each other deeply, but that does not condone his behavior in breaking multiple promises to you, whilst using your marriage for his own damn convenience to become a chess piece against his family."

My jaw drops. Worry is replaced by shock as he continues.

"Repeatedly, you have prevented his downfall and demise in the mafia, business, his status, and your relationship. While he's allowed his obsession for control to blind him when it comes to you, which resulted in hurting you for months, and to the point of accusations regarding your character that were uncalled for. Not to mention, he cut off communication with his therapist in December."

"He said he was going to go back."

"Well, he hasn't. I doubt he ever will at this point. The only one within your relationship who seems to be adjusting and communicating to help it survive is you."

My heart feels like it's breaking. "Isaac—"

"He hid information from you, which concerned you, and then ordered us to keep our mouths shut. More like threatened, which he does frequently. Given his reputation and inability to control his anger we, of course, listened and didn't push him. Even while he kept killing and torturing those you've done your best to forget. If he'd just been honest with you from the start about his family, what he's planning, and has done, then what happened last week may not have."

A knot forms in my stomach, bringing a sick feeling.

"Over the course of the last few months, he's lost much of my respect given his attitude not just as a boss, but as your husband." Isaac's words, though not entirely directed at me, sting as tears gather in my eyes. "And you, Miss Autumn, I fear your constant forgiveness and loving nature has been taken advantage of. I know he loves you, but at what cost when you have to take his place as the Mafia Don due to his actions?"

"I didn't *have* to do that. I *chose* to."

"Which you wouldn't have needed to do had he spoken the truth instead of hiding it."

"What do you want me to do? Yell at him? Punish him?" My words come out sharp as the knot worsens, turning from hurt to anger. "Divorce him?"

His jaw works. I concentrate on not throwing the vase of lilies at him.

"No," he finally answers, but the hesitation weighs heavy. "I want him to be honest with you. To not use you in his schemes as a final attempt to maintain his obsessive control."

I gape at him. "You honestly can't believe he's...*using* me?"

"I have known him for almost a decade." Blue eyes flit over my face, frustration lining them. "Perhaps, he's changed a little, but no one...especially him, changes from a man who's obsessed with control to not caring about it. Not that quickly. He's never been truly attached to anything or anyone outside the MC or the empire he built. He may understand people, but mostly how to use them, not for companionship."

"Why..." I clear my throat, torn between wanting to cry or scream, "...are you saying any of this?"

"He wasn't in that meeting with you." My stomach drops as I slump back against the table. "That wasn't you in there, that was *him*."

Everything feels heavy, my mind scrambling to make sense of all this. It feels like a hurricane that won't stop.

"He didn't watch you go to bed alone, night after night," he continues. "How you busied yourself, bettering the hotel, and then taking away any praise you deserved by dishing out money to his employees."

My mind screeches to a halt. What the fuck? I didn't want praise for that, I wanted to help people and assuage my own damn guilt. I look up at him, brows pinching together. This has been festering for months, and there's something about his tone that creates a prick at the back of my neck. A deeper anger.

"You had to flee the city *again*, because of him, and then return to save his businesses, reputation, and even his damn money. It's one thing to help him on hard days, but entirely another to relinquish what you had left of your old life. It jeopardized your safety. You even killed a man for him, for god's sake."

A sharp breath leaves him as he steps back, pacing as he breathes heavily. He rubs his head, while I look down at the ground, not believing what I'm hearing. We're quiet, the silence consuming as he paces.

"Love is not enough to sustain a relationship," he states, stopping. I look up at him through my lashes, almost glaring. "I worry in his attempt to wreak revenge on anyone he seeks, he will get you killed or worse."

"You don't think he knows that?"

"I think he believes he's God."

A scream claws at my throat, to tell him that when it's only Leo and I, he's just a man. A man who's been beaten, broken, betrayed, and who's held the world on his shoulders against his will. Shackled with responsibilities that he both chose and didn't. Or to tell him, some nights he's that boy crying over the phone to his parents to save him. How much he hides behind that scowl, while on his knees begging for forgiveness.

No. Leo doesn't believe he's God. His back tattoo flashes before my eyes. I know who he thinks he is—a fallen angel, cast out and hunted by angels and…demons.

"Miss Autumn, I love you."

My entire body goes still, staring at Isaac in horror. Oh, fuck, NO. This is not going to turn into some unrequited love bullshit. "Isaac—"

"Not like that, what I mean is that I'm fond of you. Not just because it's my job do I follow and listen to you, but out of respect, friendship, and…love. I cannot keep watching as he…he…influences you."

"You wanted to say control," I counter.

"You must admit, he does end up controlling some of your decisions."

It's then, I feel something inside me snap. A line he finally crossed that he shouldn't have. I stand fully, straightening myself as I press my arms to my sides to hide the shaking. Anger pulses through me as I clench my jaw.

"So, you saying that I'm *capable* of anything was bullshit?"

His brows pinch, shaking his head. "That's not what I meant."

"But it is, isn't? I'm able to kill a man, but that comes with strings attached because who you saw was Leo, not *me*," I state, venom filling my words as that anger from a week ago resurfaces. "I, *of course*, couldn't have decided fully on my own…my husband *has* to have been involved. The same in deciding on using a program *I* fucking created years ago."

"Autumn—"

"No, you will listen like I have!" My voice raises, causing him to step back. "Surprisingly, I'm not some damsel who needs her hand held all the time. Just because *you* saw me at my lowest, does not give you the right to use it against me or throw vitriol at my husband. My trauma is not *yours* to use as a tool to condemn me as powerless. I am allowed to be angry and feel every damn emotion of the human experience without it becoming a weapon against the *one man* who has *never* spoken down to me like I'm a child."

Isaac's expression drops, but all I see is red.

"To you, Leo controls everything he touches; the MC, businesses, hotels, family, you, even the women he's fucked," I spit out the last word, and he almost stumbles back. "Easy to assume, that of course, he *has* to be controlling Autumn, too. Because how else could a man like that function? Here I thought that you and the rest of the Crew would never believe the mask he carved so fucking well, but apparently, he's gotten so damn good at wearing it that you fell for it. You fell for the lies and carefully placed details he's created since he was a child, who was abducted for ransom to sell back to his own father!"

I'm seething with anger, taking another step closer as my voice becomes low and threatening. "He is not God; he is a man who wants to stay with the only person who doesn't believe he's made of stone."

My hands shake in anger, body trembling as I clench my fists. Isaac stares at me in shock, while tears gather in my eyes.

"You think you're scared for me?" My words come out soft, but are filled with ire, unable to stop as my heart cracks. "Imagine the woman you love disappearing, not knowing what happened to her, and then she comes back with cuts down her legs she gave herself. And then you clean them, help heal them. Imagine telling your *men* to stay with her, but they left her alone, and you find her holding a k-bar to her wrist." His eyes widen in horror. "Imagine hearing her screams. Imagine her showing up bruised and bloodied. Imagine watching her almost break, while locked in an interrogation room. After *all* of that… then imagine listening to men confess what they did to her. How they broke her. What they planned to do. Or that your own *brother* planned and tried to rape her."

He remains silent as a tear moves down his cheek.

"I have put that man through hell, and yet he's not complained once while my bloodied decisions were on his hands," I say as my tears run down my face. "Until the day I die, I will defend him with every cell in my body, damn it."

Isaac looks away, staring at the ground as more tears fall.

"And just like you Isaac, his own love and need to protect me, blinded him. He fucked up. I know. Just as I've fucked up because not everything is his fault. You *Forgotten Demons* have your codes with women to the point I think none of you will ever willingly be angry with me, so you lash out at him. But enough is enough. I lied to you. I lied to the Crew. I deceived every single one of you and did what *none* of you could do. It's not his pride and ego that was chipped, it was *yours*."

His eyes snap to mine. Isaac's chest rises heavily as he frowns, clenching his hands like a child caught.

"You want to be mad at someone, spew your venom at me. I know *everything*, Isaac, including the fine print when he married me." A different kind of horror forms on his face. "You and every person in this city should be very thankful that I love him because *I* could turn this city into complete fucking chaos. Terrified or not, if he didn't walk through those doors, I would've eviscerated those men to remind them of the woman they didn't kill. It wasn't his anger you saw; it was mine. So, I will warn you once, if you ever speak so horribly about my marriage because of your *love* for me again..." I step closer, body shaking with wrath and pain, "...I will show you how *unforgiving* I can truly be. Am I clear?"

A numbness comes over his face, the emotions draining from him. Almost too quietly and detached, he says, "Yes, Mrs. Luciano."

My heart clenches painfully. Blue eyes haunting me. "Go home."

I turn on my heel, walking heavily to the door and step inside the apartment. Quickly, I shut the door and lock it, sliding down as I begin to sob into my hands. My body shakes as I cry, trying not to make any noise for him to hear through the door. I sob, letting out the anger and frustration as I wrap my arms around my legs. I tremble and cry out the hurt.

It seems forever before the tears start to dry, my throat somewhat scratchy and my body tired. I lay my head against my knees, letting out a trembling breath before I stumble up from the floor. My legs are fuzzy and achy as I shake them out, prickling beginning in my feet and calves. I make my way to the couch, slumping onto it and stare up at the ceiling.

A migraine begins to set in as I rub my head, throbbing as I wince. Grumbling, I get up and change clothes. I tug on sweatpants, a baggy shirt, and some blue socks. They don't give as much joy as I'd like, but they'll do for now. I go to the kitchen, staring at the cabinets. Head pounding, I lean onto the counter as I feel my body revolt at the idea of food. Great. Full blown argument, thunder dome style with Isaac and now, headache from hell. Maybe I should take a nap on the couch until Leo comes home. I glance at the clock, squinting past the pain, and realize it's barely early afternoon. Fucking crud muffins.

A knock disrupts my thoughts. I groan, not ready to deal with anyone. The knock sounds again, and the door handle jiggles. Brain foggy from the headache, I sigh and walk to the door. I unlock it, opening to reveal the last person I thought I'd see today.

Chapter 10

Bravery in Many Forms

"Your hair looks good," Jameson compliments.

I blink at him in shock, then wrap my arms around myself. "Thanks. Leo isn't here."

"I know. He's in a meeting, and then leaving soon for one with Finstrum."

Head still pounding, I peek past him to the lilies, where I yelled at Isaac. I'm not sure if I'm up for another argument the way I'm feeling.

"Autumn, are you alright?" He dips his head to look at my face.

Swallowing hard, I attempt a shrug. "Fine. What do you need?"

"May I come in?" Not sure what I'm trying to process more: that Jameson is here at all or that he asked to come in. "Leo knows I'm here."

Even curiouser.

I step aside, gesturing for him to enter and close the door behind him. He ambles into the kitchen, stopping at the counter as I try to blink past the migraine that's growing.

"Are you sure you're alright?"

"Headache." I lean back against the counter across from him. "Want anything to drink?"

"No, thank you."

He watches me a moment, and I think the headache is messing with me because he seems…softer than usual. I keep my arms wrapped around me, waiting for him to yell at me next given today's track record with bikers.

Jameson walks over to one of the cabinets, grabs a washcloth, soaks it with cold water, and then rings it out. I watch him, unsure what to do, until he comes over and places the cold washcloth at the back of my neck. I don't move as he massages it against my skin.

"I apologize for being a fucking ass of late. Well, cabrón is what Enigma used and Ringer used dummkopf. Got chewed out in multiple languages."

Okay, today is officially weird. Maybe I fell asleep and need to click my socks together three times.

"Uh, what?" I ask, looking up at him as he keeps the washcloth in place. I'm not sure of the last time I was this physically close to him, if ever, but my headache is slowly subsiding.

"I was angry. With you. I was pissed about the secret marriage, lying about how deep your involvement was with the feds, *Eleanor*, the blackmail, and then stupidly taking on those crime bosses. You handled it…well. I will admit better than most men I've met."

"Okay," I murmur, staring at the buttons of his shirt.

He gently rubs the cloth over my neck, easing more of the tension from the headache.

"A few weeks back Ringer and I had a conversation," he says.

"About?"

"That I need to 'grow up' or lose Leo."

My breath shudders, and I gently reach up towards the washcloth. "Headache is gone. Thanks."

Jameson pulls away, putting the washcloth over the sink edge, then leans against the counter across from me. He speaks quietly, "It's just been him and I for over fifteen years. People have come and gone, even some *Forgotten Demons*. Crew don't know him like I do; what he's done and sacrificed, not all of it. I trusted no one, until you. Believed you in the library that day when you said you weren't going to hurt him."

He purses his lips, hands gripping the countertop.

"But I disappeared."

"And you hurt him."

"I know," I whisper.

"Last few months, honestly, I've been waiting for you to do it again. I was willing to forgive you, try to trust you again, but then he started down this dark, vengeful path. All I could think was, 'what if he does all this and she fucks him over?' And then I heard about the changes you were making, money you were spending, and it reminded me of women who've tried to use him. I thought you were going to screw him over."

I bite my lower lip, knowing I deserved what he thought. I'd brought it upon myself.

"Then more lies, hiding, and no clue what you all signed and agreed to. I got pissed with him next. Unsure if he was giving away what I built with him, too." Jameson sighs, looking down at the ground. "I was so angry how he defended both of you and your choices, that the day after all that shit went down I told him I should go back to California. Leave."

"Please don't leave me."

My heart clenches. "Is that what this is? Good-bye?"

It's quiet. The silence stretching as I stare at him.

"I saw the will, the real one," he answers instead. He looks back up at me. "Even in death, you're going to protect him."

My chin quivers, and I nod faintly.

"I could never do that. Give him that kind of peace," he admits. He inhales a deep breath. "Read the fine print of everything else. If he dies first…it's you and I who control everything."

"We would have never taken it away from you," I whisper.

"I know that now. That like me…you just wanted him to be okay."

I swallow hard, rubbing my hands over my arms. I ask again, "Are you leaving?"

"No," he answers, a small smile on his face. "I need to grow up. Adjust to you calling the shots with Leo and trust you to take care of him. Won't agree here and there, but I'm not perfect. Still…I apologize for my shitty behavior instead of just fucking talking to you again."

"Can't blame you. I did break my promise. I lied about who I was and kept secrets. Although, you're the only one who has the balls to be mad at *me*. Get a gold star for that."

He smirks, crossing his arms over his chest.

"How'd you go from potentially leaving for California to staying?" I ask.

"Had a real conversation with Leo. No yelling, shockingly."

I snort, and then sigh with relief. One less person tearing down Leo.

"Showed me all the fucking paperwork you signed," he says, and then a softness comes over his face. "And that he told you about Gretchen."

"Who?" My brows raise.

"His ex-Dominatrix."

My stomach flips again. "Yeah, he did."

"Including what you agreed to."

A nervous breath leaves me, moving to hold onto the counter edge. Where the fuck is my day going? I stare at the ground, unsure how to respond. Why would Leo tell him? He's never told anyone about what we do. Is he having second thoughts? Why would—?

"Autumn." His voice pierces through the rambling thoughts, and I glimpse at Jameson's faint smile. "No specifics and I don't want to know, but he told me because he's happy."

While I'm torn between being happy for Leo and shock that he told his best friend at all.

"I'm the only one who knew the truth of what Gretchen did."

"What about Chesty, didn't he help…well, get rid of her?"

"Like the rest of the Crew, he knew she was a play partner who attempted to blackmail him with their sessions. They all think he was the Dom, and that the videos would've made him appear abusive. Only I saw…" he clears his throat, "…some of the videos."

"Oh."

"When she turned on him, he shut everything out. It was the final break before the rest of his walls went up, and they stayed up for years. Gabriel and his family only made it worse. Until you."

We stare at each other, and then I sigh almost in pleading exasperation. "I'm not going to screw him over. I promise. He's safe with me."

"I won't pry, but…you'll be able to give him what he needs?" He asks suddenly.

My head tilts, understanding more how much Jameson cares for Leo. Perhaps, something I should've noticed before. How deep their brotherhood was to him, even if it meant leaving.

"Yes," I answer. "Honestly? I like knowing only I can do that for him. Take care of him. I want to."

"I'll have to get used to sharing him. Not in bed…you know what I mean."

I smile faintly. "I do. You and me both."

He grabs the washcloth to wring out again, putting it on the counter as he faces away from me. He stops, then says, "Thank you for taking care of him, Autumn."

"May sound odd, but thank you for being angry with me, recognizing I did fuck up. And not entirely being mad at him."

He looks at the couches, and I catch a faraway look on his face as I move over. He frowns, but in a saddened way that makes me glance towards where he looks. For a few moments, he just stands there silently staring at the empty space. His jaw muscles tighten before he clears his throat.

"Sombra means shadow in Spanish," he states suddenly.

I stare at the couches, unsure what he's seeing.

"Bikers even outside the *Forgotten Demons* would say 'where there's The Spartan, his Shadow isn't far behind' and the name stuck. He and others hated the idea of just calling me that, so it was decided on Sombra."

As he tells me his road name origin, I wonder if he didn't like being Leo's shadow. Did he feel eclipsed by always being tied to him? He said long ago he preferred staying out of the spotlight, but some days did he regret it?

His gaze still hasn't torn from the living room. A sinking feeling looms, telling me that something else happened here. I don't think he'll tell me just yet. If ever.

"Collected all the road name origins, now?"

"Supposedly," I answer.

Finally, he tears his gaze away, looking at me. "Who you missing?"

"Leo's road name, I mean he told me, but..." I exhale sharply, "...it's partially because of what I saw at the warehouse, isn't? Him getting bloody?"

Golden brown eyes stay with mine. "Then you have collected all of them."

Something silent passes between us, similar to the understanding we had at the public library or the diner, but deeper. An agreement.

He points to the washcloth. "If the headache comes back, just use a cold compress to help relieve the pain."

"Thanks." I smile weakly, and he starts to leave.

"I'll make sure he's not out late; get him home to you."

"Jameson." He stops, flicking those amber eyes to me. "Did I fuck things up?"

"No. Honestly, I truly think you did save him. Have a good night, Autumn."

"You, too, Sombra."

Jameson leaves, and I'm left stupefied. I think I need a drink. Yeah, fuck it, I need a drink.

I walk over to Leo's liquor cabinet, pulling out a bottle of Dewar and pour two fingers worth. Some ice is added to my drink, and I sip practically moaning. Ohhh, I needed that.

Not tempting fate for another headache, I start searching through the fridge for something to eat. Close to calling Christopher, I notice something in the freezer. Oh, bless Alba. I reach in, pulling out a bag of pizza rolls.

Half the bag is devoured as I sip the scotch, watching *Dracula* starring Christopher Lee. I debate going somewhere else like to see Chiari, but wasn't feeling up to leaving the apartment. I'm slowly able to relax as I continue with my marathon of Dracula movies. I've gotten through the *Taste the Blood of Dracula* and *Scars of Dracula*, and a bit into *The Satanic Rites of Dracula* when there's a noise from the front door.

He's actually home in time for dinner.

I pause the film and step out of the television room. Leo pulls his suit jacket off and folds it over the sofa, going still when he sees me. Relief floods me that he's home earlier than usual. That he is at all. His gaze roams over me, landing on my hair.

"No wig?" He asks, slowly unbuttoning his shirt, moving towards me.

"Maybe next time." I touch my hair. "You like it?"

He stops, taking my hand as endearment spreads on his face, noticing my nails next. Leo strokes his fingers through my short hair, smiling softly. "I love it."

I wrap my arms around him, sighing as my head lays against his chest to hear his heartbeat. Leo strokes my back, easing what tension was left in my body. A shudder comes over me ready to melt into his arms.

"Check in," he whispers.

"Yellow."

His hand movements falter. "Did something happen when Jameson came to talk to you?"

"No, we're fine. We're good." I step back, keeping my hands upon his waist. His brows furrow, lines appearing upon his forehead. Faintly smiling, I press a finger over one of them. His expression relaxes. "Isaac and I argued. A lot."

"Given recent conversations with him, doesn't surprise me." His voice is cold and rough. Ah, so our argument today was not the first.

I let out a huff, falling back against his chest.

"Autumn, you rarely get angry and when you do it's usually for good reason. Whatever argument you had…I'm sure it'll be alright." His voice is quieter on the last part, like he doesn't believe his own words. He clears his throat. "He takes his position very seriously."

"Like Jameson," I murmur.

"Yes." I squeeze my arms around him, and he kisses the top of my head. "Did you eat?"

"Pizza rolls." Leo releases me, going back to unbuttoning his shirt. I raise my brows. "No comeback? No snark?"

"You ate something other than cereal for lunch. I feel that requires a bit of praise for you," he smirks, grabbing his jacket then heads to the bedroom.

"Okay, you're sassy. Meetings must've gone well." I follow him, sitting on the bed as he undresses.

"Thankfully, they did."

"Even Finstrum's?"

He pauses. "Jameson tell you?" I nod, and he hums, stripping his shirt off. "Finstrum won't be an issue, especially after practically being given two of Curione's clubs. DeLuca can be handled; he won't go against Finstrum and I. The other families are too small to risk losing their territories nor do they have the pull within the police force. If they side with Matteo, they'll lose more than they gain."

"And be blackmailed."

"Exactly."

Leo's pants come off, leaving him only in his underwear which he strips out of. Suddenly, my body squirms with need. My core clenches as I bring my legs in close as I watch his tattoos flex. Warmth spreads over me as Leo reaches up, pushing his hair back. I swear I could come right now.

Long day apparently equals a very horny Autumn to help sad feelings disappear.

More fun than grabbing a razor. Okay, dark humor, simmer down.

I shake off that thought as Leo goes into the bathroom. My throat becomes dry, stomach filling with butterflies. I'm turned on, clearly, far too aware of my body now.

Just ask him. Ask your husband to fuck you. You know the thing you should *completely* be used to by now.

I don't move.

Off to a great start. Why are some days harder than others?

I hear the water turn on for the shower.

Slower than I'd like, I get off the bed and undress. I attempt to purge the rampant thoughts in my head, wiggling my limbs and try giving myself a mini-pep talk. *I can do this.* I take a step towards the bathroom, freezing in place.

What if he doesn't want to? He's had a long day, so have I, maybe he's tired. Or what if he wants me to Top him? If that's true, I should plan something. How much thought do I even need to—?

I inwardly groan, spin around and flop onto the bed before I grab a pillow and scream into it. This should not be this hard when I've already done it! I bang my head into the pillow, huffing in exasperation. I'm half-tempted to lay down naked and hope for the best. Maybe he'll—

"Autumn?"

I yelp, instinctively throwing the pillow at the voice. It thumps against Leo's naked chest as he blinks at me. Socks, now a pillow. What else shall I throw at my husband?

A towel is tied around his waist, the rest of him still glistening from the shower. His wet hair is pushed back, droplets sliding down his confused expression. His gaze goes to the pillow and then back to me.

"I want sex, but wasn't sure if you want to," I blurt out.

He tilts his head, face softening. Nervous rambling takes over me. "Or maybe you wanted me to Top you? I didn't know what to suggest. Like do it in the shower? Bed? Counter? Or maybe, not at all, but I took my clothes off thinking..." Leo prowls towards me, "...that'd be a good start, hopefully. Then I was yelling into the pillow to help clear my thoughts, but..."

Words vanish as Leo stops before the bed, grabbing my chin and tilting my head back. A gentle smile rises on his face. "I find it endearing that you still get flustered with me."

Not what I was expecting.

My face contorts with confusion. His thumb strokes over my bottom lip.

"You've come a long way since that night in your old kitchen," he explains. "Learning to be bold, but you're still you. You, who giggles when you're nervous or flustered. Smiles unapologetically. Willing to be vulnerable with me."

As he speaks, one of those nervous giggles come out.

"There she is," he whispers, leaning down to tenderly kiss me. My breath catches, swallowing hard against my dry throat while shivers run over my skin.

Once he gives me enough room to speak, I ask, "How am I supposed to be your Dom?"

Leo trails his hand under my jaw, moving to place his palm against my throat. Calm settles through me, making the fluttering thoughts and nerves disappear with that simple touch.

"Be yourself. Don't change who you are, dear Watson. I feel safe with *you* not a caricature of something you're not. Knowing you're thinking so much on how to pleasure and love me is proof enough you'd be a good Dom for me."

My hands trail down his stomach to the curve of his towel. "So…giggling or floundering trying to figure out what to do next… you won't be turned off? Still find it…sexy?"

"Yes," he says with a smoldering smile. "We'll learn how to make it work. Together. It'll get easier as it already has been with us." His other hand lands against mine on his towel, and he leans in close so his warm breath brushes over my ear. His voice is rough and practically dripping with desire. "I want to be dominated by *my* Mistress who already ignites my soul."

A shudder wrecks through my body at his words.

Fingers tracing over his towel, I dip them under the cloth and help it fall to the ground. I keep my hands on his hips, tugging him closer as he kisses under my jaw.

"Check in," I whisper.

"Green, my dear Watson."

I pull him towards me, falling back into the bed. Leo drags his body over mine, releasing my throat as his hands move along my shoulders and waist. He hums while dipping his head lower to trail his tongue between my breasts. I grab his soft wet hair, the strands sliding between my fingers. His mouth caresses my skin, licking up my breast and then towards my nipple, tongue circling. My body jolts from desire as I stare up at the ceiling, hoping I can do this.

Be yourself.

Resolute that I can, I grab his arms and move my leg around his to flip him over. Leo easily follows where I've encouraged, landing on his back as I quickly throw my leg over his hips. I straddle him, staring down at his satisfied smirk. A giggle bubbles up in my throat as he reaches for my thighs, but I grab his hands and lean over to place them above his head. His smirk vanishes, replaced by a look of pride and…relief.

Leo's eyes smolder as he gazes up at me, while I pin his hands above his head. My fingers trace down his forearms. "So…can you keep your hands there or do I need to tie you up?"

Eyes yearning with need flash as I see the answer there. *"I want to be dominated—"*

"Stay. No moving," I instruct, getting off him and wagging my finger a little. I feel him watching me as I scramble to the closet, not at all sultry about it. Quickly, I find two neck ties and then grab lube next. My eyes flick to his growing erection as Leo remains where he is.

I straddle him again, sitting in front of his hardening cock that brushes against my ass. He groans as I lean forward, beginning to wrap a tie around his wrists. I don't quite trust myself to fully bind him, not without hurting him, so I tighten it enough to keep them together.

"Don't move your hands, unless I tell you." My voice is a little shaky, including my limbs. I hold up the other tie. Leo flicks his gaze to it. A debate runs through my head on whether to cover his eyes or not. Another idea flickers.

I must sit there debating longer than I think because Leo's words break through. "Check in."

I clear my throat. "Yellow."

"What are you unsure about?"

"Whether to gag you or not." Immediately, I bring my hand up to my mouth as I giggle at the blunt words.

Leo smiles, arms fidgeting above his head, but he doesn't stop me from covering my mouth like he usually does. Realization sparks that even though we're not in a full scene, just some kinky fun, he's going to listen whole-heartedly. At that thought I relax, bringing my hand down.

"Do you want to see or speak?" I ask.

"I want to watch you."

I know his hard and soft limits; the man doesn't have many, but he does have them. Fortunately, his limits mostly align with mine on what I'm willing to do. His big wants are being gagged, bound, impact play, or forced into positions. Complete opposite of me when it comes to being a Sub, including being gagged.

"Okay." I huff out a breath. "If you can't say red or yellow, then two fingers for yellow and three for red." He shows me he can do both with his hands. "Good...job."

Leo smirks playfully, and I roll my eyes, giggling again. Gently, I place the tie in his mouth, and then wrap it around his head twice before making sure it's secure. He bites down, already the tie becoming wet from his saliva. I'm sure he could speak if he wanted, but knowing him, he won't.

"Show me one finger for green." He does immediately.

And he says I'm a good and obedient Sub? *Willing to never be dominated again*, my cereal loving ass.

I run my hands down his chest, tracing my fingers over the ink. Slowly, I wiggle back and lift my hips over his now very erect cock. A muffled hiss comes out of him as I brush my skin across his. My thighs pin his legs together under me while I continue to run my hands over his torso, following the designs that color his stomach, chest, shoulders, and hips. I stare at the various artwork as I move down closer to just above his dick. I flick my gaze up at him, his eyes staring up at the ceiling as his hands fist and twitch.

Leo doesn't move. With every featherlight touch from me, his body tensing and flexing, he remains where he is.

Unlike the first time encountering this side of him, I wholeheartedly tease him with my fingers without restraint. He breathes deep through his nose, panting as I slide my fingers along the muscles towards his pelvis. Leo bares his teeth, biting down on the tie, grinding his jaw. A wave of pleasure hits me as I lean forward, beginning to lick up from his navel. Leo's entire body tenses, knuckles cracking as he groans under the gag. I stop in the middle of his chest, looking up at him as he stares at the ceiling and his arms shake to remain put.

Pride jolts through me. It's followed by another wave of pleasure, rushing over my skin as the power I have over him clutches me. Leo obeying me.

Air rushes out from my lungs as I trace my tongue back down the middle of his stomach. I realize how much I enjoy this—controlling him and watching him obey my commands. It's a similar high as when he tells me what to do, a different side of control. Power exchange. Oh, fuck I get it. I crave it now, wanting to tease him, but give him pleasure.

I grab the bottle of lube, squirting a little on my fingers. Leo's eyes snap down to me as I carefully grip his cock in my hands. He moans against the gag, staring at my hands as I stroke his cock with ease. His breath quickens, chest heaving as I give him the hand job and smile. He's smooth against my fingers as I pump him, but then let go completely. He mumbles against the tie, laying his head back in frustration.

"Check in, baby." His hands move, and he gives me the signal for green. "Good boy."

The honorific comes out before I can think. I freeze.

Leo's gaze finds mine. Hazel eyes lock on mine with desire and lust.

Oh, fuck he likes that.

My body thrums with need, craving him to be inside me already. Quickly, I ready his dick to my entrance and bring my hips down. Leo's muffled groans occur next as I raise my hips, moving back down as I undulate. I moan next at the fullness of him, shivering as I help myself hit the right spot inside me. Circling my hips, I go in a slow motion as I feel his cock twitch. Leo grunts as I ride him, thrusting my body against his. His face contorts with pleasure and frustration as he does his best to remain where he is. Those hazel eyes sear into me, flashing between my chest, hips, and face. The tie is soaked from his mouth, almost dripping.

I circle my hips again, lifting and slamming them back down. A pleasurable moan courses through me as my spine tenses along with my legs. Muscles burn as I continue to ride him, pressing my hips flush against his. I grind hard down on him, moaning with Leo as I place my hands upon his chest. My fingers flex as I help myself stay up, sliding them further up as I pause pushing his cock into me. My muscles clench around him as I swallow hard against heavy breathing, sliding my hand up until I come to his bared neck. Instinctively, I place it against his throat, lightly pressing down as I meet his gaze.

Burning desire. Need blazing deep. Pure relief; utter, unabashed relief fills those eyes I love. Tears gather in them as he gazes up at me, holding him down beneath me. Even now with such low stakes, there's so much liberation in his eyes that my heart clenches. He wanted…no, *needed* this.

I untie the gag, pulling it away for me to slam my mouth to his. I kiss him hard, keeping my other hand against his bare throat and tilt his head back. Leo moans against me, tongue finding mine as I ride him hard. My hips move roughly, driving him deep as I pant and kiss him feverishly. My body tenses as pleasure builds, muscles tightening as Leo arches his back while my legs burn.

I'm right on the precipice of orgasming, hoping he'll follow, when he murmurs reverently against my lips, "Mistress."

I come hard. My hands move, grasping his hair as I orgasm and gasp against his ear, "Come for me, baby."

Leo grunts as his chest presses against mine. His legs flex, hips jolting forward while his hands above his head grip the blankets as he comes next. He groans and shivers underneath me, breathing heavily as every muscle in my body clenches at the force of the ecstasy that hits me. Finally, I untense and fall onto his chest completely. My vision blurs a moment, blinking quickly as I attempt to catch my breath and reach up to pull the tie off his hands. I rest my head on his shoulder, stroking his chest.

"Move," I murmur. His arms come down, wrapping around me. Leo kisses my temple, nuzzling my hair.

"Good girl," he praises. A giggle comes out as I try not to laugh too hard. I look up, finding adoration and peace upon his face. All I want to do is hide that delicate look from the world forever.

Chapter 11

Double-Cross

I'm woken up by a phone going off. Leo grumbles next to me in bed, before I hear his hand slam against the bedside table. I glance at the clock, noticing it's almost four in the morning. He starts to settle in beside me. Phone goes off again.

"Fucking…" Leo mutters, picking up the phone this time. "Come back at eight. Fuck off whatever it is."

He hangs up, tossing the phone across the room. Leo pulls me into his arms, burying his face into my hair. I'm about to fall asleep again when I hear the door unlock. My body tenses, clutching Leo. I feel him reach over to the bedside table again, likely reaching for his gun.

"We have a situation," Jameson's voice pierces the darkness.

I instantly relax, realizing its him as I go to turn the lamp on, but Leo stops me. He pulls the blanket up. "You're naked."

A squeak comes out of me, hiding under the covers as Leo turns on the lamp beside him. "Here I thought we agreed no more interruptions, how the fuck did you even get in?"

"Ringer gave me his key."

"I'm gonna kill him," Leo mutters. "Couldn't fucking wait—"

"It can't," Jameson states.

I rub my eyes, partially sitting up as I keep the blankets over me. Leo looks ready to kill Jameson. "What is it?"

Jameson's wearing a t-shirt and sweatpants, an outfit I thought I'd never see him in. His face is grave, and I notice that he looks... scared. "Jameson?"

"Isaac's missing."

My heart drops. Leo becomes rigid.

"What?" Leo asks.

"6pm, he called Ringer, told him to take over bodyguard duty today per Autumn's request."

"No, I didn't," I rasp, body beginning to shake as a coldness sweeps over me.

"Well, he left for home, but his cellphone went dark at nine. He didn't give his final check in for the day. His apartment is empty. Not answering his phone. Around midnight, Enigma tried to track him down, in case he'd been captured."

"And?" Leo asks.

"There's no footage of him leaving the hotel. But he's not here."

I stare at the blankets, gripping them as my mind reels. I feel sick, thinking of my final words to him and our argument. Leo's arm moves over my shoulders, holding me close as the trembling worsens. What if he *was* taken? Being tortured? Killed—

"We've been trying to track him, but nothing. Thought to wait until morning, but given the abruptness and his actions of late..." Jameson's voice trails away.

I flick my gaze to him. I ask, "What actions of late?"

Jameson clears his throat, crossing his arms as he leans against the doorway. "You want to finally tell her?"

"Tell me what?" I look at Leo, more questions and fears circling my head.

Leo sighs, almost a look of defeat on his face. "Did he use *any* codes with Ringer that he may have been coerced?"

"No," Jameson answers. "Iron Buffalo and Enigma confirmed *he* turned off the phone and went dark. Never used the emergency button."

"Fuck," Leo mutters.

"Leo, what did he do?" I ask as the shaking worsens. A twist occurs in my stomach, and I want to hurl at the thought of something happening to Isaac.

"Get the rest of the Crew up to my office. We need to find him, whether he defected, was coerced, or…"

"Leo, tell me before I pull down the covers and scare the crap out of Jameson." My voice interrupts him, and he looks at me in shock. Tears form in my eyes as violent tremors overwhelm my body.

"Jameson, go make some fucking coffee." Leo's voice is rough. Jameson walks out, and Leo holds me close as his hand strokes my back. "Breathe, dear Watson."

"Please tell me," I plead, burying my head against his chest.

"The day he came to the penthouse, we argued. He insinuated I married you out of revenge against my family, that he no longer respected my position, and potentially would leave. He said he'd only stay out of respect for you."

Everything crashes inside me as I replay yesterday. Tears stream down my cheeks as I cling to Leo, guilt gripping me.

"He's pushed Jameson and my decisions a couple times these past few weeks. Not to mention, him punching Jameson…perhaps warranted, but not a welcome reaction."

"Fuck, fuck, fuck…" I mutter against his chest, crying against him.

"Breathe, sweetheart…breathe…"

Leo strokes my back as the panic attack comes full force. My mind becomes fuzzy, blurring my vision as I struggle to breathe through the vice grip around my throat. Everything hurts as the violent shaking takes over.

"It's my fault," I sob. "It's my fault…I drove him away, it's my—"

"Shhh, it's not your fault," Leo reassures me, rocking me as he tugs me into his lap. I curl around him as he cradles me. "Where did you have your argument with him?"

"Foyer."

"Sombra," Leo calls out, pulling the blankets over me before Jameson comes back. "He's locked out of everything, correct?"

"Yes, did that around midnight when we noticed he went dark."

"Locked out?" I whisper.

"Precautions, in case he decided to turn on us or blackmail. He has enough to do so," Jameson answers.

Oh, fuck I'm going to be sick. I pull away to stare at Leo in horror, my vision blurry. "He…wouldn't. No, no…Isaac wouldn't."

My heart wants to shatter; insides screaming at the thought of Isaac's betrayal. No.

"We don't know that, Autumn." The softness in Jameson's voice, laced with pain makes me look over at him. "Anyone can be bought. Even bikers."

Holy shit. It truly has been only the two of them. A scream claws at my throat, not wanting to believe any of the *Forgotten Demons* could betray us.

"Jameson, get the footage from the foyer when Autumn was dropped off yesterday afternoon. It's likely the last time he was on camera, we need to see if there's any clues of where he went or what he's planning. Everyone in the top office in thirty minutes. Autumn and I will be up shortly."

Jameson walks out as Leo holds me close.

"We'll find him," he whispers.

Just as I think my panic attack is lessening, I remember what I said to Isaac. What I admitted. Truths that only Leo knew and me. I have no remorse for what I did, but horror begins to eat me alive as I recall my final words to Isaac.

What have I done?

Not even five in the morning as I sit on the couch in Leo's office, listening to the video footage. Leo and the Crew stand around the desk, watching Isaac's and my argument.

"...yell at him? Punish him? Divorce him?" I barely recognize my own voice as I keep my knees against my chest.

The men are quiet, but I can hear some muttering under their breaths. It's raining outside, streaking down the windows. I feel sick to my stomach as I shut my eyes, knowing what's coming next.

"...carefully placed details he's created since he was a child, who was abducted for ransom to sell back to his own father!"

I wince, seeing the horror on Isaac's face again. The numbness. Was it him choosing then to leave? Had he decided it wasn't Leo who was the monster, but me?

"...what they planned to do. Or that your own brother planned—"

My fingers dig into my skin, wanting to pierce my nails through the bone. A tug pulls at me, wanting to run for the nearest sharp thing. Self-hate rolling over me.

Suddenly, a hand touches my arm and I jerk. Leo gently grabs my wrists, pulling them away from ripping into my sweatpants. He crouches before me, reaching up to stroke my hair back as he cups my cheek. "Look at me, dear Watson."

My breaths are erratic as I look upon his face.

"Good girl. You're safe," he murmurs. I shiver, gripping his hand around mine.

We're silent as the video continues, the Crew shuffling on their feet until I hear me slamming the door. More silence, and then some tapping that tells me Julio stopped the tape.

"He stands there for about ten minutes, then takes the stairs down. Doesn't call anyone." Eerie quiet apart from the tapping of computer keys. "Goes to the office downstairs until 5:30, then goes to the maid service area. That's where he disappears right after making a call, likely to Ringer."

I look up past Leo to the others, seeing them all stand there with uncertainty in their eyes. None of them will directly look at me. The ache in my chest worsens.

Leo strokes my cheek again, bringing my attention back to him. My voice is barely a whisper, "I'm sorry."

He shakes his head, leaning forward to kiss my forehead. "You have nothing to be sorry for."

"He pushed you too far, *barchën*," Rudy states with a rough voice. I look up at him, who's frowning. "Not your fault. What he said must have been simmering a while."

"That's for sure," Animal comments, stepping back as he scratches his head.

I glance at all of them, but my gaze lands on Chesty who frowns deeply. He stares down at the computer that played the footage, appearing more perturbed than the others. Jameson starts to pace, releasing a long exhale. "He may have left the city completely, if we're lucky."

"Lucky?" Julio asks, stopping his tapping on the keyboard.

"If he's still in the city, he may have gone to Finstrum or DeLuca. Worse if he decided to contact Renato," Jameson answers.

"No fucking way," Chesty mutters. Leo begins to stand up, keeping his hand on the nape of my neck.

"Alright, he was pissed, but to go to another crime boss?" Owen asks.

"He yelled and argued with Autumn," Jameson rebukes, flicking his gaze to me. "I think we can all agree he's beyond pissed, given the insinuations he threw at her."

Julio starts, "Wait—"

"Gonna have to agree with Sombra," Animal mutters.

"Same," Rudy says.

I can't believe what I'm hearing. They think he actually turned on us? That he may have even gone to Renato?

"He's more level-headed than that," Owen says, crossing his arms as he exchanges a glance with Chesty, who starts rubbing his beard.

"Yet, he thought Leo was *using* Autumn," Jameson says.

"Well…" Julio mumbles, and a couple of the Crew look at Leo worriedly. Julio holds his hands up, tilting his head at Leo. "No offense, boss, but you do have a reputation."

"So, does Autumn, but none of you are going to admit that shit," Jameson practically growls as he starts to pace.

"Arguing isn't going to help get answers or bringing up what's been done, even my own damn choices," Leo interrupts before they all start arguing again. My gaze catches Jameson's who gives me a slightly guilty look. Least I can count on Jameson to keep me humble. "Is there *any* CTV footage to track where Isaac went?"

"Don't know," Julio answers. "No footage of *where* he left the hotel, he used the blind spots."

"He didn't want to be followed and knew we'd look," Animal mentions. "Again, gonna have to agree with Sombra here."

"Can we use *Eleanor* to quicken things up?" Leo asks. Julio and Owen look at me.

"Not really," I answer roughly. "Not much difference than Julio just using what he already has."

"She's right, it'll be faster hacking into cameras where we *think* he went," Owen adds.

"Didn't show him that little disrupter you used the first time, did you, *hermana*?" Julio asks.

"No. It died with that phone when I…got rid of it."

"Could've created his own version," Owen mentions. "He is the one who found her."

"Yeah, our best tracker is the one who's missing," Julio grumbles, going back to his computer.

My brain fuzzes out as they continue talking, Owen and Julio beginning to search through CTV footage at various parts surrounding the hotel. Numbness encases me as I try to think, whilst hoping Isaac did this for another reason. Something else we're missing. Leo steps away at some point to look at a video that Isaac could be seen in.

I hold myself close, getting up and walking over to the window and stare at the city. My mind races, sifting through conversations and the last hours I spent with him. Why Isaac? *Why* Isaac? He was upset, so what would he do? What would *I* do? I want to be with

Leo. To be with someone I can talk to and feel heard. *"…imagine the woman you love…"*

"Where's my phone?" I ask suddenly, looking at Leo and then Jameson. "Or any phone?"

"Autumn—"

"Phone, please," I ask, and Jameson hands over his. It's a long shot, but I dial the number I know by heart. I start pacing, holding my cardigan close, knowing it's early as fuck.

Please pick up. After the sixth ring, she finally picks up, answering groggily, "Jameson?"

"Leanne, it's Autumn. Have you spoken to Isaac?"

"Uh, Autumn? Why are you calling from Jameson's phone? Before six?"

"Leanne, hun, just tell me. Have you spoken to Isaac since yesterday?" It's so damn quiet in the office you could hear a pin drop.

I rub my stomach, trying to stop the twisting sensation as she clears her throat. "He, uh, came by last night."

I practically hold my breath. "Is he still there?"

A door closes in the background. She huffs tiredly, "He is."

My legs give out as I crumple to the floor in relief. The windowpane is cold against my hand as I press against it. The others start to move towards me, but it's Leo who crouches next to me with his hand on my shoulder. I hang my head, trying not to cry.

He left for Leanne's.

"Autumn, what's wrong?" She asks.

"Why did…he come over?"

"Okay, if I'm not gonna ask questions about you and Leo, then I—"

"He disappeared last night, and the entire Crew thought he double-crossed us," I quickly say, slumping against the glass. Leo sits down fully with me, relief coming over his face as realization hits him next where Isaac went.

The rest of the Crew make disgruntled noises.

"What?" She practically shrieks, but whispers it. "Why would they think that?"

"Because he vanished. No note. And practically blew off work without saying a damn thing. After the last two weeks, we're all a bit paranoid. So, my first guess wasn't exactly *your* place."

"You suggested he check my security."

"Nice try."

"Okay, fine we fucked."

I hit my head against the window, but before I can do it again, Leo stops me. "After the last hour, I'm torn of being delighted y'all got together finally or not."

Jameson starts to grumble, "Did he fucking break protocol so he could go—"

"Careful," I point at him. "She's my best friend. If they want to hanky panky, that's fine by me, especially if it means no stab wounds to my back."

"Not if he's gonna break rules," Owen mutters.

"What if someone grabbed him or Leanne? How the fuck did *her* security detail not know he's there or call it in?" Jameson argues.

"Probably told them not to. Or cause he knows when they switch to evade them," Chesty answers, holding back a relieved smirk.

"I don't care, long as they're both fine, and that I didn't fucking scare him off." My shaking voice punches through the air, and everyone goes quiet.

Leo moves his hand down my back, having me lean into him. The guilt that I'd driven him away slowly vanishes, but there's still worry why he'd left like that. Or this was the first step of him leaving altogether.

"Autumn," Leanne says.

"Yeah?"

"If I'd known, I'd have called you. I didn't know."

"I know, hun," I whisper. "Are you working today?"

"No, actually planning to call in sick."

"Alright…can you keep him there? Tie him to your bed if you want."

"I might, knowing he lied to me too…" she sighs, "…I'll keep him here."

"I'll be by later, when it's not the crack of dawn. Love you."

"Love you."

I hang up, holding Jameson's phone out to him. Everyone's quiet as the rain patters against the window. I look up at Leo, who seems torn between being relieved or aggravated.

"It's official, those fuckers made us all go batshit paranoid. Scarecrow would be proud," I say, cutting the silence.

The tension is thick, not a single one of the *Forgotten Demons* say a thing. After a couple more minutes of silence, I can't stand it much longer and get off the floor along with Leo.

"Yes, Leo and I lied to you," I say, almost exasperatedly. "Yes, we have a reputation of keeping secrets and controlling outcomes. *I* lied to you for months. I'm sorry for what I did, but not why I did, especially our marriage. It wasn't because we didn't trust you, but to protect you." I glance up at Leo, who nods once. "I've played these games before, who to trust or not, and it *never* goes well. Whether they got into this inner circle or not, they've done enough damage for us to point fingers instead of seeing the truth. We *have* to trust each other again. To trust Leo and I again."

I wrap an arm around Leo as he holds me. He exhales sharply.

"We're a Club," he says, solemnly. "At the end of the day, that's what we are first. *Forgotten Demons* to the end. We can't allow outsiders into our heads, if we do, we'll tear each other apart. Be angry all you want with me or her, but trust us. Clear?"

The men exchange glances, finally nodding in agreement.

Leo cradles my head against his chest, stroking his hand down my back. He adds gravely, "Otherwise we may as well hand everything over to my brothers now."

Chapter 12

Lasting Friendships

I STAND outside Leanne's door and knock.

Rudy and Chesty wait down the hall, leaning like the bikers they are. Both of them wear leather jackets, dark jeans, and black shirts. Doesn't help their case much. Not to mention them being the two biggest guys on the Crew, mass and muscle wise.

"You've never looked more mobster 'til now," I comment.

"We're lovable," Chesty retorts.

The rest of the morning was, well, quiet enough. I stayed in Leo's office with him. We were both shaken. Not just that we thought Isaac could betray us, but the fact we went there in the first place. Paranoia was already running deep, and this just pushed it deeper. A phone call from Renato didn't help either. Owen kept giving me worried glances as Leo argued in Italian with his uncle. I could only catch a few words here and there.

The door finally opens with Leanne standing in lounge pants and a knit sweater. I give her a faint smile. "Hey."

"Hey, can we…" she glances down the hall towards the other two, "…they just gonna hover?"

"Probably. He's still here?" She nods. "I want to talk to him, before anyone else, not about you two, other things."

"He told me," she sighs, opening the door more. A grimace comes over me. Leanne grabs my arm gently, leading me inside. "Come on, you two *do* have a lot to talk about. As for the other two, do you want…I don't know coffee? Beer?"

"It's 9am," I say. She shrugs.

"We're good," Chesty answers. "Wait here for ya, sister." Rudy grunts in agreement.

Leanne hums as she closes the door. I step into her one-bedroom apartment, the living room bigger than my old one with a nice window view showing another apartment complex. Her kitchen takes up one side, whilst her bedroom and bathroom are on the other. She repainted once her landlord gave the okay, making it a sage green with white trim, matching her dark floorboards. Her place always gave a sense of peace, not to mention all the plants she keeps.

I turn to face her, both of us giving a look of longing. Not even a second later, we crash into each other, hugging tightly.

"It's been forever," I whisper her usual line.

"Only two weeks." Longest fucking two weeks ever.

We tighten our hold, standing silently. Finally, we pull away, both of us sniffling a little.

"He's still sleeping. Up late. Talk first? I've got juice." I follow her into the kitchen, glimpsing at her closed bedroom door.

I sit at her small table, while she grabs orange juice and glasses, and then sits with me. We're quiet as she pours two glasses. "Long couple weeks," she murmurs.

"You've no idea," I mutter.

"We weren't planning on sleeping together, by the way. It just…"

I shake my head. "Honestly, I don't care, meaning… I won't interfere. Kind of rooting for you two anyways."

"Really?"

I shrug. "You're flirting was obvious and obnoxious."

A snort of laughter is shared between us as I look up at my longtime friend. She smiles, relaxing into her seat more.

"He's a good guy," I say softly.

"That brings up the question…" she leans onto the table, "…you thought he double-crossed you?"

Seeing Leanne, it's like a weight has been lifted off my shoulders, I groan and lean over her table, lightly tapping my head against the wood. "Past two weeks have made us all paranoid, more than usual. Not knowing where he went or how made it worse, right into well…"

"Tony Montoya territory."

I snort at her movie reference, placing my elbows on the table and she does the same.

"Well, you weren't the only ones," she says. "He wanted to talk things out, not with mobsters or guys. He was confused and frustrated, and then it led to finding *other* ways of working through feelings. After you called, we may have had *another* talk and then…"

I gape at her slightly. "Y'all are putting the burn in slow burn."

She winks saucily, and I giggle at her.

I glance at her bedroom, waiting for the inevitable interaction with Isaac, except another inevitable conversation starts.

"He told me…everything." I go still, not daring to look at my best friend as my stomach drops. "It wasn't his intention to, I think, but with him not feeling like he could go to anyone else he told me. Said I was only person he thought would be honest about you. And what's happened."

"What'd he tell you?"

"You're a better hacker than both of us thought. Some stuff in college now makes sense like certain assignments." I gape at her, and she grins. "Kidding. Doubt you did illegal stuff back then." She looks down at her glass. "You've been married since November."

My hands go to my lap, wringing them as I try to stop their shaking. Not sure if I should be mad at Isaac for telling her or grateful he did it for me. A whirlwind of emotions tear through; shame, guilt, and worry, but also relief. I've no clue what to say. What am I supposed to tell my best friend that I lied to her about being secretly married for months? Sorry didn't seem like enough. Or the fact I wasn't even the one who told her.

"He asked how I forgave you when I found out you'd been undercover," Leanne continues. "How I forgave Leo when you disappeared. He wasn't expecting learning how angry I was with Leo." Anxiety crawls over my skin. "That I didn't trust him or thought he'd be good enough for you."

I remain quiet, heart pounding in my ears.

Leanne's hands reach across the table, gesturing for mine. I bring my trembling ones up, and she takes them with a gentle squeeze.

"The night of our first dinner, when I saw Leo be there for you, care for you...I forgave him. He was *literally* on his knees for you, not caring who saw and I realized how much I may never know what pain you still go through."

I look up, meeting her soft brown gaze.

"And I forgave you with hope and love. When I recognized that I'll never know what it's like being in your shoes. As you've learned you'll never know certain things with me." I squeeze her hands, and she squeezes back. "Forgiveness didn't come quickly, and I'm gonna be mad for a bit you didn't tell me about being married, but I know you, hun. My best friend puts the whole world on her shoulders, even if it means she hates it, she'll lie to protect who she loves."

"I did hate it," I whisper. "Everything I've hid from you. From Trix. Nan. I hate the secrets, but I...I..."

"Surviving a dangerous game."

"Yeah." I gulp back tears. "I'm sorry, it's not enough, but I am sorry."

"You didn't do it to hurt me, it's okay. I doubt it was an easy decision."

"To marry Leo? No. To keep it secret? Yes. Silver lining is not having to mail out wedding invitations."

"Hope you know we're still going to have a bachelorette party or something. At least give me the thrill of being your maid of honor in that sense."

"Maid of honor?" I smirk. Leanne crosses her arms with a serious expression. I sputter a watery laugh. "Okay, yes you would be."

"Thank you."

I sip some of my juice, putting the glass down with a heavy exhale. "Did he take the advice then?"

"I think so, especially after I brought up how I deal with different grade levels." I raise a brow. "Every grade is different in how you handle the kids. You cannot use the same tactics on kindergarteners as you do with middle-schoolers or high-schoolers. I've dealt with teachers who've tried when they've switched grades. Then you get that 1st grade teacher telling a middle-school teacher what to do, but you can't make a 6-year-old write an essay about why stealing is wrong nor taking a 12th grader's favorite toy away when they misbehave."

"Well, I'm dealing with kindergarteners then," I mutter, and she gives a confused look. "Most of those I deal with behave when you take their favorite toys aka their balls."

Leanne sputters a laugh. I shrug unabashedly.

"Anyways, it's helped me," she says after her laughter fades. "You have to do things I won't understand to handle situations. It's the fucking mafia, Autumn. If I'm surprised that you had to lie, take balls, or whatever…I'm going to need a reality check. I may not like it, but it's not going to change anything. I mean, school system isn't all sunshine either, we both saw what Trix had to go through, even then it was a *mafia boss* who gave her the money she needed."

She huffs, slumping back in her chair, and adds, "All that to say, the world sucks."

"It does suck."

She grabs her glass, swirling the contents as I flick my gaze to the very quiet bedroom.

"I don't know what it's like being married to a mafia boss…

don," Leanne says quietly, staring at her juice. "What it must feel like when he's gone. Being chased out of your home. How hard it might be to make decisions to not...die. Even with what you and Isaac have told me, I can't imagine it. Like to even have to consider marrying in secret is mind-boggling enough. So, I'll continue to hope you know how to handle those kindergarteners. Forgive you, even when I'm still angry, and to trust you."

"And I trust you, even if at times it seems I don't. It's not you, it's me."

She scoffs. "Or just paranoia?"

"Yeah, like *Sixth Sense* level." She grimaces, and I chuckle. "I'm trying my best, even if it means assuming my British bodyguard pulled a *Reservoir Dogs* on me, and I was White, he was Orange."

She gives me an exasperated look, putting her glass down.

"What?"

"How do you do that?" She asks.

"It's a classic." She snorts. "Could reference a Bond movie, then I can call you a Bond girl."

Leanne covers her face, blushing into her hands. Suddenly, she gasps and flails her hands at me to come closer. As I do, she whispers, "The things he did—"

"No!" I screech, covering my ears. "Don't wanna know!"

"Oh, come on! You've listened before!"

"Not about my bodyguard," I hiss, laughing next.

"Are you sure he's straight?"

"Is that the only subject you didn't cover last night?" I ask deadpan. "And...what?"

She shrugs, holding her hands up. "Look, he did things no straight guy has done with me, and..."

"Leanne," I warn.

"I'm just curious!"

"I'm pansexual if you must know."

We both let out a yelp, and then turn towards Isaac's voice. He stands before her bedroom door, dressed in jeans and a plain t-shirt. His hair is mussed and it's odd seeing him unshaven. Leanne makes a humming noise, and I notice her biting her lower lip. I poke her arm.

"What? You have your man to ogle, leave me be," she states. I roll my eyes at her, and then she talks to Isaac. "Sorry, didn't mean to throw you out of the proverbial closet."

"Was never in, but never found a need to bring up my sexuality in conversation," he responds smoothly, keeping his gaze mostly on Leanne. "Even Julio doesn't speak much about his, but he's been openly gay since he was twenty."

"Well, best friend is bi, and the other is a lesbian, so…not like I would've cared," I say, then clear my throat. "Not that it matters."

"You're surrounded, hun," Leanne jokes.

"Oh, darn," I say dead pan.

Isaac takes a step forward, but stops and gives a long exhale. He and Leanne exchange a look, which after she relaxes into her seat and looks pointedly at the bedroom. He gestures to said room, and asks me, "May we talk?"

I nod, standing to follow him. I glance over my shoulder at Leanne, who waves at me with a smug smile. I roll my eyes, preparing myself for this conversation as I close the door for privacy.

Her small bedroom is mostly pastel colors with deep blue accenting it, including the rumpled bed covers. Watercolor paintings of plants and flowers she's done hang everywhere. A much more put together bedroom than mine ever could be. Except the clothes on the floor, the one small detail we share.

Isaac sits on the bed, slumping a little while I remain next to her dresser.

"I'm so—"

"I apologize," he says over me.

We stare at each other.

"Isaac."

"I was a complete arsehole," he states. I shut my mouth. He runs his hands down his jeans, seeming more nervous than I am. "I overstepped boundaries, presumed situations, and…you were correct, my pride was bruised. More so when Jameson pointed out my naivety several times and I felt like a failure. Then, I became angry that you didn't include me in your plans, whilst Chiari, Mikey, and Logan knew."

"It was to protect you, all of you. Because…I knew people were watching."

"I understand that now."

Silence. I rub my arms, holding myself close as he stares down at the ground.

"I understand why you're angry, and I can't blame you," I say quietly. "Any of you, but I won't apologize for doing what myself and Leo thought was right to do to protect ourselves. But I will apologize for hurting you and breaking your trust."

"You didn't break my trust, wounded my pride and ego, but not that." He glimpses at the bed he sits on. "And I hope you know my intention to come here was not simply to sleep with Leanne, but she's the only one—"

I shake my head. "Doesn't matter. If you came here for that, talking, baking, watching bad movies…not my place to judge whatever is going on. Not going to tell her or you what or… who to do." Isaac and I both try to stifle a chuckle. "Just glad you had someone to go to. I know what it's like when it feels like you don't."

Isaac exhales roughly, sitting up more. "I was too harsh on him. I shouldn't have assumed as I did, especially regarding your marriage…something that I have no right in having a say in."

My jaw works, stomach twisting a little as anxiety goes up my spine. I take a deep breath, moving to go sit next to Isaac on the bed.

"Leo worried that I'd think he was using our marriage for more than simply wanting to." The words are heavy as they leave my mouth. "He explained everything before. Every detail, what it meant and how it could be an advantage or used against us. I wasn't wholly surprised by Jameson's reaction that…day."

"What do you mean?"

"Remember the check I wrote for the centers?" He nods. "All

that money came from Leo's personal accounts, and I've been writing donation checks to several centers every month, each averaging five thousand. If the money came from anywhere else, such as the Luciano fortune or his franchises, it'd have been suspicious. But figured with his background of philanthropy, no one would bat an eye."

"Except Jameson monitors every account."

"Yup."

"So…you pretended to be a gold-digger to throw people off?"

"Unintentionally." I give him a weak smile, and he gives me a faint one back. "We knew what it would look like, Isaac. We played along. He's the one who gave me access and never asked questions. From money to computers to using the hotel. It was *me* who used him, not the other way around."

Isaac sighs, running his hand through his hair. "I need to apologize to him. I overstepped as a biker, colleague, and…friend." I nod numbly. "But no matter how angry I'll become with him or you…I won't ever backstab either of you."

Tears form in my eyes, guilt digging at me. "I'm sorry we thought you did."

"I broke protocol. You responded as I would have given circumstances. I acted poorly last night and would be more upset if you hadn't considered that as a choice."

"Even though we lost faith in you that…quickly?"

"Within a handful of hours, we lost who we were preparing to take over Leo's position as mafia don. Many of those we trusted, screwed us over and attempted to kill us. We don't know who else may do the same. No, I don't blame them. And I have no doubt I'll have a tongue lashing when I return or if I even still have a job."

"You do."

Blue eyes meet mine. My throat tightens, threatening for more tears to come. The remnants of fear that he left or driving him away trickle back. My words are faint as my vision becomes blurry. "I thought it was my fault. I went too far…drove you away."

"No," he says quietly, touching my knee gently. "You didn't."

My chin quivers as I try to nod, hands now shaking.

"May I?" He asks, holding his arms out and I can only nod.

Isaac embraces me, hugging me tightly. Tears stream down my cheeks as we hold each other. He presses his face against the top of my head, gripping me as I struggle to breathe.

"You *are* capable of anything, no matter how many bad days or nights you have," he whispers. "I am truly sorry for carelessly using those against you… Miss Autumn."

The damn breaks as I cling to him, sobbing into his shoulder.

These past few months I've grown close to the Crew, but Isaac was another story. We've grown in more ways than one, from being the guy I kicked in Central Park, to quiet bodyguard, to friend, to a confidant I went to when things were tough. My heart almost shattered this morning, not just at the thought of him betraying me… but losing him altogether.

"I love you, too," I say faintly when the sobs subside.

He squeezes harder and I do it back. We remain there, seeming like forever as relief floods me. A knock at the door gets us to pull apart from each other.

"You two good? Or do I need to give the mobsters water or something?" Leanne asks through the door. "And do I still have a boyfriend or was that the shortest relationship I've ever had?"

I raise a brow at him, wiping away tears. "Boyfriend?"

"Didn't tell you that part, did she?"

I shake my head. He sits up straighter, running his hands over his jeans. I smile at him as I see his face contort into concentration.

"No hurting her," I lightly warn.

"Never, Miss Autumn." We smile at each other.

"Helloooo?" Leanne calls, opening the door as we stand. She crosses her arms, eyeing us. "Oh, good, he's still intact."

I snort at her, mimicking her stance with my arms crossed. "How long until you were gonna say you're dating?"

Not a lick of guilt on her face. "Once you two made up. And look…you made up."

"You're conniving, but I love you," I say.

"You're secretive, but I love you," she says with a smile.

"And I think I'm in trouble," Isaac murmurs.

Leanne steps forward, taking his hand and kisses him on the cheek. He blinks rapidly, blushing a little as she starts to pull him out of the room. "You work for a mafia don's wife and now dating her best friend…you've no idea."

I giggle at them as I watch my bodyguard soften at her touch.

Oh, he truly doesn't.

Chapter 13

Saving Friendships

Leo

LEO WATCHES THE RAIN FALL. It's chilly in his office, keeping his hands in his pockets as he looks out the window. The door opens, and he flicks his gaze over his shoulder as Jameson strides into the room. His second places folders on the desk before coming to stand next to him.

"They're back at the hotel," Jameson states. Leo lets out a long exhale. "Owen started using *Eleanor* to track down Caltz. He found a bank account still under his deceased father's name."

"Last accessed?"

"112 days."

"Is it empty?"

"A couple thousand still there."

"Monitor it." Jameson nods. "Autumn may be right. He could still be in the city."

"Even with *Eleanor*, it'll be almost impossible to find him," Jameson mutters.

"We'll fucking find him. Or at least learn who he's working with because he wouldn't have lasted this long alone."

The storm thunders outside, darkening the sky more. Leo reaches into his pants pocket, touching his wedding ring hidden there. It calms him, bringing a sense of clarity.

"Apart from wanting the Marchetti family destroyed, what the fuck else could he want?" Jameson asks.

Leo's mind flashes to the interrogation room. The seething anger in Caltz's voice as he questioned Autumn. Every time she defied him and how much more it pissed him off. The satisfaction when he thought he had her.

"It's not the Marchettis he's after anymore," Leo says.

Jameson huffs, putting his hands in his pockets. "Speaking of… how was the phone call with Renato?"

Leo's jaw flexes, and Jameson exhales sharply.

"You're still set on going to Rome? What's to stop Renato from cornering you? Or if Renaldi sides with him?"

"Renaldi won't," Leo says assuredly. "We'll wait a couple more weeks. Allow DeLuca and Finstrum to settle into their new territories. Perhaps Matteo or Gabriel will show if it gets too quiet."

"If they do? What then?" Jameson looks over at Leo, who keeps his gaze on the rain. "Leo…if we have to, are you willing to kill them?"

Hurt and utter betrayal rips through Leo's insides. All the choices he made, only to be brought to the very thing he was attempting to avoid—destroying what's left of his family.

"I don't know."

"What about Renato? Cause we're fucked if he decides to help either of them, especially Gabriel."

"If he does or tries to take what's left of my father's fortune…" Leo turns slowly, scowling coldly, "…we sever everything with the Salvadori family."

Jameson raises a brow, tilting his head. "That's not us getting fucked? Going up against the biggest mafia family in Italy?"

"Not when my wife owns the Luciano name, and has given me

the ability to bring empires to their knees." Leo strokes the metal of his ring, face becoming solemn. "And if they come after me, I have faith in Autumn and you."

Their eyes meet. A long silent agreement passing between them. Jameson clears his throat as he goes to lean against Leo's desk. A thunderous boom echoes, rain pelting the glass.

"If he goes after Autumn instead?" A darkness comes over Leo. "It's why you're keeping the marriage secret, not wholly because she inherits your grandmother's legacy. He'll target her."

Leo steps over to his desk, opening one of the folders Jameson brought in and closes it.

"Spartan," Jameson murmurs, pressing for an answer.

"You'll do what's needed." Leo's answer almost makes Jameson pale, realization forming on his face.

Leo opens a desk drawer, grabbing some paperwork when he notices the false bottom isn't reset completely. He scowls heavily.

Jameson stands. "Leo, you can't—"

There's a loud knock and Leo shoves the drawer closed. "Enter."

"We're not done talking about this," Jameson mutters.

Leo ignores him as Isaac walks in, whose expression is poker-faced as he stops near the couches. Jameson frowns, disappointment radiating from him.

"I'll handle this, get things ready for the meetings with DeLuca and Petrinolli," Leo instructs grimly.

Jameson exhales sharply, stalking out of the office, but not before growling a couple words in Spanish. The side door slams shut, and Isaac glances at where he disappeared. "Don't need a translator for that."

Leo stares at him, chest tightening with a turmoil of emotions. Slowly, he steps around the desk, aiming for his wife's bodyguard. Isaac doesn't move, placing his hands behind his back.

"I apologize for breaking protocol, disappearing, and evading security," Isaac states as Leo approaches. "Although I technically work for your wife, I understand if my job is now moot. Or that what I did is grounds for expulsion from the club due to my actions towards you and your Old Lady. Whatever your choice is, I—"

Suddenly, Leo grabs him and pulls him into a firm embrace. Isaac's breath catches, his arms stiff at his sides. Leo's chest rises heavily, fingers clenching into the back of Isaac's shirt. Carefully, Isaac brings his arms up to return the gesture. The two men hug in silence as the storm rumbles outside.

Emotions muddle Leo's mind, but he can't let go of the overwhelming relief knowing one of his closest people, and friend, isn't holding a knife to his back.

Isaac's hand lands on the nape of Leo's neck, firmly holding him as Leo shudders.

"Always brothers, Spartan," Isaac murmurs. "Since your blooded ones are fucking cunts."

Leo snorts. And then responds in a rough voice, "Always brothers."

Autumn

I lean against the elevator wall while Chiari stands across from me.

"Should I be happier that our inner circle isn't broken," Chiari starts, breaking the silence. "Or that finally one of the Crew is willing to have a relationship outside their little club?"

I snort. "Dare you to call it that to their faces, but let me grab popcorn first."

She chuckles as the doors open to the first floor, and we walk out. It's late. The hotel somewhat quiet.

"Not eyeing any of them, are you?" I frankly ask.

"No," she smirks. "Don't swing that way."

I blink, pausing a moment before we get to the security room. Leanne's right; I'm surrounded.

I knock and Mickey opens the door. I'm given his wide grin,

then am quickly pulled into a hug. "Thank fuck your plan worked. And you're okay."

"Same to you."

He steps back, nodding once at Chiari. "Ms. Pierozzi."

Logan spins in his chair, smiling at me with a wink as he pulls over another chair for me. Mikey pulls his out for Chiari, who sits and adjusts her suede jacket.

"Any movement or suspicious activity?" I ask, flicking my gaze to the monitors.

"Nothing, including since Bobby dropped the briefcase off," Logan answers, and leans down to hold up said briefcase.

"I've noticed nothing since I picked up the laptop from the café," Chiari adds. "But what about service areas? Kitchens?"

"Nope," Mikey answers next, leaning onto the table with his mug of hot chocolate. "And nada while you were gone, Autumn. Bit too quiet, honestly. Everyone's doing their jobs per usual."

"Everyone did clear the background checks," Logan says, bringing up monitors on several areas. "Maybe whoever snitched on your schedule wasn't hotel personnel."

"What about extra…personnel? Security?" Mikey raises a brow, looking at me pointedly. "Could've hacked our shit and figured out your schedule."

"We weren't hacked," Logan interjects. "Not with the firewalls Autumn put in. Wouldn't Morton notice, too?"

"They would've," I answer. Isaac, Julio, and Owen would've all noticed, especially after my first disappearing act.

"Then there's a mole somewhere," Mikey says. "Problem is who and where."

"I hate that we have *nothing* after an entire week," Chiari mutters, leaning back in her seat. "There *has* to be someone else."

"Let's go through some of the footage again, maybe we missed someone," Logan suggests, flicking the monitors back.

I stare at the monitor showing the foyer of the apartment. It's empty aside from the table and flowers on it.

Out of every person caught and interrogated, not a single one knew my schedule. Parts of it, maybe, but not enough to pinpoint where myself *and* Leo would be. It wasn't always the same. There were days I'd randomly go to the bookstore, work on bikes, go back to the apartment, or help hotel staff. Someone was watching as I've been watching the guests these past few months. Whoever it was knew to learn the patterns of the Crew *and* me in the hotel.

My eyes go to the monitor for the private elevator, and watch it flick off. It's programed to turn off when it reaches the apartment floor or further up and will turn back on when it reaches the floor underneath. Privacy.

"There's no cameras on the top floor, offices…" I say out loud, "…but there are in the private elevator. But it turns off."

"Uh, yeah," Logan murmurs. "You kinda know why."

"Leo's been in his office all day?" I ask.

"Mostly, yes," Chiari answers.

"Who has access to the space?"

"Crew, couple of managers, us," Mikey answers. "Small list."

"Anyone use it while we were at the penthouse?"

"Myself and Jameson," Chiari says. "Only he and I have keys to his office when he's gone."

"Rest is locked up," Mikey adds. "Until he comes back, but oh, housekeeping has access, too."

I go very still, blood running cold while the other three exchange looks. Housekeeping. *Hide in plain sight.* Realization must hit them next because they all start swearing under their breath.

"They all passed their background checks," Chiari breathes out. "*Multiple* checks."

"People can lie," Logan mutters.

"Well, fuck," Mikey grunts.

"Bring up the private elevator feed." Logan quickly does as I say, while I pull my phone out and call Leo.

The monitors change, moving to different timestamps beginning with when Leo and I left the hotel. We watch as normal activity commences.

The line picks up. "Autumn?"

Thank fuck we've moved on to him answering his own phone.

"The key in your desk, is it still there?" I can feel Logan and Mikey look at each other.

"No," Leo answers after a pause. Fear wiggles up my spine. "It was here yesterday afternoon."

My stomach drops, watching the few people who could use the elevators. A sickly feeling overwhelms me as horror crawls over my skin of who may have turned on me.

"Last night, around 7," I whisper to Logan. The video feed changes, images blurring until the elevator is empty. Until someone gets on, and the feed cuts off as they go up to the top floor. Someone alone.

"Autumn?" Leo asks in a hushed tone.

I stare at the monitor, tapping Logan's shoulder to freeze the frame when the video comes back. Timestamp shows in and out, ten minutes.

Isaac hadn't stabbed us in the back, but as despair reaches for me, I stare at the one who's sinking the knife into mine.

Chapter 14

Losing Friendships

DISMANTLED motorcycles from the estate are placed on the pavement. Sadness hits as I stare at what was recovered. Leo's prized soft tail, now destroyed, hurts the most.

"Sure you can salvage them?" I ask Chesty and Rudy, staring at the mess. Isaac sighs standing beside me, crossing his arms. We're quiet as the two sort through the mess of dented frames and smashed bikes. Only four were brought down to potentially run again, the rest were damaged beyond repair.

Least I'll be busy.

It's been four days. Every moment I've felt on edge, while we lured out who we thought was the mole. Bait had been laid out for them, and now was the worst part—waiting.

"We'll know more when we get into their guts," Rudy comments, scowling at the mess.

"Worried about the soft tail," Chesty mutters. "Really fucked up the engine and pipes."

I glance over at it. "Can I help with it?"

Chesty rubs his beard, shrugging. Rudy meets my gaze. "No guarantee it'll run again, *barchën*, but course you can."

"It'll be like a masterclass," Isaac comments.

"Couple of'em," Chesty mutters, bending low to look over a surviving chopper. "Gotta special order some things, which will take fucking forever."

"Special order?" I ask.

"These ain't new bikes," Chesty says. "If we want them to run even close to how they did before and keep the integrity of the original bike? We'll have to. Honestly, smarter bikers would just buy new motorcycles without the hassle."

"Here I thought you were the best bike mechanics in town," I tease. Rudy snorts.

Chesty grins. "We are, but even we have our limits. Don't worry, we're stubborn."

They start moving the bikes over to their spots to be worked on when Isaac's phone buzzes. My gut twists as he answers the phone. His face becomes serious, scowling when he meets my gaze. The others pause as Isaac hangs up with sharp huff. "Bait was taken."

"Grabbed'em?" Chesty asks. Isaac nods, darkening with ire.

Fuck, I was hoping I was wrong.

"Where are they?" I ask.

"Logan and Animal are escorting them to the top floor," Isaac answers.

"Where's Leo?" I ask, ignoring the clawing at my spine.

"Coming back from another meeting." Isaac and I exchange a look. He nods, already walking towards the private elevator.

"Chesty. Rudy. Meet Leo when he gets back? I'll be on the top floor," I say.

"Yeah," Chesty answers.

I can practically feel the heightened tension as I follow Isaac. When I turn around in the elevator, I can see the pain in both their faces. Hurt. Them knowing, as well as I, who it was.

Isaac and I are quiet as we go up. My breath is slightly shaky as I concentrate, pushing the ache down. Silently, Isaac's hand grabs mine and squeezes it. I calm a little, nodding in response before he lets go.

"You going on a date with Leanne soon?" I ask, clearly gunning for a distraction.

"Planning to."

"She likes dancing and Mediterranean food, if you need ideas."

"Thank you for the suggestion." The doors open, and he follows me through the foyer and into the apartment. "There's a jazz club I know of, I think she'd like."

"Probably, and good choice."

I head into the television room, scanning through the movies swiftly. I find the film I need, opening it and out drops the secondary key to the briefcase. Isaac snorts, bemused, as I put the movie away. "What?" I ask.

"Would've thought *National Treasure.*"

I glance at the DVD case, *The Da Vinci Code,* and then smile faintly. "Gotta keep you on your toes."

We leave the apartment and get back onto the elevator in silence. Even with the temporary light banter, I can't ignore the gnawing at my insides. A headache creeps from the back of my head.

"It's not your fault," Isaac murmurs. "None of us knew."

"I know," I say softly. "Except I'm torn between feeling hope that there's a good reason and despair that my demise has been planned from the start. It feels all too similar to Roger. The lies."

Before Isaac can say anything, the doors open, and I practically rush into Leo's office. Anxiety tugs at the back of my neck as I enter, going straight for the briefcase placed on his desk.

Isaac grabs my shoulder, stopping me before looking at what was taken. "Miss Autumn, I want to tell you to hold onto that hope, but..." those blue eyes meet mine, "...it may be a fool's hope."

I swallow hard. "Yeah."

He lets go as I approach the desk, noticing the case is locked again and open it with my key. Mila comes into the office from the side door. The two murmur as I search through the titles. Immediately, I see three missing: *The Thing, Barbella,* and *Heathers.* I open several cases to see if the blank CDs Mikey put in were taken without covers, but no.

Quietly, I shut it.

I turn to face Isaac and Mila, who's gaze is narrowed as she flicks it to the briefcase and back to me. She remains stoic, coming closer to hold out another disc.

"Footage of them infiltrating the office this morning, an hour after Mr. Luciano left," she says. "There's another angle from the secondary camera we installed if you want that as well, but this is proof enough of who the mole is."

I take the disc. "How long until Leo returns?"

"Ten minutes. On route back to the hotel," she answers.

How I wish I could turn everything off like her, but then again, I have.

There's a knock on the door, and Isaac opens it to reveal Chiari with a grim expression. She comes in, eyes almost downcast. The guilt on her face has haunted me since the security room.

"They're all here," she states finally.

I nod, taking a fortifying breath. "Interrogation room, please."

Chiari nods once, and then leaves. Isaac comes over, murmuring near my ear. "You can allow Leo to take care of this."

"It's not like Steve," I whisper, looking at him. "I need to talk… this time I need to go in there."

"Ma'am, all three could be involved," Mila says suddenly. "Should we—"

"No."

"Miss Autumn, I don't want to believe it either, but we—"

"Did they show up?" I ask, holding the disc up. "Did they help take the discs?"

Isaac's face remains solemn as he glances over at Mila. She shakes her head once. "No, Ma'am."

"Then, keep the others out for now." Neither of them move. "Isaac, please escort them."

He clears his throat before he finally walks out of the room. I'm left alone with Mila who watches me carefully. This feels worse than confronting the crime bosses. With them, I *knew* they were the villains. There was no deceit or unknowing of the knife aimed at my back. I stare at the ground, a flurry of emotions running rampant along with pain and anger.

"Mrs. Luciano." That title brings me out of the tailspin. Mila's hard grey eyes meet mine. With a roughness only she could use, she says, "You have a job to do…boss."

My spine straightens. I head for the side door and out into the small hall. Mila follows me as I come to the door, hearing a couple of shouts and then a door closing.

"If he comes back while I'm in there…" my throat feels tight, and I take a long breath, "…well, he'll do what he wants. Just tell him I'm in there."

"Yes, ma'am."

I open the door, walking into the cold, drab room. It's quiet after the door shuts behind me. The mole is strapped to a metal chair with a gag tied behind their head. Silently, I walk towards them, coming closer and there I already see the hatred in their eyes. My heart cracks.

"I didn't want to believe it was Carl or the others, people I've shared meals with, long hours with, worked alongside, or even discussed futures together. Yet, here we are…aren't we, Charlotte?"

Those green eyes narrow as she bites at the gag, mumbling something. Her hair is mussed and mostly out of its braid. She's still wearing her maid uniform, likely apprehended while preparing one of the suites.

I glance over at the table in the room, seeing the three movies she took. The key she stole sits beside them. Disappointment hits me as I step around her, untying the gag. She makes a spitting sound, coughing as I toss it aside. Charlotte quiets as I step back to lean against the table.

"Why?"

She glares at me, frowning. Gone is the bubbly girl I knew or who giggled at random things with me. Gone was the woman I joked with. A character she curated, hiding in plain sight. All those questions and wonderings about me, don't feel so innocent anymore.

"Did Alba know?"

"No," she scoffs. "She thinks this is the best gig ever. Not to mention *adores* you for some reason."

"You're one hell of an actress. Thought I was good, but you take the damn cake." She snorts. I ask again, "Why?"

Silence as she gives me a very disgusted, mean girl look.

"Leo is going to return, and you've seen the aftermath of what he's done in here," I say, ignoring the sick feeling that follows. "You know what he can do. I doubt you not having a dick is going to save you from that, so I suggest you start talking while we're alone."

She frowns, but I do see a sliver of fear seeping into her eyes. Charlotte has helped clean his messes. You'd think that would've been warning enough to not to screw him over but guess not.

"Charlotte—"

"You had *everything*," she sneers, yanking at her restraints. "Everything *I* wanted, you had. There. Happy?"

"I'd have given you anything you wanted," I argue. "Money, clothes, whatever—"

"It'd be second-hand shit! Pity crap!" She spits at me. "I still wouldn't be the fiancé of a CEO and mafia don! Why take that when I could have *everything*?"

My brows pinch, horror running across my limbs. "You wanted to get rid of me…for…"

I can't get the words out, feeling myself flung into the past as I envision Bailey glaring at me. Those hateful eyes as coffee spilled down my front. Have I landed in another version of that hell?

"Oh, please." She rolls her eyes. "Not Leonardo." I'm more confused, until she says, "Gabriel."

My face goes pale as I stare at her. I breathe out, "What?"

"Who do you think got me this job in the first place?"

"You started—"

"Six years ago in the kitchens," she interjects. "No one remembered me. Everyone thought I moved on after the hotel sold. It's a big place."

My hands clench into the table's edge. "You met Gabriel here."

"Uh-huh. He's hotter…smarter…and said I'd have everything I wanted long as I did what he said. I waited for him, too, when he was imprisoned. After Leonardo got him out, I started helping Gabriel regain his family fortune again. Then, I told him about you, and he said you needed to be gone."

Thoughts tumble, reeling to grasp reality.

"You've been working with Gabriel? So, that means…Gabriel has been calling the shots, not Matteo? It was him."

She scoffs again. "Oh no, Matteo hates you, too."

"Where's Gabriel?"

She gets quiet, pursing her lips.

Anger simmers in my gut, replacing some of the hurt as I realize I was right. Matteo had been used. He wasn't wholly innocent, but if Gabriel has been whispering in Charlotte's ear, then he was doing it to Matteo, too. He *was* out there, pulling the damn strings. Fuck.

"Charlotte." She tries to ignore me, acting nonchalant now. "He lied to you, then used you to get to me and Leo. He's lying about whatever promise he gave you."

"No…he loves *me*," she says confidently.

"Listen, please—"

"What are you going to do? Torture me? You don't have the balls." I stare at her, and she shrugs. "Leonardo doesn't hurt women."

Almost brokenly, I say, "Gabriel does."

Charlotte stares down at the ground. For a moment, I think I'm getting through to her until she looks up. Bitter coldness warped with resolve drives a chill down my spine.

She knows. And she doesn't care.

The door opens. I stand fully as Mila steps in and moves to the side for Leo to enter. He keeps a rigid expression as Charlotte looks at him, and fear flashes over her face. It seeps through her features as he doesn't say a word, moving to grab one of the chairs and drags it across the floor. Metal screeches. Both Charlotte and I flinch at the sound as he places it before her, and then starts to unbutton his sleeves to roll up. Mila closes the door, taking the jacket she was wearing off and pulls out two knifes that were hidden within. The air is heavy, and each breath feels like bricks in my chest. Charlotte suddenly looks at me with terror, eyes going wide. Leo's commanding, rigid presence pulses as he comes over to me, and then gently traces a finger along my jaw; a vast juxtaposition of what he represents right now.

"Wait in my office."

My blood runs cold at the command. The mask he's perfected doesn't shift, a callous numbness.

"Wait! No, Autumn… don't leave," Charlotte begins to beg.

"Gag her," Leo instructs Mila.

I start walking out of the room as Charlotte screams and starts to cry. Her restraints clatter against the metal chair as my own legs want to give out.

"Autumn! Don't, please, umfh—" Charlotte's voice is muffled as I get to the door, hand on the knob.

I peer over my shoulder, noticing the tears now streaming down Charlotte's face with the gag back in her mouth. She looks at me, shaking her head, but then looks to Mila who's stripped down to her tank top and holds up a knife. I turn away when Leo sits and Mila holds the knife to Charlotte's throat.

Quickly, I step through the door and shut it hard behind me. Harsh reality floods me as I stare at the carpet. That's why he has Mila—a female captain, to do what he won't. My hand trembles as I press it against my mouth, feeling the need to hurl.

I rub my hands over my face as I start walking to Leo's office. I'm on the verge of screaming or crying, fighting to breathe normally as I step through the next door into the main hallway. There, I freeze when I see Isaac speaking with Chiari, Grant, and Alba.

Shame lines Grant's features, eyes immediately avoiding mine. Chiari and Isaac both have dour expressions. But it's Alba's that makes me want to breakdown. Hers contorts into shame. She starts to move but stops as if she's unsure she's allowed to even approach. My heart aches.

I head directly to her, opening my arms. She accepts the gesture, embracing me as she apologizes. Spanish and English mix, overlapping each other as she continues, and then begs me saying that she didn't know.

"Alba." I stop her, stepping back and holding her shoulders. "I trust you. Lo sé."

She nods solemnly, reaching up and grabbing my hands. I look at Grant and Chiari next.

"She used all of us. Not your fault. I blame none of you," I whisper. Chiari nods once, keeping that grim expression. Grant is practically stone. Alba pats my hands, letting go. "I'll see you tomorrow. Long as you're done for today, go home. Por favor. Isaac...make sure they do safely."

"Of course, Miss Autumn."

I give Alba another hug, then give Chiari a nod as they head for the elevator. Grant continues to avert his gaze. The elevator doors open, and they start to get on, until I say, "Grant."

He pauses before the doors. The pride I've seen on his face long gone.

"She used *all* of us," I murmur. "You've done your job perfectly."

He straightens a little, and then does that little bow nod of his. "Have a pleasant evening...Mrs. Luciano."

I stare as they leave, doors closing. Almost in a daze, I go into Leo's office and sit down in his chair. My gaze lands on the briefcase. I open it, but stop. I instead pull the other disc out and I insert it into Leo's computer to play the video. The screen flickers, showing the secret camera Enigma installed three days ago, pointed directly at where the briefcase was placed. I watch Charlotte come in to clean, then bring out the key she stole from his desk, using it to steal the three cases, and hides them in her work cart.

I shut it off, taking the disc out and toss it across his desk. Anger churns along with disgust. I stare, recalling those first moments in telling myself if I wanted dirt on someone was to become a maid. How that thinking got me to formulate all that blackmail. I was so concentrated of my own plans, I missed her entirely. The headache worsens, making me feel sick.

The violation of my life pierces through me, knowing how involved she once was. Every day and hour we spent together. For fuck sakes, she did my fucking laundry. The friendship I believed was real, became only a means to an end. For *Gabriel*.

Once more that bastard has leached his bloodied foulness into my life. Every facet and crack seem to be filled with the vileness that's him. How much more would he take? Who else will he destroy to get what he wanted?

Through Charlotte, they'd endangered more than just me and Leo. The hotel staff. The Crew. Innocent people who worked here. She threw away their safety and friendship because she wanted *my* fucking position but with *Gabriel*? Fury trickles over me, hands shaking as I recall the bitterness in her eyes. *She knew.*

"You knew!"

Betrayal, that feeling I knew all too well squeezes tightly. My privacy twisted into a weapon to harm me and those I cared about.

"—private fucking information, to the police without my consent!?"

Before I can stop, I stand and grab the briefcase to throw it. It cracks against the window, echoing with a sharp noise as it busts open. Movie cases tumble out, scattering across the floor. I stand over them, each breath heavier than the next as my hands shake. Tears stream down my cheeks. Where else will be tainted like my apartment? *Blue Java*? *Luna Stella*? The estate...the hotel...the motorcycles...what else will they get their hands on and devastate?

A hand touches my shoulder. I spin with a shriek, attempting to hit whoever grabbed me. My wrists are grasped before I can. I come face to face with Leo who looks at me with a too calm expression. I gulp in breaths, staring at him through blurry vision.

How fucking long had I been standing here?

"Breathe," he says softly, loosening his hold on my wrists.

My hands drop, slumping to my sides as I try to regain my breath. There's a pain along my spine and my lungs hurt. Anxiety drives itself deep as I start to flick my gaze over him, searching for blood.

"Autumn."

"Is she dead?"

"No." My gaze snaps to his. Leo carefully steps closer. "I'm sending her to California, making her start over."

Knowing her fate should calm me, but it doesn't. The panic attack continues to climb, crawling over my skin as my hands shake, reaching for his shirt. I numbly open it enough to see the tattoos on his skin. He doesn't budge as I trace my fingers over the ink, trying to ground myself with something I know is real.

"Autumn, Mila barely hurt her," Leo tries to reassure me. "Fear of pain was enough for her to talk. I'm giving her a chance to start over, but I won't be as merciful if she tries again. She gets this once."

Leo cups my face, gently tilting my head back to look up at him. Everything is blurry as it hurts to breathe. I finally whisper brokenly, "Red."

He picks me up, carrying me to one of the couches to sit as he cradles me against his chest. Leo rocks me as the sobs finally come. I clutch him, trembling as I heave for every breath. My brain becomes fuzzy, making the edges of my vision dim.

"She...was in...our home," I gasp between sobs. "A lie...she told..."

Leo keeps me in his arms, holding me as I sob over another crack in my heart.

In this moment, I understood more than ever why Leo made sure our marriage was secret to *everyone*. I cry harder, hating that his instincts were right and how devouring that paranoia could become.

Chapter 15

Oil and Water

I GRUNT, trying harder to get the wrench to move. With a sigh, I let go staring at the chopper I've been helping dismantle. Three more were brought down for parts. I wipe my hands over my jeans, and then try to get the nut to move once more.

For the last three nights this is what I did. I could barely stand being in the apartment. The walls felt caved in. A crawling sensation would follow like a shadow. I wanted to go back to the penthouse, but Leo and the Crew wanted me to stay at the hotel. The ping-pong feeling is beginning to feel tiring.

Even some evenings with Mikey and Logan didn't stop the constant anxiety. I decided on the garage, helping the bikers was the better distraction. Seeing Nan the other day, and then Trix, both of whom I had to lie to, just heightened my anxiety. It helped seeing Leanne earlier before she was picked up for her date with Isaac. I'm glad they'll get some time together. But tonight, I'm alone debating sleeping in the garage with the bikes like a good little mechanic protégé.

Okay, not fully alone.

I peek over the disheveled mess to where Michael and another mobster stand. The other guy, Igor, is shorter than Michael with more bulk. He also has short cropped blonde hair. Have I been reminded of *Rocky IV* multiple times, thinking of Dolph? Yes. Name didn't help.

The Crew are busy cause of a big meeting with the crime bosses. And I wasn't disrupting Isaac and Leanne's first real date night. Long as I stayed in the hotel where cameras were on me and Mikey and Logan watching, I was good. But alas, still need bodyguards.

Both men remain brooding as I go back to attempt in yanking off these damn nuts. It takes a few more tries, but I finally do. I go into a rhythm organizing pieces and cleaning parts. Unsure what time it is, I practically toss a dented rim aside and sit on the cold concrete. My wrench clangs to the ground as I huff, rubbing my face and remember the amount of oil and grease on them. I stop, dropping my hands. Whelp.

Footsteps sound and I look up as Michael comes over, stopping a few feet from me.

"Are you alright, ma'am?"

"Afraid if I get hurt then one of the Crew or my husband will gut you?" I try to sound light-hearted, but the slight fear on his face says otherwise. "Kidding, Michael. I'm fine."

Brown eyes flick over me nervously. He begins to turn away, but stops and comes closer. The mobster reaches into his brown leather jacket, holding out a handkerchief. It's dark blue with white stitching.

"You have…uh, grease…on your face."

I stare at the piece of cloth.

Thoughts churn inside me over such a simple gesture of comfort. Kindness that I would've taken easily before, I now wonder if it's a ploy. A game. Emotions I hadn't felt since under-cover keep me from grabbing the cloth. Never did I think I'd come back to this spot again, wondering what was real or not.

Faces flash. Roger. Dr. Wilson. Carl. Charlotte.

Self-hate rises as I ask quietly, "Are you going to betray me next?"

He goes deadly still. My eyes meet his.

"No, ma'am," he answers. "You do scare me, but no."

"I scare you?" My brows lift.

"Sometimes." The hand with the handkerchief drops to his side. "Not enough to…backstab you or say I will."

I snort. Yeah, guess he wouldn't tell me.

"Even after what I did in that meeting?" I mutter, looking over at the chopper.

"Rossi was a disgusting pedophile." His words have me look back at him again. A flash of alarm comes across his face. "You were right to shoot him."

"And Curione?"

His jaw tenses a moment. "It's a kill or be killed world, ma'am. And you're a pretty good shot."

I tilt my head. "The day I met you…" I start off, clearing my throat, "…when you commented on how I took care of that guy, you were serious weren't you? It was a compliment."

His gaze flashes towards Igor, who watches us with narrowed eyes and a frown.

"It was, ma'am," Michael answers. "You, uh…fucked him up good."

I laugh under my breath. That night feels forever ago, a lifetime almost. Beginning to rub my head, I stop realizing I've made more of a mess. I stare at the gunk on my hands, and in my periphery watch as Michael holds out the handkerchief again.

Different faces flash. Cheryl. Rob. Dr. Maxwell. Alba. George.

Some strangers, some not. Where would I be if I'd ignored their kindness? If I hadn't taken that chance. I think I'd be in New Jersey…dead on Roger's floor. Well, that's a sobering thought.

Finally, I take the cloth from him, wiping my face. I rub where I've touched my skin, attempting to clean my face. Michael remains quiet as I wipe off the grease, holding it back out for him to take. He does.

"Thank you…Michael."

He nods, then folds it up carefully before walking away to join Igor.

I glance over the pieces of metal and rubber, what all could be junk. A mess of what's left behind from someone's cruelty, but not all lost. Pieces still work. Not entirely new, but could be used to build again. A small laugh leaves me, thinking of those first sessions with Dr. Maxwell. Right…vulnerability.

I stand up, brushing myself off and look over the *Pink Floyd* shirt I'm wearing. I step away from the chopper, moving over to Leo's once beloved soft tail. Gathering some tools, I start to investigate the wiring harness of the bike. Most of it needs replaced, and I start working on certain sections. I fall into a rhythm, perhaps a long while until footsteps sound behind me again.

"Want to see something cool?" I ask, knowing it's Michael.

"Of course, ma'am, but you did inform me to tell you when midnight came."

"Sorry, used to long nights…likely not going back up anytime soon." I look up from where I crouch, hands all up in the bike. He stands straight, flicking his gaze to the motorcycle I work on. "Alright staying up late?"

"However long you need, ma'am."

"Not a real answer." I'm almost surprised he about got me to laugh.

He's quiet as I double-check some wiring to ensure it's good.

"I'd like to see something cool, ma'am."

I glance over my shoulder, smirking at Igor. "What about your quiet counterpart?"

"He's a stickler for rules."

"Oh, he is gonna hate me," I mutter. Michael snorts some laughter, and I look up to see him partially smile. My own forms. A sense of relief following.

Happiness in the oddest of places. Even with a mobster. Well…I guess I am now, too.

"Step back," I tell him, and he does as I stand over the bike. I lean over, tugging some wires up and check connectors before I hot wire the engine hoping it'll turn on. The engine struggles a second before it rumbles alive. I stare down at the bike, smiling broadly.

It turned on. The bike can still run. It sounds like shit and probably won't make it twenty feet, but it runs. Hope flickers inside my chest.

"Didn't know you could hot wire, ma'am," Michael says over the loud engine.

I smile at him, then shrug.

His smirk turns into a grin. I turn the engine off, wiping my hands over my jeans as I glance at Igor. He hasn't moved, standing there with a scowl as he watches. I shake my head, sitting back on the ground to go back to work.

Michael starts to walk away, until I say, "You can stay…if you want."

I keep my gaze on the motorcycle, trying to ignore the rise of worry in my chest.

"Not a mechanic, ma'am. I don't even know how to drive."

"Me neither, apart from riding."

"Common for New Yorkers, I guess."

"Not originally a New Yorker," I state, glancing up before I grab a rag to wipe my hands. "From the Midwest. Small town."

It's quiet, apart from the noise of me working. Michael steps back to his position next to the bike. His hands go into his pockets, and then he asks, "What are you doing?"

I smile and start talking about the bike. A sense of calm comes over me as Michael listens to me explain the parts of the model. All the lessons I had with the Crew, coming forth. The anxiety I've felt for days, fades with my small bit of normalcy. The tenseness down my spine slipping away as Michael listens intently.

I'm removing the bike's tail lights when SUVs start pulling into the garage. Michael steps back as I stand fully as they park. Doors slam open, and I watch Jameson and Owen leave for the other elevator, along with a handful of others. Leo comes around one of the vehicles, talking to Julio and Drew before he sees me. They walk away as he strides towards me, every step commanding authority. Michael steps further back, hands behind his back as Leo's rigid expression remains intact, flashing his gaze to him.

"You're relieved. Report to Animal," Leo's voice cuts through the air. Michael nods his head, swiftly walking away and joins Igor to follow after the others. "You're up later than usual."

I give him a confused look.

"It's almost 2AM," he says, and I almost guffaw. I glance at where Michael and Igor disappear onto the elevator. Well, crud muffins.

"Didn't realize it was that late," I murmur, tossing my rag aside and exhale roughly. "Got caught up teaching I guess."

Leo gives me a soft look. "I apologize for not being around as much the last few days."

"It's alright, I've made some good progress. Soft tail runs by the way." I nod at it. "Engine sounds like it has a bad case of pneumonia, but it runs."

His gaze moves to where it sits. Somehow his expression becomes even gentler.

"Well, since you're back, ready for bed?" I ask.

Leo pulls his eyes away from the motorcycle, stepping closer. I anticipate him kissing me, leading me to the private elevator, but he doesn't. Instead, he leans down and picks me up as I lightly yelp in surprise. A giggle comes out next as I hold onto his shoulders.

"Take that as a yes," I say.

"We're going home," he states, turning and heading towards one of the vehicles.

"Leo, the elevator—"

"*Our* home, my dear wife." I blink at him, something squeezing my chest as he kisses my cheek. I lay my head against his shoulder, body becoming lax.

L eo may be the first mafia boss to declare a weekend off that doesn't involve the aftermath of a potential kidnapping. Hopefully, it doesn't turn into *Weekend at Bernie's: Luciano edition.*

It's the next morning, and I'm staring at my omelet wondering if I'm hallucinating that Leo said we're staying here this weekend. I poke my thigh with my fork. Nope real.

He finishes with the sizzling bacon, placing it on a plate as he continues explaining the past week in a collected tone. "One of Rossi's captains is taking over as boss, Angelo Impastato. He's worked through the ranks."

"What happened to Petrinolli?" He flicks his gaze up. I nod slowly. "Barely two weeks, already sleeping with the fishes? Damn." I try to joke.

"Some aren't cut out for it," he says, turning the stove off. "Impastato will be easy enough to oversee. He's got some sense, which is why he's survived and thrived. He'll do what I suggest, along with Finstrum, to keep his foothold. He's ambitious, but also cautious."

I nod as he comes around the counter, sitting beside me as he pulls over his coffee mug.

"So…surprisingly, not much worry from crime bosses then?"

"Not here in New York."

I hum, distracting myself as I munch on some bacon. Well, at least there's that. We're quiet as we eat, until I look up and meet his gaze. He puts his fork down, grabbing his mug with a knowing smirk.

"Us and our breakfast talks," I say.

"We can change the subject to something else. Mafia politics will still be there."

"Such as?"

"Leanne and Isaac dating for one." He's so monotone when he brings it up, a sputtering giggle comes out of me. "I'm surprised you caved so quickly to it."

"Not my place to tell anyone who to date, even my head of security," I answer. "Besides, you didn't watch them flirt, make googly eyes at the other for months. Glad they did something before Trix and I intervened."

Leo raises his brows, and then hums under his breath. "Hadn't realized he liked her at all."

I chew on some egg, slowing as his brows pinch together. "I'm with Isaac every day, you're not. It makes sense."

"Well, the Crew doesn't bring up much on whether they want to pursue relationships or not. Not regular conversations for us. Never has been."

"Do you want them to? I mean, to find relationships?"

"I want them satisfied with life," he answers. "Much like you, I'm not going to say who they should date or not. Although, I guess times could change where they'll choose their person over work. I'd be quite the asshole if I forbid that while I have a reputation of ignoring work to spend time with my wife." He pauses, raising a cheeky brow. "Whom I married in secret."

"And declaring a weekend off," I muse.

"Yes." He sips his coffee, placing it back down. "The only time I may say something will be in regards to their own safety."

I smile softly, reaching over to grab his left hand and kiss his knuckles. He's wearing his wedding ring, like myself. I'm certain whenever we're home, we'll wear them until we can outside of here.

"Time may come for each of them to find someone or perhaps not," Leo continues, before going back to his breakfast. "So, I'll hope for the best between Leanne and Isaac."

"Thank you," I murmur. He smiles softly, both of us quiet a moment.

"Although, there's one relationship I may give more words to," Leo says grumpily.

"Who?" I ask around a mouthful of bacon.

"Jameson and Carrie." My fork clatters to the counter in surprise. "As colleagues, I mean. Their professionalism is waning more often than I'd like. Causing more issues than there actually are."

I purse my lips, and wonder if there's *another* reason they fight so often. "Maybe they need to fuck it out," I state.

Leo sputters next, almost coughing up his coffee as he wipes his mouth. He shakes his head, and I give him a grin. "Just saying."

"I highly doubt that," he responds. I shrug. "If that was the case, they'd have done it four years ago, not while putting another hotel up."

"How is the Boston hotel going?"

"Well enough. Carrie has been busy staving off reporters about the potential 'break-in' of the *Italian Lily*. The hotel has also been delayed in opening due to contractor issues. She's becoming more tenacious, and Jameson…rarely agrees with her approach."

From the one time I've met her, I believe it.

"She's vying for a big event to promote the hotel," he continues. "Such as a big wedding or some *other* happy announcement."

I stare down at my plate. Yup, I know what that means. Never have I thought more about being unable to get pregnant than the last three months. "She's insatiable, huh?"

"Autumn, I'd never agree to anything like that. Our marriage, our privacy, and life won't ever be used like that." His hands grasp mine, caressing his thumb over my skin. "Her job is PR, and she's good at it, but she doesn't call the shots. Jameson and I do regarding the hotel franchise. If she wants promotional events, then they can be galas or banquets like every other damn hotel opening."

I feel weird at the idea of being used as promotional material for a hotel in another state. A concept I would've never imagined or approached. Damn, Leanne's analogy works wonders in several areas.

Leo reaches over, touching my chin to look at him. I stare at his face, reaching to stroke his jaw. There's a tiredness there. Hazel eyes flick over me, silently reassuring me.

"What happens when people learn the truth?" I ask quietly, and his face becomes stony. "That I can't get pregnant? Especially… your brothers or Renato? That's what they want, isn't it? Heirs."

"Autumn."

"Probably why Renato continues trying to control you…got the potential to make heirs, more than Gabriel. What happens—"

"It won't change anything." Leo grasps my face, making me

look into his eyes before panic sets in again. Panic seems to come far too easy of late, crawling over my skin with every thought and worry. Subjects I haven't truly worried about it, jumbling around in a mess.

"You're worth more than that," he continues. "You are *my* wife. I told you that I will gladly burn it all to the ground if you asked it of me. All I need is you. Nothing more." He leans in, lips brushing over mine. "You are a Luciano now. They will not *ever* take that from you."

His mouth presses against mine, kissing me lovingly. My hands reach for him as he grabs my waist, tugging me out of my chair to straddle his lap. My legs squeeze around him, while his hands roam down my torso. The kiss becomes deeper as I feel him slip his hands under my shirt to trail across my skin. His lips move to my jawline, and then against my neck as I grip his shoulders. I lean into him, laying my head against his shoulder as he wraps his arms around me.

"Thank you," I whisper. "Deep down, I know it doesn't…thank you."

"I love you, my dear wife. You'll always have me. I promise."

"I promise, too."

He kisses my temple, humming while stroking his hand down my back. My head against his chest, I listen to his heartbeat allowing the soft thumping to lull me into calm. No matter what happens, I had him. I had this man's heart that beats for me. At the end of the day, I just needed him.

I pull back, inhaling deeply before I grab his face and kiss him again. His breath hitches as I kiss him fervently, wanting to show how much I love him. Leo then grabs my wrists delicately, stopping me as he says, "There's another reason I wanted a weekend to ourselves."

I blink at him, unsure where he's going with this.

"I want a play session," he continues. "Just you and me. No interruptions."

"Okay, but I don't think I can Top, I mean…"

"Me as the Dom, my dear Watson." He strokes his thumb over my wrists. "I enjoyed you taking charge, trying it, but I think we could both use a session with you being the Sub."

I nod and he kisses me softly.

Suddenly, I break away and raise a brow. "Did you really take a weekend off to be in the playroom?"

He slowly starts to smile. "Perhaps, *Tesoro*...although, I think when I tell you what I have planned, you'll be relieved to have a recovery day before facing society again."

Shivers run over my skin, and I almost can't help a small giggle. "Oh, really?"

"Just you..." he kisses my head, "...me...", he kisses my cheek, "...and our galaxy of solace."

I sigh with relief, body melting against him as tension evaporates. Whatever conversation we just had before, vanishes as his hand caresses my back. The very thought of just him and me in our violet room giving me quiet joy.

"Yes, Sir."

Chapter 16

Galaxy in Her Eyes

SLOW, sensual music reverberates through the playroom. I'm nude, standing on the soft rug as I push my toes into the fibers. Nerves collide, coiling down to my core as Leo approaches and threads his fingers through my hair. He grips it gently, tilting my head back. He wears his usual slacks, but no shirt, just tattooed excellence.

"I love your hair this length." His words melt over me, erasing wayward thoughts and nerves in my head. Peace. "Long enough to hold, but short enough that I don't need to worry about it getting in the way." He gently directs my head to the side, placing a kiss upon my neck. "Although if you ever decide to grow it out, I'll still love it."

"Thank you, Sir." I close my eyes as he presses another kiss upon my skin.

He straightens with a knowing look in his eye. His other hand skims up the middle of my torso, placing his other palm against my neck in an easy manner. His fingers flex while my breath hitches, the rest of my body wanting to fall forward into his grasp.

"Check in," he asks.

"Green, Sir."

"No other questions?"

It was afternoon, and we've spent the last hour discussing what he had planned. Most of it consisted of me *not* knowing what he'd do, and only the elements of what he *could* use. I've no idea what order he'll go and there's potential of this being a long session. He wanted to push our comfortability, concentrating on our trust with each other. Some of the items were soft limits, but I agreed to trying a few. Even for him, some were on his soft limit list as a Dom, but he wanted us to try. Overcome fears and let go safely.

"I trust you, Sir," I whisper.

Appreciation glimmers in his eyes as he tightens his grip upon my neck. My breaths become heavy; eyes wanting to flutter close.

"What are your safe words?" He asks.

"Red and yellow, Sir."

"Remember to use them if you need," he instructs, loosening his grip on my hair. "But do not remove anything. Wait until I do."

I swallow hard, and answer, "Yes, Sir."

"Good girl," he says reverently, kissing the middle of my forehead. "Stay still."

Hands remaining at my side, I stay as he lets go and steps back. Hazel eyes roam over me, dragging slowly, as my chest rises heavy with every breath. Finally, he instructs, "Stand in front of the cross."

Nerves kick up again as I look at the St. Andrew's cross. With all the sessions we've done, it's not once truly been used with me. Legs shaky, anxiety flaring, I walk towards the structure. My gaze moves to the purple leather that covers most of the ebony wood. I stop right before it, not touching it. Leo comes up behind me, causing my breath to catch as he trails his fingers along my arm.

Silently, he nudges my body to turn around to face him. Hazel eyes watch me intently as he backs me against the X, just a breath away from skin touching. Leo raises my arms above my head. He's replaced the cuffs with thick, twisted ropes with balls on the end to hold onto. I wrap my fingers around the rope, tightening my grasp as I take another step back for my backside to touch the smooth leather surface of the cross. My breath hitches, waiting for anything to trigger from the contact. Apart from normal nerves and anticipation…nothing.

Leo doesn't move, standing before me as he watches me with fingers barely brushing down my skin. He concentrates with hardened eyes, watching me as we both wait to see how my body will react.

Satisfied, he steps away and comes back with a small silicone bullet vibrator in his hand. He leans over me, stroking the vibrator over my sex as he nudges my legs further apart. I follow the silent command as he drags it again between my legs.

"No moving, *Tesoro*."

About to reply, but my voice is cut off when he turns the toy on. I clutch the ropes as the vibrator pulses through me. His other hand, somehow already slicked with lube, is pressed into me as the bullet caresses my clit. I gasp, breath stuttering as he gently thrusts his finger and then before I know it, the toy is fully inserted inside me. It thrums low, causing my muscles to clench around the device.

"Don't let that fall out," he says, trailing his hand up my stomach.

I blink rapidly, squeezing muscles in worry that it will. Crud muffins, do I need to concentrate on that?

A smirk grows on his face as he brings his mouth to my ear. "I'm teasing, *Tesoro*. It won't fall unless you come *very* hard." I swallow hard, tingling running across my tailbone and down my legs. "Come however many times you want. I won't stop you."

Oh, thank fuck.

Leo strokes my body, brushing his fingers over my torso, thighs, and shoulders. My skin shudders and prickles with every light caress. The hum of the bullet inside me can barely be heard with the music playing, tugging me back to the scene with Leo. Fingers circle around my breasts, thumbing my nipples before he takes one into his mouth. He sucks gently, licking and tugging delicately. They harden at the stimulation, while the rest of my body starts to feel like a live wire. Breath erratic, it catches every few moments as a wave of pleasure hits from either Leo or the toy. The ropes dig into my hands while my legs shake as the tingling sensations from the toy travels up through to my navel. The feeling makes me want to bend over and moan as Leo continues to lavish my breasts.

An orgasm is already creeping towards me when suddenly the pulsing of the bullet kicks up in speed. It jolts me, nerve endings coming more alive as pleasure rushes over my skin. My sex pulses, wanting more, I gasp and try to bite back a moan. Leo's mouth sucks hard on one nipple, while he rolls the other between his fingers. I'm suddenly coming, ecstasy washing over me as my hips gyrate in time with the vibrator. Its speed is suddenly brought down again, thrumming at a leisurely pace as I catch my breath.

Leo steps back. Satisfaction forms on his face as he glides a finger through the wetness that's gathered between my legs. Deliberately, he brings his hand back up to suck the moisture off his fingers. His eyes close, and a moan releases from his throat.

I struggle to keep hold of the rope. My eyes, though slightly dazed, can't pull away from the pleasure on his face.

Opening his eyes, his hand goes back to my sex, pressing the vibrator deeper inside me. I gasp as my body jolts. He pulls his fingers out, licking the cum off once more. This time, his gaze sears into mine as he sucks them.

Every inch of me feels aware of his presence, pulsing with need as heat coils down to my core. All my thoughts are gone. Now, I can only focus on the man who's taking pride in pleasuring and tasting me.

His other hand comes up, showing off the tiny remote for the vibrating bullet. Smiling cunningly, he hits a button, and it kicks up in speed again. I gasp, hanging my head as my body tries to bow inward at the pleasure that shocks me. It hums louder inside me as I grip the ropes, struggling to remain in place as he brings the speed back down. Breathing heavy, I try to catch my breath as the thrumming inside me calms. Except it's not for long.

It speeds up again and I have to concentrate on not falling to the ground, trembling in pleasure. It courses through me. Moans are caught in my throat when Leo lowers the speed again. The cool leather presses against my body as I lean back against the polished structure, warming against me.

Just when I think I'm safe, he speeds up the bullet and I throw my head back as it goes the fastest it's been. This time a strangled groan with a scream comes out of me as an orgasm roars through me. My legs shake as I use the cross to help remain standing, until he brings the vibrations down to almost nonexistent.

Head hanging as I catch my breath; I look up at Leo through my lashes.

"Good girl," he praises. The remote control is stashed in his pocket as he walks over to the dresser, coming back with different restraints.

He unclips the rope I have in my hands, replacing it with a smooth loop of rope. Leo slips my wrist through the loop, wrapping my fingers around the top of it. As he puts away the others, I release my grasp and realize I can hang my arms without holding onto the rope. It gives the illusion that I'm "restrained" but in reality, I'm truly not.

A satin black mask then appears in his hand. My heart rate kicks up. Fear courses through my body, but it's drowned out by the blissful aftermath and comfort of the room. I still stare at the mask he holds it up.

"Check in."

The humming of the bullet distracts me enough from my worrying thoughts as I drag my gaze up to him. Leo watches me carefully with full awareness to my bodily reactions. I focus on my curiosity and anticipation instead. Trust him.

"Green," I rasp. The word feels heavy on my tongue.

"Call your safe word if you need, but wait for me to take it off. I will immediately. Understood?"

"Yes, Sir."

"What won't you do?"

"Take the mask off, Sir."

"What will you do?"

"Wait for you, Sir."

"Good girl." Leo places a brief kiss upon my lips.

The blindfold is placed gently over my eyes, and I'm plunged into darkness. My breathing automatically picks up, clutching the rope around my wrists. Leo's covered my eyes before, but not so completely in any session.

Realization hits me of much we'd be pushing our limits.

Oh, fucking crud muffins.

I attempt to settle my heartbeat when the vibrator's speed kicks up. A yelped moan comes out, and all I can do is focus on the thrumming inside me. I almost bend over again, hips thrusting into the empty air before me. The bottom of my spine tingles as my legs tremble, my sex already sensitive from coming before. And soon I am again.

I swear under my breath as it crashes over me quickly and unexpectedly. I wait for the toy to lower in speed, but it doesn't and remains at the agonizing pace pulsating. My muscles clench around the toy inside me as I throw my head back, hips wiggling as I crave for either the vibrator to come out or to just collapse into myself. It's pleasurable torture.

Suddenly, Leo's warm body is against mine. His hands grip mine, keeping me in place between him and the cross. The bullet doesn't relent while my body convulses in need of another release, chasing after anything to relieve the sensual agony. I throw my head back, moaning as Leo's lips press against my neck. He traces his tongue down my skin. Shivers escape at the chilled saliva left upon my body. I can't seem to stop my body from thrusting as each long pulse of the vibrator makes my nerves feel like they're on fire. I gasp and jolt when Leo's hand lands against my neck, squeezing lightly.

Fear kicks up my spine.

Images behind the mask try to wiggle forward from the darkness. Long past memories.

Another long pulse of the bullet makes my body lock up, my

sex clenching around it as my legs tremble. Leo's hot breath spreads over my skin. I feel him. The soft caress of his fingers over my wrist, gently rubbing his thumb where he has before. It's his hand against my throat. No one else. The body I know so well. Familiar and safe.

I can't see or touch him myself, but I can *feel* him.

Something settles deep within me. Tension not caused from the vibrator pulsating inside me, vanishes. Overcome by the pleasure, I shout as it courses through my veins. My entire body becomes alight as muscles become taut with ecstasy.

"Good girl." Leo's voice reverberates against my ear, and I swear I see stars.

I gasp when he lets go, and then gently removes the bullet. Air whooshes from my lungs, while my body thrums with bliss. Exhaustion creeps over my skin, threatening to take me down, but the anticipation of what's next keeps me standing. My legs are practically jello as I try to listen for any hints. Until, something light flutters over my breasts.

A burst of giggles come out as feathers trail over my skin. They travel over my body, causing more laughter at the sensation. The high of the bliss softens as my body feels less taut from the orgasms it endured.

"There she is," Leo murmurs as I let out another giggle.

The feathers disappear, replaced by something else that lightly pricks at my skin. I gasp at the sharpness, which trails up my arm in a singular line. It tingles over my flushed skin, and it takes me awhile to figure out it's a pinwheel. Leo rolls it over my torso, around my breasts, down towards the apex of my thighs, and then back up. I giggle when he rolls it over my nipples. I stand up on my toes, muscles clenching at the sudden arousal.

Leo continues like this, switching out different toys to drag over my skin and create new reactions. A few make me giggle, whilst others make me more aware about the hypersensitivity of my body. Leo drags, I think, a flogger's tails over my shoulders and arms then pulls away. I wait for the next item, but nothing.

I don't even feel him nearby. There's just darkness.

Music continues playing.

My heart speeds up, waiting for him to do something. Anything.

Instincts soon scream at me to yank the blindfold off. Get out. I press my back against the cross, while my breath quickens as I stare into nothing. No movement. My heart thunders in my ears, drowning out the music.

Fear crawls up my spine.

Leo always knows when I'm about to have a panic attack. Why isn't he saying anything? Doing anything? He has to know, right? A horrific thought passes that he left. Or worse, ignoring me. Thoughts jumble, worried I'll have another panic attack after already having too many this fucking week.

Dread pools in my stomach. Familiar trembling travels up my arms. Panic rises until my hands start to jostle against their restraints.

Why don't I pull my hands out? He told me not to.

The blindfold? He said to leave it and call my safe word.

Okay, Autumn, then why aren't you saying your safe words?

Those answers make me go still. I had choices to not panic on my own, why am I not using them? My mind races, searching for answers as my wrists tug against the rope again, debating saying my safe word.

I stop.

I trust Leo with everything, as my husband and partner, and… my Dom.

He wouldn't leave me. He wouldn't let me hurt myself. He'd do everything I'd ask if I just *said* to. I could easily pull my hands out, take the blindfold off, but I *want* to listen to his commands. Because I *trust* him. Especially in here.

My heartbeat starts to slow and the heaviness in my lungs vanishes. The trembling stops as I relinquish myself to the cross I choose to be bound to. I begin calming myself as I concentrate on the music, the feel of the ropes, the leather on the cross, and the lingering touches of the toys. Once more, I inhale deeply and release it as a lightness comes over me. Suddenly, I feel more freedom in this moment than I have in months.

I'm safe.

Not just that I *feel* safe, but that I *am* safe here—pseudo tied up, blind folded, and naked.

Going lax, I wait for him. It's not long before Leo's hand touches my lower stomach. My breath hitches, jolting as his fingers move down between my thighs. He caresses me below as he whispers into my ear, "Good girl."

I moan, body stiffening at the praise as he continues to stroke me. Something bumps against my hip. There's a click and I hear the hum of a vibrator, deeper in sound than before.

"Check in," he asks.

"Green, Sir."

I feel the head of a vibrating dildo press against my clit. My hips chase after it as he continues the sensuous torture and I fall right back into that blissful chasm and let go of my fears. I fall into a space of needy desire, wanting nothing else as he plays with me. The dildo begins to enter me, and my legs shake, trying my best to remain standing without fully hanging off the restraints. He thrusts the vibrator into me, going at a steady pace as he fucks me with the toy, while his other hand caresses my skin. Moans come out of me as I lean forward, and he allows my head to fall against his chest. My mouth presses against his skin, tasting him as he thrusts harder with the dildo. My breaths are quick as I fall further into that safe, sensual abyss relinquishing everything to him.

Pure paradise. The carnal nothingness that consumes me in the dark.

Suddenly, the dildo is pulled out completely leaving me gaping for him to come back. I gasp, almost sputtering in surprise. Leo quickly pulls my hands out of the ropes, picks me up and then places me onto the bed. He moves over my body swiftly, pulling my arms up and slides my wrists through different loops that feel softer than those before. Fingers trace down my arms, shoulders, and my sides. My skin feels like it's on fire, sensitive and wanting more at the precipice he'd left me at.

Leo's mouth lands upon my breast as his hand dips between my legs, stroking and teasing my clit. I throw my head back, moaning loudly at the light touches that wreak havoc inside me. The hum of a vibrator returns, except this one he places over my clit, and it sucks at me. My hips buck at the newest sensation that creates sparks along my spine. My legs shake as the toy he uses buzzes over me, making everything inside me go wild. I grip the loops, throwing my head back as my body chases after the sucking sensation, while Leo holds my body down against the velvet blankets. I'm sent into an orgasmic spiral as it all combines and clashes into wicked ecstasy. A sudden scream rips from my throat. It's not dripping with pleasure, but a full release of emotion as my throat burns with the sound.

The toy turns off.

A haze falls over me, catching my breath as I stare into the darkness. I surrender to the drowning aftermath of pleasure, going lax. Leo's hands travel up my arms, pulling my wrists from the loops. I wait for the blindfold to come off, but it remains as he picks me up off the bed. Anticipation buzzes over my skin, wanting whatever he'll give me as I succumb to whatever Subspace is consuming me.

He sits me on the massage table. The chill of the surface makes me shiver as he runs his hands over my thighs. My head rolls back as I become completely compliant to what he wants. Hands caress me. My body buzzes with need, craving for more. For him.

Anything he wanted. Needed of me.

"Good girl. Look at you, gorgeous." His sultry voice lulls me. I sigh against his touch, moaning as fingers trail along my lower stomach. "Beautiful."

When a singular finger traces lightly above my sensitive clit my breath hitches before it trails back up. I'll do anything he desires. Anywhere he wants. I'd give into Leo whole-heartedly as this darkness devours me with nothing but him. Yearning courses through my veins, *needing* him.

"Check in."

"Green, Sir," I plead, aching for him to do more. *Keep going, don't stop.*

"Ready to continue?"

"Yes, Sir."

"Hmm, I wonder should I keep the blindfold on, allow you to see?" His seductive voice teases, dripping with eroticism. "What do you think, *Tesoro*?"

A moan is my only reply.

"What should I do next, *Tesoro*?" He murmurs, placing a kiss in the middle of my chest.

His fingers venture back down to the apex of my thighs.

"Answer me, sweetheart." His voice deep and commanding.

"Please, Sir," I beg suddenly. My brain is muddled with all kinds of thoughts.

"Please what?"

My body shudders, leaning up towards his touch as he places another kiss upon my chest again. The image of him sucking his fingers, eyes glowing approval makes me gasp.

"Fuck me with your mouth, Sir." His hands go still. "Eat out my pussy, Sir."

The silence should be deafening if not for the music playing. I'm too wrapped in a blissful haze to notice how still he is. "Please, Sir, I want—"

"Red."

The word clangs through me. I straighten.

The mask is lifted from my eyes and tossed aside as Leo cups my face. I blink into the dim light, finding furrowed brows and a serious expression. In the far reaches of my mind there's worry, but it's buried deep under the thick post-orgasmic brain. I feel heavy, but in such a good way that I could slump into his arms.

Am I drunk? It's been so long since I have been, I'm not sure.

"Focus on me, Autumn." I find hazel eyes again. "Good girl."

I hum, smiling. I wonder if I did something wrong. I couldn't have, he used my favorite title. I couldn't have. Right? What's wrong?

"You're deeply in Subspace, *Tesoro*…so we're not doing that, and stopping here."

I scrunch my brows. What's he talking about? "Did I say something, Sir?"

"You asked me to eat you out."

My breath catches. I did?

Oh. I did.

"Was that…that bad, Sir?"

"No, it's never bad to ask," he says, stroking a hand along my torso before grabbing my hand. His thumb rubs across my wrist.

My throat feels thick like I've drunk molasses. A prickling feeling climbs my spine. "Why not do it, Sir?"

"No doing anything we haven't discussed before a session, sweetheart," he explains in a slow and steady voice. "Nor will we try something that's a hard limit on a whim. You're deep in Subspace, sweetheart, and I'm sure you'll do anything I ask of you."

"Yes, Sir," I immediately answer, perking up. The need to please sparks in my brain.

"You're a very good girl, but we won't do that." My face falls briefly, until he lifts my chin. "You're not in trouble, but it's time to pull back. I don't want an overly compliant Sub who's asking to do her hard limits due to too many orgasms."

"I feel drunk."

"You're not…from alcohol that is." He leans forward, kissing my forehead and I hum at the contact. "Stay right here."

"Yes, Sir."

I think he chuckles as he walks away. I tilt my head back, staring at the ceiling as the lights twinkle. The edge of the table is clutched in my hands as I lean further back for a better view of the stars. I float with ease.

Leo returns, silently instructing me to sit up. He puts lotion into his hands, and then lifts my arm to rest my hand upon his shoulder before he begins to massage my skin. I stare at him, entranced as he works his fingers into my muscles. Those gorgeous hazel eyes focus intensely as he works.

"You can close your eyes, *Tesoro*."

"I wanna look at you, Sir."

Green eyes flecked with gold, churning with adoration reach mine. He smiles gently, cupping my jaw again before kissing me softly upon the lips. Contently, I hum. He finishes with one arm, and then starts the other.

The music continues to lull me as he takes care of my body.

"You'll never leave me, Sir," I murmur as he works the lotion into my shoulders next. "You'll never hurt me." He remains quiet, moving down to massage my thighs. "That's what I realized. That trust. Promised only pleasure from your hands. You kept it." His hands still for a moment, before continuing. "Blindfolded and I didn't panic."

"I'm proud of you." He kisses my cheek. "So, very proud, sweetheart."

"Proud of you, too, Sir."

"For what?"

"Giving me time." I smile down at his hands as they massage my tired muscles. "You hate when I'm in pain. I can see it in your eyes…" they flick up to meet mine, "…it pains you."

Leo picks me up, cradling me close to his chest. I lean my head against him as he carries me to the bed. He murmurs softly against my ear, "It does pain me, because I love you more than life itself and the galaxies combined."

I giggle weakly, exhaustion setting in as he lays me down. "Declarations."

"You inspire me to be romantic," he murmurs, kissing my temple.

"I love you…my dear Leo."

A blanket is draped over me as he tucks me into the bed. Finally, I close my eyes. There's movement around the room. The music switches to something softer and faraway. Leo comes back to the bed, gently tugging me towards him. I lay my head against his chest, listening to the gentle beat of his heart.

It's safe here. This place he created for me of violets, stars, and velvet.

The last thing I hear, filled with affection is, "My dear sweet Watson."

Chapter 17

Within a Name

Do I tell Dr. Maxwell my husband is a Sub?

The question rattles in my mind as I sit across from him after going through a very long update since we last spoke. I've cried two times and we've *just* hit the one-hour mark.

It's Monday, right after our weekend off. Thank goodness Leo made sure no one interrupted us, because after that play session I was practically a pile of goo for the whole day after. Even after Leo and I talked about what happened, I'm still confused about why I asked for him to eat me out. Leo didn't seem concerned at all but asked if I wanted to move that activity off my hard limits.

I didn't. That's just the thing that boggles me. Leo thinks I was just willing to do anything to please him, and that's where my mind went. I'd felt safe enough to do something that otherwise I'd never do. One thing was for sure, it certainly cemented my trust with him given he called the safe word for my well-being.

"Autumn?" Dr. Maxwell asks.

I shake away those thoughts, coming back to the present. "Sorry."

"Alright to continue?"

"Yeah, but what were you saying again?"

"To not refer to your past self as Sarah," he answers, putting his mug of tea down.

I clear my throat. The subject itself may be why my thoughts went back to this weekend, deflecting current thoughts. A gentle knowing appears on his face as I scrunch my brows, trying to understand what he's getting at.

"That's supposed to help me how?"

"Sarah and you are the same person, always have been," he starts. "You've brought up feeling split at times when approaching decisions and emotions to explain what you're doing. You've created a divide between two parts of you. You were forced to leave a life behind, told to pretend you *had* died. Four years ago, this perhaps helped process your trauma, compartmentalizing out of survival. It was helpful...but now I think new measures should be considered."

I'm quiet as I stare down at my hands.

"When you talk about your past, before *Blue Java*," he continues steadily. "What perspective do you use?"

I clear my throat, and admit, "Usually, Sarah's."

He watches me solemnly, not adding anything more. I inhale deeply, searching my brain for answers, which feels like it *should* be an easy answer. He said perspective, not *who* exactly.

"When I talk about *my* past, I rarely say it like that. I usually say Sarah's, separating her...I mean mine...shit."

"You've taught yourself to separate the past and present in a manner that gives them two identities," he explains. "Giving it a name, you've removed yourself from your own narrative. It separates *you* from the trauma *you've* endured. I think you're coming to a point where it's no longer helping you. It's causing more uncertainty of what you want."

He pauses, leaning back into his seat.

"I'd like for you to refer to your past as *your* past, Autumn," he says. "To say the name you have now to help reconnect to who you were, in order to accept who you are now."

"I'm...I'm afraid of forgetting though. Forgetting Sarah."

"They can't take her from you." My eyes move up to meet his, warm and compassionate. "You are not relinquishing her to them. They do not own her, as they do not own you."

My hands wring each other, pulling at my fingers as worry flicks up my spine. Is that why? That out of everything taken from me, she was all I had left? All I had to protect from being ripped from me.

"You're still her. She's still you," he continues. "You've always been Sarah, reshaped into a new person to thrive. Every part of her is you."

"What if I *don't* want that?" My mind flicks to the meeting, feeling that anger that was all consuming. The gun going off in my hand. "Those pieces of…me."

"We all have parts of ourselves we don't like. For you, there was a name attached. Sarah became this entity you could attribute to blame for past decisions."

"Except, no matter what those decisions were all me."

He nods. "Much like a young boy who decided to ride a bicycle without hands and fell, breaking his arm. Or decided to get drunk before finals."

He smiles over his mug, sipping from it as I stare at him.

"Not always the well to do, therapist, huh?" I ask.

"No," he chuckles, putting his tea down. "We've all made decisions we're not happy with. Outcomes we've despised. None of this is to minimize what you've endured, but assure you you're not alone. Its life. Confronting one's past is not easy, especially when we can admit the moments we were wrong. Fully being yourself now, does not mean you'll lose Sarah…you're gaining yourself as a whole."

My leg starts to bounce, and I attempt to stop it, but it doesn't.

"Let's try something," he suggests. "Mention several things in your past, except say that *Autumn* did or achieved it."

Hands shaking next, I take a long breath and focus on what he asks.

"Autumn went to college for computer forensics," I start off simple, meeting his gaze. He nods for me to continue. "Autumn was in an abusive relationship. Autumn and Leanne became friends over a love of marshmallows and margaritas. Autumn worked undercover. Autumn…Autumn…" I close my eyes, suddenly the words almost too heavy as I sharply exhale, "…shot the man who tried to assault me. Autumn graduated with honors, and accepted into a Masters program. I was homeless. I—"

I stare down at the coffee table, realizing the change.

"Keep going, you're doing well," Dr. Maxwell says in an encouraging tone.

"I left home at seventeen," I continue, and as I do relief starts to trickle through me. Pressures I hadn't realized were still there disappear as that crack I created becomes mended. Acceptance. "I worked at the YMCA, and really, *really* sucked in English class. I started watching Nick Cage films in my teens, and they were my only comfort growing up and while…undercover. I got my first computer after working at a pizza shop for the summer. I grew up in Ohio. I had a family. My father's name was Richard. My sister Bridgette. And my mother's is…is…Charlotte."

The name is heavy on my tongue. For so long, I've not thought of them. The family I lost and was disowned by. Perhaps they never thought about me again. Yet, there's a weight I've not felt for so long.

My mind drifts, and Dr. Maxwell doesn't stop me as I continue talking.

"It was graduation day, the last time I saw them. They left that same night. My father told me he wouldn't help with my loans, and to not expect a warm welcome when I failed living in the city." I huff, a sharp empty laugh leaving me. "I couldn't be surprised that they didn't show for the funeral. *My* funeral. I only cried because Leanne was. Sarah didn't just endure that, but I did. They buried a ghost."

Silence comes as my leg stops bouncing and my hands go still. Dr. Maxwell waits.

"I never forgot," I whisper. "Deep down, I accepted that pain long before I left for college. It wasn't just going undercover, the assault, and losing the career I could've had, but I wanted to separate from…them, too."

"We cannot choose who we're born connected to," he says slowly. "But that does not dictate who we are. And some day, if you truly needed to forget some of that pain, then that is fine. Let this time be on *your* terms."

I nod, huffing again as I pull my legs up underneath me to sit. "Guess I never truly got time to understand what *they* put me through, too."

"Did Charlotte's betrayal strike deeper because of that connection in name?"

"It'd finally be a classic diagnosis, huh?" I snort. Both of us smirk. "No, I don't think so. Mainly betrayal. Although, just in case, maybe that's a discussion for another time."

"This is the first time you've brought them up fully. Your family."

"Yeah," I sigh, rubbing my head a little. "Maybe hearing so much about Leo's is uncovering what I've buried with mine."

"Or just the idea of family, which they do come in all different variations." I nod in response, grabbing my mug of tea and realize it's cold. Wonderful. "Just remember you have family and friends now who'll support and love you. *All* of you."

"I will, although I may just lock away what I lost again."

"If it no longer serves you, then it may be for the best," he says, putting his hands on the arms of the chair. "We'll pause here for today. I'd like you to continue seeing yourself as a whole: past, present, and future. Otherwise, I think you've handled things well of late."

I laugh nervously, sputtering. "Sure about that?"

"Given the circumstances, yes. Would I use the same criteria with a patient who works solely in accounting? No." We share a laugh as he stands, and I join him. "I've learned a thing or two since working for mobsters." I snort chuckle. "Advice changes upon circumstances and relations."

"You kinda sound like my best friend," I say, following him to the door. "Although her analogy consisted of kindergartener teachers not being the same as high school teachers. Different tactics in teaching."

He pauses, raising a brow. "Hmm, that's good. I may use that in the future."

I open the door, revealing Isaac and Chesty sitting in the hallway. "I'll let her know she gave you inspiration."

He pats my shoulder, then leans in close to say, "Be proud how far you've come, Autumn. Even if situations are abnormal. Not many can say they've outwitted even one crime boss."

I smile as he gives his goodbyes, then strides down the hall with Chesty. They chuckle over something as they disappear into the lobby.

"How was the session?" Isaac asks.

The one with the vibrators and blindfold or the one confronting family trauma? Don't ask him that.

"Good, but more things to work on. Surprise." Much better.

We head for the elevators, and I glance at the clock. "Weird that therapy was later than usual," I comment.

"Prefer early afternoon, instead of later?"

I hum. "Maybe just used to it."

"Odd given you're not entirely a morning person, depending on the day. And if you've had enough coffee."

I give a playful smirk as the elevators come into view. The doors to the private elevator opens, and we both stop as Trix, Leo, Jameson and Carrie walk out. Isaac and I exchange a surprised look.

I start to ask, "Did you know…?"

"No."

The most surprising thing is seeing Jameson and Carrie not arguing.

Trix smiles with Carrie as they talk, Leo being the only one who appears normal—furrowed brow with a stern expression. If he walked out grinning, I'd run back to catch Dr. Maxwell for another twenty minutes.

Trix beams when she sees me, touching Carrie's arm before heading straight for me. We hug as I slowly come out of my shock. I peek over her shoulder to Carrie, who gives a pleasant, but business-y smile. Her curly blonde hair cascades down, accenting her pale blue business suit complete with tight pencil skirt and black stilettos. Stepping back, I notice even Trix is wearing her business attire of slacks and a fancy blouse. Her braids have been pulled back into a bun.

"Didn't know you were here today," I say to Trix.

"Thought to surprise you, but Leo said you were in therapy. You just get back?"

"Uh, yeah." She doesn't need to know I have therapy *in* the hotel.

"Afternoon, Isaac. Heard your date went well," Trix greets, smiling playfully while waggling her eyebrows. She's in a great mood. Is the elevator magic?

Isaac clears his throat, blushing slightly. I hold back my smirk, seeing his light shyness around the subject. He answers, "Yes, it did."

"Hi, Carrie," I finally greet, waving my fingers.

"Hello, Miss Watson, hope you're well."

"You've met?" Trix asks, stepping back as Carrie steps forward. I forgot how much taller she is than me, not just because of the heels.

"We did when uh… the engagement happened." Words feel stuck in my throat. I want to ask how Trix knows her, and how are they getting along?

I look to Leo for answers. Anything as to why I feel like I'm in a *Twilight Zone* episode. There's someone on the plane!

Jameson speaks abruptly. "Yes, the last time Carrie spoke with Autumn, which were few words, it was her suggesting using their engagement like a reality show entertainment."

Ah, there's the Jameson I know and love.

Trix scrunches her face, glancing between me and Leo who's now moving towards me. His hand is placed protectively upon my lower back as Carrie scrutinizes Jameson.

"I was *suggesting* how best to move forward in the public eye," she counters. "Just as I've done my best regarding Patricia's ideas for the centers and combining it with the hotel for the greatest amount of success. Or I could hand over the publicity to you for the promotional launch of the *Golden Laurel.*"

"Golden Laurel?" I ask.

"The hotel opening in Boston," Carrie answers succinctly. Her tone is borderline patronizing.

"Not my job," Jameson mutters.

"Yet, you keep trying to do mine."

"Anyways…" Trix interjects, flicking her gaze over the squabbling pair, "…we were discussing the two centers that the *Italian Lily* is sponsoring."

Wait…the *hotel* is behind funding the centers?

Confusion must come over my face because Trix flicks her gaze to Leo then me.

"I thought you told her," she says.

"I was, but it seems no matter what surprise I have for my…" his voice softens, the touch of his hand upon my back stilling before finishing, "…fiancé, I never end up being the one to tell her."

"I'm sorry, I shouldn't have mentioned it."

"It's okay," I say, leaning into his touch as his fingers caress over my shirt. "Just glad things are going well."

"Yes, they are. Besides, Mr. Luciano is not one for discussing business with those in his personal life," Carrie comments, beginning to step past me. "Informing you is just out of curtesy."

A tiny prick hits the back of my neck.

A phone goes off, and Jameson pulls his out to answer. He gives Leo a look, then turns on his heel to get back onto the elevator.

"Intolerable man," Carrie comments low, glaring at Jameson before turning back to Trix. "Patricia, it was a delight meeting you.

I'm looking forward to working together. You're a breath of fresh air. You could have a career in PR."

"Thanks. I'll see you in a week or so." Trix smiles softly.

"Mr. Luciano, I hope you consider my suggestions. Mr. Morton." Isaac barely gives her a nod in reply. Carrie walks away as her heels click over the marbled floor.

I'm half tempted to yell 'bye!' at her but decide against it.

Leo's body becomes less rigid. I ask, "Fun meeting?"

"Not quite," he answers.

"She's persistent," Trix comments, shaking her head. "Takes the heat off my back, but does she and Jameson always argue like that?"

"Always," Leo and Isaac mutter together.

Trix hums, and then looks to me. "Getting the feeling you two don't get along?"

"Don't know her well enough to really say," I reply. Trix folds her arms, nodding.

"I'm impressed with what you've done, Trix," Leo says suddenly, wrapping his arm around my waist to pull me closer. I lay my head against his shoulder, practically feeling the last of his tension vanish. "I trust Carrie in what she does, but your ideas are more feasible without taking away from the mission statement you have for these centers. I'll take them more into consideration going forward."

"Thank you." Her expression sweetens looking between us. "Want to grab some dinner? Non-business like since Autumn's back from therapy?"

Leo checks his watch, and then looks at Isaac with a frown. "Unfortunately, I have another meeting to attend."

"This late?"

"Yes," he answers promptly. "Why don't you and Autumn enjoy dinner at one of the hotel restaurants? Comped, of course."

"I'm beginning to think I may never have to pay for my own meals or drinks with you, Leo," Trix teases, and I blink at how comfortable the two of them seem together. "Not complaining; just an observation."

"So, I've been told," he murmurs.

I tilt my head, smiling at him as I hear the mirth in his voice even with his face still stern. He meets my gaze, giving a faint smile. I ask, "Will you be late?"

"Hopefully not." He bends to kiss me briefly upon the lips, humming a moment before pulling away. He gives his farewell to Trix, walking to the elevator with Isaac following in silence.

"Think Isaac left cause he didn't want more questions about Leanne?" Trix muses once the doors close.

"Maybe," I murmur, unsure of what kind of meeting it could be. I shake off the unease, turning my attention to Trix. "Where would you like to eat?"

She hooks her arm through mine as we head for the main stairway to go upstairs.

"You choose. I'd melt for this hotel's food," she laughs under her breath. "I remember Carrie mentioning she helped hire the best chefs in the city, and after that one dinner, I believe her."

"I'll tell Chef Giulia that."

"Of course, you know their names," she chuckles. I shrug. "Want to tell me your true thoughts about Carrie?"

"She's good at what she does," I say, shrugging. "Even if her ideas seem…well…"

"Uncouth?" I give her a knowing look. Trix sighs, "She knows what media outlets want, unfortunately it's that. Her and Jameson really don't get along, huh?"

"Pretty sure Leo would hire someone else, but since she's not scared of him or Jameson to do anything to promote his businesses, well…not gonna replace her. I'm positive he likes her spine of steel."

"As a woman, I appreciate that."

"Carrie's spine of steel?" I ask as we get to the elaborate stairs of the hotel that lead up to the next level.

"No, Leo. That his ego or pride aren't fragile enough to be

shaken because it's not a man who brought up an idea. Or even himself. Another positive side to the meeting today. She's ruthless, but he allows her to do her job. On that note, could you and him continue being my benefactors for other projects?"

"Don't tempt me," I laugh.

We're halfway up the stairs when she pauses. Those warm brown eyes find mine as she smiles broadly.

"What?" I ask.

"Feels like the old days. You and me going to eat after therapy. It's just nice. Some changes, but not too much, huh?"

I stare at her, slowly smiling back as I feel a bit of warmth grow within my chest. I nod as we continue up the stairs together.

It'd been a normal business meeting, which meant Leo finished in time to join Trix and I for dessert. After dinner, Trix went home, and we spent the night at the hotel. Today, Leo was booked with meetings and I occupied my time shadowing Bobby. Early evening, Leo found me down in the break room with Bobby, collecting me to go home. After both men gave each other curt nods, we left. Leo seemed uneasy as we got to the car, Rudy and Chesty also quiet. Pulling out of the hotel garage, I squeeze his hand twice. He raises the divider, and I look at him wearily as he leans back with a long sigh.

"Check in," I ask, running my hand over his thigh.

"Green. Check in."

"Green," I answer as he reaches into his pocket, pulling out his wedding ring and slips it on. I pull mine out from its hiding place and do the same. He holds my hand up, smiling faintly as he kisses above my rings.

"My dear wife." His tone isn't sad, but something tugs at me at the wrongness in it.

"Leo?"

"I had a call with Renato today." My stomach sinks. "He

believes Matteo is somewhere in Milan, but I don't believe him. He refuses to use his own resources to keep watch or look for a 'stupid, naïve child' as he said."

Is it bad I can't argue with Renato's description?

"Jameson and the others are preparing us to leave for Rome soon," Leo suddenly adds, and my jaw drops. I wasn't sure how serious he'd been, but then again, it's Leo, but then *again*, it's *Rome*. "Nancy will have everything she needs while we're gone. Jameson will oversee Trix's centers moving forward."

"Why? It'll be awhile before…" my voice trails off, meeting his tentative gaze, "…you don't how long we'll be gone."

"Could be a weeks…or months."

I stare at him. "Can you be out of the country that long?" Fuck, can I? I'd ask about a passport, but knowing Owen and Julio, I likely have three already.

"I'll attend meetings virtually. The Crew will take care of the rest, and Mila will oversee the mobs along with Jameson. The crime bosses have been assuaged, too focused on their newly acquired territories and redoing their ranks. They may even calm more with me being gone."

"Will anyone go with us?"

"Rudolph, Drew, and Owen. Only ones who can leave the country without raising red flags." I raise my brows. He rubs his thumb over my wrist. "They have their reasons."

New lore unlocked for the *Forgotten Demons*.

I swallow hard. "Months?"

He cups my cheek, stroking it as he silently breathes with me to sway the potential panic. "Hopefully not."

I nod slightly, breathing deeply with him.

"I'll show you Rome," he murmurs gently. "Take you anywhere you want. Use the time as a honeymoon."

A sudden giggle escapes, and he smiles kissing my hand again. "Honeymoon? Between mafia family business, right?"

"Make the trip more worth it. For us, not them."

Inhaling deeply, I nod. "Okay. Where you go, I'll go."

Leo kisses me, tracing his tongue over my lips. I sigh against him as he clutches me with need. Suddenly, the car stops and then there's a knock on the divider. Leo breaks the kiss, sliding his glare towards the front of the car. I almost giggle, grabbing his chin and make him face me.

"We're home, mister. More time together, uninterrupted." I kiss him again.

I smile, getting out of the car.

Leo's door opens and closes as I come around the car, looking up at the penthouse building. My gaze comes down to the entrance when warning tugs at the back of my neck. It runs down my spine and I straighten. I glimpse to both sides, but the prick doesn't leave me even as I stare through the glass to see Xavier standing behind the main desk.

Rudy and Chesty talk with each other near the front of the car as Leo takes my hand, leading us into the building. I wait for the warning to wane, but it doesn't as we pass through the doors. I can't tear my gaze away from Xavier, who looks up with a smile. It's forced. Sadness in his eyes.

No.

"Good evening," he greets. My stomach drops as I notice him not calling either of us by name. Xavier flicks his gaze down.

Leo grunts, "Get down!"

Everything becomes a blur.

I drop on command just before gunshots sound. Leo grabs me, pulling towards the pillars as he brings his gun out. Two men stand up from behind the desk, holding Xavier hostage. Shots pop off, ringing through my head. Shouting occurs as I crouch, covering my ears as the glass doors shatter. Sulfur fills the air. Two more shots echo, and then bodies hit the ground.

My ears ring as my heart pounds, looking up to find Xavier and the gunmen gone.

"Three more incoming!" Chesty calls. "Stay low!"

Leo grasps my arm, pulling me towards the desk and I dive for cover as he shoots off rounds behind me. Glass shatters and wood splinters, stonework cracking. I raise my gaze, finding Xavier slumped on the floor with another body next to him.

Gasping, I crawl to Xavier and search for wounds. Two spots of red blossom, one at his shoulder and another at his gut. Noise blurs as I rip off my sweater, using the concealed knife in my boot to tear it apart. Xavier gasps for breath as I tie off his shoulder, using the rest to press against the gunshot wound at his stomach.

"Stay with me," I rasp, flinching as another shot echoes and there's distant yelling. Tires screech outside, along with more shouting.

Xavier's eyes flit about, finally landing on me. "I'm sorry, Miss Autumn…I'm…"

"Stop. Stop, it's not your fault." Fear wrecks through me as I press against the wound. "You're gonna be okay."

The gunshots stop. Leo's gruff voice sounds behind me. "Change in plans. Get back up here, *now.*"

I'm suddenly being pulled away from Xavier, and I start screaming. "No! Wait!"

"Autumn, they'll take care of him," Leo reassures. I realize it's his arm wrapped around me. "We need to leave. Chesty!"

Sight blurring, I stare down at Xavier who gives me a small smile. My heart clenches as Leo drags me away. Chesty comes around the corner, and my head pounds as the biker kneels next to Xavier. The roaring in my head worsens as hurried conversation happens around me. I can't focus as I stare at the crimson painting the marble floors; dead bodies strewn about. The lobby damaged with carnage everywhere.

I can't breathe. Home. They attacked *home.*

Leo suddenly grabs my face. "Focus on me, dear Watson."

Hazel eyes come into view.

"Listen to me," he instructs. "We need to leave. Xavier will be taken care of. We need to get to the airport."

"Airport?"

"We're leaving for Rome. Now."

Chapter 18

Mile High

THE CITY BLURS past as the SUV seems to go at breakneck speed, Rudy weaving expertly through traffic. Leo speaks low on his cellphone, keeping his arm draped over my shoulders. I stare out the window as the city passes. My heartbeat thunders in my ears, remembering Xavier laying in his own pool of blood. I look away from the outside that's now making me nauseous, and press my face against Leo's shoulder, questions swirling in my head.

Who hired those men? Matteo? Gabriel? The crime bosses? How long had they been waiting? They were *in* our building.

"Check in," Leo murmurs against my ear.

"Yellow."

"Breathe. I'm right here." I nod against him as he tightens his arm around me. "You've never flown before, correct?"

"Just the helicopter. How long is the flight?"

"8-9 hours."

I nod again and he kisses my head. His heartbeat isn't as frantic as mine, but it's heavy and loud. Leo smells of sulfur and sweat.

Finally, we arrive at the airport. I've no idea which one as Rudy drives us through some gates and onto an airfield. I glance out the window to see a plane with cars parked not too far away. Of course, we're not flying commercial. I swear if Rudy is the pilot, I'm suggesting a raise. The car halts and we all get out. Wind whips at my face as I stare at the large aircraft. The engines are running, whirring against the wind as I watch Rudy speak with someone then disappears onto the plane. Lights blink in the distance, and I can hear other planes. Everything blends together as I hold myself against the chill.

A hand touches my shoulder and I yelp. Jolting, I spin to find Isaac with his hands up. He gives an empathetic look as I exhale sharply.

"Couple of bags have been packed for you two," he says over the roar of the engine. He nods towards Animal who's hauling luggage onto the plane. "Otherwise, just let Leo buy you whatever else you may need."

I meet his blue eyes, gulping.

"You'll like flying," he adds, carefully touching my shoulder to reassure me. "Glad you're alright, Miss Autumn."

"Why can't you come?" I ask abruptly.

He looks past me, and I follow his gaze to see Jameson and Mila speaking with Leo. My stomach twists as Jameson gestures harshly to a couple of men, who step away quickly.

Isaac steps closer, and answers, "Promised MI6 I wouldn't step back into certain countries, unless I worked for them again. Their pay is shit."

My eyes bulge, gaping at him as he grins widely.

"And…" he adds, softening his smile, "…I don't want to leave Leanne." My heart clenches, while my chin quivers. "Forgive me for not choosing you first, Miss Autumn. But I trust the others will protect you."

I rush forward, hugging him tightly.

"Take care of her," I say, shaking a little not from the breeze. "And thank you."

"Autumn." Leo's voice calls over the noise.

I step back from Isaac, who gives me a reassuring smile. Heart aching leaving him behind, I turn and follow Leo to the plane. I glimpse over my shoulder to Jameson, who gives a half-hearted wave and worried scowl. I wave back as we get onto the stairs and climb on.

It's quieter within the plane. It's mostly a light brown with wood paneling inside. I peek into the cockpit, where the captain sits with Rudy next to him. Leo guides me into the main cabin, where there's leather seating facing each other, and couches lining the sides. At the end of the plane, I see a smaller hall and doorways. Leo sits me in one of the seats facing forward, next to the window with a table between the set of seats.

"Wait here," Leo says, kissing my cheek and goes into the cockpit.

I lean back, breathing deep as I focus on not panicking. Outside it's dark, but I can just make out Jameson, Isaac, and Mila, who all get into cars and drive off. My chest constricts as reality sets in that we're actually leaving the country.

"Good evening, Miss Watson." A feminine voice surprises me.

I flinch, looking up at who I presume is the flight attendant. She wears a deep blue suit with a green ascot. Her dark hair is pulled into a tight bun, and there's freckles on her face. Her cheekbones shimmer from the amount of highlighter she's put on.

"Apologies for startling you, must be your first time," she continues. "My name is Joyce. Is there anything I can prepare for you once we're in the air?"

"Uh…no, wait… water is fine."

"Ice or no ice?"

She slightly leans over the other seat to speak with me, and I'm honestly unsure what to do. My excuse is almost being shot and keeping a man from bleeding to death less than an hour ago. So, no I don't know or care if I want ice or not.

"Joyce, I appreciate your arrival on such short notice." Leo's voice intercedes as he approaches. "I'll take scotch on the rocks, and Autumn will take water with no ice."

"Very well, sir." She nods, smiling broader as I notice her eyes skim over his chest.

My brows scrunch, realizing Leo's only wearing his button-up, which is half undone. No undershirt, so you can see his tattoos peeking out and those reaching down his forearms with his sleeves rolled up.

She walks away as I slump into my seat, bemoaning that this evening just keeps getting better. Not.

Animal sits across from me, along with Owen, who hangs up the phone call he was on.

"Xavier made it to the hospital," Owen says, "Currently in surgery. They believe he's got a good chance."

Thank fuck.

Leo sits beside me as I stare at the table.

"How many hitmen were there?" Leo asks gruffly, reaching over me and starts to buckle me into my seat. The engines roar outside, and the plane starts moving. My chest tightens, anxiety creeping up my spine.

"Counted eight dead," Animal answers.

"Believe there's one more," Owen adds. "Enigma's tracking'em."

Leo finishes buckling me in, and then kisses my cheek. He then settles into his seat to buckle in with the other two. The cockpit door closes.

I think I wanna hurl.

"Hey, sister, guess you get to fly in style first time, too," Animal comments, keeping a jovial tone. I give a tentative smile.

Owen puts digital devices onto the table, from multiple phones to a laptop.

"What's all that for?"

"Switching out phones when we land. Gotta change up the cyber security to access secure networks." I nod along. "Due to a different country and Renato's people fucking snooping."

The men murmur with each other as I stare out the window, watching runway lights blink and pass. It's completely dark out, so I can't see any other planes leaving or landing. The engines rumble louder, and I feel us picking up speed.

Leo grabs my hand as my heart rate picks up, thumping loudly as I stare outside. The plane speeds up, and I'm not sure if we'll actually take off or fucking run into a building, until there's a bump and the nose tips up. My breath catches as I feel the plane leave the ground, moving into nothing. My stomach flips, chest squeezing as we tip further back into the sky. Unease doesn't relent as we bump and jostle in the air.

I look away from the window, feeling sick as I look at Animal with wide eyes. Leo's hand remains around mine, his thumb caressing my wrist. Animal grins, settling into his seat leisurely like it's second nature being here. His composed expression, along with Owen's, does help as we jostle harshly again. It feels like someone is trying to push the plane over.

It seems like forever before the plane isn't tipped back anymore, leveling out as it leans to make a turn and then does it again. My grip on Leo's hand lightens, but I swallow hard as my ears pop.

"I think I like the helicopter more," I rasp quietly. Leo's gaze flicks over my face, brows furrowing.

"Just wind turbulence, completely normal," Animal comments. "Slicing through air instead of hovering practically."

Owen snorts, shaking his head as he opens his laptop to work.

"What? Am I wrong?"

"Slicing versus hovering? Really?" Owen asks him.

They start bickering about verbiage, and Joyce comes back to set our drinks down. She pauses, gaze lingering on Leo as he reaches for his drink.

"May I get you anything else, sir?"

"I'll take a whiskey, on the rocks," Owen answers, and Joyce tears her eyes away from Leo with a perturbed look. Her smile is tight.

Sneaking possessiveness creeps over my skin. A part of me wanting to throw my water into her face. I'm not worried, but I hate the sinking feeling. She can stare all she wants I know he's not going anywhere. But still…why do I have to be stuck in the same plane with her for almost nine hours?

She walks away, and Leo's voice pierces through my thoughts. "Autumn?"

I attempt to shake off the heavy contemplations, staring at the table. I blame everything that's happened today for making me even care if another woman leers at him. The twist in my stomach not helping.

Leo unclips his seatbelt, then undoes mine suddenly. He pulls me up alongside him, then grunts at the other men, "Don't bother us."

Leo's voice is a warning as he leads us down the short hallway, and then through a final door. He shuts it behind us as I look around the room with a bed sitting in the middle.

Leo gently sits me down on the bed, kneeling before me as he runs his hands over my thighs. I place my hands over his, looking into his gaze and find them eerily calm.

"Check in," he says.

My face falls, unsure how to answer. Was I green? No, I'm too jittery, and feeling like crap. Maybe yellow, but maybe red? I'm not really panicking though, just overwhelmed, anxious, and exhausted mentally.

"Autumn," he says gently, rubbing my thigh. "We're alright." I nod my head. "We're safe."

I nod again, numbly. My chin starts to quiver, not knowing when this dam will break. "Who...who...?"

"I don't know, but Jameson is on it. The Crew will find out." He reaches up, wiping away a tear that's escaped. Another tear falls.

"I knew something was wrong," I whisper, and that tightness in my chest worsens. I tremble as the last of the adrenaline rush leaves, grasping for survival next.

"So did I, and you listened and took cover when I told you." He cups my face, keeping my blurry gaze on him. "Good girl. Thankfully, we came out unharmed."

Except Xavier.

I swallow hard against the tightness around my throat. As if he can read my thoughts, Leo says, "Xavier will pull through. He's a tough old man."

A shaky breath leaves me as the plane jolts a little. I grip the bedspread, staring down at the ground.

"Dear Watson…"

"Are we ever going to see New York again?" I ask abruptly, eyes finding his once more. We've had multiple hits on us in only a few weeks. What happens if they follow us to Europe?

The calmness on his face slightly dissipates. He inhales sharply and leans in to kiss my forehead. "I promise you, my dear Watson. I will bring you home. No matter what."

I fall into his touch, placing my head just underneath his chin. His arms wrap around me, kissing my temple and breathing deep as he holds me. The plane bumps again, and I clutch to him as a wave of fear flickers.

"Not sure what I'll hate most," I say as he starts to stroke my back. "The plane ride itself or the stewardess ogling you."

"Should I fire her?"

"While mid-air?" I almost chuckle against his chest. "Give her a parachute and kick her off?"

"Or I won't wear anything revealing."

"I'm not worried, mister. I'm just exhausted and…wrapping my head around us currently flying to Italy."

I huff, tapping my head against his shoulder as he runs his hands up and down my back. The familiar touch helps the sickly feelings disappear. We're quiet as the plane bumps, jerking a little as it leans to turn again. I cling to him.

I swear if I'm actually fearful of flying in airplanes, but not helicopters, I'm gonna be pissed. Maybe I should see if *Airplane!* is on here somewhere. That could help.

Leo starts to stand, bringing me up with him. He then opens some drawers from off to the side, pulling out lounge wear. He gets me redressed, and then does the same, but keeps his shirt off. Next thing I know, I'm put under the covers with him as a television starts to rise from a dresser when he hits a button.

"Well, I seem to be leveling up each time I leave the city," I murmur, and he cocks a brow at me. "First ferry, helicopter, motorcycle, and now fancy plane with TV. I'm just missing train."

He snorts as he pulls me close under the covers.

"Shouldn't you be out there?" I ask him.

"We're on a damn plane, if they expect me to do anything while flying over the Atlantic, they're insane." I burrow closer. He sighs, kissing my temple. "I just want to be with my wife."

I thread my fingers with his and feel metal. I glance down, remembering we're still wearing our wedding rings. Calmness falls over me that helps soothe my nerves. More of the anxiousness disappears when I see him pull up one of my favorite movies, and I quietly giggle. "How did you get that on here?"

"Magic, dear Watson."

I remain propped up against his chest as he pushes play for *Reefer Madness: The Musical*. It does work as a distraction for a while.

Before we almost finish the movie there's a knock at the door. Leo scowls at it, throwing the blanket off as he growls opening the door. "I said not to bother us."

"Xavier made it through surgery," Owen answers. "He's stable."

My body slumps into the bed with relief.

Leo's voice is low, "Thank you. Go away."

"Sure thing, boss." Owen almost sounds amused, closing the door.

Leo returns to the bed, tugging me back into his arms as I start to silently cry. Relief and horror mix as I clutch Leo, who holds me firmly as I tremble in his arms.

Thank fuck Leo had all these movies on board to watch. Although exhausted, I couldn't sleep. Several times I thought I would, but then the plane would bump or I'd close my eyes and see blood. Leo feel asleep, and at one point Joyce came back to deliver a meal. I had her set it to the side, and once more she lingered as he slept with the blanket not fully covering his naked torso.

I practically threw her out, feeling territorial. I'm not usually like this, but seeing someone watch him while he was basically vulnerable…well, she best thank the stars I didn't punch her.

Eventually, he woke up and ate, then fell asleep again. Glad someone was getting some shut eye. I went out and sat with the Crew for a bit. All of them grabbed some sleep or ate it seemed except me. My stomach wouldn't stop churning, and random headaches kept forming.

Instead, I did what I did best: watched movies like *Fern Gully, The Pagemaster,* and even *A Troll in Central Park.* Covered the classics.

Leo's up and moving as it feels like my brain is being pulled in different directions. He's getting dressed as I switch it up and start *Roman Holiday.* At some point, I feel him come over and press a hand against my forehead.

"Autumn, have you slept at all?"

I shake my head numbly.

He starts to gently lay me down into the bed. "Try to get some sleep before we land."

He pulls the blanket over me as I still watch Audrey Hepburn on the screen. Leo sits on the edge, stroking my hair back. He continues the comforting gesture, and finally my eyes flutter closed.

All too soon, I'm woken up by Leo, who rocks me gently.

"Sweetheart, we're landing soon," he murmurs, helping me sit up as my eyes remain closed. My entire body feels heavy and hollow at the same time. I start mumbling something even I can't decipher.

"Arms up." I do as he says, lifting them as he pulls off my sweaty shirt, replacing it with a sweater. He gets me to stand, tapping my legs to lift up to remove my pants, and then pulls on some leggings. My head rolls back, too tired to fight him. He sits me on the bed, putting socks on me and then shoes. I groan a little, stomach churning once more. Leo picks me up, carrying me out of the room. He puts me in a seat, buckling me in.

"*Barchën*…you good?" Rudy's voice sounds far away.

"She barely slept," Leo answers. A headache starts to form, and I scrunch my brows. "Did she eat with any of you?"

There's mumblings of no. A hand presses against my forehead again.

"Is she sick?" Rudy asks.

"No, I think just exhausted," Leo answers quietly. I feel him lean away, and whisper, "Have Aurelio contact a doctor to be on standby, just in case."

"Sure thing, boss," Owen answers quietly.

I mumble to myself, wanting to just fucking sleep or just slump into a pile of pillows. It's like I've been hit by a truck and my stomach hurts. Probably lack of eating.

Leo kisses my head, stroking my hair as I hear more buckles being clicked shut.

"Just sleep, dear Watson," Leo whispers against my ear. "You're safe."

I grumble in response, fading into the darkness behind my eyes. One moment we're jostling in the air, and I swear the next we're landing. My breath catches as I cling to the armrest when the plane touches ground. Leo's hand is wrapped around mine, thumb stroking over my skin. Time jumps as the next moment I feel him unbuckling me.

"Arms around me, sweetheart," he murmurs against my ear.

I wrap them around his neck, and he lifts me up, tugging my legs around his torso. His arm tightens around my waist, holding me against him as he walks us out of the plane.

The last thing I remember is Joyce's soured face and fake smile. I flip her off and she gapes at me as I close my eyes and settle back into my husband's arms.

Chapter 19

Lovestruck

I don't remember getting to the hotel. All I recall is Leo's arms around me, not letting go until I landed upon a soft bed. Unsure how long I slept, my eyes open to sunlight. I sit up, groaning as I rub my eyes. Looking around, I find myself in an elegant bedroom that's cream colored; gold and green vines painted on the walls. The bed I'm in has tall posts that reach up into a canopy where white mesh fabric flutters in the breeze. To my right is a window with an iron-cast railing and curtains that match the canopy. I step out of bed, going to the open window that brings a light breeze. My breath catches.

Buildings of sandy stone and brick surround the block. The sun is streaking through buildings that line the street with their balconies. Across the way, greenery hangs from windowpanes and railings. I glance down, noticing the street is paved in cobblestones, not asphalt. There are cafés, shops, and I think another hotel entrance as I lean over the railing. People stroll about, but not many as I gather it's rather early. It's nowhere near the chaos that's New York. I stare at the city, eyes moving over…Rome.

There's noise behind me, and I turn around as Leo slides open the double doors to the bedroom. He frowns, until he sees me and his expression softens. He wears tan slacks with a white button-up, sleeves rolled up. I glance down, finding myself in pale silk pajamas. Am I dreaming?

"How are you feeling?" He asks, coming towards me and runs his hands over my arms.

"Good. How long was I asleep?"

"We arrived late morning yesterday. You slept through the afternoon and night. It's just after 6 AM."

I blink at him. "Oh."

"Drew thinks you may have had a touch of air sickness, along with not sleeping for almost 24 hours and barely eating." He kisses my cheek, and starts to lead me out of the bedroom. "Speaking of, let's get you something to eat."

I'm led into a vast living room, same aesthetic as the bedroom. The furniture reminds me of an antique store with its floral décor. There's a low coffee table, shiny with a vase of orchids on top. A sofa of deep blue, a loveseat, and an armchair surround it. A small kitchenette is on the other side, divided by a thin counter and a nook to eat near the window. On the far left is a foyer basically, along with what I believe is another room and then the main doorway. Leo leads me out onto the balcony on the right with ornate iron railings. There's a table and chairs already set out with food and coffee.

I shall never question how he knows when I'll wake up. Even in Rome.

He sits me down, pouring me a coffee from a Moka pot. I'm given a plate with fruit, a pastry, and some oatmeal. A smile rises on my face as he finally settles into his seat across from me, lounging back with his own cup of coffee. His face is serious as he nods at the food before sipping his drink.

I smirk at him, finally eating. I gaze out at the lack of metal and glass buildings I've grown used to. We're quiet as I eat, finishing everything and even grabbing another pastry before curling up into my seat to finish my coffee.

"So…this is Rome," I say.

"This is Rome."

I notice how relaxed he is. It wasn't a great start getting here, and we're earlier than we should be, but he's…composed.

"Is this your hotel?"

"Yes. Smaller in comparison to others, but then again everything in the United States is bigger." He pours the last of the coffee into our cups equally. "It's considered a luxury hotel, even with fewer rooms, placing it in higher demand."

"How were you able to get this suite? I know it's your…" he raises a brow, and I sigh, "…*our* hotel, but wouldn't that mean kicking a guest off a reservation?"

"This one is reserved for myself and very close acquaintances."

We'll ignore him not saying family or friends.

"My wife takes precedence over anyone else, so given the joy I saw on your face at the bedroom window, we'll stay here for however long you want."

I freeze right before sipping my coffee. A smug look comes over him, and I giggle slightly. His smile grows with adoration.

"Ohhh, you're gonna be a romantic menace here, aren't you?" I giggle again from behind my cup, attempting to hide my playful grin.

Leo stands and comes around the table. I stare up at him as he takes the cup from my hands, placing one hand on the table and the other against my cheek. He leans down, kissing me sweetly as my heart flutters. I stifle a moan while soft lips caress mine, teasing me with his tongue.

"Yes…I will be." His whispered confession against my skin causes my body to shudder.

Can one die from being romanced to death? Honestly, I'll take it. Best way to go. Did he take lessons from Gomez?

"And these next few days are for us," he says, stroking my cheek gently. My brows pinch together. "Everyone believes we're in Boston. A decoy plane with Julio and Jameson left soon after we did. Apart from the Crew, Chiari, and my hotel manager here…no one knows we're in Rome."

Questions flick through me. A part of me knows he's playing a game of cat and mouse; hiding us to give the others time to catch who sent those hitmen. Perhaps surprise Renato or Matteo while here. Or diverting from being tracked by Gabriel. I shove those thoughts aside, smiling up at the man who's trying to provide me happiness in a time of uncertainty.

"You should get dressed," he states. "Unless you need more time before I start showing you Rome."

"No! I'm ready!" I scramble out of my seat as he chuckles behind me.

I change quickly, finding clothes Isaac packed and more in the closet. Some are new, and I'm presuming from a personal shopper because there are some items I don't normally wear. I choose something different, pulling on a faded jean jacket to complete the look. I meet Leo in the living room. An odd look passes over his face, eyes skimming my attire. He then smiles, takes my hand, and leads me out of the suite. I follow him down a short hall to some elevators with gold plated gates.

It may be a smaller hotel, but it doesn't feel like it.

The main lobby is extravagant with white marbled floors, carpets of intricate designs, expensive looking vases of flowers everywhere, and chandeliers. A fountain sits in the middle with a statue of a woman pouring water. On one side is the front desk area, whilst the other leads to a lounge. I stare at everything unapologetically.

An older man with greying hair and beard, politely nods to Leo from the front desk then to me, and I give him a little wave in return. Leo leads us onto the street, pausing as I stare up at the building we were in and then down the road.

My breath hitches. It's as if I've been transported into one of my movies.

Leo tugs at my hand. I smile up at him as his gaze softens.

"We'll see famous sites throughout the week, today I want to show you parts of Rome that may not be as tourist filled."

"Lead the way," I tell him.

He brings my hand up, kissing my wrist and I see his wedding ring. My heart squeezes, realizing I'm wearing mine, too. Tears threaten to come with happiness of being able to wear them publicly.

Leo walks us down the path, and it's refreshing after taking so many vehicles the past few weeks. Not to mention cooped up in apartments, hotels, and planes. A large exhale leaves me, smiling at everything around us.

Halfway down the block, my anxiety pricks. It tugs at my neck as my body becomes rigid. I move closer to Leo, tossing it up to just left-over panic from a day ago. We take a turn around a corner, passing a jewelry store when he leans down to whisper, "It's just Rudolph."

I peek up at him, and then over my shoulder. Sure enough, there's Rudy not too far away as he practically towers over people. A breath of relief leaves me as I follow Leo. Not my usual body-guard or city, can't be surprised if flickers of old anxiety return, too.

I'm not sure how long we've explored before I completely relax. Leo shows me cafes, historical landmarks, and beautiful architecture. We spend hours walking around. Every step I think I fall more enamored with it, loving the art and bits of culture. More than a few times Leo converses in Italian with shop owners or locals. A few words I catch, but I have too much fun listening to his voice.

Leo's tone becomes deeper, almost smoother when he speaks Italian. Each word flows with a preciseness that's intoxicating. Twice he caught me staring, giving a knowing smirk in response.

It's coming closer to evening when we come to a piazza where a large wall sections off what could be the backside, I guess. The other side has a tall wall with levels and trees flanking it. People mill about as we approach the main attraction—an extremely tall stone pillar with four fountains at each corner and steps in between.

Leo guides me around it toward the tall wall, where there's steps towards the top.

"That's the Flaminian Obelisk," Leo explains as he's done for every place we've visited, pointing towards the pillar. "This is the Piazza del Popolo. Those stairs and path lead to gardens and eventually to the Villa Medici."

My gaze shifts back to the obelisk and the ancient markings upon it.

"Somewhat a tourist spot, but not like the Coliseum or St. Peter's," Leo mentions, drifting a hand over my shoulder. "Want to see it from above?"

I lean my head back to look towards the top. "We can go up there?"

"Yes, just be prepared for the climb."

I give him a thumbs up as he takes the lead. It winds a bit, and we have to dodge a few vehicles. It's a bigger climb than I thought as we finally get to the top, and I shake my legs a little from the slight burn in my thighs. Leo strokes my back as I see a stone path that leads to the wide curve of a stone balcony. People gather at the edge, but groups leave and soon there's only a couple of people left.

Leo's hand leaves me as I head for the edge. My fingers grip the stone railing as my breath catches. I look out over the piazza, shadowed by streams of sunlight through clouds. Somehow it appears larger, stretching out with its vast oval shape. In the distance, I see the dome of St. Peter's, among the array of dark sandy roofs. The obelisk stands in the middle of it all, while warm rays cascade through the sky. My throat becomes tight as tears want to form.

It's beautiful. Absolutely breath-takingly beautiful.

The world suddenly feeling very free.

I almost can't believe that I am seeing this—a piece of the world so vast and ancient. I inhale deeply, wanting to sear this moment in my mind. A warmth comes over my chest. I realize how grateful I am to have survived everything to now see such brilliance that I never knew existed.

I smile.

- - -

Leo

She's wearing a sundress.

His breath had been stolen the moment she walked out of the bedroom in that dress and jean jacket. She seemed confused at his reaction, perhaps not knowing what she'd done. A sweet ache clenched at his heart as his hand wrapped around hers.

Twice she's worn a dress, both for fancier occasions. She'd never been comfortable enough to wear them for every day. Yet here she was in Rome, wedding ring on her finger, wearing a cornflower blue sundress.

Throughout the day, he watched her face alight with joy. Every time he felt her tense from the crowds, he'd distract her with something else. For her to feel the peace he'd always found here.

It wasn't home, but it was close.

As he watched her interact with a city not filled with metal and noise like New York, he vowed he'd show her California. Paris. London. Wherever she wanted.

She stands at the terrace edge, looking out at the scenery as dusk approaches. The sundress flutters in the wind behind her. He notices those dimples of hers that show when she truly smiles. His wife then turns to him, eyes shining like she was meant to be here. As if she belonged in Rome.

His heart clenches, throat tightening as the heavy emotion of his love wraps around him. For a flash, he hears the gunshots and sees the crimson on his hands. The fear of it not being Xavier's blood on the ground, but hers.

Leo blinks those thoughts away, focusing on Autumn as she rushes over to him. She takes his hand, guiding him along the pebbled path towards a fountain. She releases him to reach into the water, grinning to herself as droplets fall through her fingers.

These moments, he can forget the duties he has. For him not to concentrate on finding answers, worry over his family, or knowing Gabriel is searching for them. He could pretend none of it existed. It was just him and her.

Violin music fills the air as a street performer plays to the side of the path. The music is slow, and Leo recognizes the melody. Suddenly, Autumn stands and stares at the violin player. There aren't many people mingling as evening approaches, likely leaving for dinner or other evening attractions.

"Do you think he takes requests?" She asks.

"Depends if he has sheet music or has it memorized," he answers, pulling out his wallet. "And how much you tip him."

She purses her lips. Leo pulls out some larger Euros, putting them into her hand. "Why don't you ask?"

"Still working on the Italian," she says with a grimace.

"High chance he knows some English. He'll appreciate you trying."

"Alright…stay here. No moving."

"Sì, caro Watson."

Autumn stops to smirk at him before she goes to approach the musician. Leo flicks his gaze over his shoulder, quickly finding Rudolph not far from them. His eyes rove over the greenery, searching for any source of danger.

The music stops. Leo's eyes snap to the player as Autumn talks to him, and then places the money into the instrument's case. The musician nods with a grin, bringing up the instrument up to his chin. Instantly, Leo recognizes the music and slowly grins as Autumn rushes back to him.

She stops about a foot away, bowing low and offers her hand. "Dance with me?"

"You never have to ask, dear Watson."

"Some of us do *before* dancing, mister."

He takes her hand, pulling her into frame as he starts to lead her into a modified waltz. Stepping over the gravel carefully, they dance as the violinist plays *Musetta's Waltz*.

He twirls her, watching as her skit ripples over the ground. They continue dancing as the violinist plays it again, seeming overjoyed to play Puccini instead of a pop song cover. Autumn looks over at him, smiling as she gives him a thumbs up. Her laughter ignites a hope inside him that they'll survive what's coming. And so help him, if anyone tries to steal the light that emanates from her soul, blood or not, he'll drown them in it if he must.

Chapter 20

Fallen Angels & Demons

Autumn

I WAKE UP SLOWLY. My body turns towards the window as small bits of sun sparkle through the sheer curtains; our only barrier to the outside world. I smile, breathing deep as I witness the calm morning.

The past couple of days have felt like a dream. Leo's taken me to see the Coliseum, early in the morning before large crowds were let in. I didn't ask how he did it, but appreciated that we could walk around the ancient space by ourselves for a bit. It was larger than I thought while I stared down into what used to be the arena. Then we went to the temple ruins next to it, and then we were off to the ancient race course. He's shown me other monuments, notable places. Yesterday, we walked a bit along the river, and then explored some gorgeous churches for their art and architecture. One stood out the most for me.

Santa Maria della Vittoria.

A church that appeared simple on the outside with white stone columns. Inside it was adorned with intricate works of marble, gold, and stone. Painted ceilings. Designs carved into the walls. Finally, there was a sculpture of white with golden rods reaching down, splitting like frozen sunlight. An angel with an arrow in their hand stood above a woman covered in fabric. It was simple, yet complex as I stared at the sculpture carved by Bernini.

Ecstasy of Saint Teresa—a structure of sensual and spiritual pleasure.

There was a familiarity I couldn't place staring at it, even now unsure what it was.

An arm snakes over my waist, tugging me against a torso. The warmth of Leo's skin against mine makes me sigh. We're naked under the light cotton sheets draped over us. I grasp his hand, pressing my hips back and become quite aware of his morning wood.

His hand caresses my side, coming up to my breast and gently grabs it. As I feel his body against mine, heat grows from within spreading through me as Leo kisses my neck. Warm, moist breath drifts over my skin as he kisses the underside of my jaw, arousal growing.

"Check in," he murmurs.

"Emerald." I feel him smile against my neck.

Leo eases me onto my back, covering my body with his. He kisses my skin reverently, hands roving softly over me as his hips gently rock against mine. One of his hands moves down, teasing towards the apex of my thighs. My breath catches as a finger strokes over the hood of my clit, circling gently. I grasp just above his hip, holding onto him as my body bends towards him when a finger is inserted inside me. He works me slowly, stroking his thumb over my clit. Another finger joins the first. Leo kisses down my clavicle and back up.

Everywhere his touch is a gentle caress; delicate as he breathes against my skin.

With every movement, my body bows to him in want of more pleasure that thrums through me. My head tilts back against the pillows, breathing heavily as I stare up at the canopy above us. I gaze at the scenery painted on the ceiling, past the rippling fabric. Angels lounge within clouds amongst gold and pink streaking through pale blue skies. All of them nude with feathered wings, brilliant against the color.

Leo removes his fingers, causing me to tear my eyes away from the painting. His cock replaces them as he ever so slowly pushes inside me. I gasp while my hips lift toward him. Leo thrusts at a gradual pace before he completely fills me when his pelvis pushes against mine. His hands stroke up my torso, one massaging my breast while the other moves to grasp my hair tenderly. My hands run over his back, feeling the flex of his muscles as he thrusts again. I sigh as he touches me deep within.

He kisses above my breast, placing more towards my neck. Leo gently rocks into me, and then grasps my leg to bend it, pulling up towards my chest as he pushes forward. My body shudders, grabbing his hair and feeling the soft strands as he buries his face against my neck.

There's nothing quick or harsh of what we do.

I stare down the length of his back as the sheets fall off of him, revealing those stark tattoos. My breath hitches as I feel Leo around me. His tenderness and loving embrace. I can't pull my eyes away from the tattooed mafia boss, whom I've seen covered in blood, fucking me gently in the morning light.

No. This was Leo making love.

Realization flutters over me as his breath brushes my skin. It suddenly feels like a dream, caught in a haze that I never want to wake up from. Emotions build as my heart clenches, stroking my hands down his back. I attempt to feel every part of him, gasping at the sensuous pace. The safety and craving for him. Tears want to follow next in overwhelmed affection.

Don't you dare cry during sex, Autumn. Don't be that girl.

I swallow hard, burying my face against the crook of his neck as he plunges into me. He remains there, keeping himself deep inside, rolling his hips as he lets go of my leg to trail his hand up my thigh.

Leo pulls his head away, and I'm met with hazel eyes smoldering with desire. A slight furrow appears between his brows. He reaches up, wiping away a stray tear that's fallen down my face.

Crud muffins!

"I'm okay, nothing's wrong," I speak before he can.

Leo cups my face, body going still. "What is it, sweetheart?"

"Just..." I let out a shaky breath, touching his face next, "...just...never thought I'd be this loved."

Another tear escapes. Leo leans in, kissing where it's fallen.

"Ti amo...cara mia. Ti amo."

I smile as his hips start to move again, and I wrap my legs around his waist. He drives himself slowly into me as I put my arms around his neck. Leo's forehead touches mine as he thrusts at a leisure pace. Pleasure builds, cascading through my veins making my body tremble. I clutch him as he gently rocks into me, pushing deep.

The orgasm that comes isn't boisterous, it's slow building as my muscles lock up as ecstasy flickers along my spine. I clench around him as he grunts low and comes next. Legs untightening around him, I sigh and allow my head to fall back completely.

Leo expertly flips us over, laying on his back for me lie on top of him. His hands stroke my back as I feel his cock twitch inside me. I almost giggle at the sensation, biting my lip. We're quiet as the sounds of the city drift from outside. His chest rises against mine; fingers trailing along my spine.

He breaks the quiet, "What would you like for breakfast?"

"Whatever you want," I sigh.

"How about some omelets?"

I balance my chin on his chest to look at him. He smiles softly, continuing to caress my back. "Sounds perfect."

There's a crowd outside St. Peter's Basilica. Not surprising. We walk around the square in front of the vast church. My jaw almost drops as we step into the extravagant nave of the Basilica. Stone pillars line the seemingly never-ending church, creating arches that lead into several coves. Marble and gold are every-where. Paintings of saints and angels are depicted in various scenes. We've visited a handful of churches, but this was *enormous*.

I let go of Leo's hand, walking ahead as I stare up at the ceiling where the artwork and sculptures continue. Gold plates or perhaps tiles cover the curved ceiling, and there's a golden border with inscribed Latin. I stare at the writing, neck beginning to hurt as I attempt to translate it. Leo comes up beside me, placing his hand against the back of my head to help relieve some of the pain. I smile as I continue focusing on the ancient language.

"Can you read it?" He asks.

"Something about…praying to Peter and faith never failing, and over here…" I turn towards the other side of the nave, squinting at the inscription as I take a few more steps, "…keys to the kingdom? Heaven? Bound in heaven. Bound in earth."

"Really know your Latin," he murmurs.

I shrug, bringing my head down as he lets go. We continue walking as I glance over the tucked in coves along the sides. There're places to sit, areas for candles to be lit which flicker in the dim shadows. It's ethereal here, and yet that familiar emotion returns. Maybe I just feel small in the enormous spaces.

I shake off the odd feelings as we approach a large bronze four post structure. "I might remember some Latin, but I don't know what that is," I say.

"St. Peter's Baldachin," Leo answers.

My head tilts back again as I stare up at the golden dome above. Latin scripture is around the base with images, I'm guessing, of Peter or other saints. I catch words of keys to the kingdom and something of building a church.

"This is the pulpit or altar," Leo explains as I bring my head down. We start to walk around the Baldachin, much like others as I look at the other sculptures built into the walls. More chairs.

"What are these nooks? Or coves?" I ask.

"They're considered small chapels. Each with their own name such as Chapel of the Pieta or Chapel of St. Sebastian."

"And the candles? I doubt for ambiance."

He chuckles. "No. People may light them to honor those who've died or for prayers. To either God or a Saint. Common practice in Catholicism."

Leo slips his hand around mine as we slowly walk under the dome.

"I know you're not particularly religious, or practice that I know of," I say carefully, approaching the topic. "But…do you believe in God? Or any of what this is dedicated to?"

He exhales a long breath, while glimpsing up towards the paintings. His hand remains firmly around mine.

"I was raised in the Catholic Church before my mother died. I had believed at one point, but it's been some time since I've thought of God's existence," he answers solemnly. "How my life has twisted and turned, I find it hard to believe in the God that they…" he gestures toward the parishioners within the chapels, "…believe in. I cannot say I regard Him or the Saints as they do, for that I'm likely already damned to hell."

My mind flashes to his back tattoo. Those harrowing images so starkly inked upon his skin.

"Do *you* believe you're damned?"

"In the eyes of those here, I certainly am." Leo sighs, keeping his voice low as we walk down the far-left aisle of the nave. "I've committed crimes against God; broken the Commandants over and over again. If I confessed to a priest, perhaps my soul wouldn't be damned, except I doubt I'd ever be able to bring myself to walk into a confessional booth. My existence is perhaps the definition of damnation."

"That's not a yes or no."

He stops to look down at me with furrowed brows. Leo flicks

his eyes over me, scowling as his jaw clenches. My heart sinks as sorrow lingers in his eyes.

"I'm not sure," he finally answers. "I do not wish to confess any of my sins, for I do not feel remorse for most of them. I've accepted what I am, Autumn, and what I've done. What that means towards eternity, I don't know."

I want to tell him he's not damned. Deep down, he's a good man with a heart that's been locked up due to pain. To tell him his soul was kind and gentle, even if the world didn't want him to be. All of that must've counted towards something.

"Have you ever believed?" He asks suddenly, gesturing towards a chapel across from us.

"Grew up in a Christian household, but…not really," I answer, staring at the dark browns and golds of the chapel while candle-light flickers, illuminating the dark. "I think there's a higher power to thank, otherwise I've no real idea how I got here some days. How I survived. Fate. Maybe God. Maybe another deity that's out there. Or maybe angels or…" I pause, and look at Leo, "…demons."

His gaze meets mine, face softening.

"Since I left home," I say, gesturing up to the ceiling and paintings. "I never wanted to live my life out of fear from…this. That doing anything wrong meant I'd suffer forever. Life already sucked. I just wanted to be kind and loving because I wanted to, not because my parents told me I had to in the justification of God. Nice perk, but not enough for me. That and the world just seemed to need more empathy."

I let out a sharp exhale, grabbing his hand and rub my thumb over his wedding ring.

"And if I'm damned for the things I've done, the good I tried to do is rejected, and not seen for trying to do the right things for most of my life…" I shrug, and look up at him, "…fuck believing in a God who'd forsake me like that."

My voice is soft, almost feeling blasphemous for saying such a thing within a place that's dedicated to a god I don't believe in.

Leo's scowl disappears and those furrowed lines are nowhere to be seen. He cups my face gently. "Damned or not, as long as I have you for eternity I'd willingly burn in the fires of hell."

The ache comes back, tightening around my heart as I reach up and press his hand against my cheek. I attempt to smile faintly. "Well, I don't plan on going there, so I guess you'll have to follow me somewhere else."

"Yes, I shall, my dear Watson."

I kiss his palm, bringing it down as we begin to walk out of the Basilica. My legs feel shaky. A few times before we've mentioned religion, but not to the extent of full beliefs. It's never been a priority for either of us. I wonder if it is something we should discuss more, given that it does seem to matter to him more than me. At the moment, I decide to let it go, that there's a reason we haven't spoken of it much in the past. The subject itself was likely brought on from frequenting places of worship the last few days.

We walk back into the sunlight towards the square. Leo leads the way through the meandering crowds, approaching the obelisk in the middle. Suddenly, there's a prick at the back of my neck. My spine becomes rigid, and I stop in my tracks. Quickly, I scan the crowd. Rudy is not too far, winding through tourists. While seeing him, the anxiety doesn't relent, screaming at me.

"It's just Ringer," Leo reassures. He stands calmly next to me, waiting as I look over at the column structures that border the square.

My heart thunders as I continue searching for what's wrong. I'm not sure anything is. Maybe I'm just having an *Angels & Demons* moment. The warning tick doesn't disappear as I look to the other side, finding no one suspicious.

The last few days I've been in this daydream around Rome, forgetting how we came to be here, and who we're hiding from. Reality slams into me, reminding me that this isn't completely a honeymoon. My stomach drops when in the distance, I see a figure far away.

My heart hammers in my chest. Mind screaming.

"Autumn?"

The crowd moves and the figure disappears. Am I seeing things?

"Autumn, what's—"

"Who hired those men?" I ask abruptly, turning towards Leo.

His face becomes a mask of seriousness, brows pulling together as he tenses. I flick my gaze towards Rudy, who's begun to approach our spot. Almost too slowly, like a predator observing his surroundings, Leo looks towards Rudy. Our bodyguard stops, adjusting his shirt and moves away.

Finally, his gaze meets mine again, sharp and aware. He's not telling me something.

"Who, Leo?"

"Did you see someone in the crowd?" His brows furrow deeper, scowling harsher.

My hands want to shake, and I concentrate on keeping them still. The wiggling thought of not even being safe here in Italy tugs at me. And then I realize every place Leo has taken me were very public places. Even though we're supposed to be in Boston, he hasn't attempted to hide us from being seen. *It's harder to attack in public spaces.* The daydream I've been in shatters. I swallow hard, unsure if who I saw was real.

"No, just anxiety. There's a lot of people."

Leo glances around us, sighing as the rigidness in him lessens. Finally, he answers, "Gabriel hired them. Julio and Isaac are tracking the money transfer he sent, and they caught the only one who survived. He's dead now, but they haven't found anything yet." Leo quickly cups my face to come in close. "It was a hit on me, not you. We're safe here."

Are we? I want to ask. To scream. I want to believe him.

Instead, I nod slowly before Leo kisses my forehead. His hand grazes down my side, settling at the small of my back as he leads us out of the square.

I don't have the heart to tell him that who I thought I saw was Gabriel.

Chapter 21

When In Rome

The world still believes we're in Boston. We've been in Rome for just over a week, the last couple days Leo going back to work slightly. When he's catching up with business, hiding where we are, I sight-see or stay in the room. Thank goodness there's a television and movies. Outside of the Crew, only Leanne knows I'm here and has questions about Rome every time I call her. Trix and Nan are trickier, trying to play into the hours that would match in Boston, so I keep communication short in pretense of being busy. The only part I hate about being in Rome—more lies.

At least I've been able to phone Xavier, who's recovering slowly.

Days have almost melded together. I shove away worried thoughts, knowing we'll have to reveal we're in Rome and face his family at some point. The inkling that I might've saw Gabriel keeps returning, but I keep telling myself it's just anxiety. Just worry of being found. How many times did I think I saw Steve? Although other news that came yesterday hasn't helped shake off the concern.

Enigma found a lead on Roger.

He had entered his house with, presumably, new fingerprints

left behind. The cameras that were up had gone awry, going dark for a few minutes and then back on. Roger knew about the scrambling program I used when I left New York, but he shouldn't have had access to something like it. Not to mention, no clue why he'd go back to his the house after it'd been deserted.

Enigma and Isaac tried to retrace steps that we knew Roger had taken after my interrogation. This led to Enigma using *Eleanor* to hack into the prison Steve was at, finding footage of the guards who let him loose on "parole." Isaac confirmed them as mobsters who'd been snuck in.

Good news, this led to who Roger likely made the deal with to get Steve out, finding who those men belonged to. Bad news? It was Enzo Rossi.

Isaac traced a phone call to Rossi's mansion outside the city, five days before Steve got out. Rossi apparently had a judge and warden in his pocket that Leo didn't know about. Rossi helped Roger, but for what? He risked resources with a cop. Did Rossi know who I was? I tried to recall his face during the meeting, but don't remember if I thought he recognized me. We thought Finstrum might be involved or DeLuca. Nope, it was all Rossi. Who's dead, because of Leo and me.

Except...where the fuck was Roger?

Jameson still believes he left town completely, maybe came back to retrieve some belongings. Owen and Isaac think he's hiding undercover, trying to do what I did. Rudy thinks he's dead, those prints were left long before, but a malfunction in the camera footage got us to peer closer. The Crew's thoughts are scattered, but there are pieces we keep forgetting. Such as the message left at *Nan's Bookstore* and Roger's bank account being accessed. Roger *had* to be working with someone. Maybe a buddy from the force?

My thoughts are just as scattered while I walk through Rome with Rudy. It's late afternoon. Leo's taking care of a few meetings, and I needed to get out of the suite.

"I still think it's a red herring," Rudy suggests while we stroll past another church. "The letter, bank account, fingerprints…make us think he's alive. Wild goose chase."

"We focus on him, sure, but Rossi our main connection is dead. Unless its someone who was loyal to Rossi. But all *those* guys are dead," I counter exasperated. "Otherwise, who else would it be?"

"Then it's just him, trying to fuck with you to get to the boss," he grumbles as we come around a corner to a small fountain within a tiny piazza. "For a guy who seemed hellbent on nabbing crime bosses, odd he went to one."

"Probably didn't know," I say, walking over to the fountain and sitting on the edge. Rudy frowns, propping a leg up next to me. He's wearing slacks and a short-sleeve black shirt, which shows off his tattoos down his arms.

"Didn't know?"

"Rossi was never confirmed as a boss, just an influential man in the city who *may* have criminal ties. Like many politicians. He was one of the few I didn't turn in years ago, that's why."

Rudy hums.

I look down at my hands. "Still…pretty desperate move to get to me."

"Thought it was to get to Spartan, use you and Steve against him."

My finger rubs over my wedding band. I'm quiet as I stare at it. *"Barchën?"*

"I don't believe Roger is after Leo anymore," I whisper, looking up at my tall bodyguard. "This hiding, leaving notes, red herrings…it's all for me."

Rudy comes over, sitting beside me as he stretches his long legs out.

"Nothing I regret," I say quietly. "But damn these consequences of my choices have been hard. The aftermath. I think deep down, when I refused to leave that interrogation room, it was to protect Leo, but mostly revenge against Roger. I knew it'd piss him off, but not this much."

"He won't hurt you anymore," Rudy says, putting his hand on my shoulder.

I give him a tentative smile. "I hate not knowing where he is. What he's planning or who he's working with. If he's still that desperate, he won't pull the trigger, but I know he'll make someone else do it. And *then* take the glory."

"We'll find the slippery bastard." His hand drops to his thigh, clearing his throat. "Maybe Sombra's right, grabbed his money and he left. Said yourself he's a coward."

"Yeah. Perhaps."

We sit there quietly, the noise of the fountain behind us. A few people walk through the small piazza, disappearing around buildings.

I sigh, leaning my head back to look up at the cloudy sky. "I think I'd like to do something to distract myself from thinking about it. Can't do much on the other side of the world. And no leads of where he is."

"Let's do something for *you, barchën*."

"Suggestions?"

"What have you not done yet?"

"Hmm." I tap my chin, being a bit over the top in my thinking as Rudy gives me a small smile. I look around the piazza, hoping for inspiration when I see a store sign. An idea forms as I tilt my head.

"Let's go shopping," I say. His brows lift in surprise as I stand and laugh. "Not *that* shocking."

He gets up, crossing his arms over his chest. "Ja, ein bisschen."

I mimic his stance. "I've shopped for a fancy dress."

"Against your will."

"Was not."

"Pretty Boy said you almost panicked."

I scowl, and grumble under my breath, "Arshloch."

Rudy barks out a laugh as we start walking out of the piazza. We continue strolling, until I find a fancy boutique. He falters behind me, and I smirk when he raises a brow.

"Damenunterwäsche?"

I grin wickedly. "You said something for me."

He sighs, "Ja...ja."

My inconceivable of a giant follows me, partially reluctantly, into the shop.

I walk into the hotel with Rudy behind me, carrying my bags. I tried to refuse, but gigantic ex-wrestler biker won over short mafia wife. He let me carry one. Thankfully, the important one.

Aurelio, head manager of the hotel, meets my gaze and nods. I give one back, heading straight to the elevator and get on with Rudy.

"You're gonna surprise him," he comments.

I grin mischievously. "He's told me for months to go buy new clothes. Look. I did."

Just hoping guilt doesn't come creeping up my spine for spending the money. They were smaller boutiques, so I do feel better in that department. Not to mention, I've learned platinum cards are certainly known across the world, because two of the saleswomen almost looked like they wanted to faint when they saw mine.

The elevator doors open, and we make our way to the suite. I open the door, Rudy following me in as I hear Leo's voice drift from the balcony. Owen sits typing at the kitchenette, looking up and does a double take when he sees what Rudy puts on the foyer table. Animal comes in from the balcony and freezes next as he stares at the bags.

Okay, the world isn't ending.

I roll my eyes, grabbing the bags and start heading to the bedroom.

Leo walks in on the phone, talking, "He attempted to stiff my managers, I don't..."

He stops and stares at me as I pause just before going into the bedroom. Leo's gaze moves down to the bags, confusion warping his features as he looks back up. I give him a playful wink and saunter away. Promptly, I close the double doors and lean against them with a quiet giggle.

Worth it.

Leanne would be so proud.

I move the bags, most into the closet, but keep out the one bag I carried. The items are laid out, which consist of different kinds of lingerie that stare back at me. My gaze lingers on the bodysuits. One is a black lace with a classic deep v-neck. Another a strappy violet piece which crisscrosses over the front and back, reminiscent of shibari. Lastly, there's a deep green one that's mostly thin mesh with vines and flowers embroidered to cover the nipples and further down.

Switching my gaze between them, I debate which one to put on. Could I even put the purple one on my own? I needed help with it the first time. Hmm, maybe—

"Autumn?"

I yelp, spinning in place as I put my hands behind my back as if that'll hide what's laid out on the bedspread. I bite my bottom lip and then smile at Leo who flicks his eyes to the bed. Slowly, he steps towards me, but moves to bend down and pick up the green lingerie piece.

Have I worn lingerie with him? Yes, but only what he's gotten and for play sessions. Fanciest underwear I've ever bought were tighty-whities with a blue band.

"You bought lingerie," he states.

"Uh-huh."

"Expensive lingerie."

"Yeah."

"Because you thought *I'd* want it or because *you* want it?"

His question throws me as I tilt my head at him. I glance down at the fancy underwear, and back up at him. There's a glimmer of concern in his eyes, and I realize he's worried I did this to please him, and only him. I nervously giggle.

His expression softens as the giggles continue and I shake my head.

"Because *I* wanted to, mister. I wanted to surprise you but wasn't expecting this reaction."

"What were you expecting?" He places it back onto the bed.

"Well, first I'd be wearing one *before* you came in, probably awkwardly lay on the bed, and then have you jump my bones."

He raises a brow, fighting back a smile. "Oh?"

It sinks in that I just said that out loud. My mouth opens, then closes. "I wasn't gonna tell you that."

Leo steps closer, crowding my space as I try to take a step back. His arm quickly wraps around my waist, pulling me close and sharply enough that my hands land against his chest for support. My heart thunders in my chest as my body tingles. Leo's other hand comes up, stroking under my jaw as his eyes roam over me.

"Are the others still here?" I whisper.

"No."

Leo kisses my neck. My fingers grip his shirt, tugging as I bend towards his warmth. I rasp, "Leo."

"Check in."

"Green."

"How erotic are you feeling, dear Watson?" His words drip with carnal need, rough and wanting. I scramble for a response, mind going blank as Leo gently grasps my chin to look up at him. "We don't have our violet room, but we still can scene if you want."

I nod excitedly. Leo lifts a brow, and a giggle escapes me. "Yes."

"Good girl. Almost thought I'd have to reteach you again."

"Again?" I lightly smack his chest.

He smirks, caressing his thumb over my chin. "I want you to choose which lingerie to wear, put it on, and then seduce me."

Pretty sure my brows raise so high they reach my hairline. Seduce...*him*?

Holy cabooses, how? My seduction skills usually include tripping.

"We can roleplay," he explains. "You can be whoever you want."

"Who will you be?"

"Who do you want me to be?"

I search his eyes, hoping for an answer there. Leo caresses his thumb again over my skin.

"Safewords in place, same with limits," he says softly as some of the nerves dissipate. The strength of his arm around me and the beat of his heart against my hands calm me. "You've mentioned wanting to try roleplay. We can go slow. You can even pretend to be one of your movie characters if that's more comfortable."

"That's a lot of choices."

"All the more to have fun with." The purr of his voice makes me shiver. "Do you want to play, sweetheart?"

My breath is shallow. Roleplay. Seduce him. In lingerie I just bought. Talk about a first, and in Rome, too. Well, when in Rome? I don't think that applies to this.

Finally, I answer, "Yes."

He places a gentle kiss on my lips. "I'll wait out in the living room. Take as long as you need."

Leo steps back and releases me. Ideas and thoughts zigzag in my head, trying to think of what I want to try. Oddly, a fantasy, perhaps not entirely one, comes to mind. A narrative to take back control and honestly the thought of it does make my arousal heighten.

I remind myself it's just a game. A safe place to try it. We can always stop.

"Leo." He pauses, about to close the doors. "I know what I want you and me to be."

"Who would that be?"

There's a sudden dryness in my throat as I ignore the nervousness that builds. He may say no.

"A…mafia boss," I answer. "In a club. We're rivals."

Something shifts through his gaze and over his face, mostly of surprise. I swallow hard again, wondering if I'm going too close to reality, toeing a line of past and present.

"Leo? Is that alright?"

Another shift happens across his face, but this time closer to a burning need. A slow, dark knowing smile blossoms upon him. "Green. Mistress."

Leo closes the doors.

Oh…fuck me. Thankfully that's the goal.

Heart pounding, I give myself a pep-talk and go through my head of all the characters I've seen in mafia movies. Enemies to lovers. Sure, got it. Just don't pull a *True Lies* fiasco, Autumn.

Taking a few minutes, I decide to wear the black classic lacey bodysuit, which also has cut-out sides. Once I pull it on, I check myself in the mirror, give myself a double thumbs up and stand before the doors. Frozen.

He called me Mistress.

I frown.

What if I didn't want to play a character from a movie? Pretending to be someone I've watched dozens of times.

I look down at my hands, staring at my rings. An idea forms in my head. It reaches for a craving deep within me. One I've been scared of, but know he's yearned for. I was scared as Autumn, but a part of me was courageous. The one who sat in that mafia meeting. Who married my husband in secret. Who escaped from New York City on a Harley. The one who loves when he's on his knees.

Quickly, I go over our limits in my head, safe words, and mentally prepare for this.

When ready, I take a deep fortifying breath as anticipation and excitement flickers. I place my hand on the door handle, pretending I'm once again walking into a meeting.

Chapter 22

Upon His Knees

Slow, sensual music plays in the suite. Lamps are dimmed. The final rays of sunlight stream in through closed doors of the balcony. The deep orange rays contrast with the dark ambiance. The furniture has been moved to give more space, and an armchair faces the bedroom. I pause outside the doors, closing them behind me. He lounges back in the chair, legs spread with hands splayed over his thighs. He wears only slacks, twilight providing shadows over his tattooed skin. My eyes flick down, and something coils inside when I see it.

A rosary draped upon his chest.

Dark beads cascade down with the cross laying heavy against his stark tattoos.

"You're late," he says gruffly.

A smile plays on my lips, licking them slightly as I reach far inside myself of the person I once was. Standing straighter, I conjure up the same courage I had in that meeting. I stroll towards him, running my hand along the back of the sofa.

"A woman is never late," I respond. "Especially myself when it comes to business."

"Is that what this is? Business?" He gives a bored expression.

"Apart from?"

His head cocks ever so slightly, hooded eyes grazing up my body as I stop behind the sofa. "Personal business."

A shiver runs over me at the deepness of his tone, the roving of his eyes that sear into my skin. I trail my finger along the sofa, recognizing those pieces of him that demand obedience.

"The ruthless, renowned mafioso wanting a *personal* meeting with little old me," I say each word slowly. His jaw tightens.

"You're just as ruthless, are you not?"

A sultry smile grows on my face, playing further into the game. "I have a reputation?"

"Yes."

"Then yours is fearsome. Terrifying even." His hand flexes on his thigh. "Should I be worried, mafioso?"

His head cocks again. "Have you done anything that warrants that worry?"

I step from behind the sofa, a few feet from him as I sit on the arm of it. My legs spread like his as I carefully run my hand against my inner thigh. His eyes snap to my hand.

"As your rival, I should be, but I have a confession for you." My words are almost whispered.

"Confession?" He looks back up at me.

"You're the one wearing the rosary." I tilt my head, continuing to run my hand over my bare skin. His breathing becomes heavier. "May I confess to you? Ask for forgiveness of the ruthless, terrifying mafioso who defies the church?"

"They don't own me."

"No..." I murmur, moving both hands further up my inner thighs, "...they don't."

He shudders, growling low as his hand flexes and digs into his slacks. He deeply inhales, chest expanding as he stares at my thigh.

"If I confess, will you spare me?" I ask. "Will you allow your rival forgiveness?"

He settles further back into his chair, licking his lips slowly. Hazel eyes meet mine.

"What are your sins?" His voice is rough.

I stand, beginning to walk around his chair, trailing my fingers over the arms and to the back. Desire tickles my spine, muscles clenching as arousal starts to flood my senses. I lean down, whispering near his ear, "I confess to being a liar."

His eyes slide to me. "A liar?"

"Months upon months, hiding information." I move my head to the other side of him. "I confess to killing men and having no guilt over their deaths."

"Were they mine?" He rasps.

"No…them *I* owned."

I come around in front of him, stopping next to the coffee table. "What else?"

My foot is placed upon the surface of the coffee table, and I run my hand over my thigh again. His gaze stays on mine, but his jaw tightens. I slide it up further towards the apex of my thighs, feeling the lace fabric.

"I confess of lustful thoughts…" my fingers slip under the hem, and his eyes flick to my hand, "…over a man covered in blasphemous tattoos, ink depicting hell and demons."

"Anything else?" He practically growls when my hand goes back down my leg again.

"I confess to the worst of my crimes," I say keeping my eyes on him, as I grip onto the power I feel having his attention on me. "Not lying, not stealing millions of dollars, not shooting men, or even the sinful thoughts I have about you." His eyes snap to mine, flaring. "I'm a thief, who now owns an empire, but it's not as priceless as owning the soul of a man that everyone trembles before."

I step in front of him, just out of reach. His hands flex, fingers tensing as I tilt my head like someone who holds all the cards.

"I stole the big bad wolf from his bed," I whisper.

"Have you?" His voice grates, rough with emotion.

"I shall not ask for forgiveness for being the only one brave enough…" I step closer, placing my hand on the arm of the chair, "…smart enough…" I do the same on the other side, encaging him, "…and conniving enough to accomplish such a task."

I run my hand up his torso, feeling the heat of his skin and rising chest. A shudder runs over him, attempting to keep up his façade as I reach for the rosary and wrap the beads around my hand. Gently, I tug them so he leans forward until his face is practically inches from mine.

"The most fearsome mafioso isn't you, it's me. And I *own* you."

Shadowed hazel eyes tear into mine. I flick my gaze over him, watching for any signs to pause. I tug him closer, keeping my lips just a breath away from his. His breath hitches, hands moving to the chair arms, gripping them.

"So, do you have a confession for me before I decide your fate?" I ask, tightening my grip on the rosary.

A shift happens over his eyes, glazing over with something that makes my skin tighten with a craving for dominance. The air almost changes as the switch happens, almost rumbling between us.

"Yes…Mistress."

Finally, I press my lips against his with a teasing kiss that's too brief. His breath catches as I step back, letting go of the rosary.

"Good boy. Get out of my chair."

He stands, moving to the side as I sit where he was. The warmth left behind is almost comforting as I inhale deeply. I lounge back, gripping the arms and focus.

"Kneel," I order.

Instantly, Leo drops to his knees before me.

His hands become placed upon his thighs, palms facing up as he tips his chin down in obedience. His breathing slows, leveling out as I watch him already slipping towards Subspace. Fuck wasn't expecting it to happen that quick.

I clear my throat, concentrating on the scene I've apparently set. "What do you have to confess?"

His gaze remains on his thighs, staying silent. I reach for the rosary around his neck and tug him forward. He inhales sharply, leaning forward, but his eyes remain downcast.

"Look at me." Those obedient, craving eyes meet mine. There's no fear, but there is uncertainty. "Check in."

"Yellow." The word strained as if he's not sure himself.

I start to let go of the beads, until his hand snaps up and clasps around my fingers. He doesn't move, eyes not leaving mine. I know that look. Silent begging for me not to let go.

"Good boy," I murmur, twisting my hand a little for the rosary to tighten around his neck. It's enough of a reassurance for his hand to fall back into place. "Close your eyes. Breathe."

Leo does as I say, closing his eyes as I glance at the beads which pinch at his skin. I make my breath loud, allowing him to follow in suit and his body settles. He untenses as I take more of that control out of his hands.

Briefly, I run through my head of what I've learned and trained in with Leo. Our sessions, his tells, wants, and needs. I recall when he's been on his knees before; what he said and did. Declarations. Not confessions.

Thinking quickly, I reassess on how to keep going, determined to lean into his desires.

"Open your eyes." He does and he already seems calmer. "I know all your sins and confessions." His eyes widen slightly. "Why have you repeat them when you're already on your knees for me? No confessing tonight. Just your obedience."

"Always, Mistress."

"I know, baby." I kiss him upon his forehead. "Check in."

"Green, Mistress."

"Good boy."

I lounge back into the chair, but keep my hand wrapped around the rosary. Leo has to sit up straighter, off balance as he leans forward to make up for the short distance.

"Thankfully for you, I'm a merciful mafioso," I state, moving back into the roleplay. "I have something in mind for my *rival*. Shall we see how well you do with orders?"

"Yes, Mistress."

I let go of the beads. "Turn around. Stay on your knees."

Leo faces away from me as I watch the light play over his body. The setting sun casts long shadows over him. My eyes graze down the tattooed landscape of hell and brilliant colors of the flaming sword. I keep my legs on either side of him, moving to the edge of my seat. My chest presses against his back, making him straighten. His breath hitches as I snake my hand over his shoulder, down his torso as I feel his warm body. My other hand grabs the rosary at the back of his neck, pulling slowly.

"Who owns you?" I ask, breathing against his ear.

His hands flex upon his thighs. "You, Mistress."

I continue pulling the beads.

"Who's the only one you'll listen to?"

"You, Mistress."

More I pull the rosary towards me.

"Who is the *only* one you'll worship?"

"You, Mistress."

Rosary beads wrap around my hand as I pull gently, looking down at the strand tightening against his neck. I grip his chin, tilting his head back as the wooden beads dig into his skin, just below his Adam's apple. The cross dangling. I pull harder and he swallows, causing the cross to bob against his throat.

It's then I realize how much of a Catholic I am not.

Tugging back and up a little, Leo becomes more off balance as he tries to follow, arching into me. I keep him in this position, aware of how long I do as I move my eyes down his body. His hands remain in place, palms up, and still. He keeps his head tilted back, breathing short breaths as I glide my hand from his chin down his chest.

"I could stare at your body for hours," I admit, lightly kissing his jaw. Leo's breath shudders. "Not just because of your tattoos, which I adore, but how you practically drip masculine energy. How intoxicating your power is. Then I wonder how well you'd fuck." I smile softly, and his eyes flare. "I'm not a poet like you when it comes to declarations, baby. I'm a bit blunt."

I bring my hand up, caressing my thumb under his mouth and then tugging at his bottom lip. I let go and then swiftly lift the rosary over his head. My hand skims over his neck, checking where it dug into his skin. Satisfied he's not hurt; I lounge back into my seat.

"Stand up. Then grab a pillow to kneel on, facing away from me."

"Yes, Mistress."

He does as I say, while I inspect the rosary. The beads are made of dark wood, the string a light color, and the cross is a heavy metal. I drape it over my fingers as Leo kneels. Far away in my head, a part of me screams in fear of how easy it is to order him around. Whilst another part enjoys it. It's a power I could get drunk on, similar to what I felt in that meeting when I held those men by their throats, overcoming my terror.

I lean into this "character": a combination of my past and present.

Playing with the beads in my hand, I stare at the back tattoo once more. The blue against the crimson and fires. The skulls at the bottom with the landscape looming. Lastly, those haunting wings— damaged from struggling in battle.

For a moment, it's not powerful imagery of domination, but enervation.

An odd sensation runs over me. Within this chasm of power I feel having over him, there's a bigger need to protect him. Safeguard him. To take away decisions; to provide peace.

"Put your hands behind your back." He does so. "Good boy."

Leo shudders visibly as my own body clenches at his response. I grasp his hands, crossing them as I loosely tie them together with the rosary, cross dangling. He settles into his position as I release him and stand. I circle him, looking over him in this partially vulnerable state. On a whim, I shove the coffee table away for space. He doesn't move, keeping his eyes downcast, even as I thread my fingers through his hair.

"Where was I? Oh, yes…wondering how well you'd fuck," I say, beginning to ramble a little. "Watching how fluidly you move, striding around like this…well, *boss* who owns everything he touches. Command drips from you, and honestly I love it." I tug at his head, tilting it as I slowly circle him. "Then I find myself being territorial, every fucking time someone stares at you too long. Thinks they can touch you. As if they have a chance of fucking you on the marble you walk on."

I tug his head to the other side, and he follows obediently.

"I wasn't a territorial woman until you," I continue. "Every time I saw those familiar looks, prying eyes, I wanted to pull a gun out and shoot them. Or just shove coffee down their shirts; scalding hot." His breath hitches, but more like he's holding back a laugh. "Again, not territorial until you, which I blame your calm, steady gaze. Those tattoos that would make a lesser man cry, and thighs that could crush me. Muscles that could hurt me. I've seen how dangerous you are…the fearsome mafioso."

I step in front of him, gripping his chin and leaning his head back for his eyes to move up. They burn, glazed over in reverence and yearning.

"I didn't know it back then," I rasp suddenly, enraptured by how he looks at me. "Didn't want to admit what I felt was real, but…but I think if you really had asked me to come up to your suite that night, I'd have said yes. I'd have begged you to fuck me in hopes of experiencing how great sex was."

Leo's eyes widen, breath becoming shallow.

Pushing down the shaking that wants to develop in my chest, I lean down to brush a kiss over his lips. "Instead, I truly think I did steal your soul because of the very thought of *anyone* owning *any* piece of you, makes me want to burn cities down."

His breath catches as I place another chaste kiss on his lips. Leo's body tenses, straightening as his eyelids flutter. I place my hand on his head, keeping him in place as my heart pounds.

"Stay."

The command comes out harsh, my voice rough. I walk away, silently stepping into the kitchenette and press a hand against my thundering chest. I don't tear my eyes from him, wondering what the fuck was that. And what the fuck to do next.

Supposed to seduce him, which I've done and flipped the script, but now what?

I go through everything I've learned, trying to think of scenes I've read about. I come up blank, unsure as my hands clench as I try to think.

Taking a deep breath, I calm as I recite a few lines from *The Raven* in my head. I stare at Leo's back; the man still on his knees for me, wrists bound with his rosary.

"I only need you."

Back to the basics, Autumn.

What does he want? To be owned. What does he need? Me. What would Dom Leo do? Play to one's kinks and needs.

I glance down at my lingerie. A smile grows on my face. I strip out of the lacy lingerie and fold it long ways. Releasing a long breath, I tell myself I can finish this with him.

Silently, I walk up behind Leo and say, "Close your eyes."

He doesn't even flinch. "Yes, Mistress."

Standing behind him, I bring the lingerie up and place it over his eyes. I cover them and partially his nose, wrapping it around his head. I tie it off the best I can. Leo inhales deeply; a combined groan and sigh leave him as he smells the lingerie wrapped around his face.

I trail my hands over his shoulders, and then press my naked front against his back as my fingers trace his tattoos along his chest. He's warm, and I feel his chest expand with each deep inhale as I slide my hands over him.

"This is mine," I whisper against his ear. "I stole it, so I get to do with it how I please, correct?"

"Yes, Mistress."

"Such a good boy."

A groan vibrates low in his throat.

"For being so good, and me being a merciful boss," I start, stepping away and grab a couple of pillows to put on the ground. "I want you to fuck me like you would've that night. If you'd asked me to come up to your suite, how good you would've made me feel."

Leo swallows hard before answering, "Yes, Mistress."

My brows scrunch at the hesitation as I stand before him. I place my fingers under his chin, tilting his head back. "What is it, baby?"

He swallows harshly again, tensing, and I'm half-tempted to rip the lingerie off when he doesn't answer right away. Leo's mouth opens, but nothing comes out as I peer past the lacy lingerie and barely see his eyes screwed shut.

"Check in," I ask.

"Green."

Oh, fuck no he's not.

I grip his chin harder. I ask bluntly, "Do you need to stop?"

"No."

"Why did you hesitate?"

"I lied."

A shiver runs down my spine in warning. My mind wants to spiral, but I keep it in check as I focus on him.

"What did you lie about, baby?" I loosen my grip, stroking my fingers along his jaw and down his neck. His breath shudders, but I do notice the tension along his shoulders eases.

"I didn't arrive that night to take you to the hotel," he finally admits in a soft voice. "I didn't want to fuck you until our first date."

It's like a vice is wrapped around my heart, tightening. As gently as I can, I ask, "Why did you come back the next night?"

A tear slides out from under the lingerie.

"To see you smile one more time." The words punch through me as tears gather in my eyes. A confession hidden behind his words. "I couldn't remember the last time someone had genuinely smiled at me as you had."

I let go of him, stepping around as I undo the rosary around his wrists. His head follows where I go, beginning to breathe quickly.

"Take your pants off. Then on your knees again." Without a word, Leo follows my orders and quickly disposes of his pants. He kneels upon the pillow once more.

I kneel before him as I place the rosary back around his neck. The beads wrap around my hand, tugging him towards me. He tries to keep his hands on his thighs, but as I lean away to make him off balance, he places his hands on mine.

Face close to his, hot breath drifting over my skin, I whisper, "Then fuck me as if you could've on the ballroom floor. Show me it was all worth returning, selling your soul to me in the process, and I'll reward you with that smile."

His mouth slams against mine.

My hand almost loses the rosary around his neck like a leash as I lead him down towards the floor. Leo ravages my mouth, tongue battling mine as he reaches down to grab my hip. I control his head, pulling the rosary for him to kiss my neck. The lingerie remains tied upon his head, scratching against my skin as he licks and kisses me. He nudges my legs open as he blindly feels for between my thighs. His fingers slip over my sex, and I gasp as he touches my sensitive clit. I hadn't realized how turned on I was. I'd been so focused on him.

I grip the beads, head tilting back.

"Mistress," he begs as his cock brushes against my hip.

"Fuck me, baby," I rasp.

His cock is soon at my entrance, pushing forward. My breath hitches, feeling slightly tighter than usual, although that's probably from the lack of lube. Leo goes slow, nudging into me little by little. He grunts as he pushes more, practically shaking above me. I lift my hips, meeting him halfway and we both groan when he enters me completely. My eyes roll back as his breath becomes erratic, moving his hips as he starts to thrust. While keeping hold of the rosary in one hand, I grip his hair with the other and yank hard. He moans loudly, pumping harder.

Leo fucks me against the pillows on the floor, making some slide in different directions at the force he's going. He clutches my leg, pulling it up to reach deeper inside me. I tighten my hold on the beads as they pinch against my skin and his. He gasps, bringing his head closer as our breaths mingle together. Sweat shines over his skin, some gathering above the lingerie that keeps him from seeing me.

Ecstasy builds, tingling up my spine and down to my core, time almost slowing. I stare up at the man above me. Eyes unseeing, fucking me as I hold the string that tightens around his neck. Sweat slides down his body as the last rays of sun come into the room.

His confession of the lie. The way he kneeled and obeyed. Devouring passion as his skin meets mine.

Was *this* blind faith? Trusting someone who holds a delicate piece of you in their hands, yet could end you if they truly wanted? With every deep breath, I begin to understand the reverence. The trust. The willingness to obey for something as simple as a smile.

I was his religion; he was mine.

Blasphemous or not, we'd never care long as we forgave and loved the other.

Quickly, I unwrap the rosary from my hand, pulling it off him and toss it. The beads and cross clatter against the floor as I wrap my arms around his neck. I yank Leo close, lifting my hips to him. He clutches me harshly.

"Come for me, baby," I rasp, tightening my legs around his waist.

Leo grips me as his body goes tense. He comes with a long groan against my neck. My muscles clench around him, my body bowing towards him. I'm not entirely sure if I actually orgasm, but I don't care as satisfaction washes over me as his body unclenches. I fumble behind his head, pulling off the lingerie to toss aside. I'm met with glistening hazel eyes filled with adoration.

I smile.

His hands clutch the side of my face. Relief upon his.

I can't quite tell if he's completely coherent or not. I start going through my head on what to check, when suddenly he whispers, "Good girl."

My smile widens. In return, I'm given the glorious sight of his own. Arms flinging around him, I pull him down as he falls to hug me. We hold each other, unwilling to let go as we lay together on the floor among scattered pillows as evening falls.

Chapter 23

Wildest Dreams

Leo's arms encircle me in the warm water as bubbles float around us in the bath. I sigh, leaning into his embrace, relaxing between his legs. It's been almost an hour since we got off the floor and talked. To my surprise, Leo hadn't gone into Subspace completely and honestly that gave me some relief. Although it went well for an impromptu session without much discussion beforehand, we agreed to hold off on roleplay for now. Wasn't a first choice kink and neither of us wholly stuck to the actual roleplay. That's likely from my choice of what roles to play. Either way, we decided to hold off on trying again. Leo mentioned not worrying about him calling yellow, and I didn't push. Long as I knew he was okay, that's all that mattered to me. After that part of the aftercare, Leo suggested a bath.

The massive bathroom is lit with candles scattered everywhere, flicking shadows over the marble. He runs his hands down my arms as I lean my head back against his shoulder.

"Proud of you," he murmurs, stroking a hand over my hair as water droplets fall into the bath.

"Thank you, mister."

Leo kisses my temple and hums. We remain silent, peaceful.

Questions tickle at the back of my mind, weighing heavy on my tongue. I don't want to ruin this moment, doing something we rarely do, and after something we've *never* done.

"Tomorrow, we'll go out for dinner," he mentions, disrupting my thoughts. "You can show me what else you bought today."

"Who says I bought anything other than fancy underwear?"

"I saw the other bags, dear Watson." He nips my ear. "And I know couture better than you think."

"Caught me."

Leo adjusts his arms around me, turning me to face him. I straddle his lap as his brows furrow, slightly frowning. "What is it? Do we need to discuss—"

"No, not from earlier," I interject softly, rubbing his arms. "I don't want to ruin this."

"You'll ruin nothing."

"Cause I haven't said anything."

Leo cups my cheek. Those hazel eyes sear into mine, searching for answers. "Talk to me, dear Watson."

I inhale deeply, letting out a sharp exhale. He lets go, moving the other hand to stroke my back gently.

"How long are we going to be here?" His features soften. "Not that I hate Rome, I love and enjoy it here. It's just…going on two weeks and everyone still thinks we're in Boston. I just wish I knew what to expect. Feels like, uh…winter again."

"The moment I know something, I'll tell you."

"I know, I know." My forehead touches his shoulder as he continues to stroke my back. "It's the lack of movement that unnerves me."

"They're planning next steps like us. When I know the right time to reveal our real location, I'll tell you."

I nod, moving to completely be against his chest. He shifts further into the water to submerge us.

"Until then, we're going to enjoy ourselves with what we have," he whispers, kissing my temple. "I won't allow anything to continue stealing precious moments with you; experiencing life with you."

I bring my head up, kissing him softly on the lips. Water trickles down my skin as he cups the side of my face, kissing me deeper with adoration. Once we break apart, he cradles my head against him, whispering reverently, "My dear wife...my beautiful dear wife."

My hands smooth down over the silky material. The dress I wear is a deep maroon, a simple cocktail dress that reaches my shins with an asymmetric top. I smile at myself, taking a deep breath and liking how I look. Before I leave the bathroom, I give myself some finger guns for good luck and head out to the bedroom. Checking that my short heels are strapped on, I take a picture to send to Leanne later. She's loved that I started wearing dresses again, but even I'm not sure if I'll continue to wear them back home.

Leo's already down in the lobby, needing to speak to someone before we leave for dinner. I've no idea where we're going, only being told what kind of attire to wear. I grab my small purse as I walk out to the living room, where Rudy waits and grins when he sees me.

"You look beautiful, *barchën*," he compliments.

"Thank you, Rudy." We walk out of the suite, down the hall to the elevator. The doors open, and there stands Aurelio who nods his head at us both.

"Buenasera, signora," he greets. "Signor Luciano is in the lobby."

"Grazie," I respond, smiling as I get on the elevator with Rudy.

Aurelio starts to head down the hallway, but stops. "Oh, packages have come for you and Signor Luciano, I shall have them delivered tomorrow."

I blink, and nod. "Oh, yeah. Buono. Grazie."

He gives me a quick smile and nods his head again. "Ciao."

"Ciao." The elevator doors close, and I stare at the reflective doors. "Who'd be sending mail?"

"Sombra or Pretty Boy," Rudy answers.

"We're here long enough for them to do that, huh?"

Rudy's hand lands on my shoulder, squeezing gently. "We'll be home before you know it. Then you'll miss this place just as much."

I pat his hand just before the doors open. He lets go as we step out, my heels clicking against the shiny floor. I grin at the fountain in the middle of the lobby, scanning for Leo or one of the other Crew. My hands start wringing when I don't see them.

"He's in the lounge," Owen's voice drifts forward. He approaches from said lounge, dressed like Rudy in black slacks and a v-neck shirt. "Get the car ready."

Rudy grunts, leaving the hotel lobby.

"Who's he speaking to?" I ask.

"Bar manager." Owen shrugs. "About a discussion with Aurelio earlier. I'll tell him you're ready."

"Thanks. No rush. I'll wait here." I gesture to the fountain, sitting on the small bench next to it and grin up at Owen. He grins back, walking away.

I watch the water trickle down from the statue in the middle of the fountain. It feels tiny after seeing the Trevi Fountain, especially with the crowds that were there when we visited. Much like everywhere else in Rome. Not much different from New York. Melancholy fills my heart, missing the city that's become home.

My fingers play over some of the plant leaves surrounding the fountain, tracing the greenery. Slowly, I close my eyes.

For the past few months, Leo and I have just been going, going, going. Not many moments to fully stop and smell the flowers as it were until we got to Rome. Even then, it's been a whirlwind of seeing the sights and experiencing the city. A deep breath, and I inhale the fresh scent of water, flowers, and lingering citrus.

Why do I keep becoming restless? Isn't this better? Or perhaps

I've become too used to the stress and looking over my shoulder again.

I hum to myself, opening my eyes to stare down at my reflection. My thoughts slow as I watch the rippling water.

There're footsteps, and I know it's him. Leo approaches and I turn with a smile. He wears black slacks and a dress shirt to match. A couple of top buttons are undone, hinting at his tattoos. He hasn't shaved lately, so there's a bit of a beard on his face. Leo's eyes trail down my body as I stand, and I want to twirl for him even though it's not that kind of dress.

Leo comes close, taking my hand and kisses just above my rings. "You are breath-takingly gorgeous tonight, dear Watson."

I flashback to a time when I'd come close to running out of a restaurant, when I'd felt out of place. I smile gently, knowing this is where I should be.

"And you are incredibly handsome this evening, Signor Luciano."

His eyes shine, taking my arm to lead me out of the hotel to the car. We get inside the smaller town car, Rudy and Owen riding in the front. The city lights flicker past as Rudy drives us through Rome. I'm soon lost in staring at the buildings, and then we cross the river that cuts through the city. I glance over at Leo, truly having no idea what he has planned. It's quite some time before the car stops at an almost empty street. There are balconies with plants hanging from them and string lights. It seems like a small neighborhood nestled into the city.

"Where are we?" I ask.

"Somewhere a bit more private," Leo answers, kissing my cheek and then gets out of the car.

Oh, he's up to something.

I smirk, getting out as Rudy opens my door. I glance at the one-way bricked path, filled with old buildings lining the street and, in the distance, I can see a sliver of St. Peter's Basilica. I step carefully around the car; Leo takes my hand and then gives a look to the other two. They remain where they are as Leo leads me down the path of dimmed streetlights. Music travels through the air as he takes us to a small restaurant.

We enter the quaint space of warm brick, vines, and lit signs. The smell of fresh food hits my nose as we're soon greeted by a larger man with a dark beard. Leo greets him in Italian, and I catch a few words that mostly include welcomes, and being delighted we're here. He then greets me, kissing my cheek in greeting.

"Buonosera, signora, ben—" He speaks too fast for me to keep up. I nod my head, smiling as I concentrate on the few words I can understand.

Soon, he walks us through the restaurant towards a patio outside. Flicking my gaze about, I notice the place is empty. We come outside and then I realize we arrived through the back of the restaurant, because outside there are multiple other restaurants and bars across the street that are open. We're sat at a small round table as Leo continues his conversation with the man before he leaves us. A smirk plays on his face as we sit across from each other, and I glance at the metal fencing that surrounds the outside seating area.

"How much did you catch of the conversation?" he asks.

"Little. His name is…Giacomo?"

"Yes. He's owned this place for almost twenty years, inherited it from his father."

"Family business then?"

He nods as Giacomo returns, placing down glasses for water and a tall bottle. He says something about his daughter and bread, and then leaves again.

"Okay, mister," I say, leaning my elbows on the table. "Did you reserve this entire restaurant?" A smirk plays on his lips as he pours water into our glasses. I gasp, "Leo."

"I wanted privacy for us," he answers. "And I paid him enough to cover for any foot traffic he would've had tonight." He puts the pitcher down. "And the next two weeks."

A giggle comes out as Giacomo's daughter appears, placing bread on the table. They converse a little, and I learn her name is

Sofia. He orders wine for the table, and then the starter. I continue grinning as Leo lounges in his seat when she leaves.

"How did you learn about this place?"

"The first year I opened the hotel here. He was struggling to keep his business open, and I offered to help finance the restaurant. I've been a silent investor for years now." I tilt my head at his collected, business-like words, but hear the warmth in them. "I've done so with a few places here, small businesses, and family owned that needed help from time to time."

Sofia comes back with wine, and she's joined by an older woman, who greets Leo warmly. He stands up, kissing her cheeks as she continues to talk. Leo then gestures towards me, and I stand for her to kiss my cheeks next in way of greeting.

Soon, Leo orders for the both of us for the first and main courses. Barely being able to catch words here and there, I vow in that moment to spend more time learning the language.

They leave after the white wine has been poured into our glasses. I pick mine up, clinking it softly with Leo's. It's sweeter than I would've thought, light and airy.

"At least I don't have to worry about you ordering salads for me anymore," I muse.

He chuckles. "I think you'd appreciate what Giacomo and Isabella can cook. Their ingredients, like most places here, are fresh as well."

"I've noticed. Surprisingly, I haven't really missed takeout since we've arrived. Good job, mister." We chuckle as the street becomes busier. People eat and drink across the way, some even dancing outside the bars, too.

"When did you first visit Italy?" I ask.

"I was two, I believe. Although five is when I first remember." He picks up his wine, sipping it. "Around this time of year."

"Really?" He nods, setting his wine down. "Family didn't want to be here for tourist season?"

"That's one reason," he answers, and I swirl my wine a little.

"The other is because my mother brought me here every year for my birthday."

The rim of my glass freezes against my lips. Leo's face is calm and passive. Slowly, I put the glass down.

"Leonardo Durante Luciano." He smiles. "Would this be your birthday dinner?"

"Perhaps."

Well, that explains the secrecy and wanting a fancy date night.

"Why didn't you tell me your birthday was coming up?"

"Haven't celebrated for well over a decade," he explains, nonchalantly. "Especially after my mother died." My heart squeezes, remembering how young he was when she passed. It likely meant the rest of the childhood he didn't celebrate. "And you didn't tell me yours until two days before."

"Oh, no mister, if you can pull the 'haven't celebrated' card, so can I." I point at him as he smirks. "I just have a best friend who won't ever allow me to forget it. *And* we spent the night in together, remember?"

He holds his hands up in surrender, and I laugh a little.

"I also wasn't sure if we'd be in Rome for it," he says. "Lastly, if I'd told you, then you'd have worried about what to get me or what to do for it."

"So, you pulled a Leo and planned it yourself." He doesn't deny it, picking up his wine. I sigh, not surprised he'd do something like this. "Although now I feel slightly bad because I wish I *did* have something to give you."

"You already have."

"Don't say my love or whatever," I counter, pointing at him.

He puts his glass down, leaning over the table as he gestures for my hand. I lean closer, giving him my hand as he strokes my wrist.

"Yesterday was gift enough."

My eyes widen as he kisses my wrist, then pulls away and settles back into his seat. I clear my throat, not expecting *that* as an answer.

"We're an odd couple for many reasons," I say. "The fact we

didn't know each other's birthdays, well, that takes the cake." Pun intended.

"What does it matter? Why choose one day to celebrate each other's life, when it can be any and every day of the year. Not just one."

I tilt my head at him. A smile grows as I shake my head, knowing how Leo of an answer that was. Inhaling deep, I look at my husband as he watches me calmly like this was any other dinner for us.

My voice is soft. "It's today, isn't?"

"Yes."

I lay my left hand on the table, opening it for him to take. His hand wraps around mine as I clutch his. Hazel eyes are illuminated by the low light of the lanterns.

"Happy birthday, my dear husband."

His smile is gentle, warming my heart.

The rest of dinner is peaceful as the music from the bars play in the background. Chatter fills the air from the crowd across the path and Giacomo's family. Halfway through the main course, Leo moves his chair next to mine. We lean in close to each other, talking and laughing. My mind calms, focused on just the two of us.

At the end of dinner, Leo walks me out to the front street where couples dance. A slow rumba brings us in close, and I lay my head against his chest. His heart beats steadily as he clasps my hand against his chest, while the other rests on the small of my back. I'm so wrapped up in affection and love, I don't quite notice the tugging of anxiety at the back of my neck. I ignore the crawling sensation of being watched, brushing it off that it's from wearing the dress. I sigh against him as his hand roams over my back.

It's just us.

Leo

Elm Jed

S he's warm. Her body practically melding into his as they
dance slowly. He hadn't truly planned to tell her it was his
birthday, hoping to relieve some pain this day usually brought.
Except, he couldn't not tell her.

They turn slowly as Leo gazes down at Autumn.

Warning flickers over his shoulders, weighing on him as he does
his best not to tense. Nothing to give her any indication that something could be wrong. His gaze snaps up, catching sight of Drew at
his post for the night. He then sees Owen within the other bar,
drinking leisurely amongst others. Rudolph is with the car. No
signs of anything wrong.

They continue dancing, slowly moving as the music changes to
another rumba. Carefully, he spins her, bringing her back into his
arms. She giggles against his chest, the sound alighting joy in him.
They turn again, and something catches his eye at the far end of the
street. Someone who shouldn't be there.

Leo waits until the end of the song to suggest they go back to
the hotel. On cue almost, she yawns making it easier to lead her
back through the restaurant. They say goodnight to Giacomo and
his family, approaching the car where Rudolph waits. Leo gets her
into the car, but then leans in close to Rudolph and whispers in
German, *"Have the perimeter double checked by the other two. Someone
was watching us."*

Rudolph frowns and nods.

Leo looks back over his shoulder to the quiet street before
getting in the car, and slams the door shut.

Chapter 24

Godfather Games

Autumn

LEO STROKES MY SHOULDER, waking me up gently. I blink, opening my eyes with a groan as I stretch. Leo sits on the side of the bed next to me. It's been two days since his birthday dinner and last night I'd been up late watching movies. Prepared I was not for an early morning.

"Morning, sweetheart," he says.

"Morning," I mumble. "What time is it?"

"Almost seven. I wanted to have breakfast with you before I left," he answers, as I sit up and rub my head. Left? "Owen will be with you today. I want you to stay in the hotel until I return."

"Wait, hold on, where are you going?" I finally focus on him, pinching my brows together. His face is impassive, almost closed off. "What's wrong?"

"I have to go meet with Renato." My eyes widen. "He got word that I'm here."

"How?"

"Likely informants in the city."

"I'll go with you."

"No, you need to stay here."

"Hold on, Leo. I'm not having you leave by yourself after us hiding in Rome for over two weeks. And Renato finding out by you not telling him."

"Ringer and Animal will be with me."

"And me."

Leo sighs, kissing my temple. "Don't fight me on this, Autumn,"

"Who's fighting?" I ask, getting out of bed. "I don't want you going alone."

He gives me a disgruntled expression, standing as I start to pull my robe on.

"My uncle is very traditional, Autumn. I don't run my organizations how most mafia families run them. I've already been given disrespect for having two women so high in status." I give him a perplexed look. "Mila is at a Capo rank, and Chiari is practically a Consigliere. There've been women that high before, but not in the Luciano, Marchetti, or Salvadori families. Not to mention, you sitting in as boss. Women traditionally aren't allowed near the business, especially those who married in."

"Except he doesn't know we're married."

"And I want to keep it that way."

Holy cabooses, I need coffee. I try to make sense of what Leo's truly worried about. Other than Renato realizing we've been hiding in Rome. I don't think that's the reason.

"If he's that traditional on how things are run, wouldn't that mean he won't touch me *because* I'm a woman? Or am I missing something?"

Leo stiffens, jaw going rigid, and I *know* there's something else missing.

"As we've discussed before getting married," he says, walking to the doors. "I can't protect you as easily as my fiancé, but I will not risk his retaliation now if he discovers we're married."

Retaliation?

I follow Leo through the living room to the kitchenette. It's quiet, but the doors to the balcony are open, letting in the early morning city noises.

"Is there something else going on with Renato I don't know about?"

"I don't want him playing mind games with you next," Leo responds, grabbing a couple of cups. I stop, staring at him as he pours the coffee into them. I rub my head again. Crud muffins.

"Leo, why are you worried about him retaliating? Because we were in Rome this entire time?"

"No."

"Then…what?"

He pauses, shoulders tensing as he puts the pot down. Slowly, I walk up behind him and place my hand over his on one of the mugs. His head tilts down to look at where our hands touch. My other strokes up his back, and he shudders slightly.

"I didn't tell you everything," he whispers. "Why we needed to keep our marriage secret longer."

My brows pinch together. What would Leo have left out? Something tells me it has to do with Renato and his family. It has been a key denominator.

I step to the side, grabbing the cup of coffee and sip it for the caffeine I may need. Leo watches me, quiet as I take another sip. Looking up at him, he averts his gaze and tightens his jaw.

"Leo."

"In the last five years, Renato has tried to arrange three marriages for me. To him, I've been engaged three times to women he's selected, and I've failed every single one."

I freeze. Yup, that'd be something he'd hide. But also…what in the fucking Hallmark prince movie plot?

"I never agreed to any of them," he whispers.

Pieces click into place. It wasn't just because Leo didn't trust everyone that he protects his privacy so rigorously. Those first few months being under everyone's radar with him, wasn't only because of who he was, but to keep his family, namely his uncle, away. He'd have hounded Leo, probably did when he found out about me. Someone who wasn't what *he* wanted. And if Leo is deemed a "failure" in that area, there's a chance Renato will turn to another to accomplish what Leo could not.

"Let me guess…" I murmur, drinking more coffee, "…they were young, Italian women who had connections to family wealth, and other things?"

"Yes," he answers roughly.

"Women Renato could control?" He nods. "Because your grandmother had passed." He nods again. "And Matteo is…"

"A remanent of my father only."

And Renato's wife, Fiorella, wouldn't be able to control the Luciano fortune, being a Salvadori instead. The last Luciano matriarch was dead. Leo and Gabriel were it for that bloodline's survival.

Leo is Renato's last play for more power, and arranging a marriage, like they'd done to his mother, would do that. I knew his family was conniving, but trying to force Leo into a marriage? All while dismissing Matteo completely, too? Or worse…choosing Gabriel over Leo.

Fuck, how far is his family willing to go in trying to make him his father? Is that why he didn't tell me? He told me about women in his past, those he's *actually* had relations with and who earned him a reputation of being a heartless, fuck-boy. Love them and leave them. Yet, here he was with more shame on his face than when I'd first learned about that part of his past.

It wasn't his choice.

The secret wasn't that he'd almost been forced into several marriages, but what *I* would be walking into. The kind of people who do that, without regarding his feelings, would not regard me. People willing to take *away* autonomy instead.

I turn on my heel, striding towards the bedroom as Leo exhales sharply. His footsteps quickly follow me. "Autumn."

I go to the closet, pulling out a simple sundress and toss it onto the bed. Leo enters the bedroom, breathing heavily as he tries to get me to stop.

"Autumn, I'm sorry I didn't tell you. Please, whatever I…what are you doing?"

I pull out a jean jacket. "Deciding what to wear when I leave with you. I'll be out for breakfast after."

"Autumn, trust me—"

"Oh, I trust you, it's the rest of your conceited, damn family that I don't trust." I fling the jacket onto the bed next. "I do not trust you going without me to see Renato. Mafia rules be damned. Those values went out the fucking window every fucking time someone has tried to kill me or you in the past few months."

He stops with his brows pulling harshly together. "You're not angry I didn't tell you?"

"Why would I be angry? I didn't give a damn about the women you were with before me, I still don't, so I *definitely* don't care about those who expected you to marry them. And that you've never met." I face him, holding my left hand up. "You married *me*. Not *them*. I do not need or crave approval of a narcissistic jackass to deem me worthy of being your wife. We both know who *would* have approved of me, even if she's not here anymore, because she trusted *you*." His face falls. "But damn it, Leo, tell me these things. I won't leave you because of your past. No secrets."

He stares at me as I huff out a breath.

"I know you're used to dealing with him alone, but not anymore. Unlike the Crew, I can do things they can't." *Besides choking you with a rosary.* Let's keep that to ourselves, Autumn, you're worked up. I take a deep breath, cooling myself down as I remember who I'm mad at, and it's not him. Just frustrated. "I love you, and your family will not scare me off."

I start to turn away, until Leo's hand snaps forward to grab my wrist. I look back at him, seeing emotions warring on his face. He whispers, "I don't want him to take you from me."

"No one's taking me from you." I step closer as worried hazel eyes meet mine. "I promise. I'm here."

His forehead comes down to rest against mine.

"You and me, mister Americano," I say quietly. He snorts, then nods gently.

Leo then cups my cheek, holding me tenderly as he kisses me. Soft lips move against mine. He then speaks against them, "I love you."

"I love you." I give him another kiss. "Now, let me get changed so I can have caffeine before dealing with your uncle."

***

We drive outside the city. Land I haven't seen of Italy flashes past as Rudy drives to Renato's villa. It's somewhere closer to the coast, a little over an hour drive away. Leo hasn't let go of my hand since we've gotten into the car. He stares out the window, concentrating with brows harshly furrowed. He wears a cream-colored button-up with short sleeves and dark brown pants. He also shaved, his sharper features clearer now and his dark hair swept back. He's very much the picture of a mafia boss who should be lounging on the beach with a drink.

I'm in a peach sundress with my jean jacket and converse. I wanted to appear non-threatening, almost sweet in hopes of Renato letting his guard down. Nor was I about to be caught running in heels. Nope.

I squeeze his hand, and he brings them up to kiss my knuckles delicately. The emerald on my finger sparkles. My stomach clenches, not seeing the wedding band. Both of ours were left at the hotel. Thankfully, there's no tan line on either of our fingers to give hint to the truth.

Worry travels over me as I take a breath, looking back out at the scenery.

Rudy pulls off the main road, onto a street and then around the bend to bring us to a long gravel driveway. Groves of trees line the path and a stone wall as he continues towards a gigantic, rounded driveway that ends before a huge villa. We park with both Animal and Rudy getting out. Owen stayed at the hotel.

"Do everything I say," Leo says, and I nod.

Our doors open and we step out. I stare past Animal to the large villa before us. Tall sandy walls are erected before the mansion including iron wrought gates. Cobblestone paths lead toward the large archways of the main house, which through one of them I see a courtyard with a fountain. Flowers are everywhere, dangling from windows and gates. It's sunny today, which illuminates everything with a warm glow. If I didn't know who lived here, I'd say it looked almost magical.

Leo comes up beside me, placing his hand on the small of my back.

"Animal, stay with the car," Leo orders, before walking towards the courtyard. "Ringer."

Rudy tosses the keys to Animal before trailing behind us. The shade of the archway and small tunnel is cool as we enter the courtyard decorated with brick flower beds and sprouting florals. Trees are planted in the beds, along with others near the villa itself which reach up towards balconies with iron railings. I gaze up at the open hallways of the villa. The fountain tumbles clear blue water from a statue of two angels either dancing or fighting with wings splayed. Everything is quiet. Like eerily quiet.

"Is Renato a bigger recluse than you? Thought there'd be more guards," I whisper.

"Somewhat, but he also believes no one would threaten him. The lack of guards is to show he *doesn't* consider anyone a threat," he murmurs as we stop near the fountain. He glances over his shoulder to Rudy, who takes a stance at the archway. "But there are people roaming who will inform him we're here."

Another chess game then.

He doesn't say anything else as we wait quietly. Anxiety crawls up my spine, waiting for what seems like forever. Even though Leo explained, it feels off not seeing anyone. I guess that's the point. A familiar feeling yanks at me, and it's then I realize it's the same feeling when I was in the interrogation room. Being watched with no idea by whom.

This time I'm not sure which pieces to play. Renato's a different opponent.

Hands wanting to shake, I intertwine my fingers as I try to distract myself by focusing on the courtyard. My eyes come across a flowerbed of white flowers, intermingled with pink ones. I'm certain the white ones are the species that Leo named his hotel after.

I start to move toward them but stop, wondering if I should leave his side, even by a few feet. Without a word, Leo nudges me in that direction. His hand falls away from my back as I inspect the flowers. My fingers trail over the petals and leaves, moving to the pink ones that blossom with various shades.

"They're called peonies," Leo says softly.

I look up at him, smiling a little as his hand returns to my lower back. "You have quite the knowledge of flowers, mister."

His face remains a mask of sternness, but there's a gentleness in his eyes.

There's a sound of shoes scuffing over gravel. Leo stands straighter and I swear his presence becomes colder. I glance up at him as I straighten next, watching as a strict look encompasses him. Someone walks towards us from the direction of the noise, and instantly I know it's Renato.

He's not as tall as Leo and has a rounded gut and burly shoulders. His skin is tan with age and likely from being outside, whilst his hair and beard are black, peppered with silver. His attire is similar to Leo's with lighter colors, but wears a fedora.

He greets Leo in Italian, voice low and easy paced. Unable to understand completely, I do catch a few words.

"It…been…time, Leonardo. You were…to…alone." Don't need much translation for that.

"Buongiorno, Renato," Leo responds, positioning himself closer to me. His hand dips under my jacket. The heat of his palm seeps through the thin layer of my dress, keeping himself and I composed.

They continue speaking in Italian. They talk as I carefully watch Renato Salvadori because he's clearly watching me. His gaze skims over my attire as he speaks with Leo, voice gruff before his eyes meet mine. Under the shade of his hat, I notice he has dark brown eyes.

"This is Autumn, my fiancé," Leo suddenly switches back to English.

"Yes, I've heard," Renato says, frowning partially. "It's a wonder that Leonardo finally decided to find a potential bride. American, even."

I keep my hands folded together in front of me. Noticing he hasn't truly greeted me. I smile politely, like I had when I was a barista. "Pleasure to finally meet you, Signor Salvadori."

He cocks his head a moment as if it was the wind talking, dismissing me as he turns to Leo. "We should talk alone."

Leo's hand presses against my back. "She stays with me."

Renato tsks under his breath, placing his hands into his pockets. "Now, now she's perfectly safe here, Leonardo. No one would touch her given your…reputation of late."

I flick my gaze up as Leo's jaw tightens.

Renato speaks in Italian, "*…she know…what…done?*"

"*Yes…knows…I am.*"

"*Ahh, she…here…*" his gaze roams over me again, making my skin prick, "*…surprising.*"

Renato then makes a dismissive sound, turning his attention towards me as I keep a blank expression. I pretend as though I haven't caught the few words I have. Keeping that polite smile on my face.

"Signorina, why don't you venture the grounds, eh? My villa is vast with flowers, which you seem enamored by." He waves his hand in the direction of an archway that leads to some gardens. "We have business that is not meant for a woman's ears."

"You say it's safe, but I don't even know what your guards look like," I retort calmly, keeping that smile. "You're not alone here, are you?"

His eyes narrow briefly. "I prefer not to see my servants daily. They know to remain hidden, much how you and your *fiancé* have recently."

He wouldn't happen to have a maid named Rosie, would he?

"It's hard to get privacy nowadays," I counter, keeping my tone light.

"Sí, now go on and leave us for that. Your bodyguard will have to remain in this courtyard. Leonardo knows my rules." He waves his hand as if I'm a child.

I don't move.

The mafia boss stares at me, starting to scowl in a way that should be warning enough for me to listen. Leo remains silent, stroking my back in small circles. Although he's tender with me, the rest of his body is coiled like a snake ready to strike. His brows are pulled together with a deep frown and slight curl of his lip.

Oh, if he could, Leo would be landing this man flat on his back for how he just spoke to me. Not wanting to ruin any further moves for us, I play the game I know. "Should I give you privacy, darling?"

I touch Leo's side, ignoring Renato as I look up at Leo. Slowly, Leo's head turns towards me. His eyes piercing and dark, dissent swirling in them. He trails his hand along my arm to take my hand and kisses it gently.

"Go explore the grounds, but not too far. I'll find you after." Leo's voice is a soft command.

I kiss his hand in return, spinning on my heel. I walk away towards the other gardens. Passing Rudy, I give him a quick nod as he gives one back, remaining in his spot. Walking to the gardens, I can practically feel Renato's gaze pointed at my back.

He wants to play, fine, but he'll learn the only man I take orders from is my husband.

Leo

"**S**he is not Italian or from a proper family line," Renato says when Autumn is almost out of sight. Leo remains quiet as his uncle turns back towards the way he came. Leo follows silently, watching him as he's led to the large stone patio at the back of the villa that overlooks a grove of various trees.

Leo's hand flexes at his side, wanting to hit him for how he spoke to her. For now, they had to play the game, allow Renato to think he has the upper hand until his brothers were taken care of. He had to let Autumn handle him in her own way, and she did. She had shown Renato plainly, without argument, she won't be his pawn.

"*She is not, but it doesn't matter to me,*" Leo continues in Italian. "*Nonna wouldn't have cared.*"

"*Your grandmother was soft-hearted, especially for love,*" Renato mutters, approaching a table set with late morning espresso. Leo wanted to snort. Rafaella certainly wasn't that. "*Your grandfather would've agreed with me. She should be Italian from a proper family, not some orphan you found. Or at least understand our native language.*"

"*She's learning.*" Leo's jaw grinds.

Renato huffs with a grunt, sitting down and gestures for Leo to follow. "*Why could you not accept the girls I arranged for you? They were well-behaved. Beautiful to carry on our lineage. Long hair, too.*"

Leo pauses before sitting down, frowning. He glares at him. The silence stretches, until Renato sighs and then adds, "*You understand what I mean. She does not know her place.*"

"*Her place is beside me, whether you like it or not,*" Leo argues, sitting finally. "*I suggest you accept her because she is staying and will be my wife.*"

Renato pours some sugar into his espresso. "*Leonardo, you cannot marry her. She will not survive our way of life.*"

"*You do not know that. And your own wife, wasn't from a well-known—*"

"But she was born here." Renato points at the ground. *"Your mother would've agreed with me as well."*

"My mother *would've wanted me happy."*

Leo leans back in his chair, scowling heavily as his uncle drinks his coffee entirely. Renato puts the empty cup down and folds his hands on the table.

"And you're so happy, that you hide *in Rome? From me? Your family?"* Renato argues. An expression of boredom crosses Leo's face, unwilling to give him a crumb of what's behind his walls. *"Just as you left for California. You continue to run, yet you're saying you are happy. Or is it cowardice?"*

"My grandfather, your *father, Durante was a farmer, refugee from his home,"* Leo begins to counter, tightening his fist upon his thigh. *"No background until he met Nonna, yet he found happiness with her through everything they endured. Is he a coward as well?"*

Renato sits up straight, frowning with a slight sneer. *"It is not the same."*

Silence stretches between them again. Leo doesn't rip his attention away from his uncle, who starts to look out at the grove beside them. His hand flexes again, inhaling a deep breath as he struggles to keep his anger entirely in check.

"My mother was in an arranged marriage, look what happened to her," Leo whispers.

"The one mistake my father and I made, because your *father was a bastard, born and bred as one,"* Renato sneers, taking his hat off to firmly place on the table. *"And then he continued that legacy with that younger bastard brother of yours."*

"Riccardo was married when Matteo was born."

"It does not matter. He is neither Salvadori or Luciano. A bastard to this *family."* Renato slices his hand through the air. *"We have discussed that enough."*

Renato attempts to look unperturbed, but his scowl doesn't leave. Exhaling a long breath, Leo pours himself a small cup of espresso. Quietly, Renato watches him as he drinks it without sugar. Leo finds himself missing Autumn's coffee.

After a while of the tense quiet, Leo puts down the cup and finally says, "I need help finding Gabriel. He's causing too much trouble. Whether you approve of Matteo's existence or not, he needs to be found as well."

"Let that boy rot," Renato argues, switching to English, too. "He's a liability for both of us. As for Gabriel, perhaps it's best *you* find a way to amend things."

Leo's face darkens. "He hired men to kill me."

"La famiglia è la famiglia."

"Not if they fuck me over or send people to kill my fiancé."

"You chose her fate," Renato scorns. "You know the consequences of this life. Death is one of them. I may follow my father's values to protect *our* women, but you and Gabriel are too much like your father."

Renato's voice quiets near the end, looking towards the villa.

"Then why defend him?"

"Again…family is family."

A sinking feeling hits Leo as he watches his uncle carefully. There's a reason why he's defending Gabriel, but he couldn't place his finger on it. He wouldn't years ago, why change his mind now? "Are you helping Gabriel?"

Renato chuckles darkly. "He may be family and the eldest, but anyone with half a brain would never allow him to touch one's money."

Leo's hand flexes. It wasn't a no.

"I am a staunch businessman, Leonardo, non uno sciocco," he adds. "But…" Leo's body tenses, "…if something was to happen to you, without children of my own, my only choice would be him as a suitable heir."

"Then choose Matteo, instead. He's of the Marchetti bloodline, but he's young and proven useful in the last few years, even to you."

Renato sighs, disappointment shadowing his face.

"You are not listening. He is not famiglia. He is a *Marchetti*." Renato spits on the ground at the name, frowning as he sits back.

"A product of Riccardo's disloyalty and dishonor to *this* family. *Your* mother's family. He will never be allowed to have any part of our business or fortunes. You gave him too much attention, putting ideas in his head, perhaps I'm to blame doing you a favor having him here. He gets...*nothing*. Niente."

What sliver of love Leo has for Matteo breaks a little. No clue what he'll do with him when they see each other again, but completely cutting him out to leave him to the wolves was cruel. Especially if one of those wolves sat before him now.

Matteo had spent his entire life in and for the mafia. He didn't know anything else. As angry Leo could be with him, it was a fact he couldn't forget.

"Whatever mess you've created with Matteo, running here to Rome hoping perhaps I'll help finish it," Renato continues, waving it off like a small sibling dispute. "I want no part. For Gabriel...he is your true fratello. Give him something to be occupied with and he'll relax. It worked five years ago."

So, *he* won't do business with him, but Leo would have to? Why won't he cut him out like Matteo? Gabriel's done more damage than him.

Leo scowls. "He's not a fucking child you can ground."

"No, he's a man entitled to this business, and you took it from him. Tuo padre sarebbe orgoglioso."

"Then I'm assuming you want him alive because we're the only remaining descendants of the Salvadori *and* Luciano family lines."

"I am simple," Renato says with an impassive expression. "And while both your cocks still work, there's hope for a successor."

A snarl almost rips from under Leo's breath, remembering why he kept his distance from Renato. Why he left, not out of cowardice, but these cruel games. He's been a monster, but Renato was a different kind. One who conspired family against each other, playing them for power. He only cared about family succession.

He should've kept Matteo in New York.

"It would seem you're a step ahead of your brother, being engaged, unfortunately it's to the wrong woman." Renato's voice starts to grate against Leo's ears. "You've always been smart. Inherited your grandmother's streak of wisdom. Use it now. For if you want your future assets secured…" Leo's eyes meet his, "…it won't be getting rid of Gabriel that will help you."

"Let me guess, having a child will?" Leo's voice is low.

"Not with her." Renato stands up, placing his hat back on his head. He steps to the balcony edge, inhaling a deep breath. "You'll marry a proper woman from here, and *then* use your cock to provide an heir worthy of the family."

"Is that similarly what you told my mother after you married her off to Riccardo?"

Renato keeps his gaze on the groves, putting his hands behind his back far too leisurely, switching back entirely to Italian again. *"She did her duty. Now it's time for yours."*

"Renato—"

"Break off this engagement, and I may be…persuaded to help you. Until then, you'll receive nothing from me until you're no longer engaged to that harlot." Finally, he looks back at Leo with a darkened gaze. *"Otherwise, I'll be forced to take full control, Leonardo."*

Words are stuck in Leo's throat. Any hope of convincing Renato to accept Autumn disintegrates like wet sand.

Autumn

I sit under an orange tree. I've no idea how long it's been, and I'm half-tempted to search for Leo. My hands wring together, debating going back to Rudy. I look around, knowing I'm being watched as my spine ticks with unease. Taking each breath slowly, I get up and walk over to some flower bushes in the expansive garden. There's a balcony above me, and I tilt my head to stare at the curtains rippling in the wind. Still too fucking quiet.

Soft footsteps sound from around the corner of some trees.

A woman in a dark blue dress steps out. Her black hair pulled into a low bun. Her skin tone is close to Renato's, but not as worn. She appears around his age, perhaps younger as she approaches.

"*I…not…visitors today,*" she says.

"Buongiorno, uh, mio chiamo Autumn. Scusa, parli inglese?" My Italian feels choppy compared to hers, and she raises a brow.

"You are from America?" She asks, and I notice her accent isn't as heavy as before.

"Sí. New York."

"That means you are…" her voice trails away, frowning slightly as she peers over her shoulder towards the way she came, then looks to me, "…you are with Leonardo."

This much be Renato's wife, Fiorella. I highly doubt she's a maid.

Certain she'll find out soon anyways I say, "I'm his fiancé."

Her eyes widen, looking me over. She then gestures for my hands, and I hold out my left knowing what she wants to see. Her soft hand takes mine, and then inspects my engagement ring in the sunlight.

"Not traditional," she comments.

"No."

"He never truly was."

"It's a jewel special to me."

"He was always like that," she muses suddenly, letting go. "Compassionate. A gold heart. He is his namesake."

She steps away to gaze at some strawberry trees. I clutch my hands, gripping them close. I've no idea what to do. Do I even say why we're here? How much does she even know? Questions fill my head. I'm half-tempted to talk about the weather when she breaks the silence.

"Do you love him?"

I blink, confused a little. "Yes."

"Then do what is best for him. Leave." My heart hammers as she doesn't even look at me while she says this. She continues walking toward another patch of trees, sitting on a bench between them.

"I'm not leaving Leo, he's my…" the word catches in my throat as I rub the emerald, "…my fiancé."

"There's still time."

"I'm marrying him."

"You are not right for him."

"You've only just met me; how can you even know that?" I argue, stepping closer.

"I can see it in your eyes." She looks up, frowning as those green eyes pierce into mine. "You think this life is easy? It is not. And who Leonardo needs…is someone else, not you."

I cross my arms over my chest, gripping the jacket as I fight back the quivering of my chin. I don't need anyone's approval, but fuck when will this shit end? People not liking us together for their own damn personal reasons. She doesn't even know me enough to criticize me.

"I am *exactly* who he needs," I state, not allowing this stranger to hurt me. "I am *everything* he needs. Since I've been with him for almost a year, whereas it's likely been *years* since you've seen him…" her eyes flare, pursing her lips, "…I think I know him better than you."

"You may be willing to fuck him and spend his money, but it does not mean you know him better than *family*."

Holy fucking crud muffins.

Roaring happens in my head at her harsh language. She keeps herself composed, showing no emotions. My face however does show my shock.

"From that look alone, you'll never understand," she continues. "Already I can tell you come from a background that will make you struggle with him. Life will become too hard. It already has. This family, *our* family, is particular because we must be. And you, foolish girl, will only destroy him." She straightens where she sits. "From what I've heard…you already have."

My body warps with anger. Inhaling sharply, I frown at her and ask, "Do *any* of you care about his happiness?"

"Of course, we do."

"From what you just said, no...no you fucking don't." She glares at me, disappointment lining her face. "Every day I'm understanding more why he left years ago, because who would want to be near any of *you*?"

Shock hits her features as I turn and storm off. There's no movement behind me as I head out of the garden. Tears gather in my eyes, and I quickly wipe them away. Fuck no, I will not cry over her for this soap opera bullshit.

And I thought Bailey and Carrie were bad with judging.

Who says that to someone they just met? Who else would be that horrible? Her and Renato are a perfect fucking match. Breathing in deep, I collect myself as my hands shake. I shove them into the jacket's pockets, willing myself to keep calm as I walk back to Rudy.

When I return, he's where we left him. He leans against the stone wall of the main archway, and I join him.

"You good, *barchën*?"

"Fine," I almost snap, and then inhale deeply. "He still with him?"

"Ja." He touches my shoulder. "Want to wait at the car?"

"Not until Leo is back," I say quietly, glancing to where Renato appeared.

"He can handle Renato."

"Doesn't make any of this easier," I sigh, not liking the sick feeling churning in my stomach.

Minutes seem to tick by, until a prick hits my neck. Rudy stiffens beside me, too, standing fully as I step away from the wall. Leo appears in the archway, prowling towards us. Renato isn't far behind but stops in the shadows. Leo's face is pure wrath, twisted with anger I've not seen in months. What's more terrifying is his silent, fluid manner as he walks like a lion ready to tear into its next meal.

My heart thunders in my ears. Not good.

"Car. Now." Voice strict, Rudy starts moving at Leo's

commands. I'm frozen until Leo reaches me, placing his hand against my back to lead me out of the villa.

It's shaking. His hand is shaking.

We walk without a word, coming to the car as Rudy takes the keys from Animal. All of us get in, doors slamming shut. I flinch at the suddenness. Leo sits back as he breathes heavy, leaning his head back with a snarl. Rudy steps on the gas, rocks practically flying behind us as we leave.

"Leo?" I whisper.

"Renato kicked out Matteo, who's been in Rome the entire fucking time," he growls. "He lied. Matteo never disappeared."

Rudy mutters in German, whilst Animal grumbles low, "Motherfucker."

"Call Owen. Matteo was last seen at Renaldi's clubs, supposedly working for him now. I want a fucking meeting."

I ask, "Renaldi? Vincenzo Renaldi? Isn't that…"

"Renato's rival."

Lovely. We've gone from our own little hostile mafia war to another potentially happening in Rome. I love a double feature, but not this.

"How screwed are we?"

"We won't be," Leo answers as Animal calls Owen. "Matteo running to Vincenzo isn't surprising."

"Then what is it?"

"If one more person disrespects my wife, there's going to be blood."

Chapter 25

Unraveling

I SIT on the sofa staring through the balcony doors as Leo speaks on the phone with Jameson. Owen's on his laptop, Animal's been in and out of the room the last thirty minutes, and Rudy is with hotel staff. I've debated calling Leanne, but don't really have the mental capacity to discuss what happened. Leo brought up a bit of his conversation with Renato in the car ride. It appears we had wonderful conversations. Not.

Should I be surprised by Renato's warning that Leo has to ditch me? No. Was it on my bingo card? Also no.

A huff of air leaves me as I bring my legs up. Pretty sure the honeymoon part is over. Likely we'll have to reveal we're in Rome soon.

Doors open and close.

There's no changing his family's minds at this point, especially when all of them are saying to leave me. Deep down I don't care what they think of me, but it does hurt.

I sigh, listening to the sounds of the city. In my head, I go through sessions I've had with Dr. Maxwell and what he'd tell me. Or what Leanne, Trix, or Nan would say. Common denominator?

Don't listen to them. Don't let their insecurities and toxicity tear you down.

Besides, it's not like I'm trying to please his parents. His father would've likely hated me, too.

My finger runs over my wedding band, calming me as I feel it on my hand again. Leo hangs up the phone, entering and closes the balcony doors with a soft click.

"I need to discuss a few things with Aurelio," he says. "Owen will be with me. Rudolph should be back soon."

He comes over to the sofa, leaning over me to kiss my forehead. "Stay in the suite."

He adjusts his cuffs on the new dress shirt he wears, leaving with Owen close behind. I slump back into the sofa, flicking my gaze at the now closed balcony doors. Worry trickles down my neck, I get up to head into the kitchenette to make some coffee. I've definitely not had enough today.

I'm getting the Moka pot ready when there's a knock at the door. Before walking over, I check for the stashed guns near the entrance, and the knife taped to the wall next to the entrance. I open the door slowly and let out a sigh of relief when I see it's one of the bellboys.

"Buon pomeriggio," I greet.

"Buonosera, signora." He then speaks quickly in Italian, pointing to a package and a manila envelope on a cart. Ah, more mail from Jameson.

I nod and get him to place the package on the foyer table as he hands me the envelope. He leaves smiling.

"Grazie," I say, closing the door. "One day I'll keep up. You'd think knowing some Latin would help."

I continue mumbling, glancing over the mid-sized box. I start to pick it up but realize it's heavier than it looks. Letting go, I check the postage is from New York, except it's to me. I pinch my brows, and then glance at the envelope. It's addressed to me as well.

"Did Isaac send me something?" I head over to the kitchen,

grabbing a knife to open the envelope as I lean against the counter. Tearing it open, I pause when I notice something odd.

The postage isn't stamped over. The return address is one I don't recognize, and it's missing a postal code. My heart starts to pound as I stare at the sharpie that writes out my name and the hotel. No room number. No suite name. Upon first look, it's normal, but this shouldn't have made it through customs.

Meaning it never went through the mail.

I snap my gaze to the front door, trying to recall if I've seen the bellboy before. Yes, I have multiple times. He's nice. And it *does* look like real mail.

Hands now trembling, I fumble as I try to gently open the envelope, waiting for anything to jump out or powder to release. Nothing. Only a piece of paper, far too small for such a large envelope. Warning screams in my head as I pull it out, reading the words written in bold letters.

I WAS INFORMED YOU ENJOY MOVIES. WHICH ONES DO YOU THINK INSPIRED YOUR GIFT?

My face scrunches. There's nothing else on the paper or in the envelope. Gift? What?

Time slows as I look up at the package on the table. Stomach twisting as warning yanks at the back of my neck, I put the paper down and go to the package on the table. The postage is fake, too. No proof it went through customs. Except, there's a return address this time I recognize and I want to be sick as my hands violently shake.

Nan's Bookstore.

The letter's taunting screams in my head as I stare at the box. Like distant shouting, I suddenly hear Brad Pitt's damning words from that harrowing scene.

"What's in the box!?"

"No." Tears gather in my eyes. "No."

I race back to the kitchen, stumbling as I grab for the knife.

Gripping the utensil, I come back to tear open the package, but freeze when I see a Styrofoam box. My chest hurts, squeezing in fearful pain. The lid is taped, and I cut through those next. It's cold like there's ice packs inside.

"What's in the box?!"

My heartbeat thunders as I try not to sob or puke right there as my eyes become blurry. Hands shaking, I grip the lid's edge.

"Please…please…" I beg to whoever will listen.

Shutting my eyes, I finally rip it open and the lid clatters to the floor.

I can smell melted ice, but there's something else that makes my stomach churn. Something wrong and pungent. A smell I know—death.

Eyes screwed shut, I take a few seconds and breathe before finally opening my eyes to look at my "gift" within.

Mixture of emotions flood me. Horror. Anger. Relief.

Nestled like a fucking delicate egg in melted ice sits a severed head.

Roger's head.

I stare in horror as my brain scrambles. I stare at the wrinkles. Disheveled hair. I can tell he hadn't shaved for days before the end. Eyelids drooping, his eyes are open and forever clouded in death. His mouth is partially open, and there's something shoved inside his mouth.

My entire body starts shaking as I go to reach for it, but the bile coming up wins. Snatching my hand back, I race to the kitchen and barely make it to the sink before puking up my stomach contents. I clutch the counter, hurling as I blindly turn on the water. My head pounds and my body aches, while my throat and lungs burn. Agonized groans come from me as I grip the counter for dear life, tears streaming down my face.

Sweat forms at my temple as my body hurts from the onslaught. It feels like forever before the dry heaving stops, and I can wipe my mouth. I turn off the water, leaning against the counter as I stare at the floor. The door opens, and I wearily look up as Rudy enters.

"*Bärchen*, are you—" His voice halts as he comes to the table and looks down. Shock flashes over his features as he comes over to me. "Scheisse. Are you—"

"I'm okay, just wasn't prepared to see a severed head today," I mutter as he looks me over briefly. "I'm just shaken up. I thought it was…it was Nan or Leanne…oh, *god* I felt relief when I saw it—"

I start sobbing abruptly. Rudy pulls me against him, encaging me with his body like a shield. He holds me as I cry through the mixture of emotions, ranging from fear, horror, and relief. I've experienced some fucked-up things, but a head sent to me hits the top of the list. David Mills was right to scream.

"You can be glad it wasn't them," Rudy whispers, stroking my back like Leo would do. "Fucker was a bastard who hurt you. You're not a monster."

My breathing hitches as I nod a little.

It's awhile before he lets go, then walks me over to the sofa to sit with a pillow clutched to my chest. He starts making some calls, and although it feels like forever, I know it's barely been fifteen minutes when the other three arrive. Curse words are thrown and other mutterings as I hear them shuffle things and likely looking at the envelope, too.

Something itches at the back of my mind, warning moving along my neck. It tugs, but I feel too numb to truly listen.

Suddenly, Leo is in my field of vision as he crouches before me. He cups my cheek to lift my face. Hazel eyes meet mine filled with concern.

"I puked again," I murmur.

"I'll have tea sent up, and something to eat, too."

"Maybe get rid of the head first."

He strokes my cheek, and then rubs his other hand upon my leg.

"It's Gabriel," I whisper, and he frowns. "Charlotte knew about the movies. She must've told him."

He goes to say something, but Owen speaks up from behind, "Boss, there's something in his mouth."

Oh, right forgot about that.

"What is it?" Leo stands up as I look over my shoulder at the three investigating the head.

"We'll see soon," Animal comments, giving Owen some rubber gloves. Once on, he reaches into the box. I exhale shakily as his hand comes back out with a small piece of paper.

"A fucking note?" Rudy mutters with a scowl.

"Whole things fucked up," Animal adds. "It's like a damn, well…"

"Movie," I finish. Animal winces.

Owen walks over with the paper as the other two follow, opening it when he gets closer to Leo and I.

"What does it say?" Leo asks.

"Nothing," Owen replies.

"A blank piece of paper in the mouth?" Animal questions. "I swear if it's invisible ink…"

"Not blank, it's just a picture," Owen says.

He turns it around, showing a badly printed picture of a monarch butterfly.

The roaring in my head is long gone, replaced by what seems like white noise from a television. No more screaming. My chest constricts as new horror settles in. Long forgotten fears slithering through my veins as I stare past to the manilla envelope.

"They're mimicking *Silence of the Lambs*?" Animal asks, peering at the picture.

"That was a moth, not a butterfly," Owen says.

"What the fuck does it mean?" Rudy asks.

"He knows," I whisper, unable to tear my gaze away from the package. "He knows."

"Autumn?" Leo grabs my shoulder. "What are you talking about?"

It feels like I'm in another dimension, stuck in one of my nightmares and maybe I'll wake up. The villa never happened. Fiorella practically calling me a whore. Renato's disdainful looks. Roger's head. Parts of me want to snap; scream to wake up. I'll wake up at St. Peters with Leo, right? This isn't real, a nightmare—

Leo gently grabs my face and it's then I know this is reality.

"Dear Watson, look at me." I focus on him, but fear crosses his face as he strokes my hair tenderly. "What are you talking about?"

"The mail. Movie references. The butterfly. He knows. He used Charlotte and Roger. Gabriel knows."

"Someone else—"

"Monarch was Gabriel's code name." My voice feels distant. "When I couldn't say his name in reports, the ones I sent to Roger in…in manila envelopes in mailboxes. He was 'monarch.' Roger talked before he killed him. He knows."

I can't even feel myself shaking as Leo takes me into his arms.

It seems my past truly has caught up with me.

Not only does Gabriel know we're in Rome, but he knows I'm alive. And I'm the one who took him down.

Chapter 26

Casablanca

"Everyone's accounted for," Isaac speaks over the phone.

"How fast will you be able to get prints back?" Enigma asks.

"Half a day," Owen responds, arms crossed as he stands off to the side from the kitchen table. "Our contact has to be careful so Renato's informants in the polizia don't catch wind."

"But you believe it's Gabriel?" Jameson asks next.

Leo and I exchange a look. He answers, "Yes."

The last 24 hours have been a whirlwind. We announced that we left for Rome yesterday, having Carrie issue a publicity statement about it being a 'long-awaited vacation' before the new hotel opening. Leanne helped on my end, by telling Nan and Trix that this was a surprise trip for me and had helped Leo plan it. Otherwise, it was calm on the other side of the world. While we had to deal with a severed head and securing a meeting with a rival mafia boss.

Trouble just follows me, I guess.

"He must've smuggled the head outside the postal service. Heads aren't exactly on the okay flying list," Enigma comments.

I snort, leaning back in my chair. It's early evening, the whole day spent dealing with Roger's head and Gabriel's ominous warning. No response from Vincenzo yet. I've had enough time to stop feeling like I'm losing my marbles. Leo's hand drifts over my thigh, lightly stroking it. Animal sits across from us at the table, while Rudy leans against the counter. The rest of the Crew are on this conference call.

"Three hotel employees handled the packages, all of them thought it was regular mail," Animal says. "Someone must've dropped it off with the rest yesterday morning."

"We need to find who smuggled them in," Jameson mentions.

"And if it is Gabriel, how he found out you're in Rome," Isaac adds.

"Renato could've told," Rudy says.

"Not enough time," Owen counters. "Gabriel would've had less than two days to ship the head without being noticed. Not a lot of time to plan."

"Unless Renato already knew, and didn't say anything," Rudy argues.

"Or one of Renato's people," I say softly, and meet Owen's gaze. "Renato didn't confirm working with Gabriel, but one of his own could be."

"Perhaps someone loyal to the Marchetti family," Jameson suggests.

"We can speculate all we want, it won't help. Whoever it was, we trust no one," Leo states. "This includes Renato and his people. We've no idea who's working with Gabriel. Secure all communications, including all of you in the States."

"We should send more bodyguards," Chesty suddenly suggests. Rudy scowls. "I can fucking feel you from here, Ringer. There's only three of you to protect the bosses, even you have to admit that's chancing shit, especially if Gabriel knows where you are, and you've got to meet with Renaldi."

"He's right," Owen agrees, glancing at the scowling ex-wrestler. "Too easy to be outnumbered. People know we're here now, don't have to be as inconspicuous."

Rudy looks at me and I give him a reassuring smile. He grunts in agreement finally, while Animal shakes his head.

"Unless…you get on a plane tonight," Jameson suggests.

"Not until I meet with Vincenzo," Leo says. "And finishing things with Renato, whether it's cutting ties or making him a reluctant ally."

"No offense boss," Animal says, clearing his throat. "From the sounds of it, doubt he's gonna change his mind, unless you leave Autumn."

Leo and I exchange a look. In my gut, I'm certain Leo has been preparing to split from the Salvadori organization since winter. Apart from cementing staying in the mafia, it also meant potentially creating another enemy. In another country.

"We'll send more security," Isaac says. "Although, if it is Gabriel, we should be worried about how long he had Caltz for. And how the fuck he grabbed him."

"The clubs," Enigma and I say at the same time. Enigma chuckles as I look at the phone. "Followed your advice, *hermana*. Pretty sure I caught Caltz near a club once owned by Rossi. Too grainy of an image to confirm, which is why I hadn't mentioned it, until I got something better."

"How long ago?" I ask.

"Couple months."

"Rossi could've worked with Gabriel," Owen suggests. "Hopes of Leo losing power, he gets in good graces with Gabriel. Way of trust could've been handing in a dirty cop who he knows is after Leo."

"In comes Charlotte for more insider information," Isaac adds.

I'm feeling sick again as pieces begin to click into place. Realizing, Gabriel was playing the long game. *Hide in plain sight.*

"Gabriel grabs Caltz, which explains his disappearance," Jameson mutters over the phone. "Why hold onto him for months? If he's gonna try fucking with Autumn, why wait this long?"

"He already has been," I mutter.

"Meaning?" Chesty asks.

"Find the most recent photo of Gabriel, then send it to Nan for her to place him," I say as anxiety pricks at my neck. "Enigma, send someone to check Roger's basement. He had two large deep freezers."

"Alright, seeing where you're going," Enigma says carefully. "But if Gabriel was around, someone would've clocked him. Or a body being dragged into Caltz's house."

"Except that was before multiple people turned on us," I say bluntly, and they go silent. "He also had one hell of a mole. Charlotte was feeding him information, so she knew when I'd leave for the bookstore and return to the hotel some days. As for Roger's house, she could've done the same having access to *all* of your offices, so he could've learned how to avoid the cameras."

"Fuck," Jameson mutters, swearing in Spanish.

"Nan said it was a man with dark hair. She never met Gabriel before," I add, and Rudy starts cursing in German. "And that blip in the feed may have been on purpose, along with Roger's bank account being accessed to make us think he was still alive."

He was doing everything I would've. I don't like the sinking feeling knowing how similar we are in espionage.

Chesty grunts, "Son of a bitch."

Leo's stone still and quiet, staring at the phone with a scowl.

"We should've realized all of this sooner," Owen mutters.

"You were busy with Matteo and Renato," I say softly. Gabriel was cunning and knew how to blackmail. He was at the top of the food chain for a reason even with all his fuck-ups and being an addict, because he knew how to divert attention. "Including the mobs, while thinking a rogue cop was snooping. That's *just* the mafia stuff."

"Fine, he's been playing us," Jameson says roughly. "He could've used what he knew about you when they tried to overthrow Leo, why not? What Matteo and him did combined could've pushed for a complete takeover."

"Except, Matteo essentially has no allies, and Gabriel has a shitty past," I counter. "As manipulative as Gabriel is, would you believe an alcoholic, drug addict who lost millions if he said a random girl caused that breach? He knows that and didn't have proof."

Leo remains quiet. His hand hasn't stopped stroking my thigh, but his movements have faltered a few times. I reach under the table, grabbing his hand to squeeze and he does it back.

"I'm with Miss Autumn on this," Isaac says. "I'll check with Nancy. We'll move our searches to Rossi's old clubs, see if there's footage of Gabriel showing up. He might still be lurking."

"Doubt it," Owen says.

"Check manifests of transportation, contracted or connected to Renato and Matteo," Leo suddenly orders. "I want to know how that fucking head got here. No more than four on security, Isaac. Search Caltz's house and find the rest of his fucking body. And search Curione's businesses for footage since we know he was involved with the coup. We'll be here indefinitely, until I know what my brothers are up to or get my hands on them. Watch your backs. Jameson, we'll speak tomorrow."

There's no wait on a response before Leo shuts off the call and gets up. He stalks towards the bedroom, shutting the door behind him. The rest of us stay in silence.

Owen comes over to the table, sitting down next to Animal and leans back. "We should've listened to you weeks ago, Autumn. You knew something was wrong."

"I just knew Roger," I murmur. "He was a coward. Probably told Gabriel everything thinking it'd save him. There's a reason he sucked in the field."

"Piss poor excuse of a detective," Animal mutters.

"Well, he did get detective because of me," I murmur.

"Didn't seem cowardly in the interrogation room," Owen mentions.

I snort. "Cause he thought he had the upper hand."

"Gabriel's diabolical and takes things personally," Owen comments, rubbing his head. "We're up for a shit show."

"We won't know his motives until we find him," Rudy chimes in.

"And Matteo," Animal grumbles. "If he pisses off Gabriel next, it'll be his head in the box."

Inhaling a shaky breath, I get up from the table as the other three murmur ideas. I go to the bedroom, opening the door quietly and find Leo sitting on the edge of the bed facing the window. His expression somber. He doesn't move as I shut the door, only his left hand moving as his thumb rubs his wedding band. The breeze flutters the sheer curtains. My heart aches, wishing for that quiet morning we had back. To have been trapped in that reality instead of this one.

I go stand before him, stepping between his legs as I place my hands on his shoulders. He grabs them, squeezing gently as he closes his eyes.

"I should've left for California." My face falls as Leo looks up at me, exhaustion covering his features. "You gave us that chance, and I didn't take it."

"No, none of this is your fault. It's your family doing this, killing—"

"I executed over forty men since December," Leo admits in a rough voice. "I was so consumed by fear and anger that I've done worse things than Gabriel. I lost control. Because of it, I didn't pay attention. He knew I wasn't. He was stealing everything from under my nose. He's doing to us, what we've done to him. This is revenge for me *not* leaving." I touch his cheek tenderly as his eyes fill with tears. "I stayed because I was scared of leaving you and look what's that done."

"Leo." I grab his face with both hands. "No matter where we would've gone, he would've followed. He found us in Italy, halfway across the world, so he would've in California. None of this is your fault."

His grabs my hips, eyes almost dimming as I watch that exhaustion weigh upon his shoulders. My hands slide down to his neck, holding him gently as he looks down.

"I'm scared." Leo's voice is almost too soft to hear. The defeat in it tearing at my insides, gripping my heart. "Gabriel. Renato. Matteo. All of them want to take you from me. What if they do?"

"No. They won't." Tears gather in my eyes next as his fingers dig into me.

"I can't be alone again. I won't make it without you, I can't do this alone again."

"Leo." His eyes squeeze shut, tears spilling from them. His throat works as he fights not to cry. "Baby, look at me."

With the gentle command, Leo opens his eyes that are filled with so much fear.

"I am not leaving you," I state, clutching him. "I'm going nowhere. I promise. You're not alone."

Tears fall down his cheeks as he opens his mouth, but nothing comes out. He clamps it shut again, throat working. I stroke back his hair, and kiss his forehead, and whisper, "You can be scared right now if you need. You've always let me be scared when I needed to, so right now, you can be. It's alright. I'm right here."

His arms wrap around me, pulling me close as he buries his face against my chest. I cradle his head protectively.

"I love you," I murmur against his hair. "Tomorrow you can be brave, stoic, whatever you want. Right now, you can be scared."

Leo trembles, his breath shaky. His fingers dig into me as they had in the warehouse weeks ago. He clings to me, crying quietly as I hold him. My heart aches, hurting for him and every decision we'll have to make going forward, to fight for our future. If I'm allowed to feel every emotion openly, so can he. Except, we'll remain in the confines of a bedroom with him in my arms where he's safe to grieve for the life we can never have. A safety we may never know.

"I love you," he cries brokenly against me. "I don't want to live without you, please, I love you."

"I'm here, baby." I press my cheek against his head, blinking as my own tears fall and throat tightens. "I'm right here, my dear Leo."

He shifts his arms, having me move to straddle his lap and wrap my legs around him. Leo buries his face into the crook of my neck, clutching me as those silent tears soak my shirt. I hold my husband close, knowing the pressure he's under while trying to give us happiness. That it's still his own family we're fighting. We cling to each other as I wish that one day, we'll have the peace we crave.

I don't know when the tears stop. I'm not even sure when we in our numbed states, changed for bed and fell asleep in the other's arms.

Far later, I jolt awake. It's quiet other than the pounding of my heart, thundering into my head. Blinking, I stare up at the canopy and focus on breathing. After a few minutes, my chest doesn't feel like a freight train is on it. I glance over to find Leo asleep on his stomach, face turned away. Laying my head back, I stare at the painted ceiling when suddenly my stomach growls.

Oh, right. We were supposed to have dinner after that conference call.

"Wonderful," I murmur, silently getting out of bed. I keep one of the double doors slightly open as I look for a midnight snack.

The past 48 hours don't feel real as I open the small fridge, looking at what we have. Fruit. Vegetables. Bit of milk. Couple pastries. Okay, *now*, I miss late night ordering and want takeout.

I grab the fruit, putting it all onto a plate and sit on the sofa. I find the remote for the small television mounted on the wall and turn it on with low volume as I flip through channels. I look for the ones I've found have played movies before, and finally *Casablanca* appears and it's in English. Smiling to myself, I watch as I nibble on the fruit.

It's near the beginning of the movie. Soon, I'm humming with Sam, who plays on the piano while *As Time Goes By* plays.

Noise comes from the bedroom, and I'm putting the plate down when the doors open. Leo stands there, shoulders dropping with relief when he sees me. His lounge pants hang low on his hips as he comes over to sit with me, and then tugs me into his arms. After kissing my head several times, he gets comfortable with me to watch the movie.

We're quiet as I eat a couple pieces of fruit. I grab a grape, holding it up for him and he takes it to pop into his mouth. A piece of melon is next, but I absentmindedly hold it closer to his face as I watch the film. Leo leans in, taking the melon into his mouth directly from my fingers. I become transfixed by him as he briefly licks my fingers, then chews the fruit slowly. Leo then grabs a piece of cantaloupe, holding it up for me. I move closer and open my mouth for him to place it on my tongue. The sweetness of it bursts as I chew, somehow more delicious than the last couple of pieces. Leo then strokes his thumb under my bottom lip, then licks his fingers clean. A faint smile rises on my face as I finish eating the cantaloupe.

We continue doing that, feeding each other fruit silently as the movie plays. The night wears on as Humphrey Bogart and Ingrid Bergman tiptoe around each other. During one of the altercations in Rick's Club, Leo finally speaks.

"I don't think Renato wanting an heir is completely why he won't cut off Gabriel." I stare at the television screen, running my hand over his arm. "We're all that's left of the Salvadori and Luciano line, but his persistence of late is...odd."

"Meaning?"

"Those arranged marriages were for ulterior motives, but also because I refused to settle down. Now I am and..." he clears his throat, exhaling sharply, "...I brought up the potential of heirs with you, and he still refused."

My breath catches. I hadn't really thought about why Renato wanted Leo to leave me, but maybe a part of me thought it was because he knew I couldn't get pregnant.

"You didn't tell him the truth?"

"Fuck no." He kisses my hand. "One, not my place to discuss, even as your husband, without you present." Oh, that's kinda sweet, but also very Leo. "Two, it shouldn't fucking matter or involve him. His obsession of bloodlines is outdated."

I hum. "Why isn't he even considering leaving the businesses to whoever deserves it? Like that Captain taking over Rossi's organizations? Has your family organizations never done that?"

"Not to that level. Over the past year, Renato has been vehement that Matteo gets nothing, even as a potential heir, continuing to bring up that he's a Marchetti."

"But so are you and Gabriel. Sure, you're also connected to the other family lines, but it seems…weird how much he hates the Marchetti name, but Gabriel still uses it."

"And Renato helped arrange the marriage for my mother and father."

"I get the whole it was for business. But…why hate the name so much, *now*, then? If Riccardo had killed Giovanna, then I get it, but your mom died of cancer, right?"

Leo whispers, "Yes. So, I'm not sure either."

We're quiet again. *Casablanca* showcases its own politics and work arounds. Not wanting to keep discussing his dead parents, I move back to the live family members.

"They're all after your empire…aren't they?" I ask.

"Basically," Leo sighs, stroking his fingers over my shoulder. "Renato for more power and Gabriel for a personal vendetta."

Gabriel was the kind of man who never forgot, no matter how petty it seemed. A reality I knew too well with my own past that I've come to realize. If he sent men to assault me for not sleeping with him, what is he willing to do for what Leo and I have done?

"Where does Matteo fit in all this?" I ask softly. "Just some pawn?"

"Yes."

His quick answer makes my stomach clench. A few moments pass before I ask, "Are you still angry with him?"

"He helped hire men to kidnap and kill you, Autumn. While attempting to dethrone me, and strip away what I've built in the last five years. Not to mention his stupidity in running to Vincenzo." Leo then exhales a long breath. "So, yes, I am angry…even knowing it wasn't just entirely him, I'm not sure I can trust him again. Nor will he get a warm welcome from me."

"And if he has a chance of doing the right thing?"

He keeps his gaze on the television. "We'll see."

His arm comes around my shoulders, fingers creating circles on my arm as I lay my head against his shoulder. I ask, "Are you sure Vincenzo will meet with you?"

"Although he's Renato's main rival here, I've never had issues with him. We've been on good terms, staying out of each other's way. He can be ruthless and savvy if it gets him what he wants. He's probably heard what happened in New York and will want to make a deal of some kind."

"Why?"

"I survived a hostile takeover, killed two crime bosses, and survived another hit. I've rearranged the mafia ecosystem, as it were, in the states. And then there's my companies outside of the mafia, which have remained self-sustaining. Despite how dismissive Renato is, I can be a powerful ally."

"They know how powerful you can be, especially after the last few years. But you've never had a weakness…until me."

Guilt starts to wrap its way around me as I stare at the television. Leo touches my cheek, brushing his knuckles over my skin. Although I helped regain control of the mobs, I was also *why* they got through the cracks.

Leo built a hotel franchise on his own with Jameson. He created businesses, became a well-known businessman. Then he took over the Marchetti organizations, becoming the Head Mafia Don of New York City after overcoming blackmail after blackmail. Outside of financial success and takeovers, Leo also has a ruthless side that's willing to get bloody. He had walls and security measures that were airtight, keeping everyone in check from the empire he had built from almost nothing. A cold, strict mafia don that commanded and earned respect from even the worst of men. No Achilles Heel, until me.

Leo takes my chin, turning my head to face him.

"You are not my weakness, you are my strength, dear Watson," he whispers. "Without you, I would not be here. I am...because of you." He cups my face as something flickers over his gaze. The guilt I once saw is there a moment before it's gone in an instant. "However angry I could be with my decisions, never...*never* will I blame you. For you are my salvation."

I smile faintly, touching his hand.

Leo moves forward and his lips brush against mine. Slowly, he kisses me. Soft lips caress mine tenderly as I sigh against him. We grasp for this small reprieve after the horrid two days we've had.

Suddenly a phone rings.

Leo tears away, snapping his head towards the bedroom. My face scrunches, noticing it's past 2:30 in the morning. He gets up, disappearing to answer it. There're soft mutterings from the bedroom, until he walks back out hanging up the phone.

"Who was it?"

"Vincenzo. We meet in two days."

Chapter 27

Little Red Dress

I STARE at the little red dress hanging on the bathroom door. The mirror is covered in steam from Leo's shower. Both of us are preparing to meet Vincenzo Renaldi tonight at his night club, *Mezzanotte*. Him choosing his own territory wasn't a surprise, neither was the late meeting. It was Leo suggesting I come with him that shocked me the most today.

The raiding of Roger's house and finding empty, bloody freezers was not a shock. So now we're missing a dead detective's body, sans a head. Still nothing on how or who smuggled the head into Italy.

I use a towel to dry my hair a bit more before attempting to fight with my make-up once again. I wasn't opposed in going and would've argued to go with him. It's the whole going back into the nightclub scene that causes a worried shiver.

Leo's words from earlier today, echo in my head, *"I'd feel safer with my wife alongside me."*

Was it for his own sake? To be less nervous about tonight or did he think it'd be dangerous for me to stay here? I shake off the questions, knowing it's likely both. Or he could be worried about a meteor hitting the earth for all I know.

The shower turns off. My eyes flick to the dress again as nerves jumble. Leo comes up behind me, wrapping his arms around me wearing only a towel tied around his waist.

"You don't have to wear that dress if it's too revealing, Autumn," Leo whispers against my ear. "Other dresses you bought will work just as well."

"If we want to lean into the gold-digger narrative or for me not to be perceived as a threat, then I do need to wear it."

My gaze moves to the mirror in front of us. It's covered in steam, but I can still see the irritation on his face.

"I've done this before, I can do it again," I add. "And I have you this time."

For a moment, we just stare at each other through the mirror. He turns me around to face him, cupping my face as I watch water drip from his hair.

"You are my wife, who is cunning and smart. Remember that if at any point you're made to feel lesser than tonight." He kisses me fiercely as my hands land upon his chest. He releases me, placing another kiss upon my cheek, and then grabs another towel. "I'll leave you be to get ready."

Leo steps out, closing the door behind him. I sigh, shaking off the nerves as I finish getting ready. I stick with simple make-up but darken my eyes a little. No jewelry except my engagement ring. Spraying my hair into place, I finally pull on the dress and then some strappy silver heels. My hands smooth over the short dress as I look at myself in the mirror once more.

It's a shimmery, bold red with a cowl neck top and diamond encrusted straps. The material doesn't quite cling to my body, helping hide the skintight shorts I wear underneath. The hem of the dress hits just above mid-thigh. For a moment, I stare at myself and almost see the woman who dressed like this to get into nightclubs undercover. So much of my skin is showing, I practically feel naked, making me swallow hard. The loud color also makes me stand out.

"Just play pretend," I whisper to myself. "Another role. You can do this. Just the…mafia boss fiancé."

After one more nod and pep talk, I walk out of the bathroom as Leo puts on his wristwatch. He didn't shave, giving him a darkened shadow upon his jaw which matches with his dark attire. His dress shirt is deep maroon and silk material, more buttons are undone than usual, providing a good view of his colorful chest tattoos. He's the perfect picture of a stereotypical, playboy mob boss. And it's hot.

A blush comes over me. My breathing becomes shallow as I stare. All nerves out the window. I may never, *ever* truly get used to the sight of Leo and how handsome he is. Clothed or naked. Didn't matter.

I blink, suddenly realizing Leo's staring at me as well. His own eyes drag over my body, smoldering with desire that makes my body heat with awareness. Ohhh…fuck, we haven't even left yet.

My eyes flick to his lips, where his tongue drags over his bottom lip.

Vincenzo who? Where are we going again?

Leo comes closer, grabbing my hand and kisses my wrist. He won't be wearing his wedding band either and suddenly I really want him to.

He murmurs against my skin, "If anyone stares at you too long, I'm taking their eyes out."

I sputter out a laugh as he leads me out of the bedroom. He wouldn't. Right?

We come out to the suite where Owen waits along with Michael. Our extra security arrived this morning. And of course, Isaac sent Michael, which made me happy, but also the lovely, quiet Igor and another man, Garett. Igor and Garett will be posted just down the street from the club, who will be under Animal's charge.

I somewhat believe Leo's threat of taking eyes when both men only glance at me for a moment. Michael, however, looks *kinda* terrified.

Elm Jed

We head down to the lobby and get into the car where Rudy waits. Owen and Michael get into another car that'll follow. All of them are dressed in dark attire, looking like professional mobsters. As we drive through Rome, the city feels less recognizable as we get closer to *Mezzanotte*. It's not long before we arrive, and there's a crowd out front as we pull up. I stare out at the people, familiar nerves coming forth.

I remind myself how I navigated this world. And I was good at it.

Leo starts to get out of the car, but I grab his hand. "Wait."

He glances at Rudy, and nods for him to leave as he shuts his door. "If you're having second—"

"Will you follow my lead until Vincenzo meets with us?"

"Until?"

"From what you told me, he'll posture, even with you, right?" He pauses, but nods. "Did he give specific instructions on this meeting?"

"Just to inform his staff when we arrive."

I purse my lips, glimpsing out the window as people shout.

"When we get inside, inform one of his bartenders we're here," I say, looking back at him. "Then wait until I gesture to go to the dancefloor. Together. We stay there until he sends someone."

Leo's brows are still furrowed, tilting his head at me.

"We make ourselves not look desperate," I explain. "Waiting for him at the bar or simply standing around, he'll use it as a way to control your mood and the meeting outcome. So, we pretend like we don't care when or if he does meet with you."

"And if he sees it as a slight, and cancels it?"

"He won't," I say confidently. "He won't say no after seeing us together, because he's gonna want to meet the woman who's caused such an uproar in your family. Not to mention, it'll be out of character for you, mixing pleasure with business."

"Which will intrigue him more." I nod, hoping he'll go with this.

He looks outside, brows furrowed in thought. Finally, Leo

smiles devilishly like I've given him another idea, before kissing my cheek. "Alright, dear Watson."

Anticipation mixes with nerves as he gets out of the car, then lets me out. Loud bass and shouts hit my ears, and I swallow hard as I'm flung back to those long past days. I focus on Leo as he clutches my hand, and then places it at my back before he leans down to instruct, "Do not leave my side, if you do, Rudy follows you. Michael and Owen will roam the club."

I nod, putting on a face that's happy to be here, even as people yell as we skip the line. We approach the bouncers at the main entrance, and they nod to Rudy. I swear one of them flinches when Leo looks at him. Instantly, we're let into the club of flashing lights that spill out the doors and high windows. Tension ripples over my body, warning signals going off as we enter *Mezzanotte*.

Eyes adjusting to the neon blue and pink haze, I look up and realize it's three stories. There's a large open space for dancing, bordered by multiple bars. There are two glass public elevators in the back, where people dance and make out. Everything is glass or imitates it. The next two floors you can see into, open for those above to watch below. Both upper levels have glass railings, circling the club, the only thing between you and falling to the floor. The second floor seems close to forty-fifty feet high. Techno music reverberates, pulsing in my ears as I flick my gaze around when Owen and Michael part from us.

Unease twists as Leo guides us to one of the less busy bars in the back.

Follow the plan. Observe. Where is everything?

I glance to the back, seeing some stairs to a hallway. There are public stages with poles, where quite a few girls attempt to dance on. I clock where the bathrooms are due to the amount of girls leaving and returning. Bouncers intermingle with the crowd, wearing suits. They almost look identical to our own bodyguards.

Mobsters are consistent with attire, gotta give them that.

We get to the bar, passing a group of women who eye Leo and

laugh with each other. Some grab drinks as Rudy catches the bartender's attention, speaking with him and the guy looks up at the other floors and then nods. He calls over one of the bouncers as Rudy comes back to speak with Leo.

They talk as I scan the club. Most of the women are dressed in less than me, wearing bikini tops or mini skirts. The men are all similar with half opened shirts or mesh tops. Good to know we blend in. The music changes and I straighten, stomach twisting as I try to keep my expression bored and unperturbed by the club scene.

A woman with long blonde hair and a tiny tube top comes over for a drink, eyeing Leo and licks her teeth. I step closer, putting my hand upon his chest as I dip my fingers under his shirt. I glare at her, and she scoffs before walking away.

"Here I thought I'd be taking eyes out," Leo murmurs against my ear.

His hand slips over my dress, moving up to trace over the seam along my back.

I look up, catching him roaming his eyes down my body. I smirk, tilting my head back more as he starts to kiss my neck. His arm wraps around me protectively as he continues.

The nerves along my spine start to dissipate, distracted by Leo and his touch. As I look up, I see someone on the third floor leaning on the glass railing. He's dressed in a jacket, glimmering in the light that streaks over the space. A glass of something dangles from his hand, cocking his head as I realize he's watching us.

Vincenzo.

A flash of the past hits me. Remembering Rossi sending people to dance cages. Gabriel locking his top office. DeLuca sitting in his VIP sections, making people do disgusting things on the floor. Vincenzo's clearly no different. His club layout speaks for itself.

Classic theater—balconies and boxes above for the wealthy and powerful, while the ground floor is for the commoners.

I was right. He's going to make us wait. Prove that *he's* the one in charge here.

A couple women approach Vincenzo as the music changes, lights shifting to become bluer with red lasers piercing the haze. Vincenzo turns his attention to them, already ignoring us.

Showtime.

I grab Leo's hand, meeting his gaze as I tug him towards the dancing crowd. He gestures for Rudy to stay, following as he comes in close before anyone bumps into me. My heartbeat jumps into my throat as we enter the thrall. I turn towards him, draping my arms over his shoulders as his hands grasp my waist.

"Check in," he says into my ear, battling the noise of the nightclub.

"Green." I press my body against him, breath shaky. "Just don't let go."

My hips gyrate against his as the space fills with more fog. The club music vibrates through me as Leo's hand moves along my curves. He turns me around, keeping my arms up and around his neck as his hand slides up between my breasts and lands upon my throat like a necklace. He applies light pressure, grinding his hips against my ass.

The music changes to something deeper and slower. Leo's head dips down next to mine as I bend my body, rolling my hips with his to the beat. I tilt my head back, drowning myself in the music as I catch sight of Vincenzo again.

He's no longer focused on the women sidling up to him, but instead watching us through the chaos.

The sensual music helps as I turn my attention back to Leo, losing myself to the heat of dancing. I turn in Leo's arms, making my body flush with his as he grabs my ass. My breath hitches, body tensing as I feel my dress ride further up almost showing the bottom of my ass. Leo's forehead comes down to mine, and in the mixture of bright colors and haze, his eyes meet mine like a light-house in a storm.

I can't hear him but can read his lips. *You're safe.*

We dance closer, hips rolling together with the melodic bass. Leo's hands slide over my body, fingers tracing my skin as I drown out the rest of the club. I can ignore the smells of smoke and alcohol permeating the air. I can ignore shouts, people dancing and grinding like us. Although it's an act to make us seem unworried with Vincenzo, focusing on ourselves than him, I'm finding myself forgetting Vincenzo completely as we practically fuck on the floor with multiple other couples. Muscles clench, shuddering whenever I feel the outline of Leo's cock against my hips. Body tingling, I roll my body against his as the heat of him encases me. His hot breath falls over my skin as he turns me around, tugging me completely against him.

Breathing heavy, I flick my gaze up again. Vincenzo's gone.

I grab Leo's hand, holding them on my hips as I move, feeling his hardening cock against my ass. Oh, fuck. Leo groans against my neck, kissing the sweat that's begun to form.

Quickly, Leo spins me to face him again and crashes his mouth against mine. Neither of us caring where we are or what we're doing. He clutches me, kissing me fervently on the dancefloor as people shriek and sing horribly to the music. Shivers wreck my body as his hips grind against mine. Arousal floods me, surprising me almost. I melt against him, gripping his hips as I pull him to me. We both groan as his half-erect cock in his pants presses against my body.

For a second, we're like any other couple here. Just two people frantic for the other.

It feels over too soon, when Leo rips his head away. He practically snarls at a bouncer who's approached us with Rudy, who keeps the other guy back from Leo. The muscled man flinches as Leo puts a protective arm around me. I can't hear them as they speak, and the bouncer points above. We're led off the dancefloor, Rudy not far behind and Michael appears from the crowd. My legs are shaky, heartbeat racing as we're led to a private elevator with walls of velvet. The bouncer says something in Italian, nodding for us four to get on.

We stand behind Rudy and Michael as the doors close, Leo's

hand caressing the top of my ass while I bite back a groan. My plan worked, but now I'm horny, and we still have to deal with a mafia boss.

Son of a—

Chapter 28

Gods & Mortals

THIS IS why I worked undercover by myself—no distractions, especially from hot husbands.

The elevator is quiet as we ascend, while I want so badly to drag him to the nearest empty room. What's in the club air here? Never have I ever had these kind of thoughts before, let alone in a dress that should spiral me into a panicked mess. Every light touch of Leo's hands along my back, likely to help me stay calm, send me into a different spiral.

I concentrate on breathing when the doors open, and a couple of guards are there. They converse briefly, before Rudy and Michael get off the elevator. My mind blurs as Leo tells them something before the doors close again, leaving us alone.

"Check in," Leo asks, dragging his hand along my back.

"Green," I rasp.

"Be honest."

"I am."

"You're breathing heavy—"

I spin, shoving him against the wall as I yank his head down to slam my mouth against his. He gasps against me, grabbing the nape of my neck and waist. On their own, my hips grind against his as I moan against his mouth. I grasp at the frantic need for *anything* to help me through this erotic spell.

The elevator stops, and Leo quickly slams a button to keep the doors from opening. We continue making out, until I pull back panting. "I don't know what's wrong…"

"Nothing's wrong." Leo cups my cheek, lightly stroking his thumb over my bottom lip.

"Leo, I'd fuck you in this elevator right now if I could, and we both know how I feel about public sex. Not to mention nightclubs." I swallow hard, almost feeling dizzy.

Were the last few days catching up to me?

Smoldering eyes look me over, then he licks his lips. He gently kisses me. "You feel safe, dear Watson. That's all. We won't fuck in the elevator, but depending how this meeting goes, I promise to when we get back to the hotel."

"Holding you to that, mister," I breathe, and try to find my bearings. "Remind me never to make a plan like that again. You do it next time."

"Why?"

"Cause I'm horny!" I exclaim under my breath, stepping back and attempting to straighten my dress. Leo chuckles smugly, pulling me back to him for another kiss.

"You are absolute perfection," he says against my lips, and then releases me to straighten himself. He gives a dastardly, sensual look before hitting the button to open the doors.

Leo instantly turns into a deadly, prowling force as we step out, met by another mobster. He gives no indication that we'd just been making out in the elevator. And the dancefloor.

We follow the bouncer through the top floor of the nightclub, where there are strippers and people getting lap dances. I glance down at the crowd below. Lasers flash and the DJs yell something before the crowd goes wild. Up here feels like a different club with the luxury furniture and expensive looking bars and alcohol on the walls. We approach a glass wall with trickling water illuminated within. The bouncer opens the door, stepping aside as we enter.

It's a private space with a full glass wall that cuts off the noise from outside. There's a mini-bar with a bartender and couple of women leaning on the counter. Their eyes quickly go to Leo, licking their lips as they push their boobs together and hike up their skirts. My arousal quickly turns territorial as I glare at them, stepping closer to him.

On the other side of the dark room, lit by red and amber lights, is Vincenzo. He grins like a cat who caught the mouse. He wears several chains of thick gold, and several rings.

"Buongiorno!" He greets as he walks over.

Leo remains stoic, greeting him back. "Renaldi. Bene e tu?"

"Bene. Bene." Vincenzo gestures to me, trailing his tongue along his teeth as I catch the brown in his eyes. Yup, arousal fully gone. Nice while it lasted.

"Renaldi." Leo's voice pierces the air, making him look at Leo. "Ti presento mi fidanzata, Autumn."

Vincenzo's eyes flash back to me, roaming over my body. Leo suddenly growls, muscles tensing as he says something too quick in Italian for me to understand. They exchange words briefly before the other mafia boss chuckles.

"A woman who finally caught the eye of Luciano. God works miracles, but I would've been caught too after seeing your little show," he comments, grinning at me. "Vieni a sederti."

His voice is gravelly, like he's been yelling for three years. Vincenzo brings out a cigarette and lights it. Or like he's smoking. He sits down in one of two plush chairs beside a long coffee table. Leo sits in the other, and I flick my gaze to Leo's lap. Scenarios run through my head. It's just us up here. Vincenzo watches me closely, sucking on his cigarette as I sit on the chair's arm. I cross my ankles, remaining poised next to Leo, pretending I'm disinterested.

Vincenzo's eyes are glued to my legs as he drags them back up to my face.

Okay, plan may have worked too well, because now he's *too* focused on me.

They start speaking in Italian, due to their pace and the constant thrumming from the music outside I can't keep up. Instead, I go the route of oblivious woman as I flick my eyes over the space and back to the girls at the counter. They start flirting with two other men, who repeatedly look over at us.

A bartender brings over a drink to Leo, then places one in my hands. My stomach clenches as I look down at the orange-colored drink and can smell the sugary substance mixed with probably vodka. It's gripped in my hand as flashbacks suddenly appear.

Fuck, horniness vanished and now there's no distraction from the past blasting back.

"She doesn't drink." Leo grabs my cocktail, placing it on the table. Vincenzo starts to argue. "Unlike you, I prefer my women sober."

Vincenzo laughs, throwing his head back as he settles into his seat. I slide my hand over Leo's shoulder, who keeps his gaze on Vincenzo. Leo takes my hand and kisses it possessively.

"And tell your...dancers that I won't be playing tonight. Send them away," Leo instructs.

"Oh, come, Luciano...my treat, as always. After what I saw, the more—"

"Now. Renaldi." The strictness of his voice makes Vincenzo pause, and then smirk.

My stomach twists as Vincenzo waves his hands at his men, and then says something like they aren't needed tonight. They all pout as they're about to be escorted out. One of them comes over, trying to work on Vincenzo, but shows her ass towards Leo and smiles back at him.

"Uscire," Leo growls at her, and she stands in a huff. Vincenzo smacks her ass, telling her to leave.

There's a shakiness in my chest as she frowns and leaves with the others. The door shuts, leaving us three alone. Vincenzo grins, sitting back to sip his drink.

"Still learning Italian, signorina?" He asks me suddenly.

"Sí."

He chuckles, blowing out smoke. "Tell me, is he as controlling and rough with you in the bedroom as you are dancing?"

Leo goes rigid, face darkening as he glares at the man.

"What? Come now, she's a girlfriend with a fancy ring, eh?" He smiles, taking a long drag from his cigarette. "You've never cared before, Luciano, and you have never been so *obvious* in *my* club. Quite the show. I see why you chose her, and from the way she's assessing my private room…" his eyes meet mine, "…I doubt it's only from how she fucks."

For a moment, I think of pushing back and acting like the gold-digger persona I was going for. Except it appears, he's not buying it. Great, the one time a mob boss isn't dense. Instead, I say, "Asking for tips?"

He grins. "Ah, see? You don't…*bend* quickly, do you?"

"For him?" I nod at Leo, running my hand over Leo's shoulders deliberately. "Sí. For you? No."

"Even if I could bend you over any of this furniture? Fuck better than him? Or how about the window if you truly want an audience? Your screams will be louder than the music."

His brash words don't shake me. They're no worse than what I've heard before, but I am surprised he's saying this in front of Leo, who is unmoving and practically snarling at the other man as his free hand flexes into a fist.

Not wanting Leo to turn him into a pulp, I give one of my best customer smiles and tilt my head. "Why be with a mortal, when I'm already with a god?"

"What makes you think he is?"

"You've never had him fuck you to understand."

Vincenzo suddenly starts laughing, yelling Italian about me being quick and I think, being trouble. I glance down at Leo, who looks up at me with pride hidden in his rigid expression.

"A sexy woman, smart, not fearful to speak…ahh, Luciano it's almost unfair." Vincenzo finishes his drink, lounging in his seat. "I understand why your brother hates her."

Which one?

"Matteo talked about her?" Leo asks.

He shrugs. "Blames her for losing his *owed* fortunes. I told him he may have been raised in the mafia, but not with us families who place possible wives first; the luck to not only carry on our legacy, but to have one who's loyal to you." Vincenzo lights another cigarette, flicking the lighter shut. "Not like these whores I hire for a good time, who'll turn you out for better money or a harder dick. Gold diggers. All of them. Loyal women can't be bought."

My stomach clenches at the cigarette smoke, but also as he looks at me and smirks. "You can try to pretend, signorina, but you touch him like he is your god. You should've looked at me longer if you wanted me to believe you could be bought."

"Then I'd be gagging for the wrong reasons," I retort.

Vincenzo laughs loudly. His eyes light up. "Are you sure I can't be your god?"

Leo's silent as he reaches for his drink. I'd have thought he'd be tearing into Vincenzo for how he's talking, but there's something in his calmness like a jaguar waiting in the darkness.

"Where is Matteo?" Leo finally asks.

"Comes and goes," he answers, blowing out smoke. "He tried to turn my rivalry with Salvadori to you, but I told him *only* Salvadori. Marchettis and I have always been...bene. Capisce?" He then gets up, leaning down to grab the drink I refused. He sips it. "But, you are no longer one, are you?"

My stomach twists.

Vincenzo smiles at me. "Perhaps your new girl can help persuade me to make a deal with you...*Luciano*. Allow someone else to be her god."

My heart thunders in my chest. Did he just suggest selling me to him?

"I wouldn't trust Gabriel if I was you, Vincenzo," Leo says in a dark tone. Using his first name makes Vincenzo snap his gaze to Leo. "Nor a god, whose had enough of these games especially after you inquire after his *wife*."

The air becomes chilled almost as my mind goes blank. The

drink in Vincenzo's hand becomes frozen in the air as he stares at Leo. All joking upon his face is gone as I see fear flash over him.

Leo continues talking in Italian, his voice low and dangerous. He's explaining what's happened I think, catching words for New York, Gabriel, and killers. Vincenzo steps back, and then slowly sinks back into his seat, but not before placing the drink back onto the table.

That's what Leo was waiting on—Vincenzo putting his entire foot in his mouth.

Leo stands as I'm frozen in place, heart in my throat. He towers over me, taking my chin gently. His presence is volatile, lethal even, simmering like a volcano ready to erupt.

"Tu sei sposato?" Vincenzo rasps.

Leo's answer is kissing me tenderly, placing his hand upon my throat in a protective manner. He then straightens, gesturing for me to sit in his spot and I do so, sinking into the chair. Leo remains standing, leaning down to grab his drink.

"My wife can hold her own," Leo says, far too fucking calmly. "But if you ever talk about fucking her again, I will cut off your dick and feed it to you before I carve out your eyes."

Whatever jocularity Vincenzo had is gone, replaced by worry he tries to hide. He attempts to act nonchalant as he brings up his cigarette to smoke, hand shaking slightly. He blows out the smoke, and says, "If I'd known, I'd never have brought it up, Luciano."

"Whatever business occurs between us or concerning my brothers, my wife is off limits. I've shed enough blood for her to fill the Coliseum five times over, but an ocean will not stop me from adding you or any of your people to it."

Vincenzo's eyes flick to me. I keep a calm expression, focusing on Leo's hand that rests upon my shoulder. It grounds me as I breathe deep, knowing in this moment, even in Vincenzo's territory, Leo's the scariest man here.

Muffled bass rumbles the glass as Vincenzo finishes his cigarette, lighting another quickly as he gets up to go to the bar. I reach up, touching Leo's hand. He squeezes gently back. Vincenzo pours himself a glass of vodka, adding something before he turns around. He stops a few feet from us, cocking his head to the side at me as his eyes narrow. I meet him head on, not flinching.

"You know what he's done?" He asks me, and I nod. "Why even me with my bouts of fun, knows there are limits. I am not stupid." He gestures with his glass at Leo. "Because he's not stupid. His threats are *real*. Only mafioso I know who doesn't think with his dick, greed, or obsession for blood. So, *you* are new for me. He's never killed for a woman before." He takes a long drag, blowing out smoke. "I've seen him bloody, have you?"

Once more, I'm being tested by a man who thinks they can make me afraid of Leo like they are.

A smile comes over my face. "He didn't fill the Coliseum alone."

Vincenzo freezes, eyes flicking to Leo. He then raises his hands in mock surrender, and then takes a long drink.

"Perfect for each other." He sits back down, letting out a nervous laugh. "Leonardo Luciano married. World is changing."

"It's a secret, so keep it," Leo says abruptly. Vincenzo gives him a wily smile. "Even from family."

"Ah, there's the smart Luciano," he says. "She gets control of your organizations, doesn't she? Or until an heir is born. Smart." I ignore the pang in my chest. "Honestly, Gabriel deserves nothing. He's fucking insane."

"Thought you were…bene with the Marchettis?" I ask, scrutinizing him.

Vincenzo just smiles. "Sí…" he points to Leo, "…and he's still the infamous Riccardo's son, whether he keeps Marchetti or not."

My face flickers with confusion, which just causes him to smile more, and say, "If he said yes, Matteo told truth of you. If he said no, then he's a liar. Now we know."

I'm not sure whether to be impressed or worried about this man's motives.

"Eh, but I already knew Matteo's too stupid to control anything, not without running it into Hades," he scoffs.

"You think he's that incompetent?"

That's not the Matteo I remember, young as he was, incompetent he wasn't. That didn't add up, unless Gabriel has been whispering in his ear longer than we thought. Or Renato.

"Eh, naïve," he adds. "Thus, why I allowed him in."

"He's not a threat."

"No. Boy has no connections and can't keep loyalties. In comparison to…" he gestures to Leo again, "…or Gabriel. No. Dangerous in spending money, having others do his dirty work? Sí. Except his funds have run out."

"And he ran to you," Leo says.

"Precisely. It's all business, Luciano. I have no issues with you. You caught my bluff and you raised the stakes. Cause *you* are a good opponent, but I'm not stupid. Although your wife may be more fun."

"Careful, Vincenzo," Leo warns.

"Agreeing she can hold her own." He grins at me. "A very, sharp-tongued woman."

"What did you offer Matteo?" Leo asks, pushing the conversation away from me.

"A job. Low ranking to prove his loyalty to me, and not Salvadori. We'll see how far he gets as a foot soldier. Make him work."

"What else?"

"That's it. Except truly… il tuo fratellino è stupido. I won't disrespect your wife, she I like, but him? Given his betrayal of you. Not to mention attempting to kill her? Oh, that's an unforgivable act, and if you wanted…that information could slip to those who take matters into their own hands. Those with wives they're protective of."

Leo's quiet. Not answering immediately as Vincenzo basically puts a hit on Matteo. He'd essentially be helping Leo, given the issues Matteo's caused, but it also meant owing Vincenzo a favor. Something I don't think either of us wanted, but right now… Matteo working for Vincenzo meant he belonged to him. So, if Leo touches him, that could cause outrage. And I'm not sure Leo wants Matteo dead.

I'm starting to see why Vincenzo was Renato's rival. The man went from trying to "buy" me to putting a hit on Matteo. He's a cunning and quick.

"Why take Matteo's offer if you think so little of him?" I ask.

"Potential good soldier, he's young," he says with a shrug. "At the time, thought he was in good connections with Luciano. Could've brokered a deal by having a little extra. Don't blame me for trying to conduct business with the well-established Luciano estate."

"And to spite Renato," Leo comments. "Which is your real reason. Be honest."

"Eh, mostly. He's fucked over my shipments from Germany and Poland, I'm still pissed. And he took territory *rightfully* mine from my grandfather."

"I told you not to play poker with him."

"Sí, should've listened," Vincenzo bemoans briefly, finishing his cigarette. "Want me to hand the ragazzo over? Per un buon prezzo. Or as favor, I can take care of him for you."

"No," Leo answers. "I want you to keep him occupied. Tail him and let me know if he meets with Gabriel."

"Essere il suo tutore?"

"Your men will be."

Vincenzo snorts, sipping from his glass before putting it down. Again, he lights a cigarette and I swallow hard trying to ignore the smoke that drifts and fills the space.

"What do I get out of this? Being dragged into your dramma familiare?" The mafia boss asks cockily, lounging back with a curious look.

Leo goes to speak, but I touch his hand which causes him to pause. He glances down at me, raising a brow. I suggest, "Perhaps we could buy and *gift* territory back?"

Vincenzo hums as Leo watches me carefully, thoughts running through his head. Was buying Renato's assets then selling it back to his rival potentially making him an enemy? Yes. But that ship has likely already sailed, why not jump in completely? Especially when he realizes we're married.

Vincenzo grins, blowing more smoke and I think I may be sick. "Does she have a sister?"

I ignore him, getting up to keep my composure. Leo gives me a questioning look as I lean in and say, "I think he's a better ally than Renato." Leo flicks his gaze to the other man. "I need the restroom."

He nods, running a hand over my shoulder. "Restroom?"

"Second floor. Down the left," Vincenzo answers.

I know he said to stay near him, but I did need it and a reprieve from the smoke. I give Leo a small smile. "I'll find Rudy."

"She'll be fine, Luciano. Come let us discuss business, and if anyone tries to touch her, then I'll let you do the honors of killing them."

Leo ignores him, giving me a quick kiss. "Be quick. Talk to no one."

I walk away, remaining calm as I step out. I'm hit with loud music, the smell of alcohol, and more smoke. The glass apparently blurred the lights because my eyes ache when I avert my gaze from the lasers. Quickly, I get to the elevator. My hand runs over my stomach as another twist hits me, and then my bladder reminds me how much I need to go. I get to the next floor, Rudy and Michael not far, appearing worried.

"He's fine. Bathroom." I move where Vincenzo instructed, feeling one of them follow me as I make it to the short hall and step into the ladies' room. I finally get some relief for my bladder and lungs. A few others come in and leave as I take my time composing myself. I come out to wash my hands, sighing as I look into a mirror. Not too much of a mess from making out with Leo, but I do adjust my hair. After another fortifying breath, I step out of the bathroom to go back up to Leo and Vincenzo.

The hall is clear, but I hear something behind me. Warning ticks up my spine, and I spin on my heel. Nothing. Empty hall. Déjà vu strikes me, remembering another club and coming out of the bath-room. My chest tightens as I swallow hard.

"Get back to Leo," I murmur to myself.

I turn but freeze when I see him.

His hair is longer, touching his ears. He wears a bright red shirt, barely buttoned and wrinkled slacks. Those brown eyes sear into me as we stare at each other. His lip curls, snarling as he looks me over, right before he attacks me.

Chapter 29

Vertigo

I duck as Matteo lunges for me.

He slams into the wall, stumbling as I try to get around him. He spins, grabbing for me as I jam my elbow into his side making him fumble. Feet screaming, I sprint and come out to the main area. There's no one around as I start to head for the elevator when I see someone on the ground and realize it's Michael.

"Fuck," I mutter, running to him.

He groans, beginning to get up as I approach. Blood trickles from his head as he looks up and his eyes widen. Michael jumps up and grabs me. I yelp as I tumble to the ground, almost skidding into the wall as he slams into Matteo.

Matteo claws for me, screaming in Italian and then punches Michael. They keep fighting as I get up, running for Rudy or the elevators. Shouts come from behind, and there's screaming followed by gunshots. I crouch, covering my head as I try to move towards the wall as people panic. My heel catches on the carpet, stumbling in the opposite direction I want when someone bumps into me. Everything whirls as gunfire sounds again, drowned out by the music and flashing lights.

A woman runs into me, and I stumble again towards the low,

glass railing. It slams into my waist, the force almost making me topple over. I grip the glass, barely stopping myself from falling. I stare at the nightclub below. A scream claws at my throat as I see the crowd dancing on the very hard, concrete floor that's a good fifty feet below.

After everything, falling to my death *High Anxiety* style almost seems poetic.

My head blurs when a hand grips my arm, spinning me around. I'm shoved against the railing, remembering why I hate high heels as I lose my balance. My fingers dig into the railing, clinging to it as Matteo's hand grabs my throat.

I cough, choking as my eyes widen. I bring up a hand, trying to pull him off and while trying not to fall over the edge with the other—either get choked to death or fall.

I gasp for air. Angry eyes glare at me, frowning with such maliciousness. There's commotion everywhere on the second floor, mixing with the partying below as my head goes fuzzy and vision blurs.

"Please," I choke out, pleading with those angry eyes. "Matteo. Please."

"You won't take him from me," he rasps. For a second, the pressure on my neck lessens. I suck in a breath, while my hand wraps around his wrist. Through the darkened haze, I see tears.

"Matteo. Stop."

"*Whore,*" he growls, tightening his grip again.

There's yelling and someone slams into Matteo, knocking him off me. The force pushes me back as his hands are ripped from me. Finally, I lose the last of my balance.

Time almost slows as the ground beneath me disappears, toppling backwards. My breath catches, unable to scream from the throbbing around my throat and shock. I flail for anything to grab onto, but the railing is too slippery. I'm falling to my death.

Suddenly, someone grabs me. I'm yanked forward, head snapping back as I land against another body.

"Got you, ma'am."

Gasping, I look up at Michael as he pulls me away from the edge. His nose is bleeding, another wound on his forehead. Blood is everywhere on him. Relief fills me as he gets me on my feet.

"Thank you," I rasp.

He nods once, turning his head towards the commotion. My vision is spotty as I struggle to swallow. Holding onto Michael's arm, I look in that same direction. Men hold back others, and Vincenzo's shouting at, I think, one of his bouncers. He then hits him, pulls out a gun and shoots him. I flinch at the suddenness, the act unknown to the club below as people continue dancing. More people yell as I realize one of the men holding back Matteo is Rudy. Is Owen behind them? A headache forms as I try to focus.

"Ma'am, your dress," Michael says stepping back.

I look at him, and then at myself realizing my dress is hiked up to my hips and the strap falling off my shoulder. Thank fuck I wore shorts. I gasp, pulling the strap up as Michael carefully helps tug down my dress. Suddenly, there's an angry shout.

"Hands off her!" Leo's command punches through the noise.

I look up as Michael steps back from me. Leo storms towards us, face furious, murderous even, as I catch sight of a gun in his hand.

"I told you not to leave her."

Michael starts to speak, "Boss, she went into—"

"I don't *fucking* care! And then I turn around and see you touching her!" Leo starts to raise the weapon.

My eyes widen. Holy shit, I don't think I've ever seen him this angry. I don't think I've ever heard him yell like that. His face contorts with wrath.

"Leo—"

"He failed at his job," Leo growls, aiming his gun on Michael. No one attempts to stop him, just as no one did when Vincenzo shot his bouncer. Not even Michael.

Quickly, I step in front of Leo, and he halts. The gun tilts down when I state, "Red."

His gaze flashes to mine, flaring in worry and ire. He breathes heavy, left hand flexing at his side.

"You will *not* touch him." I try to keep my voice steady, straining from the throbbing pain. "I didn't wait for him. He fought off Matteo. He was fixing my dress, after saving me from falling to my death." I point to where I'd been, keeping my eyes on him. He flicks his gaze to where I point, fury vanishing and replaced by horror. "Look at me."

He does so as I step closer, moving the gun down fully. Leo breathes heavy as a whirl of emotions cross his face. There are whispers or yelling, I'm not sure as I tune them out and focus on him. Briefly, I catch sight of Vincenzo watching us, right before yelling for Matteo to be dragged away.

Leo's hand comes up, shaking as he clutches my face. Pure terror fills his eyes as I feel myself tremble and feel sick. I realize we're both brewing panic attacks inside. On the verge of freaking out. I place my hand on his chest, coming close as I swallow past the lingering pain.

I do the only thing I know can work.

"*Once upon a midnight dreary...*"

His eyes widen, pulling me forward as he buries his face against the crook of my neck. He says against my ear, "*...while I pondered... weak and weary.*"

His gun disappears as we continue *The Raven*, both of us calming down. Suddenly, we're interrupted as Vincenzo comes closer from behind Leo, who must sense him because he turns his head in a predatory manner towards Vincenzo. He stops, stepping back as he raises his hands in surrender.

"Signorina," he tells me. "When you're certain he won't kill me or my men. Third floor. I'll have the boy. And brava." He turns away, disappearing along with his men.

Leo presses his face against my temple, breaths becoming calmer. I whisper a few more lines of *The Raven* with him, feeling my own panic attack recede. I glance over where Michael is, his expression somber. Blood drying on his face, he mouths, "Thank you, ma'am."

My head barely nods in reply.

I've no idea how long we've been there when he kisses my forehead, stepping back. His eyes are clearer, but simmer with fury. Leo flashes his gaze to Michael, but says nothing as he raises my chin to look at my neck. He traces where Matteo's hands had been and that anger comes back full force, growling low.

"Ringer." The order is abrupt, and I'm shocked to see Rudy appear. "Take her back to the hotel with Michael. Send Animal to replace you."

"I'm not leaving," I argue, that shakiness coming back.

"I have to go deal with Matteo," Leo counters. "Or Vincenzo will. He attacked you and paid *his* men to help him onto this floor to come after you."

"I'm not going back without you." Tears start to come.

The panic attack threatens to build again, adrenaline trickling away. I'm not really in pain, not compared to what Steve did to me, just fearful of leaving Leo. I don't want to be separated from him. The thought wrecks me, making me want to breakdown. Whatever they decide with Matteo, I'll endure it, but the last thing I want is to wait in that damn hotel alone.

He clutches my face. "Autumn."

"Please, don't make me leave," I plead, grasping at his shirt.

The headache forming worsens. It's barely been a couple of hours since we got here, yet the ever-changing gauntlet of emotions, swings me from side to side. I almost died, fucking again, and the last thing I want is to be away from him.

"You'll be safe—"

"Red," I rasp.

His face falls before tugging me against his chest, wrapping his arms around me. I cling to his back, begging him silently not to send me away.

"You don't leave my side, even if it's to use the restroom again, do you understand?"

"Yes." I nod against him as relief floods me.

I don't realize how rigid I was until my muscles relax against him. Leo must feel it as well, because he sighs as he strokes my hair back. He then pulls away, but not before placing a brief kiss on my lips. He gestures for the other two to follow as he leads me to the elevator. The headache is now faint, while I concentrate on the warmth of Leo's hand.

We get to the third floor, going the opposite direction from before. The floor has been cleared. Below the partying hasn't stopped, which almost makes me sick to how oblivious they are.

We get to a doorway with two guards. Glass wall again, but it's a shiny black this time. Only Leo, Rudy, and I are let in, Michael staying outside. This room is cut off from the rest of the club with a window overlooking it and keeping the noise out. The floor is a shiny tile, perfectly clean if not for the two bodies on the floor. And chained up in a chair, sits Matteo gagged and shirt ripped to shreds near the window. Another body is being dragged to the other side.

Vincenzo lights a cigarette, flicking off the lighter as he spits at the body at his feet.

"Apologies, Luciano. Didn't know I hired cheap fuckers." He looks up, surprise flicking over him when he sees me.

He clicks his fingers, gesturing towards one of his men in the room. The guard grabs a chair from the deserted bar on the opposite side. It scrapes against the floor as he drags it over to us.

"Scuse, signorina," Vincenzo says, gesturing to the dead bodies. "If I'd known this disappointing stronzo would fuck over my hospitality, I'd have never let you leave your…fiancé's side."

He turns his attention to Leo next, who starts to roll up his sleeves. They converse in Italian, words moving quickly in low voices. Rudy steps back with the other guards, scowling harshly. Leo finishes rolling up his sleeves, then sits in the chair and gently tugs me to sit on his lap. I delicately sit, holding back a moan at the relief being off my heels that betrayed me to gravity. Leo strokes his hand along my leg.

Vincenzo snaps his fingers, placing his attention on Matteo as one of the mobsters brings over a bottle of vodka. Another steps behind Matteo, yanking his head back as he takes the gag off. The mafia boss talks, and I can't translate a thing with my oncoming migraine and exhaustion. Suddenly, they hold a cloth over Matteo's face and begin to waterboard him with vodka.

Oh, fuck.

I turn my head into Leo's shoulder, trying to drown out the coughing, choking noises. Leo doesn't flinch. He doesn't stop Vincenzo from torturing his brother. He's steady, stroking my back tenderly. I'm on the brink of second guessing on staying, when Matteo shouts and sputters. He yells something, liquid splashing to the ground. More sputtering and coughing. My heart clenches as I do understand some words.

"Leo! Fratello! Per favore!"

He doesn't sound like the man who was choking me over a railing. He sounds like a younger brother, begging for mercy.

"Stop," I whisper. "Stop."

"Fermati," Leo orders. It quiets. Leo continues in a lethal tone, but I do catch a word I know well—moglie. Wife.

Oh, Leo is *really* airing out the secret tonight, huh?

Men shift in their spots, murmuring as Matteo starts to yell again. Leo doesn't raise his voice, but practically growls at him while Vincenzo scolds the young man. More arguing, and Vincenzo hits Matteo. Suddenly, everyone goes still when Matteo repeats a name—Fiorella.

Leo's hand stops.

"What's wrong?" I ask.

"Luciano's younger brother here said you'll control him," Vincenzo answers, waving for a drink. "Just like Fiorella is with Salvadori right now."

"I don't understand."

"Renato's wife died almost five years ago in a car wreck," Leo adds.

Confusion mingles with my headache, warning tugging at my neck.

"Salvadori never remarried, or am I wrong?" Vincenzo asks.

"No, he hasn't," Leo says, adjusting for us to stand, and sits me back down. He walks over to Vincenzo, muttering something. Vincenzo waves at his guards, who release Matteo from the chair and toss him to the floor.

"I'm a cold-hearted bastard," Vincenzo splits the silence, and flicks his still lit cigarette onto Matteo. "But you don't know when to quit. Attempted a hostile takeover, failed, tried to kill your brother's wife, failed...but now you dishonor a dead woman's name, who died a tragic death?"

Wait, what?

Everything is swirling as I try to make sense of *any* of this.

Leo prowls towards Matteo. Vincenzo tsks as I grip the chair I'm on.

Matteo, bloodied and still coughing up vodka, pleads to Leo. "No, Fiorella said—"

"She's *dead*." Leo snaps his hand down to grip Matteo's throat. His younger brother claws at him weakly, not getting far as Leo slams him against the window. It rattles, while my own chest squeezes, eyes widening in horror.

He's at his breaking point.

Leo teeters towards that darkness once more, threatening Matteo with a rigid, cold demeanor that makes me feel sick. No one stops him. Vincenzo grins, leaning against the wall as he watches Leo throw Matteo against the glass and drop him.

"You came after *me*," Leo says with a dark voice. "*My* businesses. *My* position I salvaged from *your* hands. *My* money." He crouches, and Matteo flinches away, cowering. "After everything I tried to help you, is this what I deserve from you? All that I *could* forgive in time. But you came after *my* wife. Laid hands on her." Matteo whimpers. "My *wife* Matteo."

He gasps, "Leo—"

"Now you blame your actions on a *dead* woman? I saw what was left of her." Leo spits on him. My hand snaps up to cover my mouth.

If Fiorella is dead…who the fuck did I meet at the villa, then?

Matteo turns to the other mafia boss, begging, "Why… aiutame…per favore."

"No." Vincenzo takes a long drink, then spits it onto Matteo. He grins. "I'll take every chance to fuck over Salvadori, but even I wouldn't go as far as disrespecting his late wife. She was a kind woman. Your brother can chain you up in here for all I care." Matteo looks at him in horror, while Vincenzo shrugs. "Questo non è personale…sono affari."

Leo stands as Vincenzo talks, taking his shirt off. Rudy moves to take his shirt, averting his eyes from me. Something's wrong. Very wrong.

Beyond what's happening right now, deep in my gut there's a twist that screams at the back of my mind. The migraine worsens as I try to concentrate, thinking as my hands start to shake. The same disturbing feeling I felt after being betrayed, lied to, it crawls over my skin. And Leo's too angry to think clearly.

"It's time you remember how powerful your brother is," Vincenzo says, crouching to pat Matteo's face roughly. "You crossed too many lines. A hard lesson to learn."

Leo's tattoos are harrowing in the stark neon light. His muscles tense, becoming unyielding as Matteo tries to stand and plead as the other mafia boss steps back.

"She's alive," his voice rasps. "Renato is lying!"

"Cowards about to die will always tell the truth."

Everything becomes sluggish as I barely hear Leo ordering me to close my eyes. Matteo continues begging, face warped with fear.

"…weird how much he hates the Marchetti name, but Gabriel still uses it."

Matteo looks over at me. I see a young man telling me to leave. Get out. Those deep brown eyes. Like Gabriel.

Leo doesn't have his father's eyes.

"…it does not mean you know him better than family."

And then I remember—her eyes were hazel.

"Leo, stop!" I shout, standing on wobbly legs as my stomach

churns. The migraine throbs through my skull, making it hard to concentrate.

Leo moves his gaze to me, stepping back from Matteo. His brother slumps to the ground, tears running down his face as he watches me with relief and resentment.

"He put his hands on you. He almost killed you. Again." Leo's voice isn't one I know. It's dangerous and unfeeling.

Through the shaking, I step closer to Leo who's coiled like a snake ready to strike.

"Signora, I wouldn't," Vincenzo warns low.

I can see the dread on their faces. The fear. They murmur as I approach Leo, placing my hand on his chest. He's hot against my palm, burning like his wrath. My eyes shift to Matteo, who continues to glare at me. Whether I could save him or not, it doesn't stop his hatred for me.

"Just a fucking cat." I guess we're even now.

"Leave Matteo with Vincenzo," I tell Leo. "We need to deal with Renato first." Leo goes to say something. "Please. Leo."

He searches my face, then snaps his gaze to Vincenzo, and then Matteo. His brother averts his eyes, curling into himself. Leo brings his attention back to me, and those dangerous hands gently caress my cheek.

"Renaldi," Leo says.

"Luciano."

"Keep him alive. Our deal is good." Leo gestures for Ringer. "How you keep him alive, I don't care, but don't let him leave. Fuck me over, and I'll burn your organization to the ground as you watch."

"We're bene, Luciano. Unlike your brothers, I keep my promises. Capisce?"

Leo doesn't give Matteo another glance, guiding me out of the room with Rudy not far behind. Matteo, even after being beaten by his brother, calls out to him.

"Leo! Per favore…Leo!"

Rudy hands Leo his shirt, who ignores his brother's cries as he puts it on. We leave the room, Michael joining us as we walk to the elevator.

"I want surveillance on Renaldi," Leo orders. "Use *Eleanor* if you have to. I don't want Matteo disappearing before I finish him."

Rudy grunts.

I feel sick, almost wobbling as the elevator doors open. My senses blur into loud colors and sounds, head pounding. My vision starts to darken as a buzzing forms in my ears. There's a slow building of horror and hurt, warning yanking at my neck.

Her hazel eyes now haunting me.

"Autumn."

Liars. All liars. A fucked-up movie script.

"Autumn?"

My body finally gives up and collapses as everything goes black.

"Autumn!"

I'm not the only one who came back from the dead.

Chapter 30

Misericordia

I jolt awake. There's an ache in my throat as I gasp for breath. My stomach churns and suddenly bile rises. A hand reaches for me as I stumble out of bed.

"Autumn?"

I slam through the bathroom door, not making it to the toilet as I puke into the sink. It's not long before I dry heave, trembling as I clutch the marble. Nerves wrench at me, making me feel worse as I realize the truth. Cruel hazel eyes haunting me.

A hand touches my shoulder. I flinch, fumbling backwards. I flashback to last night, falling over the railing. My body feels confused on whether to puke or curl into a ball. I'm soon on the floor, panic gripping me.

Leo gently brings me into his arms, cradling my head against his shoulder as I try to stop the dry heaving that make my lungs burn. He strokes my back as I shake. Everything hurts as Leo tries to calm me.

"You're safe, dear Watson." His voice is tender. The man I heard last night long gone. "Breathe. You're safe. I'm here."

Tears fill my eyes as the trembling worsens. The constriction around my chest is painful, and I want to be sick again. "I have to… tell you something. I don't…I don't…"

"Shh, it's alright." Leo clutches my head, wrapping his other around me. "I'm sorry, I almost went too far. I shouldn't…"

I shake my head. I never *ever* want to experience last night again, but it's not what I care about right now. It's not what makes me want to scream. The potential betrayal gnawing at me. The lies. Or perhaps he won't believe me. It seems ridiculous to even think it myself. I begin to cry, wishing last night ended with us on that dancefloor. That we left.

How was all of this getting worse?

"Dear Watson, talk to me." His voice is soft.

I swallow hard, clinging to him as I try to concentrate past the gnawing at my insides. Finally, I whisper, "A woman found me in the villa…I thought it was Fiorella. I didn't know she was…was dead. She had hazel eyes. Told me to leave you." My face buries against his shoulder. "Said I didn't understand your family. Knew your name's meaning. Like she *knew* you. I thought she was Fiorella…"

Agonizingly, so very slowly, Leo's movements still. His breaths become shallow.

"Matteo was telling truth…what he knew," I continue. "The Marchetti name…why they hate it. Why they haven't…I'm sorry, I'm sorry."

"Shh, sweetheart, it's alright." He sounds calm. Too calm.

"They lied to you…your mother, I think she's—"

He maneuvers me, then cups my face to bring my tear-filled eyes to look at him. His face isn't as gentle as his voice, but contemplative as he looks over my features.

"All that matters is you," he murmurs, wiping away tears. "My father could come back from the dead, I won't care. If my mother has…so, be it." The ache worsens. "All that matters is you. Only you, my dear Watson." He kisses my cheek, and then the other. "Only and ever you, my beloved wife."

I hiccup as he kisses my forehead, lingering there.

"Leo." Confusion washes over me, not quite taking away the panic, but it does dim the anxious haze.

"I will prove that it's only you."

"You don't...Leo, you..."

"To everyone else." Those green irises flecked in gold meet mine. He strokes my jaw, and then my hair as he roams his gaze over my features. "What I am going to do will make my family the enemy. It may bring more danger, and there won't be a reliable way out of the mafia, Autumn. But...I've had enough. No more games."

I swallow hard and nod my head. I've decided time and time again it would be him I'd follow. Just as he's willingly followed me.

"Only you," I whisper.

"Are you sure?"

I nod.

He leans me back to his chest as I curl myself against him. We hold onto each other on the bathroom floor.

"My mother died when I was eleven." A piece of my heart breaks at the defeat in his voice. "If that woman was her, she's not my mother. Because mine would have never left me. Hid from me. Whoever she is now...isn't my mother."

He buries his face against my neck. Both of us quiet in the early morning before the rest of Rome wakes up.

I follow Leo into a church. His hand remains wrapped around mine as I glance at the simple brick before stepping into its brilliance. It's quiet. Tall pillars with gold at the top are there when you enter, leading up to a dome that I would've never noticed from the outside. Intricate Renaissance paintings are everywhere. A long aisle leads to the main altar, lined with plain, wooden pews. It feels like the altar is a mile away. Candles are lit, illuminating the colorful space. Our six shadows follow silently. I glance over my shoulder, all of them spreading out into a diamond shape.

Today has moved too quickly, and yet too slow. Leo was on and off calls all day with Jameson, before having another one with the Crew. He gave them all one last chance to leave, get out while they could, but of course they wouldn't. He had a similar meeting with Chiari. And then Mila. Chess pieces were moving on our part to secure assets and partnerships before Leo would break from Renato. The Salvadori and Luciano family would be split for the first time in a half a century, including the Marchetti family that was once brokered by his parent's marriage.

Leo was even planning to cut Renato off from the mobs in New York, offering to replace him concerning business. Overhearing his conversations with Jameson, we'd have to go slow to keep the hotel franchise and other businesses separate from the mafia, but it meant Leo coming out completely, and officially, as the Head Mafia Don of the Marchetti and Luciano family. Most of that concerned partnerships across seas, which I doubt anyone argued given he was offering a bigger payout to turn their backs on Renato and Gabriel. It just meant he was losing millions, numbers I didn't want to think about.

He wasn't just cutting family and alliances from his empire, but taking parts of theirs, too.

Now we're in a church, late at night and I've no idea why.

A priest appears, and Owen walks past to talk with him. It's not long before the priest gestures for Leo.

"I'll be right back," he whispers, kissing my hand and walks away. Animal, Igor, Michael, and Garett are left with me. The others disappear with the priest down one of the halls.

I pull my cardigan closer, moving my jean covered legs against the other. I'm not sure when I'll be willing to wear a dress again. I stare up at the paintings, breathing in deep as I wander down the aisle. I glance behind me, noticing Animal off to the side by a pillar, watching the entrance. Igor and Garett are on the other side, closer to the pews. Michael trailing after me.

My fingers trace over the arches of the benches as I continue slowly. No noise comes from me as I make my way to the altar. Trickles of anxiety crawl their way back, to run from a place that feels too large. Too big like I'll be swallowed up. I stare at the sculptures, stopping a few rows away from the end. Quietly, I move to sit in one of the pews.

It's practically silent apart from small noises of feet down other halls. Maybe the echo of a bird or mouse somewhere. Oddly, that thought calms me a little as it reminds me of a certain mouse. One who looked upon a tapestry, and how precious it was to him, along with a small abbey filled with creatures.

"*I am that is,*" I murmur, remembering the line.

After everything that's happened so far, the chaos and pain, I wonder how Rome did it. Go through so much carnage and destruction, almost erased and burned quicker than it was built. Yet, here was this ornate, gorgeous work that still stands. Parts of history that survived in every rock and stone. Those places like the Coliseum. The squares and roads. Churches, mosaics, and paintings. All preserved somehow through destruction. Rebuilt for…

"To use what serves us and rebuild new." I snort under my breath. Well played, Dr. Maxwell.

Shoes scuff, and I glimpse over my shoulder as Michael quietly sits on a bench behind me. Animal has moved closer, sitting a few rows back.

"You think Claude Frollo is here somewhere?" I whisper.

"Wouldn't he be in France?" Michael asks in a low voice.

I snort, then give him a faint smile. A smile tugs at his own lips, and I notice the bruising and scabbing beginning on his face.

"Thank you again, for last night, ma'am."

I turn back to the altar. "He wouldn't have…you know. He was just scared."

"If that's the boss scared, I never want to see him angry." I snort. "But…I think I was scared, too, ma'am."

My eyes go down to my hands. "Me, too."

We're quiet, and I hear small noises. The creak of a bench. Soft foot falls. Candles flickering. I breathe in what could be the last of peace I may know for a while.

"Ringer said you saved Matteo," Michael murmurs, shifting in his seat. "Why? He almost killed you…again."

"I'm gonna lose count on the attempted murder from my in-laws at this rate." My voice rasps, touching my throat gently.

"Then why? Pity?"

"We all do things in anger and pain we later regret," I answer, staring at a statue of a robed figure in blue. "Sometimes it's more blinding than love, cause you just…hurt so much. You want it to end. Problem is when you come out of that haze you realize what you've done. The consequences. Sometimes what you needed was mercy. To have anyone recognize your pain."

Michael remains quiet, shifting in his seat that causes the wood to creak.

"He's alone," I say quietly. "In pain. Young. Scrambling for anything…*anyone* to hold onto. I think I understand too well the choices he's made, no matter how awful, he's still not cruel. Gabriel, Renato, and so many others are. They make people bleed because they can, not out of hurt. Not because they're afraid." I clear my throat, rubbing my arms a little. "Besides, probably only saved him for Leo's conscious. The regret he would've felt."

"Still, you think he's worth helping? After the sh—…" his voice trails off, and I glance over my shoulder as he looks at the holy figures, "…you know."

"I cost Leo millions, years ago," I state, and his eyes widen slightly. "Who knows how many people I got killed, arrested, or livelihoods destroyed. Businesses and companies dismantled. I'm partly why he became the Mafia Don, whether my actions helped him or not, I *was* the villain. I'm not innocent. I was the dangerous one. Angry and in pain. Yet…I was given mercy. Given trust again."

Michael exhales a long breath, jaw working.

"He was left alone," I continue, looking down. "Used. Lied to. Made a pawn in a game, I doubt anyone taught him how to play. His actions are his own, yes, but…even if Leo may never forgive him, I think I can. Because I understand being so alone and hurt, that you'll do anything to survive. He's trying to survive."

Matteo's anguish flashes over my mind, telling me not to take Leo from him. Calling out to him. He just wanted his brother.

In another time, I remember nights just wanting my sister. The ache to be heard.

There's a faint sigh, and I look back up at him. "You are odd, ma'am." I raise a brow. "But I think it's incredible to even consider giving him mercy at all."

"Blame Leo," I muse, turning back to the front. "He's who showed me how far compassion can go."

I stare up at the elaborate church. Breathing in the quiet with him, and brush away silent tears.

"Hey, Michael."

"Yes, ma'am?"

"When we get back to the states, I want to talk to Isaac about adding you as one of my bodyguards. Not just when I'm tinkering in the garage." There's no response. I look over my shoulder as he just stares at me. "If you want the position, that is. But you should know it means following me everywhere in the hotel. And making sure I don't eat cereal for dinner."

He smirks. "I'd be honored, ma'am."

"Part of orientation will be watching *Face/Off*, I should warn you." I face the altar, and he snorts behind me. I smile faintly. Then I feel it—hope.

There're footsteps, echoing from a corridor. Leo appears and Michael gets out of the pew, moving away from me. Leo comes over, holding out his hand. I take it, following him closer to the altar, until he stops us and takes both my hands.

"You're not hiding Quasimodo somewhere, are you?" I teasingly ask.

"Wouldn't he be in Paris?"

I try not to laugh, envisioning the potential between him and Michael getting along.

His thumbs caress my skin, and a tender expression comes over his face. "Marry me again, my dear Watson."

I blink up at him, and then briefly down at our wedding rings. "In all the mayhem, I didn't miss a divorce hearing, did I?"

Leo smirks, raising my hands to kiss my knuckles. "We're going to say we were married in a church, late at night in Rome. We didn't want attention, just us. So, we will have witnesses…" he glances at our bodyguards and the priest that's reappeared, "…that it just happened. Not months ago."

The priest smiles warmly at us, holding a bible in his hands as he waits patiently. Owen and Rudy are not far away, much like a couple of groomsmen. Does that make Animal and Michael my bridesmaids? Oh, Leanne is gonna be mad about this.

"I'm not Catholic," I whisper.

He steps closer, voice low. "The priest knows we're married legally, and assumes we've gone through the whole marriage counseling. And that you converted. He believes this is a…formality for my Catholic upbringing."

"Isn't that kind of, well…"

Leo smirks, coming in close to whisper in my ear. "No worse than what we've already done, including that rosary, my dear Watson." I hold down a giggle as he kisses my neck. "Our union being seen as official by the Catholic Church will give my family less ammo to fight with." He kisses my neck again. "And distract from our true plans, dear Watson."

Well, we weren't following the rules anyway. Then again, such was being with a man like Leo.

I reach up, touch his cheek, and smile. "Leonardo Durante Luciano, I will marry you however many times I can. In churches, beaches, cabins, or lawyer's offices."

His eyes shine, even as his face becomes serious again. He nods at the priest, who gestures for us to come forward. Leo doesn't let go of my hands as there's talking and reading from the bible. It's surreal. Never thought I'd be married "again", let alone in a Catholic Church in Rome.

In between the long speeches from the priest, I flick my gaze to the men standing near us. Not all the *Forgotten Demons* are here, and I'm missing my best friends, but we're not alone this time. I stare up at Leo, finding him calm. He raises his hand, caressing my cheek.

"I do," he whispers.

"I do."

For the second time, I kiss Leo as husband and wife for the first time.

Chapter 31

My Heart Cries

THERE ARE clouds on the horizon. The sky not as blue as it has been while we drive once more to Renato's villa. I hold Leo's hand while Rudy and Owen sit up front. Most of the ride has been quiet. Leo's face solemn and composed. I bring our hands up, and kiss just above his wedding ring. The silence almost deafening as the car turns into the villa's drive. We pull around like we had before, parking at the entrance. Leo steps out first, adjusting his black suit jacket nonchalantly. I step out next, glancing up at what's supposed to be a sunny day, but the clouds say otherwise.

"You sure about this?" Owen asks low as he steps out. He then flicks his gaze past me to the other car. Doors open and slam as the rest of our bodyguards arrive.

"You ran the numbers with Enigma, anything I should be aware of?" Leo asks, unperturbed.

"No, just…" he sighs, and I look at the far too peaceful villa, "…you're betting millions here, Leo. Whether he takes the deal or not, you're also losing millions."

"I never cared about the money," Leo replies in a stiff tone. "It was just a thing I needed to curate businesses. Money is what *they* need. Whatever is lost, can be regained. I won't lose sleep over it."

Rudy grunts in agreement.

Leo meets my gaze, and I give him a faint smile. He takes my hand as we start to walk towards Renato's villa. The Crew follows us, along with the other three bodyguards.

We came with no real invitation. Leo demanded to see Renato, brought up potentially "listening" to his advice which got him to agree. His uncle didn't agree to extra bodyguards, all armed, including Leo, but his opinions aren't valued at the moment.

Leo is dressed like he's attending a business meeting, and so are the others. I wear jeans, a plain dark shirt, and converse. No more pretending to be someone I'm not. And in case shit hits the fan, I'm ready to run.

We walk through the first archway, and that's when I see them. Guards. They straighten, but don't move otherwise as Leo scowls at them. We continue through the courtyards. One guard does attempt to stop us, but after Ringer makes a growling noise and there's the click of a gun safety, he stops. There's murmuring from the others as Leo and I continue towards a large patio that overlooks the back half of the villa's groves and gardens. In the middle of it, sits a table with a couple of chairs. Coffee already set out. Renato stands beside it, looking out at the grove before turning towards us and frowns. Leo lets go of my hand, placing it on the small of my back. I hear our guards and Renato's spread out, taking covering positions as we stop just before the table and chairs.

"I never took you for one to lie and disregard my advice, Leonardo," Renato comments, putting his hands in his pockets. "She's not supposed to be here. *Why* is she here?"

Leo ignores him, looking down at me. "Do you want a macchiato?"

"Leonardo, you are in *my* home, you best explain yourself now," Renato continues.

"No, I'm alright," I answer.

Leo brings my hand up, briefly kissing it.

"Mi stai ascoltando?" Renato asks.

"Unfortunately, it's not hard to hear you prattling on," Leo comments, straightening himself. "She's here because I want her to be. I never said which advice I would take. I rarely play by anyone's rules and yours are no exception."

Renato glares at him. "Cosa vuoi?"

I breathe deep, keeping a calm expression as Leo talks, hand stroking my back.

"Due to the lack of communication over the past year, I've decided to cut ties with the Salvadori organization as it's proven not be a reliable partnership. This includes *all* connections and assets begun by you and my father to be dissolved. All current deals, I am revoking." Renato's face starts to turn red as he attempts to keep his composure while Leo talks. "You have two choices. One is to agree to my terms on how this transpires, and I may even sell you a few of my European based businesses at a low cost. Anything attached to the Luciano or Marchetti name you'll get nothing of. The other choice, not agreeing to my terms, I buy you out and resell to the lowest bidder."

"You wouldn't dare."

"I would."

"Dangerous games, Leonardo," Renato curls his lip, straightening himself as he attempts a smirk. "You don't have the funds to buy out my companies. Or the means to replace their revenue for yourself."

"He does," I interject. Renato refuses to look at me, until I say, "The financial status you've been made aware of was *only* the Marchetti organization's companies connected to the mafia. You've been seeing less than half of what Leo is worth, which is over 500 million outside the Marchetti fortune, and that's me low-balling due to his real estate investments throughout the year."

His small smirk falters as I give him my best customer service smile. The curled lip quivers as he glares at me with a mix of outrage and disgust. Warning flicks up my spine, instincts telling me to hide as I recognize the threat upon his face. Leo's hand caresses me, helping my smile remain intact.

"He built a five-star luxury hotel franchise," I add. "In a decade with barely anything to his name. I doubt it'll take him that long again with the partnerships he's created if he must."

"Your decision," Leo says calmly in his business-like tone. "But before the end of the month, all business ties regarding the Salvadori name to the Marchetti *and* Luciano name will be severed."

"You are *pissing* on your family's legacy." Leo remains stoic as Renato spits at him. "You can't."

"Watch me."

Renato starts to pace, seemingly trying to calm down as he mutters to himself in Italian. Suddenly, he turns to the house and his posture relaxes. He turns back to us with his rage gone from his face, replaced by something sinister. My stomach twists, warning crawling along my spine as I feel uneasy at his expression. Deep in my gut, I could feel the pieces moving on the chess board with a deadly scrape.

"Did she prompt this?" He asks, nodding towards me. "To turn on family?"

"No," Leo answers briskly. "You did."

"Me? Cosa?"

"Someone told Matteo when I was meeting Renaldi," Leo answers.

"Then it was him, who Matteo left to work for."

"Renaldi is cocky and deceptive but keeps his business quiet. He viewed Matteo as a foot solider, nothing more. A position that wouldn't have earned such information." Leo's hand stills against my back. "But a couple of Renaldi's men aren't as tight-lipped as you thought."

Renato remains apathetic, unmoving as Leo holds up his other hand and gestures. Igor approaches with a small bag and dumps the contents onto the table. Ten fingers thud onto the surface, followed by clinking noises from the rings the wearers once had.

"A gift from Vincenzo Renaldi." Leo's voice is cold, while Igor steps back again. "A reminder of what happens if you try sending another mole into his organization—that's all you'll receive back."

Renato doesn't even glance at the fingers, tilting his head and mutters something in Italian I can't understand. Leo argues back, voice low and foreboding. I glimpse to Owen, who watches Renato closely.

I catch my name being said, Renato flinging his hand in a dismissive gesture. Leo suddenly moves as he positions himself in front of me.

"You knew Matteo would try to kill her," Leo's voice is a growl, switching back to English that almost whiplashes me. "Either wanting him to succeed or that I'd kill him for you."

"Do not blame me for his actions. Blame yourself for his hatred, instead of assuming such things." Renato spits.

"Then what of Matteo speaking of Fiorella being here?" A shift happens over Renato's features. "Or is that just an *assumption*?"

The air feels charged as silence looms. Out of the corner of my eye, I can see Leo's face is barely a mask of chilling severity, edging towards rage. He scowls as heavily as Renato who meets him head on. Time stretches as the wind whistles through the trees.

My chest squeezes as the truth I was horrified to say out loud gnaws at me again. That damning truth is now written upon Renato's face.

"That *boy*…always talked too much," Renato warns, stepping towards us. Leo doesn't move but does nudge me further behind him. I place my hand at his back, hearing the noise of guns being grabbed.

"Where is she?" Leo asks.

"Fiorella's dead, my wife—"

"That's not who I'm speaking of." There's a roughness in his voice. Not shaky or trembling, but it's strained as his hand flexes at his side.

Renato stops in his tracks. His eyes almost disturbing as he remains silent.

"Where is Giovanna *Marchetti*?" Leo growls.

"She is *Salvadori*," Renato snaps back. "Not a Marchetti!"

"Is?"

Renato's jaw twitches. Finally, he clears his throat before yelling to one of his guards in Italian, *"Bring her out."*

The air is thick with tension. Leo's body tenses as I try to see his face. My hand presses against his back when I hear a noise. I look up to see the woman I met.

Her hair is pulled back into a bun like before, and she's wearing simple clothing with a cream cardigan. She's poised at first walking out of the shadows, but her face falls a little when she sees Leo. His body becomes more rigid as she walks towards us. Leo's hand flexes at his side, balling into a fist as I hear his breathing become shaky.

I'd planned to stay back, let him face her if it was true that she was alive. It was between them. Except, when his hand slightly trembles as I hear his foot scrape back, away from her as she reaches for him, I can't stop my feet. Quickly, I step between her and him as a shield.

Murmurs circle around us, low and questioning. Giovanna's crumbling, sad look disappears when she brings her attention to me.

"Step away from my son," she orders me.

"No."

Her eyes flare. Now, knowing who she is, I see the similarities he once spoke of. The greens and golds in her eyes. The high cheek-bones. I stand my ground as I find more resemblances of him on her face.

"You should not be here at all," she says, straightening herself as she gives a tone only a disappointed mother would give. "I advised—"

"Advised me?" I interrupt. "Before or after you insinuated I was a whore? No, I think you were disrespecting me when we met... Giovanna."

She slowly looks me over, disdain on her face. When she looks at Leo again, her expression changes into a grief stricken one that I want to slap off.

"Leonardo," she says softly. "Come here, *mio figlio.*"

Nothing.

The wind picks up, clouds blotting the sky out as the sun becomes more covered.

"Leonardo, she is still your mother," Renato intervenes.

"Is she?" Leo's voice is rough behind me. "The mother I remember wouldn't have left me with that tyrant. Wouldn't have faked her death, hiding from me for over twenty years."

Giovanna talks, switching to Italian swiftly. There's little guilt in her tone, and I'm assuming she's explaining her side of the story. Leo doesn't ease, his breathing still just as shallow. I reach back for his hand, and he takes it without moving from where he is behind me. Giovanna continues, and I catch words for Fiorella, his father, and Leo. I take another step back, allowing Leo to fully place his hand upon my back and his trembling stops.

Finally, she ends her explanation, I presume, looking almost pleased with herself as she smiles sadly. Once more she holds her hand out to him. He doesn't move.

I guess her story held as much water as a plot twist in a M. Night Shyamalan movie.

"Leonardo, per favore—"

"No," he interjects. "You lied to me for over twenty years, both of you. To Matteo, making him believe you were Fiorella. How long were you planning to stay hidden? Forever? Or were you waiting for the right moment to return as if leaving your children behind wasn't sinning enough? What *mother* would ever do that?"

Her hand drops, and that smile warps into a quivering frown. Renato comes forward as she steps back, placing a hand upon his sister's shoulder as she seems to cry. He scowls at Leo, as if what they did wasn't wrong. Wasn't cruel.

"Do not speak to your mother—"

"She is not my mother," Leo rebukes, stepping to the side of me as his hand remains on my back. Leo asks in a rough voice, "Does Gabriel know?"

There's no change on Renato's expression. But Giovanna's

shifts, chin quivering again. Not quite guilt, but maybe some for lying to her youngest son.

I almost feel sick, fully understanding Renato's actions. Because it wasn't all him—it was her. She pulled the strings to protect her sons in her own twisted way, but specifically her eldest son. It somewhat explained Gabriel's cockiness, too.

"I see," Leo murmurs.

"You left behind the family. Disappeared," Renato argues. "You walked away—"

"Yet, she walked away first, but when *I* returned, no truth came. All of you *lied*. The only one telling the truth was Matteo, even if he didn't know it wholly. A boy *you* scorn for his existence—"

"He is not Luciano or Salvadori," Giovanna interrupts. "He is your father's abomination, a bastard and that *whore's*—"

"Do *not* call her a whore when she died tragically while you lounged here in solitude. She was a better mother than you." Leo's voice snaps. She flinches, eyes widening at his outburst.

"He is a Marchetti! That *monster's* child!" She yells back suddenly. "He deserves nothing from our lineage."

"Then what of me?" Leo argues, hand beginning to shake against my back. "I am Riccardo's son, whether you like it or not."

"Oh, I can see that, because you have the same rage," she abruptly states. Gone is the grieving mother who cried a moment for her son, replaced by a horrid, narcissistic woman. There's so much vitriol, it's agonizing to listen to as she purses her lips at him. Discontent rife on her face. "How often do you strike her? Make her bleed on your floors like your father had?"

She did not just compare him to Riccardo like that, not after his fucking brother sent me a damn head in the mail.

I step forward, anger boiling in my veins, ready to punch her. Leo wraps his arm around my waist, keeping me back. Giovanna sneers at me hotly, while Renato looks at me like I'm a disappointment. And then Giovanna calls me, "Puttana irrispettosa."

So, I throwback in Spanish, "Pinche perra."

Blazing hazel eyes meet mine, and I give her the same. She

won't shake me. And I'll call her every insult I can think of in the four languages I know.

From the corner of my eye, I see Ringer and Animal have come closer. Owen's pulled out his gun, but so has one of Renato's men.

"You chose quite a disrespectful *child*, Leonardo, making you forget your place," Renato says, and then snaps his fingers at someone. They come over to finally collect the fingers on the table, wiping it down.

Giovanna continues to glare at me, stepping back. So much for the hope that she would've loved me. Renato sits down, suddenly, smugly gesturing for Giovanna to do the same. We remain where we are as he replaces the coffee where the fingers had been. I grimace slightly. Leo's hold on me loosens, moving his hand back to its place upon my back.

"Such as?" Leo finally asks.

"You may have left, returning from curating your own financial success, but if you cut me out, then you're only a Marchetti. Since you so wish to remind us that you're Riccardo's son. Then inherit his legacy on your own."

"Meaning?"

"The Luciano estate and fortune, in my mother's will, *must* be overseen by the matriarch of the family. Her dying wish and final testament as you might remember." Renato gestures to Giovanna, and a vile smile crawls over both their faces. "Your *mother*, my sister is still alive. So, it seems, you'll have to convince *her* to keep any of the Luciano fortune you've received through mama."

"And I'll agree to nothing while you're attached to...her," Giovanna adds smugly, flicking her gaze at me.

"Did Nonna even know you were alive?" Leo asks.

"No."

"You even lied to her?" The condemnation in Leo's voice, almost makes Giovanna's smugness crack.

"It was for the best," Renato interjects. "To make sure Riccardo wouldn't find your mother. Unfortunately, we could not tell mama of Gigi being alive. But she wanted the Luciano name headed by a matriarch as she and her mother before had. And if you were to marry…this one, well, you'd have to be approved and blessed by the current." He gestures to Giovanna and smiles. "Given the circumstances, I don't think that will ever happen."

It's quiet as I look up at Leo, who meets my gaze. His brows furrowed.

"If you want to keep the Luciano *empire*, you'll have to find another bride, I'm afraid. Rethink *your* options, Leonardo," Renato adds.

Leo's hand moves as he brings it up to brush his knuckles across my cheek. I feel the metal of his wedding ring as he looks at me with certainty; no longer hiding the ring behind me.

Giovanna and Renato little merriment in thinking they won falters when they notice how calm he is.

I smile, realizing how in awe I am of Leo's planning. The waiting for right moments and all his back-up plans. He knew Renato had an ace up his sleeve for months, and today he revealed it was Giovanna. That's why Renato *and* Gabriel were cocky in their attempt to control Leo. If they didn't get Leo to fall to his knees to his mother, then they'd just take away the Luciano name, what he built with it. Agree to them or lose everything.

Except, Leo wasn't his mother, his father, his brother, or even his uncle. No, he was Rafaella Maria Luciano's prodigy. Because damn, she was right about her own children.

"You're very behind," I say, breaking the silence. "Because he won twelve moves ago."

"Meaning?" Renato asks.

"I was here just before Rafaella died," Leo explains slowly. "I was here in Italy without you knowing. Unsurprisingly, she didn't trust you, Renato, or any other in the family to care for the Luciano estate. *Her* legacy." He looks over at Giovanna's paling face. "Although…I wonder now if it was *you* controlling the strings this entire time, revenge not just against the Marchettis, but your parents for arranging the marriage you'd come to hate and run from. I wonder how you'll make your brother pay…mother."

Renato sneers at Leo silently, while Giovanna's eyes widen.

"Nonna changed her will." Owen steps forward enough to hand Leo a folder. "It states when I married, my wife would be solely in charge of the Luciano name and fortune. You likely never noticed because we had to share the estate until I would. She trusted only me. Believed in me. Even when I told her the likely-hood of me marrying at all was a fool's errand." Leo pauses, looking over at me. "I planned to just give it all back after I helped Matteo become the Mafia Don. I would've walked away completely, taking what I built only. But Nonna, as always, was right. Much like my wife."

The chairs scrape on the stone patio. Movement snaps all around us as Ringer moves closer, guns drawn. I keep my attention on them before us, while Leo's posture changes to his more commanding presence.

Renato spits, "Liar!"

Leo suddenly tosses the folder, papers flying out towards them. "Read it yourself."

Giovanna sputters, "Impossible, you are not married—"

"We were married before God the night before. Our marriage is recognized by the church," Leo says calmly. "Whether with your approval or not, Autumn is the main proprietor of the Luciano name, and everything owned by it." Leo turns to Renato. "I wondered if those arranged engagements were because of the will, but no, you were just greedy."

Renato sneers, scowling in disdain and then mutters something in Italian.

"She will *never* be part of this family," Giovanna rasps, staring at me in horror. "It does not matter—"

"You're right it doesn't," Leo continues low. "Because you're still technically deceased. Why would I need permission from a dead woman? Your approval means nothing."

She gapes and Renato sputters, face turning red.

"Let me finally introduce myself," I state, letting go of Leo as I move towards her. The sky darkens, storm incoming as I approach Giovanna, who remains in her spot. I smile.

"I am Autumn Watson Luciano, your son's wife. And there's one thing you and I have in common."

"A last name you *stole*?" She hisses.

"No. Remember you *died* as Giovanna Maria Marchetti, unless you got a divorce beforehand." Her eyes darken. I come closer, and whisper, "You're not the only bitch who came back from the dead."

I step away as her face reddens with anger. There are footsteps as Leo takes my hand, leading me back to him.

"You have until the end of the week to decide, Renato," Leo states as his uncle is too fuming to respond. "I'd like a final week with my wife before we leave for the states. Your time is up after that. Both of you."

Leo turns away with me, hands gripping the other. My heart pounds, thundering through my body as the wind picks up from the storm. There's yelling behind us as Giovanna screams. For a moment, I think she'll chase after us to drag Leo back from his she-demon wife, but she doesn't. Neither of us look back, disappearing into the courtyard.

My hand squeezes his and he does it back as we approach the cars. The Crew splits away, getting the vehicles ready to make a run for it before Renato or Giovanna decide on any rash retribution before we leave.

Leo opens the car door for me, and the engines turn on. I flash my gaze to his as I get into the car, finding only furrowed brows and a stern expression. He starts to follow me into the car, but pauses when Giovanna shrieks again in the distance.

"You owe her nothing," I say.

He meets my gaze, and gets into the car, shutting the door as the wind howls.

Chapter 32

Black Widow

It's POURING rain when we enter Rome again.

For once, I don't hate the grey that seems to surround the city as we drive. We're quiet in the car as the wipers swish in the background. I stare out my window, replaying so many moments in my head. The day we were actually married. Getting the credit cards and seeing the paperwork. Small moments of Leo explaining things as I had to help sign things away, because he'd already given me all control. For months I had to pretend that I wasn't in charge of assets worth millions. Not even Jameson knew.

Our marriage did many things, not just protecting him and I in multiple ways, or him keeping access to that much money, but it protected Raffaella and Durante's legacy. From their own children apparently.

We pull up outside the hotel.

"Leave us," Leo says suddenly. Owen and Rudy get out in silence as the rain taps on the roof.

At the same time, we say, "Check in."

I smirk at him as our hands intertwine, moving closer.

"You're the one who faced their supposed dead mother today, you first," I say quietly.

His thumb strokes over my wrist. "Green."

"Leo," I say softly.

"I mourned my mother years ago. I made my peace, I've been to therapy, talked long hours about her, moved on. It's been over twenty years. I don't want to spend any more of my time chasing a ghost."

I reach up, my hand cupping his cheek as he looks at me. My eyes search his face, hidden under his mask I see the pain. Buried deep and not wanting to come out, because then it'd be real. A pain I understood in some capacity. Building a life for a certain purpose and then watching it crumble in your hands.

"You knew!"

I swallow hard, taking a deep breath. "Be honest, Leo."

His eyes shift away, jaw muscles tightening under my palm. He then closes his eyes, breath becoming shallow as I stroke my thumb over his cheek.

"I wanted to reach out to her," he whispers. "A part of me, that young boy, wanting his mom to hold him again. For a moment to just fall for the lies, so a long-time wish could be real. Except, that life was stolen from me."

A tear appears in his eye, slowly falling down his cheek. He blinks, bringing his gaze back to me as he touches my hand. "How much did you understand from her explanation?"

"Not much at all."

"Renato and Fiorella helped fake Giovanna's death, pretending that she got cancer. Her casket in the U.S. is empty after they tricked my father with a body double. He swore he'd never walk on Italy's shores again, so it was easy to hide her here. She said she left because of how violent my father became, which is true, but she wasn't my father's only victim. She knew that."

My stomach twists as he admits a piece of his past. I had guessed that Riccardo likely hurt Leo or Gabriel growing up, but he never quite confirmed it. Until now.

"He mostly calmed when he met Angelina, Matteo's mother,"

Leo says. "She was young and a spitfire, even if she didn't care for Gabriel or me, but she stayed." His eyes become downcast. "In Giovanna's entire explanation, there wasn't a single apology for leaving her children behind."

"It won't change anything, and it's not me you deserve to hear it from, but I'm sorry, Leo. I'm so sorry."

He tugs me over, and I climb onto his lap to hug him fully. His arms wrap around me as I cradle his head against me. Rain pounds upon the top of the vehicle. Leo reaches up, clutching the back of my head.

"When we get home," he says roughly. "I want you to take over the *Italian Lily*. It's become more yours than anyone else's now."

I pull back to look at him. The meaning behind his words, weighing heavy in knowing why that hotel was built. It was to his heritage itself, but also to her and his grandmother. I muster up a faint smile, and nod. But then I hold his face between my hands and speak to him tenderly as he's done with me.

"I will replace every touch that has wronged you, any part of your body and soul will be replaced by my love for you, my dear Leo." Hazel eyes soften. "Where there was pain, there will be pleasure; where there was fear, there will be comfort. I promise with everything that I have, body and soul, my dear husband. We will make it out of this mess alive, and together."

My statement is soft, almost too soft against the rain falling.

He takes my hands, bringing them down between us. Leo kisses my neck, my jaw, and my cheeks while speaking between each kiss.

"We will ride together. Dance in ballrooms. I'll show you California. I'll show you London, Paris, wherever you want. We'll have cereal for dinner. Watch movies late at night. Memorize the contours of each other's bodies." He comes to my lips, and murmurs against them. "We will live, Autumn. For every moment they stole from us."

I kiss him affectionately. His breath hitches as he holds me in the quiet as the rain falls.

"I love you, my dear Watson."

"I love you. You can mourn her, again. It's okay."

He shakes his head. "When all of this is over. When we're home again, then I'll grieve what was lost. Until then, it's making sure we return." He kisses my nose. "You didn't answer the check in."

I chuckle, willing to wait until we get home to help him move on. "Green, mister."

He nods, kissing my cheek and then pats for me to get off as he goes to open the door.

"Honestly, neither of them were that scary," I admit, and he pauses. I shrug. "Know five mafia bosses who are way scarier."

"Am I one?"

"Oh, yeah terrifying. But Al Pacino tops the list." He raises a brow. "Survived all *Godfather* movies and there's *Scarface*."

"No more mobster movies for you." He smirks. I gape in mock horror, glad to see a little joy on his face as we get out into the rain. We rush into the hotel from the downpour as we enter the lobby.

Owen approaches, walking out of the lounge of the hotel. Igor, Michael, and Rudy all stand at the entrance with frowns. Aurelio rushes over, murmuring to Leo and I watch his eyes slide towards the lounge.

"How long?" Leo asks.

"Hour or so," Owen answers as Aurelio steps away to greet some other guests coming in from the rain. "Bartender says he's been quiet and paid for everything but won't stop smoking."

Speaking of mafia bosses.

"Be prepared to shut down the lounge," Leo mutters to Owen, taking my hand as he leads us to the lounge.

Leo strides past our guards. There's barely anyone in the lavish, comfy space. The main bar is empty, apart from one bartender who cleans glasses and flicks their gaze to a section of chairs facing each other. A tendril of smoke comes up from the chair facing away.

"Not Al Pacino," he grumbles, walking us over. There are some patrons, sipping their late afternoon aperitif.

We come around the chair, finding Vincenzo Renaldi grinning

smugly as he lounges back in the red leather seat. He blows a puff of smoke, and I clear my throat from the smell. He wears a white, silk dress shirt paired with an embroidered suit jacket, the lapels encrusted with gems. New necklaces hang from his neck, along with several rings.

"Buongiorno, Luciano. Your hotel services are excellent as always. Class act."

"No smoking," Leo replies gruffly.

"Scuse." He finishes the cigarette, flicking it into his empty glass. He then makes a show of wiping his hands off.

"Matteo still alive?" Leo abruptly asks, expression strict.

"Sí, I keep my promises." Vincenzo leans back in his seat. "I am here because I come with information that I found interesting, and well…" his eyes move to me, smiling, "…how can I refuse an opportunity to potentially make the deal of the century?"

A shift happens over Leo as he slides his hand to the nape of my neck protectively. Coiled tension ripples over his body. Vincenzo likely isn't here to truly start something, but his presence is still unnerving, coming straight into a lion's den by himself.

"Go to our room," Leo murmurs to me.

As I start to leave, Vincenzo says, "Oh, no Luciano, it's your wife I think I should have this conversation with."

"Careful, Renaldi," Leo warns. "I've had a long day, and my patience is thin especially regarding her."

"Remember? I like her." He looks at me, still smiling. "Even to help keep secrets I've just learned of. And perhaps help me understand why body parts were sent to me for confirmation of them."

I glance at Leo, who meets my gaze briefly.

Vincenzo moves his attention to Leo. "Your brother, Gabriel, contacted me. I thought he wanted Matteo, and I was curious to how much he would outbid you, so I humored him. But no…it seems Gabriel doesn't care what happens with your little brother. Poor ragazzo, can't catch a break, eh?"

We remain silent as Vincenzo takes his time finishing his cocktail that doesn't have a butt in it. He licks his lips, putting it back when he finishes. He's definitely one for dramatics, and slowly reminding me of an Arkham villain I never wanted to meet in real life.

"What did Gabriel want, Vincenzo?"

Vincenzo's face pulls together in thought.

"He brought forth some information, but I didn't believe him with his history of lying, you see." He cocks his head, looking up at Leo. "Until he sent me papers. Papers wrapped around body parts, like fresh steak from the meat markets, of a headless polizia."

Fucking crud muffins. Found Roger.

"Your older brother is twisted, Luciano."

"I know."

"Worse than I remember. Perhaps it was that short time in prison." Vincenzo then looks at me, and my stomach drops. "Which you're to blame for, aren't you, Sarah Marie?"

<hr>

L eo didn't want to chase his ghosts, but I kind of wanted to blast mine in the head.

I think I've become more violent of late.

Vincenzo walks into the suite, but not ours. Leo moved the conversation away from the public eye, having us go upstairs to a suite that's more modern than ours. My body buzzes with anxiety as Leo strides in beside me behind Vincenzo. There's a weight on my chest as my mind reels into overdrive.

Leo shuts the door with the Crew outside guarding the entrance. Vincenzo goes to the wet bar, pouring himself a drink as he places a couple of glasses on the coffee table. He grins at Leo, then sits in one of the chairs. Leo and I exchange a look.

"Join me? As long as your marito approves, that is?" Vincenzo begins, opening the bottle he grabbed.

Leo remains standing behind the sofa, furrowed brows and all. I step around to sit in the chair across from Vincenzo.

"I don't need his permission, even with you," I respond,

noticing it's a bottle of Dewar. Slightly poetic. I grab one of the glasses, pouring myself a little.

"Hmm, thought you didn't drink…signora." Vincenzo's voice is low, watching me as he tilts his head.

I lean back into my seat, reminding myself Leo is right behind me. The Crew just outside.

"Special occasion," I respond, letting it stay on the table.

"To speaking with the *real* wife of Leonardo Luciano." He raises his glass.

"What do you want? Because I thought you weren't one who wouldn't openly try to piss off my husband."

"Who says I am?"

"Me."

"Oh, no, no, no, you've got me wrong, signora." He shakes his head, lounging back as the storm rattles the windows. Raindrops streak down the glass. "To explain. I grew up in this world, much like Luciano. Done and seen things that would make grown men cry. Our world you do not trifle with, and yet *we…us*, him and I have enemies that make us stay awake at night. And you it seems…" he points at me, making a clicking sound with his mouth, "…are one of them."

"Think I'm that scary?" I smile carefully, willing to go along whatever route he's taking. I'll take him over the Salvadoris.

"I wondered why he married *you*, especially after my little package from his brother. To spite said brother? Means to an end? Except, Luciano has never used women, not like that, so why you? You're bellissima, but I've seen, well…prettier women. Even ones he's fucked. Unless the god is you, and not him."

His gaze suddenly becomes cautious, looking past me. I glance over my shoulder at Leo who gives him a severe scowl.

"Oh, I assure you he is," I say, grabbing the glass of scotch and glimpse at the amber liquid. My mind yells to keep a cool, clear head. Don't with the alcohol. The glass remains in my hand.

"But you are, eh? Perhaps, capturing him being the final stage of your plan?" My brows pinch together, unsure what he's getting at.

"Seduce the great Leonardo Luciano, then take what's left of Gabriel's power?"

I almost want to laugh. So much for him not thinking I'm a gold digger.

"No," I answer.

"No?" He raises a brow, sipping his drink.

"I didn't even know he was in the mafia until a few months into dating. No clue who he was. No intention of going back to the mobs. I could've left everything behind. All of it, and never be found again."

"Why didn't you?"

"Amore." He cocks a brow again, swirling his drink. "I'd fallen in love with the man I was supposed to be taking down."

Leo's hand suddenly is upon my shoulder, the warmth of his palm spreading through me.

Vincenzo hums to himself, and then says, "And you…Leonardo, still brought a black widow into your web, knowing she could kill you?"

Leo is silent. A crack of thunder comes from outside. I flick my eyes to the pouring rain, swallowing hard against my dry throat. My fingers rub over the smooth glass, wanting to shove Vincenzo into what he's getting at. I doubt it's our love story.

He suddenly finishes his drink, reaching for the bottle to pour a bit more.

"I was unsure why Gabriel decided to tell me," he suddenly speaks in a low and serious tone. My gut tightens as I watch him. "Revenge. Power. Such games I can play, but when they are my own, not others. Rules I swore to my father I would never break."

"Such as?"

Those dark eyes meet mine. "There was smugness in Gabriel's tone. You know it. Don't you?" The weight on my chest worsens as I barely nod my head, forcing myself not to be flung into the past. "It reminded me too much of men my father warned me about. Those *enemies* that keep us awake. Especially when I realized what else he sent me wrapped around those chopped up body parts."

"What?" I clutch the glass; almost afraid I may break it. Please don't let Gabriel send more fucking body parts my way.

With his glass in hand, he gestures to me. "You're the one who got away."

I stare at Vincenzo, and an emotion shifts over his gaze. One I knew too well—pity.

"After Gabriel was released, he visited Italy briefly. We met for drinks, old time sakes, but he had this scar on his face." Leo becomes deathly still behind me, his hand rigid upon my shoulder. "I asked him if it was from prison, he said it was from a bitch who refused him, but she got what she deserved in the end."

A flash of screaming. Glass shattering. Pain radiating up my arm.

"Sarah Marie Mitchell." His voice is slow, enunciating each part of my old name like a dagger to my chest as he leans forward. "The only woman I know to survive Gabriel Cesare Marchetti."

I knock the fucking drink back.

"Burned the pictures, for your sake and mine, signora," he continues. "Although one could barely tell it was you. A miracle by God you're alive."

"No. Spite," I rasp, putting the empty glass down.

Son of a nutcracker, Gabriel even has that. My mind reels wondering how Roger even fucking got those records. Fucker probably kept them for himself.

"Did you see them, Leonardo? Is that why you didn't punish her for infiltrating your empire?"

"He hasn't..." My voice trails away when Leo's hand leaves my shoulder.

I look over as Leo's expression shifts. His jaw tenses and the scowl he wears deepens. He averts his gaze from me, but across his face I see it. Haunting pain. I stare at him with shock.

"Oh, he has, signora," Vincenzo murmurs.

Leo finally brings his gaze to mine. His eyes feel like they should be vacant with how hollow and melancholic they feel. A simmering darkness that won't leave you, and a handful of guilt. Shadows. *My* shadows.

"When?" I rasp.

"The estate," he answers.

Suddenly it hits me why he lost control. Why he left Steve in that room. Why he tortured the last of the men who assaulted me. Gone after every single person who hurt me and haunted my steps. It wasn't just that he heard what they could've done, wanted to, thought of, or even had…he'd *seen* what they did. What they left of me.

"I understand why you filled that Coliseum with blood, Leonardo," Vincenzo says. "Nothing will make us see red more. You can never trust a man who delights in making women bleed."

"So, you didn't make a deal with Gabriel, then?" I ask, turning my attention back to him.

"Remember, I'm not stupid, signora." He puts his drink down. "No, I thought out of the goodness of me that you should know your little secret isn't as secret anymore. But…" he raises his hands, folding them in his lap with a shadow of a smile, "…I could help keep it."

Ah, there's the endgame. Blackmail.

"You sure have a knack for seeing how far you can get without him killing you," I say bluntly. "Threatening me isn't really going to help you."

"I would never threaten you, signora." He makes a clicking noise, shaking his head. "No, a suggestion of business between… *friends* in helping secrets stay behind closed doors. *I* may understand what you did, and what do I care if you fucked up the American mafia? Do it again if you so wish. But if those across the ocean discovered their esteemed, mafia don married a polizia sympathizer, well…his reputation could be in jeopardy."

Menacing, agitation crawls under my skin. Perhaps it's because someone is trying to use what I'd done against me against Leo. To make me a puppet as Roger had tried.

I look over at Leo, something silent passing between us. I hold my hand up for him to come back over and he kisses my wrist tenderly. Softening my expression, I try to relay to him that I'm not mad he'd seen the photos. If there's one thing I knew at the beginning of us, it was how paranoid and detailed he was in finding information. Honestly, not surprising, and probably should talk about it, but not right now, especially in front of Vincenzo. My hand cups his cheek as his expression becomes tender.

"Do I tell him or you?" I ask.

"You," Leo answers.

"Tell me what?" Vincenzo asks.

"Do you know how I fucked over Gabriel?" I ask.

"You infiltrated his businesses and many others. Selling out to the feds." He leans forward, grabbing his glass.

"I was a hacker and about to start my Masters' when the police recruited me. The cop sent to you was my ex-handler." He pauses before taking a sip. "I created something that allowed me access into any mainframe without being detected. It's best used when you know what you're looking for in servers, banks, camera feeds, business networks, you name it. I went into those clubs to locate where it was best to unthread their webs. Like you said...black widow."

Vincenzo tilts his head, fascination flickering.

"Back then, I had to be physically closer to where I wanted to hack, not anymore. It's now versatile to the point I can hack into any computer network from the 90s to today's technology. Just need good internet connection."

His eyes narrow, watching me closely. "But you sold it. I saw the documents."

"They got a dupe." I smile, while his starts to disappear. "You saw the photos. I trusted no one, not even the police. What they got was a self-sabotaging program. No bene." I grab the Dewar, pouring some into my glass. "So, you can guess who has the *real* program."

Vincenzo takes a long drink from his glass, flicking his gaze to

Leo. I pick mine up, swirling it a little as Vincenzo tries to smile at me again. "You, signora?"

"No..." I hold the glass up for Leo, "...him."

Vincenzo becomes very still.

"You said you know what he can do on his own," I say, slightly loving the fear in Vincenzo's eyes as Leo takes the scotch. "So, signor, if you want to try blackmailing me that's what you're up against. I gave my husband the power to drain your accounts, and you wouldn't even know until it was too late. Or better yet, give the polizia everything. I bet they'd love to lock you up forever." I grin politely. "Your move, Vincenzo."

A moment passes, thunder crashing outside.

Suddenly, Vincenzo laughs, throwing his head back as he gets up and puts his drink down. He speaks in Italian, quickly talking as he points to me. Leo doesn't respond, just sips the drink I gave him.

"You are a more fascinating opponent than him, no offense, Leonardo," he says, switching languages again. "Ruthless beauty. Oh, you two will be fantastic *gods* to work with." I give him a puzzled look. "Come now, your partnership with Salvadori is waning, you need someone else in Italy to do business with." He gestures to himself. "May I propose me?"

Vincenzo may give me whiplash. He has a twisted and weird way of doing business. Still better than a head in the mail or parents back from the dead. The bar was low.

"If you ever learn to stop putting your foot in your mouth, Renaldi," Leo interjects. "Then you'd learn I was already planning to do so."

Vincenzo's smile broadens. "Oh?"

"My organizations will be cut from all Salvadori enterprises," Leo continues. "The Luciano fortune and name is now under the control of my wife. I was prepared to move on without connections in Italy, but there can be discussions to maintain lucrative cash flow for us both."

I take the cue, getting up as he takes the seat I left. Vincenzo's eyes go alight, flashing between us as I stroke my hand over Leo's shoulder. Respect, I think, comes over his face. His smile still wily, but softening.

"If you want to keep any chance of having such a business relationship…" Leo frowns at Vincenzo, lounging back with glass in hand, "…keep my wife's name out of your mouth. Otherwise, I will help the police disembowel you and then sell everything you own back to Renato as penance."

Vincenzo almost seems to wave him off, unbothered. "No, I would never dream of it. I have too much respect for your wife." I cock my head at him as he sits back down. "I enjoy the dramatics to learn *why* and *who* potential business partners are. You can learn a lot about someone when certain options are given. No one wants a *weak* partner."

He becomes serious again, watching me as he finishes his drink.

"And what have you learned, Vincenzo?" I ask quietly.

"You truly do not bend," he answers with a solemn expression. "No woman should ever endure such cruelty as you have. I am sorry that was done to you. And glad you found a…*god* who's as unbending as you."

Odd understanding passes between us. A flicker, and I think I see the real man behind the discord of his antics. The moment passes as Vincenzo quickly switches back to his relaxed persona again.

"Luciano, you have to admit your family is fucking insane. Starting with Gabriel, who in my opinion, you should take care of soon. He's escalating. Sending body parts to people? Does he think this is a movie?"

My stomach twists. Time for me to leave.

I squeeze Leo's shoulder, and he gives me a look and then to the doors. I bend down to kiss his temple, relief flooding that I can go scream into a pillow soon.

"Ciao, signor. Don't keep putting your foot in your mouth," I say.

"Ciao, signora! Pleasure talking with you and may we have

many more intriguing discussions in the future." I get to the door and hear him say, "I'll help you kill Gabriel for her sake."

I step through, closing the door behind me. The Crew all look at me as I give a long exhale. "He's fine. Just one or two of you stay here."

I head to the elevator, hands beginning to shake.

"You alright, *barchën*?"

"I need fucking ice cream." And a pillow.

Chapter 33

Rocky Road

I WANT to take a nap for a month, but a pint of gelato will do for now. Rudy hands it to me, and I smile before I stab it with my spoon.

"Long ass day," I murmur.

"Ja."

We stand at the balcony doors, watching the storm outside. The gelato does help bring down some of my nerves. I want this day to be over. I want this week to be over. This entire year actually. My mind jumbles trying to concentrate on each piece of news. Giovanna and Renato's betrayal. Vincenzo's chaotic way of conducting deals. Gabriel sending body parts. "*…like a movie.*"

A shiver runs over me, not from the gelato, as I recall what Vincenzo said and another flash of the past. A scar, huh? I don't remember that part.

"*Barchën?*" Rudy asks, touching my shoulder.

I shake off the thoughts, and I look up at his concerned face. "You know what I would love?" He grunts in reply. "Three days working in the garage with rock music playing. Each day a bike ride and greasy takeout for dinner."

He chuckles. "Good plan."

"Just have to get home in one piece."

"We will. And we'll do that as soon as we get back."

I have another bite, sighing as the rain pours. "Hopefully, cause I'm not having as much fun arguing with mobsters. Surprise, surprise. But given the circumstances, I guess I should get used to telling off mafia bosses, huh? Pretty good record today. Three already."

Quiet again, until he asks, "Are…you fine staying in the mafia?"

I freeze with the spoon in my mouth. I look up at the big man, who tilts his head in question. Blue eyes calm and gentle.

"Yeah, as frustrated as these people make me, yeah," I say softly. "Not the life I would've bet on having, but I've accepted it. But… what about you? It was never the Crew's intention to stay."

"Neither was yours."

"Touché."

"Spartan and you would never keep us prisoners. If we truly wanted to, we could leave."

"Why don't you? Maybe go after bigger dreams?"

He smirks, shaking his head. "No, this is what I want."

"Really?" I eye him teasingly.

"I lived a full life before him," Rudy says roughly, crossing his arms over his chest. "All I care about now is the club. I'm content being a *Forgotten Demon*. Good with driving his ass around, and now yours, *barchën*." He shrugs. "Good at being a mobster, too."

I snort. "Maybe we both are."

He glances outside. "I need to check with Igor and Garett. Hopefully, the boss doesn't take too long with that anarchic gangster."

I laugh under my breath. Yeah, that's a way to describe him. "Well, it's good weather for me to sit back and watch a movie. So, I'll do that."

"Call me if you need, *barchën*."

He starts to leave, heading for the door. Something tugs at me, melancholic like as if I need to start gathering answers before the end. I suddenly ask, "Ever gonna tell me what that means? Your nickname for me?"

He stops, turning back to me with a quizzical look. "You haven't looked it up? With all the language learning?"

I shake my head, walking over to put the gelato down on the counter. "I figured you didn't tell me for a reason, and if it was special to you that I wouldn't pry. It'd have felt…wrong to find out without you wanting to tell me."

The all-around driver, ex-wrestler, mobster looks at me tenderly. Rudolph slowly walks back over, towering over me as I tilt my head back to see his face. Surprise flicks over me as he cups my face gently, placing a kiss on the top of my head.

"It means 'little bear' and is a term of endearment for someone we like, but for me…someone I cherish who's a fighter."

I stare up at the first *Forgotten Demon* I met.

Rudolph, the first one whom I learned their name and spoke to. I remember the confusion on his face when I thanked him outside the *Italian Lily*. The usually quiet, frowning giant to everyone else. And then I remember the first time he called me barchën after that long ass day in the café. Before bike rides. Before late night talks with Isaac. Before knowing the truth.

"Danke," I whisper. "Rudy."

"Willkommen…*little bear*." Another affectionate kiss is placed upon my hair. He squeezes my shoulders gently, smiling as he turns away. "Ah, you should know it's commonly used with men." I snort laughter. "Figured you wouldn't care."

I shake my head as he winks, leaving the room.

Tears gather, and I quickly wipe them away. I put away the gelato and go sit on the sofa bringing my legs up as I lay my chin on my knees. And then oddly, my mind goes quiet. It becomes blank as I stare out at the rain. I wait for the anxiety to come from yelling and confronting people today, but it doesn't.

For now, I'm fine. Or perhaps I've reached the numbed-out part.

Every few moments, it seems like the storm will let up, but then it continues raging.

Sighing, I start looking for the remote when I hear the door open. I jolt slightly, turning as Leo closes the door behind him and removes his jacket.

"How'd the rest of the meeting with Harvey Dent go?" I ask.

"Who?"'

"Vincenzo. He doesn't seem to be off his rocker enough to emulate Joker." Thank goodness.

He sighs heavily, coming over to sit next to me. "Well enough, given the start of that conversation."

"Seriously, I think he has a death wish."

"He's never been the straightforward type, sometimes helpful and sometimes… extremely annoying." Leo leans back, placing his arm over the back of the sofa behind me. His leg comes up, crossing over the other casual like as if he just got home from a regular meeting. "Renaldi's organization will replace Salvadori's. He'll get a bigger cut in profit margins, but it won't put us in the red and I'll continue business in Italy and Europe without Renato. Just smaller payout for us."

"Why does something tell me it's still a lot of money?"

"To the average household, yes. To a CEO of multiple companies and businesses, still yes," he smirks. "But no more buying buildings on a whim."

"Oh, whatever shall you do," I tease, smirking back.

He reaches over, stroking back some of my hair. "I should've told you—"

I shake my head, grabbing his hand and not wanting to think about it. "It's alright. I was a mess at the time, and the few weeks after. Probably best you didn't because I think I would've spiraled more knowing that the photos still existed."

"They don't," he murmurs. "Enigma and Isaac helped make it all disappear. What Gabriel received likely came straight from Caltz."

Yup, one last thing to use against me. I exhale shakingly. "Thank you."

Leo's arm moves around my shoulder, tugging me against him as he loosens a long breath.

"What's the next step?" I ask.

"We wait. Enjoy what time we have left in Rome, then go home."

"Pretend we're on our honeymoon after we *just* got married the other night?" I slide my gaze to him.

He whispers, "We're just a pair of newlyweds."

I giggle quietly, laying my head against his shoulder. His other hand sits on his lap, and I put my hand into it, holding it gently. We sit quietly as the storm continues.

"Vincenzo's throwing a party," Leo says suddenly, and I blink rapidly at him. "To celebrate our future collaborations, and our marriage. It was a party already happening, but he wants an excuse for us to show face."

"A visual of us being on his side and not Renato's, I'm guessing?"

"Exactly. I told him yes."

Nervous laughter bubbles up. Good for Vincenzo's partnership, even better to give the finger to Renato. A public display of severance.

"There'll be a lot of people, just as a warning," he says.

"Not surprised. But hey a party to basically spite your family more? Sounds like the perfect gift from him," I muse. "Better than other gifts."

He rubs his thumb over my wrist.

"You were incredible in there with him," he says, and a flicker of pride pulses through me. "You've always had a spine of steel, unwilling to bend, but I am proud of you, Autumn." Tilting my head, I catch his eyes that are filled with adoration. "Not to mention standing your ground against my family, even calling Giovanna a bitch."

"She started it."

The tone of my voice makes us both suddenly laugh. I press my face against his shoulder, unable to stop likely from pent up nerves.

Our laughter finally subsides, and I grip his hand as I look up at him. Exhaustion lining his face, but less worn.

"I'm proud of you, too, Leo. None of this has been easy, for either of us, but I know especially for you. It's not easy to have your life turned upside down and twisted after putting so much work into a future that may not be."

He listens to me solemnly, and then looks out the balcony. His brows furrow, mouth working a little.

"I didn't want to stay in the mafia in fear of becoming like any of them, especially my father," he says quietly. "Giovanna can be added to that list now. The other night, I almost was my father with Matteo." He closes his eyes tightly. "I realized I *am* very capable of becoming any of them. Always have. And hope that as long as I always have you, my dear Watson, I will not."

"You don't need me for that, Leo."

"Yes, I do." His voice is rough as he opens his eyes. Hazel irises become misty, almost numb. "For now. Because for the first time in my life, I don't mind being the ruthless mafia boss. To burn everything to the ground if I must. The only one keeping me from doing so is you. Not because I don't trust myself, but due to me having enough."

He leans in close to place his forehead against mine, breath tickling across my skin.

"I am tired, dear Watson." The strain in his voice makes my heart ache. "But having you beside me helps me remember the compassion you see in me. No matter how ruthless I can be."

Lips press against mine, kissing me reverently. So much of me wants to tell him that he's always been kind and compassionate. All those pieces were there before me, and it's what helped me fall in love with him. Except now, those aren't the words he needs. After facing fears and nightmares that have come true this past week.

Right now, the merciless mafia boss just needed to know he's loved, and that his heart is protected.

Chapter 34

Jupiter Descends

Yeah, I needed a month-long nap.

I stare at myself in the mirror, glancing over my attire for Vincenzo's party tonight. It's been five days since the mafia boss shit show. Leo and I have tried to "relax", meaning attempted to make the best of our last week here. Even with 2-3 guards following everywhere, we've been on edge. It's odd that we've been here for just over a month. Doesn't feel like it as I glance at the suitcases already packed for us to leave the day after tomorrow.

Feels like a year since we left the U.S.

And Nan just made it feel longer.

I glance at the phone in my hand. She's leaving for Georgia. Permanently.

With a sigh, I put the phone away and grab my corset. I'm wearing black silk pants with a matching blouse, cuffed sleeves, and a slight cowl-neck lining. The under bust corset is maroon velvet. My outfit chosen by Leo himself, including the fancy sandals instead of heels. Thank goodness.

I stop with corset in hand, staring at the bed. At first, I thought Nan's phone call was just to give her opinion about Leo and I getting married. A few jabs here and there about him being secretive and trying to act nonchalant about the situation, including us being gone for so long. I didn't tell her anything like us lying about being in Boston, but then she brought up her recent trip to Georgia. Someone else is pregnant, her grand-nephew is starting pre-school, and something about a girl's trip. That's when she admitted she's moving.

Her voice was solemn bringing up that she liked the weather there more. To be around her family and help them as more babies come into the picture. I could hear the craving for a normal life. The softness there, but also the fear. Nan knew she'd never have the peaceful life she wanted in New York.

I couldn't blame her. And I didn't have the heart to take that away when she had the opportunity to take it. Honestly, I think the only reason she ever stayed was because of the guy who was fleecing her, otherwise she would've left years ago and took me with her.

Except, now *she's* leaving.

After Steve broke in, the cameras fucked with, the letter, and me being chased out of New York…deep down I knew she would never feel safe again, even with the renovations and security upgrades. She became distant, literally and figuratively. I understood, but it hurt. I know she loves me, but a faint pain is there.

My thoughts are brought back to the present when Leo enters the bedroom, adjusting his dark dress shirt. He hasn't shaved, stubble shadowing his jaw. He pauses when he sees me, and I hold up the corset. He comes over, taking it from me and places it around my body as I bring my elbows up. He helps adjusts its position, bringing my arms back down before he starts lacing me up.

"Who was on the phone?" He asks as I hear the ribbon slide through an eyelet.

"Nan."

"How is she?"

I swallow hard. "Fine."

Leo's hands slide over my body, smoothing down the velvet before tightening the corset. My breathing slows, closing my eyes as I feel the constriction around my torso. Peace from the compression seeps through me.

"Nan's moving to Georgia. Permanently," I say quietly. Leo's fingers continue working. "She said she'll talk with us when we get back, but she…is giving the bookstore to me. "

"Are you okay with that?"

"Yeah. Was a dream at one point, taking over for her, but never thought she'd actually leave New York or the bookstore entirely." I sigh as he tightens it further down. "I can't blame her."

Leo ties off the lacing, tucking away the end pieces beneath my corset. His hands glide up to my shoulders, resting there as he kisses my head.

"People change," he murmurs.

"I know." I reach up and touch his hand. "She wasn't going to tell me yet until we returned, but…we'd been gone so long she wasn't sure when we'd be back. It sounds like she didn't want to wait."

Sighing, I walk away to finish getting ready. Leo pulls on his shoulder gun holster, pulling on his suit jacket to conceal them. He checks his cuffs as I check my hair, and then grab my small knife and hide it under my corset against my ribcage. It disappears completely as I slide my hands down the velvet material. Leo comes over, pausing me to cup my cheek.

His eyes search mine, brow slightly furrowing. I take his hand, kissing his wrist.

"I'm alright. I knew it was coming. She's been slowly stepping back…just didn't think it'd be this soon. And I think she's mad we got married, too."

"We'll talk with her when we get home," he says softly. "If you want."

I shake my head. "She wants peace, her family, and to feel safe again. Her life, not mine."

He inhales a long breath but doesn't say anything more as he kisses my cheek. Leo takes my hand, leading me out of the room. I shove aside the unsure feelings of change, focusing on his hand around mine as we leave for Vincenzo's party.

Vincenzo's villa, one of many apparently, is just outside of Rome. The place is huge as it feels like we're pulling up outside a castle. A long drive leads to the main entrance, past a maze of hedges, groves, and side paths I'm guessing for employees. Once parked, and I step out with Leo, I look up at the three-story building. It's massive with bright lights illuminating the stonework. There are dozens of cars, lined up to be parked by valets as people enter the villa. Our other car with the rest of our bodyguards pulls up.

"Keep your heads on a swivel. Only hover," Leo instructs Michael.

"Yes, boss."

Michael, Igor, and Garett will be the only ones inside with us tonight. Owen's taking care of last-minute details before we depart. Rudy and Animal are in the other car but will be leaving to oversee sending Matteo back to the states tonight. We knew Vincenzo would have his own security, I can plainly see that just looking at the entrance and the dozens of his men standing around. Leo was one of the few allowed to even bring his own. Otherwise, it's just hundreds of fancily dressed people.

Leo takes my hand as we head inside. There's a large courtyard that leads through another archway, and then doors to a grand foyer entrance.

"What is this place?" I ask.

"Vincenzo's favorite villa, although it's constructed more like a fortress or castle," Leo answers, glaring at one of the security guards who quickly looks away. "He uses it for large parties like this for the...*elite* as it were."

"Meaning?"

"Government officials will sometimes have parties here, along with other big hitters."

"For a price and protection?"

He flicks his gaze to me, and I nod in understanding.

More people are seen mingling, moving with us towards the inside. The grand foyer has two large staircases leading up towards he second floor, winding up into a large circular balcony. Everything is extravagant as I note other hallways, one I see towards the back outside. Honestly, it seems like Vincenzo was trying to modernize a palace that once stood during Rome's height of success, merging modern and renaissance art.

Tingling of warning goes up my spine as my eyes slide towards the guests and servers. Instinctively, I step closer to Leo. We go up the stairs and then another set that leads us to the rooftop terrace.

If I thought below looked like Roman times, this took the cake.

Columns line the sides, decorated in gold and vines, between them are fires burning in bronze bowls. Red and violet sheer curtains drape above us, rippling in the breeze. People fill the space, dressed in suits and gowns. Tables are adorned with decorations and flowers. There are stone railings bordering the entire rooftop that you can see out towards the groves, maze, and gardens of the villa. On the left and right, there's walkways to smaller terraces just as brightly decorated. There has to be over a thousand people here. One hell of a party.

"So, did he really love *Gladiator*...or am I stereotyping?" I whisper to Leo.

He snorts. "You saw his club. He's excessive with his show of power and influence. And he loves showing off to visiting *friends*."

"How Commodus of him," I say sarcastically. Leo snorts, but keeps his stoic expression.

A shout comes from the side, and I flinch. It's Vincenzo, who quickly comes over to greet us. From there, everything blurs with the party. Everyone mostly speaks Italian, making my head swim as I try to translate what words I catch, but then stop when

French, Portuguese, and another language I don't recognize are spoken next. Most conversations are geared towards Leo, thankfully. There are also congratulations on our marriage, but I catch snide looks and narrowed gazes, too. Women try at times to fawn over Leo, but get taken aback whenever he glares at them. Vincenzo seems to enjoy witnessing it, waving them off as I stay next to Leo.

From time to time, I look around and find our three bodyguards who are stationed around the party. Garett and Igor appear grumpy each time I see them, while Michael between his serious scowls will give me a half-hearted smile when I look in his direction.

While mingling, I note more hallways that lead to other stairs or rooms. One to the bathrooms I presume, and servers keep reappearing from the other terraces. My anxiety runs over my skin. I breathe, telling myself to relax and I'm just on edge due to the very large and loud crowd.

I don't dare to stand too close to the terrace edge or end up near it.

While Leo speaks with a couple of other men, I look up and notice it's a full moon. I continue staring up at the night sky, feeling him caress my skin as I sip my sparkling water. Another souring in my stomach hits me, yanking at me.

You're in a party of mobsters and jealous women, that's why you're on edge.

"Check in," Leo whispers next to my ear.

I look at him, finding concerned hazel eyes that flick over my features. "Green."

He takes my left hand, kissing it adoringly and there's some murmurs and chuckles from the group he's been talking with. Leo stands straighter as he turns his head towards Vincenzo in a menacing manner. The others in the small group, step back, but Vincenzo doesn't move. He just grins merrily. He says something, waving them away and they leave.

"He's going to scare away potential partners, signora," Vincenzo muses.

"Then they're not good enough to do business with," I retort sweetly.

He grins broader, chuckling to himself as he sips his drink. "You both shall be missed when you leave Italy. You'll have to visit soon. Don't take as long as usual, eh, Luciano?"

"If you make the trip worthwhile," Leo rebukes.

"Of course, but you must admit Italy herself is reason enough to be admired from up close, not a distance." He gestures to the night sky and gardens beyond us, but his gaze stays on me. "All her glory should be revered."

He winks at me. Kiss ass.

He switches to Italian, speaking quickly with Leo as he gestures to the party. I go back to star gazing and then out to the large maze. Why wouldn't I be surprised if a minotaur statue was in there somewhere?

A breeze shifts, blowing curtains towards us. A scent drifts under my nose, a musky one with the lingering smell of stale cigars and a spicy cologne I can't place. My mind sparks, blaring in warning as I glance towards where the wind comes from. Just guests. Bodyguards in black.

"I'll be back," Leo murmurs against my ear. "Stay within our security's sights."

I nod, forcing a smile as he follows Vincenzo and two other men. Important looking men. All four head towards one of those hallways, and I'm assuming they want to discuss something privately.

I place my drink onto a wandering waiter's tray, then glance back out to the gardens. I must admit, everything here is beautiful. Music plays, switching to something more upbeat. Warning flicks over my skin again. I look over my shoulder. People are dancing and there's more than before. I'd caught word about fireworks going off sometime tonight, something Vincenzo does for every party. Remembering that, I move away from the terrace edge and start to walk between some of the columns.

The music gets louder, people chattering and laughing as I stop near a table with desserts. I flick my gaze, seeing Igor has moved. Michael looks at a group of women talking. My gaze keeps moving, and I glance towards where I'd been. My stomach drops. Warning screams as my breaths become shallow, telling me I should've listened to my damn gut.

His head slowly turns towards me.

How the fuck did he get in here?

I turn and head down between the columns. I weave through people, and someone shouts right before there's a boom in the distance. Fireworks go off, glittering as popping noises fill the air. The sky becomes alight as I scan for Leo or Vincenzo. Which hall was it again?

My mind spins, flailing to think, except fear overtakes it all. It blurs my thoughts as I pick up my pace. I rush towards one of the halls to the stairs but come upon a huge crowd coming up to watch the fireworks. I step to the side, searching for one of our bodyguards, but can't see them. They're lost to the crowd and movement, booms muting out the cheers.

I try to skirt past some people as the crowd thins, soon realizing it's the wrong hall I needed to find Leo. I turn around, determined to find him, but run right into someone.

"Scuse," I say, backing up, but rough hands grab my forearm.

Cold terror slides over me as I rip my arm out of their hold. I look up and find dark brown eyes.

I forgot how big he is, tall and broad like a heavyweight bouncer. His black hair is grown out, swept back with too much gel and a beard. His skin is worn and overly tanned, like he forgot to use sunscreen for months. There's a scar above his right eye, cutting through his thick brow.

The past flickers as I finally remember a glass bottle flying; my hands cut from grabbing it too hard.

He looks down at the hand that had touched me, and then brings it up to slide his tongue over his palm. I feel sick as he gives me a sinister smile that makes my blood run cold.

"Still a fighter, eh?" His voice is raspy and deep, threat lacing it. "Marriage hasn't tamed you yet...Sarah."

My hands tremble as I take another step back. Pops occur above, pinks and yellows burst through the sky behind him. It adds a chilling ambiance as I swallow hard, gripping every ounce of courage I have.

"Buonasera, Gabriel."

Chapter 35

Olympus Falls

GABRIEL'S GAZE moves down my body, dragging his eyes with a vicious darkness. He takes another step towards me, and I move back. Fireworks continue to burst, keeping the crowd's attention.

"Enjoy my gift?" He asks.

Snippets of the past ram into me. Pieces I've blocked out, forgotten on purpose, come rushing back as Leo's older brother prowls towards me.

"Not original."

"What is now these days?" He says, stepping to the side to block my view of the party. I keep my hands to the side, not daring to grab my knife yet. Wait, Autumn, wait.

"What do you want?"

"Now who's unoriginal, Sarah?"

"Don't say that name."

"Oh, but your handler had *so* much to say about you…Sarah." He chuckles low. "He fucking hated you. But you lasted longer than him. He caved within a few hours. A pity *he* was your handler. Disgraceful, begging coward."

My chest hurts, heart pounding.

"You last longer than Steve, too? He was always a greedy, cock-sucking twit. How long did my brother work on him before he squealed?"

I flick my gaze to the stairwell, which feel too far to make before he caught me.

"I'm getting what I want, girl," he warns, and the smile disappears. "I'm getting everything back what my brother and you took from me. Because it wasn't just him screwing me over, huh? Even now…Mrs. *Luciano*."

My mouth remains shut even as I want to scream. Yell. Anything, but my gut tells me to stay silent. Don't give him anything. Wait.

"My brother is going to pay," he continues, beginning to slide his hand into his suit jacket. Movement occurs behind him, and I do everything to keep my facial expression the same. "He will beg me like a beat dog to its owner before I'm done with him. The Marchetti *and* Luciano fortunes will be *mine*."

"Never," I rasp.

"Says his Achilles' heel." My breath shudders, trembling moving up my arms. I allow myself to show fear, looking horrified at him. "Tell me, Sarah…how long will *Leo* last before I break him?"

He pulls out a knife and there's a blast from the fireworks above. Cheers follow as the sky lights up. Suddenly, Garett rushes up behind Gabriel to grapple him. They come barreling towards me in a wrestling match as I stumble to the side. I barely make it out of their way before Gabriel flips him over. A scream is caught in my throat when Gabriel jams the knife into Garett's neck, blood pouring out. There's gurgling as he rips it across his throat brutally.

I run into the crowd as another firework blasts, but it shakes the building. The shouts of excitement change to terror as another blast booms. Columns start to fall, and I realize it's not fireworks, but explosives in the villa. Sparkling fireworks still shine over the terrace, while gunshots fill the air next. I crouch as a blast rocks the terrace, causing another column to crash to the marble floor. People scream and run as the party is turned into a war zone. There's a grunt behind me, and I glance back to see Igor fight Gabriel next.

The knife is knocked out of his hands, but Gabriel's too quick. I stare in horror, frozen as Gabriel gets a hold of his head and there's a scream. He then twists his neck, giving a deafening snap as Igor slumps to the ground. Gabriel stands over his body with a menacing expression.

People shove past, running for the stairs. Michael is suddenly beside me, and shoots towards Gabriel, who ducks behind the mob of terrified guests. Michael grabs my arm, shoving me.

"Run!"

"Michael—"

"Go! Now!"

I scramble as Michael goes after Gabriel. People scream, trying to escape the bloodbath. I work my way through the stream of people, aiming for the other stairs as the building shakes from an explosion. Stones fall as I make it closer, but then see two men dressed in all black standing far too still as they search the crowd that shoves for escape. One sees me, points and starts in my direction. Spinning around, I race back, but a hand grabs my arm. I scream, dragged back towards another hall away from the chaos.

More hands grab me, yanking at me as someone rips at my hair. I scream again, but it's useless against the cacophony of terror. I rip my arm down, breaking from one of them and jab an elbow down. And then again into a groin. The first guy bows over as I use the disruption to punch the other guy in the nose. He stumbles, stunned mostly as I break free completely. I run, coming around a corner and fear shakes me as I see it's a dead end.

I turn, grabbing the knife hidden under my corset as they come around the corner. Both snarl at me, one of them pulling out a gun. The other snaps his hand out, tugging the firearm down.

"He wants her alive."

"Can be without working legs."

"I ain't fucking losing money cause you're pissed your balls were busted," the first one growls, then looks at me. "Come on now."

"Fuck off!" I spit, flipping the blade in my hand as I get ready to defend myself.

The other chuckles. "Oh, look, someone's had lessons, eh?"

Another blast shakes the building, shots ricocheting. One man lunges forward, and I swipe at him nicking his arm. He yelps but is quick to snap back and knocks the knife from my hand. I kick below his knee but I'm knocked off balance and tumble. My body lands hard against the ground, knocking the wind out of me. My eyes widen as the mercenary might let his buddy shoot me now from the way he glares at me. I scramble back on all four limbs, my corset digging into my hip as they come for me.

"No!" I scream with all my might, panic driving me as I search for anything to help.

Suddenly, a shot rings out, closer than any of the others have been. The one pointing a gun at me seconds ago, abruptly slumps to the ground with a gasping sound. His weapon clatters to the floor. The other turns, reaching for his weapon and dodges the next bullet fired. He doesn't get far before his head snaps back, falling to the ground dead. Breathing hard, I stare up at Leo who snarls with violent rage. He shoots the other in the head.

My voice is caught in my throat as he comes to help me. My legs shake as I start to stand, but then see more men coming around the corner. One of them brandishing a knife.

"Leo—!" I shriek as he spins to face them.

I stumble back in sheer horror, bumping into a wall as my body stiffens. Time slows as I watch Leo fight. He's swift even as his gun is knocked from his hands, quickly going into hand-to-hand combat, punching and snapping one's neck with a frightening crack. He's vicious, pulling out his other gun and shoots him in the chest twice. Two more come around the corner, and he shoots one in the torso, making him drop to his knees. The last one, dodges Leo, trying to knock the gun from his hand again. Abruptly, Leo lets go of it, stunning the other as he crouches, grabs the knife from the dead man, and jams it into his knee. The man howls, stumbling as Leo then thrusts it into his jugular.

My stomach clenches. I finally shut my eyes, trying to ignore the sounds. But I can't escape them as I listen to Leo kill the men who'd come after us. Too quickly, the noise mutes.

The fireworks have stopped. Screams are distant, likely anyone who could escape from the terrace is below. Clinks of brass hit the floor. And then heavy steps come toward me, and a hand touches my shoulder.

I jolt back, snapping my eyes open. Leo.

"You're safe," he says in a rough voice. "I'm here. You're safe."

His hand is placed against my cheek. I nod, trying to remember how to breathe as I notice the blood upon his hands. Freckles of crimson on his face.

Holy fuck. Leo just took out six men by himself.

Leo steps away quickly, dips down towards the men he killed, grabbing the knife and another gun. He turns holding his hand out to me. I take it as he leads me around the corner towards the stairs I'd been aiming for.

"No," I abruptly say, stopping him. "They were waiting for me there. The other stairs."

He takes my direction, and I follow him back through the main terrace where bodies and crumbled stone lay everywhere. Body-guards and guests lay dead. There's more shrieks and the building trembles as another explosive goes off.

Did Gabriel bring a fucking militia? And how did he hire them?

We quickly get to the other stairwell, and I almost trip over my own feet when I see Igor's body. Everything hurts as I remember his scream and the snap of his neck. I then see a man slumped against a wall with his throat slit. Another with his head twisted wrong. And then one of the women who'd sneered at me, gaping towards the sky with blood all over her chest.

Panic starts to take over as I realize I don't see Michael anywhere. I stumble right before we get to the stairs, tugging on Leo. "Wait, Michael…he—"

"He's dead, Autumn. They all are."

I freeze, staring at him in horror. So badly I want to fall to my knees, scream and cry. Michael's final shout to me, shoving me away as he went after Gabriel, who had just killed our other body-guards. My heart pounds in my ears.

"Autumn. Look at me."

"He killed them," I gasp, gripping my hair.

"Dear Watson, look at me."

Leo clutches my face, making me look at him. He holds his eyes with mine, speaking steadily, "Listen to my voice. We have to leave. Focus on getting out of here. Do you understand?"

I whimper as the darkness tries to close in. Blood. Crack of bone. Igor's screams. Gabriel licking his hand.

"My dear wife, focus on me."

Get out.

"You know how to help us get out."

Get out.

"Focus on me." *Escape. Run. Focus.* "My dear Watson."

The darkening edges around my vision start to disappear as I focus. I swallow hard, nodding my head. I keep my gaze away from the bodies.

"Okay. Okay." I nod, concentrating on Leo. Come on, Autumn, escaping is your specialty. "Down the stairs to the second floor, then we find a backway to the cars. Not the main entrance, it'll be a bloodbath with everyone."

Leo takes my hand, rushing us down the stairs where there's leftover carnage from the stampede, more bodies. There's shouts and another blast, lights flickering as glass shatters. We get to the landing, and Leo suddenly raises his gun and shoots. I look as a mercenary goes down.

"Get behind me," he says, keeping the gun up.

I follow closely as he slowly goes down the stairs, and then checks both sides of the hall when we get to the next floor. He starts to take us down one of the halls, and I flick my gaze over the balcony down to the grand foyer. It's anarchy as people shove to get out, fighting each other, everything in disarray. The mercenaries

I see aren't stopping them, instead focused on Vincenzo's men and destroying the villa.

Leo leads us down the hall, and I see a shadow of someone coming. He pushes us back against the wall, surprising the mercenary and punching him, then stabs him in the chest and then neck. The knife is yanked out, and he starts to keep going, but I grab his arm.

"Something's wrong," I whisper. He gives me a "no shit" look. "Meaning they're not stopping people from leaving. And they weren't stopping them when the blasts first started.."

His brows scrunch.

"Why bomb this place and have it still standing? Think like Gabriel."

Leo flicks his gaze towards the main entrance, and then back where we came. His gaze comes backs to me. "He rigged the cars."

And like a damn movie, a blast occurs from out front, which causes bloodcurdling screams to erupt.

"They were forcing everyone outside," I whisper.

"He's trying to trap us here."

I grab his hand and yank him back where we came. He doesn't question me as we go back up the stairs to the terrace. I ignore the bodies and destruction, weaving through them as I continue past where he'd killed those other men. I don't stop, putting all my energy into my instincts and to fucking follow them without second thought. We get to one of the other terraces, and I see billowing smoke from the front of the villa.

"What are you looking for?"

"Back service entrance. Servers kept coming from this area, so there's gotta be a stairwell that goes directly to the kitchens. Another backway."

Leo glances around with me, and then nods towards the stone railing at the far end. We run that way, and sure enough there's stairs down along the side of the building. More blasts rumble, likely every car going off if they start the engine.

We get down to a back courtyard, one side is the entrance for the kitchen and the other to the back gardens. Hand clutching his, I run over the stone gravel through the archway and into the barely illuminated gardens. It's almost peaceful back here, untouched by the destruction as we pass fountains, stone paths, and trees. Finally, we come upon the maze entrance and there's shouts behind us.

Leo takes the lead next, taking us into the dark maze. Our feet barely crunch over the pebbles as we go further and further into the dimly lit winding paths. Men shout, not far from behind us. Leo suddenly grabs me, putting me into a corner as he covers me with his body, ducking his head. It's dark enough, I can't see his face as I grip his shirt. His breaths are quiet, but ragged as I concentrate on keeping mine soft. His arm slowly snakes around me, holding me close as we listen to the men inside the maze.

Panic begins to curl its way around me again. Every crunch of their boots deafening. The murmur of their voices. My corset squeezes around me as I press my face against his chest. Leo silently pushes us further into the scratchy bush walls, trying to remain hidden in the darkness.

I concentrate on the compression of the corset, fighting to remain calm. Every soft exhale feels damning as their voices echo in the night. Every second stretching forever.

Their voices are quiet, but I catch one of them saying, "Stupid maze. Should've stashed our shit closer."

"I ain't letting my bike get caught in that mess."

"You're the—"

Something beeps, and their footsteps quicken as their voices disappear.

We don't move, even as another blast comes from the villa. Distant yelling.

"Find the bikes," I whisper.

"Autumn—"

"I know how to hotwire. We need to find the bikes."

Leo finally steps away, taking my hand and we make a run for it. I'm not sure how Leo is able to easily navigate the maze, but I'm guessing it's not his first time in here. We start to get to the end, and he slows us down.

"Stay here. Stay down." He hands me a gun, and then disappears into the darkness.

I crouch against the bushes. When I hear a grunt, I close my eyes and wait. There's a soft thud, and then another one. When I hear footfalls on the gravel, I snap my eyes open as Leo returns. Quickly, I get up and follow him to where several vehicles are parked. There's a driveway that leads to here, probably for the gardeners.

We search through the vehicles, and then I see them. Three motorbikes.

"I need a knife," I tell him, and he yanks one out from his belt. I rush over, debating which one, until I see the Ducati. Perfect.

"I'm going to make sure they can't follow us." Leo strips his jacket off, walking away.

I get to work on the wires, hoping I remember everything Isaac has taught me about the motorbikes. It's hard with the lack of light, but there's just enough moonlight to see. Low popping sounds, and I briefly glance over my shoulder to just make out Leo puncturing various tires. Right when I'm sure I've got it, I stop hotwiring, not wanting the engine noise to attract anyone until we're ready.

"Do you know how to ride this?" I ask when he comes back as he tugs off his dress shirt, revealing his undershirt.

"Yes." He pulls his shoulder holster back on. "Bond and I used to race in California, because it pissed off Jameson."

"Should turn on."

He walks past, stabbing the other two bikes to deflate their tires. When he comes back, he gestures for me to turn around. "Don't move."

Swiftly, the laces for my corset are cut and tossed into the bushes.

"Shirt off," he instructs.

Knowing what he's doing, I take it off and pull on his dress shirt, buttoning it up. He tosses the rest of our clothing into the darkness. He then grabs two of the three helmets, and thankfully they fit. Leo gets onto the bike, straddling it as I finish hotwiring. Thankfully, the engine roars to life.

I get on behind him, wrapping my arms around his waist as he touches my knee. "Good girl."

The bike's engine rumbles beneath, but nowhere near what any of the Harleys feel like. Within moments, the bike is moving as dirt and gravel kick up behind us. The path is bumpy as I hold onto him, until we finally get to the main driveway and speed off. Leo races us away from the carnage as I look back, seeing only fire and smoke.

The wind stings at me as he speeds on, heading for Rome. Briefly, he touches my knee, stroking it a little as I loosen my grip slightly and adjust to the high seat. My entire body is flush against his, leaning with him like one body. The countryside zips past us, and it's not long before we're back in the city and he's weaving through traffic at breakneck speed. Breath catching, I have to close my eyes a few times as he takes tight turns and zips around vehicles.

It's a stark difference from when I raced out of New York City. I hadn't been going nearly as fast. Nor had I used such tight turns at dangerous speeds. Leo does it with ease, maneuvering like a pro. I hold onto my husband, the biker of more than fifteen years, as he navigates us through the streets of Rome.

It takes me longer than I care to realize that he's zagging through the city to throw off anyone who may be following. My heartbeat finally starts to calm, even as we leave the main part of the city and head towards the outskirts. He opens the throttle suddenly, picking up speed as I try not to shiver against the wind. After a while, he starts to slow, and I peek over his shoulder to see us coming upon an airport. We take a quick corner, going a back way, and weave through vehicles until we come upon some buildings and chain link fencing. I half expect him to ride us directly onto the runway, but he stops, and shuts the bike off within the shadows outside of a hanger.

He takes off his helmet, putting the kickstand down, and then helps me off as I take my helmet off next. Leo starts to move carefully along the wall towards the fence that separates us from the airfield. I stay behind him in the shadows and then follow his stern gaze to where a private jet sits with a couple of cars around it. A few men stand around, seemingly waiting.

"Back up plan?" I whisper.

"In case something happened, a plane was chartered ready to leave tonight."

"A plane that's not yours," I add.

"Correct."

We watch quietly, and I'm unsure of what he's waiting for until another car shows up on the airstrip. It almost happens too quickly. A shootout occurs, the sound of gunfire ricocheting, almost not audible from the roar of the plane's engine. I watch as one of the men duck into a car, speeding off as the men who showed up get out. They're dressed like the other mercenaries.

"Gabriel's predictable," Leo mutters, pulling out his phone from his back pocket.

"Leo, did you know he was—"

"Renaldi and I knew he was in Rome, which is why we were shipping Matteo out tonight," he interrupts, flicking his gaze to me as he puts the phone to his ear. "I didn't want to worry you and hoped to be out of Italy before he found us."

"I think I already knew anyways," I murmur.

His jaw tightens, about to say something, but then focuses on his phone call.

"We got out. Update." There's muttering on the other side, and I'm pretty sure I hear Enigma or Jameson. "Airport is compromised."

More mumbling, and Leo's face darkens.

"Cut all communications with Renato. Shut it all down."

My stomach sinks. That's where Gabriel got the funds to hire those men. All those explosives. Knowing where we'd be. I stare at the runway as the men who arrived get on the plane. Or Giovanna told him.

Leo's face contorts into concentration. "We're down three men. No, all dead."

Dread fills me. More mumbling and muttering.

"Where's the rest of the Crew?" I ask.

"Another airport. They were attacked right after Matteo's plane took off. Their gunmen are dead, but our chances making it there without being tracked is too slim."

The plane's engines turn off.

"Were they mercenaries?"

"All of them worked for the Salvadori organization," Leo answers bluntly.

My body feels numb. I hear the ricochet of gunfire. My throat tightens, knowing they just killed the pilots. I knew they'd retaliate, but holy shit, they're killing people left and right.

"We need out of Italy. *Now*, Enigma. An airport to fly out where they can't track us." His brows furrow as I look away from the plane, a shiver running down my spine. "Latina's airport is all military; he may have people…"

Leo keeps talking low with Enigma and whoever else is on the phone. The past hour or so tugging at me as it sinks in how fucked we may be.

"Autumn." I blink, coming out of my thoughts. The phone is at Leo's side as he glimpses past me to the plane. "Can you stay awake for a few hours more?"

"If I have to."

"We can ride to either Naples or Pisa. Naples is shorter, but Renato may have people waiting if he's willing to go that far. Pisa is further, but the Renaldi family mostly owns that city."

"What about the Crew?"

"They're already going in opposite directions. Decoys. They're splitting, and then heading directly back to the states."

I swallow past the lump in my throat. "We're not going home… are we?"

Leo shakes his head. So, the running continues.

"Whatever you think is best. I'll stay awake."

Leo brings the phone back up to his ear. "Pisa. Set up a vehicle switch. Use *Eleanor* to wipe everything on our routes and those that could coincide so they can't track us. Shut down parts of Rome for all I care."

He hangs up, stalking towards the bike and I follow. I feel sick again, glancing over my shoulder as the men now stand around to wait for us.

"Dear Watson." My foggy brain, ragged with uncertainty and fear, tries to focus on Leo. He cups my cheek, stroking his thumb over my skin. "We will make it home. I promise."

Gabriel's voice echoes in my head. *"How long will Leo last before I break him?"*

"He's coming for you," I whisper, tears finally brimming my eyes. "Gabriel. He's…"

Leo gently hushes me, pulling me into his arms he presses his face against my hair. "I know. He won't win, Autumn. Don't let him into your head…not when we've come this far."

Trembling, I nod and hug him back.

"We need to go. If you think you may fall asleep, tap three times."

"Okay."

He kisses my forehead, and then dips his head to place one on my lips. He hands me the helmets, then kicks up the stand to roll it further down the way we came. We get to the far end before he straddles it and tries to start the engine. It doesn't turn on.

With shaking hands, I go back to the bike's wiring. Hoping it'll turn on, fearful it won't, the engine finally roars to life again. Relief fills me as I give him his helmet and put mine on. Leo then helps me onto the seat behind him again.

"Good girl. You know your bikes," he says loud enough for me to hear.

A fragment of pride flashes as I hold him tight, and he rides us out of the airport and into the night.

Elm Jed

Once more, I feel the pattern of my life click into place, shad-owing me—fleeing a city. Again.

Chapter 36

Goodbye, Rome. Hello—

IT'S LATE when we switch bikes at some random shop. A middle-aged man greets us, taking the Ducati and helmets. We're given clothes to change into: jeans, boots, shirts, and jackets to ride safer and warmer. Thank goodness, because even though it's summer, the night is chilly, worse going the speeds Leo's been taking.

We're given either a Bonneville or BMW, but I'm too exhausted to double check. We're soon off again into the night as the engine revs underneath us. Leo squeezes my knee, and I do it back around his middle as I remain close to him even if I don't need to on this model like the Ducati.

The engine rumbles as we ride north to Pisa. Anxious thoughts still swirl, adrenaline wearing off as I focus on the vibrations of the bike. It's not a Harley, but it's enough to help calm me as I try to process what happened and lies ahead. The breeze rushes past as I turn my head, staring out at the coast we ride alongside. The full moon glistens over the water. It could almost be a peaceful night ride.

Horrendous as this night has been, it's comforting to have Leo with me this time escaping a city. Two times in a row. New record.

At some point, I have to focus to stay awake as we approach

Pisa. Leo easily guides us towards the airport, and I'm soon blinking as we approach it. We come upon a small airfield where there's a smaller private jet sitting on the runway. Someone meets us, and it's a whirl of quick conversations as the bike is turned off and handed over to someone else. My eyes have a hard time focusing as we get onto the plane.

It's much smaller than the other one. White leather seats and two areas to sit in. One with chairs facing each other, and the other with sofas sectioned off with a curtain. It feels more luxurious. I slump into one of the seats pulling my jacket off as I lean back tiredly.

Please don't let me get sick again.

Leo's gone for a few more minutes, talking with the pilots before he comes back and tosses his jacket off next. He instantly starts to buckle me in as the doors of the plane are closed.

"No hostess this time?" I ask.

"No. Only us and the pilots."

"We can trust them?"

"Yes. They're Renaldi's people. And his plane." Explains the fancier feeling.

He gets into his seat next to me. "How much do we owe him?"

"Only message he left for Enigma was his apologies to you for a terrible leave of Italy." I lean my head back as the plane starts to move. "I think he likes you too much."

"Good thing for him he's across an ocean."

Leo takes my hand, running his thumb over my wrist. "There's no bed this time, but we can sleep here or on the sofas."

"How long is the flight?"

"About three hours."

So, we're going somewhere else in Europe I'm assuming.

"Fingers crossed I don't get sick again."

He brings my hand up, kissing it as I hear the engines rumble. It pauses in moving, and other noises come from the cockpit.

"How are the other three?" I ask.

"Animal and Ringer got to their planes with no issues. Iron

Buffalo will get to his in an hour. All three were followed, but Renaldi took care of it."

"Guessing between our plane and helping them, he's not pissed at us."

Leo shakes his head. "His anger is with Gabriel and Renato. He's declared his own war with them. Given the destruction caused and civilians killed, he has every right. The Salvadori name can die with Renato and Giovanna. Renato crossed a stupid line allowing Gabriel to hire his men. He's likely learning that now."

"I thought they were mercenaries."

"It would've been worse if they were." Well, that's comforting. Not. "And Matteo's plane has been diverted to Atlanta, and then he'll go to New York." I flick my gaze to him, anxiety flipping in my stomach as the plane starts moving again.

Leo's gaze remains forward, exhaustion pulls at the corners of his eyes. He swallows hard, letting out an exhale.

"I doubt Matteo had any part in tonight, but if he ever does touch you again, I may kill him. When we finally get home, I don't want you near him." Leo's voice is rough, his jaw tightening as he brings our joined hands up to kiss my knuckles. His eyes finally meet mine, and I hate seeing how tired and pained he looks. The last few hours weighing on him. "When I heard you scream, for a moment, I thought I lost you."

My chin quivers, trying to give him a reassuring look. I kiss his knuckles next, squeezing as the plane starts to move quickly. The seatbelt sign blinks, and I loosen a shaky breath as the plane races forward to fly off. My stomach flips as we lift into the air, and I stiffen entirely at the odd sensation.

We're still tilted upward when he moves the armrest between us, giving me the ability to lean into his side. He kisses my temple as the plan jostles. I grip him tighter, wishing it was the helicopter or to be back on the bikes.

Unable to stay quiet as we glide into the sky, I abruptly blurt, "I watched you kill multiple men. How'd you even…I mean, I know how, but…"

"An entire life of training." He strokes my leg, keeping his face against my hair.

"Childhood?"

"Partly. A requirement of my father." Explains why Gabriel was so lethal, too. "Then later with Isaac, Owen, and Julio. At first it was because I'd be this hotel mogul, potentially targeted, but also paranoia if Gabriel came looking."

"Good instincts."

"Good instincts yourself."

I scoff, going rigid once more when the plane bumps.

"I fucking froze and almost..." I huff, rubbing my free hand over my face.

Leo pulls my hand away, tilting my chin towards him gently. "What you saw would've made anyone freeze or panic. You witnessed a massacre; you're allowed to be scared."

"You didn't."

"Training, remember?" I purse my lips, recalling Chesty saying something similar. The Crew *did* have training from military to police work, for specific situations like what happened tonight. To know how to act, whereas I hadn't. Just survival instincts. Yet, the shame was still there.

"You were targeted, chased, and attacked while explosives were going off, and surrounded by death, Autumn," Leo says slowly. "Even those trained for the worst situations would've needed a moment." He strokes his fingers over my cheek as I shakingly inhale. "You got us out, helped us not get caught. You hotwired a fucking Ducati. Fought off those men, too. Nothing for you to be ashamed of after what you saw."

"I watched him kill them," I whisper. "Igor and Garett. And then Michael..."

"I know. If it wasn't for Michael, I wouldn't have gotten to you in time." He kisses my forehead. "Their job was to protect us. They did. Remember that."

I nod against him. We're quiet as the plane starts to ease from its jostling, and the seatbelt sign turns off. Leo undoes our seatbelts, helping me over to the sofas. He pulls a blanket out from the overhead compartment, closes the privacy curtain completely, and then finds some water. Leo then pulls off my shoes and his, settling us onto the sofa under the blanket together. His arm goes around me, holding me close.

My head hurts, aching and throbbing along with the rest of my body. Leo's warm against me as he breathes deeply, stroking my arm in a comforting manner.

"Try to sleep, dear Watson." His voice is rough, breathing deep against my hair.

Somehow, even with the nightmare we lived through tonight, my eyes close as I feel his body go lax. We fall asleep, finally leaving Italy behind.

The next twelve hours felt like a warped montage of exhaustion. I was jolted awake by the plane when we landed, and we were quickly escorted off. I barely remember anything as Leo got us onto a train. Guess I can finally mark that off my mode of travel. We arrived at our destination, both fatigued when we fell asleep in our hotel room.

My eyes snap open, a tightness around my chest when I wake up again. Hand reaching out, I feel Leo beside me in the bed and I calm. Slowly, I sit up and groan. Headache is barely there, but it faintly throbs. My body is sore. At least I didn't get sick this time flying.

I glance out the window beside the bed, which shows a pretty view of London.

We're in a hotel owned by an acquaintance of his, non-mob related. I pull my legs in, wrapping my arms around them as I try to breathe after whatever nightmare woke me up. There's barely any sunlight, making me guess it's early or just really fucking cloudy.

Leo mutters in his sleep, turning over and runs his hand under the covers. He touches my leg, and then my hip. I look over as he lifts his head a little, and roughly asks, "Nightmare?"

"Yeah. I'm gonna start some coffee. Go back to sleep," I whisper. He makes a noise, putting his head down. I lean over to kiss his head before getting out of bed.

Our room is more modern than in Italy. It's not a fancy suite, simple compared to Leo's hotels. Different luxury hotel vibes. The furniture is more minimalist, dark colored and rigid, the rest of the room a light amber with touches of blue. The bed is just around a corner from the living room space and kitchenette, where there's a breakfast nook to eat. I glance through the cabinets, thankfully finding stuff to make coffee. I half expected to only find tea honestly, glad to be wrong.

I put on the kettle, pulling out a French Press and get the coffee together. It's not long before I have a cup and am sitting near the window, staring out at a cloudy London.

I definitely have a knack for unexpected travel.

First New York when I was seventeen, then New Jersey, Rome, and now London. In a year, I've accidentally become well-traveled. College Autumn would be stoked.

As I drink the coffee, my mind wanders going over the last 24… 48 hours. Week. Month. Two months. Shaking my head, I slump back into the chair and groan inwardly. *Oh, don't do that you'll land yourself in Arkham, Autumn.*

"Can't change it. Focus on now," I murmur to myself. "Like the fact that you're in a foreign country with your husband, running from his maniacal older brother who essentially caused a massacre. Okay, not helping."

I grumble to myself, putting my coffee down and hold my head. "Deep breath. You're safe. The others made it back home. You're safe. For now…"

My head goes onto the table.

Suddenly, there's a soft knock on the door. I pinch my brows together as I look up. It's barely 6:30. Maybe Leo ordered an early ass breakfast…or the mobsters here are nice enough to knock before tearing through a door. The knock occurs again, and I briskly get up and walk over to the bedside table next to Leo. I grab his gun as he stirs a little, while I go back to the door. I hold it ready at my side as there's one more soft knock.

My heart pounds, chest shaking as I exhale steadily.

I unlock it, getting ready for whoever is on the other side, except I'm not when I open the door. Familiar blue eyes greet me, and a smirk when he notices the gun in my hand.

"Decided to shoot me instead of kicking me in the balls this time, Miss Autumn?"

Chapter 37

London Town

QUICKLY, I put the gun aside to fling myself at Isaac for a hug.

"Thank fuck you're alright," he murmurs, clutching me tightly.

"What are you doing here? You can't…how? When?"

"If you think any of us were going to allow either of you to be in a foreign country without back up of some kind, you need more tea."

"It's coffee." I step back, letting him into the room.

"My point exactly. I haven't spent months teaching you how to make a proper cup for you *not* to make it in my home country."

"Sue me."

He smirks, placing a briefcase and another bag onto the table near the door. He's wearing jeans and a long-sleeved shirt, very casual. Isaac starts for the small kitchenette, glimpsing towards the bed around the corner where Leo sleeps. I grab my coffee mug, coming over to stand near him as he starts refilling the kettle.

"Flew in a few hours ago," he explains. "Leo knew I was coming, you must've been asleep when we told him."

"Probably."

"Well…" he looks over his shoulder towards Leo again, "…him getting rest is for the best. As for my being here, it's *other* European

413

countries I'm not quite welcome in. I'm not exiled from England. Yet."

He better not be lying about the MI6 thing.

"How's Leanne?"

"Worried about you, but also was the one who said I should be the one to come. I think my nerves we're getting to her." He puts the kettle back into place, turning it on. "But she's safe."

"How are you two? I don't want to pry, but I could use some good news. Something uplifting, even a funny date." I clutch the mug. "Anything, even if simple."

His smile turns tender, turning away to grab his tea of choice.

"Given the circumstances, we've been good. Leanne is wonderful, incredibly smart, and almost too intuitive. I've not had many good relationships due to jobs and lifestyle, so she's the first I've felt this…communicative. Not to mention, her ability to make me feel like one of a kind."

I smile back as he goes through the motions of making himself a cup of tea. He finishes, turning around to lean against the small sink towards me.

"She may get mad at me telling you first, but I'm sure she'd like you to know," he says, and I raise my brows. "I admitted I loved her a couple weeks ago, and she reciprocated the feeling."

I slap my hand over my mouth, almost spilling my coffee as I try not to be loud enough to wake Leo. He chuckles at my predicament trying to stay quiet.

"How dare you do that when I can't be loud." I point at him.

"But her reaction to you trying not to wake your husband may be worth it."

I smack him.

There's a grumble as Leo stirs in the bed. Well, not very successful.

"Is he wearing pants this time?" Isaac swears under his breath when I shake my head, and he turns away as Leo gets out of bed.

I glance over at Leo's nudity, hiding my grin behind my mug. Leo grabs a pair of pants, pulling them on before walking over.

"You're early," he tells Isaac.

"Figured she'd be awake, even with the time difference."

Leo grunts, coming up beside me. His hand strokes through my hair, and then leans in to kiss my temple with a sleepy sigh. I almost want to shove him back into bed. Apart from the plane ride, he was up for over 24 hours, not to mention riding for hours at night and getting us to this hotel. Knowing he won't, I gesture to the coffee, and he pours himself a cup.

"No tea, boss?" Isaac jokingly asks.

Leo glares at him, then goes to sit at the table near the window. "Why are you so early?"

I go to sit next to him, Isaac remaining by the sink. "Items to discuss before you're on and off the phone with Jameson and others."

"Such as?"

"Perhaps, wait until you finish your coffee. Or had breakfast."

"Might as well dive in, not going anywhere," I say with a sigh. "Can't be that bad, after the last…" Isaac's face turns into a worried frown, "…or not."

Leo sips his coffee, putting the mug down with a clatter. I can't help a small flinch, my shoulders rising at the noise. Leo flicks his gaze to me, right as I stare down at the table. Oh, good, those reactions have decided to rear their ugly head. He reaches over, gently sliding his hand over my shoulder. I let out a soft exhale, placing my hand over his as I give him a tentative smile.

"We'd rather know than wait," Leo says gruffly.

Isaac sighs, relenting to our demand and puts his tea down. "After being missing for the past week or so, Charlotte was found dead. Police were keeping it on the down low, because they thought she was a victim of a serial killer, except when they found her body nothing matched their MO."

Leo's expression darkens with a frown. While horror slithers over me.

"What?" I rasp.

"We thought giving her a new identity would've kept her safe, to start over in California," Isaac admits. "Apparently not."

"How was she found?" Leo asks.

"Construction workers on a job site. Single bullet to the head, but there were marks on her wrists from being handcuffed, including her ankles." He clears his throat, averting his gaze from me. "There's evidence of sexual assault, and she was dressed in nothing but a silk robe. She was also put in messy make up that looked from the 80s, and her hair was permed."

A scene flashes through my head. My chest feels heavy, bricks laying on it. I ask, "What color was the robe?"

Isaac frowns, but goes over to the briefcase he brought in and brings it over, opening it. He flicks through the papers, shuffling them.

"Light purple, lavender with, uh…"

"Pink lining," I finish.

Leo's hand drops from my shoulder, rubbing his face in frustration. Isaac looks between us, putting the papers down. "Miss Autumn, how'd you know that?"

"*Scarface,*" I answer. "Honestly surprised I remembered that detail, but Al Pacino has been on my mind lately." Leo's hand falls to the table. "That's what Gina wore, Tony's sister, after he thought she betrayed him…marrying Manny in secret. Although it wasn't Tony who killed her."

"Well, that's not all," Isaac clears his throat. "Before she died, someone carved *Sullivan* into her back."

I stare down at my mug, thoughts racing going through movies, and I feel sick when I make the connection. "*The Departed,*" I whisper.

My thoughts whirl, beginning to blame myself for what happened to Charlotte. Except, she chose to help Gabriel. Believed him. Much like…those characters. It wasn't mine or Leo's fault what Gabriel's done, pulling every trigger. It didn't make it easier as a sadness comes over me, pitying her that she received that brutal of an end.

"He's really banking on me knowing my movies," I whisper.

"Gabriel would've had time to go out there, and then to Rome," Leo says, exhaling sharply. "Barely, but the timeline fits."

"Caltz was understandable to get rid of, but why Charlotte? Or is this just a sick message to you both?" Isaac asks.

"He's cleaning up loose ends," Leo answers, picking up his mug as he becomes far too calm.

"Loose ends?" Isaac asks, grabbing his tea.

"Caltz was Autumn's handler, and got Steve out, both who screwed up getting rid of Autumn. Charlotte ruined his inside mole operation by getting caught. We took care of Curione and DeLuca who fucked up his coup."

Basically, we helped him. Fuck.

"All of them had information that he wanted, and he doesn't want to share," Leo adds. "He loses valuable control that way."

"Matteo could be on his hit list then," Isaac suggests. "He was part of it all."

"Not to mention him knowing about Giovanna, and going to Vincenzo," I whisper. "He's tried to kill him before, too. What if he finally does?"

Leo's jaw works, brows pulled together in concentration.

"If that's so, then we keep Matteo under lock and key," Leo instructs.

"He's already at the warehouse," Isaac says.

"The warehouse?" I ask.

"Can't take him to the estate, still compromised," Isaac explains. "Nowhere else will have enough space for security to watch him *and* look for Gabriel. Maybe if we put him into an apartment somewhere."

"Why not the hotel?" Both men exchange a look, confused by my suggestion. "Security is practically doubled there. Use a room on a random floor. It's big enough, that when we get home, we won't interact either. And…Gabriel probably won't think Leo will keep him there."

"Then what? Give him a job?" Isaac asks incredulously.

I shrug.

Isaac blinks at me, and then looks up at the ceiling. There're his thoughts on that. Leo's face becomes deep with concern, brows furrowed.

"Look, better than just 'locking him up' or whatever," I say, sitting back and wrapping my arms around myself. "It can be something menial to keep him busy."

"Perhaps it's because I wasn't here, Miss Autumn…" Isaac starts, and then clears his throat, "…and I will be blunt. He tried to kill you, and this time with his own hands." My hand wanders up towards my throat, tears threatening to come. "You're quite a forgiving person, but you don't need to be now."

My fingers trace over where his hands were, an ache falling over me as my jaw clenches. I stare at the coffee mugs, chest tightening.

"There's no penance for you to pay for his wrongs," Isaac continues softly. Leo's chair creaks as he shifts in his seat. "You don't need to save him for your sake or Leo's because what Gabriel's done. Young or not, he's made his decisions, and is grown enough to understand them. You do not *have* to give him forgiveness, Autumn. You're not a monster for not giving that."

Tears silently fall down my cheeks. Heart hurting as I recall my conversation with Michael, similar to this. Grief overcomes me, wrenching at me as I struggle to fight back the tears. Leo goes to touch my shoulder, but I flinch away and hug myself closer. I continue staring at the table as I feel him drop his hand.

"Autumn," Leo says my name gently.

"Michael asked why, too." My voice is quiet and shaky. "In the church, he asked why I stopped you. He didn't understand either, after fighting Matteo off." I inhale trembling. The pain finally catching up to me. I wipe away some of the tears. "I asked Michael to be a permanent bodyguard when we got home, cause he…he… fuck." I bury my face with my hands as I try to think of the right words, why I didn't want to throw Matteo to the wolves, but the sudden grief blurs my head.

There's a stillness from them, neither saying anything as I try to collect myself. I wipe my face roughly, letting out a trembling breath.

"He's been fucked with, lied to, and used. I want to give Matteo a chance, and maybe giving a semblance of mercy or compassion like I've been given…" I finally look up to see Leo's solemn gaze, "…maybe he won't turn into a monster like Gabriel. Renato. Or even Giovanna."

Leo closes his eyes, brows pulled together as his face contorts with different emotions.

"Miss Autumn, this might be because Michael and the others were killed, to save—"

"And?" I snap back, looking at Isaac. "Alright, fine, I want one less person dead. Whether I want to save Matteo out of guilt or not, why not have one less person added to the bloodshed?"

"He's betrayed us multiple times. Backstabbed us. What happens when he does it again?" Isaac asks.

"You believe in him that little?" I ask almost brokenly, tears still coming down.

Isaac gives him a sympathetic look. "You believe in him that much?"

Leo's still quiet, rubbing his fingers over his forehead as he lets out a long exhale. I look over at him, watching as he silently fights with himself. Ire and pain lining his face.

"He hesitated," I whisper, and Leo goes still. "Gabriel didn't, but Matteo did. For a moment, he stopped. Maybe it's a fool's hope, but it's something."

Leo finally meets my gaze again. They're aggrieved and unsure.

"His life doesn't need to be decided right now," I say, swallowing hard as I wipe away more tears. "If you keep him in that warehouse, he'll harbor more resentment towards us. Strip a room to bare essentials. Have him work with Bobby, who's not attached to the mob, but knows who he is. He helped me. He'll teach him a thing or two. Start there."

I feel Isaac watching us as silence fills the space. I knew I was asking a lot, putting faith and time into someone who could back-stab us *again*. Except, I couldn't let go of this gut feeling. I don't want him to have the same fate as Charlotte or Roger. I don't want to see those pictures.

Slowly and carefully, Leo holds his hand out, reaching for me. This time I place my hand into his, shaking a little, as he squeezes it gently.

"I don't want you near him," Leo says gruffly.

"Okay," I say softly.

"Do what she suggests, Bond. Tell the others. If he gets out of line, lock him up."

Leo brings my hand up, kissing it. My body calms a little, less shaky as relief floods me, but still mixed with grief.

"Order breakfast," Leo continues. "And make sure your room is to your liking. I need time with my wife before we get into any other business."

"Sure, boss."

Leo stands, pulling me up with him. His hand grips mine as I follow him silently to the bathroom, where he closes the door. He turns the shower on, then faces me to cup my cheeks with both hands. He opens his mouth to say something, but nothing comes. My chin quivers, but I silently nod to the hot water as he wipes the last of my tears away.

Without words, he and I undress and get into the shower. He faces the water first as I come up behind him, running my hands over his back and around his torso. I hug him, pressing my body against his as I lay my cheek against his spine. I shudder, trying not to suddenly spiral due to the last 24 hours. The terror, agony, and loss.

Leo turns around as the water pours over us. Those hands I've watched kill, tenderly stroke my skin before he gently kisses me. He's affectionate in his caress as I cling to him for that small tether. There's no hesitation in him as he touches me, holding me close. We're silent as we wash each other's bodies, grounding ourselves in this moment to feel in control again.

We're alive.

———

The rest of the day was thankfully quiet. Leo took some calls, but by late afternoon, he shut off all communications and just laid in bed with me. Both of us getting more rest.

The next day, Leo went back to his usual business self, handling issues with Jameson and apparently Carrie. He sent me off with Isaac to explore London while he stayed back to deal with things unrelated to the mafia chaos.

Early afternoon, it started raining when we reached Regent Park. Isaac has already shown me the Globe Theater, the Palace entrance, and a few other touristy spots. The distraction somewhat working. Now we sit at a café that overlooks the large pond, although they call it a lake.

"You know as someone who's from a state with a *very* large lake," I start as the rain comes down harder. "Pretty sure that's a pond."

"Careful calling it that here," Isaac muses.

"Yet, you call the *ocean* a pond," I tease, and he smirks.

I sit back, watching the rain as I stir my tea.

"What do you think of London?" He asks.

"Nice. Bigger than I thought," I answer, smiling. "Although I think I'd like to finally visit a new city without reason of escaping someone."

"Cannot blame you there. Did you at least enjoy Rome?"

"Yeah. Enough that if Leo and I never go back, I think I'd be content."

He hums, solemn as he adjusts in his seat. Again, he's wearing casual attire with a black t-shirt, cardigan, and jeans. I'm almost matching, but have a jacket instead. The rainy weather has made it chillier.

"I wouldn't blame him if he never returned because of what happened," Isaac says quietly. "Quite reprehensible what his family did. I've heard of some dastardly things of family affairs, but lying about one's living status for over twenty years is quite a feat."

I swear Isaac's accent is stronger here. I grin softly, finding comfort in the small familiarity.

"Even though I did that to my family, too?"

"Not the same."

"You sure?"

"Miss Autumn, they didn't even come to your funeral nor cared what happened to you. Leo was a child, who loved his mother. You *died* to protect yourself and others. Giovanna did it selfishly. Perhaps for good reason given her situation, but then *that* reason dissolved when Riccardo passed. If it was solely because of her husband, why not come forward after he died? To continue living a lie, not attempting to be with your son again? I truly believe it was for more reasons than she's led you on to believe."

Okay, got me there.

Still, hope Dr. Maxwell is ready for more three-hour sessions. I know *I'll* need them.

I change the subject, not wanting to stew on it longer. "So, does your family know you're alive or was that part of your... retirement?"

Leaning my elbows on the table, he smirks at my subject change.

"They know I'm alive. We already had a sordid relationship before I joined the military, worse when I joined MI6, disappearing a lot. When they learned I'd gotten a US dual citizenship, they practically disowned me."

"Ahh."

"I love the country I was born in, but it became not for me anymore. Much like yourself with the hometown you left behind."

"I left a state, not a country," I muse. "But guess we all do move on, even if it's not what we thought it would be."

The rain lightens, drizzling over the pond as people still jog and walk through the park. Barely any umbrellas in sight. I sip my tea, watching the quiet ambiance as it slowly reminds me of Rome. It's quaint, but not home.

"Any idea how long we'll *actually* be here?" I ask softly.

"Hopefully not long, but for now, it's safer for you two. No other mafia to speak of." I raise my brows. "There's mobs and underbellies, of course, but not like Italy or America. Names such as Marchetti or Salvadori don't have the same impact. Different ecosystems as it were, who don't want to be caught up with others. Leo has better connections with them, as well."

"That doesn't entirely keep us safe, though, does it? If he turned Vincenzo's home into a massacre, I doubt the mobs here will stop him."

"Yes, but he doesn't know you're here. And if he does learn…"

"We run to another country." His eyes meet mine, giving me a sincere look.

I sigh, leaning back as I look out over the…lake. Falling rain disrupts the water, creating circles.

"Grateful as I am being safer here, I'm ready to go home, Isaac. I thought I missed it when I was in New Jersey, but not this much. I really just want to be home."

"You will, Miss Autumn." We share a faint smile as the wind picks up.

"Well, until then, might as well enjoy London," I say and then huff at him. "But, uh did Mary Poppins lie to me, because why aren't there more umbrellas around?"

Chapter 38

Butterflies

It's early evening when I return to the hotel room. Isaac split off in the lobby to talk with a manager, and then to his room for the night. It's still raining outside as I pull my jacket off, noticing Leo sitting at the small table facing the window. His chin is propped in his hand, and I peer closer to see no phone in it. The folders are closed on the table. Everything is quiet.

Once the door shuts, he twists in his chair and gets up. "How was London?"

"It's pretty, but also wet. Reputation stands strong, and it's a bigger city than I thought." I answer, locking the door and hanging up the jacket as I pull my boots off. "How'd meetings go?"

"Well enough." He picks up the folders, walking them over to the desk near the bed. "I'll be free to be with you tomorrow. Promise."

I give a small smile. "It's alright if not. You've got a lot on your plate." He exhales sharply, sitting back down at the table. "Speaking of plates, we had a small dinner, but do you want to go get something?"

He shakes his head, and I nod as I walk to the kitchenette. I glance over the couple of mugs, noticing housekeeping came through due to the lack of mess. Humming, I run my hand down over my hip, thinking on how to spend a rainy night in. Well, television and tea sound nice and simple.

I turn my attention to Leo to ask what he wants, when I notice his lowered gaze. The exhaustion that's been constant on his face for over two days diminishes as his eyes roam over me. His legs spread slightly as he lounges in the chair, focused on me. I go still, noticing the usual slacks he wears and button-up that's barely closed.

My chest feels flustered suddenly, breath shallow. "Leo?"

"Check in." His voice is rough. Those hazel eyes reach mine, simmering with want.

Surprise flicks over me, heartbeat quickening. The rest of me feels flushed as heat travels across my skin. Tingling desire roams, almost foreign after the last few days, like when we first dated. Butterflies and all. I'm unsure of my reaction, maybe just from the tumultuous events, but I answer, "Green."

"Why'd you hesitate?"

"Uh, surprised."

"Why?"

I look down, seeing the very normal, casual clothes I'm wearing. Nothing fancy like I've worn in Rome. No sundresses, corsets, silk blouses, or tiny red dresses. Just…average. It shouldn't matter, but I keep my mouth closed unsure if that's even why.

My hands rub against my jeans, trying to think as Leo stands. He practically saunters over, body lithe and fluid as the air feels sucked from the room. My stomach flips again, butterflies going rampant as he stops before me.

Suddenly, I'm in the bookstore. Leo flips through pages of the book in his hands. The quiet music in the background, standing close to me. The smell of his cologne I've given up learning the name of. The commanding presence he always had that was alluring and mysterious. Lastly, green eyes mixed with golds and browns like faraway forests.

Leo's fingers stroke down my cheek. I'm brought back to the

present, staring up at the man who's consumed me every moment since that day.

"It's been a long week, if you don't want to, it's alright, dear Watson."

"Watson. The last name is Watson."

"Very well...dear Watson."

Why am I flashbacking? Even so, it causes a nervous giggle, and I shake my head. Leo's brows furrow, creating those lines on his forehead. I smile, reaching up to touch them and his expression relaxes.

"I want to..." I finally answer softly, "...just, some reason I... have butterflies like I used to."

"Used to?"

"Like whenever you'd come into the coffee shop." His hands slide down my torso, thumbs stroking just above the seam of my jeans as he steps closer. "Those first dates. I'd always get this fluttering feeling in my stomach. Nervous."

Leo dips his head, pressing his face against my hair as he inhales deeply. I close my eyes as he nudges his nose against my cheek to the underside of my ear, and down my throat. He then kisses my skin delicately, murmuring against it, "You gave me butterflies, too."

I giggle. "No, I didn't."

He pulls back as I open my eyes, finding seriousness in his. My brows raise, mouth opening. "Oh...I did?"

"How else would I have felt about a woman who laughed when my coffee was spilled on her?"

"Look at that weirdo?" He smirks, slipping his arm around my waist. "What *were* you thinking?"

His other hand slides to the nape of my neck, holding me as my breath hitches.

"That I finally felt alive."

Leo kisses me, clutching me as my hands grip his shirt. I sigh against him as he kisses me tenderly, lovingly as his hard body presses against me. The fluttering continues in my stomach, traveling up with growing desire.

He reaches down under my ass, lifting me up against him. My legs wrap around his waist as he continues to kiss me fervently, mouth sliding over mine. Our chests press against the other as the kiss becomes more frantic, a yearning that's deep as his hands grip me. He starts to walk us over to the bed. I tighten around him, sliding my hands up to grasp at his hair as he groans against my mouth.

Slowly, he lays me down onto the bed and blankets me with his body. He grabs my hands and pulls my arms up. His fingers become interweaved with mine as he pins me against the bed, the weight of him sinking me further into the covers. Leo kisses me deeper, tongues wrangling as his pelvis rubs against mine. I can feel his erection, breath hitching as my hips involuntarily move up towards him.

I gently nudge my arms, and he quickly lets go to start moving his hands along my sides. I reach back up, grabbing the back of his neck as we continue to make out. Fingers trace under the hem of my shirt, and then slide under to pull it off me smoothly. Swiftly, he takes my bra off next. I work on the last of his shirt buttons, yanking it off and tossing it aside.

For a few moments, I stare at the ink covering him. Leo sits up onto his knees, legs on either side of my upper thighs. My hands continue to caress him, fingers trailing after roses, fire, and weapons tattooed upon him. Leo's head tilts to the side, watching me while shadows play over his face from the dim light and rainstorm outside. Intense eyes filled with need gaze down as I trace the artwork. Muscles flex when I hit certain spots.

His fingers start to move over my own torso, following small scars before coming up to caress my breasts. He skims over my skin, up and then trails his fingers down the middle of my chest. When he gets low enough, my hips kick up from the sensation. A smirk comes over him as he does it again, making a giggle escape me as he leans down to glide his tongue between my breasts to the base of my throat.

Leo kisses my neck, placing more up to the underside of my jaw. His breath skitters over my skin. "How do you want me, dear wife?"

Another kiss upon my neck. I rasp, "You inside me."

"Like this?"

He sucks on his fingers momentarily, then unbuttons my jeans to dip his fingers under them and my underwear. He strokes me before his fingers slowly push inside me, causing my breath to hitch. My hips rock, wanting more as he gently thrusts his fingers while his thumb circles my clit. My breathing picks up as I continue to wiggling my hips to his movement.

A whimper leaves me as his fingers brush my inner walls, hooking up and then scissoring gently. Muscles contract around him as he sits up again on his knees, darkened eyes watching me. He twists with two fingers, adding a third which makes my body shudder and back arch. My legs are trapped under him as I reach for the blankets, clutching them as he brings me closer to the precipice of coming.

"Like this, dear Watson?"

"No," I plead. "More."

"More?"

I moan as his thumb flicks over my clit. "Leo. Please."

His hand suddenly disappears as I'm on the brink. I gasp in shock as he gets off me and pulls his pants off. He then makes quick work of tugging my jeans and underwear off. I'm still breathing heavy as he pulls open the bedside drawer, grabbing some lube before crawling back on top of me. His fingers slide over my sex once more, before he nudges his cock at my entrance. It's not long before he gradually plunges into me.

A satisfied groan is what I give at the fullness of him. The closeness and connection as he pulls back, driving himself deeper. Leo's hips meet mine as I reach for him. His hips roll against my pelvis, and I moan into his neck, back to cresting towards bliss again. He moves fluidly as his cock hits the right spot, and my muscles clench around him as I come. My body tenses as I clutch at his back with a death grip. Leo groans against my ear, holding me still as my hips gyrate against him.

Pleasure travels over me, tingling as my legs and body trembles. Leo abruptly pulls out of me, gently flipping me over to face the window. Rain drips down the glass, drizzling against the foggy surface as he pulls me up onto all fours. His hands run up and down my spine, caressing my skin. He carefully stops at my shoulder blades, pushing down my front. I press my chest against the bed, keeping my hips up as he continues to stroke my skin with reverence.

Soon, the heat of his body engulfs mine as he leans over to kiss along my shoulder blades and spine. I sigh at the light touches, listening to the rain as he lovingly worships my body. Hot breath drifts over me, causing shivers as his lips press upon my skin.

A moan leaves me when he enters me again, going deep with his cock. I grip the blankets as he starts to steadily thrust. Leo clutches my hips, pulling me back to him firmly as he fucks me from behind. I whimper with need as he stretches me, rubbing against sensitive spots due to the position. My skin tingles as the core of me ignites and spreads through me with bliss.

Leo's hot chest covers my back, damp skin slides over me as he snakes his hand to my throat. He grips it gently, hips moving faster with a fervent pace. Every few times, he pauses long enough to push himself deep inside making us both moan. My muscles tighten, grasping for pleasure as my head starts to swim. His other hand comes over mine, fingers threading together in a tight hold as he slams his hips into me again.

"I love you," he rasps against my ear. "Fuck, Autumn, I love you."

"I love you," I respond breathlessly.

His hips jolt forward, and I'm thrown into ecstasy. We come together, almost overwhelmed as I silently scream into the bed. Leo clutches me, tightening around me as pleasure explodes from the bottom of my spine as everything tenses. Leo groans against my ear, breaths short as his body shakes, grinding himself into me. His hand releases my neck, sliding his arm under my torso to keep me close as he kisses my sweat sheen skin.

Outside rain pounds against the window. We remain there, clutching each other as I feel him soften inside me. It's comfortable. Warm, even when our skin dries all I feel is his warmth. I watch the storm, staying present for this. Savoring this moment in the chaos together.

Finally, Leo pulls out and picks me up to carry me to the bathroom. We're quiet as we shower together, washing the other with small smiles and tender touches. He rinses the soap from my hair as I kiss his chest, and then lay my head against him to hear his heartbeat. His hands rove down my spine as the water streams over us.

We finish, taking our time, and Leo orders food to be delivered. We then cuddle up onto the sofa to eat as I find a show, *Would I Lie to You?* to watch. For a few hours it felt like everything outside this moment had been a nightmare. That we'd waken up and were on our real honeymoon in London.

Except, like many times before, the calm didn't last.

It's late into the night when we're woken up by a call that our nightmare was indeed real and not finished.

Renato's dead.

His body was found in *Mezzanotte*, hanging from the second floor for the entire club to see. His ankles were nailed together, while his arms were stretched out nailed to the concrete all the way to his biceps, naked and covered in whip marks. Across his chest, carved likely before his death was: *Veritas Aequitas*. His head was gone, a rosary hanging from where his neck should be, stapled to his skin to not fall off. The head was soon found in Vincenzo's private room, propped upon the bed with the pillows.

It's 1am as I stare at the crime scene photos. I'm in shock, I can't even feel horror at this point from what I'm looking at. Leo and

Isaac sit at the table with me, all of us quiet while the storm continues outside.

"Cause of death could be blood loss or beheading, too hard to tell until the autopsy," Isaac mutters. "But they already know he was dead before the attack."

"He probably refused to help Gabriel. That's what he got in answer," Leo says darkly.

"The head placement is *The Godfather* obviously," Isaac murmurs, then points to the obvious crucifixion symbolism. "Is the other reference from *Passion of the Christ*?"

"Doesn't fit the other movies he's used," Leo answers. "Thrillers, mainly."

"What about the Latin on his chest?"

"*Boondock Saints*," I say, easily recognizing the phrase the brothers used. "Lot of Christian symbolism in the movie." I then look up at Leo, slowly remembering more of the plot through my numbed state. "Tell Vincenzo to leave Rome. They kill a character of the same name who's part of the mafia. If he did this to Renato, who knows what he'll do to Vincenzo for agreeing to work with you."

Isaac mutters under his breath, rubbing a hand over his face.

"We'll send a warning. See if he listens or not," Leo says in a rough voice.

We're all quiet, staring at the photos in disbelief that Gabriel actually killed Renato. Not to mention, in such a brutal way and for so many to see. The rain taps on the window like an omen.

"Not sure if I should be impressed or…horrified that he knew you'd catch that," Isaac murmurs.

I look out the window, finding my grave expression in the reflection.

For the first time in my life, I really hated movies.

Chapter 39

River Thames

Vincenzo finally left Rome after I scolded him. At first, he wouldn't listen to Leo, refusing to be scared by Gabriel. His villa was destroyed, barely standing, and dozens of his men killed along with civilians. He wanted revenge and penance. Frustrated, I may have ordered him to leave Rome. He wasn't safe. I'm not sure if he believed my reasoning due to the clues left behind, but I think he believed my fear for him.

Did I care that much about him? No. Did I want to see what horrific desecration Gabriel would wreck onto his body? Bigger no.

The next three days were radio silence.

Only Isaac kept in contact with anyone, completely cutting off communications for Leo and me. Carrie published that we were in Paris for our honeymoon after having our small, intimate wedding in Rome. At least I didn't have to take any calls, lying about where we were. Again.

The Crew was doing their best to track down Gabriel. Renato's estate was in disarray from what we heard. Leo wants nothing of what's left of it. With Gabriel still alive, it likely goes to him, until then there's nothing we can do about it. No word of where Giovanna is or if she's even alive.

Now the only question was, would he go after Vincenzo first or us? Or the wild card, Matteo?

This morning, Isaac told us that Jameson was suggesting we head to another country to keep moving until they found Gabriel. No one wanted us in the states until he was gone. At the moment, Berlin and Prague were at the top of the list. Never thought I'd be disappointed in traveling to other countries. Leo and I both needed to think on it, so we decided to take our daily walk.

The River Thames is on one side and the Tower of London is on the other. Isaac shadows us through the late morning crowds of tourists that travel in groups. I glance over at some as they head into the entrance for the Tower. We take a turn up a road, walking past the stone walls.

"In all honesty, how long do you think you can continue the honeymoon excuse for the rest of your companies?" I ask, moving closer to Leo's side.

"However long I want." I squeeze his fingers playfully. He glances down at me, and I raise a brow. "Jameson will be able to handle it, along with Owen and Julio. Chiari will take care of the hotel, like the others I'm never at. Basically, they can self-sustain without me constantly at the helm."

"Is that what you've been preparing for?"

Leo looks away, voice softer, "Often as I work, I never wanted my businesses to depend solely on me. For them to survive if anything happened. It's somewhat why I have the Crew."

My stomach flips a little as I inhale a long breath. Had he always been ready in case Gabriel snapped or was it because of something else?

I want to ask, but decide not to push as we continue walking up the slight hill. We take a turn down a road where more shops are. A tingling runs up my spine, and I flick my gaze over my shoulder. Isaac isn't far behind, pretending to enjoy the sights.

"We have choices of where to go next, but if you had somewhere that you wanted more, where would it be?" Leo asks.

"Home," I answer. I feel him look down at me, and he gently places his arm around me. "Prague sounds nice though."

We're quiet for a bit. We've walked like this every day, picking somewhere random in London, talking. We'd take the tube and then just amble around the city. Today we decided to walk along the Thames. As we venture further from the river itself, we come upon smaller streets and less traffic along with streets of cobblestones. It's busy around us with tourists and just those who live in London.

"We'll get home soon, dear Watson. I promise."

"I know," I sigh, leaning my head awkwardly against his side. "Never thought I'd miss New York so much, yet here I am."

"Never thought I'd miss it either."

I tilt my head up, and he meets my gaze briefly. He leans down enough to kiss my head, moving his arm down to his side to grab my hand again.

"What are you wanting for lunch?"

"Hmm, well we could do fish and chips again." Leo snorts at my suggestion. "Or pick a random pub. Isaac knows a place with really good chicken tikka masala."

"The upside of traveling is that you're no longer suggesting cereal," Leo muses.

I gently push him, and he smiles at me.

There's a sudden shout nearby, and we both turn towards the noise. It's just someone yelling at another for their bike almost hitting them. They're loud, garnering attention, but it's a quick argument as the crowd goes on as it has been.

I notice Leo's hand had gone to his firearm, hidden under his jacket, but he eases back as we continue walking. We come around another corner and that tickling sensation comes back, worsening. Dread fills me. Spine stiffening, my eyes flash to the side. I clear my throat softly, trying to look over my shoulder nonchalantly.

There's no Isaac.

I look forward, heart beginning to race.

Leo leads us around another corner, and I glimpse back again.

Still no Isaac.

"Leo…"

"I know. Keep walking. Stay within the crowd." His voice is low as we maneuver closer to more people.

Leo's hand grips mine as we act like our bodyguard didn't just disappear; our *ex-MI6* bodyguard didn't just fucking disappear.

"The argument was a decoy," I whisper.

"Do you have your phone on you?" Leo asks. I nod barely. "Knife?" I do it again. "There should be a station about two blocks from here. Take it to get to Kings Cross."

"I'm not leaving you—"

"You run when I tell you." His voice punches through me. "Go to the address we discussed with Isaac."

"Not without—"

"I'll find you in Edinburgh."

"Leo."

"Autumn, do as I say. What we planned."

Except that plan was to run together. His hand grips mine, almost shaking as I chance a look to see him staring ahead with his jaw muscles tight.

"Leo…"

"I love you," he says as we come to an intersection. A chill hits my skin when he lets go of my hand. "*Run.*"

My heart and soul scream as I sprint, obeying his command as I've done before. Instinct drives me as I bolt through the crowds, racing for the tube. There's no noise behind me, no gunshots or even yelling. I keep running, fighting back tears, but right as I should take a turn for the station, I go the other way.

I try to recall the maps I've looked at with Isaac, memorizing parts of London. Unfortunately, it's not set up like New York or even Rome. I come to an intersection I'm unsure about, glancing at the street signs. I take another turn as I try to find a way to double-back behind Leo, unable to leave him or Isaac behind. Anxiety runs up my spine as my heart clatters in my chest.

My hands shake as I come up through a small street, recognizing I'm back to where Leo and I had just been. He's nowhere. The tingling sensation yanks at me with warning. Slowly, I back away, looking in multiple directions for him or Isaac.

Shit. SHIT.

"Get to King's Cross," I mutter, turning around.

Suddenly, someone grabs me. I'm nabbed from the crowd of tourists not paying attention to anything around them as they talk loudly or play music. I'm pulled into a more deserted side street. There's honking from cars and buses, people yelling as I let out a shout. Too much noise for anyone to notice as an arm I don't know wraps around my neck. Panic consumes me as something soft muffles my screams, trying to shake my head. I can smell something that's wrong. The tightening around my neck worsens as my vision darkens.

No.

My mind is frantic, struggling to break loose.

No.

Everything goes black.

Chapter 40

Mrs. Cowboy

My head fucking hurts.

Each of my senses taking too long to get back online. It throbs while my stomach flips, squeezing like I've been sick for hours. My mouth is dry as a musty smell fills my nose. Too slowly, my body goes on alert as I feel the cold hard ground beneath me. Concrete. My cheek lays against it as I start to slowly lift my head. It smells of wet fabric and dirt.

I clear my throat, coughing out dust while attempting to get up on all fours. My arms fumble under me and I fall hard against the concrete, making me groan. I try again, blinking through blurry vision, dark spots everywhere as I try to focus where I am.

Abandoned building probably. Has to be with the bare concrete walls. Mess of construction left behind with paint cans and ripped tarps. Planks of wood damaged from moisture. Drywall half up. I blink more, shaking my head a little as I try to make sense of where the fuck I am.

Concentrate, Autumn. You were abducted in plain fucking daylight in London. *Definitely* not on my bingo card.

Fuck the bingo card, get moving.

I cough again, throat burning as I finally stumble to my feet. My feet sting, cold as I realize my shoes and socks are gone. A shiver comes over me as I look around. I see a window as I shake myself again, trying to be more alert as my head pounds.

I stumble to the window, fingers biting into the edge as I look down. It looks like I'm roughly four to five floors high. I'm in an abandoned office building. Or something that would've been. I stick my head out, trying to see where I might be, but it seems whoever abandoned this place did the same with the area below. Rain drizzles over my face, helping me wake up and concentrate.

I pull my head back in, muttering to myself. "Get your bearings. Get moving."

More of me wakes up as I shake my limbs out, body still feeling tired and sore. My chest then constricts with oncoming panic, anxiety crawling over my skin as I see the only way out is through a doorway with the door ripped off at the hinges. It's not extremely dark inside, just dim from the clouds outside.

"Seen enough movies for this shit," I grumble, allowing anger and annoyance to come forth. Better than curling into a ball crying and panicking.

I wipe at my face, brushing off dust and dirt. Then I finally look myself over, finding my jacket gone and wearing a tank top that's not mine. The fuck? I pat around my pockets, finding my knife gone, too. I check the smaller pockets of my jeans, thankfully still mine, and find my emergency key knife tucked into my front pocket. I let out a sigh of relief for the tiny weapon, opening it and closing it quickly. It's something.

I press it hard against my palm. It helps me focus as I start to head for the door. My feet pinch from the concrete and debris as I walk. I come to another hallway, lights hanging from the ceiling with bare wires. As I go, I listen for noises. I come to a large room with pillars, wires hanging from the walls, more abandoned wood and materials. Stepping forward, I jump back as I accidentally step on a loose screw. I hiss under my breath, bending down to rub my foot as I glare at the mess before me.

Through the foggy confusion of my brain, clues begin to click.

I'm in a destroyed office building. No socks. No shoes. A tank top that's not mine. A floor under construction covered in glass and debris.

How did Gabriel get fucking *worse*?

"Yippee-ki-fuck you, asshole," I mutter, carefully moving towards one of the doors that could lead to stairs.

I need to get the fuck out of here before he decides to raise the damn dead or come out with a ghost face mask. The photos of his other victims flash over my mind.

When I get to the door, I try to open it, but it won't budge. My heart rate picks up, looking around the place. There are two other halls, and there's more windows mostly covered by tattered tarps and plywood. Maybe I could tie the tarps together to climb out of a window. I glance up, debating pulling a John McClane and crawl through the HVAC. Thoughts scramble, looking at the materials around, when suddenly there's a noise from one of the halls.

There's a knot in my stomach, wanting to hurl whatever is left in my stomach as I swallow hard. Another noise, and I think I hear chains rattling.

Panic starts to grip me again.

"He's trying to fuck with you. Don't let him."

My voice is quiet as I nimbly step over junk towards the other hall. Lightbulbs barely illuminate it, haphazardly strung up, causing shadows as the long hall twists to the right. Pale light comes from the other end. I blink, trying to adjust to the odd lighting, head swimming as I see tarps hanging on the walls. With a slow breath, I tiptoe over shards of glass and nails, but then notice it's not tarps.

My eyes widen as horror fills my veins and I feel cold.

Papers are pinned up. Not papers. Pictures.

They're stills taken from paused moments likely from a video. Blurred edges of motion. Bad lighting as if the camera was hidden. I want to be sick as I look from picture to picture, anger washing over me next.

"I'm gonna kill him," I hiss under my breath. "So, help me, I'm going to kill you Gabriel."

Every photo is of Leo either being fucked by a woman or in a compromising position. Gagged. Tied up. Wearing a cock cage. Hand cuffed to walls or crosses. Being beaten. Or on his knees.

I slowly step forward, breath shaking with anger as I stare at one where he's on his knees. He's blindfolded, ball-gagged with his hands tied behind his back. I see a shadow of a woman with a crop in her hand. His ex-Mistress. The one who blackmailed him. Right as I'm about to be so fucking angry with her, I see other photos tucked in with the rest.

Instead, it's her in all those positions, but she's crying. There's blood covering her, spattered across her vulnerable naked skin. And as I step further down the hall, I see the photos of her dead body. Horror rolls over me as I clutch the knife in my hand, seething at this fucked-up funhouse Gabriel's created. His twisted version of "truth, justice."

There's rattling of chains and a grunt, and then a shout quickly cut off.

I go still. Another grunt.

Warning yanks at me. Skin prickling as I grip the pocketknife, stepping carefully through the mess in the hall. Glass is everywhere, and I'm careful not to cut my feet up. Quietly, I come around the corner and hop to the other side of a pile of nails, peeking around the wall.

Get out.

I want to puke. Scream.

Get out!

I don't move, unable to look away in terror.

It's a large room with few windows which look like just holes where a wrecking ball has hit. Rusted chains are strewn about, along with metal pipes and planks of wood. In the room is a gigantic fucking hole with metal rods sticking out. I glance up at the ceiling, crumbling from what fell and likely made the hole. But in the middle of it all, stands Gabriel with a knife in his hand. He wears slacks and tank-top covered in blood.

RUN.

My instincts scream for safety.

Except, the only reason I'd ever stay in the same damn room as Gabriel is strung up in chains—Leo.

Chapter 41

Wretched Comedy

LEO'S WRISTS are bound by rope, held high above his head looped and tied to a hook hanging from chains. His feet are bare and tied as well, wearing only his slacks. His toes barely touch the ground as blood drips down his sides, creating a small puddle. He's covered in cuts, crimson streaked all over him. His lip is busted, cuts across his face, and there's blood trickling down his head.

I want to run to him; get him out.

Gabriel starts to turn, and I hide behind the wall. My heartbeat thunders into my head, making the migraine that was disappearing come back as I try to think. Hands shaking, I press them to my sides as my legs feel weak. I want to fall to the ground going through potential scenarios in my head. There's a pained grunt and I hold back a sob.

Shit. Shit. Think, Autumn!

Too big of space, no way can I surprise him. Can't sneak up. If I come out right now, I've no clue what his plans are. Kill Leo immediately, then me? Or kill me, then him? My mind scrambles through the fear as it shakes me. I slowly edge away from the room. Quietly, I tiptoe back over the glass, eyes coming back to the photos with despair.

What does he want? It repeats in my head. I stare at a photo of Leo tied up similarly how he is out there, but he still touches the ground, and his head hangs back.

It clicks.

Control.

The movie references. Setting all this bullshit up. Each piece to fuck with me, not to outright kill me, not even when I saw him at the villa. Fuck, he even took his time with the others he killed. I flashback further to those days in the clubs, how he reveled being in power. He's feeding his own ego, which means it's his weakness.

A plan formulates. It meant getting close to him, but it may give us a chance. Inhaling a shaky breath, I close my eyes a second and focus.

Get out. Don't stop.

I get to work. I tiptoe over the glass, wincing at some cracks in the concrete that pinch at my feet. Carefully, I grab some of the planks of wood and place them at the hallway entrance. Too slowly it feels, I pile them, but I'm able to remain silent. Quickly, I grab nails and lay them out face up just a foot from the wood. I then memorize my surroundings, noting items I can pick up as weapons.

Chest tightening like a heavy lead ball is inside me, I carefully hop over the small trap, going back down the hall. I get to the middle, looking once more at the photos of Leo. My heart clenches, promising myself I'll get him out. I close my eyes, breathing deep and force my past self to be here. To be numb. To be vindictive.

I grip my tiny knife, and then inhale once more before I let out a bloodcurdling scream that echoes off the walls. I gasp when I finish screaming, and there's a stillness from the other room. Until Gabriel laughs.

"Don't enjoy your gift, Sarah?"

I step down the hall, careful with each step. There's no sound of him walking towards the hall. Good, good.

"Come on, *sister-in-law*, join us." I get nearer, stepping over the glass and hiss as I step on a screw instead. I shove the key knife into my back pocket. "Or I come to you…Mrs. Cowboy."

Fuck. Too slow.

My feet hurt as I rush to the end, scraping against the concrete as I stumble into the room. Pounding vibrates through my head as I look up, coming face to face with Gabriel who stands like a cocky asshole, flashing his large butcher knife. Leo's eyes widen with horror.

"You had her here?" Leo's voice is rough, alarmed.

"Oh, worried what I did when I left you?" Gabriel licks his lips, flicking his gaze over me.

My stomach churns. Fuck I already want to be sick. How long was I out for? How long has he been hanging there?

"Autumn, run," Leo orders weakly.

"Oh, no, no, she's not going anywhere, are you?" Gabriel flashes his knife again, stepping closer to Leo with the point at his abdomen.

I step forward. "Stop!"

His smirk grows, pressing it further and I see blood seep as I move closer.

"Gabriel, fucking *stop*!" I scream, and he does. "Whatever you want—"

"Give me anything to save him?" Gabriel brings his hand up, grabbing Leo's chin roughly before jerking it towards himself. "Hear that? What do you think she's willing to give me?"

Leo tries to yank his head away.

"What *do* you want?" My voice trembles, shifting as I ready myself to run if he comes for me. My eyes flick to the chains and other random objects in the room. The pipes and boards are too big.

"You both to suffer." He lets go of Leo, playing with the knife as he takes a few steps towards me. Leo yanks his arms, trying to escape as the chains rattle. Gabriel keeps his gaze on me, looking disappointed as he points the knife back at his brother. "Careful, Leo. Talk or struggle too much, and those fantasies will be *very* real right here."

Leo abruptly goes extremely still. Terror I've never seen before on his face.

I swallow hard, concentrating on each breath as my skin starts to feel hot. Anxiety shaking me.

"Like the photos?" He asks me.

"Seen better," I rebuke, pressing my hands against my thighs. He steps towards me, and I step to the side.

"Did what I could with the pictures left. Apparently, the films were all burned. He must've scared her good, cause she refused to give them to me. Until after some…" he holds up the knife, "…edge play changed her mind. You're welcome in getting rid of her."

"Where'd you send her body parts?"

"I kept her in once piece. Fishermen may find her in due time."

Whether I hated her or not, she didn't deserve that. Nor Charlotte, Renato, or fuck, even Roger.

I keep stepping to the side, pretending to stumble a little as Gabriel circles with me.

"You two were harder to grab, but he…" Gabriel points back at Leo, "…was easy when I showed him your limp body. Would've crawled through glass to get to you. Pathetic."

"Says the one chasing us around Europe. May I suggest watching a movie?"

"I enjoy a good primal chase," he jeers, then points to the scar on his face. "You and I have had the longest game."

My eyes flick to Leo, who's working his bloodied fingers against the rope. He swings a little, but not enough to cause noise.

Play dumb. Feed the ego.

I tilt my head at Gabriel. "Have we?"

"Need me to connect the dots…Sarah?" I don't tear my gaze away as he continues to prowl, now seeming to enjoy this idea of circling with me. Stalking me.

"What dots?" *Keep him talking. Always the downfall of the villain, let him do the damn monologue.*

"I knew Leo was up to something. The famous lone bachelor suddenly wasn't fucking anything that moved. But him and his paranoid ways…" he tsks loudly, as I back around the edge of the hole and hold back a grimace when I step on rubble, "…not even allowed near hotel staff. Thankfully, you're a bleeding heart. Charlotte suddenly didn't have to do any digging at all. You made it easy."

"I thought she was a friend."

"That's what makes *you* pathetic."

"Why kill her? Cause she left?"

"She got fucking caught! What use was left of her, apart from fucking? Even if she received such good intel on you." His tongue runs over his teeth, and disgust fills me. "You're the perfect fuck, eh? No chance of little heirs running around. That why he kept you? No chance of babies popping out?"

My chest shakes, flashing back to that afternoon I said I couldn't get pregnant. Fearful realization must cross my face because he grins sinisterly.

"Oh, she told me. Everything from movies, that stupid bookstore, to no screaming kids." He laughs suddenly. "You must fuck like an expensive whore for him to want to keep you."

I glare at him, chin quivering as I hear Leo behind me move. I don't dare look back at him as I keep circling with Gabriel.

"How'd you get Roger?" I ask roughly, trying to keep him on me.

"Late at night. Too easy. Dumb fuck. You really should be thanking me. I've killed everyone who's fucked you over, too. You should be on your knees thanking me, sucking me off."

His tone darkens, sliding his eyes over me possessively.

"Yet, aren't you the one who hired all those men to kill me?"

"You mean Matteo?" He smirks. "He so desperately wants to be loved by his big brothers, it was easy to convince him. Renato already hated him, making Matteo believe he'd get rid of him, child's play. And hate you? The little, broken gold digger, fuck toy who'd steal *everything* from us."

A sinking feeling hits me. "It was all you," I breathe out.

"Matteo and Renato were the easy pawns. I thought the other

mob bosses would be harder to convince, but then my little brother decided to make our father proud. Blood pouring onto the streets of New York. Easy to convince them to look for new leadership. You see, he's not the only one who knows how to get what one wants out of people's wishes."

Gabriel comes back around to Leo, smacking his cheek harshly. Leo grunts, body shuddering. He sneers looking at Leo.

"We learned from the same father. Same world. He just tries to be more holier about it. Always has." He grabs Leo's chin, yanking to look at him again. "Too bad our mother didn't trust you. Guess she was right. You had too much Riccardo in your blood. I look like him, but you *stink* of him. Deceptive cocksucker."

"You kill her alongside Renato?" I ask.

"I'm not a monster." Liar. "Renato fucked me over. A liability and obsolete. An old man who'd never part with his money, even if it meant his downfall. No, my mother is still alive."

He steps away from Leo, and I breathe easier seeing his hands off of him.

"After you two, next will be Renaldi for turning his back on me. And then Matteo to rid the world of his stupidity. Probably Leo's little biker buddies, too. Then she and I can live peacefully, in total control of *all* the fortunes *you* stole from me."

"How Oedipus of you," I mutter.

His face darkens, lip curling as he steps directly at me. *Oh,* struck a nerve and *there's* the kink in his armor.

"Will you rejoice by fucking her next when we're dead?" I taunt, moving quicker as he stalks me.

He snarls, hand gripping his knife. "Oh, no, I'm going to fuck *you,* slut. I'm going to pin you against the concrete floor, rip your clothes off, and put this at your neck. All while making you stare at *him* while I do."

My gaze flicks to Leo, who's face contorts with anger and horror as blood gathers at his wrists.

"I won't finish there. I'll silence your smart remarks by fucking your mouth so hard you'll never speak again," Gabriel continues, panic runs over me. "Perhaps I'll make you suck him off while I fuck you from behind. That's what you did when I sent those men after you, right? A real pro."

Anger splits through me. "Bastard," I spit at him.

He sneers, stopping in his tracks.

"And then I'm going to do what I told him I would when you arrived…" the menacing smile on his face makes my blood run cold, "…remember the ending of *Leaving Las Vegas*? I wonder how hard he'll be when I make him fuck your dead body."

"You sick freak," I rasp.

The grin worsens. "Be a good girl. Maybe I'll kill him quickly for you."

The pet name clangs through me. Overprotective, violent wrath floods my veins as I growl at him, straightening ever so slightly.

Game on, motherfucker.

"Is that what you call Giovanna when you fuck her? While she calls you Riccardo right before coming?"

Gabriel's face turns red, and he charges.

Chapter 42

Inferno

I ᴅᴜᴄᴋ down and swing my leg towards his shins when he's close enough. He grunts, stumbling forward as I swipe my arm to knock the blade from his hands, stepping on a sharp rock. The knife clangs to the ground as I fall forward, pain jolting my body. Survival kicks in, along with flight as I scramble away from him and grab debris. As he comes for me again, I fling the stuff into his face. He sputters with a yell as I get up, punching him, which makes him stumble over his own feet. My hand throbs as I run out and down the hall.

My feet scream, biting with pain as I step on glass. I yelp, stumbling towards the wall and rip off pictures as I try to keep going. Gabriel bellows from behind as I push past the pain and get to the end, barely jumping over my trap.

Wild thoughts run through my head as I aim for one of the boards, feet bleeding.

Distract Gabriel. Kill him before he kills you.

There's a yell as I scramble for a board I can pick up. I glance over my shoulder when he howls, tripping over the boards and steps on the nails. He still charges for me as I bring up the wood, swinging. I hit him square on, but it doesn't take him down as I swing again. He grabs it, ripping it from me and makes me tumble backwards. Gabriel is suddenly on top of me, pressing the wood against my chest to crush me. It feels like something snaps inside, cracking, pain radiating through me.

Raging eyes meet mine. *"You little cunt!"*

I bring a leg up, and I'm able to hit just behind his knee, pushing him off-balance as I shove forward with all my might. He falls to the side as I jam my heel into his crotch. He roars in pain as I scramble to all fours, grabbing a piece of rubble and come around to hit him hard in the dick.

His scream vibrates the walls and my head. I go to hit him again, but his arms swing and knocks the rock away. I reach for anything, getting hold of another plank of wood, and swing back at him as he grabs for me. This time I make contact with his head. Gabriel falls to the ground, moaning into the concrete floor as I clutch the wood and run.

Agony slices through my feet, making me whimper as I stumble back through my little trap. I rush down the hall as fast as I can, finding it difficult to breathe.

"Fuck, fuck..." I swear under my breath. Pain courses up through my legs feeling like I've run through an entire hoard of legos.

Gabriel groans down the hall when I get to the other room. Fuck I should've hit him twice.

"Autumn," Leo rasps.

Pushing past the pain, I sprint to Gabriel's knife and then to Leo. He's too tall for me to reach his hands, not without hurting him while in a rush. Instead, I get to the ground, cutting the rope around his ankles.

"Autumn, get out—"

"Not fucking leaving you!"

His ankles are undone as I hear Gabriel tear off pictures, huffing and swearing. I grab my smaller knife, open it and practically climb Leo to shove it into his hands. Sticky blood clings to me. For a split second, our gazes meet in terrified hope.

I hear Gabriel's approach, ripping my attention away from Leo as I jump away and grip the larger knife. Gabriel runs at me, and I swipe down. It catches his arm, but it doesn't stop him. I move away from Leo as Gabriel charges again, and I swipe. This time I just miss his arm and he grabs mine, twisting it. I cry out, dropping the knife as I kick at him. He pushes me suddenly, and I fall back only a few feet from the hole. Agonizing pain screams through me as I quickly scramble back from him over the rubble.

Except, Gabriel lands on top of me, grappling me to the ground as the concrete and debris scratch against my skin. He starts to yank at my pants as pain pulses from my insides.

"Want to play rough?" He tries to unbutton my jeans as I squirm, continuing to fight him. "Fine, bitch!"

I kick at him, screaming as I shove and try to get away from underneath him. I can't get to his shins or knees again, trying to hit at his vulnerable points. Suddenly, he flips me over, and my head bangs against the concrete.

There's a quick shock of pain. My brain fuzzes as I see black spots and that snapping feeling in my chest I'd felt earlier happens again. Something cracking. My breath catches as he pins me, shoving my face into the dusty concrete. I try to catch my breath, but keep breathing in dust, struggling for air. He tugs at my jeans, attempting to pull them down as panic surges.

"No!" I scream hoarsely.

My body trembles, starting to go numb as that survival tactic I'd used for years rears its ugly head. *Go numb.*

"No!" I scream again.

Don't fight.

His hand grips my hip, pulling down my jeans.

No!

"Little fucking—"

Abruptly, Gabriel is off me. There's a grunt, a thud and sounds of quick breath.

I scramble, pulling my jeans back up and look over my shoulder. Leo punches Gabriel, grappling him to the ground with blood flying. The men fight as my head swims, pain pulsing through every fiber of me. My thoughts are jumbled, distorted. Agony cuts through my chest as I groan, forcing myself to get up as I hold my side. Pain sears through my leg as I stumble towards some chains near the edge of the hole.

There's a clang, and I watch Gabriel's knife slide and tumble over the edge. It clinks when it hits the floor below. My hair stands on end when I hear another grunt. Through the foggy pain, I turn towards the other two and watch Leo slump to the ground. He's barely moving, and horror fills me.

"Always won those fights growing up. Glass stomach," Gabriel comments, spitting out blood. It trickles down from his nose and mouth. "Or maybe it's from being tortured for hours."

I bend down quickly, grabbing a chain, honestly unsure what to do with it. I can't seem to think as my vision darkens on the edges and it's getting harder and harder to concentrate. Gabriel blurs a little as I blink, clutching the metal as it bites into my hand. Everything hurts.

Gabriel comes closer as I stumble back, my heel finding the edge of the hole and I glimpse behind me. Panic rushes as I see it's a two-story fall to rubble and metal. A flash of fear hits me. I face Gabriel stepping away, giving myself more slack of the chain.

"Gonna go *Ghostrider* on me?" He jeers, spitting out blood again.

Suddenly an idea flashes. Through the pain comes a moment of clarity. I focus not willing to give up. Leo starts to get up, rope still wrapped around his hands.

I look at Gabriel as he stalks me. He won't win. I won't fucking let him.

"Go to hell," I snarl.

I tense as he charges for me again, then at the last second move to the side and swing the chains. He tries to grab for them, but I entangle him as I bring them up, grunting with all my strength. My feet slip in doing so, both of us going down as my body lands hard against the concrete. More pain pierces me, making tears spring to my eyes. Air punches from my lungs as I fight through the agony, wrestling with Gabriel to wrap him in the chains. He's too focused on trying to get to me, grappling me as we get closer to the hole's edge. Soon, I feel the pinch of the concrete edge at my shoulder blades.

A gasp leaves me, head throbbing and swirling. My head hangs over the side, and I see the long fall. Gabriel pulls the chains off of himself, but is quickly dragged away. I hear Leo grunt, pulling his brother away from me. While Gabriel's distracted by him, I fumble to get up and grab the chains again. Gabriel hits Leo hard, knocking him down as he starts to get up and kicks him in the stomach. I toss the chains over Gabriel's head as he turns for me. I move aside, yanking down on the chains that are left, and he stumbles. He yanks at the chains as I kick behind his knee again, luring him back to the hole.

He yells, swearing and reaching for me as I yank the chain down and toss it over the edge. His hands grab me as the heavy metal links slide over the concrete, jolting Gabriel's body at the sudden weighted pull. I shove him with all I have, and he tilts backwards. His face reddens, falling over the edge. He flails for the metal rods, but misses as he disappears and there's a nasty ripping sound. The chain goes taut from the ceiling, a crack resounding through the space as my body starts to give up, falling next.

I'm grabbed and yanked back before I join him. My body thuds against another, landing as my vision blurs. Arms wrap around me, clinging to me through blood, sweat, and grime. Everything's fuzzy as dark and white spots flicker over my vision. Still, I glance over the edge where the chain dangles. Gabriel's limp body swings, head almost ripped off. Dead.

"Oh, fuck," I mutter, stomach revolting.

Leo clutches me as I look away. My hands move over his bloodied skin, finding cut after cut as he hisses in pain. I flinch at my own radiating from my chest, head, limbs, and feet.

"Leo." I don't know if I'm shouting or whispering.

My head rolls back. He starts to move us, grunting as I whimper at the flashes of pain. It's the only thing keeping me awake. I'm lain down, while my chest aches sharply. My eyes try to stay open as hands move over me, touching gently. My feet throb likely shredded up.

"I think…cracked…ribs," I whisper, trying to concentrate as Leo's face appears above me.

His face is covered in blood, streaked down his neck. He finally gets the rope on his wrists off, and I see his skin has been ripped off around his wrists and forearms. Oh, fuck.

"Autumn, stay awake," he murmurs.

"Hard…to." I swallow against my dry throat, more of me feels cold and numb. "Need…a nap."

"Not now. Keep your eyes open, sweetheart," Leo tries to order me with a shaky voice. Something's wrong. There's fear in his voice.

I feel him stumble up. My body feels heavier and heavier. Head pounding down through my spine. Slowly, I remember this feeling. The cold numbness. Body shutting down. The exhaustion pulling at you. I've been here before.

Leo returns, and I'm able to just make out a phone. Something rings and there's talking, but I can't make it out.

"Phone?"

"He wanted them to find our bodies," Leo responds, putting the phone down. "Autumn, focus on me."

Everything is going dark as the pain beating through me seems to vanish. I try to focus on him, but it's harder every second. Hands gently grip my face. "Don't leave me. Don't let him take you from me, too."

"Not leaving," I whisper. "I promised."

Something wet hits my cheek. Another drop.

Leo's tears fall upon my face as he clutches me, hands shaking against my skin. "Sweetheart, stay awake."

So, damned tired. Was it like this last time? Knowing I was dying, but I was terrified back then. I'm not now. I can't be this calm if I'm dying, can I? No, I just need to sleep.

Beeping. A clicking sound. Muffled voices.

Lips press gently against my forehead. "Don't leave me. Don't you dare fucking leave me. I need you."

It hurts to breathe. Each breath harder.

"Autumn." His voice is distant. My eyes close completely. "Open your eyes."

I can't.

"Open them, Autumn."

I'm so sorry, my dear Leo.

His voice shakes. "Dear Watson…please…"

A limpness reaches over me as I succumb to the darkness and exhaustion, finally escaping the pain. The last thing I hear is Leo's heartbreaking scream.

Chapter 43

Purgatorio

Leo

THERE WAS ONLY PAIN.

It choked him from every direction. That dark well dragging him further and further. All he could focus on was Autumn.

Her closed eyes. Far too still body. The deafening silence as his hands trembled clutching her face. Pain radiates over him from the cuts, throbbing as his wrists and forearms burned from the ropes that ripped his skin off. Agony wanting to yank him under, exhaustion threatening next, but he couldn't tear his eyes away from her.

He could barely feel the faint breath from her nose. The weak heartbeat in her chest. The only flicker of hope for him.

Anguish tears at him, blending with flashes of the last 24 hours. His focus becomes skewed as he struggles to concentrate on Autumn. *Get her out. Get her home.*

Leo's thoughts jumble, merging with the torture he endured for hours. Dripping of blood. Gabriel's taunts. The slow burn of the knife dragging across his skin. Her soul crushing screams.

461

"I'm going to fuck her in front of you." Gabriel's words echo as his vision blips. He can see him masturbating in front of him, coming all over her shirt.

Horror plunges deeper.

"No!" Autumn's terrified shrieks as Gabriel was about to rape her. *"No!"*

Leo shakes his head. Moments jump from one to the next as if he's living in a nightmare. Too slow. Too fast.

The phone ringing. Jameson's shouts through the building. Rudy swearing. Cars pulling up. Ripping pictures down, and the smell of fire as they burned them. Wait…how is Jameson here? He called Enigma. Isaac was here, not—

The smell of fresh rain hits as he stumbles outside. Vehicles. Flashing lights. Arguing and yelling, most of it from him. Terror buries him as he blinks, feeling heavy as the next moment of clarity jolts him.

He's aiming a gun at a woman.

Leo breathes heavy, holding it over Autumn's body on a gurney. Jameson is trying to calm him down, while Rudy tells two others to stay back. It's drizzling as they stand outside the abandoned building Gabriel dragged them to.

The woman's brown eyes are calm as she holds her hands up.

They were about to touch her. Take her to the hospital.

"She's going home," Leo says in a rough voice. "Plane. Now."

"Your wife may be in a coma," the woman says. "We need her to go to the hospital. Both of you."

"No."

"Leo, Autumn needs medical help. You both do," Jameson tries to convince him. "We'll take care of the hospital—"

"So, fucking help me, not even you will stop me, Sombra," Leo growls, dizziness swamps his vision as he shakes his head slightly. "I am taking my wife home."

"Then allow me to help you get her home alive," the woman says. "We will get her stable, check for internal bleeding, brain damage—"

The gun trembles. "No one touches my wife. *No one.*"

He doesn't feel like himself. Pain unravels while the dread worsens. The only constant thought is to protect Autumn. Get her home.

"Mr. Luciano—"

"She has a DNR," Leo states. The others go still. "And a *very* specific LST."

"What the fuck do you mean…" Jameson's voice trails away as horror comes over his face. "Fuck."

"That doesn't mean we can't check her vitals or see what else we can do," the woman reassures, briefly glancing at Jameson. "What's her medical history?"

Leo feels himself sway, catching the gurney with his free hand to stay standing. It jolts pain up through his arm. Everything hurts. Pulsating as he tries to focus.

"Medical induced-coma," Leo answers, voice rough. "Assaulted, multiple lacerations, broken bones, her uterus ripped from her." The woman's eyes widen. "Medical procedures *she* didn't want."

It could be minutes or fucking hours, but in the next blink, the woman is closer with a calm expression. Her soft voice almost soothing the raging turmoil inside him.

"You have full control of her medical decisions?" Leo nods. "Then that won't happen, and *I* won't let that happen. Let me do some tests, nothing invasive, and then I'll help you get her home. But please…let me make sure she *does* make it home *alive*. Not to mention you. Those wounds on your arms can fester and you'll lose your ability to use them or your hands entirely. That's why you're struggling to hold the gun up."

He doesn't move, keeping the gun on her and yes, struggling to keep it up as pain slices through him. The woman doesn't budge, not showing any fear. Once more he can hear Gabriel's voice, saying he's worse than him. His hand drops with the gun.

"No intubation."

"Very well."

"I go with her. Everywhere."

"There may be rooms you can't enter, but I promise as a doctor and woman, no harm will come to your wife under my care."

He nods, closing his eyes briefly. Next blink he's in the ambulance. He sits across from the doctor with Autumn between them. Another medic near the front. The doctor looks up as he shakes his head, confusion filling him.

She says something about Autumn's pulse, but all he hears is, "…your wife wants to be here, Leo."

Torment clutches him as he looks down at Autumn, an oxygen mask over her face. He closes his eyes again, searing this image of her into his memory.

For the next 24 hours it's like that. One moment he's somewhere, and the next he's somewhere else. Hospital rooms. Doctors. Medical staff. Jameson trying to speak with him. Almost starting a fight with a nurse who stitches up his cuts. Another who tries to mend his wrists and forearms, but he keeps scattering things onto the floor. Only that woman doctor can touch him without repulsion. It's a blur of noises, colors, and pain.

And then words clang through him as every test comes back. Cracked ribs. Her feet cut and destroyed, possible stress fractures. Spinal contusions. Brain swelling. Coma.

Soft words explain everything to him, something about no internal bleeding and her brain still functioning. Another shift happens, and he's at the airport getting on the plane before exhaustion thrusts him under.

Gabriel's taunts and torture follow him. Disgusting fantasies as he cuts away at Leo. He never escaped. His brother clutches his throat as he licks the blood off his fingers. *You thought you could run from me again?*

Leo's eyes snap open, breath shaky as the nightmare disperses. He's on a plane. He glances around, finding Autumn on a gurney next to his seat, the woman doctor on the other side. Slow, trembling breaths release as he realizes this is reality. Gabriel is dead. Autumn killed him.

"You're alright," the woman says gently. "So is she. Stable, as much as I hate her flying right now."

He looks over at Autumn who has IVs in her chest and arms, breathing quietly on her own. His hand slides over to hers which lays on her chest, gripping it. Somehow, by a miracle, they both still have their wedding rings on.

Leo kisses her hand, then notices his forearms are bandaged tightly. He pats himself in other areas, feeling more bandages and where stitches are. All underneath a shirt he has no recollection of.

"Can you make a light fist with both of your hands, please?" The doctor asks gently.

Tiredly, he looks down and does it with his left and then his right. He struggles a bit as if his hands are too stiff.

"They're still working, good," she comments. "You shouldn't need a skin graft, but have them checked regularly as they heal. Get some sleep. I'll watch her. Don't worry."

"You kept your promise."

"You kept yours by not shooting me."

Leo lays his head upon the gurney, trying to get close to Autumn. He doesn't want to sleep, fearful of the nightmares that will come. To feel trapped once more as he had hanging from those chains. He remains awake, staring at his wife.

"She doesn't need to have a feeding tube, perhaps safer not to, given the contusions in her spinal area," the woman says gently. "But with only IVs, there are complications that can arise. Something tells me you aren't taking her to a hospital when we arrive in New York, so you'll need nurses around the clock to prevent said complications or her health declining."

Leo's silent, stroking his thumb over Autumn's hand.

"She may also need help with oxygen, which you can use a nasal cannula or even a BiPAP to not intubate her. It's all possible to stay within what she wanted, but there's far more risk by not taking her to a hospital."

He should do everything to keep her alive, but he couldn't break his promise. Remembering the relief on her face when he said he'd protect her in health and sickness. Promising she'd never endure what she had in the hospital before, which meant potentially giving her up. He couldn't bear the betrayal he'd feel if she woke up in a hospital again. To not be home. To want to die instead.

"No hospital," he murmurs.

"Are you prepared to turn your home into an ICU then? Because she will need it." Leo barely nods his head. She sighs. "May I suggest some physicians who can help you?"

"Why not you?"

"I have no visa. And not certain that I should even be on this plane right now, but I couldn't in good conscience leave you or her yet."

"You won't need a visa."

"I'm unsure who you are exactly," she says quietly. "But I can't. I have a residency, a life…to go back to. But I can help you set up something for her."

Leo slowly looks up, finding those calm brown eyes. "What's your name?" She blinks at him, confusion over her face. "Everything's jumbled." He swallows hard. "I can't remember much of the last…however long it's been."

She rubs her temple. "I knew I should've made you take a CT scan. You likely have some head trauma if you're having memory issues."

Leo doesn't say anything, just watches her. He clings to Autumn for any semblance of relief from the torment that's continuous in devouring him.

Finally, she answers, "Dr. Howell. Sara Howell."

His chest constricts, squeezing as he looks away and murmurs, "Sara. Thank you."

Four

A rguing. That's all he recalls. Voices tumbling together as they fought with him, telling him to take her to a hospital. The constant barrage. Insinuations that he's "insane". Nancy chastising him for what felt for hours, until Chesty escorted her out of the penthouse. Leanne about the same, throwing frustrated curses, tears in her eyes as Isaac had her leave.

"Leo, she'll die!"

The Crew even argued. Pushed. All of them.

He wouldn't budge. Alone in his decision as he succumbed to a numbness that felt familiar and foreign at the same time.

Dr. Howell helped set up a makeshift hospital room in the television room of the penthouse, making sure it was safe and sanitized for Autumn. A large bed faced the television screen. Monitors tucked to the side, along with all the items needed for her sustainment. He stared at Autumn as she laid there, barely hearing Dr. Howell's explanations on how to care for her. Reassuring him and everyone else.

He's not sure when she left. All he could recall was the gentle touch of her hand before she was gone.

The pain that radiates through him is numbing. He watches Autumn, listening to the faint beep of the monitor. He sits in a chair that's next to her bed, holding her hand as he caresses it with his thumb. She isn't cold, but isn't truly warm either.

"Leo," Jameson's voice drifts through the nothing. "I have two more nurses lined up to interview."

"Triple check their background."

"The doctor recommended by Dr. Howell will be up later this afternoon." Silence apart from the beeping. "I want them to check your injuries, too. You've ripped open several stitches, and your bandages need replaced."

"No."

"Leo—"

"You weren't supposed to be in England," Leo suddenly says, his voice rough and dry. He can't even remember the last time he's eaten or even drank water. "Only Isaac."

"Who'd been shot in the shoulder, drugged, and beat up," Jameson almost snaps back. "A damn ocean isn't going to stop me from going after my best friend when I've learned he's been kidnapped."

Leo's head is heavy, throbbing as it has been the last couple of days as he looks over at Jameson. He's not dressed in business attire, wearing just jeans and a shirt. Worry passes over his face. Pity even.

Did he look that broken again?

"She'll wake up," Jameson says.

Leo goes back to watching Autumn.

"I'll get you something to eat." Jameson steps out.

With every silent, harrowing moment, Leo wishes Jameson is right. That his dear Watson will come back to him again.

<hr />

Five

"He won't eat," Jameson whispers from just outside the doors. "I don't think he has in days."

Owen replies, "I could hold him down, you—"

"Fucking touch me, and I break your wrists," Leo grumbles, stroking Autumn's hair.

Three nurses have been chosen to regularly care for Autumn, along with washing her and keeping up with physical movement to prevent bedsores. The doctor recommended by Dr. Howell will come in every other day as well. Her bandages are new. His aren't.

Leo's only left this room for the bathroom, even then he almost spiraled into panic; that she'd be dead when he returned. The monitor silent.

"You're slowly killing yourself," Jameson says in a strained voice. "If not from eating, then your injuries will." Leo ignores him. There's mumbling, and then Jameson questions, "What happens if you die, and she wakes up? What do you want me to tell her? That you gave up?"

Leo just stares at Autumn, unable to move. The raw emotions filling every crack. What's left is gnawed by an ever-growing loneliness and helplessness, digging at him as he watches her sleep. Unsure she'll wake up. Unable to reach her.

"Culo, tonto…" Jameson's voice vanishes. Both men disappearing.

Leo leans back into his chair, somewhat feeling that pull of hunger. It's nothing compared to the grief that keeps him in that dark well. He can almost feel himself looking up from the bottom, bloodied and too far away to climb out. What's the point if she doesn't wake up?

Sleep pulls at him next.

And like every time he closes his eyes, he's haunted by Gabriel's jeers. The knife dragging over his skin. The smell of concrete and rust. Rattling of chains.

"I'll kill her and—…Renato cried, didn't know he could. The first bullet—…Tears as I—…" Punch. Rip. "Fucking weak, stupid—…what do think she'll sound like—"

"Where is she, Gabriel?" Laughter. "Gabriel."

"Fucking bitch!"

Leo jolts awake, panic surging as he grips the chair. His body trembles violently as he stares at the shelves of movies. His heart thunders in his chest, pounding up through his head. Everything hurts, scratching at him as he feels the tug of his stitches and twist in his stomach.

"Señor." A familiar voice comes.

Breathing heavy, he looks over and finds Alba standing with a tray in her hands. Her gaze falls upon Autumn, frowning. She then places the tray on the bed next to Autumn's feet, leaving the room.

Leo looks at the tray, seeing soup, bread, and rice. His stomach clenches, hunger yanking harder at him as Alba comes back. She places a small table next to him, moving the tray there. She's quiet as she then grabs a chair and sits in front of him.

"You need to eat, por favor." Leo stares at her. Every inhale feeling like work. She purses her lips, grabbing the bowl of soup, and then scoops some to hold up to him. "Eat."

Leo just continues to stare at her. She brings the spoon closer to his mouth.

"Alba—"

"When she wakes up, I will tell her how stubborn you were. Worse than her." She holds it closer, voice softening. "Por favor… mijo. Eat."

Tears form in his eyes as his throat tightens. Alba waits patiently. Finally, he leans forward for her to bring the spoon to his mouth. He's slow in swallowing the chicken soup, and then she does it again.

Quietly, Alba gets Leo to eat.

———

Six

He can't breathe.

The wall presses against his back as he struggles to catch his breath, feeling like bricks are on his chest. His arms burn, bandages falling off as panic surges through his veins. Terror grips him as his skin feels like it's scorching. Something crawling over him.

The nurse who'd tried to change his dressings, backs away with fear on her face. His vision blurs, black spots appearing as the world around him fuzzes out.

More people come in. He blinks, thinking he sees Jameson or Alba. Both? Someone comes closer. Hands. A flash of Gabriel shoves at him. Bombs going off in his ears. Gun shots. The cut of a knife.

"…*make you fuck her while she's dead. Her cold, pussy around—*"

They come closer, and Leo flinches back. He presses further against the wall, growling under his breath. "Fuck off, Gabriel."

The man standing before him pauses. Suddenly, someone else appears and speaks softly.

"Leo. It's Trix. You're home right now. Autumn's next to you. Look over."

His head dips down, finding Autumn in the mayhem. A calmness washes over him as he shakingly moves towards her, leaning down to press his face against her hair. He inhales, finding small comfort.

"You're home." The voice continues, floating through the carnage of his mind.

He blinks. A bit more clarity as his arms ache more, throbbing. He holds them up, noticing bandages have been ripped off, showing the bloodied wounds underneath. Another flashback of hearing Autumn's screams, and he wants to puke.

"Let's get new bandages on, okay? Will you feel safer if I do it?"

Leo looks over. Trix smiles faintly, gesturing towards the chair. His breath quickens again, the idea of being touched repulsing him. He grimaces with a frown, feeling the bile almost coming up.

She steps a little closer. "Just me. Trix. See?"

His body shudders as he stares at her, slightly shaking his head as his vision clears more. As if moving through sludge, he gets back to his chair and sits down. Trix pulls a chair over carefully, and something is placed on the table beside him.

"Do you want me to change them?" She asks again.

"I don't want anyone…touching me," he rasps, voice not wholly sounding like himself.

"How about if Alba takes care of your bandages?" Leo looks up at Trix, who keeps a calm, faint smile. He shakes his head. "Okay, but we need to take care of your wounds. I won't hurt you. He can't hurt you."

Leo's face becomes more severe, brows pulling together.

"They told me what happened," Trix says gently.

"Fuck, Trix he'll spiral don't…" Jameson starts to speak, but she holds her hand up at him.

"He needs the truth right now. Not lies. Honesty. Right?" She asks, keeping her eyes directly on Leo.

"They fucking told you?" Leo mutters, anger beginning to grow next. "She didn't want—"

"I already knew," Trix says quickly. She brings her hands down.

Confusion fogs his mind again as he shakes his head, and then holds it. He winces from touching the stitch upon his head, wrist and forearm on fire.

"Let's talk while I rebandage your arms. Give you some relief. Just us." Trix suggests, and then waves whoever is in the room out.

There're footsteps, and then the door closes. Silence, apart from the beep of Autumn's monitor. Leo moves his gaze to her, staring in hopes she'll look at him. Smile at him. That they'll be alright. She'll take care of him. *"You're safe, baby."*

"Leo."

He drags his eyes over to Trix, who holds her hands open to him again. She's patient. Waiting until he finally moves, arms trembling as he holds out his right one to her. He flinches harshly when she gently takes it, undoing the bandages carefully.

"I told Autumn who you were," she starts explaining softly. "The hotel mogul. I knew quite a bit about you because of you funding *Luna Stella*. Took a bit of digging, but I could see how powerful you were. And how kind given your list of philanthropy. That's all she ever spoke about. Your kindness."

The old bandage is taken off, and she grabs something to clean the wound. Leo won't look at it, stomach churning. He hisses when she touches it.

"After she disappeared to Roger's and came back disappearing *again*…of course, I knew something was off. Not to mention our dinner, but how you helped her that night, I couldn't care. Yet, I noticed things. Small stuff. With her. Leanne. Even you." She takes a deep breath in. "And doing some more digging, I saw a last name that I remember being in her paperwork years ago."

"Marchetti." The name is ragged upon his tongue. She nods. "How long?"

"December. I should've just talked to her, but I was worried after you got engaged. And was gone for work, and then Roger disappeared."

"Wasn't me."

"I know. They told me, including who did it."

She starts to rebandage the right arm. Anger flicks through him as he clenches his jaw, chest feeling heavier.

"I was scared for her, to go back into a world that I'd seen hurt her," Trix says somberly. "Break her. Almost killed her. But the loneliness that followed her for years, finally left when you came around. Even with the lying, well…I watched her lie to Leanne and Nan for years so they wouldn't know horrible truths. Nightmares. She has this habit of protecting the people she loves a little too… fiercely."

"Go to hell." Leo swallows hard; Autumn's voice echoing.

She finishes wrapping his arm, and then holds out her hands for the other. He hesitates, and her hands drop.

"They don't know how bad it was," she whispers, tears glistening in her eyes. Leo's face begins to crumble as they fall down her cheeks. "Those weeks in the hospital were horrendous. I couldn't save her from it. And watched as they just… took from her. Ignored her cries. How she hurt herself more, trying to escape as they… " she clears her throat, "…but you…knew. What that did to her."

Hot tears slide down his face next. They don't feel real as they fall. Throat tightening as that torment pulls at him. Loneliness and fear. "Yes."

"Thank you." Leo looks at Trix, who smiles sadly through her tears. "For protecting her. You listened when no one else had. Even if it's terrifying."

Carefully, Trix reaches for his left hand, and he jolts at the contact. She waits, and then tries again gently, gripping him as she says, "You are not selfish or some kind of asshole keeping her here. You are being completely selfless by trying to abide by her wishes. Four years ago, even now, I think she'd rather die than be back in a hospital. It's scary right now, not knowing, but I truly think you're doing the right thing. No hospital is going to magically wake her up."

More tears fall from his eyes, sobs wanting to escape as his chest trembles. "All I feel…is failure," he murmurs. "Weak. Guilt."

"You are not a weak man, because one who is could never do what you are doing. You are surviving, while trying to be strong for your *wife*. Only an honorable man who loves his wife, so dearly…" a sob breaks out of Leo, "…would risk so much to give what she's asked. Once begged for. It's not easy, but she trusted *you* to listen. Because she loves you, Leo."

Leo weeps, breaking down as Trix holds his hand tenderly. He covers his face with the other, clutching himself as he cries.

"She'll wake up. We have to believe that. Have hope. Give her time."

"I miss her," he gasps. "I need her."

"I know. Hold onto that hope. For now, hold onto that, not despair. Do everything to keep her comfortable."

A darkness fogs his brain as he eventually stops crying. Minutes, hours later, who knows. Trix rebandages his other arm. She then checks his other injuries, cleaning some areas as he sits numbly once more staring at Autumn.

"I'll talk to the others," she tries to reassure.

"No. Let me be the villain. It's what I deserve."

"Leo, you are not."

"Until she wakes up…if she does…that's all I'll be." Resignedly, he looks over at Trix's sad expression. "It's fine. Please."

With a deep breath, Trix finally nods her head. "How about I get you something to eat? Alba made potato soup. Smells good."

"Fine."

"We can even put on a movie. You have a favorite Autumn and you liked to watch? Could be comforting. For you both." She starts to leave the room.

He glances over at the shelves. "*Face/Off.*"

Nine

Leo pulls the blanket back over Autumn. He helped give her a sponge bath after her physical therapy, a daily routine that's starting to take form. The nurses care for her other vitals, but he helps care for her alongside them, even with their mutterings of complaints.

Movement comes from the doorway as he leans over to kiss her forehead, stroking her hair back. Everywhere his body still hurts, a constant ache that never leaves. It drains him constantly. Although he's less disorientated than the days before, his thoughts are still constantly fuzzy.

"Boss," Isaac's voice comes.

He looks over at the man with bruises on his face, arm in a sling. He holds up a phone. "Renaldi." Leo starts to ignore him. "Michael's alive."

The name echoes through Leo, causing his breath to catch. Brows furrowing with confusion, he holds his hand out and Isaac places the phone into it.

"Vincenzo," Leo greets.

"Leonardo, how is she?"

"Breathing."

"Better than not. Straight to the point. One of your men was found in the rubble, alive."

"His throat should've been slashed."

"Oh, it was, not enough to kill him. Nor the two bullets, and another that grazed his head," Vincenzo clears his throat. "Wasn't going to tell you unless I knew he'd live, but he needs another surgery due to complications. It's risky, capisce?" He pauses, making a humming sound. "Do I allow surgeons to try…or is it a waste of time? Your choice. Your man."

Leo gazes down at Autumn. His heart clenches. Flashes of her crying, admitting she wanted Michael as a bodyguard. Standing between him and the gun.

"Do it," Leo answers.

"Very well, hopefully I'll send him back not in a casket."

Nothing else to say, Leo begins to hand the phone back to Isaac, until Vincenzo says, "Did the motherfucker suffer? Gabriel?"

The snap of chains. *"Go to hell."*

Leo's jaw clenches as his mind tries to go crawling back towards the haunting memories.

"She hung him with chains." Leo's voice is distant.

"We all owe her," Vincenzo says, clearing his throat. "She'll wake up. She's a god. She has to. Ciao, Leonardo. I'll try to send your man back alive."

Leo holds the phone out, and Isaac takes it. He moves past in a zombie like state to the shelves of movies.

"Anything else?"

Isaac clears his throat. "Leanne wanted to come by this afternoon to see her."

"Fine."

Leo's fingers move over the movie titles.

"We're certain Matteo called Gabriel. Used a guard's phone."

Gabriel's sneer. Licking his blood off his fingers. Ejaculating onto her shirt. The drag of a knife. Screaming. Leo recoils, shutting his eyes harshly. His stomach knots, grimacing.

"Bobby still with him?"

"Yes."

"Keep him working in the hotel."

"Leo—"

"Do it."

"Bloody hell, Leo he—"

"She wanted him in the hotel." Leo's rebuke is harsh as he looks over his shoulder at her. The constant beeping of the monitor. "Keep him there."

There's more muttering, but Isaac leaves and Leo can hear him talking with another. Likely Jameson or Alba. Perhaps Trix. Alba moved into a guest room upstairs to be here 24/7.

He grabs a movie, putting it into the player. He goes back over to Autumn, kissing her head. Leo lingers there in hopes she'll open her eyes. To wake up. To move.

Nothing.

He sits down, keeping her hand in his as *Pride & Prejudice* starts to play.

Twelve

"She's arriving in ten minutes," Animal says, coming around the corner.

Leo adjusts his shirt, nodding once with a solemn expression. Animal disappears as Leo looks over at Autumn. The haunting quiet pressing down on him. Inhaling shakingly, he kisses her forehead as the sudden fear of leaving even for a short time emerges. Again, terror grips at him, telling him to stay.

What if she wakes up? What if the monitors turn off? What if—

He shakes his head, clearing his throat and gives her another kiss. "I'll be back, dear Watson."

Straightening, he walks out of the room as dread claws at him, making every step harder. He has to do this. He agreed for her to come. Waste her time more than his. And a part of him needed to see with his own eyes that Giovanna was still very much alive.

He needed to see his mother one more time.

Jameson and Animal wait for him near the door as Alba cleans the kitchen. Leo diverts his path, walking towards her.

"Go sit with her, please," he murmurs.

"Sí, mijo." She pats his cheek gently, then smiles gently. "She will be fine." Leo nods barely, and then watches as she walks away, stepping into Autumn's room.

"Leo," Jameson pulls his attention back to them. "We can take care of this; you don't have to."

"Yeah, boss, maybe it's not best—"

"She's my mother...." his stomach clenches, suddenly feeling sick, "...she won't leave otherwise."

Inhaling sharply, Leo straightens himself once more and walks out of the penthouse that he hasn't left in almost two weeks. He's silent, frowning as he stares at the ground of the elevator as they go down. He can feel the other two watching him, but ignores them.

He didn't want to meet with her. Or even have her in the states, but she's been causing problems in Italy. He'd given up the Salvadori organization to Renaldi, but Giovanna wanted it. Claimed it. Apparently, *she* wanted to be a mafioso now.

The elevator stops, doors opening as he steps out into the main lobby. Xavier stands at his old post, arm still in a sling. All of the Crew and Mila are spread out in the lobby, glancing between Leo and their unwanted guests.

Giovanna stands near the entrance with three guards behind her. Leo stops a good distance from her as those around them, settle into positions. It's quiet as she narrows her gaze at Leo, frowning with disappointment.

"Where's Gabriel?" She finally speaks.

"Is that what you wanted?"

"He deserves to be buried—"

"Nowhere."

Her face contorts into fury. "Give me my son."

"The one who killed your brother?" She straightens. "The same who tortured me and kidnapped my wife?"

"He was still my son."

"So was I."

A morsel of remorse almost passes over her face, but she quickly schools her expression. "Where is he?"

A coldness comes over Leo. Worse than before as it mingles with resentment and disgust towards her pleading for Gabriel like he hadn't been a monster.

"You'll never find him."

"How dare you—"

"He killed and tortured your brother. Do you not care about that?" She's quiet, shifting on her feet. "Or you helped him."

Her eyes flare.

They're silent as Leo's heart starts to pound in his chest. A deep pain forms as he looks at Giovanna, unable to ignore the pull to have what he's wanted for so long—his mom.

"And who, Leonardo, killed Gabriel?" She questions.

The knife clanging at the bottom. Chains snapping.

"My wife."

Darkness settles over Giovanna's face as she takes a step forward. Mila moves closer, scowling harshly at the woman.

"She's still alive?" Giovanna asks next.

"Hope she wasn't?"

"Well…when she dies it will be my concern. I am the only heir—"

"You won't receive a single penny from the Luciano estates." Leo's voice is sharp, the knowledge of what Autumn decided to do giving him a sense of pride, but also melancholy.

"I have every right—"

"Autumn is the sole decider of the fortune and every business attached to the Luciano fortune," Leo explains, placing his hands into his pockets as he relinquishes to that stony rigidness. "When she dies, most of the fortune will be divided amongst numerous charities. The rest of the businesses will be dissolved, and what's left will receive the same treatment under my supervision."

Giovanna's face turns red, fuming as she clenches her fists. "She can't!"

"As the rightful *matriarch* she can decide what she wants." Leo dips his head, becoming more menacing. "Your plan with Gabriel of killing her would have backfired. Neither of you would have received a thing. Because if he'd succeeded in killing us both, everything that *I* own would be split equally with my motorcycle club. Then they could decide to continue what I have begun or dissolve it all."

There're murmurs from the Crew. Leo ignores them, knowing the only one who knew those plans were Jameson, who remains stoic beside him.

"You selfish—!"

"My empire was never yours, Renato's, or Gabriel's to ever touch. And I assure you…you never will."

Ire twists upon her face, glaring at Leo. Except, even with that faint pull of wanting his mom again, give in to the want, it was easy to bury it beneath his bitter misery.

"You're lying," she insinuates.

"That's your specialty, not mine."

"You were just married in another country. She came back in a coma. There's no fathomable way you could've signed—"

"Autumn has legally been my wife since November." Leo's statement is merciless as Giovanna slowly pales. "Marrying in Rome was a facade to lure out Renato's plans. And you." She gapes as shock covers her. "You lost…mother."

Quickly, her seething anger returns as she scowls.

"I have no claim to the Salvadori fortune and want none of it. Fight with Renaldi for what's left of the scraps Gabriel left behind. Beg him for Renato's body if you want. I don't care. What belongs to me, and my wife will never be yours. Go back to Italy where you so *desperately* wanted to be. You wasted your time coming here."

Leo starts to turn away, heading for the doors.

Suddenly Giovanna spews at him in Italian, *"Ungrateful, deceitful boy! You are Riccardo's son! And like him you'll be a widower, left alone to suffer as you deserve!"*

He stops.

Leo's numbness is quickly replaced by the rage and torment that's gnawed at him for weeks. The terror that haunts him. Nightmares digging at his brain with no relief in fear of Autumn's stillness. Her heart finally stopping. *Alone.*

He snaps.

In the next blink, there's gun in his hand and it's pointed directly at Giovanna's head. He doesn't know where he grabbed it or how he ended up in front of her. There's commotion around him as people swear and other weapons click into place. There's a ringing in his ears while darkness blurs at the edges of his eyesight. Leo glares at Giovanna, hand almost shaking.

"Did you just wish my wife death?" He rasps, hot vile rage coursing through him.

Giovanna almost flinches but holds her ground. Surprise upon her face, but mostly smugness. Leo blinks, seeing Gabriel there instead.

"Be like your father. You'd make that *bastardo* proud," she taunts.

Leo clicks back the safety.

"Sir." A voice breaks through the chaos. He's not sure if the noise is from those around him or within his own mind. Leo glances over to where the voice came, finding Xavier with a concerned expression. "I don't believe Mrs. Luciano would approve. For your sake."

Leo flicks his gaze over Xavier. The anger inside him begins to cool as he puts the safety back, bringing the gun down. Slowly, one last time, Leo looks at his mother, scowling heavily. And then in a bitter voice he says, "I'm *exactly* what Riccardo wished for. So, if you ever come back to New York...no one, not even my wife, will stop me from sending you to hell with Gabriel and him."

He turns on his heel, shoving the gun at whoever is closest. His steps are heavy as he gets to the elevator, getting on and making the doors shut before anyone else can join. The ache comes back, squeezing his chest as panic sets in. His hand rubs harshly at the feeling, ripping open his shirt, struggling to breathe as the sudden need to see Autumn engulfs him.

She needs to be alive. What if she's not—

The doors open and he almost sprints out to the penthouse

door. He slams through, rushing to the television room and clutches the door frame as he comes around the corner. Autumn's there, still in the bed with Alba next to her who rises from her seat.

"Mijo? Por que? What happened?"

The monitor beeps.

He slumps back against the wall, breathing erratically as he shakes his head and steps to the side of the bed. His eyes flash over the monitors, going over ever vital.

"She's alright," Alba says quietly. "We had a nice conversation about dinner, which I'll go start, now that you've returned."

"Gracias," he murmurs.

She walks out of the room, passing him.

Instinctively, Leo's hand reaches out. Except, there's only air.

Alba gone from the room. He glances down at his hand in mid-air, reaching for someone. Something. Alone.

He clenches it into a fist, walking around the bed to Autumn's side as he leans over to press his forehead against hers.

He whispers brokenly, "My dear Watson."

Sixteen

He'd fallen asleep while the nurses moved her limbs and checked all her IVs. Leo slept on the couch, no one daring to bother him except his nightmares.

Giovanna's screams from across the villa. Him at her supposed deathbed, crying for his mother. Wanting his mother. His father. Anyone to comfort him. All he heard were screams. Then came his own from the scorching pain as he fought to get loose. Gabriel's sneers, echoing in his head. His plans to—

"You fucking bitch!"

Horror grips him as he's forced to watch Gabriel yank her pants down, and then—

"No!" Leo sits up on the couch, sweating profusely as his heart pounds. It's dark as the panic ensues when he realizes he can't see Autumn.

He stumbles up, tripping over the coffee table as he practically crashes into the room. The faint beeping of the monitor, once haunting, now the only thing reminding him she's still here. His hands fall upon the edge of her bed, clutching the blankets as he crumbles to his knees. His thundering heartbeat drowning out everything as he feels nauseated.

Leo buries his face into the blankets, gripping them. Every breath agony. The helplessness gnawing at him deeper and deeper. *Alone.* It swallows him up as he falls deeper into that dark well.

"Red…red…red."

Leo's voice is faint as he repeats the safe word.

No movement from Autumn. No noise. Nothing.

His body rocks in silent suffering. The night wears on as his cries are muffled by her blankets. It's too long before the paralyzing aftermath settles in, wrapping around him as his tears stop. His throat hoarse.

He falls completely to the ground, kneeling as his hands clench achingly. Isolation twisted with desperation, Leo suddenly brings his fists up and slam them into the ground. Pain radiates up through his arms as quiet tears fall.

"Please don't take my wife," he begs, voice drifting to no one. "Please. Don't take her. Please."

His forehead touches the ground. His pleas vanishing into the night, left only with silence in response.

Joints creaking and limbs heavy, he drags himself back up, stumbling to his feet. Leo makes it over to his usual chair, slumping into it. Exhaustion weighing. He focuses on her; the softness of her skin as the bruising heals on her face. Her hair showing signs of where it's been colored. Faint freckles. Every soft breath as her chest rises.

"Wake up," he begs in whispers. "Wake up, sweetheart."

Silence greets him once more.

Leo doesn't move. Unable and unwilling to go back to sleep.

Finally, he gets up and goes to the shelves. He doesn't take long finding a movie, putting it in as he goes back to his post next to her. He reaches over, taking her hand to caress his finger over her wedding band. Gently, Leo lays his head down next to her as *The Princess Bride* plays.

Twenty

The penthouse door opens and closes.

Leo watches *The Muppet Movie*, ignoring the murmuring that's become constant white noise. Jameson talking to Alba. Trix talking to someone. The Crew that stops by. All of them muttering about him. About Autumn. About the state of things.

Her fluids had to be adjusted. Something about her glucose levels.

Leo glances over at Autumn.

Each day the gnawing worsens. Slowly, a part of him gives up. To tell them to let her go. He'd just follow her wherever she went.

He relinquishes himself to the numbness. The loneliness. The helplessness that threatens to drown him. The only reason he doesn't give in is her. A hope of her smiling again. Her eyes meeting his once more. His only solace within her silent presence as he continues to play movie after movie. He sits and watches them with her, eating when Alba tells him to, and then goes back to helping take care of her. Yet, it's not enough.

Nothing matters. His hotels could burn to the ground, he wouldn't know or care.

There's another voice. Deeper. Someone comes around the door, stopping as their hands go into their pockets to look at the television screen. Dr. Maxwell then looks over at Leo.

"Mind if I drop in?" Leo responds with a confused frown. "I wanted to come say hello." He gestures to the chair on the other side of Autumn.

Reluctantly, Leo nods his head.

The doctor walks over, settling into the seat and then smiles faintly at the shelves of movies.

"She told me about her collection, but it's a sight to see. Must have taken her days to organize it all," he comments.

Leo continues rubbing his hand over Autumn's, trying to pay attention to Kermit and Fozzie Bear. The movie plays as the two of them sit. It's Leo who finally breaks the silence between them.

"Have you come here in hopes of getting me to talk?"

"Getting you to? No. Only if and when you're ready," he answers calmly, and looks over at Autumn briefly with a soft look. "And I'm sure I'm not the person you want to talk to. I quite miss our discussions. She's come a long way, mainly to be there for you."

Leo frowns, chest starting to ache as he looks over at her. Melancholy flooding him.

"And perhaps knowing she's such a good listener, if I sit right here…." Dr. Maxwell sighs, settling back into his chair, "…maybe ask Alba for some tea, you'll tell her what's going on. What you're feeling."

Leo inhales a shaky breath, going back to watching the movie. He constantly looks over at Autumn, while Dr. Maxwell watches the Muppets. Leo doesn't speak even as it ends, putting in another movie. He's still silent when Alba does bring Dr. Maxwell tea. It's over an hour into *Clue* playing, his emotions twisting inside him, that he finally clears his throat. He refuses to look at the doctor as he starts speaking.

"I'm scared I'm killing you," he rasps. "But I'm more scared of harming you. Breaking your trust."

Words filled with fear, guilt, and loneliness pour out of him.

But finally…Leo talks.

***

Twenty-Three

Leo places paperwork on the kitchen island, alongside a few other folders Jameson brought over. Doing the bare minimum to keep things from completely crumbling.

Alba is upstairs cleaning and doing some laundry, while Nancy is visiting with Autumn. The now too familiar panic of not seeing Autumn starts to rise. He walks over to the television room as Nancy pats Autumn's hand, standing up.

"Leaving?" Leo asks.

She nods, still refusing to speak to him. The one who's been arranging for people to come visit Autumn was mostly Trix and Alba. Leo ignores her cold attitude as always, moving to the shelves to pick out a movie. Nancy stops at the door.

"I should've never let you in that day." Her voice slices through him. Leo goes still, keeping his gaze on the row of 90s action films. "I should've listened to her, turned you away. Whether I'd fallen in debt or not it would've been better than this. You've been nothing but trouble for her and dragged her into a life that…" she gasps, inhaling quickly, "…would kill her. She didn't do that. You did."

Leo glimpses at his wedding ring.

"You still have nothing to say? No apologies? Just your stubbornness and selfishness that will have her rot and die on this bed?"

Every word cuts deeper and deeper. Words that shouldn't matter, but re-enforce themselves with his own guilt and self-hatred.

"Are you admitting it was for selfish reasons then?" Leo asks roughly. "To have me pay off your debt, not for what she wanted… but to solve your own problems?"

"How dare you!" She exclaims under her breath.

He turns towards her slightly, finding Nancy's angry face.

"Given your reasoning, you're just as much to blame. Except I arrived to be with her, while you used her for my money."

Nancy gapes, face paling and then going red. He didn't care how angry she was, knowing she'll likely never approve of him. Her tune had changed the moment he paid off that building, and he noticed. Not fully caring before, until now, wondering if that was her plan from the beginning. Pay off her debt, then have Autumn leave him, knowing he'd never harm her because of Autumn.

Suddenly, she's in front of him, slapping his face. It's hard enough to snap his head to the side. It stings, almost welcome with the torment that consistently follows him. He stares at the movies as she seethes.

"*You* did this to her. You brought this horrid fate—"

"Nancy." Alba's voice interjects. "It's time for you to go. Señor Luciano is tired. The nurses will be checking Autumn's fluids soon. Por favor. Another time."

There's some scuffling and muttering as Nancy leaves at Alba's request. He doesn't move. The sting dissipating as voices return in his head. They scream and yell. Call him names. The chasm that is their insults are vast, thrashing against his ears as they once did so long ago. Before this mess. Before Autumn.

Alone.

He reaches for one of the movies, but it clatters to the floor. His hands suddenly too stiff as he clenches his fist. Suddenly, he's not here, but holding a door open. Autumn trying to push it close. Her kitchen. The ice cream flying and landing on the counter as she looks so exasperated. He might've loved her already. Perhaps that's why he desperately wanted her forgiveness. And then he held her. The warmth of her body.

Someone touches him, and he flinches. He turns towards Alba as she looks at him somberly. She gently touches his cheek where Nancy hit him, pursing her lips as she bends down to grab the fallen movie.

"Voy a hacer café." Her voice is tender, giving him the DVD case. She pats his arm softly, walking away.

He glances over at Autumn and slides back into that numbing loneliness again. He puts in the movie he dropped, flexing his hands as he goes to sit in his usual spot. Leo takes Autumn's hand.

The Fifth Element starts playing.

Twenty-Five

Water drips over his skin. Leo dries himself after his shower, pulling on lounge pants. There's a soft knock at the bathroom door. He opens it, and there's Alba. Leo walks over to the counter where his bandages are, sitting on the stool they've kept in here. As they do every night, Alba takes care of his wounds. All the stitches were finally out, but his forearms and wrists still needed a lot of attention. Alba rewraps them gently as he focuses on not flinching away. His body recoils, still not comfortable with anyone touching him. Finally, Alba, looks over his head injuries. The bruises slowly fading.

Once finished, she gently pats his shoulder. "Dinner will be ready in fifteen minutes. The nurses should be finishing up with Autumn soon."

He nods as she walks out.

Leo pulls on a shirt carefully, briefly glancing at himself in the fogged mirror. He's lost weight from lack of eating and movement. Alba and Trix had him start walking around the penthouse for some semblance of exercise. He notices the dark eye circles that seem permanent, skin pale from lack of sun, mottled, aging bruises in random spots. His lip was healing, not swollen, but the cut was still visible. His beard unkempt from inconsistent shaves.

His hand swipes down over the glass, walking out. Noise comes from the kitchen as the smell of beef and vegetables fill the air. Leo pauses at the bedroom entrance, gaze moving to the door of the playroom.

Silently, he approaches the door. He stares at the doorknob, bringing his hand up, but stops. A deep ache, yearning for relief forms. It drags him as he can practically see himself at the bottom of the well, looking up at the faint light that's too far and doesn't feel real. Hand trembling, he presses it against the surface, scraping his fingers down as his head hangs. The misery worsens, constricting around him as every breath is a struggle. He leans forward, forehead touching the door as the pain of shoving his hand against the wood starts to form.

Leo closes his eyes. Unable to open the door since they arrived home. Unable to look at it. An emptiness that shouldn't be there while she still breathes. Yet, every day he felt haunted.

"Only you can remind me that I can be gentle and loving…"

Tears gather in his eyes.

"You help me feel safer, and you deserve it, too."

For over a month, he hasn't felt it. The paranoia he once constantly had, trickles back more each day without her.

Alone.

"La comida está lista, mijo. Vamos!"

Leo drags himself out of his thoughts. He steps away from the door, hand falling back to his side. He'll burn the room to ash if she never wakes up.

***

Twenty-Seven

I't's raining.

The hour is late, everyone else asleep or gone from the dark penthouse. Leo remains the only one awake, sitting next to Autumn as *The Swan Princess* plays. Weariness hovers, wanting to sleep as his exhaustion deepens. Except, even with the movies playing he can't shake the voices in his head. The nightmares that follow. Horrifying images and then the terror of waking up, and the monitors silent.

Scenes of heartache come across the screen as Derek yells for Odette. Fights the beast for her. And then holds her, begging for forgiveness.

Leo stares ahead as tears fall easily from his eyes. They worsen as Odette awakens, hugging Derek. Through his blurry vision, he looks over at Autumn, finding nothing changed. Sorrow, painful and unending grips him as he stumbles out of his chair. He's on the verge of collapse as he gets to the doorway, clutching it for support as the tears fall. Heavy sobs wrecking his chest as his knees give out, struggling for air. He lands hard upon the floor, shaking him, but not enough to distract from the isolating torment.

No matter how long he sat with her. No matter saying his fears out loud to her with Dr. Maxwell. No matter the wishing at door-ways. No matter who blamed him, accused him of selfishness. No matter the physical pain.

Autumn still wasn't here.

She's out of reach like in the interrogation room. A glass wall where all he could do is watch. Except this time, he was the one spiraling. The one feeling the threads untethering. Fists hitting that glass wall, begging to break through.

"Red!"

He clutches his face, breaking down in want of one simple thing —his wife.

For her to hold him. To talk to him. To sit with him in the dark. To cry alongside him. To come around the corner in socks. To burn eggs. To make an Americano. To nervously giggle. To kiss him. To smile.

"Dear Watson…" he rasps between sobs, pleading for her as the suffering threatens to drag him fully under, "…Autumn."

Helplessness overwhelms him. He's alone. He's alone. He's—

The beep of the monitor changes. The slow beat, picking up speed.

Like a hand reaching down into the well, Leo looks up through tear filled eyes. He waits, listening. The beeping fluctuates again.

His head snaps over his shoulder looking back at the monitor, watching her heartbeat change. Leo stumbles towards her bed, rasping, "Autumn."

His hand grabs hers once more, watching the monitor, hope flicking like a faint flame.

"Autumn." He squeezes her hand. "My dear Watson."

A finger from her other hand twitches.

Leo's eyes widen, unsure of what he was seeing. Until that finger twitches again.

"Autumn." Leo repeats her name, pressing his forehead against hers. His tears falling upon her face. "Wake up, sweetheart. Come back to me, *Tesoro*."

Autumn squeezes his hand.

Chapter 44

Paradiso

Autumn

I don't remember waking up.

I do remember confusion. Anger. Fear.

People tried to calm me down. Maybe ripping something out of me. Flashes of the past came reeling back. The fear of being in the hospital or stuck in that abandoned building.

But I remember his voice. His hands. I could feel his wedding ring against my skin, gripping me. Moments of his face above me. Hazel eyes.

Leo.

Familiar voices drift like a distorted symphony. And then flickers of where I am. Confusion filling me when I see rows of movies. A television screen. Home.

How?

Time feels unreal as it seems like every moment I open my eyes, something new is happening. Someone else is talking. Being moved and wanting to scream. I think I do, because every time I think it, Leo's voice comes back again. His hands touching me, the only thing calming me.

He'd never put me in harm. He'd never—

Until there's finally quiet. Slowly, my mind begins to catch up to the present. It feels like I'm one of my computers rebooting and coming back online. Air gently blows into my nose.

I open my eyes. I'm in the television room. Blinking some more, I try to reach up to touch the tubing around my face. There's IVs in my arm. My shoulder…chest.

"That needs to stay, Autumn," Leo's voice drifts as his hand brings mine down.

"Leo?" I ask in a rough voice.

I'm able to focus better as his face comes into view. Faint bruises. He hasn't shaved for days, perhaps longer. Dark circles under his eyes. He almost looks gaunt. What happened?

"You're safe, dear Watson." His voice is raspy, bringing my left hand up to kiss it. "You're home, sweetheart."

I feel my brows pinch, and then there's movement at the doorway.

A woman walks in with chestnut hair and a light sandy skin tone. She's taller and wears a pleasant smile as I notice a stethoscope around her neck. She goes to the other side of the bed.

"Hello again, Mrs. Luciano," she greets, voice warm with a heavy English accent. "I'm Dr. Howell. I was who oversaw your tests and primary treatment before coming back to the U.S. You seem more awake and coherent today, which is a good sign of you coming out of the final stages of your coma."

"England?" I ask, clearing my dry throat. "Why are you here?"

"It appears I'm the only physician your husband trusts," she muses, giving him a look and then over to the monitors next to me.

I glance at Leo, where there's not a lick of guilt on his face. I whisper, "Did you kidnap a doctor?"

"No."

"He…" she pauses, "…*inquired* I come for a week. The hospital in which I have my residency, gave me leave after someone gave a *very* large amount of donations to two of their departments."

Dr. Howell diligently checks my oxygen, every IV, and catheter she calls them, and then does something briefly over my eyes for movement. A part of me wants to recoil from her, but she speaks in a comforting tone, telling me everything she's about to do. Leo never leaves my side.

"Um...I'm not sure if you already told me," I say, as she finishes. "How...how long was I...I asleep?"

She looks over at Leo, who clears his throat. My head rests back as I feel a tug of exhaustion. He strokes the side of my face, and then he answers my question. "27 days."

My breathing slows, eyes widening. That's why the bruises were faded. Him having a beard. Why he looked worse than when I came back from New Jersey after a week. Holy fuck I was in a coma for a month.

Panic starts to grip me.

"Autumn." Dr. Howell brings my attention to her. "I know it's scary, realizing how long you've been asleep, but you're awake now. Your vitals look good. Oxygen is a little low which is why we need this." She gestures to the thing propped into my nose. "In all honesty, it's quite a miracle there's not more damage or complications that could've occurred. You're very lucky."

Knowing how I got here, doesn't feel like it.

"How did the...how? Why?"

"During the first tests, and I'm assuming the only testing allowed..." she glimpses at Leo, "...there was some swelling of the brain from the blunt force trauma you endured. There were also high levels of a drug that I believe was part of the cause for the coma as well. I've been informed of your medical history, and this wasn't your first coma or trauma you've survived, am I correct?"

I slowly nod my head.

"The brain is a peculiar thing. My own theory is that with the head trauma coupled with the number of injuries your body took, it was trying to heal itself. Perhaps, remembering the first time. In the medical field we place people into medically induced comas to heal faster. It could've done it on its own without the help of proper drugs. Not a solid theory, mind you."

"What injuries did I…do I have?"

"There's a good chance most of these are healed or almost are," she answers, turning to grab a folder. Leo gently squeezes my hand, and I do it back. My head swims already from the information, but I want to know. Need to. "Several cracked ribs. Stress fracture in your right foot. Sprained ankle in your left. Severe damage to the soles of your feet; we had a lot of glass to take out. Scrapes, cuts, and bruises. And a spinal contusion along with a lower back contusion due to harsh physical impact."

Panic spikes again, as I glance down at my feet and wiggle them.

"You still have movement and feeling in your limbs, which is good," she explains. "In a few weeks, you'll learn more on where your mobility is. You'll need to go through quite a bit of physical therapy for the coma alone."

"So…no running in the marathon this year," I try to joke.

She smiles. "No."

I look over at Leo, who watches me like I'm gonna disappear.

"I do have a request," Dr. Howell asks.

"Sure, doc," I whisper.

"Although you're awake, that doesn't mean you're entirely out of the woods. I want to advise you to get a series of tests again. CT. MRI. X-Ray. Blood tests. To ensure there are no lingering complications that haven't been caught here at home. You're also on TPN." I give her a confused look. "Total Parenteral Nutrition. Meaning these IVs and catheter instead of a feeding tube. The tests will give us a better idea of where you are in the healing process to move forward."

My heart starts to pound, and the monitor I'm hooked up to kicks up. The beeping intensifying.

"Autumn, you don't have to," Leo says quietly, holding my hand tighter.

"I will be with you the entire time or your husband will be," she reassures me. Her face becomes grave suddenly, whilst trying to be understanding. "At least a brain scan to ensure the swelling has gone down. Your husband has already done a superb job in ensuring your best interests, so anything you don't want we won't."

"Do I…I have to stay there?"

"Normally, I *would* advise you to," she says gently. "But…this is a peculiar situation. Remarkably, Mr. Luciano's instincts have proven to be true in regards of your health. As long as nothing major appears endangering your health, then you can come home. The hospital will try to make you stay, but you can refuse treatment. Unless your husband wants to donate money again to shut their traps, which will likely work, too."

I'm starting to understand why Leo flew this doctor in from England.

I look down at myself, trying to think through a fog of emotions and whirling concerns.

"I know this is a lot to digest," Dr. Howell adds. "But this decision should be done soon."

"Can I have a moment with my husband?" I ask quietly.

She nods, stepping out of the room and even closes the doors.

"Autumn, if you don't want—"

"Thank you," I murmur. I turn my head, looking over at Leo as his face remains solemn. "I know it must've been hard, and I'm so sorry."

"No, I promised you."

My eyes move over him. I see the exhaustion. I've no idea what he's been through while I've been asleep. Here, but not really. And the thought of leaving him completely tears at my soul.

"I'll do the tests," I say.

"Autumn."

"I have you. I'm not alone this time." I squeeze his hand. "I can do it."

A smile pulls at my lips, and Leo's face starts to crumble. His hand trembles as he reaches to cup my face, and I kiss his palm. The pain upon his face worsens.

"I'm here, Leo," I whisper as tears glisten in his eyes. "I'm here, baby."

He leans close to kiss my forehead, moving down so that his mouth is a breath away from mine. "Dear Watson, my dear Watson."

My heart aches as he finally kisses me, like he's afraid I'll vanish. He's tender. Almost too soft as if I'm too fragile. Leo pulls away and places another upon my cheek.

"I love you. And I've missed you," he murmurs.

"I love you, Leo."

Not long after, we call the doctor back in to get me to the hospital.

At this point, I'm convinced my brain refuses to remember anything about medical treatment. The hospital visit is a blur as if a part of me just shuts down or numbs out from instinct of fear and disdain for it. I barely remember the tests, going into the machines that make my heart race as doctors try to soothe me. The smell of cleaning supplies. The random sounds from other patients or rolling gurneys. Leo constantly there, and I think Trix, later on, too. Or maybe I'm just remembering the past.

The swelling of my brain has gone down. Most of my injuries were healed or on their way. There's still concern about the contusions, mainly in my lower back. All I really remember is to rest and heal.

I'm transported back home and faces blur next as those come to see me. The Crew. Leanne. Nan. Fragments of their conversations. At some point, maybe hours or days later, time seems irrelevant, I ask Dr. Howell about it. This constant memory loss. She said it can be a symptom from the coma or even the damn contusion or just the head trauma in general. Basically, brain may be fickle for a bit.

It's perhaps two days after the hospital visit as *Teen Wolf* plays on the screen. Dr. Howell is finishing some things for my "charts" at home for the nurses that'll be here constantly.

"Sure Leo can't convince you to stay?" I ask, taking a liking to the doc.

She grins, putting the paperwork down. "I have a residency I like, and a life in England. Could be considered too career focused, but it's still mine."

"No, I get it. Just thought I'd try. Rare for me to find medical people I like."

"Well, you're in good hands. And it seems Dr. Maxwell will fight for you as well."

He came by yesterday briefly to say hello.

"I haven't asked, but…" I start to say, and she turns back to me, "…what's your name? Well, first name. Like to know the person who agreed to fly across the pond to help me."

She smiles warmly, coming closer to the bed. "When I'm not being someone's doctor, I'm Sara."

I stare up at her brown eyes. A warmth fills me at this odd fate. The universe playing an odd joke on me. I grin, almost chuckling a little under my breath.

"Usually, I don't get that kind of response. Been told it's a common name even in the U.S," she teases.

"No, it's…just a long time ago, a woman named Sarah saved me." I grin back up at her. "So, it's almost poetic. Feels like fate you were the one to help me this time."

Her expression softens with a genuine understanding. "She must've been quite important to you."

I continue smiling. "She is."

Dr. Sara Howell finishes, and not long into the day she says her goodbyes before leaving for the airport. It's quiet in the penthouse as doors close and the day nurse leaves. My night nurse will be around in about an hour.

Alba makes dinner, and I hate smelling it knowing I can't have it yet. I'm gonna have a long list of meals I want when I can fully eat again.

Leo comes in, sitting down as *Con Air* plays next. I'll be able to rewatch my entire collection at this rate. He takes my hand as he always does.

"How are you feeling?" he asks.

"Tormented by the smell of Alba's cooking," I answer, grinning over at him. He doesn't grin back. "I'm alright, Leo."

He sighs, rubbing his face with his other hand. I've noticed the bandages around his wrists and forearms. I've thought to ask to look at the injuries, but haven't had the heart to. Weariness stretches over his face once more.

"I'm sorry, you were just making a joke."

I reach over to the remote, pausing the movie.

"Talk to me," I tell him.

"You've been in a coma. You're still healing, and don't need unnecessary stress."

"I'm gonna be healing for quite some time, and it's not unnecessary if it's something you need to talk about."

He looks down at the ground, gripping my hand like a lifeline. I wonder how many times did he do that while I was asleep? Holding onto me?

"Leo, look at me," I say softly, and he does, eyes glistening with tears again. "I know I wasn't here. That you were scared. And maybe felt alone, but you're not. I'm here." I swallow hard, taking a long breath, thankful to have the oxygen thing out of my nose. "We both went through something...horrible."

His jaw tightens, swallowing hard as he lets out a shaky exhale.

"You flinch when someone touches you," I say softly as he watches me with a sliver of guilt. "Do your injuries bother you or are you in pain?"

"No." He shakes his head, looking down at his hands. "I don't like...want anyone to touch me. Unless I have to because..." he holds up his free hand, "...of these."

"Because of what happened?" He looks back up at me with

haunted eyes. Every so slightly he nods his head. "You're okay if I touch you?"

"Always."

Fuck it must've been torture for him. I remember how I withdrew from everyone all those years ago. It was like things crawled over my skin when someone would touch me.

I glance down at the bed I'm on. It's large, bigger than any hospital bed I've seen or been in. Carefully, I try to move over. No luck, too weak.

"Autumn, what are—?"

"Help me move."

"What?"

"To make room for you."

"I'm not sure—"

"Been breaking rules and protocols, might as well add husband lying next to me as one of them." I try to scoot again, wincing a little. Finally, Leo helps maneuver my body over as I glance at the IVs still in me, firmly in place. I then pat the open space for him.

Leo carefully gets into the bed next to me, curling up on his side and gently lays his arm over me. He adjusts my pillow to lay his head next to mine, folding his other arm up between us. His body shudders, but calms instantly as he partially holds me for the first time in over a month.

"The nurse coming in will be disgruntled," he murmurs as I turn on the movie again.

"Sounds like you have experience, don't worry so do I."

Already, I can feel the tension leave his body with every passing moment being next to me.

"You're safe, Leo," I whisper, and his breath catches. "We both are. You got us home."

Leo finally relaxes after so long of being on alert. Myself easing, knowing he's still here.

"I'm so proud of you, baby." My voice is gentle as I keep my eyes on Nick Cage. Not long after, I hear Leo fall asleep. He breathes deep as I settle beside him.

Elm Jed

A bit of time passes, and Alba peeks in with a tender expression. Relief upon her face. She whispers, "The nurse will be here soon."
"Distract her for thirty minutes?" I ask. "I'm sure I'll survive."
"Sí, señora." She winks, closing the door behind her.
For a bit longer, Leo sleeps next to me as I watch *Con Air*.
We're home. Finally.

Chapter 45

Long Days Ahead

Fuck this. Fuck simple tasks. Fuck the damn nurse who won't leave me alone.

It felt like forever being weaned off the TPN, but I finally got to the point of being off completely. It also meant a lackluster diet temporarily. The IVs were out, along with the catheters and I could start using the bathroom on my own. Been no issues with my bowels or whatever yet, except me wanting to throttle the nurses.

Tonight, was no exception as I my body recoils from the nurse, refusing to get out of the wheelchair and onto the toilet. I was supposed to use the bathroom, and then try taking a shower. But at the rate I'm going, that's not happening. Especially with Nurse Ratchet not giving me space to use said toilet in peace.

There're safety rails now, meant to help me. I can admit I'm still pretty weak in the strength department, even to pull my own pants down. I knew I still needed help, but a stubbornness rose as panic surged when she suggested tugging my shorts off for me.

I remain in the wheelchair, unmoving as she crosses her arms.

"You're a fall risk, I need to help you," she argues, and then flicks her blonde hair over her shoulder. Something about that movement agitates me more. She's a newer nurse after the third one quit. Apparently, I'm an intolerable patient. "You let Natalie help you."

Anger, frustration, along with a semblance of shame build. I've been cleaned and taken care of for a few weeks, but I felt sick and didn't want her to touch me. Repulsion hits me again as she reaches once more.

I flinch back. "Don't...touch me."

"You're being unreasonable, Mrs. Luciano."

"Leave Bridget, get my husband."

"He isn't qualified—"

"This isn't a fucking hospital; this is my *home*." I spit out, barely recognizing the venom in my voice. I start to tremble, stomach clenching with bladder hurting as the need to use the toilet rises. Panic starts to form, making my chest hurt. "So, yes he is."

"You'd rather shit in front of him, than a nurse?"

Am I allowed to kill my nurse?

I close my eyes, jaw clenched as a roaring happens in my head. "Get my husband."

"Seriously, you're paying me—"

"Go, Bridget."

"You're being unreasonable. This is my job, not his. I know what I'm doing."

"Go get empathy lessons," I snap.

She scoffs and suddenly there're hands on me. "You're acting like a damn child—"

The moment she touches me, trying to yank me up, my body locks up. I wince as pain spreads through me, legs giving out as I fight her off and the chair rolls back. Fear strikes me, remembering someone else grabbing me. Yanking at me. Falling.

A terrified shriek tears from my throat, *"Leo!"*

Suddenly, she lets go, swearing under her breath as I crumble to the ground. I land on the tile, pain spreading through me. And then my bladder releases, unable to stop it as I piss myself on the floor. My mind tears back to the interrogation room, and I dig my fingers into the smooth floor. Tears threaten to come, building with shame and disgust.

There's heavy footsteps and the door slams open, making me flinch.

"Get out," Leo states, coming towards me.

"Mr. Luciano—"

"Alba, get her the fuck out before I make her." Bridget shrinks at Leo's menacing voice. I press my face into the ground as he approaches. Muttering and swearing occurs before the door closes.

"I'm sorry," I whisper through tears.

"Sweetheart, are you hurt?" His hands stroke over my head as I shake it. "I'm going to move you."

"I'm covered in my own piss, I don't want—"

Leo pulls me up, carefully sitting on the floor to bring me into his lap. My hands shake, burying my face into his chest.

"I didn't want her to touch me," I rasp, skin crawling as I feel the wetness along my legs, soaking through my shorts and now his pants. "I couldn't...I'm sorry...I'm a shitty patient."

"No, you're not. She should've listened to you," he murmurs.

"Explain the other fired nurses," I say with a hiccup as his hand strokes my back. "I'm awful to work with."

"You're not with me."

"Because you're Leo." I cover my face with my hands, wincing at the aches in my hip. My stomach hurts, and I know I'm not done needing the bathroom. Except, I may not care if I soil myself further.

"Sweetheart, I'm going to help you clean up, alright?"

"I need...the toilet...I...fuck." My voice shakes. "But I don't... don't..."

His voice becomes firm and gentle. "I'm going to help you up onto the toilet, while you go, I'll take care of the floor. And then I'll help you clean up."

"You're not a...a...Daddy Dom," I say almost too quietly, folding more into myself.

Leo tenderly takes my chin. "Look at me, dear Watson." I do as he wipes tears way. "Good girl." A whimper comes out of me, heart clenching. "No, I'm not, but I have been your caretaker many times. A role I pride myself in with you. If that means helping you with this, then I gladly will." My chin quivers, staring up at him as more tears form. "Just bodily functions. I've already put plugs in you, not much different and I won't put you in a diaper. Promise."

I snort, feeling a semblance of humor.

"There she is," he whispers, kissing my temple. "Are you okay if I help remove your clothes?"

I nod, and he gives one last stroke over my back.

"Let's get up then." Leo moves, crouching behind me to help me stand, but my legs give out. He easily keeps me up, positioning me before the toilet. "Turn around. Arms around my neck."

I do as he says, holding on as he removes my shorts and underwear. He then gently sits me down on the seat. My ruined clothes are tossed into the hamper, and then he grabs a towel to soak up... well, my puddle.

Embarrassment floods me suddenly, and I cover my face with my hands to hide another sob. Never mind, put me back into the bed with the catheter.

"Hey." He pulls my hands down, crouching before me. "Nothing to be ashamed of. You fell and needed to go. Your body is still adjusting and healing, Autumn."

My throat hurts as I nod.

"Take as long as you need. If you need me, say your safeword." I nod again, the only response I seem to be able to give. He kisses my temple, before stepping away.

I close my eyes, concentrating on the need to go and not that Leo is in the room with me. Some relief does come as he diligently washes the floor. I still haven't gone, gripping the rails in hopes of doing so before this century ends. I hear him finish, and I grimace at the fact I still haven't gone, but know I need to.

Quietly, Leo stands beside me, moving his hand over my shoulders and down my back. A shiver runs along my spine, limbs still shaking.

"You're safe, *Tesoro*," he says.

Finally, I go.

A flash of embarrassment comes back, feeling myself redden, but it's quickly gone as Leo strokes my head. It feels like forever I'm on the damn toilet, not wanting to see this next part as I shut my eyes harshly. Leo's patient, helping me clean myself and flushing the toilet. He's diligent in cleaning our hands next, before stripping my shirt off and getting me into the shower to sit me on the newly installed seat.

"I'm going to undress, and then we'll take a shower together. Do you need a towel to sit on?" I shake my head, bringing my arms around me. He steps over to turn on one of the showerheads, warm steam filling the space. "Give me a minute."

He steps out, pulling his shirt and pants off to toss into the hamper next. As he gets undressed, I realize this is the first time I've seen him completely naked since London. There are cuts every-where, new scars and some of his tattoos have become disjointed. He's lost weight, not as muscular as before. He removes the arm bandages, revealing where his skin practically was ripped off around his wrists. More scarring up his forearms.

Most of it seemed healed. Why was he—?

He didn't want to be touched.

My eyes fill with new tears, realization of how badly he'd been tortured, not just from the physical. A gnawing hurt engulfs me. I hold myself tighter.

"Autumn." I look up at his face as he walks over, coming into the shower to crouch before me. "I'm alright."

"He hurt you," I whisper.

"You stopped him. Made sure he never will again."

My chin quivers, nodding slightly.

He cups my face, tenderly stroking his thumb over my skin. Standing up, he closes the glass door, turning on the other shower head above. He uses the detachable head to rinse me off and then him. Leo's careful and thoughtful on how he helps wash me and then himself. I start to relax as the smell of piss leaves, replaced by soap and cleanliness.

I still want to break down.

Leo puts my arms around his neck, moving me up to wash and rinse my back.

"Breathe sweetheart, you're safe," he murmurs. "Today's just a hard day. I've got you."

His voice is soothing as I lean into his touch.

We finally finish, and he sets me down, and then turns off the water. He quickly wraps a towel around his waist, and then grabs another to wrap me in. I focus on the care he's giving me, clinging to knowing that he covets this. To not spiral into feeling like a burden or more broken.

It's barely been weeks. I've got months to go. Fuck, probably longer. I can't give in now.

Except, that's all I wanted to do.

Leo picks me up, carrying me out to the bedroom. He places me on the bed, and I press my fingers into the covers, longingly looking at it. My mind drifts as Leo brings the wheelchair out. He then, walks over to grab a set of pajamas for me. He has me raise my arms, putting the shirt on me and then helps me into the shorts. Lastly, he slides a pair of fuzzy socks onto my feet.

"I need to finish cleaning the bathroom, and then get dressed," he says, stroking my damp hair back. "You look exhausted, so I'm going to lay you down until I'm back."

I nod my head.

Leo easily helps me lay upon the once familiar bed. I breath deep, appreciating the softness. My "hospital" bed was comfortable, but it wasn't this. It wasn't Leo's and my bed, even though he's spent numerous nights next to me. My fingers press into the blankets, wondering the last time he slept in here. It smelled clean, but I wouldn't put it past Alba to regularly wash everything, slept in or not.

A melancholy fills me, wishing to sleep in here, yet there was also a fear. We haven't slept in here since before Rome. Would it feel the same? Nothing did. It was all different. My thoughts tumble as I stare up at the ceiling, emotions muddled.

Leo returns dressed for sleep, giving me a soft look. "How are you feeling?"

"Tired. Really don't want to…go back to the room suddenly. I know I have to."

Gently, Leo helps me sit up, crouching before me again. "No, you don't."

"Leo."

"You're off the IVs, monitors, and catheters. Basically, in the rehab part, so there's no reason for you to stay in there if you don't want to. Bathroom is closer here, too."

I swallow hard, dread nagging at me as I whisper, "I'm not sure if I'm…ready to be in…*here* yet."

His hands roam over my thighs, trying to comfort me as a tear falls down my face. He reaches up, catching it.

"Then I know where we can sleep tonight." Leo stands, picking me up again. My chest pinches a little, but I ignore it as he walks us of the bedroom.

My breath hitches as he steps in front of the playroom door, opening it. The lights flicker on, stars in the ceiling. Leo carries me over to the bed, laying me down. Everything smells of light lavender and touch of vanilla. He goes to the drawers, pulling out the velvet blanket to drape over me, and then props me up on some pillows.

"Stay right here." He kisses my forehead.

He walks out of the room, and I hear muffled voices. Not long after, he returns rolling the wheelchair in, and sets it next to my side of the bed. The door is shut, and he gets into the bed with me, pulling the covers back to slip us both under them.

"The bathroom is closer, and there's safety rails on the toilet in here. But wake me up if you need to go," he instructs gently, settling me against him.

"When were you in here last?" I ask.

"Three days ago. To clean and set up for you." He kisses my forehead. "I didn't have the heart to walk in here while you were… not here."

I tilt my head to look at him fully. Calm hazel eyes meet mine, a peacefulness that hasn't been there since I woke up. Those tears begin to return, refusing to be ignored. They fall as Leo hugs me gently against him.

It sinks in. What we endured and how long we'd been separated from home. From everyone. From even each other. The amount of change, and how much more will come. The suffering. The loss.

My breath shakes as I gaze up at the ceiling. It feels like forever since we've been in here.

The one place that hadn't been touched by all the carnage. The destruction and betrayal. The hurt and torment. It remained untarnished, remaining as our true safe haven. Our real home.

Leo strokes my head as the tears finally dry. We settle further under the blankets. I concentrate on every long breath of his, soft and comforting. I turn my head to look at him, finding his gaze in the dimness. Leo caresses the side of my face, tender and loving.

"I don't want another nurse," I whisper. "But that means more work for you."

Leo shakes his head, pressing his face against my hair as he speaks softly. "I'd rather take care of you, knowing how to better than anyone else. You have always been mine to care for, especially now." He inhales unsteadily. "I couldn't…when you were asleep. I couldn't do anything…" he clears his throat, swallowing hard, "…you're not a burden, never will be…I want and *need* to take care of you. As long as you're comfortable with me."

He kisses my temple, lips lingering there as my chest constricts.

"I only trust you…" my voice fainter, almost sounding scared, "…only you listen."

"Then I will happily take care of you." Leo leans back enough to cup my face, meeting my gaze once more. "My Tesoro. My wife. *My* dear Watson."

I nod, burying my face against his chest. We hold each other close in the quiet, violet room. Just two people hoping to find peace again in the aftermath.

Chapter 46

Penthouse Fever

Jameson's arguing with Leo in the dining room.

I bring my book down, sitting in the living room after a long PT session. Leanne and Trix were here as well, supportive as always, before having to leave. My days were filled with PT mostly, along with other medical check-ups. It's been well over a month since I've woken up. Although my mental state in healing was getting better, I could feel myself itching to leave the penthouse. I used a wheelchair around the place, which was almost as fun as sliding in fuzzy socks.

That was kinda my goal—skating in socks without falling over instantly.

The therapist said to make a goal and I did. Never specified.

Jameson's voice becomes agitated, switching to Spanish as they argue. Leo has been slowly going back to work, mainly just attending selective meetings in his office upstairs. He shuts everything down when 4pm hits.

Putting my book aside about hot firefighters, I scoot and transfer myself to the wheelchair. A loud exhale leaves me as I settle in, grabbing the push ring to roll myself towards the dining room. Even though I was making progress physically from the coma and trauma to my spine, there was so assurance I'd walk on my own again. Still too early to tell. The docs wanted us to be aware that a wheelchair could be part of my daily life. This, of course, meant Leo special ordered one.

It was a shiny black with a low backrest, no handles or arm rests, a big difference from the typical hospital one I started with. Easier brakes to use. This one was smoother to handle as well. My own little KITT, except it doesn't talk back.

I come down the hall, peeking into the dining room where papers and folders have been scattered over the table. Leo stands with a rigid expression with his hands in his pockets. Jameson's arms are folded across his chest, dressed in business attire. Leo's in slacks and a long-sleeved shirt.

Jameson catches sight of me, walking around Leo to approach. "I need you to talk some sense into him."

I raise my brows, wheeling myself into the room. "About?"

"That he can leave you here, and nothing bad will happen." Our track records haven't exactly been great for that to be a truthful statement. I must show it on my face, cause Jameson sighs. "Just to go to the *Italian Lily*."

"Why does he?"

"Renaldi is arriving in New York tonight, and staying at the hotel."

"Yeah, I know." He wanted to talk with Leo in person and deliver something. Or escape Giovanna for a couple days.

"Wouldn't you rather him meet Leo at the hotel, than here? Not to mention for safer protocols."

"Thought nothing bad will happen," I smirk, and Jameson gives me a look. Okay, not a joking matter and he's not in the mood. Dark humor will help me; it will not with Jameson.

"It's more professional, and to keep affairs separate," Jameson continues to argue. "Not to mention, he hasn't left this building in over two months."

"You know he's standing right there."

"Yes, and I can feel him glaring at me."

I glance past Jameson, and sure enough Leo is.

"Over three months he's not made any physical appearances for meetings in person. It's been a tough couple of months, but he still has responsibilities and businesses to run."

"Jameson—"

"Talk to him." His voice lowers as his gaze meets mine. I see the worry and frustration from having everything on his shoulders. And if there's one person who hates being in the spotlight more than Leo, it's Jameson.

I exhale heavily, flicking my eyes to the hall. Jameson takes the hint, walking out of the dining room. Leo stares at the ground, jaw grinding as his body becomes more rigid.

"I'll be fine if you're gone for a few hours, Leo."

"I don't want to leave you," he says hoarsely. "Even if I know, rationally, you'll be alright. I can't…won't be that far from you."

"Okay, then I can go with you."

"You know that's risky, health wise. You're rehabbing well, but that's because you're *here*." His gaze meets mine, concern heavy. I move closer.

"I can stay in the office, where I won't have to move much or tire myself out," I say softly. "The bathroom should be big enough for the wheelchair, but I'll need help using it if there aren't any safety rails installed yet." I clear my throat, thinking about other necessities. "But there's the apartment below, which Isaac and Chesty have already equipped for what I need. Has a bed and everything."

Leo grunts out a breath, pulling one of the chairs out and sits down. He leans back, rubbing his hands over his pants. "I forgot about the apartment."

A sudden giggle comes out of me.

"What?" He asks.

I get closer so my knees bump with his. "I just remember a time where that apartment is where you always were. Tables turned."

He smirks weakly.

"I'll be alright in the hotel, Leo," I reassure him again. "One of the Crew will stay with me if I go to the apartment or Alba—"

He shakes his head. "She won't go back. Apart from not working for me in that manner anymore, she doesn't want to be there. We discussed it while you were…asleep."

"Ahh." I haven't dared bring up Charlotte around her.

Leo's hands fidget, shaking a little. He's quiet, averting his gaze from mine.

"Hold your arms up please." He gives me a confused look but does as I say. I roll back a little, implementing the brake as I give myself enough space. I then grab his arms, easing myself up slowly so I can shuffle forward and land on him. Leo swiftly grabs my legs, pulling them over his to sit across his lap. My head lays against his shoulder as his arm wraps around me. I rub my hand over his chest, gently caressing him as he places his head upon mine. Gradually, Leo stops trembling.

He has small panic attacks like this. Similar to mine. Although he's been mostly in caregiver mode with me, which seems to help, there are still these moments. Ones where I know the dynamic shifts ever so slightly, allowing him to lean on me. Honestly, it made me feel better that we could balance each other. It chipped away at my "am I burden" thoughts.

"Are you worried about me leaving the penthouse…or you?" I ask gently.

He inhales sharply, swallowing hard as I continue to stroke circles on his chest.

"Both."

Leo holds me tighter, clutching me as the trembling comes back a little. I trail my hand up to the nape of his neck, holding him gently.

"I was terrified, too, years ago," I say softly. "Never wanted to leave my apartment again. So many what ifs. Everyone went back to normal it seemed, but I just couldn't for so long. Coming right out of something traumatic and horrendous will feel like that. A dark cloud you can't get out of. I don't want to push you to leave before you're ready, but I think it may be a good idea that you try. To slowly start moving back to a…new normalcy."

"I didn't think I'd be this shaken," he murmurs. "After everything, horrors I've dealt with…this time I don't feel…okay enough."

"Leo, trauma isn't something you compare, even with your own." I lean away, cupping his face to look at me. "You were physically, mentally, and emotionally tortured. Not just that…day. You do not need to be okay right now."

He brings his hand up, stroking my face gently. "I should be the one comforting you, you're the one in a wheelchair."

"It's not the end of the world of me being in one." Leo gives me a look, and I sigh. "It's new reality for me, yes, but not…something devastating. Yeah, some days I really want to run or dance or just jump…" I swallow hard, giving him a small smile, "…but I can hope to, one day. Even if I don't, I can be thankful to be moving at all. It's gonna really suck some days, but I'll be okay. And rolling around in KITT is easier than your office chairs."

We both give a slight chuckle.

"And this is a two-way street, mister. Comforting each other." I move my hand back to his chest, rubbing there again as I feel him become less rigid. "And I am scared, too. It's just the last time I felt utterly alone. No clue how to go forward. Just survive. As much as some days I may feel that now, I know I'm not alone. There's a future to work towards, even if it's hard and terrifying. I have you. We have each other."

Leo places his hand over mine against his chest. His heart beats underneath it, but not at as erratic. He takes a deep breath, nodding gently.

I glance down, noticing the bandages that still cover his wrists and lower forearms. He finally admitted to me he wants them hidden. Not out of embarrassment of others seeing it, but for himself. A stark reminder of what he'd been subjected to. I've asked Dr. Maxwell for help, and he said time, and then we'll work on self-acceptance.

"We'll go to the hotel tomorrow," he says.

"Are you sure?" I also knew seeing the hotel again wouldn't be easy after the whole ordeal with Giovanna.

"Yes, putting it off may only make it fester." He kisses my cheek. "I may shut down or become…cold again."

"That's okay. We'll come home and then decompress. Watch a movie."

He smiles faintly, stroking my hair back. "I love you, my dear wife."

"I love you, my dear Leo. We'll get through this."

He kisses me briefly, before laying my head against his shoulder so he can cradle me in his arms. My hand continues to stroke his chest, helping calm him.

"I want you in here, but at the same time I don't," Leo comments, moving around his desk.

I lean my head to the side, looking underneath the desk. Part of me wonders if I could fit. He must tell what I'm thinking because he snorts as he places paperwork onto the desk. He leans against it crossing his arms. "Not under the desk, Autumn."

I grin back. "Could be fun."

"I'm never going to *hide* you under my desk like some secret rendezvous."

"Not even as roleplay?" I wink cheekily.

He raises a brow. "You're getting bolder."

It's probably because I've finally escaped my penthouse tower.

It was such a relief to get outside, even with the summer heat, and to see people again. We haven't seen many today, but it was more than just the usual handful. So, today being with Leo in his main office has made me cheeky and flirty.

"Because racing around in your office chair wasn't?" I tease.

"Different kind of bold." He drops his hands, coming over to bend down and place a kiss upon my temple. "If he looks at you wrong, I may shoot him."

I reach up, placing my hand against his neck. "Vincenzo's a harmless flirt. You're my *god*, remember?"

A smile tugs at his lips, and then he kisses me briefly upon the lips. It's sweet and affectionate, but that's it. That's all they've been. He straightens, turning away to glance over paperwork. I bite my lower lip, trying not to let a different worry claw at me.

I've been cleared for sex. Was I expecting it this soon while healing? No. I figured we both needed time, but there wasn't even anything sensual or flirty apart from a quip here or there. It's still very comfortable between us, such as platonic cuddling in bed. Light touches. Holding each other. Nothing beyond that. It reminds me of those early months of dating. Odd how it's, well, flipped.

I take a deep breath in, shaking off the worry I know I don't need. Things are just different. It's not me. Just like it hadn't been him. He just needs time like I did.

"I'll stay over near the couches, let him hover by your desk," I say, moving myself to the area.

"Autumn, there's something I need to tell you." I stop, spinning around to face him. He's been mostly stern throughout the day, hiding fully behind that mask of his as his hands go into his pockets. He comes around the desk, jaw working. A glimpse of different uncertainty.

"Oh, no don't tell me Vincenzo did something and that's why he's here."

"No, unfortunately, he's been a valuable asset." A snort is my response to that. "It's about what he's delivering. I didn't want to tell you unless I absolutely knew for sure the outcome."

I blink at him, now fully confused. "Leo, what are you talking about?"

"They found Michael in the rubble…alive."

Everything goes blank. What?

"He had to go through multiple surgeries. Chance of survival was slim. Renaldi wasn't going to go forward with it, but I told him to." I stare at Leo, breath becoming short. "After meeting with him today, I was going to tell you, but he probably would've said something."

Words want to form in my mouth. Ask questions. See if I was dreaming.

Suddenly, there's a knock at the door.

"Not now," Leo calls out.

The door opens anyhow, and Leo practically growls towards who enters. It's Vincenzo wearing one of his embroidered suits and a silk red shirt. Embellished as ever, but it's hard to concentrate on him as my mind whirls. Flashes of that night. Screams. Explosions. *"Run!"*

"Buonasera, Luciano. Buonasera, signora, a wonderful surprise to see you," he greets, putting his hands into his pockets as he grins leisurely.

"He wouldn't wait in the hall," Chiari steps in, looking agitated as she glares at the other mafia boss. I can see Isaac and Jameson just outside, exchanging glances.

"I've already been waiting for months, can't blame a man for not being patient," Vincenzo says, grinning at her and tries to wink. Doesn't sway her.

"Vincenzo," I say with a rasp.

He steps closer, flicking his gaze over me. I can feel Leo step closer, imposing and territorial. Vincenzo tilts his head to the side, flashing his gaze to Leo briefly. His face softens and tells me quietly. "Your man is outside, waiting for orders."

My eyes widen, and without another thought I grab the push rims and move. Vincenzo steps aside as I roll past, aiming for the door. I can hear him behind me chuckle, "Ah, well already knew I wasn't her favorite, eh Luciano?"

Chiari steps aside, keeping the door open as I come out to the hallway. Isaac nods his head to the side, and I snap my gaze to the right. My heart almost stops when I see him. Michael sits and waits in a chair. He turns his head with a nervous expression. Slowly, I go towards him as he stands and straightens himself.

A large bandage is across his neck, moving down underneath his shirt. His head is mostly shaved, and along one side I can see a gruesome scar. Another across his forehead. I stop, staring at him as he remains in his spot.

There's a hush behind me. I stare at the man I thought was dead.

He goes to say something, but stops, mouth working. I move closer, leaning my head back to look up at him. He shifts on his feet.

Finally, he says in a much rougher voice than I remember, "Is that bodyguard offer still open, ma'am?"

My heart clenches, tears threatening to come as my throat tightens.

"How healed are you?" I ask quietly.

"I can move," he answers. "Nothing too extraneous yet, so I doubt I can chase you, especially now that you have the advantage with wheels."

A tear runs down my face. His face drops more.

I put the brake on the wheelchair, starting to get up.

Michael moves forward, panic coming over him as he tries to stop me. "Ma'am, wait—"

I stand, grabbing his arms and fall into a hug. My legs struggle to stay upright as I hold tightly around his chest. His breath hitches, arms up and away from me.

"Thank fuck you're alive, and yes it's open." My words are muffled. I know he still hears me when his arms finally come down and hugs me back before my legs give out. He keeps me up against him, holding firmly.

Tears fall as I openly cry, not caring who's watching, even Vincenzo. Michael breathes in shakily. "Thank fuck you're alive, too, ma'am."

Chapter 47

New Wild West

LEO'S VOICE MINGLES, along with Chiari's and Owen's in the background. I sit across the couch, legs propped up as I switch between reading various books on the basics of business. Figured with the whole inheriting a fortune and businesses, I should learn *something*. My days of being a simple barista were over.

There's a grunt, and I look over my shoulder as Jameson leans back in his seat across from Leo's desk. Chiari's tapping away on a laptop, and so is Owen.

It's been like this the past week. Me sitting on the couch, occupying myself in some shape or form while Leo works. A few times I've left to go see friends within the hotel, but no more than an hour. Leo's slowly moving back into his work routine, but I could tell when he becomes overwhelmed, eyes almost glazing over. He becomes quieter and rigid in his seat. When it seems to not let up, that's when I say I'm tired and we head home. Funny how no one wants to disappoint the woman in the wheelchair.

I snort to myself flipping another page. Yup, I have my cards and not afraid to use them if it meant protecting Leo's sanity. And mine.

I try to concentrate on my book. Boredom certainly nags at me, almost every day. I have physical therapy almost every other day, but most of my time was spent reading or watching movies. Wasn't exactly well enough to go gallivanting to work on bikes, clean rooms, or bug Grant when bathing alone exhausts me.

An idea sparks suddenly, wondering how fast I could race down the halls in the wheelchair. Definitely faster than the rolling chairs. Although, I'm certain I'd give the hotel staff and Leo a heart attack if I did.

I sigh softly to myself, putting the book down and move my legs a little.

Chiari suddenly walks by, giving me a smile before leaving the office. Not far behind is Jameson, he only gives a nod before disappearing. Leo then strides over, pushing my books aside to sit on the coffee table next to me.

He glances at the books. "Bored?"

I shrug, giving him a half smile. "Your meetings aren't exactly entertaining."

"Won't argue that," he murmurs, brows pinching together as he glances at my wheel chair. "Go to the apartment or visit whoever's working. I have a handful of meetings and work to get through but will be done in time for dinner."

I raise my brows. That's four to five hours away.

"I'm not that paranoid or dependent on you being near, I swear," he murmurs.

I take his hand, squeezing it. "It's fine, Leo. I haven't read this much since college, and my professors would be *ecstatic* that I'm finally reading about business." He smirks. "I can stay."

His jaw tightens, and then looks over at where Owen works. Leo brings his gaze down, and then exhales roughly. "I need to relearn how to do this again. If I need you, then I'll call."

The emotions war over his face, lines of uncertainty merging with determination. I squeeze his hand again, rubbing my thumb over his skin. Wonder if this is how Leanne felt the first time I went to work, scared, but knew I needed to take the next step.

"Ok, but if you need anything, mister," I warn lightly, pointing at him. "You call. I'll zip my way back up here."

He leans in, kissing my cheek briefly and stands. I sit up more as he brings my wheelchair closer and I maneuver myself onto the seat. "Maybe I can see which halls I can go down the fastest."

Leo pauses, amusement finally flickering over his gaze. He leans down again, kissing me on the lips before pressing his forehead against mine. "Dear Watson, do not potentially cause yourself more harm. Otherwise, I *will* become insufferable."

I think of giving a retort, but hold back seeing distress in his eyes, I hold off on it. Not the time.

"I shall remain in the speed limits, mister Americano. Promise." I cross my heart with emphasis.

"Thank you." He strokes my hair back, standing fully as I start rolling away. "Have Isaac and another Crew member with you."

I give a mock salute as I get to the door, remembering how much I *don't* like doors. Especially large heavy ones. I raise my hands, gesturing to the barrier I've struggled with the most being in a wheelchair. Apart from stairs. And small bathrooms. And tall counter tops.

"Given I've reached my nemesis, I may need them," I say.

Owen chuckles, and I scowl over my shoulder. He smirks as Leo opens the door, and I give a wave, heading for the elevator. About to contact Isaac for bodyguard duty, the elevator doors open and there he is.

"Did you sense a shift in the force?" I ask.

"Owen." He holds his phone up and gestures me into the space. "How long has he let you out today?"

I give him a look, and he gives me one back that we both know he's right. I shake my head, rolling onto the elevator, and spin around. "Rest of the day."

"Really?"

"He's trying. So, fingers crossed no panic attacks for either of us."

"Very well, where we off to?"

"Basement. Just past lunch, Mikey or Logan may be here. Could find Bobby, too."

The doors close and we start to descend. He taps onto his phone, and says, "Ringer will meet us down there."

I nod, pursing my lips. Michael won't be on bodyguard duty for a bit. He's not quite well enough to fully be in action as it were. Until then, it's been mostly Isaac, Ringer, Chesty, and Animal doing their normal rotations. Except, it's always two or more of them, even in the hotel.

"The doubled security is just paranoia, right?" I ask him. "He hasn't really talked much about…stuff."

"Things have been calm, but do remember that your life has been threatened, multiple times, including here," he answers, shifting on his feet. He adds in a lower tone, "And that one of those people work here."

Right, a little detail I seem to always forget.

A couple weeks ago, Leo and Jameson finally told me it was Matteo's doing that Gabriel found us. Apparently, he'd overheard a quiet conversation while on the plane to the U.S. about us being in London. He then stole a phone from the bodyguards he was with, using it to contact Gabriel. Enigma was able to track it to that phone, and it was thought security had told Gabriel, but they didn't even know we were in London. One afternoon "conversing" with Jameson, and Matteo admitted what he'd done. It was easy to assume that not only Leo, but the rest of the Crew blamed Matteo for what happened to us.

Except, they never confirmed he was still *in* the hotel.

"Matteo's still here?" I ask.

Isaac lifts a brow. "You didn't know?"

"Not a subject I bring up, and although not said otherwise, I'd figured after the whole stealing a bodyguard's phone, would've put him in the warehouse and no one told me."

"Personally, I think that's where he should be," he mutters.

Great. Yeah, the kid fucked up, but he was just shipped to who knows where by his other brother who let another mafia boss waterboard him with vodka. And then threatened to kill him. I'd be vindictive, too. Fuck, I *have* been.

"Where does he stay?" I ask.

"I'm not sure—"

"You better tell me before I roll over your foot a hundred times," I warn, giving a light glare.

He sighs as the elevator doors open. "6th floor. Standard room that's been stripped down to nothing and without many amenities."

"Is he working with Bobby like I suggested?" I haven't been able to see him, yet. Now I understood why one reason I may not have. Damn my frequent headaches and little memory lapses, otherwise I'd have noticed sooner.

We move out of the elevator and into the hallway.

"Most days he's scheduled with him. Days he's not, he's difficult to work with and complains like a child."

"He grew up in a wealthy, mafia family, not surprising there," I murmur. The doors close as I stop, and glance down the hall where the maid's quarters are. "I know it was my idea for him to work here, but…how is he still here?"

"Because it was your request. And unless you say so, Leo will comply." I rub my head a little, small migraine forming. "Although, I shall admit him working here does make it easier to monitor him, frustrating as he is." I look at him with a small frown. "He's a liability, and myself and the rest of the Crew would rather have him gone."

I fold my arms over my chest. "He's just a kid, Isaac."

"He's almost 23, not really a kid anymore."

"Yeah, one who had to grow up before he was ten," I argue. "At 22, I just graduated college and was making all kinds of mistakes. Recently for him, he was dragged into a mafia family war. Interrogated by one brother, lied to by the other, practically sold to another mafioso, and then shipped back to a country he hasn't been in for years. I'd be sour, too."

"That's no excuse for his actions which almost killed you and

Leo," Isaac counters, folding his arms over his chest next. "He was selfish, and should've trusted Leo—"

"Leo *hurt* him," I interject. "Tortured him basically. Whatever reasonings we give and why, anger this or that, expecting him to be okay is ridiculous. Not to mention, Matteo was lied to *for years* by Renato, Giovanna, and Gabriel. I wouldn't know who to trust anymore either."

"Miss Autumn—"

"I'm not excusing his behavior, but he should be given an actual chance to make his own decisions that won't manipulate him into situations to just survive."

"What do you suggest then? Send him to another state?"

"I think sending him away may be the worst thing. He'll feel like a burden or a piece of property."

"He is and has been a burden."

I hang my head back. Yup, hello, headache.

Okay, very obvious Isaac and probably the rest of the Crew hate him. They have been dealing with him longer. Then there's the whole partly why I was in a coma, almost drove Leo to insanity because of it, and getting us both abducted. But in earnest, I don't think Matteo knew Gabriel was planning that, especially hurting Leo.

I sigh, bringing my head back up. "What if I talk to him? I doubt he'll listen to you or Leo, but—"

"You cannot be serious."

"What?"

"He hates you."

"Oh, no *Gabriel* hated me."

"He tried to kill you."

"Very aware, I was there."

Isaac groans, rubbing his temple as the elevator doors open. Rudy walks out, immediately, narrowing his gaze. "*Barchën*, what are you doing to Pretty Boy?"

"She wants to talk to Matteo," Isaac answers.

Rudy frowns, crossing his arms like Isaac. Where's Michael when I need him? He'd go with my chaotic plans.

"Not alone, okay?" I argue.

"Did you forget—"

"Kill me. Yes. We've established that. All of you keep reminding me of when I was almost choked to death and pushed over a railing."

"Exactly," Rudy grunts.

I meet his gaze, and a twinge of guilt is there. I sigh. Right. He didn't save me. Michael did. No doubt shame he's held since that night.

"You should just have him sent somewhere," Rudy adds. "Boss will listen to you if you say it."

"Because that clearly worked the first time," I say deadpan. Rudy doesn't change his expression, scowling as Isaac looks away with a frown. "We can't keep sending him away as an answer. That's not a solution that's just pushing away responsibility."

"Miss Autumn, he's not your responsibility."

Anger flourishes, quick through my chest. I sit straighter in my chair, acting as if I wasn't so much shorter than them at the moment.

"Yes, he is." My voice is sharp. "I'm married to Leo. We are *equal* partners in regards of the Luciano and Marchetti fortunes, companies, and anything else attached to those names. *I* am the matriarch of the Luciano name, whether I am walking or rolling down these halls. Not to mention, who will be the owner of this hotel by the end of next month. But most of all, I am Matteo's sister-in-law, whether he likes it or not. Apart from Leo, I'm what's left of his family. So, for the love of Nick Cage, let me talk to my brother-in-law."

Both men stare at me. Finally, they exchange a look, and a voice comes from behind Rudy.

"He won't do anything to her."

We turn, and see Bobby standing there wearing cargo pants and a dirtied work shirt. His hair has grown a bit, pulled back into a small ponytail. His beard is longer, too. He faintly smiles at me, coming over as he glances at the other two wearily.

"Hey, kiddo, good to see you finally."

"Hey, Bobby."

"What's your top speed on that thing?"

"No clue yet," I shrug before he bends down to give me a hug. He stands and glances at the other two again.

"Matt is in the lounge, finishing lunch." My brows pinch, and he chuckles. "Been calling Matteo that. But yeah, I think you should talk to him. Start somewhere."

Isaac starts to speak, "It's not exactly your call—"

"Isaac, I may be in a wheelchair, but that will not stop me from kicking you in the dick again." His eyes widen. "Bobby's spent the most time with him. Pretty sure he's the one who *can* make that call."

Isaac clears his throat, bringing his arms down. "And what of your promise to not go near him to Leo?"

My heart clenches as I narrow my eyes at Isaac briefly. Low blow. "I'm pretty sure with you two, Bobby, and whoever his guards are...I'll be fine. Safety or health wise. *And* I'll talk to Leo."

Isaac's jaw flexes, and he looks away disgruntled. Rudy looks just the same.

"Pretty certain they just worry about you, kiddo," Bobby says softly. "So do I, which is why I wouldn't agree unless I knew you'd be fine."

I rub my hand over my face, briefly black spots venture over my eyes as I shake it off and hope the faint migraine leaves. Great already wearing myself out with this.

"I need to try," I tell the other two. Isaac looks over at me. "If he tries anything, you can hang him upside down by his toes, okay?"

Isaac snorts, while Rudy grunts. After a minute, they finally agree, and we follow Bobby down the hall. The two remain behind me. We're quiet as we get to the maid quarters, where a few do say hello as we pass. A few other workers greet me, and I smile to each until we get to the back lounge. Rudy goes ahead first, checking the space before I follow with Isaac directly at my back.

Two guards stand behind Matteo, who sits at one of the corner tables. He's wearing a plain shirt and cargo pants, much like Bobby. He looks up, disappointment coming over his face when he sees Bobby isn't alone.

I stop a few feet away, while Bobby sits in the chair next to Matteo. The younger Marchetti brother glares at me, flicking his eyes to the other two. Briefly, I glance at his bodyguards, remembering one with Michael at one point.

"What are your twos names again?" I ask.

"Ron, ma'am." The one with a ginger beard and shaved head says. He nods his head to the other with dark hair pulled back. "Levi."

"I'm sorry about Igor and Garett," I say. Both their grumpy expressions soften, nodding their heads slightly.

"At least Michael made it," Ron says.

"Thankfully, yes."

I bring my attention back to Matteo, whose face is scrunched together. Without the flashing lights and dimness of Vincenzo's club, I can see his features more clearly. He has a bit more squarish jaw than Leo, deeper brow bone that makes him look older than he is. His hair is mussed, dark brown and slightly curled. Clean shaven and smooth. His brows actually come together similar to how Leo's do. He's just…young.

Suddenly, I'm not sure what to say. How to start. The others shift in their spots as he and I stare at each other.

Then I inwardly thank Bobby as he nudges Matteo's shoulder, who frowns at him next. "Shouldn't you tell her somethin?"

Matteo rolls his eyes. Bobby grunts, which elicits a reaction I wouldn't have expected from Matteo. He stops, and actually looks sorry for doing so. Like he doesn't want to disappoint Bobby.

Finally, while staring at the table, Matteo says, "Sorry."

Surprise flicks through me. Bobby gives me a little shrug, and I'm glad I listened to my gut.

"Thank you," I respond softly.

Matteo then slumps back into his seat, crossing his arms like a sullen child. Whelp, that was short-lived. "What do you want?"

"Watch the tone," Levi warns under his breath.

"Still working on Matt's manners," Bobby comments casually, giving him a cocked brow. "To be less of a gloomy mobster."

Matteo slides his gaze at him.

He acts like a teenager who didn't get to play video games for a week and who doesn't really want to listen to anyone. Apart from Bobby, but even that doesn't seem concrete.

I let out a soft exhale, folding my hands into my lap. Matteo glimpses over me, and offhandedly remarks, "So, you a cripple now?"

Yup, needs work on the manners part.

Bobby swears under his breath, and I feel Isaac and Rudy ready to twist the kid into a pretzel.

"No thanks to you," Rudy rumbles. Matteo flinches a little, keeping an eye on the very pissed off ex-wrestler that's more than twice his size. "Arshloch."

"Don't go saying that to people, okay?" I tell Matteo. "It's outdated and offensive."

He shrugs, acting indifferent.

Alright, getting him to talk or believe me isn't going to work on a first conversation. Nothing I say is going to convince him to listen to me. He's been lied to and used. Words won't mean shit, but actions might.

"Wanted to know if you need anything," I say, and he narrows his gaze. "I'll give you one thing in your room. Something to help pass the time between working hours."

Confusion flits over, and he looks at Bobby, who just gestures for him to talk to me. Matteo sighs, still acting sullen. It's like he's *trying* to be a spoiled teenager, but it's coming off…strange.

He mumbles finally, "Television."

"Just the monitor so you can watch the black screen? Fun," I say sarcastically.

"No," he grumbles.

"Video games then?"

He scoffs, "Non gioco."

"Just asking."

He shoves his arms over his chest together. "Movies."

My interest has been peaked.

"What kind? I can add a streaming service or give you cable."

"Non mi importa," he mutters, shrugging.

Is he switching to Italian because he's frustrated or more comfortable? That thought lingers as he avoids my gaze, lips pursed as his jaw works.

"Better tell her," Bobby says. "Or she'll only give you Cartoon Network, which you hate."

He shrugs, giving Bobby a bored expression. Bobby gives him a look, gesturing for Matteo to answer me.

"Whatever you put on there, better than nothing," Matteo says.

"So, Cartoon Network?" Matteo glares at me. "You said movies, so what kind?"

"You probably can't get them, doesn't matter just…cable's fine."

"Matt," Bobby warns, but there's also encouragement in his tone.

"What? Why tell her when she's just gonna give me anything else but that?" Matteo questions.

Ah, gotcha. Not a spoiled teenager. A kid who's been tormented and fought for attention, only to get nothing in return.

"Qualunque film tu voglia," I say slowly, and he finally looks at me again. "Promessa."

Matteo narrows his gaze, frowning at me as if he just realized I can speak Italian. Finally, he answers, "Western Italiani."

"Westerns?"

He scoffs. "You probably only know *The Good, The Bad, and The Ugly* anyways."

Isaac and Rudy both snort.

"Well, *Fistful of Dollars* is a favorite, iconic theme and can't forget that whistle," I say, and Matteo pulls his brows closer. "But

My Name is Nobody is, uh bene, and *Once Upon a Time in the West* is just memorable for the opening."

Matteo just stares. I smile a little, and add, "Also have *Death Rides a Horse, The Great Silence, Django*, and dozen more you can borrow from my collection. I'll have them delivered to your room tonight. Capisce?"

I look over at Ron and Levi, who both look surprised. "He still has a TV, right? Didn't get ripped off the wall?"

"Still there, ma'am."

"Okay, thanks." I grab my push bars, ready to leave and keep things short.

"Grazie." Matteo's voice is almost too soft to hear. I stop, looking over my shoulder and that flicker of hope ignites in my chest. "Just, uh…grazie."

"Whether you like it or not," I respond. "I give a shit about you. Even if the others don't like it." His eyes meet mine. "Ti perdono."

"Perché? You're in a wheelchair cause of me."

"No, I'm in a wheelchair because of Gabriel. You don't get his sins." His face falls. "No matter how hard you tried or were almost convinced, you're not the monster. I've met them. I've fought them. But only you decide what you turn into."

I catch Bobby's face, who winks at me as I turn and leave.

Chapter 48

Brotherly Secrets

MY MOVIES ARRIVED SAFELY to Matteo, but I haven't spoken or seen him since. It's been over two weeks, but I knew to be patient and hope that olive branch will be a start. I do know he's been less frustrating with other hotel staff. That's a start.

I wave to my occupational and physical therapists as the elevator doors close.

"Would you like to get some lunch, ma'am?" Michael asks.

"Think I'll go up and see if Leo wants to eat together, I haven't seen him all morning," I turn my chair around, going back into the apartment.

Michael follows after me silently but stops at the bedroom doorway as I grab clothes to change into. I wasn't fully sweaty from PT but felt sticky enough to change.

"Can you check in with Isaac to see if Leo is upstairs?"

"Yes, ma'am."

I roll into the bathroom with clothes on my lap, closing the door behind me. It takes longer than I care to change my clothes, legs shaky, but I'm able to do it without much fuss. I can stand for a bit on my own but I've noticed either a numbing sensation or pinching pain along my lower back occurs if I stand too long. I'm able to walk around the apartment sometimes, holding onto things, but it's like my body and brain aren't on the same wavelength most days. My therapists suggested I start using forearm crutches soon, mix it up with the wheelchair depending on my pain levels and movability.

I slump back into the wheelchair, already winded. I toss the clothes into the hamper, rolling KITT out of the bathroom. I find Michael in the living room with Isaac.

"That was quick," I comment, smirking.

"He's in a mood," Isaac says by greeting.

I look at Michael and then the door. He takes the hint. "I'll go run some errands, ma'am. See you after lunch."

"Thanks." Although slowly becoming my full-time bodyguard, Michael wasn't privy to certain conversations.

He leaves, and I gesture for Isaac to continue as I go grab some water.

"He had multiple meetings with crime bosses this morning, and Finstrum is currently upstairs for one," he says.

Explains the early morning. "How long until that's done?"

"Twenty minutes? Maybe longer?" I grab the glasses that have been brought down so I can reach them. "Carrie is supposed to be here later, which Chiari has been instructed to keep her busy until Finstrum is gone. Which has only made Jameson grumpier."

Oh, fun. I get water from the fridge, then spin in place to face Isaac. "Is that it?"

"Giovanna tried to contact him today." The glass freezes at my lips. "She's still asking for Gabriel's body."

Never gonna happen.

Leo had him cut apart, and then buried where Giovanna's body should be. He had her grave dug up, finding an empty fucking coffin. Not even her body decoy was there. So, he buried Gabriel where his mother was supposed to be. Right next to Riccardo and his second wife. The pettiest I've known Leo to be.

"So, that hasn't helped," Isaac mentions.

"Well, I'll head up, check in with him," I say, taking a few sips and leave the glass on the counter.

I start to leave the apartment, and Isaac abruptly asks, "He's still seeing Dr. Maxwell, right?"

My gaze shoots over my shoulder to him. "Yes. He and I have check-ins every week to make sure he is, along with myself."

Isaac nods, and then leads the way, keeping the door open. I see the worry etched on his face as I move past, heading to the elevator.

"Is there anything else I should know?" I ask, pressing the button.

"No, just...he's off today. Along with Jameson. We've all noticed."

"Just a bad day. They happen."

He nods, but his scowl doesn't tell me he's fine with that answer. I ignore the tightness in my chest, and the worry in my gut. Come on, Autumn, you've had bad days. Plenty lately, too. Just three days ago you had a small breakdown.

The doors open, and we get on. "How about you help me with some ideas?"

"Such as?" He asks.

"OT wants me to do an activity outside of just normal PT. So, you know, a hobby that's not watching movies."

He thinks a moment, doors closing as we go up. "Swimming?"

"Eh, not a big fan."

"Bicycling?"

"If it doesn't have a rumbling engine, I don't want it." We both smirk.

"What about dancing?" I look up at him, delightfully surprised. "It can help with balance and movement. You could take weekly lessons."

"Not a bad idea."

"You could do it with Leo. Get him out of the office."

Isaac and the Crew must be worried if he's suggesting weekly dancing dates.

"I like that idea, get us both out of the hotel and penthouse," I say with a smile, and Isaac slightly relaxes.

The doors open, and we come out to the hallway; Leo's office doors are closed. Down the left I see Rudy standing on guard, next to Chesty. There's a handful of others I don't recognize.

"Why don't you wait in his office?" Isaac suggests in a low tone.

"Yeah," I murmur, moving to the doors. Isaac opens it for me and then walks away to the others.

I get into Leo's office, but stop when I see Jameson on the couch with his head hung low. It takes him a second to get up, trying to act like he wasn't lamenting on the couch. His face is scrunched together, jaw working as I see frustration along his face. "Autumn."

"Was gonna wait here for Leo, but I can go somewhere else."

"No. Come in."

I move my wheelchair forward, closing the door and coming closer to him. He sits back down again, almost seeming defeated.

"Long day?"

"You could say that," he mutters, running his hand over his face. Jameson places his elbows on his knees, looking down at the ground. "If you could just make sure no one comes in or tell anyone."

"Okay," I say softly, sitting back more in my chair. A tiredness I've rarely seen on Jameson is there. It's been a long couple of months. He's been holding down everything here and took care of business while I was in a coma. The man needs a vacation for half a year at this point.

"How are you?" I ask gently.

"Need a damn ride." Or just that.

"Could go spend a few days at the estate. It's clear now. Maybe take some of the Crew who damn sure need it. We can handle things for at least a week, I swear."

He shakes his head. "No. Can't leave Leo alone yet."

"He's not alone."

I go still as Jameson looks at me. His frown deep with melancholic eyes. Something else is wrong, obviously digging at him.

"What is it, Jameson?"

"Just a long day."

"Bullshit," I say, leisurely crossing my arms over my chest. "Something's on your mind. Get it off your chest, I'll listen."

His eyes flick over me before shaking his head, leaning back.

"If you don't want to talk to me, okay, but it's alright if you're *not* alright."

I give an encouraging smile. There's noise outside the doors, but then it quickly disappears.

"It's been a rough few months," I sigh, rubbing my hands over my jeans. "Hell, last year."

"Yeah…it has been. A year." Something in his voice, makes me cock my head at him. "Tomorrow is a year since Leo met you."

My eyes widen at Jameson. One, how did *I* not remember that? Two, how does *Jameson* remember that?

"How did you remember the date?"

He stares down at his hands, flexing them. "Shit would've been a lot different if he hadn't."

An uneasy feeling moves through me, stomach flipping. "Jameson, why do you remember the date?"

His eyes come up, and there's hurt. The kind that cuts deep.

"You can't tell him I told you, alright? I know he hasn't. Why he's acting…" he shakes his head, and sighs, "…I don't know what happened weeks before he met you. Maybe it was something simmering, and I hadn't noticed."

I nod along, rolling closer.

"Right before he met you, deals had gone wayward, work was erratic. Renato was being a dick. So was Matteo. At that time, Gabriel was screwing with Leo's hotel in Florida. But it was our usual issues." He swallows hard, clenching his hands. "The night before he met you, I went to the apartment to talk about something. When I opened the door, he was…was sitting in the living room with a half a crystal of scotch gone." My memory flashes back to a quiet night, walking in on Leo staring at the fireplace. "I'll never forget the image. Burned into my fucking brain."

Jameson's voice strains, hands starting to tremble as he stares at the ground. He clears his throat, and says, "He had his Colt Revolver. Same fucking gun he used to kill your rapists months later. The barrel was in his mouth. Safety already clicked back. He stopped. We both did. All I could fucking do was stand there. No guilt on his face. No shame. No anger. He was just…done."

I stare at Jameson, feeling like bricks are on my chest. Tears want to work their way up as sorrow digs deep; an understanding I knew too well to get to that point.

"I wanted to see you smile one more time." Oh, fuck. His "confession".

"Couldn't say a damn thing when I finally grabbed the gun, putting it away along with the alcohol. Told him to sleep it off. Tomorrow would be better. He wouldn't say a thing but went to bed. I slept on the couch, no idea what the fuck to do. Next day he ended up in that coffee shop when you were there. That night, I skipped two meetings to get back to his apartment when he would, hoping I wouldn't find him too late."

Jameson's voice catches as he tries to clear his throat.

"New bottle of scotch. Almost empty. Gun on the table. He looked…perturbed. Confused. Thinking so fucking hard staring at that fire. Then he just got up, said something about needing to go back to the coffee shop. Went to the bedroom and shut the door. The next night he had a to-go cup next to the scotch and gun. Every night that week, I checked on him and slept on the couch. Every night, with the small window he had of being left alone, that coffee table had liquor and a gun on it. Until a couple of days before you showed up again, I caught him spinning the revolver." His hands go to his hair, rubbing harshly. "I didn't know what the fuck to do. Should've called his therapist. Told Chesty who's dealt with this shit before. Or Owen or Enigma. Anyone. But I fucking couldn't. It felt too personal to tell them…even if it meant losing him. His privacy was all he fucking had at the time."

Tears slip down his face. Gently, I reach forward and take his hand. He grips it, shoulders shuddering.

"I didn't know what to do, Autumn. My best friend…brother wanted to kill himself. I hated that I couldn't blame him."

Finally, I realize why Jameson was the way he was. The questions he had for me. How angry he was when I left and broke my promise. The coldness at that diner, willing to do anything to help his friend. Why he kept Leo busy. Those times he came in unannounced, checking in. Jameson responded how Leo had when I started cutting again, that fear pushing him. He was waiting to find Leo like that again or being too late.

"When did he stop? Bringing the gun out?"

"Three days after you reappeared," he answers. "Making every excuse to go to that shop every day. Can't tell you how many meetings he skipped or was late for." He wipes away the fallen tears. "I don't know why it was you who saved him, but I'm sure fucking glad you were. Even if I was an ass half the time."

"I didn't save him."

"Yeah, you did," he murmurs, looking over at me with glistening eyes. "You gave him a reason to keep living when the rest of us couldn't."

I squeeze his hand. "Jameson, it's not your fault. You were and *are* enough. A true, good friend that stuck by him."

He clenches my hand, tears rolling down his face.

"You still stopped him. You helped save him, too. Not just when you were two punk kids working at a rundown hotel. I wish I could do half the shit you do for him."

He snorts, sniffling hard as he wipes his eyes again. "We both remember but aren't saying anything. He likely feels guilty cause if he had, well…" he shakes his head, "…if you didn't wake up, Autumn, he would've killed himself within the hour you died."

My throat tightens. I try to breathe in, but it's like my lungs want to burn. "Deep down…I think I knew that, too," I whisper, and he meets my eyes. "And probably why I made sure to wake up."

I clear my throat, trying to push away the sobs that want to come as I smile faintly. "Thank you for telling me, I won't say anything. And thank you for always being there for him when I wasn't. He'd have never trusted me unless you had taught him that."

Suddenly, Jameson hugs me. I'm slightly taken aback with surprise, not sure if we ever have in the past. I move my arms around him, hugging him tightly as he shudders a breath.

"If you need an early day, that's okay," I whisper. "That's a lot to hold onto."

"Feel better telling someone." Jameson pulls back and then places a brief kiss on my cheek. Another wave of shock ripples over me. "Gracias, hermana."

"De nada, *hermano*." I gently pat his shoulder.

Jameson then gets up, shaking off the emotions as he adjusts his suit. He's mostly put together, but his eyes are a bit red. He starts to say something when there's commotion outside and the doors open. The last possible person myself or Jameson needed right now strides in as I bemoan inside.

Carrie walks in like it's her damn office with Chiari behind her, looking ready to throttle her.

"I told Mr. Luciano we'd meet—"

"In ten minutes," Chiari interrupts, exasperated. "You can wait that long."

"Except, he's avoided all my phone calls. We're less than a month away from the *Golden Laurel* opening, and we're behind schedule. Not to mention the gala—"

"Carrie, get the fuck out," Jameson mutters, expression going numb. Chiari and I both blink at him in shock. Yup, they argue, but he *never* swears in front of business associates or clients.

"Excuse me?" She asks. "You don't—"

Jameson glares at her, and the woman actually stops. Her all-business attitude slips as a flash of hesitation moves over her face.

"Leo will meet you downstairs, in ten-fucking-minutes. In thirty. Or an hour. Doesn't matter," Jameson continues, and Chiari looks at me with worry. "It's been a busy few months given his *wife* was in a month long coma and now rehabilitating, along with himself after being abducted. You're good enough at your job to not need your hand held. He told you what he wanted, so fucking do your job."

Chiari blinks rapidly, seeming torn of stopping Jameson from tearing Carrie apart or letting it happen. Even Carrie tilts her head at him briefly, looking him over with disdain and curiosity.

Suddenly, she kind of dismisses him, by looking over at me. If she thinks I'm saving her from barging into Leo's office, I am the *wrong* person to ask.

Her professional manner comes back.

"My apologies, Mrs. Luciano. I hope you're doing well, and that you received the flowers my assistant sent. I do hope your recovery is quick and smooth."

Maybe I'm being petty, after almost being used like a prop with her or because she upset Jameson more, but I respond, "I'll likely never walk normally again or without a mobility device, so we'll see. And I already told Laila thank you for the flowers."

She stands straighter, inhaling deep. Composing herself with only a sliver of embarrassment, she says, "Mr. Luciano made it clear that he will *not* be attending the gala or the centers' opening that Patricia has spear-headed. I want to make it clear for public relations, it's within his best interests that he does attend these events after being gone for so long. Perhaps, *you* can tell him the importance of that, Mrs. Luciano."

"I'll be attending the center openings with Trix, so you'll have one Luciano there," I retort, giving a sweet customer smile.

"It would be best—"

"Chiari, has there been a hotel opening gala thing for every one?" I interrupt, now *definitely* being petty.

"Yes."

"How many has Leo attended?"

"Only the *Italian Lily*," Jameson answers. I look over at him. "The reopening after he bought the building. He's usually too busy."

"Or just simply avoiding social events," Carrie retorts.

"That's why he hired you," Chiari chimes in, smiling ruefully as

Carrie slides her gaze to her. "So, he *doesn't* have to attend them. If you're so good."

Carrie scowls, lips pursing as she tries to maintain a professional attitude.

"What if I make you a deal?" I ask, and all three snap their attention to me. "Since I'm planning on already being at one event, I can attend the *Golden Laurel* gala, too. You'll have *one* of the Luciano faces there, take it or leave it."

Carrie briefly looks me over, her mouth quirking. "Will you still be in the wheelchair?"

"Perhaps, but if you're thinking of where I *think* you're going… don't," I warn, voice becoming steely. "My predicament is not yours to twist and use like a fucking farce, are we clear?"

Jameson crosses his arms, pride coming over his face as her little smirk leaves.

"Yes, Mrs. Luciano."

"Great, want the deal or not?"

"Your attendance may not—"

"How about an announcement that I donated large amounts to five homeless centers in Boston?" I interrupt and her eyes slightly widen. "Since I was already planning it, you can even announce a donation of $100,000 worth of scholarships to the Universities that Trix's centers are being opened at." That almost makes her face crack. "Would that work?"

Not to mention an extra fuck you to Giovanna. And it's something I think Leo's grandmother would've wanted to see the money go towards.

"You've certainly adapted the role of his wife, haven't you?" She asks.

"You have no idea," I say.

She purses her lips, then says, "Very well."

"Given your worries have been quelled, I'll tell Leo you don't need to see him," Jameson adds, and she glowers at him. "Unless you have other concerns, which I think Autumn can take care of from here on out."

"Apparently. We'll be in touch, Mrs. Luciano." She starts to leave as Chiari steps aside.

"Carrie," I call out, and she stops. "*Never* enter my husband's office unannounced again. He won't fire you. But I will."

Suddenly, she smiles, which almost unnerves me. "I'm going to like working with you."

Carrie leaves with Jameson close behind as she murmurs something to him, and he grumbles before they disappear.

"That wasn't too territorial wife, was it?" I ask Chiari.

"Nope, absolute perfection. I thought Jameson was going to kill her."

"Me, too, except now *I'm* gonna have to the be one dealing with her."

"For everyone's safety, that actually may be for the best." Chiari exhales sharply, giving me a soft smile. "He'll be back soon. Finstrum just left."

"Thanks," I say, starting to turn towards his desk. "Maybe I'll ask Trix how to handle her, since they get along."

"Perhaps, and that reminds me before I go." I look over my shoulder. "You wouldn't happen to know if Trix is seeing anyone do you?"

My face almost goes slack, and I shake my head a little. She smiles coyly, leaving. The door shutting behind her. Son of a nutcracker, did what I think just happened…happened?

I shake my head, rolling over to Leo's desk and I notice the oncoming storm clouds. I stop, rubbing my hand over my face for just the last thirty minutes alone. Whiplash was one minor way of describing it.

As the sky darkens, I wait for Leo. The once bright afternoon now filled with grey skies. The door opens, and Leo enters as he shuts the door behind him. I give him a reassuring smile as he walks over, taking his suit jacket off.

"I was going to see if you wanted to have lunch together, but maybe you'd like to play hooky instead?" I ask.

He snorts, placing the jacket over a chair. "Heard you took care of Carrie."

I shrug.

Leo places his hands on my shoulders and kisses my forehead. "Thank you."

Quickly, he averts his gaze, pulling away to sit in his chair. "I have several more meetings to attend this afternoon, including one in…" he glances at the clock, "…twenty minutes."

I watch him as he runs his hand over his jaw. Weariness tears at him, and there's still the rest of the day to go. Once more, he's shoving himself into work.

"*Yellow.*" Remembering Rome, that word echoes in my head.

I roll forward, bumping my knee into his. He looks up, dropping his hand as I gesture for him to hold his arms out. He does, helping me get up from the chair and sit upon his lap. Leo helps me adjust, leaning back as he presses his face into my hair. He breathes deep as some of his rigidity disappears.

"Hey, it's going to be a year of us meeting tomorrow," I say gently. "We should celebrate. *Patch Adams* style."

"Meaning?"

"Instead of a pool filled with macaroni, let's do lattes and Americanos."

Leo chuckles softly against my ear. He then clutches the side of my head, nuzzling his face into my hair.

"How would your doctors feel about that?" he asks.

"Well, they want me to have a physical hobby. Swimming in coffee could be one."

"Perhaps something else."

"How about dancing?" I ask, pulling back enough to look him in the eye. His hand moves down, stroking my back gently as the tiredness on his face eases. "Isaac suggested it, by the way, can't steal his idea. We could…take lessons together. Maybe fool a teacher or two that we know nothing." He smirks, lounging further back. "Make it a weekly date."

Leo's eyes soften, running his hand now over my legs. He has a bit of a more serious look, brows furrowed in thought. "How about a couple times a week?"

"Like your thinking, mister."

Leo moves in to brush his lips against mine. It's tender and sweet, but brief. I give him a faint smile.

"I love you, my dear Watson, and thankful you caught my coffee without a net."

"I love you, Leo, and so am I."

Reaching up, I wind my arm around his neck, holding him close as the rain starts to fall.

Chapter 49

Sweet Revenge

I'M RETHINKING my bargaining skills with Carrie.

I attended the opening for the *Golden Laurel*, which went well. Mostly. Leanne was my date, ecstatic to fly a private jet to Boston, plus Isaac was already going with me. I thought it'd go smooth because I'd only be gone 24 hours. Leo assured me it'd be fine.

Except it hadn't.

In the middle of the gala, I got a call from Jameson. Leo was having a panic attack to the point of not knowing where he was and repeating Gabriel's name. I helped calm him down over the phone, while leaving early with Michael and Rudy to New York. Isaac and Leanne helped take care of Carrie's disgruntlement. To be honest, I thought I'd pass out at the amount of people and kept excusing myself to the bathroom.

So, rethinking further deals with Carrie, top of the list—no parties.

The *Golden Laurel* opening was last month. A lavish party filled with over-the-top decorations for the dark marble and gold hotel. This party however was decked out in balloons and decorations, but not to the same degree.

Elm Jed

I sit back in my seat with water in hand, looking around the array of people. Trix's center opening was a success, although not hers technically. Same with the other two opening in the spring semester. Haven't agreed to attend yet, although I may shove past my fears for Trix. Carrie not so much.

I'm sat at one of the back tables, by my request, the space filled for the dinner being held in the large auditorium that'll hold future events for students. A *free* space for displaced students, mostly women and others in marginalized communities, who have nowhere else to go. Almost all of it funded by Leo and me.

Sipping my water, I see Leanne and Isaac together, talking to some educators. He's not on bodyguard duty today. I wanted him to be here with her, and he looks all proper and posh in his three-piece suit. Leanne wears a gorgeous dress of pale blue and silver jewelry. Her smile is the icing on the cake every time she looks at him, and he smiles back. They're an adorable couple and I get giddy inside every time I see them.

Water put down, I slide my chair out and grab my forearm crutches, deciding to take a stroll. My hands grip the now familiar handles, moving away from the table. I remain near the wall, trying to be unseen, but most don't even recognize me.

I glance over my shoulder, finding two of my shadows—Chesty and Michael. Mila is overseeing from a distance, stoic and such.

While walking, I notice Trix in a crowd of people. Next to her stands Chiari, holding her hand gently. Trix wears a gown that sparkles with oranges and yellows. Chiari wears her usual suit, but with a silky white blouse underneath her jacket. Her hair is down past her shoulders. I smile at them, still getting over the fact they've been dating for almost a month. They complement each other well.

I'm the least dressed of the bunch. I'm in slacks, wearing loafers hidden under the fabric with a simple shiny blouse. Nothing flashy with my pixie cut hair styled by Lisa, and nails to match by George. My little stylist team.

I tried to wear a dress for the *Golden Laurel* opening but

panicked and almost broke out in hives from the anxiety that gripped me. Leanne was with me, and we both decided for me to wait before trying again.

Rome might be the last time for them.

There's a sudden pop that pierces through the noise. People exclaim, and then laugh.

My body goes on alert as I grip my crutches, spine stiffening. My legs shake, ready to collapse beneath me as fear pulses through me. Everything quickly starting to close in as there's a tightness around my chest.

"Just a balloon." Chesty's voice sounds from the side. Something touches me, and I flinch almost tripping. He holds his hand up. "Breathe, sister."

There's laughing and talking around me, people unbeknownst to my growing panic. The cacophony almost too loud as a ringing starts within my ears. *Pillars falling. Blood. Screams—*

I try to focus on Chesty's face, concern lining his features.

"You're not there," he says softly.

I swallow hard. "Michael."

Chesty moves to the side as I blink, trying to focus enough to recite the first few lines of *The Raven*. And then Michael is in my vision, who approaches and carefully places a hand over my crutch's cuff. I focus on him, eyes flicking to the large scar across his neck, mottling his skin.

Igor's screams. Blood on Leo's face. Gabriel licking—

"We're not there, ma'am," he says quietly.

I blink. I nod slowly, breathing in deep as I see Michael before me. *He's alive. We're not there.* He squeezes my arm a little, giving me a comforting smile.

"What's wrong?" Mila's voice appears.

I jolt again at the suddenness, and curse at myself for now being jumpy. My chest shakes as I inhale slowly, trying to calm. I glance over at Mila as she approaches in her pressed suit, dressed like Chesty and Michael. I'd feel better if all of us were in jeans or boots.

"Small scare," Chesty answers.

"From?" She asks.

"Just a fucking balloon," I add, shuddering a breath.

Another reason I may not be able to keep doing these events. I thought my anxiety was bad before, it's gotten worse. Crowds in general could easily drive me into a panic, that even some dinner evenings with Trix and Leanne I've almost passed out thinking someone is going to blow up the building. Or get shot. Or my bodyguards get killed. Or I'll be abducted. My anxiety had choices. I've found one of the few people who can touch me while in a panic attack, besides Leo, was Michael. Not sure why. Perhaps it helps my brain to see him alive or it's the shared experience from that night in hell.

I knew my trauma from the last few months would linger and haunt, even with Gabriel, Renato, and so many gone. Except one, who was still working in the hotel. Matteo wasn't the cause of any of the flashbacks though. We've had two other conversations, brief, but it was something. One about Henry Fonda in *My Darling Clementine*, an American Western he actually liked. The second conversation was mostly him just asking a singular question, *"were you really homeless?"* Leo knew about them all, and was okay with those short conversations, long as I wasn't alone with Matteo.

I shake my head, coming back to the present as Mila looks me over carefully.

"I can have the perimeter rechecked if you want, ma'am," Mila suggests.

"I'm fine. Just need a breather." I nod at Michael who let's go of me.

"Do you need to sit down again, ma'am?" Michael asks.

"No, I just got up."

"Are you sure?" Mila asks next. "Perhaps—"

"Concern is weird on you. Quit it," I tease her, and she almost smirks.

"Just doing my job, Mrs. Luciano." We give each other a

knowing look, and then her phone rings. She steps away, taking the call.

"She's getting sassier," I comment.

"That's her sassy?" Michael asks, perplexed. I shrug.

Chesty snorts, folding his arms over his torso. "We can leave if you want. You showed face and dinner was served. Checked off the list for Carrie."

"Not going until Trix's speech. I'm better now, just needed a minute."

I shift on my feet, moving my crutches as I take a few steps forward.

"Maybe you should sit down," Chesty suggests.

"Seriously? I just stood up. I can last another thirty minutes, even longer with Flotsam and Jetsam here." I wiggle my crutches.

"Out of all the things to name them, why eels?" Michael asks, always intrigued by my naming choices. I have another wheelchair, a foldable travel one, I call Optimus.

"They help get the job done," I say with a snarky grin. "And they're actually sea terms."

His face scrunches. "That makes less sense, ma'am."

"Don't try to get her to make sense," Chesty mumbles.

I playfully glare at them, walking away and getting closer to Trix's group without really being seen. Anxiety travels up my spine again, warning flicking. I glance around, trying to reassure myself.

There're no explosions. Everyone's fine.

Taking another long breath, I start to head for Trix and Chiari, when someone catches my eye. I stop, wondering if I'm seeing a mirage. It can't be. She turns and holy crud muffins, yup it's her.

Chesty pauses next to me. "Is that who I think it is?"

"Uh-huh."

"Why is she here?"

"Guessing the older man and woman next to her are her parents. Likely donors for the university. Maybe they're alumni."

I stare at my ex-coworker who's in a pink sparkly dress. Her blonde hair is down, curled like it always was. Bailey appears bored, standing next to her parents while she drinks champagne and wrinkles her nose at it. Her father is speaking to one of the administrators.

Suddenly, Leanne and Isaac appear. "Autumn, that blonde pain in the ass—"

"I see her," I interject, trying not to cause attention, turning away. "Okay, maybe I do need to sit."

Michael guides me back towards our table, the others following me. Leanne asks, "What is she doing here? Thought she hated the idea of college."

"She did. Maybe her father changed her mind, she could be starting this semester," I answer, noticing Isaac's slight scowl as he exchanges a look with Chesty. "Okay, so what, Bailey is here. The girl isn't gonna try to start a firefight."

"Should I be worried, ma'am?" Michael asks. "Am I missing information on someone?"

"Old enemy. Harmless unless she has a coffee in hand, if so, grab a net." I make it to our table, easing down into my seat and flex my hands as I put Flotsam and Jetsam aside.

"Should I escort her out?" Michael asks, looking at Isaac for answers.

"Son of a nutcracker, she's not a mobster," I say, exasperated and almost wanting to laugh. Well, least some of my anxiety went away. Leanne sits next to me, Isaac beside her.

"Oh, come on, use your powers and take her out," Leanne muses, glaring over where Bailey disappears into the crowd.

"Perhaps just let the girl wander, Miss Autumn already got her revenge, darling," Isaac says, smoothing his hand down her arm. "From spilling a latte on her to marrying Leo and being happy."

"I love you, but not good enough," Leanne rebukes and Isaac snorts laughter. I chuckle with him.

After the past year or so, Bailey was the least of my concerns. I *am* happy, even with hiccups here or there. Life was different and I had to move about the world differently, figuratively and literally, but I am happy where I ended up.

Chiari suddenly appears, and says, "Trix is about to give her speech."

Right then, Trix and the event organizer get on the small stage, bringing conversations to a hush. We all sit quietly as Trix talks, thanking everyone for attending and those who've donated to the center in hopes of its success. Someone else talks about the future of the center, my mind blanking out at times as I blink and drink some water to help focus. Except I can feel a migraine forming and a pinch up my spine.

I whisper, "Michael?"

Michael leans down next to my ear. "Yes, ma'am?"

"You have my medication?"

"Pain forming?" I nod, and he steps back to grab it.

"You, okay?" Leanne asks.

"Normal stuff, just something to help," I whisper as another speaker comes to the microphone. Michael returns, putting some pills in my hand as I grab my water.

"Proud of you for not being as scared of medications to help you," she murmurs, flicking her gaze to the front.

I give her a small smile, before knocking back the pills. A smidge of pain trickles over my spine, almost making the forming headache worse as I take another sip of water. I blame the noise and chaos. I'm here longer than I was at the gala, so maybe I've found my limit.

Trix comes back to speak again, smiling as she finishes and looks in my direction, "And lastly, I should fully thank the one for making this center happen." Oh, shit. "They're the one who funded this entire project, who wanted to relieve stress for those who are less fortunate and to give people that chance." Oh, crud muffins. My entire body stiffens, knowing what's coming as Leanne and Isaac snap their gazes to me. "Not to mention, there are *twenty* new scholarships for students in the arts, history, and writing."

"Or maybe this could be sweet revenge," Leanne murmurs under her breath.

Trix gestures towards me. "Please help me give thanks to Mrs. Autumn Luciano."

The crowd gives applause, people turning towards our table as Leanne and Isaac join in. I remain seated, already hating this as I give a little wave. Worry tightens over my skin, not wanting eyes on me as my chest constricts as I force a grin. Chesty and Michael step a touch closer, and in the corner of my eye I see Mila moving towards the entrance.

I know Trix wanted to make sure I got the recognition for helping this place happen, but it doesn't mean I don't like the fanfare that comes with it.

A photographer comes by, snapping photos. Someone else starts to approach, along with another to come over to greet me or likely ask about donations for their own projects. I've heard about this song and dance with Leo. An older gentleman tries to approach, and Chesty steps between with a short shake of his head.

"No conversations at this time," he says.

"Oh, please, I'm one of the—"

"Mrs. Luciano, pleasure to have you—"

"Mrs. Luciano."

I think I'm gonna black out. This is a nightmare come to life as my smile almost slips. My eyes swing to the front, and I see worry on Trix's face.

Can I go back to being chased by mobsters? I'm allowed to hit them with skillets.

Trix starts to head back to the microphone, likely to pull attention back to her as worry gnaws at my stomach. My heart pounds, darkness edging around my vision. I look over my shoulder at Michael, who meets my gaze as I give a singular nod.

"I'm sorry," he says, coming closer and helping me grab my crutches. "But Mrs. Luciano cannot answer any questions if you—"

There's a sudden screech from the microphone, feedback splitting the noise. Everyone stops and there's a hush as their attention is now on the stage again.

My heart almost stops when I see him standing there, relaxed in his usual black business attire. His hands are loose in his pockets, expression neutral with a slight furrow in his brows. Trix stands off to the side, relief on her face as Leo instantly takes command of the room. His face becomes a hint stricter as all attention is given to the reclusive hotel mogul.

"My wife and I are humbled by your response," he says in that collected tone of his. "Her work in providing better and safer spaces for students is important to her, and myself. Education should be more readily available to those less privileged. My wife has a degree, but I do not. Learning comes in many forms, and for those looking for it at colleges such as this one should be given the ability to do so without fear. Without looking over their shoulders. Without worrying where to sleep or eat."

His gaze comes over to me, and my heart flutters as I give him a soft smile.

"People should be able to create and learn while thriving, not surviving. We hope this is a start for better lives and futures. Thank you for your support, but all gratitude should be given to Patricia Fuller. It was her idea, ingenuity, resilience, and care that this is a reality. She's the one who should be given all the praise." He nods at Trix, who comes forward. "Now, the crowd invading my wife's space, step back immediately."

They listen, and damn do I wish I had that superpower.

Leo leaves the stage, Trix taking the mic again, but I don't hear her as I just stare at Leo who expertly navigates the crowd. I notice two more guards at the entrance next to Mila as he approaches, making the rest of the people part from the table.

"We'll see you, looks like your knight in shining armor arrived," Leanne whispers, kissing my cheek as she and Isaac step away.

Leo strides over as I smile up at him. He places his hand on the table before me, leaning down to kiss me gently on the lips.

"You weren't supposed to be here," I say quietly.

Hazel eyes meet mine. "I couldn't let you do this alone again."

"Thank you." I touch his arm, squeezing gently. "But I am

starting to get pain flare-ups and would totally not be against being whisked away in your arms."

"Very well, dear Watson." He steps back, giving me room to grab my crutches. He remains close as we start to leave, except we're stopped once more by people. Leo gives me a side glance, and I give him a small nod I'm alright.

He pauses only for a few conversations, Mila and Chesty staying close. Michael lingers on my other side. Leo's much smoother at ending conversations than me. We're close of escaping the masses, when he stops and asks, "Is that who I think it is?"

I follow his gaze to find Bailey and her parents approaching. Bailey almost gawks, but her expression changes when she looks me over. Annnnd now I'd like to punch the smugness from her face.

"Yup," I grunt.

"Boss, would you like me to derail them?" Mila asks, sliding her narrowed gaze towards them.

"No," he says low. "I think it's finally time we have a conversation."

My eyes go wide, looking over at Chesty who doesn't look at all perturbed. Mila allows the man and his wife to approach, Bailey lingering behind as she pushes her chest out. I want to roll my eyes. Honestly, thinking she wouldn't try with a married man was a fickle hope.

Bailey's father introduces himself, attempting to shake Leo's hand, but Leo doesn't take the bait. He then introduces his wife, and then practically hisses at Bailey to come closer.

"Mr. Luciano, I've always been—"

"Bailey, do you still work at *Blue Java Café*?" Leo interrupts.

She blinks, instantly flirting harder with the routine I knew too well. Her smile is plastered on, fingers twirling through her hair, and she angles her body to show off. Good to know not everything changes.

"I do," she says way too warmly. "I absolutely love getting to know people, and I certainly miss getting to know you."

She's fully ignoring me, and I almost want to groan at her.

"I'm not sure how you know each other," her father says, glancing between them. "But yes, she'll continue working while going to college for business."

My brows raise. Business? That's a plot twist.

Leo ignores him, talking directly to Bailey. "Are you still bullying your coworkers?"

His blunt question makes everyone pause. Michael stiffens, while her parents look aghast. Bailey's father starts to argue, but Leo over talks him.

"Or harassing customers? Perhaps getting coworkers fired for petty, immature reasons while you fucked others in the back of the shop?"

Totally forgot I told him that, and now I fully remember doing so. And then shock hits me that Leo said 'fuck'…in public…outside the mob.

Bailey's face falls, reddening as she starts to glare at me. Her mother gasps, while her father sputters angrily, "Mr. Luciano, that is quite an accusation—"

"Your daughter sexually harassed me when I was a customer at the café," Leo continues, and I have to concentrate on not staring at him next in shock. "She also bullied, harmed, and got my wife fired even though she was a diligent barista for almost three years. Surely *you* would remember because you helped threaten the management to fire her, including not allowing your daughter to be reprimanded after breaking several health code violations by using the kitchen like it was her bedroom. All due to you preserving your name and stock attached to the café."

I'm realizing now that *I* may have moved on, but Leo may not have. Then again, he didn't get to dump coffee on her.

Her father flusters, turning red as her mother gawks. "I well-well, you know…now, these are serious accusations—"

"They are," Leo counters as more people seem to listen in. "Thankfully my wife is forgiving, who asked me not to pursue legal actions at the time. But I'm sure there's…" Leo scowls at

Bailey, who at least steps back, "… security footage of your daughter's behavior, from how she's treated coworkers and customers. For I doubt *you* stopped after Autumn left."

Bailey visibly gulps, eyes wide with fear and shock. She turns to me, "Autumn, you can't let—"

"Mr. Miller," Leo states, and her mouth shuts. "Your firm was on the docket to represent two of my companies. I'm afraid it'll be your responsibility to inform them that none of those will proceed further. Not to mention your stock will become obsolete once I buy the café and replace every worker I think *won't* fit the criteria of who I'll want. Perhaps that will teach you that there's bigger sharks, but most certainly that you are *not* nor *ever* will be one."

He pales while his wife looks near of fainting. People murmur, already gossip starting in whispers. Bailey looks around frantic, switching from fearful to shaken socialite. For a moment, she looks like she'll attack me, but Michael and Leo dissuade her.

Leo's voice becomes low, addressing her one final time. "May this be a reminder to *you*, Bailey. I will not tolerate any disrespect towards *my* wife. She may have moved on from your abhorrent treatment of her, but I have not. Come within fifty feet of her, and you'll spend the rest of your days remembering that warning."

He turns his back on them, leaving them blubbering as he guides me out of the place. I catch Leanne grinning, giddy while Isaac tries to hide his smirk. Trix is not far either, fully shocked while Chiari appears unruffled. People whisper as we leave, Mila and Michael keeping others away. A few do try to approach as we come outside, where Rudy waits with the car. There's another one of our cars with Animal behind the wheel.

Leo helps me in, then goes around to his side. He gets in, shutting the door promptly. I stare at him, surprised not of him practically destroying Bailey's father's career essentially, but basically threatening her. He looks over at me, adjusting his jacket.

"Too far?" He asks.

I slowly start to smile. "Nah, long time coming."

"Should've called her out on her behavior a year ago."

"I asked you not to remember?" I reach over, grabbing his hand. "Same with buying the café, but…guess it doesn't count with me not working there anymore, huh?"

His expression softens, shaking his head gently. He then brings my hand up, kissing my knuckles. "I'm sorry I wasn't there earlier."

"You showed up right on time, mister," I whisper, leaning closer.

He cradles my face, tenderly kissing me. I gently press forward, desire trickling through me as I feel his warmth, and frankly turned on by him putting Bailey in her place. My lips press harder against his, while my hand slides up his thigh. Leo's breath hitches, and then he pulls back just enough to break the kiss and remove my hand from his thigh.

"Red." The word is barely a whisper upon his lips. His breath picks up, eyes shut tightly. "I'm sorry, Autumn…"

"Leo, look at me," I whisper, gently touching his face. He opens his eyes, soft and vulnerable. "I love you. And if anyone understands needing more time, it's me…your dear Watson. I should've asked before pushing for more. I'm sorry."

"Please don't apologize." His breath is shaky as I caress my thumb over his skin.

I watch as that commanding man who'd been in that center disappear beneath my hands. All because he wasn't ready for sex or activities attached to it. He still hides the scars on his wrists and forearms with arm sleeves under his shirts, unable to look at them. The hurt in understanding that kind of pain and guilt makes my heart clench. His eyes stay on mine.

"You are not broken," I whisper. "You are my dear Leo, whom I love to be with. Laugh with. Cry with. And who'll always be there for me. Like today. I will be patient not because I have to, but because I want to. I love you. It's alright." I bring my other hand up, placing it on his chest, and his free hand goes on top of it. "What do you need, baby?"

"Just to hold you," he whispers.

I nod, maneuvering to be closer to him as he wraps his arms around me. His face becomes buried against my neck. I lay my head against his, looking out the window on his side.

"I love you," he says against my skin. "And I'm proud of you today."

"Thank you. Proud of you, too. Good boy, telling me red." I stroke his hair as he shudders, body going lax. I take comfort in soothing him, preferring to be in the quiet than the noise of any party out there.

Chapter 50

Cage Madness

It was a relief to finally ride again. Not cleared to do so on my own, but I'll never complain being Leo's backpack.

My favorite season has come bringing changing leaves, sometimes a breeze, and more reason to have coffee. Today the weather is especially nice as we rode through the hills of New York. The first time in a long time for me; my first ride since Italy.

It was sweet music hearing the rumbling of the engines, laying my head against Leo's back as the club rode to Snake Eyes' bar. We rode one of his newer bikes, a classic dark green roadster with a comfy backseat. A smile was on my face the entire time.

We made it to the bar, taking our time through the winding curves and hills. The big biker greeted us outside when he heard the engines, grinning large as he shook his head at the club. His face fell only a little when my cane was pulled out attached to Leo's bike, my crutches were left at the estate. He relaxed when he saw me smile, both of us waiting a moment before Leo nodded his head for us to hug. About an hour here, I asked Ikemba for a dance. He seemed unsure, until I assured him I could do a slow dance or two, long as I could lean on him.

Isaac was right about the dance lessons; they've been good for

Leo and me every week. The only downside was us not quite finding the right instructor yet. We've bounced to three different ones already, hopefully the current sticks.

It's later in the afternoon when it feels like something crawls up my neck. I shiver, glancing over at the others near the bar or playing pool. We're all clad in jeans, boots, and club vests. The shiver comes back again, and I grab my cane and head for the door with a gesture to Animal that I'm going outside. He nods as I step into the warm afternoon air.

I walk down the row of bikes that belong to another club, and then get to the *Forgotten Demons'*. Calmness reaches me, making me realize that even in a bar that I'm comfortable in, is still too busy. Some days, I just felt myself waiting for bombs to go off. To be grabbed. Gunshots to go off.

My hand grips my cane, the pulsing pain helping ground myself briefly. I call the cane Rhonda, so when I need it, I just say, "help me, Rhonda." Chesty and Animal thought that it was hilarious, meanwhile I received confusion from Isaac and Jameson.

I approach Leo's bike, stopping to brush my fingers over the handlebars. The past month or so I've been able to help a little on the destroyed bikes with the others. There's hope for them to run again, but I guess like me they're gonna need more time. Nor will run the same.

I bemoan inside myself at the weird analogy, sighing as I run my fingers over the headlight.

"Already missing it?"

I yelp, jolting as I spin and bump into the bike. I start falling, but Leo swiftly grabs me before I can as Rhonda clatters to the ground. Gasping, I clutch his leather vest as he holds me against him.

"You alright?" he asks.

"Apart from almost knocking out a row of motorcycles? Peachy." I press a hand to my thundering chest as Leo bends down to grab my cane, handing it over before stepping back.

"Why'd you leave the bar?"

"Crowds," I say, giving a partial sad smile. "Even here they make me antsy. Today's a nice day to admire motorcycles anyhow."

Leo looks over the motorcycles. "You'll ride one on your own again."

"Being your backpack is good enough for now." I give him a brighter smile.

His hands go into his pockets, brows pinching together as he watches me. There's a slight frown on his face as I can practically see the thoughts in his head swirling. The past couple of days he's been quieter than usual after his latest session with Dr. Maxwell. A day later he proposed the group ride. Knowing there's something on his mind, I shift on my feet to adjust my weight. I then glance past him to the bar's entrance, finding only a long row of bikes.

"What is it, baby?" I ask gently.

A faint smile tugs at his lips, almost sad.

Finally, he reaches for my free hand. He leads me to the side of his motorcycle, getting on. Leo then helps me swing my leg over to sit on the seat with him, facing him as I straddle his lap. He leans my cane against the side, placing his hands on my hips to keep me balanced.

A strike of desire ripples over me, feeling him against me, but I ignore it. We're coming up just over six months without sex or anything within that regard. Not since London. I'm ready to try, but not him. Those unspoken ghosts followed too closely. I've spoken a few times to Dr. Maxwell about it, mostly on what to do. He said patience and reminded me our relationship was never built on sex in the first place; our desires have grown along with us, and to take each day at a time. Much like I had for myself.

My eyes flit to his covered wrists and forearms. He's wearing a long-sleeved shirt made for riding. Underneath, I knew he wore sleeves that would keep those scars covered. My quiet thoughts are broken when he finally speaks.

"I held a gun in my mouth the night before I met you."

Surprise he finally told me squeezes my chest, but I focus on keeping my expression calm.

He exhales a sharp breath, meeting my gaze as he runs his hands over my thighs.

"I'd felt like a failure," he admits, speaking low. "No matter what I did, I kept coming back to the same place. I was becoming someone I despised. Hated it all. And the people I *did* care about, I felt like I'd taken away their lives and hopes. It was just always about the mafia, business, Renato, Ga—..." he clears his throat, "... the moments I felt alive was riding with the club, but it was too far in between. I was hollow."

His hands stop at the top of my hips.

"I changed the Will for everything we built to be given to the Crew. Let them leave or stay, decide what they wanted. The rest... Luciano name, Marchetti would be given to Renato and Matteo. Since it's all they cared about, complained about, or wanted." Leo pauses, bringing a hand up to stroke my cheek. "Then I met you."

Solemn eyes meet mine as my heart pounds.

"Jameson found me," he says. "He didn't say a damn word, just took the gun and alcohol, told me to sleep it off. I planned to finish the job the next night, do it while I knew he was in a meeting. But... I couldn't get your face out of my head. How easy you smiled while covered in coffee and foam. A small piece of me just wanted to see you again. One more time. Just one more time before I..."

His hand drops, staring down to the pavement. Gently, I take his hands, holding them close. I ask quietly the question I've wondered since Jameson told me, "In Rome...you admitted you weren't planning to take me back to the hotel to fuck me, but just wanted to see me again. What were you planning for that night?"

"Have an Americano, then blow my brains out." My throat tightens, trying not to cry on something from well over a year ago. He didn't do it. He's still here. I hold on to that as his breath catches a little. "But I talked to you...and then I couldn't get the sound of you saying my name out of my head. When I came back you were gone, and I couldn't do it until I knew you were okay."

"And then I appeared through a window, waving at you with a mop," I whisper.

"Most beautiful sight I'd seen in days." Hazel eyes meet mine, guilt lining them along with old pain. "You asked me those first dates, why you and honestly, Autumn, I have no fucking idea. All I knew is that I wanted to smile. I hadn't in so long. Every moment I felt less of a failure. I just didn't want to die anymore, not if you were around. And I apologize for not telling you sooner."

"Thank you for telling me," I say softly. "But don't apologize. For having low moments, having those thoughts, or not telling me. Whether you told me right after, weeks later, months, or longer than now…you're still here and that's what matters." Tears blur in those hurting eyes. "I love you unconditionally, every piece of you. You're not a failure. You're not broken."

I bring my hands up, cradling his face as I caress my thumbs over his skin. He gives me a weak smile, and I give him one, too. I say the words that I understood in needing to hear, to make it this far after almost not being here at all.

"You have always been more than enough, Leo. I am so proud of you, and so grateful that you took that chance of living again. You are the very best thing to have ever happened to me, because of you I learned how to live again, too. My patient, strong, loving husband."

His chin quivers, and that small movement makes my heart crack. I tug him to me, cradling his head against my shoulder as he wraps his arms around me. He buries his face against my neck, holding me tight as I feel his chest shake as he inhales short breaths. Leo's hand strokes along my back, and I hug him tighter.

"I love you," he murmurs.

"I love you." I kiss his head.

We stay there until I feel a numbness along the bottom of my spine and into my hips. I shift a little, and Leo pulls me up closer onto his lap. I squeeze my legs around him. We pull apart enough to smile at the other as he strokes my cheek, and then my hair back.

"Is that what's been on your mind the past few days? Telling me?" I ask.

He nods. "Dr. Maxwell said if I was tearing myself up about it, that I should. And…" he clears his throat, letting out a soft exhale, "…to suggest doing a couple of sessions together."

I raise my brows. He's never brought it up with me.

"Not as a couple's session," Leo explains. "But he thinks some subjects I may finally open up about with you in the room…if you're alright with that."

"Of course." I rub my hand against his chest, reassuring him. "I really am proud of you, Leo."

"I don't know how you did this on your own. Some days, if not for you or Dr. Maxwell, I'd splinter apart."

I take a long breath, looking past Leo as I see the sun's rays lower in the horizon. Bright streaks of colors through clouds. "Honestly, I don't know either sometimes. But that's kind of what survival and healing is. You do what you must."

I look back at him giving him a smile. "It does get easier, even when there are bad days," I say softly, reaching up and lightly run my finger down where that line between his furrowed brow is. It vanishes. "You push through those shitty days, and wait for the next sunrise."

Leo brushes his fingers over my cheek again, his gaze tender. He says again, "I love you."

I place my forehead against his as our breaths intermingle, closing my eyes. Slowly, Leo tilts his head for his lips to touch mine. It's almost like the first time, mouths meeting tenderly as our lips join at a warm caress. I start to pull away, not wanting to overdo it, until his hand slides up to the nape of my neck. My breath hitches, arousal blossoming below as his other grips my hips against his. Leo presses further, kissing me deeper than he has in months as my body shudders at the touch. I want to moan, melt into him after so long. My hands glide over his shoulders, back up to wrap them around his neck.

"Autumn," he breathes against my lips, going back in like a man starved. The kiss becomes fervent, giving in to the desire as Leo definitively takes that next step. We make out like teenagers on his bike, hips pushing against his as we become hot and wanting.

A wolf whistle pierces the air.

Leo immediately rips away, growling at whoever is interrupting us. I can't stop the sudden giggle, finally seeing that familiar disgruntlement of being disturbed upon his face. He slides his gaze to me, almost softening perhaps realizing it, too.

I look over my shoulder, finding, of course, the Crew there with amused faces. And slight fear.

"If you're gonna do it on the bike, least do it behind the bar like a gentleman," Iron Buffalo comments.

"Careful," Leo warns.

"Easy, Spartan, just joking," he adds, crossing his arms over his chest with a smile. "Besides…you adore us."

"Not right now," Leo grumbles, holding me close. I rub my hands over him, grinning.

"We gonna do what we planned or yer gonna stay out here, makin'out like kids at prom?" Chesty asks, puffing out smoke from his cigar.

"Y'all don't need us if you're playing Duck, Duck, Goose," I retort, and half of them laugh, while the other half look more concerned. I shrug. "Fine, Sardines."

Enigma and Animal burst out laughing. Ringer shakes his head.

"Well, Spartan?" Sombra asks.

Leo pats my hip, helping me off the bike as Enigma comes over to help and hand me my cane. I get onto the sidewalk with Leo behind me, facing the rest of the Crew. I give them all an odd look, realizing we're staying out here.

"Okay, gangsters, what are you up to?" I ask.

Ringer walks over to his motorcycle, pulling something out of his saddlebags as Sombra starts talking.

"Never had special rituals or ceremonies, we just get to the point. We make a decision and go forward. Couple weeks ago, the *Forgotten Demons* had a vote in changing some club by-laws. It was unanimous across all our chapters."

Butterflies form in my stomach, fluttering as I adjust my weight as I stand. Leo places his hand on the small of my back, giving me extra support.

"Proven you're more than just Spartan's Old Lady," Ringer adds.

"Eres nuestra hermana," Engima says with a smile. "Good mechanic, too."

"We know you'll wear it with pride," Iron Buffalo says, grinning with the rest.

"From escaping mobsters to hot wiring bikes, you're a biker, Miss Autumn," Pretty Boy Bond states.

Ringer holds out what he got to Sombra, who takes it and comes closer to hold it out to me. "Don't need some probationary stage or what the fuck ever…you earned this fucking patch."

I take it, opening the new black leather vest. The *Forgotten Demons* patch is on the back, but across the shoulders it says *New York*.

"You're the official first New York member for the *Forgotten Demons*," Sombra says quietly.

I stare at the leather, Leo reaching past me to help turn it over so I can see the front. A *Member* patch is on it, below a smaller patch says *Old Lady*. I smirk, but my chest shakes with emotion.

"You're a full member," Sombra says, meeting my gaze as they fill with tears. "Can vote and everything. Whole club voted for women to be part of the club, not just as Old Ladies. You're the first."

I look down again, speechless as I find a road name patch: *Cage Madness*.

"Pretty Boy suggested the madness part, given how many times you've watched the damn movie," Sombra comments.

"And can recite the songs," Chesty adds.

"Hey, it's a good movie!" I argue.

They exchange looks, grimacing while a few roll their eyes with amusement.

"And it seemed wrong not to include your tiny obsession with Nick Cage," Animal teases.

I shrug. "He's an expressive actor. The beginning scene of *Face/Off* is iconic."

"More like deranged," Chesty comments.

"And creepy," Engima adds.

"Don't start with me." I narrow my gaze.

"Yeah, Cage Madness works perfectly," Iron Buffalo chuckles.

"Gonna put the vest on?" Enigma asks, waving me on.

Handing my cane to Leo, I take off the one I have on, pulling on the new one. It's perfect. I grin, smoothing my hands down before I take Rhonda back. I catch Leo's look of pride and affection.

"Was this your idea?" I ask.

"No. Given slight conflict of interest, I stepped back to let them all decide," he answers. "Ringer proposed it."

My gaze moves to my inconceivable giant with those blue eyes. He winks, but not before brushing away stray tears and smiles. "*Barchën.*"

I give him a nod back.

"Well, good news she didn't say no and took the vest!" Animal yells.

"Cage Madness is part of the Crew and *Forgotten Demons...*" Chesty states, looking over at me with a feral grin, "...officially."

He lets out a shout, along with the others who give their celebration. They all take their turns of hugging me or patting me on the back. Once through, we start to head back into the bar to celebrate me as a new member. Leo puts my old vest into his saddlebags, walking back into the bar alongside me where Snake Eyes waits.

The biker glances down at my new vest, grinning from ear to ear. "Congratulations, Cage Madness."

"Thanks, Snake Eyes."

He glimpses at Leo, and chuckles, "The Spartan and Cage Madness. Perfect pair indeed."

Snake Eyes then calls out to the bar for a free round to celebrate. There are shouts of elation as I walk in as a *Forgotten Demon.*

Chapter 51

His Emerald Fire

THE ENGINES TURN off outside the country estate. Quiet, early evening falls as the motorcycles are put away. We head inside, most the Crew aiming for the kitchen and talking about relaxing for the rest of the evening. I stop in the foyer, watching them as they joke around. I reach up, touching the leather vest with gratitude and pride.

Soft footsteps come up behind me, and I look over my shoulder at Leo.

"Should we bet on who's gonna suggest poker or a movie?" I ask.

"They can do whatever they want," Leo murmurs, leaning close to my ear as his arm winds around my waist. "Check in."

I blink, surprise and arousal flooding me at his words. My breath catches, finding burning hazel eyes on me. "Green."

He swiftly bends down, picking me up in his arms. A soft yelp leaves me as he heads for the stairs as I wrap my arms around his neck. The others are too preoccupied with each other to notice as Leo strides across the catwalk. The only one I catch looking is Jameson, who smirks before going back to the others. Leo carries me into our bedroom, shutting and locking the door behind him. He then puts my cane aside and takes me to the bed, sitting me down.

He's silent as he takes his vest off, and I follow suit. He hangs up both, and then takes his boots off. I remain quiet, watching him as he comes back to remove mine and sets them aside with his. He abruptly stops a few feet away, hands flexing at his sides. Slowly, I stand and undress to just my underwear. Leo's eyes roam over me as I run my hands along my thighs, sitting back down, waiting for him. I want to walk to him, but I know in three steps I'll collapse without any help. Yearning builds as I watch him, waiting as he feels too far away.

Except, he doesn't move. Swallowing hard, I see his chest rise heavily with each breath.

"Check in," I murmur.

"Yellow."

Silently, I hold my hand out to him. Thankfully, he steps forward. I pull him down to sit next to me, and then climb over to straddle his lap. I run my hands over his chest, feeling his thundering heartbeat. His hands flex at his side, but he starts to breathe easier.

"I'm gonna take your shirt off," I whisper. He nods. "Words, Leo."

"Alright," he responds quietly.

Smoothing my hands over the bottom of his shirt, I touch his skin underneath as I slide under the hem. His breathing shudders as I move the fabric, slowly drawing it up until he has to raise his arms for me to pull it off. His breathing is still heavy, not necessarily in anticipation of sex, but I know of fear.

Gently, I run my hands over his torso and up over his shoulders. Our bodies have changed since the last time. He hadn't gained much of his muscle back, still thin from not eating normally and working. Mine, I have some weight gain in attempt of being healthier after the coma. Then there's spots of marred skin; my feet are scarred, along with my back. He has his own scars, some of them making his tattoos disjointed from being cut through. Lastly, there were still the sleeves on his arms, covering his wrists and forearms.

We've seen each naked plenty of times over the months, but not like this. Not like lovers again.

His hands shakily go to my thighs, moving his fingers over me in soft motions. I continue running my hands over him, beginning to trace his tattoos as I've done before. His hands move up to my torso, gliding over my skin with a tender caress.

Gently, I move my hands to one of his arms to start peeling off the sleeve. He freezes, watching me as I roll it down. Halfway there as the worst of the scars begin to show, he stops me and shuts his eyes as his body shakes.

"Yellow," he rasps.

I let go, letting him roll the fabric back up. He clutches at his arms as his face contorts. I tenderly grab his face, and say, "Okay, we'll keep them on. It's alright."

"I'm sorry."

"Leo, it's okay. Look at me." His eyes snap open, desire slowly being washed out by fear and uncertainty. "If you're not ready, it's alright."

"No." His body trembles, hands now grabbing my thighs to keep me where I am.

"Leo—"

"I want my wife," he says, bringing a hand up to cup my face as I move mine down over his chest, soothingly stroking him. "I want *you*. God, I have wanted sex with you for months, missing that part of us." Tears form in his eyes, grasping me harder. "I can't let him take that part of us. I just…"

Leo leans forward, pressing his forehead into my shoulder as his hand moves to clutch the back of my neck.

His heart pounds under my hands, almost in unison with my own that thunders in my chest. Tears form in my eyes. I go still as memories, moments flood me in a matter of seconds as Leo murmurs, "How did you do this? How did you make it stop?"

Fragments flash. *"One day it'll be your turn."*

Those feelings of guilt and being a burden as he helped care for me. *"Focus on me."*

It was never a scale of who could love more than the other. *"You'll take care of him."*

Those fears became manageable not wholly because he loved me. *"Good girl."*

He made me feel safe.

After over a year being with Leo, working on myself, getting stronger and even forgiving myself…I can be what Leo has been for me the moment he recited Poe with me.

In a gentle voice, I start reciting *The Raven* as I smooth my hands over his back. I stroke his skin as I speak. My own worries melting away as I focus on him; to help him get through this difficult hurdle. One I understood far too well, and how scary it is.

I'm halfway through the poem when Leo starts to recite it with me. Warm breath drifts over me as he speaks. When we finish, he's finally breathing normally and not shaking. I lift his head, cradling his face with one hand while I smooth his hair with the other.

"You're safe," I whisper, leaning in to kiss his forehead. "You're safe." I continue saying it, kissing him upon different places of his face. Finally, I come just a breath away from his mouth, and say, "I'm here. Focus on me, baby."

I press my lips against his, and his breath hitches. Its slow, affectionate, and sweet as I slide my hands down his neck and shoulders. Leo begins to rove his hands over me, kissing me deeper and deeper as his body becomes less rigid.

Leo's hands move behind me, pulling me closer for our chests to press against the other. He's warm as I clutch his head, kissing him as desire builds.

"Check in," I say against his lips, nipping softly at his bottom lip.

"Green."

"Good boy," I say easily, smiling as his eyes meet mine. The fear dissipating, replaced by want and yearning. "Tell me what you want."

"You. I want you," he breathes out.

"You have me." I kiss him again. "Put me on the bed."

Arms wrapped around me; Leo spins us so that my back is against the bed while he's on top. He continues to kiss me, moaning as his hands roam my body. I gesture for him to take my underwear and bra off. He does so with need upon his face.

A hand starts going up towards my neck, but he stops himself. I grab him, placing his palm at my throat. He stares at me, and that panic starts to form on his face again.

"Focus on me," I say gently. "I'm safe, Leo. So are you. Only pleasure from your hands, right?" My voice seems to calm him as his hand lightly presses against my neck. "We're safe. It's just you and me. You and me, mister."

Leo's body lays over mine as he comes down to kiss me. His jean clad hips brush against mine, causing a shiver to run over me. Relief floods me, the craving for this, for him finally coming to fruition as I revel in his touch.

He breaks away from the kiss, sliding his hand down to caress my breasts next as he kisses my chest. Another shudder runs over me as he strokes my skin. Soft lips trail down as he explores my body as if it was the first time. I reach for his head, gripping those soft strands as he moans against my stomach.

"Check in," I ask.

"Green."

"Good boy." He moans at the honorific, clutching my sides. "Take your pants off, baby."

He places one more kiss above my belly button, getting off the bed to yank his jeans, chaps, and underwear off. I sit up, moving over to the bedside table and desperately hope he still has lube in the drawer. There is and I pull the bottle out as Leo climbs back onto the bed.

"Sit in the middle," I tell him, and he does while furrowing his brows. I smile gently, putting some lube in my hand as I toss the bottle aside, and go to him. Carefully, I wrap my hand around his cock to slick it up, which makes him groan.

I wipe the rest through my sex, straddling him once more, but on my knees to hover above him.

"Autumn, I don't want you to wear yourself out," he says gently, grabbing my hips.

"I'll be fine for a bit. It's good PT," I lightly tease, and then place my hands on his chest, looking up at him through my lashes. "You can help control the pace and how deep, and if you need to stop then you can easily hold me, okay?"

Realization begins to form on his face, making his brows unfurrow, eyes widening. He swallows, inhaling a sharp breath as I grab his cock. I stroke him a few times, and he groans while gripping my hips.

"Ready?" I ask. He nods, jaw clenching. "Words, Leo."

Amusement flashes over him. "Yes."

"Good boy," I praise, kissing him briefly.

He chuckles.

My heart flutters at the small sound.

Finally, I sink down upon his dick. He stretches me, what once was familiar coming back. My breath stutters as he groans, both of us inhaling sharply as I move a bit. He lifts my hips, and I'm sunk fully upon his cock. I clutch his shoulders, eyes closing as the arousal flourishes into pleasure. Oh, son of a nutcracker, I almost want to cry being this close to him again.

I start to move, but Leo holds me in place. "Wait."

I sink further, allowing my legs to relax. We both groan at the small movement, but I wait for him. Leo's hands run over my back, down over my hips, and back up again. He comes to my breasts, squeezing them as I hang my head back and close my eyes. He flicks over my nipples as I make sounds of pleasure. His hands disappear, and I open my eyes, finding him slowly peeling off one of his sleeves.

"Leo, it's okay, you can keep them on," I say, placing my hand over his.

"I want them off…" he says roughly, moving his gaze to mine, "…nothing between us."

"Okay," I whisper.

He starts to roll it more but stops at the same spot as before. Carefully, I place my hand over his and help him take it off together. His chest shakes as we do the same with the other one, tossing the sleeves aside. His scars come into full view, mottled skin around his wrists that are a pinkish color moving up his forearm.

Leo stares at them, and I grab his hands, placing them on my thighs. I move my hips a little, circling them once and he groans. I then grab his face, making him look at me instead of the scars upon his arms.

"Focus on me," I say, circling my hips again and his breath hitches. "We're safe, Leo. Only you can touch me. We're safe. Only us."

Tears gather in his eyes, and some begin to form for me as well. I clutch at his back, bringing us close as I move my hips slightly. Leo's body shudders, hands moving to my ass as he grips me and my breath hitches.

"Check in," he murmurs.

"Emerald."

Leo lifts my hips, then pushes them back down. We groan, the noise intermingling as he does it again and I grind against him. Our breaths pick up, finding a rhythm to work together. A hand comes up to clutch the back of my head, keeping our bodies flush as he pushes into me. Sweat forms, clinging to our bodies to help slide us together.

He suddenly stops, and I'm about to check in, when he begins to lay me upon the bed. Leo places me gently, keeping us connected as he roams a hand down my side, hips, and thigh. He thrusts gently as I grab his neck, moaning into his shoulder as I'm wrecked with pleasure. Desire strikes through me, tingling up my spine and through my bones. My legs shake as I feel myself on the verge of coming, the need and craving to be together after so long.

Leo places both of his hands at the side of me. I pull him closer as he continues to thrust, grinding his hips against mine. He groans, bringing his head down next to mine as he grips the sheets.

One of his hands move to cup my face, and he brings his head up. His movements falter when his eyes come to those scars again.

"Focus on me," I say gently, reaching up as my back arches towards him. I take that hand, keeping it in place as I tenderly kiss his wrist. And then again. "You're safe. We're safe."

My heart clenches seeing that flicker of fear, hating it. Anger simmers beneath the desire, despising what was done to him. To make him fear himself and us. I'm determined by the need to love him and cherish him. Protect him.

I reach up with my other hand, stroking his hair back as I pull him down to me. I kiss him fervently, relaying all the love in my heart for him. That we made it.

His hips grind against mine and my legs shake as another shudder of bliss hits me.

"I love you," I say against his lips, clutching his hand against my jaw. "I love you, baby."

"Autumn."

My hand goes down to his ass, grasping him as I grind my hips up. He groans against my mouth, and his body goes tense. Mine does next as the orgasm pulls at me, pushing me over as my entire body goes taut with a much-needed release. Leo breaks the kiss, grunting into the bedcovers next to my head. We cling to the other, covered in sweat and panting heavily.

Finally, his body starts to go lax over mine, barely holding himself up from crushing me. He brings his head back up, sweat along his brow. I smile up at him.

"I'm so proud of you," I say softly.

His chin quivers as I watch a torrent of emotions move over his eyes. Relief. Love. Hope. Unbelief. Emotions I knew too well. The aftermath of just a mixture of everything as you feel a weight lifted off.

"Come here." I reach up for him, my own emotions threatening to overwhelm me. Leo wraps his arms around me, falling over to the side. We hold each other firmly.

Leo silently cries against my skin. I focus on Leo for my own well-being as I remind myself he's okay. We're okay, even as I cry quietly as well.

After a while, our tears dry. Both of us clinging to the other. I feel him stroke his hand over my back.

"I love you," he whispers. "And so, fucking thankful I have you, my dear Watson."

"I love you, my dear Leo."

I rest my head on the bed, coming face to face with him as he does the same. Leo strokes my cheek, calm moving over him. His gaze flickers to his hand, movement pausing again.

"We can put them back on," I say gently. "However long you need."

Carefully, he brings the hand down between us. "I don't want them to be a constant reminder of my failings."

I take his hand, stroking my thumb over the scars gently. His face flinches a moment, but he doesn't stop me. "Would you like to know what they remind me of?"

Leo's brows furrow with uncertainty, but nods.

"That you won," I answer. "Just like my own, that you survived. You fought. You walked away, and he didn't. That you got us home." My breath becomes shaky as I kiss his wrist. "That you saved me from enduring a pain you knew broke me. That my husband, a man I love deeply, protected me…and kept his promise. You kept your promises, Leo."

He places that hand against my cheek, glistening eyes flicking to those scars and back to my face. He pulls me back against him, embracing me with his warmth.

"My dear Watson," he whispers against me. "My dear wife."

It's much later when Leo pulls me up with him, carrying me to the bathroom to shower together. About halfway through, my legs almost give out and he catches me before I hit the ground.

I think of asking him to get my crutches or wheelchair, but he just picks me up again. I don't have the strength to argue with him, wanting his closeness. Putting us both in robes, he settles us into the chairs near the balcony to watch the starry night. We cuddle together in silence, wrapped around the other. My fingers softly caress the scars on his arms.

His lips brush against my ear, and whispers reverently, "Good girl."

I smile, turning my head to kiss him lovingly as I feel a crack inside me mend into gold.

Chapter 52

A Fistful of Chances

I can't breathe.

My hip hurts from hitting the ground and my hands sting from trying to keep hold of my crutches. They're on the ground next to me as I clutch my head, constriction around my chest as the panic attack grips me. My vision blurs, a migraine drowns out the voices around me. Everything trembles, making my muscles hurt as darkness forms at the edge of my vision. I feel sick, scooting back in an attempt of hiding further. My back touches a hard surface and I cringe away as a sob works its way up my throat.

Thoughts scramble as it feels like I'm splintering. Why is this happening, why—?

We'd gotten back from the estate a week ago, and I've barely slept. A nightmare last night. I stayed up watching movies, until Leo woke up to make breakfast. I couldn't remember them. Just a constant crawling, something far buried in my mind underneath numbness. We came to the hotel. Leo had meetings. I was helping Grant. Normal day. Until…

A door had slammed. Guests were yelling, upset, being thrown out of the hotel. Blood. Smashed mirror. Cigarette smoke. And then the cologne. That scent thrusting me back to the smell of wet concrete and rust.

My stomach churns, folding more into myself as I remember his laugh. The pictures. Gabriel tearing at my pants. Snap of chains. Leo's screams.

"Gabriel, fucking stop!" No, no, no…not Leo…not—

Someone touches me, and I hit him. There's noise as I rock in place, shaking my head as the torrent of memories flood me.

"Want to play rough? Fine!"

"…fuck your dead body…"

"Open your eyes."

"Autumn. You're not there. Breathe." A deep voice tries to comfort me. Chesty? Rudy? More voices collide as I rock myself, trying not to hurt myself or another.

Leo. I need Leo.

My head spins as people talk. "Keep…she'll…violent…call Leo…clear."

I screw my eyes shut, hoping it'll end. It'll pass. It's been months since I've had a flashback like this turning into a violent panic attack. Fuck. Anger churns, hating it happened over a messy fucking room.

"Twenty minutes," someone says.

Fucking crud muffins.

I barely remember I'm in the hallway of the hotel on some floor. Shit. I need to get calm enough to make it to the apartment. My head pounds, making me want to hurl as I groan against my legs. My nails dig into my thighs, which ache, a numbness forming at the bottom of my tailbone.

"Shit, shit," I mutter, panic now occurring that I hurt myself. Frustration and pain rolls over me. I don't want to set myself back with healing from a stupid fall.

It sounds like they're blocking off the floor, keeping people away from the newish owner of the hotel having a damn meltdown.

My heart pounds into my ears. Another round of memories

bombards me—cracks in the concrete. Pillars falling. Screams. Dust in my nose. Pain splitting through my feet and Leo's groans. That final *crack*. Waking up.

Tears run down my face, wanting it to end. *Make it stop.*

There's a scuffle and some arguing. I flinch from the raised voices, hiding my face. More arguing, and then Bobby's voice, "Let him go."

Someone sits next to me. Sitting like me, silent.

"He's gone. You made sure of that."

I recognize the voice. Struggling to breathe I turn my head. I sniffle as snot starts to run down my face, gripping myself harshly. Matteo adjusts where he sits, grabbing something and holds out a handkerchief. I stare at the blue cloth.

"It's clean. Was Bobby's," he murmurs.

Arm trembling, I take it to wipe my nose. I clench onto it as I lay my head on my knees. Matteo mirrors what I do.

"How…" I swallow hard, voice rough and throat hurting from sobbing, "…do you know?"

"Room smells like his fucking cologne."

The noise around me has subsided, turning to whispers. There's still the roaring in my head, and I flinch as another memory slips through.

"I never killed anyone," he admits softly, which makes me open my eyes. He shrugs nonchalantly. "Leo wouldn't allow it. Gabriel, well, always go to them first."

"Hey, no bringin' that fucker up," Chesty warns.

Matteo glares past me, then brings his attention back to me. "Sorry."

"It's not the name," I whisper shakingly. "It's what he did. Almost did."

Matteo's face becomes a pained, guilty almost as he slumps more. We stare at each other, him sitting much like me as my muscles ache and exhaustion yanks at me. Tears still fall as more of me feels numb.

Then almost quietly, Matteo murmurs, "Era...davvero un mostro."

My chin quivers as I can just make out tears forming in Matteo's eyes. I can only nod. We remain there as I feel some of the panic vanish. Memories returning to the dark crevices of my mind. A part of me wants to reach out, hold his hand. Perhaps for me. Perhaps for him.

Suddenly, Matteo gets up in a panic, holding his hands up. "I didn't touch her."

There's movement, quick footsteps as I turn my head as Leo approaches. He scowls, practically growling at Matteo as he comes to me. He crouches low, expression instantly concerned. "Check in."

"Yellow."

His hand strokes my hair, glancing down at the handkerchief I clutch. My body starts to tremble again, feeling heavy and confused. I then whisper, "I can't feel my legs."

"I'm going to pick you up," he says softly. I nod just before he eases his arms around me. "You're safe. I've got you."

Leo picks me up easily as I go limp in his arms and put my arms around his neck. He kisses my head, holding me close.

"Chesty, tell Jameson to head the meeting with the investors. Have Owen cancel my other two," Leo speaks. "Rest of you finish your duties. She's not some sideshow attraction."

"He was only trying to help," Bobby comments. Leo stiffens. "Seemed it did."

A deafening silence comes over the hall. Through the fogginess of my head, I can't tell if it's because Bobby said something, Matteo is here, or just the commotion in general. I then realize why Leo may not be moving yet.

He hasn't seen Matteo since Rome. It's been over six *months*.

"He did help," I whisper. Leo turns his face towards me, face stern and scary to anyone else.

He looks back at the others. "Get back to work," he orders. "Chesty bring up Flotsam and Jetsam later."

Leo turns, walking us to the private elevator. We're quiet as he gets on, the doors shutting us off from the rest.

"Any feeling coming back?" He asks.

"Tingling."

"Likely sat too long, constricted blood flow. Did you fall?" I nod. "We'll ice it, then."

He kisses my temple when the doors open. He takes me into the apartment, sitting me carefully onto the couch. I adjust how I sit, wincing at the pain along my hip. Leo comes back with an ice pack, water, and some of my medications.

I take them, grimacing as I swallow. Leo then has me lay on my side, putting a pillow between my legs and sits down. He lays my head on his lap, putting a pillow there first as he holds the icepack where I'd fallen. His other hand strokes my hair as I finally find it easier to breathe.

"Check in," he asks.

"Greenish yellow," I mumble, feeling like shit.

"Chesty mentioned you hit Grant. Flashback?"

I nod as he takes the icepack away, beginning to stroke my side and thigh. I close my eyes, sighing as I concentrate on him.

"Talk about it?" He asks, and I shake my head. "Do you know what triggered it?"

"Cologne," I mutter. "It smelled like…yeah."

Leo exhales sharply, not faltering in his soft caress. Everything just aches as I start to feel my legs more, wiggling them a little. My body is heavy, while my throat is sore and feels swollen.

"How are you feeling?" he asks.

"Sore. Feel my legs. Head hurts."

Leo carefully helps me sit up, getting up again as he grabs the ice pack and goes into the kitchen. I hang my head, divided between wanting food or a long bath. He comes back, pulling me over his lap to stretch my legs out. I look up at him as he places a warm washcloth against the back of my neck, massaging the warmth there.

I smile softly as he gives me a gentle look, stroking his hand over my leg. We're quiet as he holds me, helping the soreness go away the best he can. It seems like forever before he breaks the silence.

"What did Matteo do?"

"Sat with me. Recognized the cologne, too. I think he just... understood. Or was trying to." I hold my hand up that's still holding the handkerchief, dropping it over on the coffee table. "He's not the same person, Leo. Just like you and I aren't."

He inhales sharply, but then there's a knock at the door. Leo calls out, "Enter."

Chesty comes in carrying my crutches, setting them against the counter. He gives a nod, and then leaves. We stay there silently.

"Check in," he says.

"Green, just tired and achy."

He pulls away the washcloth, tossing it onto the coffee table. I lean against him. Leo takes in a long exhale, and then asks, "Do you want...do you want a relationship with Matteo? As in-laws or friendship?"

I swallow hard past the dryness of my throat. "Yeah, I do. If he's willing."

Gently, I pull away from him to look at him. His face is neutral, barely any emotion as I notice that cold mask of his. His eyes though do betray him of guilt and concern.

"Will you be okay with that?" I ask softly.

"If it's what you want," he says roughly, continuing to stroke my back.

"Leo."

"I want to speak with him first." He clears his throat, adjusting in his seat to pull out his phone. "But I...I need more time."

"Okay."

Leo briefly calls Chesty, instructing him to bring up Matteo. There's some grumbling on the line before Leo hangs up and goes back to cradling me in his lap. Finally, there's a knock. Leo calls out for them to enter again, and in comes Chesty with Matteo close behind.

Surprise flicks over the young man's face when he sees the apartment.

"Wait outside, Chesty," Leo instructs. Chesty gives us a weary look but listens as he scowls at Matteo before leaving the apartment.

Matteo stands near the counter with his shoulders hunched. Leo carefully moves me off his lap, placing me back on the couch as he stands to face his brother. Matteo folds his arms over his chest, holding himself close. He does it like he's protecting himself, fear and unease on his face.

"Why were you on that floor?" Leo asks suddenly in a rigid tone.

He clears his throat before answering. "Bobby was replacing a bathroom fan, needed help. Wasn't following her." Leo only scowls at him. "Everyone kept arguing while she was freaking out. Felt I should've done something."

I snort. Leo glances over to me. I shrug, cause he's gotta admit that when he's not around, protocol or whatever, the Crew turn into worried mother hens.

"Thought someone could just..." Matteo shrugs, "sit with her."

Leo's brows furrow, staring at the ground. Matteo clears his throat again, looking at me. "You, uh, get those a lot?"

"From time to time," I answer, seeing him trying to keep his focus on me; not on his brooding, scary brother. Yeah, don't blame him, given the last time they saw each other, Leo was letting him be waterboarded. I shiver at the memory. "That's been the worst in a bit."

"Because what...what happened in London?"

"Today, yes. Sometimes...because of Rome." Wide, guilty eyes find mine. "Sometimes because of New Jersey. Interrogation rooms. Cold streets. Dingy clubs. The harbor." His lips press together harshly. "Or a life long before New York. I have options."

His brows scrunch together, jaw moving in thought.

Leo finally starts to move, taking his suit jacket off. Matteo stiffens, almost flinching from the simple movement. Leo is slow and deliberate as he unbuttons his sleeves, rolling them up to reveal his scars. Matteo's eyes go wider, confusion and horror warping.

"What happened...?"

"Gabriel," Leo answers roughly. "After torturing me for hours, I almost ripped my hands off when he tried to rape and kill my wife in front of me."

My stomach clenches, a tremor running over my chest. Matteo goes pale, arms dropping to his side as he steps back.

"I'm sorry," he says abruptly, staring at Leo's hands. "For everything. Le chiedo perdono. Mi dispiace. Not listening to you...not believing you, trusting you after..." he runs a trembling hand over his face, "...Gabriel was a monster. You warned me. And I...I never wanted that to happen. Lo giuro, I didn't know he would—"

"Except it did, and you are to blame for him finding us."

"I never wanted him to hurt or kill..." he shakes his head, hands starting to shake. He looks nothing like the man who tried to kill me, hell, barely the one I saw in the lounge as I see the torment across his face. "Autumn...mi dispiace. I thought..." his breathing picks up, "...Gabriel and Renato kept saying you were gonna make Leo leave. I didn't want to be left alone again. Perdonami..."

Those words pierce me. My voice and Leo's from the past echoing in my head.

"Enough." Leo's voice cuts through the air, silencing Matteo, who sniffles and wipes at his nose. Leo's words are cold. "I don't forgive you."

Matteo's face crumbles. My own heart cracks faintly. Fuck.

"But my wife does." Leo continues in that strict and numb voice. "And she wants to try to have a relationship with her brother-in-law, so I won't damn you, but I do have rules you will follow. You even fucking think of hurting her, I'll cut you apart." Matteo grimaces, but nods. "You'll continue working this hotel until I say or her. Only person who outranks me is your sister-in-law, we clear?" He nods. "Words, Matteo."

"Yes, sir."

There's a twist in my stomach. Leo's still hurting, carrying a different pain than Matteo or me. It would be a while, perhaps never, for him to forgive.

"If you don't fuck up or cause trouble, then I'll consider removing your guards," Leo adds. "Try anything, *anything*, I send you back to Renaldi who'll do with you as he pleases. Capisce?"

"Yes, sir." I hate seeing how broken Matteo looks, beaten down and rejected.

"I have to go discuss some matters with Jameson. Stay here and talk with her. There's still going to be guards outside the door. So fucking behave," Leo warns, walking out of the apartment.

Matteo flinches away when Leo passes him. He doesn't even look back at me as the door opens, and I see the pinch of light from the foyer before it closes.

Well, didn't exactly give Matteo a choice, but here we are.

It's a couple minutes before Matteo speaks, wiping at his nose again. "He hates me."

"No, he's angry," I answer, wishing I could get up, but my legs will give out underneath me. Damn crutches are by Matteo. "He's still working through things, but I don't believe he hates you." Matteo stares at the ground, sniffling again. "Do you hate him?"

He shakes his head. "But I want to."

"Do you hate me?"

He finally looks up with teary eyes. "Not anymore."

I give him a soft look. "I won't make you have a…relationship or whatever. If you don't want it, that's alright."

"He'll kill me if I don't."

Quietly, I say, "He's scary, but he's not Gabriel."

He frowns, chin quivering a little.

I lean forward, grabbing the box of tissues and hold them up for him. "I'd bring them to you, but my legs are out of commission and Flotsam and Jetsam are over by you." His brows pinch together with confusion. "The crutches."

Matteo glimpses at them. "You named them?"

"I have a wheelchair called Optimus, and my cane is Rhonda." More confusion. "Helps me cope."

He blinks, and sniffles again. Once more I hold up the box, and he rolls his eyes. Ah, there's the sullen teen attitude I know. He starts to walk over but stops, grabbing my crutches and brings them over to lean against the coffee table. Stiffly, he takes a tissue.

"Grazie."

I lean back, sighing as I wince at a pinch of pain along my tailbone. I adjust, and then gesture for him to sit. One, to help him be more comfortable after being threatened by his older brother. Two, it's weird if he's just standing.

After a minute, he finally does, but a good foot away.

We're quiet as I run my hands over my thighs. I wait to see if he'll talk or just ask to leave. He grabs another tissue, wiping his nose and puts the discarded tissue down.

"Will he ever...trust me again?" He finally speaks, voice low as he hangs his head, elbows on his knees.

"Depends on what you do. But I don't know."

"Do you? Is that why you want..." he waves his hand between us, "...or is it some way to make a happy family?"

I snort, leaning back into my seat more. "No, you can't force a family to get along. As someone who'll never talk to theirs again, I know that's not always doable. And no...I don't necessarily trust you." He starts to turn away, perhaps glaring at the windows. "But I want to, which means communicating and getting to know the other."

"Why do you even care? I almost killed you. Tried to."

"I know how terrifying being alone can make one desperate. And you, Matteo, just wanted your brother." His shoulders tense up, still not looking at me. I swallow hard, holding back my own tears as I see too much of myself in him. Too much of Leo from months ago. "And sometimes those thoughts and voices in our heads can drown us. To the point, we don't know what reality is anymore. Who to trust. Even ourselves."

Matteo looks down at his hands, beginning to wring them as I watch him try to cover his wrists. Like he can imagine Leo's scars on him instead.

"I'm willing to try, Matteo," I say softly. "If you are, too. I know I'm not Leo, and I'll never try to be him or replace your brothers. I just…don't want you to be alone."

His breath hitches, continuing to wring at his hands. "Was it you? The girl…hiding in the cans at the harbor?"

"Yeah." My voice is rough as I watch him, hoping my tears don't betray me. He nods barely.

Silence again, stretching before us as the air feels heavy. I'm unsure if I'm doing this right or anything right. I could be off my rocker for wanting to try with Matteo. Or too-soft hearted. His cries for Leo when we left him in Rome haunt me. The pain in his eyes trying to choke me. The hurt. The anger.

"Yeah…I'll try," he finally says. "No one other than Bobby wants to be near me anyways."

I sit up a little, feeling a trickle of hope as he agrees. "When were you hugged last?"

Brown eyes snap to mine. Confusion contorts his face, and then a sliver of pain. He tries to shrug it off.

"Do you want one?" I offer. He just stares at me. "Doesn't have to be now. Just thought—"

"Yeah."

Turning a bit more towards him, I open my arms. It takes him a moment, but he finally moves and tentatively puts his arms around me. He's extremely careful, like he may break me. Don't blame him after Leo's threat. I hug him tighter, smoothing my hand down his back. His breath hitches as we hug, slowly becoming less rigid in my arms. I feel his shoulders shake as I feel the familiarity of him trying not to cry.

He's similar to Leo in that way.

Unsure what else to do, I say the words I hope he needs. "Mi dispiace, Matteo." He goes still in my arms. "I'm sorry you've felt alone and isolated, and for being used so much you didn't know what to believe anymore. And I'm sorry neither myself or Leo were there."

A tremor happens over him as he hugs me tighter. I clutch his head, holding him. I wait until he's ready to let go, unwilling until he does first. Slowly, he moves away from me. Until I grab his face briefly and kiss his forehead.

Matteo stares at me slightly, slack-jawed at the gesture as I settle back into my seat alongside him. He clears his throat, grabbing another tissue to wipe his face.

"You're a really forgiving person, you know that?"

"So, I've been told," I muse. "I'm a pain in the ass like that."

He snorts, rubbing his face a little. "So, uh, how does this work?"

"Well, let's start with…why do you like Italian westerns so much?" Movie topics—tried and true for me.

"Dad used to watch them with me." I smile as he shrugs.

I glance over my shoulder at the television room. "Open to other genres?"

"I don't like the romantic crap."

I resist the urge to roll my eyes. "Fine, how about action films?"

Matteo looks over at me. "You got those, too?"

"Oh, enough to start a museum." A bigger grin forms on my face as he looks at me curiously. "How do you feel about Nick Cage movies?"

Chapter 53

Violet Worship

LEO's on the phone as he cooks breakfast. I watch him as I glance through the paperwork for *Nan's Bookstore*. She officially moved down to Georgia early autumn. I'm happy for her. Besides her leaving, more changes will occur to the store, such as renovating the space next door to be a café, connecting them. It's a large project, but Leo and myself believe in the future plans I have for that block and the next one over.

Most of my time was spent taking care of the *Italian Lily*, apart from being the owner, I've taken over parts of Chiari's job of the more…illegal side of things. It kept me busy, and it meant Chiari finally took shorter hours, which Trix loved. Although Chiari would've anyways if Trix asked, just as Isaac worked less hours for Leanne. Better balance. It was for all of us, well…most days.

I close the paperwork that would ensure Nan's and Finn's legacy. Briefly, I glance over my shoulder to look at the snow swirling outside. Leo mutters over the phone, pulling my attention back to him. He turns the oven off, putting everything onto our plates as he stops and glowers at the counter.

"It's a quick interview, that's it, Jameson, you can handle that,"

Leo says. "Carrie knows what she's doing. And then you can avoid her for the next month. Adiós."

He hangs up, rubbing his temple as he slides his phone away. Past few weeks he's been busy with the *Golden Laurel*. Jameson's mostly been in Boston since Christmas to take care of issues, fighting with Carrie about everything. On top of that, two of DeLuca's captains were killed by some smaller rival gang. Leo has nothing to do with it, except getting a headache from them. Not to mention Vincenzo and Giovanna are essentially at war with the other in Italy. Again, not involved, but it didn't stop the headaches.

His shoulder tenses as he grabs the plates, setting them in our spots. "I should've sent Owen or Julio."

"It'll be fine. He's just not used to interviews," I say. "And Carrie loves pushing his buttons."

He grunts, sitting down in his seat as he rubs his face. I reach over, gripping his leg to catch his attention. He looks over, and he already looks tired. It's not even nine yet.

"Why don't we pull a Ferris Bueller today?" I suggest, smirking a little. He gives me one back, grabbing my hand to bring up and kiss my wrist. "They'll survive for a day."

He hums, staring down at breakfast.

Carefully, I get up and run my hands over his thighs. I step between his legs, continuing to run my hands up his sides. That finally gets him to bring his attention back to me.

"No work today," I state, keeping my eyes with his. Slowly, I feel his rigidness vanish as he nods. "We'll silence our phones. I'll tell Xavier no interruptions and inform Owen and Chiari as well." He nods again, taking longer breaths as he strokes his hands over my hips. "Then we'll spend the rest of the day in the playroom."

A calmness already settles over Leo as pride and elation flick over me as power shifts. I grab his face, thumbs brushing over his skin.

"Just you and me. Do you want that, baby?"

Hazel eyes simmer with need before he leans forward, kissing me gently. "Yes, Mistress."

I lock Leo's wrist in place to the St. Andrew's Cross. I double check he's secure with the padded leather cuffs. They're the only ones he's willing to wear, and I refuse to use metal cuffs. I crouch, securing his ankle next, and then move to the other side. My hands slide up his naked leg as Leo submits to the restraints, relaxing against the cross. He's naked apart from the cock cage chastity belt he wears. It's leather, small buckles around his half erect cock to pull up against the leather front. My hands slide over his buttocks and his breath hitches as I check that the anal plug attached to the belt is seated well in his ass.

The room is dimly lit as the lights sparkle in the ceiling. I have a few more lights brought up in the areas I plan to move to during the session, along with items already there. The rest are on a small wooden, tiered cart. I can easily move it around the room, after the rug has been rolled up. It also has a hook for a singular forearm crutch in case I need it. My wheelchair, KITT, is in the back corner of the room. I doubt I'll need it today, but we always keep them nearby. Leo can also undo his cuffs on his own in case my body physically gives out.

I step back, glancing at the resin floor that shimmers within the violet room. I get to the cart, bringing it closer to Leo. It has every-thing I want and need from toys, wipes, emergency shears, and first aid. My gaze flicks over myself as the low hum of the music vibrates through the room. I'm wearing lingerie from Rome, the strappy one. I've found myself staying within the Domme/Mistress role when I wear them.

Over the course of the last few months, our power dynamics have evolved and strengthened as we've worked through new kinks and triggers. Dr. Maxwell also helped once we finally admitted we were both Switches and realized he's been in the BDSM scene for decades. I wasn't surprised after the books he suggested, but Leo was.

Most of our desires and needs hadn't changed, but a few things had to be adapted. Such as my physical disabilities, especially on bad pain flare-up days. Leo wanted to be tied up and bound, but due to trauma it had to be more specific for him. He still could easily slip into Subspace knowing I was the one in charge, and with that came his full Submission in being used or fucked.

I grab the first flogger, twirling it in my hand easily after months of training. Leo's breath picks up at the sound of the swishing tails. I twirl them more.

"Check in, baby."

"Green, Mistress."

"Good boy," I praise, and then snap the leather tails along his shoulder.

Leo doesn't flinch. He rarely does from the first couple of floggers. The sound of the leather hitting flesh saturates the air. The rustling joining the smacks and Leo's breathing patterns.

Jolts of excitement move through my body as that sensation of control thrum over me. The off feeling of hitting him is distant, while I focus on him for small tells of where he's at physically and mentally. He hums at the light flogging.

I stop, moving closer to run my hand over his skin. The heat of him already invigorating and tantalizing. My fingers trace over the wings of his tattoo, and then a singular finger drags down his spine to slip under the hard leather of the belt. His breath hitches as I pull a little, then let go. Smiling, I kiss the middle of the flaming sword.

"Do you like when I touch you?" I whisper.

"Yes, Mistress," he rasps.

"We've barely started, and you're practically panting, baby," I tease, kissing his spine again as I move a hand to his front. He jolts when I faintly trace a finger over his strapped in cock. I do it once more, and his breath hitches.

Done with my teasing, I step back and switch out the flogger for one with braided tails. I swing the flogger, testing the weight. It snaps in the air, and I notice Leo's hand clenches. His ankles clink where the locks are.

"Check in," I ask.

"Green, Mistress."

I twist my wrist, flinging the tails forward. They snap at the isolated spot at his shoulder. His breath hitches as I do it to the other side, moving down to his ass. I'm careful where the belt is, not hitting him directly over it. I continue the pattern, moving to various spots. A satisfied groan comes out of him as I continue, going back up to his shoulders. Leo's head hangs as he exhales heavily. I give one last hard snap across his ass, and he grunts.

Dropping the flogger onto the cart, I grab a pinwheel and roll it down his spine. He arches his back, cuffs clinking against the cross' hard points. My other hand runs over where I hit him, noting slight redness in some spots. I rub his shoulders a little as I continue to distract him with the pinwheel rolling over his skin. I have it follow the length of leather to his front, his body jerking as it rolls just below his belly button. A shudder leaves him as I roll it back towards me, following the outline of his tattooed wings, which ripple as his skin reacts to the metal wheel.

"Mistress," he pleads.

"Tired of me teasing you?"

"No, Mistress."

"Don't lie," I say softly, kissing his shoulder.

My hand slides up to the only other thing he wears: a thick, dark leather collar with three silver rings in the front, two in the back. I lightly yank on a ring, making him bring his head up.

"Do you want more pain, baby?"

"Yes, Mistress."

"What else do you say?"

"Please, Mistress. Please, more."

"Do you want to be used?"

"Yes, Mistress." His voice beseeching.

"Who do you belong to?"

"You, Mistress."

"I'm the only one allowed to use and touch you like this." My hand moves down, going back to lightly trace a finger over his cock. He jerks, shivering at the touch. "All mine, right, baby?"

"Yes." He breathes heavily, jaw going slack as he shuts his eyes. *"Mistress."*

"That's my good boy. All *mine*." Another shudder goes over him.

I step back to put the pinwheel away, shivers running down my own spine. That primal, territorial feeling I get comes like a wave. A need to give him what he needs, knowing he feels safe with me, supplementing what I want—control.

Grounding myself, I pick up the last flogger. The smaller tails of it clink together from the small metal beads embedded in each tail. I grip the handle, swinging the flogger to recall the heavier weight. Just in case, I grab my forearm crutch to keep my balance. Leo's head remains where I lifted it to.

"Check in," I say.

"Green, Mistress."

Stepping closer, I twirl the flogger to just brush over his body. His skin ripples at the contact as I do it again and again. Each movement a taunt as I flick it. His fingers flex in anticipation, shifting on his feet. I wait until he's entirely still before I allow the flogger to crack against his ass. He lets out a sound of relief as I do it again and again. Then change to the other cheek. I hit him hard, paying attention to the reddening of his skin and his pace of breathing. I move higher upon his back, the beads cracking. The sound echoes through the space. A moan slips out of him as I bring the flogger one last time across his ass.

Quickly, I grab the leather paddle next. Moving the crutch aside, I step beside Leo and bring the paddle down onto his ass. My other hand grips the other side of his hip as I hit him again. Leo hisses under his breath as I paddle him, moving to the other cheek as I run my hand across the heat of his skin. I spank him, noticing his toes curl as I smack his thighs next. His breath quickens as I mark his skin, then hit inside his inner thighs. Leo's grunts and moans merge with the echoes of the leather paddle hammering his skin.

I give one last hard smack, and his body practically vibrates. My hand moves to the front of him, feeling that his cock strains against the bindings. He groans as sweat forms at his brow. His eyes close, brows furrowed in concentration as his jaw clenches. I notice as his dick becomes less strained as his erection softens.

"Hard time focusing there, baby?" I taunt, sliding my finger over it again. He grunts, wiggling in his restraints.

I barely stop the giggle in my throat as he smirks without opening his eyes.

"I'll stop teasing. Not that cruel, am I?"

I run my hands over his reddened ass before I smack his cheek. He grunts.

In my defense, he asked for more pain.

Putting the paddle away, I unlock his ankle restraints, and then his arms. He moves where I put him, and then I hook my finger through the middle front ring of his collar. I bring his face closer to mine, making him off balance with the sudden movement. His eyes are almost glazed over, but there's pure euphoria on his face.

"Good boy, you barely moved today."

"Thank you, Mistress."

"Ready for more?"

He breathes out in relief, "Yes, Mistress."

"Did you think I was going to stop there?" I smile softly. His eyes are filled with pleading. "We've barely started, baby." I pull him close for a chaste kiss.

Finger still hooked in the ring; I lead him over to the area next to the bed. A bar hangs from a couple of chains hooked at the hard points in the ceiling. I can easily move the height of it by using a pully system on the wall, but I already know it's at the height it needs to be. I already double-checked it was secure.

I bring him over to the hanging bar where there's a cushion.

"Kneel." He does so, eyes downcast in submission. "Raise your hands." He obeys as I clip his cuffs onto the bar just above his head. I make sure he adjusts on the cushion, body straightening to be in high submission mode even with the cock cage and plug inside him.

I run my hands over his shoulders. His hands placed just

outside of his shoulder points. My fingers tilt his chin back as far as he can go with the leather collar.

"Check in, baby."

"Green, Mistress."

I run my hand through his hair, and he closes his eyes as I caress him. Whenever I bring him over here, I take my time, waiting to see if it elicits any flashbacks. Usually, long as I have him in a cock cage, a plug, gag, anything of the like he's alright. Something to help keep his mind present.

Leo settles more into his position, breathing more evenly.

I whisper against his ear, "Fall as far as you want, baby. I'll catch you."

Every breath makes his chest expand. I step back, letting go as he tilts his head forward again, eyes downcast. I go grab my cart, rolling it over and then lock the brakes to keep from moving. Now to debate what to use next.

Unlike me, Leo never wants to know what I may use. He wants to submit completely in that way; to use him as I please. If there's anything he's not feeling, he'll safeword.

I grab some nipple clamps, clinking them in my hands. His breath hitches as I circle a finger around his pecks, and then lightly pinch one of his nipples. He inhales deeply as I carefully position the clamp, screwing in the sides. It tightens around his flesh, causing him to groan. I do the same to the other.

Silently, I step away and grab the gag with a leather bit. Leo's eyes flick to it as I step in front of him.

"Show your signal for yellow." He brings up one finger on his left hand. "Show your signal for red." He brings up two fingers. "And what's for green?" He makes a fist, putting his thumb under his fingers deliberately. "Good boy."

Carefully, I reach around him as he opens his mouth to take the bit. The straps go around his head as I snap them together. I check the tightness, and then his jaw moves a little from the gag. The music playing in the background shifts to something deeper and darker in tone as I grab a riding crop. Leo's eyes widen with anticipation.

Without any heads up, I smack the riding crop against his torso. I do it again to his other side, hitting at specific spots. Leo moans against the bit, saliva collecting around his bottom lip. I trace the crop around the nipple clamps, moving it down the middle of his chest. I watch as his body shudders, awaiting what I do next. Pleasure of my own flourishes, but never the same like when he Tops me. Being Leo's Dom, I felt something entirely different—a flourishing ecstasy of power and admiration, purpose enshrined.

His nostrils flare as I swat at the nipple clamp next. He grunts against the bit as I do the same with the other. The riding crop comes down onto his thigh, making him sit up straighter as the chains above rattle. A shiver runs down my spine, but I ignore it as I move around him to continue the onslaught of hits to his skin. Every other smack, I drag the riding crop along his skin, watching the glistening of sweat form.

"Check in." He makes the signal with both hands for green. I kiss his head, and he moans in response.

The low vibrations of the music echo as I leave the riding crop on the cart. I can hear his breathing pick up when I grab the bamboo cane next. I slip my hand through the leather strap at the end, gently smacking it against the palm of my hand. It fucking stings even just from that.

I hate this thing, but he loves it.

I remind myself of that fact when my eyes meet his. Hazel eyes sear into mine, completely overrun by desire and yearning. His body is practically slack, chest heaving as he hangs from his restraints. I doubt he fully remembers his cock is strapped up or there's a plug in his ass.

I walk around to step behind him, adjusting how I stand before I raise the cane. Without warning, I bring it across his back. There's a small whistle of it pulling through the air before it makes impact. Leo grunts at the contact. I do it again, moving lower. He grunts, chewing at the bit every time the cane lands. I crack it against the top of his ass, and he shifts on his knees as his back arches a little.

Coming back to his front, he shifts on his knees as I bring the cane between his thighs and quickly rap it between his legs. He sits up straighter at the noise which for a split second, overpowers the music. He does his best to fix his kneeling position, becoming rigid. The bamboo cane then taps lightly underneath the nipple clamps. I then grasp one of the clamps, tightening it. Leo whimpers, body trying to rise.

"Check in." He gives the signal for green. Although I believe him, I still ease the clamp back, not wanting him overwhelmed.

Instead, I bring the cane down over his thighs. It whistles, cracking into the air. Leo's grunts follow the next three times I do it. His chest rises heavily with every quick breath through his nose. My own become heavy as I watch him. Turned on in a way that's indescribable.

Using the end of the cane, I lift his head to look at me.

Hazel eyes brimmed with tears meet mine, pleasure and release filling them. Euphoria in the pain. Freedom. Sweat drips from his brow down the side of his face, mingling with the saliva that slides down his chin from the bit. I remain there, keeping his head tilted back in that uncomfortable position to look at me.

Again, that territorial feeling returns, wrapping around me with a thickness. It combines with the intoxicating power of having him in this position willingly. Wanting to be here. Leo in his most coveted, revered position—on his knees for me.

For a moment, I wonder if this is what he'd always wished for. Every time he'd fallen to his knees before me. Every gentle word. Every touch. Every pleading in his voice. The worship upon his face. All of that reverence in his gaze now. Leo stares up at me like I was his god. To be owned and coveted in this way that no one else could achieve. Quite frankly, it was fucking arousing knowing it was me.

Although I understood months ago of what he wanted, it slides more into place of what Leo had been craving and searching for—

complete submission, relinquishing his dominance to someone who'd never truly harm him.

I put the cane down, and then undo the gag. Leo moves his mouth around as I set the gag aside, grabbing a cloth and gently wipe away the saliva that's dripped down his chin and neck. Tossing that away, I then carefully massage his jaw.

"How are your arms and knees feeling?"

"Fine, Mistress."

"Cock and ass?" I smirk.

"Desperate, Mistress."

"Oh, really?" I lean in closer. "For?"

"You, Mistress."

"Hmm, well I was thinking of pegging your ass..." he groans needily, "...but I think I'll use your mouth first. Just a bit longer in this position. Can you do that?"

"Yes, Mistress."

"Good boy."

I kiss his cheek, and he whimpers at the contact. My heart squeezes at the sound of his neediness. I give another kiss, trailing a few more down his neck just above his collar. I slip a finger into one of the rings to tug him closer. My lips reach his, kissing him deeply as we both moan at the contact. His tongue moves over mine, desperate as I kiss him harsher. Arousal sparks inside me as I pull away.

"Ready for more?"

"Yes, Mistress," he responds quickly.

"Good boy."

I go to the cart, bending down to grab my options. He likely hasn't noticed I'm already wearing the harness on my hips; slightly hidden amongst the other straps of the lingerie I wear. Turning around with a cheeky smile I hold up the two silicone dildos. Leo's restraints rattle.

"Mistress." His voice is pleading, almost begging.

"Deciding. Cause whichever one isn't in your mouth goes in your ass." One is slightly bigger than that other. Either dildo can be secured into the harness I wear, which he is now noticing I'm already wearing with a heated gaze.

I decide on the light blue one with a gradient of deeper hues. His eyes are fixated on me, breathing harshly with the clamps hanging from his nipples and his cock straining against the buckles. I step right in front of him, ready to grab the bar to help keep me steady. If at any point I feel a numbness or tingling in my legs, that's my cue to back off and reassess.

Directly in front of him, I attach the dildo to the harness and my breath hitches at the chilled bottom that rubs against my pelvis.

"Mistress," Leo begs again. "Please."

"You want my cock in your mouth, baby?" I rasp.

Leo responds by opening his mouth, tongue flattening and sticking out. Using one hand to guide the dildo towards his mouth, I grab the middle ring of his collar and tug him forward. His eyes close as I rub the end of the dildo along his tongue. Slowly, I have his saliva coat the dildo before I slip the toy entirely between his lips. Letting go of his collar, I grab the bar and gently thrust my hips towards him. Leo makes a small gagging sound, and I ease back. Sounds of his slick mouth fill the air.

I let go of the dildo, grabbing the top of his head to grip his hair. Carefully, I yank him forward as I thrust. From just the movement and pressure against my sex, I moan as Leo grunts around the dildo. My hips rock as I slowly fuck Leo's mouth.

"Look at me," I rasp.

His eyes snap open. Euphoria floods them as he sucks on the dildo, cheeks hollowing out with every long draw. Both my hands go to his hair, widening my stance. Leo's eyes stay with mine, saliva dripping down his chin while his lips are glistening wet. A shiver runs down my spine.

I'm not sure if I'll ever be alright with him eating me out, but sucking my fake cock was a turn-on I never had on my bingo card until a few weeks ago when we first tried it.

"Check in," I ask, watching his hands as he makes the signal for green. "Ready for me to fuck your mouth?" He groans, making the signal for the green again. "Are you certain?" I tease, and his head bobs in a nod as I almost pull the dildo out of his mouth.

Remembering how deep this dildo can go without hurting him, I grip his head and push forward. The force of it presses against me, and I gasp as I do it again. Leo takes it, mouth slurping as I thrust towards the back of his throat. He gags and I pull back, driving forward again. Leo grunts, wet noises permeating the air as saliva drips down his chin.

Leo makes a sudden choking sound, and I immediately pull back for him to breathe through his nose. The same noises are made when I plunge the toy back into him again. There's a twinge in my back, and I instantly pull the dildo out of him.

His gasps fill the air as I catch my breath along with him. His hands flex in their restraints as I straighten myself, pulling the dildo off the harness. Leo pants, watching me with more need than even before.

"Ready to move, baby?"

"Yes, Mistress," he rasps.

I unclip the restraints, massaging his shoulders once I do. My finger slips through the middle ring of the collar again to tug him to his feet. He stands up a bit unbalanced, quickly correcting himself. I let go of him, and a flicker of fear moves over him.

"Grab the cushion, while I move the cart." He does as he's told, following me over to the spanking bench.

The bench has been turned around for me to use it a bit differently today. I have Leo place the cushion before the bench, facing the structure. A flicker of pain moves over my tailbone, and my breath hitches in pain as I grab the cart for support. A quick of wave numbness hits my lower spine, legs shaky a moment, but then disappears.

"Mistress?" Leo doesn't move from his spot that I've placed him in, but his head does tilt to where I am.

"I think I fucked your mouth too hard," I chuckle, straightening myself. Once I'm sure I can stand and walk okay, I come up behind him to run my hands over his sides. "Guess I'll have to fuck your ass another time."

A shudder runs over him, almost like disappointment.

"Don't worry, baby, I have a back-up plan. What kind of Dom would I be, if I didn't?" He grunts amused. I slip my hands around his front, tracing over his cock. "I think it's time we take it out."

Leo groans as I run my finger over it again, his dick pressing against its cage.

"Turn around." I instruct, and he faces me with craving on his face. "Hands behind your head. Legs apart." He goes into the high protocol stance, showing all of himself to me.

Slowly, I start to release his cock, buckle by buckle. He doesn't move, but I can see the muscles move in his jaw, shoulders, abs, and even his dick. I finally release it, and he holds back a moan as he becomes erect. I have him turn around, unbuckling the sides of the belt to take off the front part. I place it on the cart, telling him, "Bend over."

He does, giving me better access to safely remove the anal plug. Leo releases a sound mixed with relief and discontent. Briefly, I grab some wipes to make sure he's clean and the plug. He stands back up, facing me still with his hands at the back of his head. Carefully, I clean his cock and balls next. A sound is caught in his throat as I take my time, and I smirk.

"Sit on the bench. Spread your arms out."

Leo does, taking his seat gingerly on the padded leather of the bench. I go to one hand, locking his cuff to one of the hard points of the contraption. I do the same on the other side, keeping his arms completely open and spread.

"Open your legs," I order. Leo opens his thighs, sitting up straight. Kneeling on the ground, I pull forward the spreader bar I hid under the bench, attaching his ankles to each end. Leo's breath picks up as I feel him watching me with anticipation. Without warning, I push his legs further apart and he grunts as I lock the bar in place.

Lastly, I reach under the bench and pull up straps to wrap over his upper thighs. I tighten them, making him stay seated where he is. He wiggles a little, likely from the soreness of being spanked and caned earlier.

I stand, looking over him as he's restrained to the bench, limbs spread. His dick is hard, jutting straight up after being caged. Leo's eyes are hooded as he stares at me, while I take my time to look over him. Stark tattoos and scars in the dim light of the room. He can't move, not unless he wants to drag the bench from its spot while fighting a bar that'll widen his legs more.

"You've been such a good boy," I whisper, stepping between his open legs. My heart clenches suddenly, looking down at him as he gazes up at me. I flick the nipple clamps and his body twitches.

I step back to the cart, grabbing one of the lacey lingerie pieces and the bamboo cane. Watching him carefully, I approach with his eyes searing into mine. Swiftly, I bring the cane down over one of his upper thighs. He grunts, closing his eyes as I do it to the other one. His dick remains erect, and Leo pulls his lips in as he whimpers under his breath. Satisfied with his reaction, I set the cane aside, folding the lingerie in half.

It's similar to the one I wore in Rome. I prepare to wrap it around his head as I've done before but pause before him as he opens his eyes, and they widen. A soft limit for him is blindfolds. He's prone to panic attacks if he can't see me. Given the lace is thin, he could see through it, and it may mirror what we'd done in Rome.

I hold it up, and his breathing picks up. "It's thin lace, even folded, you'll be able to see a little."

He swallows, sudden fear rippling through him. I bring it down, moving closer to cup his face and stroke his cheek. Leo rasps, "Yellow."

"You need to see me, baby?"

"Yes, Mistress."

"Good boy for telling me." I kiss his forehead, and he relaxes. "Then I'm putting it in your mouth."

"Yes, Mistress."

I place another kiss on his temple, moving a hand down to a nipple clamp and flick it. He twitches, and then I tighten it. He jostles in response. I do the same with the other. He then visibly relaxes more.

"Better?"

"Yes, Mistress."

"Open your mouth." I fold the lingerie again, putting as much as I can into his mouth. He groans, jaw moving as he practically chews on the fabric. "You should be able to spit that out if you need, otherwise use your hand signals."

He makes the signal for green in his left hand.

I can do this. I'm in control. You've planned this for weeks.

My hands run over his thighs. Leo shudders under my touch as I trace over the scars on his stomach and the lines of his tattoos. His skin prickles as I pull over the cushion to kneel on before him. Leo mumbles something against the lingerie in his mouth, restraints jostling. I flick my gaze to them, seeing no hand signal.

My hands move over to his cock, ignoring the distant worry in the back of my mind.

I'm in control.

I flick my eyes to every restraint. He can't touch me. He can't force me. He can't do anything. I'm in utter control and *he's* at *my* mercy, not the other way around.

"You once told me you could live the rest of your life without your cock being sucked," I whisper, and Leo's legs twitch, making the spreader bar open a bit more. He groans as I look up at him under my lashes. His eyes are blown wide as he stares down at me. "I don't think you deserve such a fate."

I stroke his cock once more as he mumbles just before I dip my head closer. My tongue traces over where my fingers had been teasing him. Leo's body goes rigid, head leaning back as I do it again. Stomach clenching, and telling myself I can do this, I bring his dick into my mouth. I go as deep as I can, sucking on him as he sucked on my own. Leo groans, restraints clinking and straining.

The worry vanishes as I keep going, realizing into each second he truly can't do anything. I focus on Leo as he moans, hips wanting to jut up, but are stopped due to the spreader bar and thigh restraints. I take him deeper, hollowing my cheeks as I try to remember how to do this. Leo doesn't seem to mind given his cock has been caged most of the afternoon.

His words are muffled by the lingerie in his mouth as I bob my head, gripping the base. Leo's moans become louder, arms flexing as he trembles. I lick him one last time, popping his cock out of my mouth while I continue to work him with my hand. I stand, moving my hand over his slicked member as I reach up and pull the lingerie from his mouth.

"Mistress," he whimpers, sweat covering him as I see him awaiting my command.

"Come for me," I finally instruct, and then tug off one clamp and then the other. Leo lets out a bark of release, body spasming. His cum coats my hand, dripping to the floor, as I help him ride the orgasm out. His face twists with pain, pleasure, and relief.

"Good boy…" I kiss his jaw, "…my very good Leo."

He pants as I sweep his hair back, and then kiss his temple.

"Good girl," he rasps.

Smiling, I kiss him on the lips.

After that, I release him from all his restraints, taking the cuffs off completely. Finally, I take the collar off after I instruct him to take a shower. While he does in the playroom's bathroom, I clean up the areas used. Setting aside toys to sanitize and putting away others in the dresser. Almost done, I have to stop as that twinge of pain comes back near my tailbone, followed by a wave of dizziness.

My hand clutches the handle of my crutch, leaning into it. Leo comes up behind me, naked with only a towel around his hips as he wraps an arm around my waist. He kisses my neck, then helps me finish cleaning. Lastly, I put cream on some of the more marked areas of his skin.

It's not long before we're in the television room, starting up a newer Nicholas Cage film. Chinese takeout is on the coffee table, and there's ice cream waiting in the fridge. We're dressed in comfortable clothes and fuzzy socks as I tug the blanket up. Leo adjusts in his seat with a heavy sigh.

"Didn't tucker you out, did I?"

"No, my ass hurts."

I immediately start laughing at the deadpan in his voice, unable to hold it in as I practically fall over. Leo grabs me to pull me into his lap, smiling down at me with his eyes shining.

"Oops," I say.

"No, I enjoyed every fucking moment." He takes my hand, kissing just above my rings. "Knowing you'd take care of me, in every single way."

I kiss his knuckles next. "Always, mister Americano."

"Always, my dear Watson."

I settle into my husband's arms, content and proud of how far both of us have come.

Epilogue

A Few Years Later

CALIFORNIA SUNRISES REALLY ARE MAGNIFICENT.

Light bathes the hills, casting long streaks of colors across the valley and lake far in the distance. Colors of blue mingling with purple and shades of oranges. It's gorgeous.

I sit in the lounger on the patio of Leo's getaway house, which sits about a couple hours away from the city. Perfect place to stay for a weekend away from the chaos. Or to have alone time before catching up with the rest of the *Forgotten Demons* for our annual ride along the coast.

The sliding doors open next to me, and I smile up at Leo who's fully clad in his leathers; chaps and all. Just as I am. Both of us already wearing our club vests. We wanted to get an early start before meeting with the others.

"It gets more beautiful every time I see it," I whisper as I look out at the horizon.

"That's what I think whenever I look at you," he murmurs, dipping down to kiss my neck.

A giggle comes out of me. I'll never tire of his smooth, suave lines.

"Think I'm like a sunrise?" I ask.

He hums, stepping past me as he places his hands in his pockets. I watch how the light falls over him, casting a warm glow on his features. "You're more brilliant than a sunrise."

"Well, mister…" I smile, emotion wrapping around me as he turns back to me, gentle and open, "…you're a dawn I always look forward to waking up witnessing."

"Now who's being smooth?"

"Learned it from the best."

He smiles. My heart soars and clenches at the same time, knowing how long it took to get to this point of openness. The cold mask Leo had worn daily was gone, no longer burying him down in that deep well.

There were still some bad days. Some were good. Some were chaotic, and stressful. Just like some days I could easily get out of bed, and others I needed KITT. But some were calm. Most were happy, content, and hopeful in moving forward. Even as the head mafia bosses of New York. We didn't leave; those plans long gone.

My past self would never believe it.

Honestly, I didn't hate it. I had the Crew. Chiari. Bobby, even Matteo. I had the entire staff of the *Italian Lily* who were constantly under my protection. I had Leanne. I had Trix. But most of all, I had Leo. My dear husband who still whispered his devotion to me every day. The man who was still healing, like myself, but together.

"We should get going, if we want to meet up with them on time," Leo says.

I look out once more at the beautiful sky, and smile.

"It's like watching a sunrise. I don't know what I'm going to get…but there's going to be light. And I don't want to miss a second of it."

"Autumn?"

I blink back tears, smiling as I shake my head. "Just an old thought."

I grab Rhonda, getting up from my seat. My arm crutches are what I use most days, but they're a bitch to travel with. So, Rhonda it is.

Leo's hand lands against the small of my back as we head through the house, locking up as we come out to the driveway where our two motorcycles sit. Leo's riding one of his Larry Knucklehead choppers that he keeps out in California for longer distances. It's silver and gold with long braids hanging from the handlebars. My own is a custom soft tail Harley that Rudy, Chesty, and Animal built for me. It has two wheels in the rear, much like a trike with the rest of the body a soft tail frame. I can't ride a two-wheeled bike without injuring myself further, so extra wheel it was for me to ride on my own. I loved it. It was a replica of Leo's prized soft tail, colors and all, which I got running again.

I gaze back at the house. Leo tilts my head over to look at him, forest green eyes flecked with gold and browns meeting mine. "We'll be back again."

My heart flutters. Those butterflies I only get for him flourishing.

"I know. Hey…" I place my hand on his chest, and he grabs my hand, stroking his thumb over my skin, "…are you happy?"

Leo smiles gently. "Yes, my dear Watson. Are you?"

"More than I thought I ever could be."

His hand goes to my neck, gently cradling it as he kisses me. I sigh against him, clutching at his vest and that happiness makes me float.

We're interrupted by the sounds of rumbling engines, splitting the morning silence. We pull apart as the *Forgotten Demons* pull into the long driveway, lined up with mischievous grins.

"Told you, they'd be smooching!" Animal yells over the noise.

I roll my eyes, while Leo glares at them. "We told you we'd meet later."

"Wanted an early start before meeting up with the rest of the club," Sombra answers.

"Morning too beautiful to waste!" Chesty yells, grinning large.

"Vamos, Cage Madness!" Enigma calls, revving his engine.

Laughing, I look out at the entire Crew.

Jameson, Sombra.

Isaac, Pretty Boy Bond.

Rudolph, Ringer.

Owen, Iron Buffalo.

Waylon, Chesty.

Julio, Enigma.

Drew, Animal.

Lastly, I glimpse up at The Spartan. My mobster. My husband. My everything.

He smirks, before we put our helmets on, getting on our bikes as the rest start riding out to the road. My motorcycle and Leo's add to the noise of the roaring engines, vibrating through my body. The world is overwhelmed by the thunderous sounds, and my grin gets bigger as I ride out with Leo behind me. We come out of the driveway, onto a road that winds its way back down the coast. I speed up the bike, catching up to the group as the engine roars beneath me as I steer around a bend and into the glorious light of the sunrise. I briefly glance over as Leo rides up beside me, straddling his chopper with ease. My favorite sight.

We ride alongside each other. The feeling I always get from riding, whether as Leo's backpack or on my own, flourishes— freedom.

Opening the clutch with my dear Leonardo at my side, I say with a grin,

"Let's ride."

The End

Afterword

I have no words and yet too many to properly give a lasting
goodbye on this series.
So, let's do what Autumn would likely suggest.
Give a proper movie send off.

Walks off, pumps a fist into the air, and go into a freeze frame.
"Don't You (Forget About Me)" by Simple Minds

Acknowledgments

Is this how Oscar, Emmy, Tony award winners feel like? Trying to go through the whole list of who they're thankful for? Phew, least I won't have music urging me off stage….instead you'll probably just close the book. WHELP.

Thank you to friends and family who answered multiple questions on multiple subjects from motorcycles to living in New York City to how to properly tie up someone without nerve damage.

Thank you to my sister, Sam, for listening to me and breaking down in your living room to making me watch *Centaurworld* to calm my ass down.

Thank you to my mom for everything from being the main reason why I started writing all those years ago to giving me those break days of crocheting and watching random BBC game shows. (Okay, mainly *QI* and *Would I Lie To You?*)

Thank you to my husband who dealt with many a breakdown, long rants, getting me to eat and drink water, and being the best re-supplier of coffee when I needed it. I love you and I appreciate you.

Thank you to my editor, LJ, for helping me trust in my writing again. If not for you, my anxiety would've ruled over this entire damn project.

Thank you to my Lemon, who always kept urging me to go forward and pushing past those "limits" I thought I had.

Thank you to my author bestie, Mariah, for being the BEST cheerleader on social media. You've always made me feel included and appreciated. (I still want to grow up to be like you one day)

And my biggest thanks…

To my readers, who stuck to me like caramel when the nights got hard, I give my full appreciation and gratitude towards. If not for your love for Autumn, Leo, and the *Forgotten Demons* this series wouldn't have been finished. Thank you for the kind messages and sharing your own stories of growth and achievements. Those moments mean the most to me. Thank you.

Books Also By Elm Jed

Paranormal Mafia

Mafia, Murder, and Mayhem Series

Vinny the Vampire & Me

Sweet Cheeks & Her Mob Boss

The Wolf Boss & His Darling

The Werecat & Her Lone Wolf - A Novella

Memories of the Underground - Volume One

The Goth & The Housewife - A Novelette (Standalone)

Suspense Romance

My Dear Watson Series

My Dear Watson

My Forgotten Demons

My Emerald Fire

My Dear Leo

About the Author

Elm Jed is an award winning author, who mostly writes mafia, paranormal, and suspense romance. They are a disabled, queer, Marine Corps veteran, who's been writing since they were ten years old with a degree in Theatre. Their books focus on mental health awareness and giving readers a space to feel seen in different ways from disabilities to understanding their queerness.